Title: Patch

Series: Steel Archangel's MC, SAFC3 (Book 3)

Cover by: JG Designs

Formatting by: Becky Hodges

Edited by: Franklin Beck

Contents

Dedication

To my loving husband and children. Thank you for believing in me and supporting me <3

To my alphas and the Steel Archangel's men they licked before I wrote their stories.

This one's for you Mary <3

Acknowledgements

To my readers, thank you for joining me as we learn more about the men and women who make up the Steel Archangel's MC where the members are possessive, protective alpha's who will do anything to protect their woman and partners. Women and partners who are kickass and strong in their own way, whether they realize it or not.

To my PA (the Goddess of PA's) Becky Hodges, I can't say enough how much having you as my PA and friend means to me. You are my rock, my sounding board and I love our gab sessions—especially when they result in five book ideas. For those who don't know, those sessions started the premise for Cannon & Atlas (yup—got more ménage coming up), Devil, Beast and two second generation books. I don't know what I'd do without you girl! You are the best and I love ya girl <3

To my Alpha Team, there aren't enough words to thank you all enough! You all have been a tremendous help when I've hit roadblocks. You've been there when I needed to bounce ideas around, character inspiration, and so much more. Thank you for your support and keeping me going <3

To Cassandra and a friend who wishes to remain anonymous, I can't even begin to say how grateful I am for looking over my translations! Thank you, thank you, thank you! (and so many more, lol) You helped me in my hour of need, and I can't express much I appreciate you both for all of your help! You are both lifesavers <3

To my editor, formatter, and cover designer, thank you all for everything you did to help make Patch into the book that it is. I loved working with all of you <3

Reading Order & Other Works by R. Knight

Steel Archangel's MC

Thor & Dragon (SAFC1)
Timber (SAFC2)
Patch (SAFC3)
Patch & Mary: A SAMC Christmas to Remember (SAFC3.5)
Reaper (SAJC1—coming soon)
Smoke (SAFC4—TBD)
Cannon & Atlas (SAJC2—TBD)

Children of Prophecy

Hell's Lost Princess, Book 1
Book 2 (coming soon)

Shifter Royalty

Mates, Book 1

Spirits, Book 2

Book 3 (coming soon)

Standalones

New Beginnings

This is in the process of being rewritten and rebranded. Link will be coming soon

Content & Trigger Warning

This book is intended for a mature audience aged 18+. It contains foul language, violence (including torture and murder), adult situations, body shaming (not from MC), fat shaming (not from MC), underage sex (consensual at age 17), kidnapping, human trafficking, grooming, abortion (while no abortions take place, there is talk about a side character possibly getting one), and mentions of rape (does not go into great details but there is talk about the situation).

There is no cheating and there is a HEA. Each book can be read as a standalone, but it is best read in order as the story builds on the members and their women/partners in the Steel Archangel's MC.

Steel Archangel's MC Members

Forest Creek Chapter (SAFC)

Ryan Gilbert (Thor)—President
Reed Thomson (Phoenix)—Vice President
Nick Gilbert (Dragon)—Enforcer
Alexander 'Alex' Carter (Ryder)—Sergeant at Arms
Elijah Anderson (Tripp)—Secretary
Liam Caldwell (Timber)—Treasurer
Noah Banks (Judge)—Road Captain
Levi Gilbert* (First Lady)—Unofficial 2nd Enforcer
Jaxon 'Jax' Witlock (Smoke)
Luke Morgan (Patch)
Malcolm Hart (Bones)
Michael Adams (Gunner)
Aiden Hunt (Axe)
Owen Burke (Bear)
Troy Simpson (Colt)—Prospect
Drae Black—Prospect
Alexei Petrov—Prospect [pronounced ALEX-AY]
Sasha Petrov—Prospect [pronounced SAWSHA]
Ethan Mills—Prospect

Old Ladies

Levi Gilbert*—Old Lady to Thor & Dragon
Mae Caldwell—Old Lady to Timber

Children

Lindsey Joy Black—Daughter to Drae Black

Steel Archangel's MC Members

Junction Creek Chapter (SAJC)

Anthony 'Tony' Leyton (Reaper)—President

Isaac Lopez (Devil)—Vice President

Kai Miller (Punisher)—Enforcer

Leon Foster (Razor)—Sergeant at Arms

Tyson Manning (Smithy)—Treasurer

Grant McGee (Beast)—Secretary

Adam Collins (Loki)—Road Captain

Cole Thornton (Python)

Hunter Beck (Doc)

Ragnar Miller (Odin)

Duncan Goodwin (Atlas)

Theodore 'Theo' Harris (Cannon)

Drake Olsen—Prospect

Nathan Flynn—Prospect

Old Lady

Astrid Miller—Old Lady to Odin

Translation Glossary

Below you will find the glossary list for the translations that will appear in *Steel Archangel's MC: Patch*. You will also find translations for the first four times the foreign word/sentence appears in the body of each chapter so that you won't have to repeatedly flip back to this glossary list.

If you see an error with any of the translations, please remember that I am human and do not speak these languages, though I do love their cultures. I have researched, talked to friends, and tried to get these translations as close as possible to being accurate, but again, we are human and may miss something.

If you do spot something that needs correcting, please reach out to me via email rather than reporting the issue and I will work to get it corrected (author.r.knight@gmail.com). Thank you for your patience and understanding <3

Greek

Please keep in mind, that Greek and English have many differences, one of them being that the Greek do not capitalize words like 'mom', 'grandma' when they are talking to them or about them. Another is that the Greek language has declension cases (nominative, genitive, accusative, and vocative and to further complicate it, there are masculine, feminine, and neuter nouns).

As a note, the Greek translations here do not include the declensions cases (nominative, genitive, accusative, and vocative or the masculine, feminine, and neuter nouns)—those will be seen in the body of the paragraph for each chapter since the Greek words will alter slightly depending on how they are being used in a sentence.

Please note that a word could have the same ending for more than one case in the Greek language. For example (see below), 'dad' and 'dads' have the '**ας**' ending is for the masculine nominative case, whereas the '**α**' ending is for the masculine genitive, accusative, and the vocative cases. Same for 'grandma' and 'grandmas' where the female nominative, accusative, and vocative cases have the '**ά**' ending but the female genitive case has the '**άς**' ending.

Μαμά / μαμά (mama = mom)

Πατέρας / πατέρας (pateras = father/dad)

Γιαγιά / γιαγιά (giagia = grandma)

Παππούς / παππούς (pappous = grandpa)

Γιαγιά και παππούς (giagia και pappous = grandma and grandpa)

Παππούς και γιαγιά / παππούς και γιαγιά (pappoús kai giagiá = grandparents)

Παππούς και γιαγιά' / παππούς και γιαγιά' (pappoús kai giagiá' = grandparents')

Προπαππούδες και γιαγιάδες / προπαππούδες και γιαγιάδες (propappoudes kai giagiades = great-grandparents)

Εγγονή / εγγονή (eggone = granddaughter)

Εγγονός / εγγονός (eggonos = grandson)

Θεία / θεία (theia = aunt)

Θείος/ θείος (theios = uncle)

Θεία και θείος / θείακαι θείος (theies kai theioi = aunt and uncle)

Κορίτσι μου / κορίτσι μου (koritsi mou = my girl)

Λουλούδι μου / λουλούδι μου (louloudi mou = my flower)

Του λουλουδιού μου / του λουλουδιού μου (tou louloudiou mou = my flower's)

Άγγελος / άγγελος (aggelos = angel)

Σε αγαπώ (Se agapo = I love you)

Κι εγώ σ' αγαπώ (Ki ego s' agapo = I love you, too)

Φοβάμαι (Phobamai = I'm scared)

The below Greek only appears in the body of the chapter:

Έχουμε την πλάτη σου, λουλούδι μου (Ekhoume ten plate sou, louloudi mou= We've got your back, my flower)

Πάντα σε αγαπούσα και πάντα θα σε αγαπώ (Panta se agapousa kai panta tha se agapo = I've always loved you and always will)

Το ξέρω, αλλά δεν είσαι μόνος πια (To xero, allow den eisai monos pia = I know, but you're not alone anymore)

Υπόσχομαι ότι θα είμαι δίπλα σας σε κάθε βήμα (Yposkhomai oti tha eimai dipla sas se kathe bema = I promise that I'll be by your side every step of the way)

Το γλυκό λουλούδι του τίτλου μας (To glyko louloudi tou titlou mas = Our sweet little flower)

Είναι εντάξει (Einai entaxei = It's okay).

Είναι στο πλευρό μας (Einai sto pleuro mas = She's on our side).

Παίξτε μαζί (Paixte mazi = Play along).

Spanish

Mi madre (My mother)

Compañía de mi madre (My mother's company)

El libro de recetas de mi madre (My mother's cookbook)

Las recetas de mi madre (My mother's recipes)

Padre (Father)

Mi Padre (My Father)

La casa de mis padres (My parent's house)

Mi hermana (My sister)

Mi hermanita (My younger sister)

De mi abuela (My grandma's

La memoria de mi abuela (My grandma's memory)

Abuelo (Grandpa / Grandfather)

Mi abuelo (My grandpa / grandfather)

De mi abuelo (My grandpa's)

La cara del abuelo (Grandpa's face)

Los ojos del abuelo (Grandpa's eyes)

La casa de mi abuelo (My grandpa's house)

Tía (Aunt)

Tío (Uncle)

Mi tíos (My uncles)

Tu padre y tu tío (Your father and uncle)

Tus tías y tíos (Your aunts and uncles)

Abuelo y mi tios (Grandpa and my uncles)

Bebés (Babies)

Niños (Kids)

Mi niña (My girl)

Mi sobrina (My niece)

Mis sobrinos y sobrina (My nephews and niece)

Familia (Family)
Mi familia (My family)
Su familia (Their family)
Nuestra familia (Our family)
Nuestras Familias (Our families)
Mi precioso capullo de rosa (My precious rosebud)
Hola (Hello)
Sí (Yes)
Gracias (Thank you)
Buenas noches (Good night)
Bastardo (Bastard)
Estúpido (Stupid)
Mierda (Shit)
Daga de oreja (Eared dagger)
Mi daga de oreja (My eared dagger)
Muro ancestral de nuestra familia (Family's wall of ancestors)

German

Suchen (Search)

Bleiben (Stay)

Russian

Да (Da = Yes)

Обычный (Obychny = The usual)

Заставим их извиваться (Zastavim ikh izvivatsya = Let's let them squirm)

Series Song Inspiration

Man of Steel by Brantley Gilbert
Tough Town by Brantley Gilbert
Who Hurt You by David Morris
Warriors by Imagine Dragons
Simple Man by Lynyrd Skynyrd
Ride the Wind by Poison
Miracle by Shinedown
Monsters by Shinedown

Patch Song Inspiration

Rest in Peace by Dorothy
Roots by Imagine Dragons
You Tella Tale by Just Surrender
Simple Man by Lynyrd Skynyrd
Good to You by Marianas Trench
Words as Weapons by Seether
A Symptom of Being Human by Shinedown
Cut the Cord by Shinedown
Get Up by Shinedown
Face Down by The Red Jumpsuit Apparatus
Your Guardian Angel by The Red Jumpsuit Apparatus
Get Out Alive by Three Days Grace
Here Without You by Three Doors Down
Never Too Late by Three Days Grace
Painkiller by Three Days Grace

Synopsis

Mary

My life was a perfect dream. I had an amazing family, supportive best friends, and a boyfriend who adored every plus-sized inch of me.

In a single night, my blinders are ripped away. The mirage has evaporated to expose the nightmare hiding beneath.

Nine years of abuse. Nine years of having to relive the worst betrayal a person can withstand. Nine years of poison whispered into my ears, corrupting my

vulnerable heart. Nine years of existence with only my precious babies to tether my sanity.

And then my world twists once more.

Patch

Nine years ago, life was almost perfect. Then a single moment stripped away my dreams. My only hope and salvation was my relentless search for answers.

For her. My Siren.

My prayers are finally answered, but you know what they say: be careful what you wish for. Mary may have returned to me, but she's no longer mine. The life that was supposed to have been ours, the family that we'd planned… it was supposed to be with me. Not him.

However, nothing is as it seems. A tangled web of truths wrapped in lies and betrayals runs deep into the underbelly of our city. It'll take an army to get to the bottom of it all, to have a chance to pick up the pieces of our shattered dreams and build the life we'd once dreamed.

It's a good thing we have not one, but two armies at our backs.

Chapter 1
Mary

Ten Years Old

We've been stuck in the car for eight hours and I'm so ready to get to our new house. We left early this morning at 6 am. Normally with it being summer, I would have hated getting up that early, but I was too excited, anxious, and nervous to sleep much last night.

I was able to nap a little during the car ride, but not much because our car is jam-packed full of so many boxes that I'm squished into a very small space in the back seat. It's so bad that whenever we stop, I have to squeeze my hand behind a heavy box just to buckle and unbuckle my seatbelt. The corners of the boxes dig into my side and shoulder, which I know I'll be feeling for a while.

There are also boxes underneath my feet, so I've been sitting with my feet resting on them, knees bent, for the entire trip. I have just enough room to the right of my legs for my backpack filled with my pencil case, notebooks, a couple of books, and a few puzzle books—*Mad Libs*, word finds, and *Sudoku*. The only movement I can really make is to slightly lean to my right to rest against the door, but doing that for too long makes my side hurt. To say I need to stretch is an understatement.

Πατέρας (Dad) had tried to convince Mom to let the movers take part of what's loaded in our car, but she wouldn't hear of it. She just kept saying that *'I'm a kid and will bounce back in no time from the cramped quarters.'* That she needed all of her stuff and didn't want to wait for the movers to show up, especially if they got delayed for some reason.

My size also doesn't help with the cramped quarters because I'm not a skinny kid either.

Mom's family has Scandinavian and Spanish roots. However, Mom mostly takes after my grandmother with her Scandinavian roots rather than my grandfather's Spanish genes. Mom has short, brown hair that she bleaches blond, is fairly tall, and has blue eyes. Both Grandmother and Mom are rail thin, something Mom desperately wanted me to inherit from their genes, but that didn't happen. Or at least not yet. My weight has been an issue for both of them for a few years now.

Πατέρας (Dad) is a big, tall man with green eyes, medium-dark olive skin, and black curly hair. Not like ringlets curly, but curlier than just wavy hair. If that makes any sense. He's not skinny by any means, as he has a bit of a tummy, but he isn't overweight.

His family is Greek, so food is very important to them. As my **γιαγιά** (grandma), **πατέρα** (dads) mom says, food is our family's love language. **Γιαγιά** (Grandma) has been teaching me to cook for the last couple of years and already, the cookbook she gave me the first time we cooked together is chock full of our family's recipes as well as a few that I've created on my own. Also, anytime she teaches me something new, she makes sure to bring the recipe cards along for me to put in my cookbook.

I mainly take after **πατέρα** (dad), both in personality and looks, which includes that I'm big boned and heavier than most kids my age. I also got his silky, black curly hair, which I like to keep long. My olive skin isn't dark like **πατέρα** (dads) it's more of a light olive skin tone, which I think is in part because Mom's skin is pale. Whenever she's outside for too long, she'll end up burning but will never tan. However, my blue eyes are from Mom. No one in **πατέρα** (dads) family has blue eyes. Just me.

Both of my parents have glasses, though my mom usually wears contacts, and they've had them since they were kids. That pretty much doomed me in that department, as I've already been wearing glasses for over two years.

"Just another fifteen minutes or so," I hear **πατέρα** (dad) say and then notice that the radio has been turned down.

As the words register in my brain, my head pops up from my *Sudoku* puzzle just in time to see the sign for *'Welcome to Forest Creek'* go by outside my window. Turning, I look up at **πατέρα** (dad) and find him watching me in the rear-view mirror. His gaze darts to the boxes that surround me and it's then that I notice the creases around his eyes, which brings to mind this morning's argument and how much he protested, even as Mom kept packing in box after box. In the end I told him it was okay, however, we both knew that I was lying. I smile at him, trying to ease his worry, and as he smiles back at me, some of those creases around his eyes lessen.

Quickly, but carefully, I stow my stuff back into my backpack. I've always been a stickler for keeping my books in as good of a condition as possible, which includes my puzzle books.

Pushing my black wire glasses up, I look out the window again. I've visited Forest Creek a lot over the years, but very rarely was I awake for the trip, or if I was, I wasn't able to see out the window much until now. Both of my parents grew up around here, but for some reason had moved to western Iowa before I was born. Now, they're moving back home, and both sets of my grandparents are excited to have us closer again as they also live in Forest Creek.

Pushing up on my seat so I can see better, I can feel a wide smile pulling at my lips at what I see. There are a lot of cute little stores along the main street and my jaw drops when I see the awesome playground at the park. Twisty tunnel slides, swing sets, teeter totters, jungle gyms and so much more. There are a ton of trees littered around the edges and I can see them being fun for playing hide and go seek. I can't wait until we can visit the park!

As **πατέρας** (dad) drives through town, I bounce in my seat, both with nerves and excitement, as I take in everything that's in my new town. I chew my lip nervously as we pass the school. I wonder if I'll make any friends this time? Or if I'll just be bullied again by most of the students like at my last school?

After a few minutes, Mom points out her window to the right. "Oh, there it is. Mulberry Lane."

Πατέρας (Dad) puts his turn signal on and when we turn onto Mulberry Lane, my jaw drops at how big the houses are on this street. I know **πατέρα** (dad) said he was offered more money for his new accounting job than he was getting at his last job in Iowa, but is it really enough to afford a place so big? Mom got a position as a teacher at the high school in town, but I know from their many arguments that she doesn't get paid a lot. Her family comes from money, but for some reason,

Mom had to give up her trust fund a long time ago. Or, at least, that's what I heard from their many, and loud, arguments.

We've rented small two-bedroom houses and apartments my whole life and I have been told time and time again that I couldn't have things I wanted because my parents were pinching pennies. Almost everything I own is second-hand because *'I'm just a kid and am going to outgrow my clothes and things quickly'*. That's something Mom has told me repeatedly over the years when I beg to get at least one new outfit or new shoes or a new backpack at the start of each school year, but it's never happened.

To say I've been on the receiving end of jokes and bullying because of my clothes and belongings is an understatement. That bullying got even worse when I had to start wearing glasses and when I started to become heavier than the other kids. And I'm only going into the fifth grade. I have a feeling that the bullying will only get worse as I get older.

Though, I will say, the worst things that I've heard have been from my own mom.

She doesn't get why I can't lose weight so that I can fit into her 'perfect family picture'. I've often caught her giving me disapproving looks when I go back for more food at dinnertime. Even if it is healthy.

"Here we are," **πατέρας** (dad) says in a sing-song voice.

"Oh, look. A few kids are out playing in one of the yards across the street. They look like they could be your age, Mary," Mom says, as she points out her window again.

I turn and look out my window to see a girl and two boys playing together. My heart sinks a little when I realize what Mom is probably thinking when I see them playing kickball.

'Maybe these kids will encourage you to pull your nose up and out of a book long enough to work off some of the calories you shove into your mouth.'

And I know she's thought it because I've overheard her muttering it under her breath or when she doesn't realize I can hear her when she's on the phone with Grandmother.

Needless to say, my mom and I aren't very close. I'm very much a Daddy's girl.

Πατέρας (Dad) pulls up in front of a large two-story house with white siding and black shutters. Tomorrow, the moving truck is supposed to be here with the rest of our things.

Opening my door, pick up my bag and carefully crawl out of the back seat. Standing, my left leg goes out from under me almost immediately, which has me stumbling as I realize it's fallen asleep. Leaning against the car, I shake out my leg, hating the pins and needles feeling that's rushing up it.

Shoes slapping against concrete have me looking up and my eyes widen when I see the three kids Mom spotted running toward me.

"Hi, I'm Allison, but you can call me Alli if you want," the little girl says, her voice bubbly and excited.

She's about my height with short, straight black hair and hazel eyes. She's a little skinnier than me, but I also realize she's a bit bigger than other girls our age, but still smaller than me. Though, that thought has me instantly feeling bad because I know those were Mom's words in the back of my mind noticing and saying that about her. I feel my cheeks heat slightly with embarrassment, but I still manage a small, awkward wave.

"Um, hi. I'm Mary. Mary Catarino."

I try not to cringe at how shy and unconfident I sound, and I hope that they don't pick on me like so many kids have in the past. Despite my mom's mean words, I am happy with my body just the way it is. However, I do wish I could be more confident.

"This is Luke and his cousin Brady. Do you want to come play with us?" she asks me and I turn, looking hesitantly at the boys next to her.

Luke has blond hair that's shaved short on the sides, but the top is long. He has it styled so that it flips over to one side and it's long enough that it almost reaches his jaw. His green eyes sparkle with happiness and excitement and his smile is wide. Then I realize he's about a head taller than I am and I start to get nervous again. Especially when I see that he's fairly muscular for his age. Well, at least compared to the boys that went to my old school.

My gaze slides to Brady, and I can see the family resemblance in their faces. Brady wears his light brown hair short and, like his cousin, he has green eyes and has a similar build to Luke.

Okay, my nerves are kicking in more. The memories of those older boys at my old school shoving me and pushing me down while calling me names are coming back full force.

"Um, I have to ask my parents," I mumble.

"Go ahead, Sweetie," Mom's sickly-sweet voice comes from behind me, startling me and making me jump slightly. "We'll put your things in your room for the time being."

"**Κορίτσι μου** (My girl), how about you go up and pick out your room first?" **πατέρας** (dad) says as he walks down the sidewalk and back toward us. He must have just unlocked the door. Seeing that I haven't moved, he smiles widely at me and when he tilts his head toward the house, silently encouraging me to go inside. It's then that his words fully register and I feel like my eyes bug out so much they're practically about to fall out. Thankfully, my possibly new friends don't make fun of me for it. Or that I probably look like a goofball with how wide my smile is. I've never had a chance to pick out which room I wanted in the previous places we've rented before. But then my heart sinks and my smile fades when I hear Mom's scoff and **πατέρας** (dad) frowns as he shoots her an irritated look.

"I thought we already decided she was going to be in the room next to us."

It's not a question, more like a statement with the way she says it combined with one of her signature irritated slash disappointed glares directed at **πατέρα** (dad). He sighs and shakes his head slightly.

"No, you decided that, Dear. This is the first time our Mary has had the opportunity to pick a bedroom out, and we are going to give her that. The only room that is off limits, beside our room, is the main floor study. That way I'm not keeping either of you up come tax season when I have to work extra-long hours."

Turning toward Alli and the guys, I give them a small smile that I hope doesn't show how nervous I am as I silently pray my mom won't say anything embarrassing in front of them. "I'll be back down in a few minutes," I tell them as I pick up my bag and turn around, quickly walking down the sidewalk.

Turning the doorknob, I push open the front door and my jaw drops at how beautiful the house is. There are hardwood floors throughout the rooms that I can see and a mostly open floor plan where you can see nearly everything in the dining room, kitchen, and living room.

Then my nose wrinkles.

Everything's so... white.

That's one thing I've come to hate thanks to the houses and apartments we've rented in the past. We couldn't change the wall color in any of the places and every single wall was always white. Maybe I can ask **πατέρα** if I can paint my room at some point?

Hearing footsteps on the walkway, I quickly head upstairs, figuring that's where the bedrooms are, and peek my head in the first room. It's really big, so I'm guessing it's supposed to be Mom and **πατέρα** (dads) room.

The next room is bigger than my parent's room has ever been in the past and there are two windows in here. The closet is small, but definitely not the smallest I've had.

However, the last room takes my breath away. There are three windows in here where I can see the woods in the distance and I know now that's why Mom wanted this room for her hobby and reading room.

Biting my lip, I try to decide what to do. Choose this room for me and have something I want for a change? Or pick the other room because I know Mom wants this room? Hearing raised voices, I step quietly toward the door and it quickly dawns on me that Mom and **πατέρας** are arguing downstairs. With the house being so empty, I can easily hear their voices carrying upstairs.

"Why did you tell her she could pick her own room, Nikos? We already have everything picked out for where it's going! Things were purchased with that in mind," Mom hisses.

"Eileen, stop. We've already had this argument a number of times and I'm putting my foot down on this. This is the first time that Mary has been given a choice like this, and she is going to get it. Both of us have had those chances growing up, but she hasn't. This move is the start of something good for all of us. We don't have to scrimp by anymore. We're going to go and get Mary some new clothes, shoes, and school supplies before school starts next week. You and I both know that she's been picked on and bullied constantly at school because we've had to get her second-hand clothes her whole life. That ends now."

Mom huffs again. "I don't see why we need to waste money on new clothes for her when she has enough that fit her just fine. It's a waste and the money could be put to better use on other things."

Wait, that's part of the reason why I could never have new clothes or shoes? A loud sound comes from downstairs, like the sound of a hand landing hard on a counter, and it makes me jump.

"That's a fucking lie, Eileen, and you know it! Her clothes are too thin. Her pants are too short. She's self-conscious because of the length of the shirts you *insist* she wears, even though she hates them. Stop trying to impose your clothing style on her because we both know she doesn't like that for herself. And anytime I've tried to buy her what she wants, the clothes mysteriously go missing or shrink in the wash. Enough is enough."

"Well, it wouldn't be so hard to dress her if she would stop gorging herself all the time and lose some goddamn weight."

I swear I hear a growl of some sort from **πατέρα** in response to the disgust in Mom's voice.

"Why does her weight bother you so much? My whole family is big. While yes, a few are overweight, most of us are tall and big-boned. We've been big our whole lives, even though most of us eat fairly healthy. Stop being so harsh on her and just let her be a kid. You keep going at this and you're going to give her a complex or an eating disorder."

"Well, at least that would be one way for her to lose weight," Mom mutters, and my heart breaks even further as I blink back tears.

Why does she hate that I'm heavier than the other kids so much?

Another slap on the counter has me jumping as I cling to the door.

"Enough, Eileen! You will do no such thing. Stop pushing your ridiculous expectations on her and just let her be herself."

Not wanting to hear anymore, I shut the door and I wince when it shuts harder and louder than I meant to. Digging through my backpack, I find my notebook, a black sharpie, and some tape. I quickly make a sign and tape it on the door, *my door*, before shutting it.

Hurrying down the stairs, I can't help my glare at Mom, and her lips pucker as she shoots me one of her many disapproving looks. Turning toward **πατέρα**, I give him a tight, small smile, which he returns. After hearing them argue so much, a lot of it being in front of me even though I know that's something **πατέρας** hated letting me see, I know almost all of his tells. Mom's too, for that matter.

"I've picked out my room. I'm going to head across the street to play if that's still okay?"

His smile softens as he nods, but judging by the sympathy in his eyes, I think he heard the door slam and knows that I heard their argument. "Of course, **κορίτσι μου** (my girl). Be home by suppertime, okay?"

Nodding, I head to the front door, but when I open the door and am about to head outside, I hear Mom clearing her throat.

"No goodbyes for me?" she asks, and I turn, narrowing my eyes at her.

"**Γιαγιά** (Grandma) taught me that when you don't have something nice to say, don't say anything at all, so no, I don't."

Her face puckers even more and she glares at **πατέρα**, even though she's the one that is in the wrong. However, I also know that she hates how close I am to **πατέρα** (dads) family. Mom doesn't get along with them at all, so it's always awkward when we have family gatherings. Another thing that she doesn't like is that I speak Greek, which is why I only speak it to **πατέρα** and his family, and not with her. However, I know **πατέρας** loves the fact that I've been learning Greek.

I turn to head out, but then pause, looking over my shoulder again. Hearing her earlier words and what she's said in the past has something in me finally snapping, wanting to push back and stand my own ground.

Turning back around toward my parents, my spine straightens and I hold my head up as high as I can, mustering up the strength to go against my own mother. Hopefully, I won't end up grounded because of this. Or have to endure one of her 'punishments' again.

"You know what? No. I'm going to speak up because I'm tired of how you treat me. I like myself the way I am. I know I'm not a very confident person right now because of things I've heard over the years. A lot of it I heard from *you* or overheard you talking about me. I know there will always be bullies and I'm trying to get better at handling them. I know that's something you're worried about for now and when I get older." Pausing, I narrow my eyes at her again, which has her visibly bristling.

"However, why can't you accept that, for the most part, I'm happy and just be happy *for* me? Why can't you support me? Instead, you constantly criticize every little thing I do and try to turn me into a mini you. I don't like the same styles of clothes you do or the things you eat. Other than reading and liking to paint my nails, we don't share any other likes or hobbies.

"You're always on me about my weight, saying things no mother should ever say to her daughter. The only thing I'm allowed to drink when **πατέρας** isn't home is water and absolutely no snacks. You make me eat one measly scrambled egg for breakfast and for lunch it's always small, disgusting, dry salads with no protein and no dressing.

"Why do you think I eat so much when **πατέρας** comes home for supper? You don't give me enough to keep me full. Probably not enough to keep *anyone* full, for that matter. Why do you think I've been having lightheaded spells all the time? And then when I do eat more at supper, you give me disapproving and disgusted looks as well as muttering under your breath about how I'm shoving so many calories into my mouth. You know that's the one meal you can't control what I eat because **πατέρας** is home, but if he has to work late? It's another small dry salad with no protein or dressing.

"Why can't you accept that I'll never be rail thin like you? If you can't accept me for me, then at least, take a lesson from **γιαγιά** (grandma) and don't say anything at all."

By the end of my rant, **πατέρα** face is redder than I've ever seen it before as he glares hard at Mom.

I know it's a cowardly thing to do, but I can't take any more arguing. Turning, I slip outside, shut the door, and jog across the street as I try to push the whole thing to the back of my mind.

Chapter 2
Luke

Ten years old

I frown when Mr. and Mrs. Catarino's backs turn to carry some boxes into their house.

Just going off first impressions, I already don't like Mary's mom. How she looks down her nose at Mary while wearing her sky-high heels, skinny jeans, and fancy-looking shirt. Not to mention her gaudy jewelry, of which she wears a lot of. Mr. Catarino is dressed in jeans and a t-shirt. He seems pretty cool and laid back so far.

My frown deepens when it sinks in that their clothes are so much nicer and newer than Mary's. Why doesn't she have nice clothes like theirs? Her gray t-shirt is so thin that we can almost perfectly see the white tank top underneath it.

Mary seems sweet with her heart-shaped face, bright blue eyes, long black curly hair and cute as heck black frame glasses. She did act sort of shy, but I don't know if that's how she normally is or if it's from moving to some place new. Yeah, she's a bit on the bigger side, but I'm guessing she took after her dad more. The guy looks like he could fill in for the Jolly Green Giant or would be an awesome basketball player if I hadn't seen him tripping over air a couple of times.

A tug on my t-shirt has me turning around and both Brady and Alli nod toward Alli's house. Both of them look concerned about something and I'm wondering if we are all thinking along the same lines. With one last look at Mary's house, all three of us cross the street again.

"Okay, I don't care what you two think, but I am making Mary one of my best friends. Based on her mom, I think she might need all the girl power she can get. I know we just met her, but I already don't like her mom," Alli says as she wrinkles her nose and crosses her arms. She juts her chin out at us, daring us to disagree with her.

I can't help my grin, but before I can say anything, Brady does.

"Agreed. She looks like she could use all the help in the world. Her dad seems cool, but her mom seems mean," he says as he shakes his head.

"Same. Besides how she talked about Mary, something just seems wrong with her. I mean, why wouldn't she want to let her daughter pick out her own room if this really is the first time she's been able to? Unless she's one of those self-centered spoiled moms like all the rich kids' moms at school."

They both nod in agreement.

"And if her mom's this unhappy with just a room decision, what else is she putting poor Mary through?" Alli asks as she looks over her shoulder, a worried expression on her face.

That thought has my gut twisting and the urge to protect her increases. Glancing over at Brady, I know he's feeling the same when he turns and gives me a look.

Brady and I have always been close. So close that if you didn't know he was my cousin, most people assume we're brothers. Heck, once someone even asked if we were twins since we always seem to know what the other is thinking and the fact that we look so much alike.

I'm about to say something when the door to Alli's house opens. Turning around, a smile forms when I see her mom, Meghan, coming out with a tray holding three lemonades and a plate of cookies.

"Here you go, kids. Let me know if you need any more to drink. It's going to be a scorcher today and I don't want any of you to get dehydrated," she tells us as she shoots a pointed look my way.

I squirm under her gaze because I'd done just that a month ago, though I hadn't done it on purpose, of course.

"Mom, can we get another glass and a few more cookies? I invited the new neighbor girl, Mary, over to play with us."

Meghan looks behind us toward the street and nods, but then frowns. "I'll be right back," she says quietly and I turn slightly, looking over my shoulder.

Mary's walking toward us, but her shoulders are slightly hunched, and it seems like she's curled in on herself some.

Alli bounds over to her, sliding her arm through Mary's. She looks up in shock, but then gives Alli a small smile.

"Mom just brought out some lemonade and cookies. Would you like some?" Alli asks her.

Mary chews on her lip nervously, looks over her shoulder, and then it's like she comes to some sort of decision. Turning back toward us, she nods, giving us a shy smile. "Yes, please."

Meghan comes out at that point with another glass of lemonade and a second plate of cookies. She sets them down and stands, smiling at Mary.

"Hello and welcome to the neighborhood. I'm Alli's mom, Meghan Thatcher."

Mary gives her a shy wave. "Hello and thank you. I'm Mary Catarino."

"Have some lemonade and some cookies, Dear. Let me know if you want more to drink. Like I was just telling the others, it's supposed to be a scorcher today and I don't want any of you to get dehydrated on me."

"T-thank you," Mary replies as she shyly reaches for a glass.

Not wanting her to feel like all the attention is focused on her, I reach for a glass, too, taking a large gulp of it. I sigh, feeling relief from the cool liquid as I set down my glass and pick up a cookie. The sound of a giggle has me turning toward Mary. She points to her lip, and then a few seconds later, Alli's giggling along with her.

I wipe my mouth, feeling lemonade on the top of my lip, and can't help my grin.

Their giggles seem to bring a light to Mary's eyes, which has a part of me angry that it wasn't there before. I'm surprised I'm feeling so protective of Mary after just meeting her, but then again, she does remind me a lot of Alli, both in personality and size. Though, Mary is a little bigger than Alli, not that that matters to any of us. However, in the past, both Brady and I have stood up to bullies on Alli's behalf. They had been bullying her because she was bigger than other girls our age.

A commotion and raised voices from across the street draw my attention, but I'm thankful Mary doesn't turn around or take notice of them. Instead, she grabs a cookie as she and Alli start talking.

I listen to my friends and cousin with half an ear but focus on watching Mr. and Mrs. Catarino across the street out of the corner of my eye. Mrs. Catarino is fuming as she hastily grabs things out of their car, stomping around in her insanely high heels and wildly gesturing with her free hand as they argue. I can't hear everything but from the sounds of it, Mr. Catarino is really angry about how Mrs. Catarino has been treating Mary and forcing an unhealthy diet on her in the hopes that she'll lose weight.

That has my anger rising. Chancing a look at Brady, I know he heard the same things I did, judging by the fierce look on his face.

Both my dad and Alli's dad work at the hospital in town. We've heard countless stories about accidents, patients they've saved, scenarios they've seen, and things like that. Though they don't mention anyone's name. My guess is for privacy or something.

However, there were a couple of their topics that always made me mad on the patient's behalf. Those that forced other people into doing what they want, like the parents of one of dad's patient—a kid who had developed an eating disorder because of comments the parents made about her weight.

Or another similar scenario where the patient's mother denied her food because in her mother's eye, she was too fat and she didn't need to eat as often as everyone else in the house did. The mother did it so much that her daughter's organs started shutting down and she eventually died. I heard from Uncle Sam that her mom was arrested shortly after the girl was admitted to the hospital. The dad had no idea what had been happening since he worked long hours, and I feel for him. Losing a child like that and that it was caused by someone he loved had to have done a pretty nasty number on him.

Another is where someone close to the patient was physically abusing them and had the patient lie about how they were hurt. Brady's dad, my uncle Sam, also had input on that from the law side since he's a cop. He's seen the abuse happen firsthand a number of times, as well as other things that send shivers down my spine.

Some may say our parents shouldn't be talking about such things with us, but all of our parents want us to be aware of our surroundings as well as the good, the bad, and the ugly that's in the world. There is no 'sweeping things under the carpet' in any of our households because it might be a hard or uncomfortable conversation. While all of our parents have taught us to accept ourselves for who we are, it was really our moms that drove that way of thinking and acceptance home. That no matter what color a person's skin is, what gender a person identifies as, who someone loves, what someone's size is, all will be accepted as guests into our home and as friends.

Our moms all work at the school here in town. Pre-k through seniors are all in one very large and multi-floored building. Alli and Brady's moms are teachers, and my mom is a counselor. Some may think that having a parent as a teacher or counselor can be awkward, and they are right, but it's kind of cool in a way as well. It also helps when we get stuck on a homework problem and they have a way of walking you through it to help you understand how to solve it. My mom loves to help kids discover what they're passionate about and give them a safe place if they are having trouble with something in their lives.

However, a side effect of having so many adult conversations with our parents means that we don't exactly act or think like many other kids our age sometimes. It's made it harder for us to relate to other kids and it keeps us somewhat separated from them at school. That and we talk and think about things differently than the other kids do. We notice more about what's going on around us because of what our parents have told us about in the past.

I shake off those thoughts and refocus on my friends and cousin.

"So, what kind of books do you like to read?

"Some of my favorites are *Black Beauty*, the *Black Stallion* series, *Little House on the Prairie*, the *Babysitter Club* series, and *Charlotte's Web*."

"Oh, those are some of my favorites, too!" Alli darn near squeals as she bounces up and down on her toes in excitement, her face lit up with a huge smile. I can see them both curling up together and reading in the near future.

"You both need to read *Goosebumps* and *Captain Underpants*," Brady tells them, rolling his eyes.

This has the girls giggling more, but then Mary nods. "I have, but I wasn't going to list all the types of books I like, and I didn't know if you and Luke read or not."

I nod along with Brady. "We do, but probably not as much as you girls. Though we both have a fair amount of comic books."

Alli squeals and hops up and down. "When you're all moved in, can I see what all books you have?"

Mary's cheeks heat, but she nods. "Yeah, as long as I get to see yours, too."

"Of course! What else do you like to do for fun?" Alli asks her.

Mary's cheeks heat a little more. Is she embarrassed? Or has someone made her embarrassed of her hobbies before?

"I like to draw and sing. Do puzzles and paint my nails. Things like that. What about you guys?"

"Luke and I love playing soccer, reading comic books, and playing video games."

"I'm more like you. Reading, puzzles, painting my nails. Sometimes I'll kick the ball around with the guys or play video games with them, but I'm usually sitting on the swing reading while they play," Alli says as she points to the large porch swing behind her.

Over the next couple of hours, we play, talk, and get to know each other better. We find out that Mary's in our grade, fifth grade, and that she's in the same class as all of us.

"You'll like Mrs. Eddington. She's really nice and hardly ever raises her voice," Alli says and Mary's shoulders relax, almost like a weight has been lifted off of her shoulders.

"I'm so relieved you guys are going to be in the same class as me. I was so worried I'd be the new kid, again, with no friends and immediately shunned by everyone."

I'm about to say something when I hear someone coming up behind me. Turning around, I see Mary's parents.

"**Κορίτσι μου** (My girl), care to introduce us to your new friends, her dad asks.

Huh. I wonder what those words mean? And what language is it?

Mary turns around in surprise and then scrambles to her feet, rushing to hug her dad.

"**Πατέρας** (Dad)! Guess what? Allison, but you can call her Alli, Brady, and Luke are all in the same class as me this year," she tells him excitedly as she points each of us out.

His smile widens, but for some reason, her mom's lips thin even more. "That's wonderful, **κορίτσι μου** (my girl)! Nice to meet you kids. I'm Nikolaos Catarino, but you can call me Nikos, and this is my wife, Eileen."

Mary's smile fades some. "Is it suppertime already? I want to hang out with my new friends some more."

Somehow, Nikos's smile grows even bigger. "Actually, while you were playing, Brett and Stephanie invited us over to their house for a barbeque to welcome us to the neighborhood."

I grin at that and the girls cheer before they start talking excitedly. I'm glad that my parents invited them over. Brady's parents, my Uncle Sam and Aunt Ellie, will be there along with Alli's parents, Curtis and Meghan Thatcher. Hopefully, all of our parents will be able to get along, because then we'll be able to hang out with Mary more.

Authors of the book titles mentioned in this chapter:
Black Beauty by Anna Sewell
The Black Stallion series by Walter Farley
The Little House on the Prairie series by Laura Ingalls Wilder
The Babysitter's Club series by Ann M. Martin
Charlotte's Web by E. B. White
Goosebumps by R. L. Stein
Captain Underpants by Dav Pilkey

Chapter 3

Mary

THE NEXT MORNING, I wake up eagerly and climb out of my sleeping bag. I'm using a small air mattress for my makeshift bed until the moving truck holding the rest of our stuff arrives today.

Digging through my bags, I pick out my nicest, but also comfiest clothes since I know from experience that I'll have to try everything on when we go shopping today. Once I'm dressed, I walk across the hall to the bathroom that, thankfully, is all mine unless we have guests. For the first time ever, we have more than one bathroom in our house. Which is good because Mom takes forever getting ready. Downstairs, there's also a half-bath, which is another bonus.

After doing my business, I wash my hands, brush my teeth and hair before tying up my hair into a ponytail. As I'm getting ready, my mind wanders to last night after we got home from the barbeque.

My parents had sat down with me and **πατέρα** (dad) told me that things were going to change from here on out.

For the better.

No more was Mom going to control my meals for me. If she tries to do it again, I'm supposed to tell him and he'll put an immediate stop to it. Mom looked like she wanted to spit nails at that, but I couldn't care less. Her 'nutritious' torture was finally going to stop.

I know Mom has it in her head that she's always supposed to look prim and proper and that she shouldn't have an ounce of fat on her. Something I'm almost positive Grandmother drilled into her since she was a kid, since Grandmother's the same way. But **πατέρα** (dad) said he wouldn't tolerate her treating me the same way. He also apologized repeatedly for ignoring or brushing off what I had tried to tell him about the meals in the past before I eventually gave up. He was almost in tears for how sorry he was for not listening to me or to my concerns.

Today, though, he said I'll be going shopping with **γιαγιά** (grandma) and that Mom would not be going. Wanting to spend some more time with my new friend, I had asked if Alli could come with us. After Dad talked with them, I couldn't contain my shriek of happiness when he said that both Alli and her mom, Meghan, would be able to join us.

Πατέρα (Dad) also said that since his new job pays so well, that I won't ever have to wear thrift-store clothes again unless I want to. So, this year, I'm getting all new clothes, shoes, and school supplies. To say that I was ecstatic would be an understatement. I'd never had anything new before, except for some of my books and maybe when I was a baby, but I'm not counting the last one. Once again, Mom had glared at him, but I didn't care. I'd finally be able to get the types of clothes that I wanted instead of wearing whatever she picked out for me.

Giving myself one more look over in the mirror once I'm done, I bound down the hallway and stairs, excited for what today will bring. Halfway down the steps, I grin when I see **πατέρας** (dad) in the kitchen and that he's cooking breakfast. Glancing around, I don't see Mom, so she's probably still upstairs 'primping'. I'm not sure what she all does, but it shouldn't take *that* long to get ready. Sometimes she's in the bathroom for an hour or more, which was extremely annoying when there was only one bathroom in the house.

"Morning, **πατέρας** (dad)."

He turns slightly and smiles brightly, but I can see the tightness around his eyes and my good mood fades a bit. Were they fighting again after I went to bed last night?

"Good morning, **κορίτσι μου** (my girl). Are you excited about today?"

I bounce on my toes in excitement and do a little twirl, my long hair fanning out around me. "Yes! I can't wait to introduce **γιαγιά** (grandma) to one of my new best friends! Meghan's also really cool and she made some really good homemade lemonade for us yesterday. I want to ask her how she made it so I can try and make it with **γιαγιά** (grandma)."

Last night, **πατέρα** had said that in addition to going with me today, **γιαγιά** (grandma) is also going to stay for supper tonight. After we're done shopping, we're going to go to the grocery store to get supplies for whatever we're cooking tonight. When I talked to her on the phone last night and had asked what meal we were going to cook, the only thing she'd tell me that it was going to be a surprise. I'm hoping it's a new recipe.

Πατέρας turns off the stove and dishes out some eggs and bacon onto a plate for me with some toast he's already made up. My mouth waters at being able to eat like this again, and I immediately dig in. He makes his own plate and sets the pan back down before pouring us both some orange juice.

"I've got the rest of the week off to settle into the house. Before we get everything put away in your room, I thought maybe we could go to the store tomorrow? Pick out some paint and maybe a few decorations? You can personalize it however you want. The guys even offered to help me paint it so we can get you settled in quicker."

"Seriously?" I ask, not believing what he's saying, and I'm sure my eyes are bugging out right about now.

I have never been able to decorate my own room before. Mom's always done that. If I hang anything up that she doesn't like, she'll take it down as soon as she sees it before destroying it and throwing the 'offensive' item away, her words not mine. Then I'd get at least an hour-long lecture on needing to be a prim and proper lady even if my body doesn't fit her image requirements.

The only things that she's 'allowed' are if a relative gives me something that goes on the wall or a shelf. Well, as long as it's in 'good taste'. There have been a few things that I've hidden in the back of my closet, hoping for a time in which I'll be able to put up whatever I want on my walls.

This all came out last night during our *very* long talk and to say **πατέρα** was furious was an understatement. He had no idea that Mom had been doing all of this behind his back.

Πατέρας chuckles, bringing me out of my thoughts, and I notice his smile widening. "Seriously. I know how much you hated all those white walls growing up—I wasn't fond of them either, but you know how Greek families are about wanting one color for the walls. I also hate that you were forced to have decorations you didn't want," he says, scowling before he shakes his head and continues. "We'll get your room all set up, so it's a sanctuary for you and so that you're ready for when school starts. I don't want you getting behind on your homework just because you can't find something you need for an assignment. You know how seriously I take your schoolwork."

Hopping down off the stool, I run around the counter and hug his waist tight, burying my face into his side. Well, as much as I can without ruining my glasses. "Thank you, **πατέρας**," I whisper.

He sets his fork down, grabs me under my arms and hoists me up, holding me tight. I wrap my arms around his neck and try my hardest not to cry. His large hand rubs up and down my back.

Heels click on the hardwood stairs, but I don't make any move to let him go. Mom sighs heavily, and I can't help but tense up. I can practically feel my body folding in on myself as I prepare for what I'm almost positive is going to be an uncomfortable conversation. I don't know if **πατέρας** can feel the change in me, but if he notices, he doesn't say anything.

"Mary, you're too big to be held like that. Get down and act your age," she says harshly, and then she sucks in a sharp breath. "What are you doing giving her carbs and fatty bacon? It was bad enough that she had all that red meat and those dinner rolls last night. At least she ate her vegetables, but they were covered with oil, so it probably negated all the positives."

Πατέρα (Dads) arms tighten around me and I worry about what's going to happen next. I've witnessed many of their fights over the years, and I've often wondered if they'll get a divorce. When I was over at Alli's house yesterday, I pretended not to hear them, but I heard everything they said when they were unloading the car. If they do get a divorce, I know Mom will fight tooth and nail to keep me, even though she can't stand the sight of me, just so she wouldn't have to pay **πατέρας** a nickel.

How do I know? I overheard her telling Grandmother those exact words. Confused as to what she had meant, I'd talked to **γιαγιά** about it. While I could tell she didn't want to talk about it, she did explain what a divorce meant and what Mom had meant. Hearing **γιαγιά** explain everything had made my heart break even more.

On top of that, ever since **πατέρα** got his new job which led to our move, their fights have been getting worse and worse. When they were looking for a new house, they argued constantly on which one to get. Before bed one night, I overheard **πατέρα** say that he was putting his foot down and told Mom that we were going to be getting this house and not whatever house she had wanted. That we didn't need anything that big because it was just the three of us. I never saw what house my mom had wanted, but if I were to guess based off comments she'd been making, it sounded a lot like my grandparents' house, which is what **πατέρα** had called a mini-mansion one time after visiting them.

That's another thing I've overheard her talking about on the phone with Grandmother. Well, two things—the house and the fighting, which eventually led to talks about divorce. They think they were being so secretive, only talking about those topics when **πατέρα** wasn't home, but they didn't pay any attention to me.

Like usual.

I heard everything they talked about since Mom never fully closed their bedroom door and always had the calls on speakerphone. Even if I was in my room with the door shut, I could hear everything they said since the walls were super thin in our last apartment.

Πατέρα (Dads) chest vibrates as he growls in frustration, which brings me out of my thoughts.

"Eileen, enough. We've had this discussion and you are no longer allowed to starve our daughter like you have been. Also, you will no longer decide every little aspect of her life. I can't believe you've been so controlling and manipulative to your own daughter. That ends now. If it doesn't, you won't like the consequences."

Mom huffs, looking down at her perfectly manicured fingernails. "If you're going to eat that trash, then do it quickly. I'm taking you shopping since your father thinks you need different stuff, even though it's a waste of money."

"Eileen," **πατέρας** hisses, but Mom just rolls her eyes at him and waves him off.

I can feel anger radiating off him and I squeeze my arms tighter around him, hoping to comfort him some like he comforted me. Pulling back, I frown up at her, relieved when **πατέρας** makes no move to lower me to the ground. I need his support right now and I think he knows that.

"I'm not going with you, I'm going shopping with **γιαγιά** (grandma), Alli, and Meghan today. If you were there, you would just try and force me into the clothes you want to see me in. I want shorts, leggings, jeans, t-shirts, tank tops, hoodies, tennis shoes, and flip-flops. I don't care about fancy, frilly and tacky things, dresses, or those kitten-like heels you try to force me into. That's not me."

Mom's scowl deepens, but **πατέρας** hugs me tight and kisses my cheek. I turn, looking at him and he reaches up, lightly grasping my chin.

"Then that's what you're going to get, **κορίτσι μου** (my girl). **Γιαγιά** (Grandma) has instructions on what is needed and I've sent her a copy of your school supply list. Now, it's your decision whether your mom goes with you or not. There's going to be no judgement from either of us on that," he pauses and levels Mom with a hard look. Once again, her lips press into a thin line, her eyes blazing as she glares daggers at him.

Πατέρας (Dad) turns back to me. "**Κορίτσι μου** (My girl), what do you want?"

Swallowing hard, my words are barely a whisper as I once again try not to cry. "I don't want her there. She'll just ruin it and make everything about her like she always does. She'll say mean things about me when I don't fit into the clothes she picks out. I want to have fun with my new best friend and if Mom's there, then it won't be fun."

Πατέρας (Dad) nods. "Then she won't be there. Besides, I could use the help here. Not to mention, it seems like I need to have another talk with your mother."

He's about to say more when the doorbell rings.

Turning, I see Alli peeking through the windows that are on either side of the door. I squirm in **πατέρα** (dads) arms. He lets me down and I run to the door.

"Alli!" I cry out as she shouts my name back and we immediately hug each other.

"I hope we're not too early?" Meghan asks as she walks in, smiling at us.

"I just have to finish eating my breakfast and then when **γιαγιά**, which means 'grandma', gets here, we'll be ready to go!"

Last night, I'd told Alli, Luke, and Brady about **πατέρα** (dads) side of the family at the barbeque and they were really interested in my big Greek family. They even asked me to teach them some Greek words.

"**Γιαγιά**, grandma. **Γιαγιά**, grandma," Alli repeats quietly and slowly. I smile, nodding when she pronounces it correctly.

Bounding back to the kitchen, I climb back up on my stool, ignoring Mom's sputtering as her and **πατέρα** talk quietly, and continue eating my food. Alli follows me and sits next to me, telling me about the shops that her mom usually takes her to. I'm so excited to get new clothes that I'm practically vibrating in my seat.

A few minutes later, I'm done and as I put my dishes in the sink, the doorbell rings again.

"**Μαμά** (Mom)," **πατέρα** (dads) voice echoes happily through the empty living room.

Seconds later, I can hear them having a short conversation in Greek, but I tune it out for right now. With an excited squeal, I snag Alli's hand and rush to meet **γιαγιά**, hugging her when she opens her arms for me.

"**Λουλούδι μου** (My flower), it's so good to see you. And who is this?" **γιαγιά** asks as I pull back.

"This is Allison, but you can call her Alli. She's one of my new best friends! She lives across the street from us. Later, I'll see if I can introduce you to Luke and Brady. They're cousins. Luke lives next door to us and Brady lives next door to Alli. Their parents are all friends too, and I got to meet them last night when they invited us over for a barbeque. Oh, and guess what? We're all going to be in the same class this year!"

Γιαγιάς (Grandmas) eyes soften as she smiles at me and then she beams up at **πατέρας**. "I'm happy you've already found friends," she says as she looks down at me and hugs me tightly again.

Then I notice her stiffen slightly, and I know she must have spotted Mom. They've never gotten along after my parents got married, but then again, that isn't much of a surprise. From what I've heard, Mom had fooled them all into believing she was someone she wasn't. After the wedding, Mom slowly revealed her true colors to everyone but **πατέρα** from what I've been told. From experiencing my own issues with Mom, I'm pretty sure they're right. However, I think **πατέρας** finally realizes what type of person she really is.

"Eileen," **γιαγιά** says politely but coldly. Though, her voice sounds colder than it usually is toward Mom. Did **πατέρας** talk to **γιαγιά** about what Mom has been doing? About their fights lately?

"Maria."

Γιαγιά looks down at me and smiles. "**Λουλούδι μου** (My flower), are you ready to go?"

"Yes! I can't wait," I reply, bouncing on my toes.

Laughing, she looks up at **πατέρας** and they have another quick conversation in Greek, but I pay them no mind. However, I do notice **πατέρα** giving **γιαγιά** what looks to be his credit card. Alli hugs me and with her excited chatter, I'm able to block out Mom and focus on just being happy for once.

"Okay, let's go dears," **γιαγιά** calls out. Alli and I run outside and into Meghan's SUV. When we talked last night to her, Meghan offered to drive since she knows some good stores to go to. With Alli being a similar size as me, though a bit smaller, she must know where to go to get clothes that would fit my body.

After buckling in, I glance back at my house and my smile fades when I see my parents yelling at each other through the living room window. I don't know how everything's going to go now that 'the wool is no longer pulled over his eyes' as **πατέρα** said last night. I just hope that whatever they decide, I want **πατέρα** and me to be happy. That and I pray that Mom doesn't get custody of me. Not that long ago, I'd given up on any true mother/daughter relationship with her. All of her harsh words and actions toward me have made it so that I no longer feel anything but anger and hate toward her.

"**Λουλούδι μου** (My flower), it will all be okay. You'll see," **γιαγιά** tells me and I give her a small smile in return, hoping she's right.

Chapter 4

Mary

One Week Later

Nervously, I sit beside Alli in the backseat of her mom's SUV. We're on our way to school for our first day, but that's not the only thing I'm nervous about.

Last week, when we got home from clothes shopping, Mom was nowhere to be found. **Πατέρα** (Dad) had sat me down along with **γιαγιά** (grandma) and told me that he and Mom were going to be getting a divorce. After we had left to go shopping, my parents got into a huge screaming match that lasted hours. He didn't tell me everything, but apparently between what happened the first day we arrived and that morning, he learned a lot about how she's been treating everyone the past few years. When his family would tell him about things she'd done or said, he hadn't wanted to believe them since he'd never witnessed it himself, so he had brushed off their concerns. However, he said that the things she said during their fight confirmed that his family had been right all along.

The fight finally ended when **πατέρα** (dad) gave Mom an ultimatum. That she either needed to change and be a loving and supportive mother and wife or to leave and never come back.

Without another word, she grabbed her purse and what she had brought with us in the car, called a car service, and went to her parent's house.

Πατέρα (Dad) said that as soon as she left the house, he called **παππού** (grandpa) Harris and asked him to draw up divorce papers for him. I hadn't known it, but this wasn't the first time **πατέρα** (dad) had talked to **παππού** (grandpa) about the papers, so it didn't take him long to get them done. Then later that afternoon, **πατέρα** (dad) asked me to repeat everything I'd already told him so that **παππού** (grandpa) would know as well. By the time I was done, I could almost imagine steam coming out of παπποὐ (grandpas) ears at how angry he was at how Mom had been treating me.

The papers were served to Mom the next day.

Παπποὐ (Grandpa) is a well-known lawyer in this area and from what my πατέρα (dad), γιαγιά (grandma), θείε και θείο (aunts and uncles) say, you never want to cross him on a good day, let alone in a courtroom.

The same day Mom was served the divorce papers, πατέρα and I went through every box we'd moved with the help of γιαγιά (grandma), παπποὐ (grandpa), and a few of my θείων (aunts). Everything of Mom's was boxed up and set aside for her in the garage. It helped that we were doing the unpacking of our things and then repacking Mom's things at the same time. There was less hassle, according to what my θείες (aunts) had said. The boxes and packing materials were already there, so there wasn't any need to dig out supplies or go and buy stuff. If we opened it up and saw it was all her 'gaudy shit', θεία (aunt) Selena's words not mine, it got rewrapped if πατέρα didn't want to fight for it. Though, I know from what πατέρα said, Mom will probably argue about some things that she might want or won't want him to have. Even if she doesn't want it herself.

According to παπποὐ, because of her trying to starve me to 'help' me lose weight and my lightheaded episodes, Mom isn't allowed anywhere near me and isn't allowed to step foot in our house. Though, πατέρα and παπποὐ made one exception in that she can come and pick up her stuff, but that she couldn't enter the house. It also had to be supervised, so Brady's dad, Sam, came over since he's a cop.

Πατέρα (Dad) ended up getting a restraining order against her because of what she'd done to me and the things she'd said during their fight. He wouldn't tell me what she had said, but θεία (aunt) Catherine said it must have been bad if παπποὐ advised him to get the restraining order.

Unfortunately for Mom, that means she can't keep the job she just got at the school, since that's where I'm enrolled. I feel guilty about that part, but if things were as bad as πατέρα and παπποὐ said, then I'm not sure I want to be around her at school. I don't know what she'd try, especially with not knowing what she threatened to do.

As for our house, I didn't know it, but it's only in **πατέρα** (dads) name. Not both of theirs, which **θεία** (aunt) Sofia says is how it's usually done with married couples. Apparently, **παππού** advised him to only put his name on the paperwork since he qualified for the house loan on just his income alone. Because of that, Mom has no claim to it. Or his car. Her car had been brought up along with the moving truck, and even though Dad paid for most of it, he said he wouldn't fight her for it. Since hearing that the house and car were only in **πατέρα** (dads) name, I've often wondered if **πατέρα** had suspected that things might go south in the near future.

Shaking my head, my mind wanders to a couple of days later and how things changed after Mom left with the last of her things. It was calmer for **πατέρα** and me, but I know he misses her. Or at least, the woman he thought she was. I've overheard him crying each night about her. Asking what or where he'd gone wrong? How did he not see who she really was sooner? Why did he marry her?

After one really bad night, I shuffled downstairs for breakfast, and noticed **πατέρα** (dads) red-rimmed eyes, which probably matched my own.

*"***Πατέρας** *(Dad)? Do you... Do you regret having me with Mom?"*

Instantly he shut off the stove and a few seconds later, I was wrapped tightly in his arms. After a few moments, he leaned back and brushed my hair out of my face. "Never. You are the one decision I will never regret. I'm guessing you heard me talking to myself last night, huh?"

Sniffling, I nodded.

*"***Κορίτσι μου** *(My girl), I'm sorry that you thought I regretted having you. No, what I regret is that I didn't see through your mom's act sooner. I could have saved you a lot of heartache if I had. The only thing I'll thank her for is giving me you."*

I wrapped my arms tightly around his neck and we held each other as we both cried.

After that, things got better for both **πατέρα** and me. I know he still has moments where he still questions himself and Mom, but I think he tries to hide them when they happen. If I do happen to see him breaking down, or hear it, I don't mention it.

Γιαγιά (Grandma) stayed with us for a few days and was happier than I'd seen her in a long time. However, I think a part of that is because **πατέρα** had asked her if she could set up the kitchen like how she used to have hers. I had thought our kitchen was similar to hers when I first saw it, but he confirmed it and said that was part of the reason why he chose this place.

Πατέρα (Dad) said that he had always loved how easily it was to move around **γιαγιάς** (grandmas) kitchen when he used to cook with her. With how important food is to them, **γιαγιά** (grandma) was beyond pleased to help set up our kitchen and help stock whatever we needed. Well, after hugging **πατέρα** for a long time and making him bend down so she could pepper his face with kisses. I giggled a lot at that, which turned into a bigger giggling fit when **γιαγιά** skirted around the island and did the same to me.

While **πατέρα** set up his office that was off the living room, **γιαγιά** and I worked in the kitchen. One thing I like about his office is that if the French doors are open, you're able to see almost all of the living room and kitchen. Something **πατέρα** took advantage of while we all worked so he could easily check in on us or we could ask each other questions about where to put stuff.

Πατέρα (Dad) had only closed the French doors once since we moved in and **γιαγιά** told me it was because he had to call the HR person at his new job to notify them that my parents are getting a divorce and that Mom will soon be off his insurance. Not to mention let them know that he was now a single parent, but that he had a support system in place for when they were at their peak during tax season or if illness hit.

It took a while, but by Saturday, we were all unpacked and settled in. **Πατέρα** (Dad) and I hung out together this past weekend, and I enjoyed having him home and to myself. We didn't have to worry about Mom ruining our movie marathon with complaints about both of us eating popcorn with extra butter on it or that our choices in movies were boring or childish. Or that we ordered takeout pizza so we could keep watching the movie instead of stopping to cook.

"We're here," Meghan says in a sing-songy voice, and I shake my head, pushing those thoughts away for now.

Seeing the school in front of me brings back all those first day jitters to the forefront as Meghan pulls into a parking space. Since she and Ellie are teachers here, they brought us kids in over the weekend so that I could get a feel for the school and where things were. Also, for where their classrooms are for if I ever needed one of them. Since Stephanie wasn't able to join us, they showed me where her counselor's office was as well.

Alli reaches over and slips her hand in mine, squeezing it slightly. "Don't worry, everything's going to be okay. You've got me, Luke, and Brady on your side. You aren't alone."

I nod, giving her a small smile even though I'm still worried about what the other kids will say about me. I look better than I ever have in the past with my new clothes, new sneakers, new supplies, and new, durable backpack that isn't duct taped or sewn back together repeatedly.

Climbing out of the SUV, I hoist my heavy backpack onto my shoulders. I had missed the school supply drop off date, so I have to carry all of my supplies in with me.

Meghan heads inside to get her classroom ready, and Alli and I sit on a bench outside chatting until they open the doors to the students. I haven't seen Luke or Brady yet, but maybe they're with their moms in their classroom or office.

Once we're allowed into the school, Alli guides me through the halls. Even though I'd recently walked the halls, I was still forgetting some stuff. When we reach our class' cubby area for our coats and bags, we hang our stuff up, and I rehoist my backpack onto my shoulders as I follow her into our classroom.

Luke and Brady both wave when we come in, and I wave back before walking toward Mrs. Eddington's desk with my bag of required tissues and a few other things. She's got light blond hair that's got a fair amount of white in it that's pinned into a bun at the back of her head. Her smile grows as I approach her, and I think my friends may have been right. She seems like a really nice teacher.

"Um, hello Mrs. Eddington. I'm Mary Catarino and I'm new here. I missed the supply drop off date, but here are the things you asked for on the list."

She smiles again at me and nods, taking the bag from me. "Thank you, Dear, and welcome to Forest Creek. I'll get these put away." She pauses and nods to Alli, who's still standing by my side. "I see you've already made a friend. Did you by chance show her where the class' cubby area is, Alli?"

Alli nods her head, her ponytail bouncing at the action. "Yes, Mrs. Eddington."

"Thank you, Dear. Now, how about you both take your seats? Class doesn't start for a few more minutes, so that should give you enough time to put your things inside your desk, Mary. Don't worry about your backpack. You can take it to the cubby area when it's time for recess."

I give her a genuine smile, glad to have a few minutes to set things up rather than digging through my bag all morning. "Thank you, Mrs. Eddington."

She nods and gets up, going to a cupboard in the back of the room. I look around for my name tag and sigh inwardly. Apparently, Mrs. Eddington had set us up in alphabetical order by our last names, so I'm right in the front row. I notice that the others are more toward the back of the room.

I plaster a smile on my face, hoping it covers my nerves, as I walk to my desk and start putting my things away. Luckily, I finish right as the bell rings.

The morning goes really well, and I can confidently say that I love my teacher! Morning recess was fun and I spent it playing with Alli, Luke, and Brady. No surprise there. I can't believe how fast I've become comfortable around them, but I wouldn't change a thing.

We're standing in the lunch line, and I just grabbed my tray of food and am about to head to a table when I feel like someone's watching me. I look around, but no one is staring at me that I can notice.

"What's your fat ass doing here?" a voice sneers from behind me.

Confused that a kid would curse in school, I turn around to see who it is and who they are talking to, and immediately wish I hadn't.

It's my cousin, Isaac.

My good mood instantly vanishes. I had completely forgotten that him and a few of my other cousins on Mom's side of the family go to this school.

My stomach tightens as my heart sinks. Out of all the cousins on my mom's side, Isaac is the worst. He's a downright bully, and he isn't afraid to hurt people. Something I know from personal experience. I just pray that being at school will prevent him from hurting me. Physically, at least.

I hold my head up high, hoping that none of my nerves are showing. "We moved here and I go to school here now."

"Your pathetic, wussy-assed dad should have left to head back to Iowa and taken you with him last week after what happened. I don't know why Aunt Eileen shunned the family business to marry that low life in the first place."

What? Family business? What's he talking about?

Shaking my head, I put those thoughts out of my mind for the moment. "Whether you like it or not, we aren't leaving. **Πατέρας** (Dad) and I like it here, so if you don't like it, tough. Nobody said you had to come over here and talk to me."

Apparently, that was the wrong thing to say. His face turns red, and he pushes me, trying to knock me down. He's only a little over a year older than me, but he's always been stronger than me.

Arms wrap around me, catching me while someone else takes the tray out of my hands before my food or drink can spill on me or the floor.

"Back off, Isaac," Luke says in a hard voice that sends a chill down my spine. I look up at him, realizing it was him that caught me, but he doesn't take his eyes off Isaac.

Refocusing on Isaac, he shrinks back at the sight of Luke standing at my back before straightening. "Ah, so the fat-ass has found some poor old shmuck to back her up, huh?" he pauses and then smirks at me. "This isn't over, bitch. I'll make your life a living hell if you stick around here."

He turns around to leave, but his steps falter when he sees an adult standing behind him, arms crossed and staring down at him. My focus had been entirely on Isaac, so I hadn't even seen him approach.

"Starting fights on the first day of school, eh, Isaac? Well, how about we go into the office to have a little chat? I think a phone call to your parents is in order." The man pauses and looks past Isaac toward me, his eyes softening slightly. "You must be Mary. We only have a handful of new students this year, but you're the only girl among them, so it's a little easier for me to remember your name. I'm the elementary principal, Mr. Reese. I had approached you to welcome you to Forest Creek and overheard everything."

My cheeks heat in embarrassment and he gives me a small smile, though I do notice a lot of kids watching us, which makes my cheeks heat even more.

"No worries, Mary. You aren't in any trouble. However, I will need to let your father know about what has happened. Now, if you will excuse young Isaac and me, we need to have a little chat."

Mr. Reese places a hand on Isaac's shoulder, and carts him off, all while Isaac is sputtering about how it should be me in trouble and not him.

When he's out of sight, my body sags as my limbs start to tremble. My mind starts reeling as memories from the last time I saw Isaac bombard me.

"Crap, Mary!" Luke curses, and then he guides me to a nearby chair. Immediately, Brady and Alli are also by my side.

"Talk to us, Mary," Brady says softly.

"He's my cousin on my mom's side. He and his parents are mean, but thankfully we don't see them often. Well, at least before. Last year, Isaac was picking on me at a family gathering at my aunt's place and pushed me off the play set that was in the backyard. I fell and broke my arm.

"Isaac told them that I had been the one instigating everything and that he pushed me to get me off him. No one believed me when I told them my version of what happened except for my uncle Mateo, who had said he'd seen the whole thing. Aside from Isaac's father, Uncle Carlos, talking to him, he didn't get punished for what he'd done.

"Later, I'd overheard Uncle Carlos and Uncle Diego telling Isaac that if he's going to pull a stunt like that to make sure no one's around to rat on him. Then they both gave him pointers on what he should have done instead. Out of all my family on my mom's side, Grandmother, Mom, Uncle Diego, Uncle Carlos, his wife Gianna, and Isaac are the ones that treat me the worst."

All three of them get angrier, but then they surprise me by wrapping me in a hug.

"No one's going to get to you with us around," Luke says, and the others voice their agreement.

I don't know what I did to deserve friends that are so supportive, but I'm thanking all my lucky stars that I met these three last week.

A few hours later, I'm playing with the others on the playground during the last recess of the day when the kids around us go quiet. Looking around at them, I'm confused until I turn around and see a group of kids approaching us. They look a year or so older than us.

"Well, well, well. What do we have here?" a boy says, who appears to be the 'leader' of their group.

"Looks like the three freaks have added a fat blob as a fourth freak," another boy sneers.

The others step closer to me, but I'm frozen in shock by their words. After a few moments, I shake it off and look at them closer. They're calling me fat? Three of the seven kids in front of me are bigger than I am, including the leader. And I'm not trying to say that to be mean.

The two girls with them look down their noses at me in the way that only a spoiled rich girl can. "You're just a waste of space and air. You're so pathetic that you can't do anything right. It's no wonder your mother gave up on you and left you and that worthless lump she married, but at least she's back where she belongs now."

My heart breaks at that, and it's then that I know Isaac must have set these kids on me. It already hurts enough to know that Mom's love for me faded once I started taking after **πατέρα** more and more in the looks and personality departments as the years went on.

I've seen the pictures. When I was a baby, I was slightly chubby, but as a toddler, I'd lost the baby weight and was thin, like Mom. In the pictures, Mom had truly seemed happy at that point. You could see it in her eyes. But somewhere between ages four and five, the weight started coming back on, even though I was still pretty active. The number of pictures of me thinned, and when Mom and I were in the same picture, her smile never met her eyes.

Internally, I shake myself. Mom must have gone back to her parent's house and cried that it's all our fault rather than taking the blame for what she's done.

"Well, at least I don't have to suffer her poison anymore. However, I'm guessing that your parents are still pouring their poison into your ears, judging by how you're acting."

One of the girls visibly recoils at that, but then her eyes narrow at me along with the others.

"And what would you know? You're nothing. Not a blimp on anyone's radar. You think these three want to hang out with the fat-ass nobody that got cut off? You're delusional. They just feel sorry for you and that's all you'll ever get in life. Pity," the other girl says.

"You're better off killing yourself to save yourself the heartache. You're a fat-ass and that's all you'll ever be. A nobody that everyone pities," one of the boys responds with a sneer.

"You're wrong," Brady says beside me. "Mary isn't a waste of space, and she isn't a fat-ass. She has friends. *Real* friends."

"If you haven't looked at your so-called friends, three of you are even heavier than Mary. What? You think that it's okay to act like you are just because you three are spoiled rich boys? You're all hypocritical jerks," Alli says as she takes my hand and squeezes it.

"A person's size does not define them, even if you've all been brainwashed into believing that. It's their heart that matters, but I'm pretty sure yours are all raisins, since you're acting like little puppets for Isaac and your rich parents. Go back to your caviar and fancy cars. We don't need your filth around here," Luke says from behind me as he places a hand on my shoulder, squeezing it slightly.

The lead kid scoffs. "You think you're so special cause your dad is a doctor? You'll regret talking to us like this."

"No, we won't, William, but you might. You think you can rule the school just because your daddy is one of the richest men in town. He didn't earn his wealth; it was handed to him. He never had to work a day in his life, and it shows. Listen good, you little puppets. Mary is with us, and we won't tolerate you picking on her like this. Or do you want a repeat of kindergarten?" Luke asks him.

The boy who I now know is William pales significantly, but he quickly masks it. "We'll see about that," he says with his nose in the air before turning and walking away. His groupies soon do the same.

My body sags slightly when they are further away and Alli wraps me in a hug.

Looking over my shoulder, both Brady and Luke are still watching the other group retreat.

"Um, what happened in kindergarten?" I ask, and then Alli's body shakes against mine with her giggles.

She pulls back and wipes at her eyes. "They decided to make me their target that year because I was bigger than all the other girls. Luke, Brady, and I have been friends since we were in diapers. They stood up for me and Luke got into William's face, telling him to back off. William got so scared; he peed his pants in front of the whole grade at recess."

"So, they're also in fifth grade? They look older than us."

Brady nods. "Yeah, they are. It's just how they're made up that makes them seem older than they are. All their parents run in the same circle, so they've also known each other since they were babies."

"Unfortunately, I don't think we've seen the last of their nastiness, but don't worry, Mary. We've got your back and we won't let them hurt you," Luke says as he looks straight into my eyes.

Something in his eyes makes me believe him and for once, I finally feel like I belong.

Truly belong.

Chapter 5
Luke

Seven Years Later

Taking a deep breath, I knock on Mary's door. As I wait, I pull at my suit collar, uncomfortable as heck, but it's a necessary evil since tonight is our homecoming dance.

The door opens and Nikos smiles at me. "Come in, Luke. Mary said she's almost ready."

I step into their living room and stand awkwardly as I look around. I can see elements of Mary everywhere. She loves art and her dad has several pieces, both hers and ones they bought, on display throughout the house. Not to mention, their house is now full of color, which is surprising because normally, Greeks stick to one color on the wall. However, I suspect that Nikos did it for Mary, despite what his culture norms. That had happened in the weeks after they moved in and they practically erased all the white walls in the house. Though they did start preparations on a big garden in their backyard. I quickly learned that Greeks like to grow their own food as well as canning as much as possible come harvest time.

"Hello, Luke. My, you look handsome," **γιαγιά** (grandma) Maria says as she air kisses my cheek so that her lipstick won't rub off on me. Normally, I get a full kiss on the cheek and I'm glad she didn't do that tonight.

"Thank you, **γιαγιά** (grandma)."

She beams up at me, her eyes watering slightly. Brady, Alli, and I took to calling her 'Grandma' years ago, but she still gets worked up about it at certain events like this.

"Would you like anything to drink?" Nikos asks me, and I shake my head.

"Thank you, but no, I'm good."

It's then that I hear heels on the stairs, and I turn around.

Mary comes into view, and I swear my mouth drops and my heart stops beating.

She's wearing a strapless teal dress that has a corset-like top. The bottom of her dress is flowy, with some sort of sheer fabric overtop the silky-looking base layer. Her long black hair is half-pulled back with a few strands loose around her face, with the rest of her curls flowing down her back.

"Mary..." I pause, swallowing thickly. "You look gorgeous."

She blushes as she carefully descends the stairs in her heels. Last week I had heard her tell Alli that she's been practicing with them since she never wears heels. I wish she would wear them more often. I've seen her practicing, and the combination of her in the heels and her skinny jeans... Fuck, do they make her legs and ass look gorgeous.

"Thank you. You look rather handsome yourself."

I'm in a black tux with a white shirt, a teal waistcoat that matches her dress, shiny black shoes, and a pocket square that also matches the color of her dress.

When she steps into the living room, I nervously open the container holding her corsage and slide it over her bare wrist since she has a bracelet on her other one. She takes mine out of the container and pins it on my lapel, smoothing it down with her hands before looking up at me.

Fuck, with the way she's looking at me, I wish we were alone so I could kiss the shit out of her. We've been going out for the past two years, finally taking that step from friends to lovers.

"Well, turn around, you two. Let us take some pictures," **γιαγιά** (grandma) says excitedly.

We pose for a few pictures inside and then go outside to pose for a few more by the limo we rented. Once Nikos and **γιαγιά** (grandma) realize that Brady and Alli are also ready, and that their parents are also taking pictures of them near the limo, we pose for even more pictures with them and their dates. Brady's date is our friend, Angelina, or Lina as she likes to be called. Alli asked another one of our friends, Sean, to be her date.

Finally, we're released from taking pictures and we climb into the limo to head to the school.

A few hours later, I'm barely able to contain myself. Not to mention it's getting harder to hide my erection. I press a chaste kiss to Mary's lips as we slow dance, just quick enough so that hopefully none of the frickin' teachers jump on us, but enough to sate me a little longer.

I was wrong. So wrong.

That kiss just fanned my desire for her even higher.

"Want to get out of here, Siren?" I ask her, using my nickname for her that's a nod to her beautiful singing voice.

She shivers and goosebumps erupt across her skin. She looks up at me from beneath her long lashes as she flushes. "God, yes. Please, Luke."

As the song ends, I guide her out of the gymnasium and out into the cool fall air. She shivers again, this time from the cold, and I shrug off my jacket, draping it over her shoulders before guiding her to my car that I'd left here earlier today.

Half an hour later, I pull up at the hotel room that I'd rented in the next town over, hoping that we can keep our night a secret from our friends and family. Shutting the car off, I turn to her, threading my fingers through hers. "Are you sure you still want to do this, Mary?"

She flushes again and nods. "Yes. I've been looking forward to this ever since we decided to take the next step."

Grinning, I lean forward to kiss her, but she presses a manicured finger against my lips. "Once we're inside. You'll mess up my lipstick if you kiss me now and I don't want to go in there with it smeared all over."

A growl escapes. "Sexy little minx," I grumble and she just grins that sexy little grin of hers.

Getting out of the car, I walk around and open her door, offering her my hand. She takes it and after shutting the door, I grab our bags out of the trunk.

Within minutes, I've got the hotel key and unlock our door. I step aside to let Mary in first, and when I close the door behind us, I flip the lock, and then spin her so that her back's against the wall and my lips crash down on hers.

I press into her and she gasps when she feels how hard I am for her.

For months now, we've been doing a lot of heavy petting as we make out, and I'm about to burst at being so close to claiming my girl.

She moans into my mouth, and after a few moments, I pull back, kissing down her neck to her gorgeous cleavage.

"You've been fucking teasing me with these beauties all night, Siren."

Mary whimpers as I trace my tongue along her cleavage and along the edge of her strapless dress.

"Luke."

Fuck, her breathy moan and my name on her lips turn me on even more.

My girl is fucking gorgeous, and I love *all* of her curves. She's still heavier than most of the girls in our school, but I don't care. So, what if she wears size sixteen or eighteen jeans that make her ass look incredible, her thighs are juicy, her stomach is rounded, and she wears a 42C bra? That's just more for me to love. And fuck, do I love this woman. Also, I know her sizes because I've looked at her tags. Mary has a quirky sense of taste and loves humorous t-shirts, so I needed to know what size to get her whenever I found one.

"God, you're so sexy, Baby. I have to get you out of this dress. I need to worship you."

She whimpers again and then turns, lifting her hair up off her shoulders. I find the hidden zipper and lower it down, biting my lip when I see her wearing a white corset beneath it, white silk panties, and I nearly swallow my tongue when she steps out of her dress.

Fuck me... she's wearing a garter belt hooked to sheer stockings.

Mary shyly smiles, but I can tell that she's relieved at my reaction. "I thought you might like them."

"Like them, Siren? I love them. You look so fucking sexy in them."

My eyes rake up and down her gorgeous curves before meeting her eyes. "On the bed, Siren."

Not taking my eyes off hers, I lay her dress over a chair and I'm surprised when she pouts.

"Nuh-huh, Mister. You're wearing way too much clothing for me to already lay down. Now it's your turn."

Her hands slide up my chest as she reaches for my tie. She loosens the knot and tosses it on the nightstand. Next, her hands nimbly unbutton my waistcoat and then my shirt before sliding it off my shoulders and tossing them on top of her dress.

Looking into my eyes, she goes to her knees and slips off my socks and shoes, setting them aside. Her hands glide up my legs and a moan escapes me when she cups my length through the slacks.

"I think we need to relieve a little pressure before we get to the main event," she purrs and reaches for my belt.

I wrap my hand gently around her wrist, stopping her. A part of me is worried because she hasn't done that yet and I don't want her to feel pressured to do it. "Are you sure, Mary? You don't have to. I can jerk off and paint your gorgeous body with my cum instead."

"I want to try, Luke. I want to please you and make you feel good."

I've never been able to say no to her, and fuck, with that look in her eyes, I can't bring myself to say it now. Nodding, I release her hand, and she undoes my belt and unzips my pants. I quickly step out of them, taking my boxers with them and she licks her lips as her gaze roams over me, her eyes darkening with lust.

One of her hands grip my hip and with her other hand, she reaches out and wraps her fingers around my length. At her hot touch, a hiss slips past my lips and I can't help tilting my hips, which has my cock sliding through her hand. A bead of precum oozes out the tip and she tentatively licks it off, humming when it hits her tongue.

"Fuck, Mary," I damn near yell when she suddenly takes me in her hot mouth. I reach out, resting one hand against the dresser to steady myself as my other hand goes to her head, my fingers threading through her hair.

She bobs her head as her hand pumps my base. Every now and then I feel a little scrape of her teeth, but I can't bring myself to care. She feels too good.

A strangled noise comes out of me when she sucks harder and she hums as her other hand lowers, teasing herself.

"Fuck, you're so hot, taking me like this and teasing yourself. Work that clit, Siren. Get yourself nice and wet for me. I can't wait to lick your pussy."

She hums again and I give a tentative thrust in her mouth. She stills and lets me fuck her mouth. When she gags, I pull back slightly, but keep thrusting since she doesn't stop me. Her eyes water and I wipe them away with my thumb.

"I'm so close, Mary. If you don't want to swallow, you need to tap my leg or pull back."

Mary tightens her grip and when I go deeper in her throat, she frickin' swallows.

"Fuuuuck..." The action tips me over and has me cuming down her throat.

When my dick finally stops twitching, she licks me clean and I'm already back to a semi.

Looking down at her, I smirk. "On the bed, Siren."

She quickly stands and throws off the comforter and sheets before sitting on the edge. She reaches down to undo the buckle of her heels, but I stop her.

"Nope. I want you to wear them when I claim my woman."

Her eyes sparkle and she leans back, putting a pillow under her head. Leaning over her, I kiss her, not caring that I can taste myself on her.

I nip her lip and kiss down her throat, sucking on that spot at the base of her neck that she loves.

"Luke," she moans, as I make my way down her chest.

"Time to take this off so I can tease your gorgeous tits."

My fingers go to unhook the buttons down the front of her corset, but she pushes my hands out of the way. "Your fingers are probably going to be too big for these little hoops and buttons and I don't want to break them. I hope to wear this again someday," she says with a wink, and fuck, I'm back to being fully hard again at the image.

Her fingers start to undo the buttons at the top, but I'm impatient. My hands go to the bottom and start unhooking them, but she's right. I only get a few undone before she catches up to me.

She sits up and I pull the corset out from under her and immediately latch onto a nipple while my fingers tweak her other one.

"Luke!" she cries out, her hands going to my head to keep me where I am. She fucking loves having her nipples played with, it makes her so wet.

After a few minutes of playing with her nipples, I kiss my way down her stomach and take my first lick of her pussy, humming when her juices hit my tongue.

"Fuck, I love the way you taste," I growl out before devouring her.

I wring out three orgasms from her before I pull back and slide on a condom.

Crawling back over her, I kiss her and love when her hands slide through my hair.

"Are you sure you want to keep going, Mary? We can stop here or I can go back to wringing out as many orgasms from you as your body will allow."

A shiver works through her, and then her arms tighten around me.

"Claim me as yours, Luke."

Notching myself at her entrance, I slowly slide in, giving her time to adjust to me.

When I reach her barrier, I lean down, kissing her. "You ready, Mary?"

I know I'm checking in with her a lot, but fuck, am I going to hate this next bit. I hate causing Mary any sort of pain.

She takes a deep breath and nods, pulling me back down for a kiss. Keeping my eyes open as I kiss her, I reach down, tweaking her nipple and she moans deeply into my mouth. When I feel her body melt against mine even further, I quickly thrust, breaking through her barrier and fully seating myself in her.

Tears prick her eyes, and I brush them away when they roll down her face.

"I'm sorry, Mary, but from here on out, it'll be good."

Even though it kills me, I don't move, waiting for her to tell me it's okay to move.

After a few moments, she rolls her hips, and I pull back before slowly thrusting back in. Gradually, I increase my pace.

"Oh, my God. You're so big. I love how you feel inside me."

My chest warms and I lean down, kissing her. "You feel fucking fantastic. So tight and squeezing me like a vice. I'm not going to last long this first time, but I'll make it up to you next round."

Her hands claw at my back. "Harder, please."

Leaning up on my hands, I quicken my pace and go deeper.

"L-Luke!" she cries out a few moments later, and she clamps down hard on me, taking me over the edge with her.

My arms shake, and I almost collapse onto my elbows, but I try to keep most of my weight off Mary so I don't crush her. I capture her lips, and we lay there for a few moments, just kissing as the tremors leave our bodies.

Reluctantly, I pull back to take care of the condom. "Be right back."

Tying off the condom, I toss it in the bathroom trash and wet a washcloth. I should have brought some from home, not thinking about this step, but oh well. Quickly, I clean up Mary and then myself before pulling the blankets up around us. Mary rolls over, resting her head on my shoulder and I wrap my arm around her.

"I love you, Mary."

She looks up at me, a look of pure happiness on her face and I see her love shining back at me through her eyes. She kisses my chest and looks back up into my eyes. "I love you, too, Luke."

Chapter 6

Mary

LAYING IN LUKE'S ARMS, I'm fighting off sleep after we made love another couple of times. It's nearing eleven o'clock, but I don't want to sleep. I want to stay in Luke's arms. To not go back to the real world.

Unfortunately, right as my eyes close, my phone rings. Groaning, I roll over and grab my phone off the nightstand, getting nervous when I see who's calling.

"Shit, it's my **πατέρα** (dad)."

Luke's arms tighten around me as I answer it.

"Hey, **πατέρας** (dad*),"* I say, hoping my voice doesn't sound too nervous.

"Hey, **κορίτσι μου** (my girl)*."*

I frown at hearing the hesitant tone in *his* voice. Casting a nervous look at Luke, I sit up. I very rarely hear my dad nervous. *"What's wrong?"*

He sighs and my heart drops as I clutch the blanket to my chest, balling it up in my fist.

"I debated calling you at all, but after talking to **μαμά** (mom) *and the others, I decided I'd rather have you hear the news from me before you hear it from someone else."*

*"***Πατέρας** *(*Dad*), you're scaring me. What's wrong? What happened?"*

Luke sits up and tightens his arms around me. Glancing up at him, his gaze locks with mine, and I know whatever it is, he'll be by my side to help me through it.

Πατέρας (Dad) sighs again. *"There's been a really bad car accident in town. Your mother was one of the victims."*

Even though I've rarely had contact with Mom over the years because she's refused to accept me for who I am, I still didn't want her to die. A tear escapes at knowing there will never be any more chances for her to be in my life.

"You said one of the victims. Were there more?"

He clears his throat and my heart sinks to my stomach. *"There were two other cars. One was an elderly couple. The wife lived, but the husband didn't. The other car..."* He pauses again, taking a deep breath. *"Sam and Ellie were in it. They're both alive, but really banged up. I'm at the hospital with them."*

I toss off the blankets and make a beeline for my duffel bag, throwing on clothes. Luke must have heard what **πατέρα** (dad) said because he's doing the same.

"We'll be there soon. Is Brady already there? Alli? Curtis and Meghan? Brett and Stephanie?"

"The parents are all here. They're on the phone right now with Alli and Brady."

"Okay. We'll be there soon. ***Σ' αγαπώ*** *(*I love you*),* ***πατέρας*** *(*dad*)."* I bite my lip to keep it from trembling and crying.

He takes a shaky breath. "**Κορίτσι μου** (My girl), **κι εγώ σ' αγαπώ** (I love you, too). *See you in a bit."*

Hanging up, I toss my phone on the bed and finish pulling my clothes on.

As soon as they're on, Luke wraps me in a hug. "They'll pull through, Mary. Both of them are tougher than nails."

Numbly, I nod as I gather everything, making sure neither of us leave anything behind and within minutes, we're in Luke's car, speeding back toward Forest Creek.

Twenty minutes later, Luke and I burst through the doors of the hospital and I head straight to **πατέρας** (dad). He wraps me tightly in a hug.

Pulling back, I wipe my tears and then I'm wrapped in Alli's arms.

"I know you didn't get along, but I'm sorry about your mom, Mary."

My throat tightens and I squeeze her back harder.

"What are you doing here?" a familiar voice seethes from behind me.

Turning around, my already numb heart shrinks from the hatred on Brady's face. My best friend's face. Hatred that is directed at me.

"What? Why wouldn't I be here? Sam and Ellie are hurt." Though, I purposefully make no mention of my mom. That box I'll unpack later when I'm home alone.

"You're not wanted here," he says as he looks down at me, his lip curling slightly.

"Brady! Your attitude is uncalled for. Mary wasn't the one that caused the accident," Meghan chides him.

Luke wraps an arm around my shoulders and it's only then that I realize I'm trembling.

"I don't care. Her mother," he says, spitting the word, "almost killed my parents because of Dad standing up against her family's business."

"Brady," Stephanie, Luke's mom, chides him again.

"But you're my best friend. I want to be here for you and your parents," I whisper, my heart breaking even more when the hatred in his eyes intensifies.

"Not anymore. Leave. All of you." Then he turns on his heel, walking back toward where I'm assuming his parents' room is.

"Don't mind him, Sweetie. He's just in shock. He'll come around when he realizes it was Eileen's fault, not yours," Stephanie says as she and Meghan both pull me in for a hug.

"So it's true then? Mom caused the accident?" I ask when I pull back a few moments later, wiping my eyes.

Πατέρα (Dads) face falls, which is all the answer I need.

"What did he mean by Sam standing up against Mom's family? She said they were in the fashion industry."

All the adults share a concerned look and **πατέρας** (dad) steps forward. "Maybe we should have that conversation at home, **κορίτσι μου** (my girl)?"

My gaze darts between each of them, and when I look at Alli and Luke, they both have a slightly guilty look on their face and my stomach sinks further. Crap... How can they know what **πατέρα** (dads) talking about and I don't? About my own mother and her family?

"You both knew and didn't tell me?" I asked, and they both flinch at the hurt and betrayal in my voice which is probably showing on my face, too. "So, everyone else is allowed to know the truth, but I wasn't allowed to? Why?"

Stephanie clears her throat. "It wasn't on purpose. We thought you knew, but a hospital waiting room isn't the place to have that discussion."

Looking over at **πατέρας**, he looks guilty, and I barely feel myself nodding in agreement. Whatever he has to say doesn't sound good and they're right. A hospital waiting room isn't the right place for a sensitive discussion.

"Come on, Mary, I'll drive you home," Luke says quietly as he takes my hand.

After taking my stuff upstairs to my room, I grab a water bottle and sit down at the table across from **πατέρας**. He runs a hand through his hair which draws my attention to the gray that's recently started to show at his temples. Now that I'm looking at him, he seems to have aged years since I saw him earlier this evening.

Sighing, I take a sip of water. Capping it, I find myself picking at the label—a habit I've always had—as everything that everyone said earlier runs through my mind.

"First of all, what happened tonight? Will Sam and Ellie really be okay? Why does Brady hate me so much now?"

Πατέρας (Dad) sighs as he rubs a hand over his face. "From what we were told, your mom tried to t-bone Sam and Ellie's car, but it wasn't a true t-bone. At the last second, witnesses saw her car pull to the left, so it mostly hit the front tire instead of hitting Sam full-on. I'm not sure if it was on purpose or if she changed her mind and decided not to hit Sam head on at the last second.

"Sam's injuries are, obviously, worse than Ellie's. His left leg is broken, and he had to get a few stitches from the glass. Ellie broke her arm. Both of them have concussions, bruising, and minor cuts from the glass shards."

I swallow thickly, my eyes stinging with fresh tears.

"The reason why Brady's upset is because of a note that was found in Eileen's car. It said *'This is what happens to those that stand against the Vasquez family.'*"

I frown, confused. "But Mom's last name is Delgado. Not Vasquez."

Πατέρας (Dad) sighs again. "After we divorced, I found out Eileen lied to me. To us. Vasquez is her real maiden name. She had paperwork drawn up to use Delgado as an alias to keep us from knowing her heritage." He pauses, making sure to look right at me. "Your mother is the daughter of a very powerful Spanish Don."

Not blinking, I stare at him, not believing what he just said. "She's a mafia princess?"

Πατέρας just nods, not saying anything.

Slumping in my chair, I play with the label on my water bottle again. "And she never gave any indication of who she really was the entire time you two were together?"

Πατέρας shakes his head. "No, she didn't. Every time I met with her family; they always said their name was Delgado. Hell, even their company here in town is under her father's first name but listed as Delgado, not Vasquez. Why it is, I'm not sure, but Sam thinks her father has multiple aliases that he has money and property listed under. Not just in Wisconsin, but also in a few other states."

"How did you find out she lied about her name?"

He runs a hand over his face, and then gets up, walks over to the bookcases surrounding the TV and kneels. He shuffles through the photo albums, and I frown when he pulls out their wedding album. Walking back to the table, he flips through the pages and when he turns it around toward me, it's a picture of him and Mom on their wedding day. On one page, it's a picture of them both with his family, and on the other page, it's one with them and Mom's family. I pick up the paper that was stuffed in between the pages and unfold it.

It's a printed-out news article.

> *Diego Vasquez, implicated in a human trafficking ring around the Great Lakes coastline, was released on bond on November 15th, 2006.*

I stop reading the article and stare at the black and white grainy image. Then I look up at the picture at the top, confirming that it's Uncle Diego.

I'd only met Uncle Diego a handful of times before my parents divorced, for which I was grateful. He traveled a lot for business but the few times I did meet him, he always seemed cold and detached. Every time he talked to me, his words were clipped and if I didn't listen, he'd start talking in rapid Spanish at Mom. From his tone and his looks, it seemed like he was yelling at her because of my behavior.

I look at the pictures again, just to make sure it isn't his twin brother, Uncle Mateo, but it isn't. While, yes, they are identical, you can tell just by looking in their eyes who is who. However, if need be, their tattoos and birthmarks are more ways to tell them apart. Uncle Mateo is a complete one-eighty from Uncle Diego in almost every aspect. He's quiet, reserved, and always looked at me with kind eyes. He doesn't talk much, but whenever he did, I listened. Uncle Diego is loud, has a huge ego, and he always looked at me with hatred and thinly veiled disgust.

Finally, I look up at **πατέρας** and he nods sadly.

"I talked to Sam when I found that a couple of months after we divorced. He unofficially confirmed what I had suspected. Eileen, your mother, is... was a Vasquez."

"But if they're such a powerful mafia family, why'd they have Mom go after Sam and Ellie? Wouldn't they have used one of their goons?" At least, that's what I've always seen in the movies. I know movies are usually not realistic, but not having known a mafia family before and how they operate, that's all I have to go by as comparison.

Πατέρας shakes his head. "I don't know, **κορίτσι μου** (my girl). We might not ever know."

I bite my lip as I process everything.

A few minutes later, I can't keep it from trembling. "So, one of my best friends hates me now because my mom hurt his parents and is a Vasquez? When did he learn the truth about her?"

Πατέρας frowns. "I think he found out tonight, just like you. That's the only thing I can think of. I'm not sure when Luke and Alli found out. Us parents were trying to keep all of that mess from reaching you kids. To let you grow up without that cloud hanging over you."

"But I'm a Catarino, not a Vasquez."

The corner of **πατέρα** (dads) lips lifts into a small smile at that. "That's right, **κορίτσι μου** (my girl), but others may still think you're connected to them because of who your mother was. I hope Brady will come to see that you had nothing to do with what your mother did or her family, but only time will tell on that. Seems even in death she's still fucking with your life."

I say nothing to that, even though I agree with him. Over the years, Mom has tried numerous times to derail special events in my life and remind me that I'd always be worthless so long as I remained heavier than others my age.

The first one that pops into my mind was my golden birthday, when I turned fourteen. Mom crashed the surprise party **πατέρας**, his family, and my friends had planned for me. It was obvious that she was drunk as she shouted obscenities at the top of her lungs. Once again, my weight was at the forefront of her hateful and hurtful words. Then she started blaming me for something her family had denied her. For not fitting into their perfect and rich lifestyle. At the time I had no idea what she was talking about, but now it clicks. She must have meant the Don, her father, was the one that denied her something.

Was being a grunt man, I mean woman, part of her way to gain his trust or whatever she had asked him for?

I rub my temples, my head throbbing as I try to sort all this out.

"I'm so sorry, **κορίτσι μου**. I should have told you this a long time ago, but I thought if you didn't know, that it might protect you."

Not being able to take the guilty yet also concerned look on his face anymore, I get up and round the table. He holds out his arms as he scoots his chair back from the table, and I sit on his lap, sinking into his embrace. I haven't sat like this with him for years, but right now, I kind of need the closeness. This night started out so good, and once again, Mom's managed to ruin two special events for me. A part of me wonders if she planned for this to happen tonight, the night of my homecoming dance.

"Thank you for trying to protect me and finally telling me."

"I'll always do what I can to protect you, **κορίτσι μου**. You're my little girl."

Taking a shuddery breath, I will myself not to cry. At least not until I'm alone in my room. Sighing, I can only hope that things with Brady will improve. He's one of my best friends and I don't want to lose him because of Mom's mess.

Chapter 7

Mary

Seven Months Later

"Um, Mary," Alli says as I turn from my spot on her bed and stuff the last of my schoolbooks back in my bag. I look up at her since she's now standing by the side of her bed, her fingers tug and twist the hem of her shirt, something she does when she's nervous.

"What's up, Alli?"

She blushes, then whirls around, grabs a bag from under her pillow and thrusts it in my hands.

I stare at it in confusion, but then through the thin plastic bag, I can read the words on the box that's inside.

A pregnancy test.

"I wasn't going to say anything before in case I was wrong, but then I kept thinking I should say something because you keep wondering why you're so tired all the time, have no energy, you feel bloated, you've been complaining that the school lunches are never big enough anymore, so you've taken to bringing your own." She pauses and takes a deep breath. "Mary, I think you're pregnant."

I try to take in her words, but my mind keeps freezing on the word 'pregnant'.

Yeah, what she said is true, but I've been getting my period still. Though, they're always hard to track because ever since I've started getting my period, they've been light and the time between cycles is erratic. I've tried tracking it in the beginning, but there were times where I went months with only the barest hint of spotting before getting a true, but light, period again. I haven't tracked my period in years though. Could I really be pregnant?

I shake my head to clear my thoughts when I realize Alli's been talking to me this whole time.

"I'm really sorry. I've been stressing about this for a couple of weeks, and I hope you don't think I'm being a shitty friend, but I was just worried about you."

Stuffing the test in my bag, I open my arms for a hug. She comes over immediately and hugs me tight.

"I don't think you're a shitty friend. You're an awesome friend who looks out for me."

She pulls back, wiping a tear away and it dawns on me that she must have been stressing pretty hardcore to be this worked up.

I smile, hoping to put her more at ease, though even I can feel that it's shaky. "I really do mean it. Thank you for being an awesome friend."

She worries her lip as her gaze drops to my backpack, then she looks hesitantly back up at me. "Will you text me?"

"I'll tell you tomorrow." She pouts and I give her a 'come on' look. "Alli, your dad has a rare evening off and you guys already have things planned to go out to dinner and the movies afterward. I'm not going to interrupt that for you."

She huffs. "What if I text you when we get back home? Will you tell me then?"

Relenting, I nod. "Okay, text me when you're back in your room and then I'll tell you as long as I haven't already crashed for the night."

Giving her one last hug, I shoulder my bag and head downstairs.

Seeing Alli's mom in the kitchen, I give her a little wave. "Goodbye, Meghan. Have a good night," I call out as I cross the living room.

She smiles back at me as she loads the dishwasher. "You, too, Sweetie. See you later."

Putting my plate in the sink, I wipe my hands on the towel and clear my throat, hoping to dislodge the lump that feels like it has been there since Alli muttered those four words.

'I think you're pregnant.'

I'd barely been able to choke down my food. Thankfully, **πατέρας** (dad) seemed preoccupied with something from work because it's tax season, so he didn't notice I was on edge. At least I don't think anyway.

"I'm going to head up to my room to study some more."

He looks up from his phone and finishes swallowing the bite he'd just taken. "Okay. I've got to finish some accounts tonight, so it'll probably be a late night."

"Still covering for your coworker?"

He nods as he swallows a drink of juice. "Yeah. No one blames her for suddenly needing to go back home because her mom is in the hospital, but the timing sucks."

I walk over and give him a hug from behind. He pats my arm and tilts his head up. I lower mine and he kisses my temple, just like he does every night.

"Just in case you crash before I head to bed."

Turning, I kiss his temple in return. "**Σε αγαπώ** (I love you), **πατέρας** (dad)."

"**Κορίτσι μου** (My girl), **κι εγώ σ' αγαπώ** (I love you, too)."

The familiar balm of how close **πατέρας** (dad) and I have become ever since Mom left washes over me as we hug. I mean, we've always been close, but her leaving brought so much more peace to our lives. I hardly ever get into trouble or do things I shouldn't, so he's more of a best friend than my **πατέρας** (dad).

Giving him one last squeeze, I pull back and head upstairs.

In my room, I stare at my bag sitting next to my desk like it could bite me.

Taking a deep breath, I grab the pregnancy test, keeping it in the grocery bag just in case **πατέρας** happens to come upstairs, and quickly walk across the hall to the bathroom.

Setting the test on the counter, I open it and read the directions.

My hands shake and my heart starts beating harder. I set the test down on the counter and stare at it.

Is Alli right? Could I really be pregnant?

My shaky hands go to my stomach and I swear I feel a flutter.

Taking a deep breath, I look up at the test on the counter.

I can do this.

I may be eighteen and wasn't planning on having kids for a few years, but if this test is positive, I know he or she will have the best parents.

Exhaling, I take the test out of the individual packaging and follow the instructions before capping it and laying it down on the counter. I barely get the timer set because my hands are shaking so much.

Washing my hands, my gaze stays glued to the test and after drying my hands, I can't help wringing my hands in worry.

I can do this.

I can't do this.

I can do this.

I'm only eighteen! We took all the precautions. I'm on birth control and Luke always wore a condom. I know they aren't always foolproof, but we had hoped to get married after we graduated and then once we both had our degrees, him nursing and me teaching, then we'd start having kids.

Hearing my timer go off, I shut if off without looking at the test.

Squaring my shoulders, I close my eyes and give myself a good shake.

If the test is negative, we'll just have to be more careful.

If the test is positive... If it's positive, then I'm going to put on my big girl panties and do what I need to for my baby. This may be happening a little earlier than we planned, but sometimes, nature just wins out. And deep in my heart, I know Luke will be there for me regardless of what happens.

Cracking open my eyelids, I peer at the test.

Pregnant.

Fuck............

Grabbing some toilet paper, I wrap up the test and hide it at the bottom of the trash bin. Picking up the box and instructions, I stuff them back into the bag and quickly run back into my room, making sure not to slam my door in the process so that **πατέρας** won't think anything's amiss.

Flopping down on my bed, my hands instantly go to my stomach.

This can't be happening...

Closing my eyes, I let myself have a mini-panic attack as I think back over the past few months. I'd been feeling off since October when I really think hard about it, but I just thought I kept catching the flu or something. Repeatedly. I mean, a lot of kids have been sick at school.

The night of our homecoming dance was the start of Luke's and my relationship getting more serious. While we both wanted to get married after we graduated high school with a small ceremony, both of our families wanted us to wait until after college. I get what they're saying, but we both want to get married sooner rather than later. We both know that our studies will take up most of our time, but the urge to start our little family with just the two of us is strong for both of us.

Luke wants to follow in his dad's footsteps into the medical field, but not as a doctor. He wants to be a nurse. I want to go to school to be a teacher. To help kids as they grow. To build and nurture the foundation blocks their parents started. To help guide them as they grow older.

Groaning, I scrub my hands over my face. Then a thought sobers me and drives home that our previous plans for our little family just being the two of us, is now the three of us.

Wait... How far along am I?

Grabbing my phone, I ignore the fact that my hands have started shaking again and look up the information for a women's clinic nearby. Luckily, there's one in the next town over. Until I know more, I don't want my entire family finding out just yet. I dial the clinic before I can chicken out.

Ten minutes later, I've got an appointment for tomorrow at 8 am, not caring that I'll be missing a couple of classes. I need to know how far along I am and if the baby is healthy.

Crawling into bed, I pray that either the test is faulty or that I only just got pregnant. Graduation is at the end of next month, and I had planned to start taking summer classes at the local college to get some of my gen-eds out of the way. Not to mention at a cheaper rate.

My hand goes to my stomach and I freeze.

Pressing a little harder, I feel it again and then bolt upright in bed.

Oh, fuck...

How the hell far along am I that I can feel the baby moving? That was the baby... right?

I lunge for my phone on my nightstand, but then pause.

I can't call Luke just yet. He and Brady are still at school working on the sets for an upcoming play, but since I wasn't feeling well, I didn't stay after with them like I normally would. Not to mention things are still pretty tense between Brady and me.

Shaking my head, I send a text to Luke, asking him to call me when he's done and back home.

I'm about to plug my phone back in but then hesitate. Gripping it tightly, I try to calm my nerves.

I need to tell **πατέρας**.

Pocketing my phone, I cross the room but right as I open my door, I hear the sound of glass breaking downstairs. Maybe **πατέρας** dropped a glass or something? Hopefully, he didn't cut himself in the process.

When I get to the top of the stairs, my frown deepens. All the lights are out down here and when I get to the base of the stairs, **πατέρα** (dads) nowhere to be found. His office is dark. I look back up the stairs toward **πατέρεα** (dads) room but the door is open and the lights are out as well.

I hesitate, wondering if I should call someone. Maybe Sam? I don't want to turn on the light and give myself away if there is an intruder inside. Then a muffled noise catches my ear and my worry increases that something happened to **πατέρας**. Worry ends up being my deciding factor and quietly, I sneak forward while scanning my surroundings.

Another muffled noise and a thud come from the living room and when I peek around the corner, my entire body starts trembling.

Πατέρα (Dads) laying on the ground in a pool of blood. Everything else is forgotten as I stare at the growing pool of blood under him.

"**Πατέρας** (Dad)! Oh, my God. **Πατέρας** (Dad)," I cry out as I rush to his side, putting pressure on the wounds in his chest. His bloody hands raise, clasping my arms, and then he tries to push me away.

"Run, ...**koritsi**... **μου** (my girl). D-Diego... here... w-wants... you... To... take... you... R-run..."

"No, **πατέρας**. I need you. Especially now." I push forward, putting pressure on his chest again, but the pool of blood around him continues to grow. So much blood. Tears stream even harder down my face.

"You must... go... **Σε... αγαπώ** (I love you)..."

"**Πατέρας** (Dad), no!"

His hands fall limp from my arms and his chest stops moving.

"**Κι εγώ σ' αγαπώ** (I love you, too)," I whisper and a sob escapes me as I bury my head against his shoulder, crying.

"Well, isn't this touching," a cold voice sneers from behind me and I spin around, only to find Isaac and Uncle Diego pointing guns at me. **Πατέρα** (Dads) words come back to me, and I can't help but put a hand to my stomach, even though it wouldn't stop a bullet from tearing through me. Fuck... What am I going to do? How am I going to get away from them?

"Why are you doing this? Why did you kill him?" My throat is tight, but somehow, I choke the words out.

"Easy. He didn't do as he was ordered to," Uncle Diego says with a shrug of his shoulders as if he was discussing some mundane topic like the weather instead of my **πατέρα** (dads) death.

No.

Murder.

"What did you order him to do?" I ask through gritted teeth as my mind whirls, trying to figure a way out of here. If I can just get outside, then I can run to Sam's house. I curse myself for not texting him earlier when I first thought about it.

Uncle Diego's and Isaac's faces turn lecherous.

"To hand you over, of course. Being a Vasquez means it's time to do as your Don orders. Now that you're eighteen, you are to take a husband to further the Don's goals. It's all been arranged and by midnight, you'll be in your new owner's clutches. Don't worry. Your little surprise won't negate the deal. In fact, it earned me even more money," Diego says with a sadistic look on his face.

I stumble back, my feet slipping in the pool of **πατέρα** (dads) blood and I land on my ass as I stare up at him.

He's insane. Completely insane if he thinks I'm going along with this hair-brained plan. And how does he know I'm pregnant? I only just found out myself. At least I think that's what he means by 'little surprise'.

"No. No, I'm not going with you. And I'm not a Vasquez. I'm a Catarino."

Uncle Diego sighs and waves his gun as he looks over at my cousin. "Isaac."

Isaac slips his gun into the back of his pants and stalks toward me, the lewd expression deepening on his face. "Time for some fun," he sneers.

I stumble to my feet, but once again, I slip again in the pool of blood on the floor. Bile rises in my throat, but I push it down. Finally, I get to my feet and run into the dining room.

"Gotcha," Issac says when his hands wrap around my hair, pulling me back against him and then he roughly grabs my arms and throws me across the room.

A cry of pain escapes when I hit my head on the corner of the coffee table. Black dots dance across my vision as I try to force my limbs to scoot backward and away from Isaac.

I can feel a trickle of blood run down my face, but I ignore it. Scrambling to my feet, my foot slipping slightly before I gain traction, I run toward the patio door as Isaac laughs darkly from behind me.

He's toying with me, I know it, but I still need to try and get away from them.

My hands fumble with the lock, the blood on them making my fingers slip before I'm wretched away and thrown against the wall. My shoulder smashes into something and I cry out as I feel glass digging into my skin.

"Isaac! You're damaging the merchandise," Uncle Diego hisses.

"Well, I wouldn't have had to if your sister had been able to train this overweight brat right the first time. Same for that idiot of a so-called husband."

"Regardless, you're still damaging the merchandise. You better hope he doesn't ask for a discount, because if he does, it's coming out of your share," Uncle Diego says nonchalantly.

I feel Isaac's body tenses against mine and his eyes harden as he stares down at me. He grips my chin hard and pulls his gun out from behind his back. He pushes into me, shoving the barrel of the gun into my stomach, and I bite my tongue to keep from crying out again as the glass pushes deeper into my shoulder as my mind whirls with how to protect my baby.

"You're going to come with us, or I'll end this bastard's life right here, right now. Then I'll be going house to house. Killing all your little friends and their families. Next I'll have some fun with Alli and Mandy before killing them, too. I'll have some fun with you. But you, you would die last after seeing the life fading from every person you've ever loved or cared about. So, what's it going to be?

Come with us? Or watch us torture, rape, and kill your family and friends before being killed yourself?"

His dark tone sends a chill down my spine and my hands automatically go to my stomach. As if sensing I'm beyond stressed, I can feel his or her little feet kicking. Looking between the two men, I know they'll do it. I'll just have to bide my time until I can make a run for it.

Isaac must see the defeat in my face, because he grins, and the darkness in it sends a shiver through me. He yanks me forward and a cry escapes me as I feel the glass digging through my skin again, as well as his tight grip on my arm. The pain from the glass rips through me, sending black dots dancing along my vision again, and Isaac takes advantage of my distraction to wrench my hands behind my back.

The pain in my shoulder intensifies at the action, making me cry out again. Something plastic is wrapped around my wrists and then I hear the sound of a zip tie as he tightens it, the plastic digging deeper into my skin.

Duct tape is slapped over my mouth and I look up to see Uncle Diego smiling down at me like he's won the lottery and considering the fact that they're selling me to someone, he probably has.

"Nighty night, dear niece."

My eyes widen as he brings a needle forward, but with Isaac holding me, I can't get away. I feel the prick of the needle in my neck and my eyes start to get heavy.

The last thing I remember is looking at my **πατέρα** (dads) body one last time before my eyes finally shut and darkness consumes me.

Chapter 8

Luke

I FROWN AS THE phone rings again and again. However, instead of hearing Mary's sweet voice answering the call, I get her voicemail for the fifth time.

"Maybe she went to bed, son. You said she's been feeling sick lately," Dad says as he nurses his whiskey.

"Maybe... I'm going to walk over. Make sure she's okay. If she is asleep, at least then I'll know she's okay."

Dad gives me a weird look, but nods.

Thing is, though, I don't think Mary's sick.

She's put on a bit of weight the last few months, but I don't know if she's noticed it or not. She's also switched from coffee to tea suddenly. Not to mention she gets nauseous around spicy smelling food.

I think she's pregnant, but I've been trying to figure out exactly how to bring it up to her. Surely, she'd tell me if she knew, but maybe she doesn't know. I've learned over the past few months that her periods have always been light and erratic ever since she started getting them, so it wasn't like she could rely on them to let her know.

Pocketing my phone, I grab my keys, slip on my hoodie, and head out into the night. Mary had given me a spare key a while ago when we both had decided we wanted to marry after we graduated. Thankfully, graduation's only a couple of months away. I already have her ring picked out and it's sitting in my sock drawer, waiting for me to ask her the night we graduate.

I take a deep breath and instantly regret it. It's early April and the brisk air has me shivering. I start jogging down the sidewalk, careful not to slip on any black ice, and head over to her house next door, eager to check on Mary and get out of the cold.

When I reach her door, I pull out my keys, ready to unlock the door since all the lights are out when I suddenly stop.

There's broken glass, glinting in the moonlight, in the flower beds below the large living room window.

My gut churns and I inch forward, looking into the window. Instantly I stumble back, tripping over the flower bushes and landing on my ass in the snow.

Hands shaking, I pull out my phone, and dial the one person who I know can help with this.

"Hey, Luke. Saw pictures of how the set's coming along—," Uncle Sam says before I interrupt him.

"Uncle Sam. Nikos, he's... he's..."

Instantly, Uncle Sam's tone changes. *"What's wrong? Where are you?"*

"Mary's house. I went over to c-check on her because she wasn't answering her phone. She... She asked me to call her when I got back. The window's broke a-a-and I can see Nikos on the floor..."

Tears stream down my cheeks, and soon there are hands on me, startling me.

"It's okay, Luke. Sam's going to call it in," Aunt Ellie says softly as she wraps her arm around me, and I notice Brady's behind her but keeping his distance.

Wait.

When did they get here? Did they run over here as soon as I called?

"Mary wasn't answering her phone. Oh, shit, Mary! Mary, where are you, Siren?" I yell as I jump to my feet and strong arms band around my waist.

"Son, it's a crime scene. You can't go in," Dad says, and logically, I know it's true, but I have to find Mary.

"You don't understand. I need to find Mary. She's pregnant."

His arms go still around me, but he doesn't let me go. Uncle Sam looks at me over his shoulder, his phone glued to his ear as he pauses, keys mid-air and I realize he was going to unlock the door with my keys. I must have dropped them when I fell. I can see him tensing even more at my words. He nods and holds up a gloved finger before pulling out booties, slipping them on over his shoes. He pulls his gun out and then he's gone.

I stare at the door, willing my Mary, my Siren, to come running out toward me, but she isn't the one that appears next.

Uncle Sam emerges and shakes his head while motioning me forward. Dad finally lets me go, and I numbly walk forward.

"I'm sorry, Luke, but she's not here. Nikos is, unfortunately, already gone. There are signs of a struggle inside. I pulled up my security system to see if it caught anything," he pauses as he sighs, running a hand over his face. "I'm sorry, but Mary was taken out of the house, unconscious, by two men. We'll find her, Luke."

He shows me the video and I know one of the people in the video, but not the other two. Though, I do notice similarities between the two men. I could also tell the driver was smaller, so maybe it was a woman? Regardless, as soon as the two men toss Mary unceremoniously into the trunk of their car, they get in themselves. Before their doors are even shut, the car takes off. I stumble backward when it stops.

Blood rushes through my veins and I see red. Turning, I stare Brady down, pointing at him.

"Did you have anything to do with this? You wanted her gone the minute you found out her mom caused your parents' accident. Don't you dare deny it because I've heard it out of your own fucking mouth. You've been buddy buddy with Isaac, her fucking bully and nightmare, for months. Did you have a hand in this?" I'm damn near yelling at the end of my rant, but Brady just looks worried, which instantly has the pit in my stomach growing even further.

"No, I didn't, asshole. Yeah, I'm pissed at her because of what her mom did, but I would never sink to this extreme." He steps forward, and it takes everything in me not to launch myself at him. But he's been my best friend since forever, so I know when he's lying.

And right now, he isn't.

Still, I can't help but flinch, my muscles tensing, when he places a hand on my shoulder. Thankfully, he doesn't say anything about it. Things have been extremely strained between us ever since the night of the accident seven months ago with how he's been treating Mary. He may be my cousin, my blood, but I'd choose Mary over him every time.

"We'll find her and then you can give her the ring you've been hiding for the past few months."

His lips kick up a little. How did he know I'd bought a ring? The next thing I know, he pulls me in, hugging me tight. Small arms circle around both of us as Alli joins us, however, I don't know at what point she came over here.

"They'll find her, Luke," she says as she squeezes me tighter.

Fuck, I hope so. And I hope it happens quick. I'm scared about what those assholes will do to her when they find out she's pregnant. I don't want to lose my woman or my baby.

A few hours later, there's a knock at our door. Instantly, I'm up off the couch and walking forward, yanking the door open.

Uncle Sam stands on the other side with two other cops behind him. He looks exhausted, but he gives me a small smile. "Can we come in, Luke?"

Swallowing hard, I nod and step back, letting the three of them in. Mom comes in from the kitchen and twists her hands in front of her nervously.

"Would any of you like some coffee?"

Uncle Sam gives her a small smile. "Yes, please, Steph."

She disappears and Uncle Sam turns to me. "Let's sit down and I can fill you in on some of the things we found out."

I gesture toward the living room, since that has more seating. After retaking my seat, I notice one of the cops frowning at Uncle Sam, but he doesn't say anything. Uncle Sam huffs at him and he rolls his eyes.

"Relax, Wolfe. Luke is Mary's fiancé and father of their baby."

Officer Wolfe's eyes narrow at me. "A little young to be engaged and bringing a baby into the world, aren't you?"

His condescending tone has my hackles rising and I stare back at him, clenching my fists so I don't do anything stupid. "We've known we wanted to get married for over a year, so no, neither of us thinks it's too early. When you know you've found your other half, you hold on to her with everything you have."

Officer Wolfe frowns at that for some reason. "How can we be sure you didn't just send her off or cut her loose as soon as you found out she was pregnant?"

Anger runs through my veins, but Sam replies before I can. "Luke's alibi checks out. He was at the school working on the sets for the play. His phone records were double checked and verified. Multiple people confirmed hearing Mary say she was going to head home because she wasn't feeling well. She stayed over at a friend's house, studying, until her father came home from work. We further confirmed that Mary hasn't been feeling well the last few months. With the home test confirming that she is pregnant, that's probably why she was feeling off."

Reigning in my frustration and anger, I look over the other two officers more closely. Then, Officer Wolfe's words come back to me. I frown as my gaze goes back to Officer Wolfe and then the other guy before settling back on Uncle Sam. "Why were they thinking I'd cut her out of my life? I love her. I'd never do that."

He sighs, but before he answers, Mom comes in with coffees for them. He takes the cup and nods. "I know you do, but we have to look at all the angles." He pauses and takes a sip of his coffee. "I called in a favor with a buddy of mine to look into things on the dark web."

My chest tightens as the pit in my stomach grows. "The dark web? ...What'd he find?"

Uncle Sam chews on his lip as he stares down at his hands for a few moments before finally looking up at me, his eyes are filled with sympathy.

"There's a website where people can post what they're looking for in a person. Like a want ad. There was one matching Mary's description, and it was marked 'fulfilled' half an hour ago." He pauses as he takes a deep breath and exhales shakily before his eyes harden and the muscles in his jaw clench. "There are also rumors about Mary needing to fulfill her duties to the family since she's come of age."

I'm out of my chair so fast, my hands buried in my hair as I take deep breaths while trying to rein in my anger. After a few moments, I turn back to Uncle Sam. Questions burning inside me.

"Did it say who posted the want ad?"

Uncle Sam frowns. "My friend is trying to trace that as we speak. Same for the rumors to see if they're valid or not."

"You realize I know who one of the people is that carried her out, right? From your security footage?"

Uncle Sam sighs. "Yeah, I know and I know him, too. Same for the second guy. We can't ID the driver. He or she was keeping their face hidden the entire time."

I pause at that. "Who?"

The muscle in Uncle Sam's jaw ticks again.

"We aren't—" Officer Wolfe starts, but Uncle Sam cuts him off.

"Diego Vasquez."

My blood runs cold at his name. "U-Uncle Sam... Mary showed me a news article clip that Nikos found—"

"Not too long after he and Eileen divorced. About her true origins. Yeah, he showed it to me, too," he says as he stands, walks over to me and lays his hand on my shoulder. "We won't stop looking for her, but I need to be honest with you, too."

The pit in my stomach grows at the look of fear and frustration on his face, but there's also determination there, too.

"The only ones we've found from the human trafficking ring that we think Diego is associated with are the ones they let us find and every single time, it was too late to save them. They're either already dead or they end up dying shortly after finding them. We've never been able to infiltrate their ranks or find clues as to where they keep or how they move their victims."

I swallow thickly. Determined not to let Mary end up that way. "I'm not going to stop looking for her."

Uncle Sam nods and squeezes my shoulder. "I know, Luke. We'll keep you updated as much as we're able to."

Movement behind Uncle Sam draws my attention and I frown when I see the other two officers sharing a look. Unease swirls throughout me, because it's not a look of concern or worry on their faces. They wore smug, arrogant smirks. It only lasted a couple of seconds, but I saw it.

Uncle Sam heads toward the door and the other two officers move to follow him.

I purposefully move so that I'll be able to see who the other officer is.

Moments later, he passes me on his way to the door and I can finally read his nametag.

O'Grady.

I'm going to be keeping my eye on him and Officer Wolfe. Something doesn't sit quite right with me about them.

Determination fills me once again as my anger simmers just below the surface. Tomorrow I'm going to head out to the edge of town. There's another group in town that might be able to help me. I'd known for a long time that I wanted to join their ranks. Mary was a little worried before since there is a danger element to it, but I'll do whatever it takes to bring my Siren home.

And to do that, I need to start prospecting with the Steel Archangel's MC.

Chapter 9

Mary

Ten Weeks Later

Another contraction rips through me, and I grit my teeth against the pain. Stephan [STEE-VAN] had finally driven me to the hospital when my contractions started to be two minutes apart, but until then, I had lain in agony on the bed while he worked in his office.

For eight fucking hours.

The jackass even had the nerve to yell at me to keep my voice down so that he could concentrate on his work when I kept crying out in pain.

The night Uncle Diego and my cousin, Isaac, kidnapped me and killed my father was the worst day of my life.

I woke up in a room that almost mirrored a prison cell, just without the concrete and bars. In their place were sheetrock, tiles, and a locked door that I wasn't able to pick with my bobby pins. Granted, there was a pedestal sink, a toilet, and a shower, however there were no walls separating any of them. For the shower, there was just a half-moon rod with a clear plastic curtain attached. There also wasn't a divider between my bed and bathroom area, so I always had to be careful of slipping on wet tiles since the shower curtain hardly kept the water in the shower where it belonged.

Without any windows or a clock, I had no concept of time and quickly lost track of the days. Later, I'd found out that I'd been held in that room for a month with no outside contact except for doctor visits, which I later found out were bi-weekly. However, even those were held in my cell and the doctor never said a word to me. Never asked how I was doing or feeling. Nothing. My food was delivered through a slot in the door and promptly shut. Even when I yelled after them, no one would come back or talk to me.

I had begged the doctor in the beginning to help me, but all that got me was reduced rations. They also limited my shower privileges in that they controlled the water flow to my shower. Almost immediately, I learned that I was only allowed five minutes and the only way I knew that was during the second shower, I counted out the seconds since I had no clock until the water shut off. And five minutes is if it was a good day.

Then, I was moved up to the main floor and into another prison cell, but with better furnishings. The carpet felt heavenly under my bare feet after spending so much time in the cold room downstairs. There's a soft, queen-sized bed that felt like I was getting a hug with a navy blue bedspread and sheets. On the other wall was a dresser with a matching desk and nightstand.

Relief flowed through me when I saw that I had a window, but I quickly found it was sealed shut. I was surprised to see a cute little crib nestled in the corner with a diaper changing table next to it, but then it dawned on me that a man like Stephan probably wasn't going to lift a damn finger for anything in the house. Or to help with my son. I was going to have to do everything myself. Tears had pricked my eyes, but I had waited until I was alone before letting them fall and mourning all that I had lost because of my mother's family's greed.

A couple plusses to no longer being in that basement cell was that my meals improved, which was a relief because I'd been feeling extremely weak near the end of my stay in that first room due to the reduced rations. Another was that I was allowed longer showers, but I never dawdled, not wanting to have them reinstate the five-minute rule.

The same day that I was moved upstairs was also the day that I was informed that I was married to Stephan Hayes. Well, it had happened the day after I was kidnapped, but I wasn't informed until that day. Of course, everything was forged. There was never a chance for me to say I didn't want this. I didn't have a wedding, let alone say, 'I do'. Not that I wanted one with Stephan.

That first day upstairs was also the day that I met Stephan for the first time, as well. While he was good looking with his blond hair, hazel eyes, and his fit, lean body, he wasn't my Luke. It also didn't help that I got a bad vibe whenever he was around or when I would sometimes catch him staring at me.

I was also never allowed to leave the house, and if I did, it was only with Stephan. I have, and still am trying to think of ways to be able to escape. Unfortunately, the asshole somehow always knows when I'm thinking about escaping because then he reminds me that if I even tried to disobey him or leave him, that he would kill my baby before sending me to be used as a plaything for his boss' underlings.

I'd found out really quick that Stephan is part of a human trafficking ring, even though he's a cop himself. And not just any human trafficking ring. The one my uncle, Diego, has ties to. I have no idea if my grandfather, Antonio, knows about it, but for some reason, I almost believe that he doesn't. Nothing in the past gave me an inkling that Grandfather was sleezy like that. Then again, appearances can be deceiving.

Stephan actually boasts on a regular basis that he 'saved' me from that sort of life when he bought me. In his words, for that alone, I should be grateful to him for anything and everything that he does for me and my 'bastard child' as he calls my son.

Asshole.

My son wouldn't be that if my so-called family hadn't kidnapped me. By now, Luke and I would have already eloped.

Pain sears through me again and I grit my teeth to stop the cry of pain I so desperately want to let loose. I don't want Stephan taking out his anger on me or my soon-to-be-born son. Asshole knew I wanted an epidural, but I should have known that he wouldn't let me have anything for pain relief. By the time I got admitted, I was too far along to get one.

"I know it's going to be difficult, but on this next contraction, I need you to not push. The doctor will be here in a few minutes," the nurse says, and I groan in exhaustion.

My throat is so dry. Shakily, I reach my hand out to the cup of ice chips on the bedside table. I knew Stephan would be parking his ass down in the recliner as soon as we got in here and wouldn't help me in the slightest. Which is exactly what he did as he continues working on his laptop. Even the nurse has side-eyed him multiple times. At least she's refilled my little cup for me as needed since I'm so exhausted I can't lift the pitcher.

Suddenly the door opens and a man whom I'm praying is the doctor steps in with a gentle smile on his face.

"Hello, Mrs. Hayes, I'm Dr. Greene. Let me just wash up and you'll soon be meeting your son."

"Mary, please." I give him a tired and small smile in return, but really, it's that I hate that Hayes is my last name now. A moment later, I wince in pain as another contraction hits and again, I fight my body so that I don't push like the nurse had requested.

Moments later, the doctor steps between my legs and it's only then that Stephan closes his laptop, but he doesn't get up. Instead, he crosses his arms across his chest as he watches the doctor's every move. Then he gives me a sharp look, reminding me of his threats.

Internally, I roll my eyes. There's no way I'd be stupid enough to risk my son's life when I'm so vulnerable. Even if I did manage to get away from Stephan, there's no way I'd be able to physically run after just giving birth.

That and I have no money.

Well, I know I'd be able to request a new card from my bank back in Forest Creek, but I'm sure Stephan would cut it up as soon as it arrives in the mail. Just like he had my last one cut up. I was surprised when he had shown it to me, which meant he or someone else had gone through my house, making me wonder what else they had taken. He took great glee in cutting up my card and telling me that I was only allowed whatever he deems fit and that I was to stick to whatever budget he gives me, otherwise there would be severe punishments. I'm also almost positive the asshole drained my account before cutting up my bank card. He's crooked and greedy enough to do anything to get his hands on more money. And that's only after knowing him a little over two months.

The doctor clears his throat, bringing me out of my thoughts.

"Alright, Mary. On this next one, I want you to push. I can see the baby's head."

Weakly, I nod before getting some more ice chips. Though, as soon as they touch my tongue, I instantly regret it as I almost choke on them. Another contraction hits and I can't stop my cry of pain as I push as hard as I can. God, I wish Stephan would have brought me sooner so that I could have had an epidural.

Black dots dance across my vision as the pain intensifies, but I refuse to give in. I will not leave my son unprotected around that asshole.

"His head is out, so give me one more big push like that last one on the next contraction, Mary. Come on. You can do this."

His encouraging words give me strength, but I also don't miss the side-eye he gives Stephan as he sits stoically in the recliner. For what seems like the millionth time, I wish it was Luke at my side instead of Stephan. There's no doubt in my mind that Luke would have been the usual supportive, loving husband that's also eagerly awaiting the birth of their child.

When the next contraction hits, I push hard again and then I hear it.

My son, crying, for the first time.

Dr. Greene places my son on my stomach as the nurse helps to clear his airway and clean him.

I brush my hand across his little cheek and I feel like my heart is trying to beat its way out of my chest. He's absolutely perfect.

He's got my black hair, but I think it's too soon to know if it'll end up being curly like mine or straight like Luke's. I continue running my finger along his cheek and wonder if he'll have inherited his daddy's stunning green eyes. His little fingers curl around my finger and tears start to fall down my cheeks.

"Dad, do you want to cut the umbilical cord?" Dr. Greene asks.

My breath hitches as my gaze snaps over to where Stephan is still sitting.

A look of disgust comes over his face for a second, and I lower my gaze. I know he hates that he wasn't the first to claim me or put a baby in me, but it's not like that's my fault. I'm here against my will.

Stephan sighs as he gets up and follows the doctor's instructions. Then the nurse whisks my son over to be fully cleaned up and check him over.

After a few minutes, she places him in my arms once again. "Congratulations, Mom. What's his name?" she asks excitedly.

My stomach churns at having to give my son a different last name, but it's the only way I'm allowed to choose his name. Not to mention keeping him with me. Stephan had told me multiple times that he wouldn't be raising a son that didn't have his last name. It would put a stain on his reputation. So long as the last name was Hayes, and that I didn't name him or any future children after any of my relatives, I'd be able to name him whatever I wanted.

"Asher Lucas."

She smiles brightly, and I can't help but return it.

The nurse helps me with getting Asher to latch on, which he does after a few attempts. She then wheels over the table and places a piece of paper and pen down in front of me.

Asher's birth certificate.

I glance in Stephan's direction, but he's already back on his laptop. Since Asher is nursing on my left breast, I should be able to fill out some of the paperwork while he nurses. Picking up the pen, I start filling it out, but I leave the father's name blank. There's no way I'm putting Stephan's name there, but I also know he won't tolerate me putting Luke's name down. That would just earn me another beating or more verbal abuse. However, the worst is when he shows me multiple pictures of Luke being intimate with other women.

At that thought, my chest tightens and I swallow my sob.

It killed me seeing pictures of Luke having sex or getting a blow job from someone other than me. I'm still holding out and trying to believe that the pictures are fake. There's no way Luke would cheat on me. We love each other too much.

Thinking about that has me filling with dread for when the doctors clear me to be able to have sex again. With the looks Stephan's been giving me, I'm afraid that's when he'll finally end up forcing himself on me. So far, he hasn't touched me sexually, but if he's serious about keeping me under lock and key, it's inevitable that it'll happen. I just hope that when it does happen, that it's over quickly. The less he touches me, the better.

The nurse frowns when I hand her back the document. Then she does something I wasn't expecting.

She pulls out a piece of paper from her pocket and holds it where Stephan can't see it. Or at least I think he can't see it.

Are you safe with him? I can help you if you need to get away from him.

My breath hitches, and at that moment, Asher stirs in my arms and I look down at him.

I want so badly to accept this woman's help. For a moment, I dream about being reunited with Luke. Him holding his son and me in his arms.

Asher fusses and I switch him in my arms, trying to get him to eat from my other breast. Nibbling my lip, I lower my gaze and nod. With all the threats Stephan has already given me, I know he would destroy her, her entire family, and her friends if she helped me. I can't risk all of them.

I'll try to find a way out of this somehow.

On my own.

Chapter 10
Mary

Nine Years Later ~ February 2023

Carefully, I tiptoe down the hallway toward Stephan's office. I peek out around a corner and when I notice the coast is clear; I round the corner before pausing and covering my side as I swallow my hiss of pain.

Three days ago, on Valentine's Day, I received my usual 'present' from Stephan, which entailed him drunk off his ass and beating me until I was black and blue. I could have sworn he broke my wrist, but it was only badly sprained per the ER nurse. My wrist, a swollen right eye, which thankfully didn't swell shut, and a couple of bruised ribs were the worst of my injuries. Compared to my holiday 'presents' in the past, I got off easy this time.

However, this time, something different had happened.

As I was laying in the hospital bed in the ER, resting, Stephan answered his work phone and had a conversation right there in the room. In the past, he's always been so careful not to take phone calls around me. He would usually take it to his office or step outside.

The only thing I can think of for why he took the call this time, was that he thought I was asleep.

Whatever the reason, I heard the entire conversation. At first as I heard his Chief swearing him out, I thought I might finally be getting some help. That someone finally noticed.

But that hope was immediately dashed when he started calling my beating an 'incident'. That he should have been more careful.

Half of the police force here in Credence, Wisconsin are dirty and are on some crime lord's payroll. However, it seems that even the criminals get tired of the heat and inquiries from the hospital staff. Not to mention the few good cops when I heard that they were starting to suspect that Stephan was beating me rather than me being insanely clumsy.

I mean seriously. Who falls down the stairs almost every month and ends up in the ER? I'm surprised we haven't lost our health insurance by now. Our rates must be astronomical. Not that I've been allowed to see a bill since everything went to automatic withdrawal from Stephan's checking account. I haven't seen the bank statements either.

My mind wanders back to his Chief's words. In the past, whenever people at the station or around town start questioning things too much, it means change. That Stephan's mafia boss, who unfortunately is my very own grandfather, Antonio, orders him to move to whatever town he needs Stephan's help on the police force. For the past nine years, we've lived in five different towns in Wisconsin, including Credence, where we are now.

Based on that phone call and some things Stephan has said in drunken rants this past year, I think he's getting on Grandfather's last nerve. Ever since around a year ago, Stephan's beatings have been more violent and for trivial offences, like not doing something fast enough or the meat I cooked was too dry. I had to bite my lip hard that time. I know how to cook and there was never a time that the meat was too dry. Obviously not all of his beatings lead to ER visits, but like I said, I'm probably in there at least once a month or so.

However, all of those beatings that lead to ER visits meant that Uncle Diego and Grandfather have had to cover things up more than they've had to in the past when it would just be four or five times a year.

Taking a deep breath, or as deep as I can with these fucking bruised ribs, I push those thoughts out of my mind, and continue to quietly creep down the hallway until I'm just outside Stephan's office. Thankfully, he kept the door slightly ajar tonight, which will make it easier to hear him. It's almost midnight, so the kids are safely tucked away in their beds. I would have been too if I hadn't seen the text message on Stephan's phone earlier saying that one of my uncles was going to be calling at midnight for his next assignment.

His phone rings, and like the lazy asshole he is, he puts it on speaker. Internally though, I'm doing a fist bump in support of his laziness. I'll be able to hear the entire conversation now.

Stephan thinks he's cowed me into obedience and that I'd never consider eavesdropping on him. So much so, that over the past three years, he's gradually become more and more lax in how he handles his 'side businesses' for lack of a better term. Except for that night in the ER, he still takes calls away from me, but it's no longer behind closed doors with his phone pressed tightly to his ear. Like tonight, he leaves the door open slightly and has been using speakerphone during his meetings. Which has made things easier for me.

Little does he know that for the past few years, I've been eavesdropping a lot on him so that I can learn their operations better. I knew from the get-go it wouldn't be a simple escape. Stephan has eyes and ears everywhere it seems because of the things he says when he beats me. If it was just me, I'd take the risk, but it's not just me anymore. I'd never chance my babies being hurt because I didn't find out as much information as I could about the situation.

As the years went on from Stephan buying me, the more I played along, the more he allowed me freedoms to go places without him, like to the grocery store, to one of the kids' doctor visits, or taking the kids to a park. Though, I think he has someone shadowing me because he knows if I speak more than the usual 'hello', 'thank you', or normal polite conversation that happens when someone sits down next to you. Or answering 'yes' to the usual 'did you find everything you're looking for' kind of questions cashiers always ask you. If I do speak more than that to someone, I end up in a crumpled heap on the floor that night after he's done 'administering my punishments'. Uncle Diego's voice coming through the line brings me back to the present.

"This is your last chance, Hayes. Your next assignment is in Forest Creek. The cops are getting a little too bold in their efforts to bring us down."

Stephan sputters at Uncle Diego's words, but I'm frozen to the spot. We're going back to Forest Creek? Hope starts to build in my chest at the thought.

"Boss, wouldn't it be a little suspicious for us to move there? That case is still open."

"Then you better make sure that insolent wench knows her place and will only answer in favor of the family. She needs to make everyone believe that she left willingly and married you by choice. That's the only way this will work. If it doesn't, you're done, Stephan. You've been getting on the Don's nerves the past year with your

inability to keep that wench and those little leeches in line. I don't need to remind you what happens when the Don decides that you are of no use to him."

Stephan clears his throat and I can imagine him paling at Uncle Diego's threat. *"No, no, you don't."*

"Good. Boss has some jobs you'll need to do to make up for your fuck-ups. We'll be in touch."

The call ends and I start to make my retreat back to our bedroom. As I crawl under the sheets, my mind goes to Luke and my heart clenches.

Over the years, Stephan has taken great joy in constantly showing me pictures of Luke being intimate with other women. He knows how much it hurts me to see the love of my life not caring about me and not looking for me.

However, the worst are the stretches of time where he'd show me those pictures daily if not multiple times of day. That, in and of itself, is torture. That I have proof of what he's done, or supposedly done, on my phone. After showing them to me, he texts me the images and I'm not allowed to delete them. I know because I tried in the beginning. I'm not sure how he knew that I deleted them, but he did and the punishment that night actually ended up earning me a hospital stay. Not in the ER, in the actual hospital.

I've long given up hope that Luke waited for me, and I know it's going to be painful if I see him on the streets or in the stores when we move back to Forest Creek. To know he's close, but to never be able to reach out to him. I still love him and in all honesty, I don't think I could ever stop loving him. Though if he's moved on with someone else, I think that would be the worst. It might kill me seeing him in love with someone else and possibly with kids of his own.

My mind wanders to Brady's dad, Sam. If he's still on the police force, he might help me, but then I shake my head. If anything were to happen to Sam because of me, I'm almost positive Brady would kill me for sure this time. I haven't forgotten what he'd said to me when the others weren't around back in high school after the accident my mom caused. The harsh words of hate and bullying that he'd spewed were almost as bad as Isaac's version of bullying.

Shaking my head, I sigh, knowing there's only one place I can go if the kids and I manage to escape.

My **παππούς και γιαγιά'** (grandparents') house.

I'm hoping that **παππούς** (grandpa) is still alive and that his lawyer's license is still active. He'd help us get free from Stephan. I wish I'd been able to check on social media or the internet about my family over the years to see how they were doing, but there's no way Stephan would allow me to do that. I know our laptop has tons of tracking software on it. Looking them up would just be inviting more pain and I try to not do that as much as possible. It's bad enough that he beats me for no reason at all anymore.

My mind goes to that fateful night where my life no longer became my own. That night, I was cut off from my entire family and friends, except for my cousin, Isaac, Isaac's dad, my Uncle Carlos, and Uncle Diego. I've seen the three of them many times since then and they always rub it in my face that I'm the black sheep of the family. That I was sold off like cattle to further the Don's goals like the worthless reject that I am.

Sighing, I shake my head. I should stop referring to them as my family because of what they've done. True family would never have done that. I should have stopped considering them family years ago, but even though they're all assholes, I hadn't wanted to cut that last tie to my family at the time. I wasn't ready to. Now though, I'm done. I'll figure out some way to escape and get **παππούς** (grandpa) the evidence I've collected so far.

With that thought, I close my eyes and try to get some sleep.

A soft finger pokes my cheek and I groan, not wanting to wake up yet. My body still aches from Stephan's beatings, and I pray I'll be able to do everything around the house I need to today. At least it's Friday and a no school day for the kids.

That means I don't have to go anywhere.

A finger pokes my cheek again and I crack my eyes open to see my little cutie, my youngest and only daughter, Cassie peering up at me. She bounces on her toes, which causes her little blond curls to bounce along with her. Her hazel eyes sparkle as she smiles up at me, showing off the gap in between her teeth that she lost two days ago.

"Mama!" she cries out, her smile widening when she realizes I'm awake, but then it melts into a frown as she scrambles up into bed with me.

Carefully extending my arm, she takes the cue and gently lays her head on my arm, snuggling into me. They've seen me hurt multiple times over the years, even though I try to not let them see.

However, my oldest son, Asher or Ash as I like to call him, has unfortunately seen me at my worst too many times to count. It's him that helps doctor me up when I'm not able to reach my wounds. Well, for the ones that aren't severe enough to warrant an ER visit, that is, which is most of the time. He's also taken on a protector role with Isaiah and Cassie to get them quickly out of the room, especially if I redirect Stephan's rage away from any of them and onto me.

Stephan tries to limit where he hits me so that my clothes can cover my bruises. On the rare times that he hits my face, I try not to go out until they are healed. However, I can't do that anymore since Cassie's in pre-school. Whereas Ash and Isaiah take the bus, I have to drop off and pick Cassie up each day. Those days, the only way to hide the bruises is to cake make-up on and style my hair just so to help hide them.

"Is it still bad, Mama?" she asks me in a quiet whisper.

I don't sense Stephan in our room. Glancing up at the clock, I realize it's seven o'clock, and internally I groan. Stephan's going to be mad when he gets home tonight since I didn't have breakfast and coffee ready for him before he left. Honestly, I'm surprised he didn't beat me and wake me up to make it for him. Normally, he would have.

Pushing those thoughts away, I lean down and kiss Cassie's forehead. "A little, but it'll heal."

She twirls my long black curls around her fingers, her little forehead wrinkling as she thinks.

"What are you thinking about, Angel?"

Her little face falls even more, and she sniffles. "Why does Daddy hurt you? Hurt us? Doesn't he love us? I've seen the other dads at pre-school, and the other kids are always happy to see their daddies. The daddies hug and kiss their kids.

Our daddy doesn't do any of that unless he's apologizing after he hurts us or if he wants something from us."

My heart breaks as a little tear falls down her cheek. She's way too young to be this observant, but then again, living in this type of environment changes you. Taking a shaky breath, I wipe away her tears. "I don't know, Angel. I don't know."

Personally, I think he gets off on what he does to us, not that I can tell Cassie that. More than once he's left after giving me one of his 'punishments' and the next day, I have to wash away the evidence from his clothes. The stench of strong perfume. Tacky, pink lipstick stains. Neither the perfume or the shade of lipstick were ones I wear. Though, if I do wear anything, it's usually lip gloss rather than lipstick. Not to mention that I never would have done said gesture to Stephan to begin with.

Even though I don't love Stephan and didn't want to be his wife in the first place, it still hurts that he isn't faithful to me. That I'm not even allowed to speak to other men, but he's allowed to go off and sink his pathetically small dick into other women. Or maybe it's average and I'm just comparing him to the other dick I've seen, which is Luke's. Thinking about the other women, I pray that whoever he's seeing is willing and that he isn't raping her. His escapades are also why I regularly get tested to make sure he doesn't give me some sort of disease.

Shaking off those dark thoughts, I kiss her forehead again. "Let's get up, Angel. After I get ready, I'll make breakfast. You can go ahead and put your cartoons on in the meantime."

Cassie nods, gets up, and kisses my cheek. "Love you, Mama."

"Love you too, Angel."

Cassie bounds out of the room, hollering to her brothers that they can watch cartoons. Smiling, I gingerly sit up when my phone rings. Reaching over to the nightstand, I unplug my phone and my body sags as I groan loudly in the now empty room.

It's Stephan.

Swallowing another groan, I answer the call.

"Hello, Stephan."

"About time you woke up."

My cheeks heat, but then I stamp down my nerves at his arrogant tone. *"I'm sorry about that. I must have forgotten to set my alarm before going to bed last night."*

He grunts and fear coils in my stomach. Does he know that I eavesdropped on him last night? Regardless, I don't speak as the silence stretches. I learned that lesson early on.

Finally, Stephan clears his throat. *"Chief notified me this morning that I'm being transferred, so we need to get things packed up and get ready to sell the house. I'm also picking up some extra shifts to help with the costs. You'll have to be the one to research and work with the real estate agent this time. I've already called them, so they know what I want our house to go for. The agent will be calling and emailing you information later today."*

Shock courses through me. He's never let me handle anything with the selling and buying of our previous houses. Why is he doing it this time? Is this one of his tests?

"O-Of course. I'll look online to get a head start. Where are you being transferred to? Is there anything specific you want me to look for?" I gnaw on my lip as I wait for him to answer.

"No more than $300k, and make sure there's an office for me. I'd like to be out in the country, but we might not be able to do that this time with the short notice."

"Okay." I wince internally at his preferences. If we're out in the country, he can get away with more because there'd be no neighbors to hear my cries of pain.

He pauses and, even though I already know where we're going, I wonder if he's going to tell me himself or if I'll have to wait for the real estate agent to say something.

"Forest Creek. Tonight, after I get home, you and I are going to have a little talk about the move. Things need to be different there, and there will be a few more rules that you'll need to obey."

Ice slides down my spine and I wonder what exactly he's going to demand. I have a rough idea from what Un... I mean, Diego said, but who knows if Stephan will use the opportunity to make my life even more miserable than it already is with him?

"Okay, Stephan."

He grunts in response and then the line goes dead.

Well, guess I better get ready.

Still, a thrill goes through me that I'll able to pick our house this time around. Well, mostly. I know Stephan will ultimately get the final say since he's never allowed me to get a job, so I have no money of my own.

Smiling, I gingerly slide out of bed. I'll take this little freedom because I know it'll be a long time before I'm ever allowed another one.

Chapter 11

Mary

One Month Later

Biting my lip, I swallow my cry of pain as the car lurches over yet another pothole that was obscured by the snow.

It's dark.

It's snowing.

And it's nearing one o'clock in the morning.

The kids are all buckled into their seats in the back seat. There was no way I was leaving them home alone with Stephan. Especially after a night like tonight.

Not only has Stephan seemed to be getting worse since getting news of the transfer, both in attitude and the severity of his beatings, but two weeks ago we'd moved into our new house in Forest Creek. While we weren't able to get a house in the country like Stephan wanted, our yard is fairly big, so the neighbors' houses aren't right smack dab against ours. If it were a perfect world and my husband didn't beat me, I'd think it was great that my neighbors weren't so close yet the kids could still play with other kids in the neighborhood.

However, since that's not the case, I really would have preferred them to be closer to us. Unfortunately, I don't know our neighbors well enough yet to know if they are under Stephan's or my so-called family's thumbs or if they'd be able to help and watch the kids at a time like this.

Yesterday was St. Patrick's Day and Stephan had come home a few hours ago, drunk as hell and reeking of a brewery. I swear a gentle breeze could have knocked him over.

Still, he was stronger than me and I'd been pretty much defenseless against him since he took me by surprise, hitting me up alongside the back of my head. My vision swam, and I was seeing three of him for a while. It also didn't help that my body still hadn't healed from his 'present' three days ago on my birthday. Well, four days now since it's after midnight.

I should have known tonight would have been no different from all the St. Patrick's Days in the past. However, I had thought I'd have more time if he truly was going to heed Diego's words that I'd overheard a little over a month ago. That he'd try to not draw attention to himself.

Well, that attention is unfortunately going to start because I *have* to go to the ER.

I'd heard my arm snap twice when he'd been kicking me with his boots. Those fucking steel-toed boots. I swear he keeps them just for the purpose of beating me and inflicting even more pain. My body is littered with more bruises than I'd seen in a long time. Not to mention that it hurts to breathe deep. However, I don't think he broke any of my ribs, but that's just by comparing my current pain to past scenarios. I've had both bruised and broken ribs in the past. Multiple times.

A groan slips past my lips as another bump sends a new jolt of pain up my ribs. My mind travels back a couple of days to his last beating on my birthday. I don't know how I'm going to explain the older bruises that have already started to turn a little yellow-ish green. Hopefully, they won't ask to examine my body.

By the time I pull up at the hospital ten minutes later, black dots are dancing across my vision. Taking a deep breath, well as deep as I can right now that is, I grab my purse off the passenger seat and Ash starts urging Isaiah and Cassie to get out of the car. I bite back a sob when I see that Ash has prepared a bag for them and I know it will also contain some coloring books and crayons, toys, and snacks. I hate how fast Ash has been forced to grow up. He should be able to be a normal nine-year-old kid. Not nine going on twenty-one.

Cassie's little hand slides in mine, and I give it a squeeze as I lead us into the hospital.

Minutes later, I'm settled into a chair in the waiting room. Cassie is curled up on Ash's lap and I raise my good arm, running my fingers through his hair.

"Thank you, Ash, and I'm so sorry that you've had to grow up so fast. Too fast." My throat tightens with emotion as I try to blink away my tears.

He looks up at me, giving me a small smile, but it doesn't escape my notice that his eyes hold so much pain and sadness. "I don't mind, Mom. I'll always take care of you."

Carefully, I bend forward, trying not to wince as I lean down to kiss his forehead.

"Mary Hayes," a voice calls out and I gingerly rise, slinging my purse over my shoulder as I cradle my arm to my chest. Standing, my kids follow me and when we're through the doors, I almost freeze in place, but I force my body to keep walking.

It can't be.

I lower my head so that my hair can somewhat shield me, but one of my worst nightmares has come true.

Luke's here.

My Luke.

And he's an ER nurse.

Thankfully, the nurse leads me into the next room, and I quickly turn, giving the nurse's station my back until the door shuts. Without even having to ask, Ash pulls the curtain shut so no one can see inside the window. A habit from being in the ER so many times in his short life, though only one of those times was it him that was injured thanks to Stephan. The rest were for me. His gesture has more tears threatening to fall and later, when I'm alone, I'm sure I'll break down at how I'm failing them as a mother, even though I'm trying to find us a way out.

"So, it says here that you fell down the stairs and broke your arm?" the nurse asks me and I nod.

"Yes. We have just recently moved to this area, and when I got up to use the restroom tonight, I guess I was remembering our old house's layout. Instead of going down the hallway, it ended up being the stairs."

The nurse looks skeptically at me, but eventually she nods.

I force my body not to sag in relief that she believed my lie.

Or at least is pretending to believe it.

Either way, I'll take the small win. Lord knows I only get a few of those these days.

Three hours later, the nurse confirms that my ribs are just bruised and not broken. I've also been fitted with a cast and I couldn't help the small smile when Cassie pouted that I didn't pick the purple or pink cast. I'd chosen plain white so that, hopefully, it wouldn't attract more attention to it.

Not being able to resist it, I pull her close as I kiss her forehead.

Then I freeze.

The nurse must have reopened the curtains when I was wheeled down to get an x-ray, because Luke's at the nurse's station and staring straight at me with a shocked expression on his face.

I'd texted him thousands of times over the years once I'd found out that Stephan had kept my old phone and was still paying for it to have service. It was weird, but I couldn't resist not taking the chance that he might still want me. His silence, coupled with all the pictures over the years, had finally broken me. That he was able to forget about me so quickly and move on with his life without me in it.

Something snaps in me, and I turn away as anger runs through my veins.

He'd said he loved me and wanted to marry me.

But not even two weeks after I was kidnapped, Stephan had shown me the first picture of Luke having sex with another woman. I have no idea how Stephan got the images, but I didn't, don't, care. Not anymore. The only thing I really want to know was if Luke had even been faithful to me before I was kidnapped, but I'm not going to ask him. Especially not right now.

There's also no way I can tell him that he's a father.

Stephan would kill him if he tried taking Asher away from us. To suddenly not have one of his sons around, even part time, would bring 'shame' to Stephan's reputation and I know what happens when Stephan feels either he or his reputation is threatened.

Thanking the nurse, I take my discharge paperwork and prescription, tucking them into my purse. I'll get it filled tomorrow.

"Come on, kids, let's go home."

Cassie's asleep on Ash's lap, so I carefully kneel down and pull her into me, settling her on my hip. The nurse gives me a look that says I shouldn't be carrying her with bruised ribs, but I shake my head before she can say a word. It's not like Ash can carry her for long distances.

Ash opens the door, and I purposefully don't look at the nurse's station. The kids follow the nurse, and I'm right on their heels as we leave the ER and head out into the night.

It's not until we're on the road and the hospital is in our rear-view mirror that I finally let myself relax slightly.

I had worried that Luke would try to stop us or catch up to us, but thankfully, he did neither. Even though I hadn't wanted him to do anything, a part of me breaks that he didn't even try to talk to me.

Half an hour later, I pull up to our house and into the garage. I pray that Stephan's still passed out on the couch, but I know that as soon as he sees my cast, he'll flip. It happens every time that I have to go to the ER, but especially when I have to go when he's already passed out and isn't able to be with me. He feels he needs to go with me to make sure I stick to his stories.

Getting out of the car, I open the back door and pick up Cassie's sleeping body, ignoring the jarring pain that shoots through me. Ash and Isaiah come around and my heart breaks when I see the look of fear on Isaiah's face as he stares at the door leading into the house.

"Mom, if he's awake, give me Cassie, and I'll get her and Isaiah to their rooms," Ash whispers to me.

Once again, my heart clenches at what I'm putting them through because I haven't figured out enough about the people Stephan has watching over us yet to make our escape. I need to know how many patrols and their shifts before I can make a break for it, but so far, I haven't been able to find that out yet.

"Let's go to bed. Tomorrow morning, stick to your rooms for the most part until I come for you," I whisper in return.

They both nod and as quiet as possible, I open the door and we sneak through the house. I can hear Stephan's snores coming from the living room, but unfortunately, we need to walk right past him to head upstairs.

Thankfully, I'm able to get the kids tucked into their beds. Quietly, I shut Ash's door and turn, intent to head to my room. However, as soon as I look up from Ash's door handle, I stumble back in fear at seeing Stephan looming over me with murder in his eyes.

His arm lashes out, grabbing a handful of my hair, and I bite my lip to keep from crying out and waking the kids while he drags me to our room.

When he reaches our room, he throws me inside and I stumble, but somehow stay upright while he shuts and locks our door.

The snick of the door locking sends fear and ice down my spine. His worst punishments happen when he locks the door.

Fuck, fuck, fuckity, fuck.

"Why can't you ever behave, Mary? After everything that I've given you, done for you. This is how you repay me? Running off with my children and that bastard in the dead of night?"

Swallowing, I will my voice not to waver too much. "I had to. My arm and wrist were broken. I don't think they suspect anything. I made up a lie about how I got this house's layout confused with the last one. That I thought I was headed to the hallway and instead fell down the stairs."

I stand there, frozen, as he stares at me.

Minutes pass, but it's probably only seconds, even though it doesn't feel like it. My stomach sinks when I see his face darken.

"You still embarrassed me and will have to be punished."

Fuck, I hope this doesn't land me right back in the ER.

Chapter 12

Patch

It's her.

My Siren.

My Mary.

Here in Forest Creek.

Only now, she's got three children, and I don't miss the obnoxious ring on her left hand.

Though when I look in her eyes, all I notice is pain, sadness, defeat, and shock.

Confusion runs through me when her face turns into an angry snarl and she turns away, using her hair as a curtain so she can't see me anymore.

Why is she angry with me? I've been searching for her these last nine years. Every time I got close, I suddenly lost her and then I had to start all over again.

It doesn't help that none of the houses she and her husband have lived in these past nine years were under their real names. They've been using aliases for their mortgages and bills. Aliases that were most likely provided for them by the mafia.

"Is that...?" Alli asks as she walks up beside me.

"Yeah, I think it is," I reply just as quietly. I don't want to spook Mary as she hurries out of the ER like the fires of hell are on her heels.

Still, I notice that she's got a cast on her arm and is limping. Is she hurt anywhere else? What all did that fucker do to her this time? The need to know what he did flares through me, but I force the feeling down.

Uncle Sam was able to procure dozens of ER logs from each town they'd lived in for her case. Her asshole husband is beating her, but because he's a cop and tied to the mafia, he gets off with the lightest of punishments every single time. If he gets any punishment at all.

"I'm going to take my ten-minute break. I know it's early, but...," my voice trails off and I pull my phone out of my pocket, my fingers already bringing up Uncle Sam's phone number.

Alli squeezes my bicep. "Don't worry about it. I'll cover for you." She gives me a worried look that says she saw the same things I did about her injuries and is worried about her, too.

Turning on my heel, I place my call and he picks up on the second ring.

"Everything okay, Luke?"

"I'm not sure, but you need to keep that cold case on the top of your paperwork pile for the foreseeable future."

He's silent for a few beats, and then I hear a door close. *"What have you found?"*

He knows I've been trying to find her on my own as well as having Smoke, our chapter's resident hacker and programmer, looking into it as well. *"She was here. Tonight. In the ER."*

He inhales sharply. *"Are you sure it was her?"*

"Positive. I can see if Smoke can get a picture from the security system if you want?"

"No, I think I'll pay Curtis a visit at work and see if he can get it. That way it's all on the up and up."

Nodding, I bite my tongue. The need to get Mary away from that asshole is intensifying, but he's right. If we want to nail him, and have the charges stick, he needs to get the information. Not me.

"Do you know what she was in for?"

I sigh heavily, running my hand through my hair. *"Well, she walked out of here with a cast on her left arm and wrist. I don't know if she had any other injuries, but she was limping. I'm sure Curtis would be able to get you her file. You know I can't pull it up since I wasn't her nurse."* Pausing, I stare down at the floor tiles and try to calm my racing heart and anger. *"She had the kids with her. All three."*

"Well, then, that proves part of what we believed. That they're all still alive. That their deaths were all a scam."

"I've got to get her away from him." My voice is barely a shaky whisper, but he still hears it.

"You know as well as I do that a victim of abuse won't escape his or her abuser until they are ready to. Until they can be sure, or at least mostly sure, that they can be free. And that's if *they are ever ready to leave. From the reports I was able to gather, he's a master manipulator and could have been feeding her lies all these years. We have no idea the extent of everything he's told her, so she may not believe any of us in the beginning. I wouldn't put it past him to make her think we all forgot about her."*

Exhaling heavily, I scrub my hand over my face. *"Well, that would explain why she looked so pissed when she saw me."*

A heavy sigh comes over the line. *"It'll take time for her to come to terms with everything. Are you sure you don't want to leave this to me? For me to be the one to talk to her first."*

Immediately I shake my head, then realize he can't see me. *"I need to do this, Uncle Sam. She's my everything. My Siren."*

He's silent, but I can almost see him nodding and stroking his short beard. *"Then just keep trying to get through to her. You and I both know that she'll end up in the ER at some point again in the near future. There's no way that asshole's going to change his MO just because he's back where it all started."*

I grit my teeth at the thought. Thinking back to the reports of everything she's endured at the hands of that asshole has me wanting to go hunting, but he's right. *"I'll do my best, but it'll all depend on if she'll even talk to me. I'll rope Alli in on this in case she comes in on her shift and I'm not here."*

"Wouldn't hurt since they were so close. Especially if that asshole did feed her a bunch of lies about you. However, if the two of you do this, you both *need to be on the lookout constantly. If he catches wind that you two are trying to take her and the kids away from him, you'll both become targets. Just like the ones in the past. Don't make me be the one that has to break that news to your parents and sister."*

My chest clenches at that, but there isn't anything I wouldn't do for my Siren. And my parents and sister know that.

"We will. Promise."

Later that night, I lay in my bed at the clubhouse, staring at our homecoming picture on my phone. A few moments later, I flip to the images from tonight that Smoke got for me. Among them is one where he was able to get all four of their faces visible. It was when they were in the waiting room. Yeah, I know I said Uncle Sam should be the one to get it for his paper trail, but that sure as hell wasn't going to stop me from getting one for myself.

Sure, Mary's a little heavier now than she used to be, but having three kids will do that to a woman. Honestly, she looks even more beautiful than before.

The only thing that would make her even more gorgeous would be if her blue eyes were sparkling again. Right now, even in the pictures, you can feel the weight of her pain, sadness, and defeat. But especially her pain.

I hate those looks on her. She should never have had to endure the things she's had to over the years.

Broken bones and ribs.

Bruised ribs.

Sprains.

Concussions.

Eyes swollen shut.

Not to mention countless black and blue bruises.

And who knows the amount of emotional and verbal abuse he's put her through as well.

Hell, whenever she was pregnant, I'm almost positive that the asshole brought her into the hospital when her contractions were too close together on purpose. By the time she got admitted, she was too dilated to get an epidural. She gave birth to all three of her kids without pain meds.

However, only one of her kids' birth certificates didn't have a father listed.

Her eldest son, Asher.

The other two, Isaiah and Cassandra, both have Stephan listed.

I zoom in on Asher in the picture and feel my chest tighten even more.

Asher looks just like I did back when I was a kid, if you were to replace his black hair with my blond hair. Hell, it's even styled similar to how I used to wear it at that age. Did she do that on purpose? Or did he choose the style himself?

Is Asher my son and not Stephan's?

Was I right all those years ago that she was pregnant before being kidnapped?

Chapter 13

Patch

Three Months Later

Like I've been doing these past three months, I make another loop around the nurse's station, making sure to check in on the roster at the front check-in desk, then with the receptionist, and then finally with the triage nurse. Each time, I verify if Mary's name is or is not on the list. I'm sure the other nurses and receptionists think I'm crazy, but I don't give a fuck. Though I think one of the triage nurses suspects I'm watching for someone specific, but so far, she hasn't said anything to me.

The last time Mary was in the ER, it was a little over a month ago on Mother's Day. I hadn't been working, but Alli had been.

My body tenses as I recall what Alli had told me about their conversation. Somehow, Alli had convinced Stephan to step outside so that Mary could be examined. He knew it was hospital policy, but he was fighting it. That, in and of itself, is a red flag we watch for in potential abuse situations.

"When I asked Mary if she remembered me, she cut me a glare that could have killed, Luke. Said that she'd never forget those who forgot about her. Abandoned her. Walked away from her." Alli pauses and gives me a sympathetic look. "Or those that ripped out her heart and shredded it repeatedly these past nine years."

I could only stand there, shocked, as I stared at Alli's sad face.

Somehow, I manage to shake myself out of the shock. "What do you mean, ripped it out and shredded it? I've been spending every spare second looking for her and my child."

Once again, Alli gives me a sympathetic look. "When I pressed, she finally showed me pictures that her husband's been sending her about you. There were a lot of them.

Probably over a hundred, if not more." Her cheeks flame and she looks everywhere but at me.

"What were the pictures about?" I ask, even though I probably know based on Alli's reaction.

"You having sex with other women as well as you getting blow jobs," she whispers.

My heart drops at this new level of low that this asshole's been putting her through. I'll admit, I've given in a handful of times over the years where I slept with someone else or had a bunny suck me off. I could probably count the encounters all on both hands and that's for the last nine years. In total. Each time, I felt absolutely terrible about it. Like I was cheating on Mary.

"You and I both know how many times I've done that, so to have more than nine or ten is a lie. Fake."

She knows because we've talked about it before in the past. She caught me once as I sat on my parents' back deck and stared up at the windows next door that had been Mary's bedroom all those years ago. I was drunk and pissed at myself for stepping out on her the night before. It was the second time that it'd happened.

I bared my soul that night to Alli. Afterward, she made me swear that I was to come to her if it ever happened again rather than get shit-faced and beating myself up even worse than I had been.

Alli nods. "I know, and I told her. She didn't look like she believed me. I told her about you and Sam looking for her all these years. That whenever you guys got close to finding her, she moved. When I told her Brady started looking as well, once he got his badge, she really looked skeptical.

"She told me she texted you hundreds if not thousands of times once she found where her old phone had been hidden. Same for me, but I told her I never received them. I even showed her. Hell, I kept my number the same all these years just in case she called." Alli shakes her head and the defeat on her face has my chest aching.

She takes a deep breath, but I can tell she's trying hard not to cry. "I don't know what else to say. What to tell her that will make her believe that she wasn't forgotten or abandoned," she says, the last words choked as tears start falling down her cheeks.

I pull Alli into my arms and hold her as she cries. "All we can do is keep trying. Somehow, I'll get her and the kids away from that asshole. Just keep trying,

Alli-bear." Using my nickname for her from when we were kids has a small laugh escaping her, just like I had hoped.

As I stared up at the night sky that night after my shift ended, I swore I'd do everything I possibly could to convince Mary to believe me. That everything Stephan has told her is a lie.

Sighing, I shake off those thoughts and duck into the check-in station, then freeze when I look over the list.

Mary's name is on it.

And she signed in ten minutes ago.

My head pops up and I anxiously scan the waiting room. I finally find her tucked into a dark corner as if she were trying to hide herself. Next to her are her children, and it doesn't escape my notice that Asher looks devastated as he watches his mom.

Picking up her clipboard, I read over her information and my blood boils when I connect the dots to what's really happened. Then I look at the triage nurses' notes for who will be coming back next. Thankfully, it's Mary.

"I'll take this one, Sally," I tell the receptionist and she gives me a nod before going back to entering information into our system for another upcoming patient.

Backtracking to the nurse's station, since I have to pass it to get to the hallway leading to the waiting room, I'm not surprised when Alli rushes over to me, a worried and anxious look on her face.

"She's here, isn't she? You look like you could murder someone."

I grit my teeth and nod as I try to stamp down my anger over her being hurt again. I can't approach Mary if I'm like this. If I do, I might scare her and possibly the kids. She might not realize my anger isn't directed at her, but rather toward her asshole husband.

"Take a deep breath, Luke. I'm here if you need me, okay?" Alli looks up at me expectedly and I jerkily nod my head. She gives me a hug before going back to her station.

After a few moments, I'm able to tamp down my emotions enough to where I think I can keep myself under control. Exhaling heavily, I leave the ER and head down the short hallway to the waiting room.

"Mary Hayes," I call out and her head snaps up at my voice, shock written all over her face.

My chest tightens when I see her blank her emotions a second later. She carefully stands and Asher takes her trembling hand in his. She whispers something to them and they all nod. The youngest, Cassie's, lip trembles and Isaiah tucks her into his side as they follow their mom.

"Right this way." I turn and grab my badge to open the doors, but freeze when not just Mary, but her kids too, all flinch and jerk away from me.

Motherfucker is a dead man.

Deciding not to draw any attention to their reactions, I scan my badge and once the door closes behind us; I notice the tremors running through Mary intensify a little more. Even though I want to pick her up and carry her into the closest available room so I can help ease her pain quicker, I don't. I don't want to scare her off right away. Nor do I want any of her husband's cronies to possibly see us, either. That's the last thing I want is for Mary or the kids to be beaten or hurt because of something I do.

There are rooms that are closer to the entrance of the ER that are open, but I lead Mary to the back of the pod, where there are multiple rooms open on either side of it. With how skittish they all are, maybe they'll be more open to talking if there's even less of a chance someone will hear them.

Opening the door, I step inside and after they are all in, I close it. "Feel free to have a seat, kids. Do you want me to get you another chair so all three of you can have your own seat?" I ask as I crouch down in front of them, trying to make myself smaller.

The youngest, Cassie, whimpers slightly and buries her face in Asher's side. His arm tightens around her as he stares defiantly at me. "She's shy, but she usually sits on my lap if she can't be with Mom."

Nodding, I stand and step back. All three of their little bodies slightly relax and I bite my cheek to keep my anger off my face. "No problem. Let me know if you change your minds." Pausing, I turn to Mary, who is now sitting on the examination table. I had meant to say everything after getting her fixed up, but instead my mouth decides to overrule my head. "Hello, Siren."

She stiffens, and her eyes harden as she glares at me. "I'm not your Siren anymore. Please leave. I want a different nurse," she says, her voice as hard and icy as her eyes.

Glancing at the kids, I notice that Asher's eyeing me warily and my gaze goes back to Mary. "I swear to you, Siren, I've been looking for you for the past nine years. As soon as I got close, as in physically on my way to you, you'd be gone by the time I got there. In fact, as a just in case I ever saw you again after you came in here a few months ago, I took some pictures of some of my notes so you can see the proof for yourself."

Digging into my pocket, I unlock my phone and bring up the photo album for her to see before handing her my phone. "Do you want me to do my examination while you look through that, or wait and do it after?"

Hesitantly, she takes my phone with her good hand since her other is still in a cast. Normally, she should have gotten it off a month ago, but when she was here last month, it was re-injured when she fell, so the doctor decided to recast it.

Mary gnaws on her lip as she stares at me. It takes everything in me to not reach out, to caress her lip and gently pull her abused lip free like I used to do when we were dating. Finally, she glances down and opens the album. Taking a deep breath, she swallows thickly. "Wait please. I need to know. After all these years, I need to know. I can deal with the pain for a little longer. It's not like I'm not used to it," she replies, her voice barely a whisper.

Rage boils in my veins at her words, but I try to stomp it down as much as possible. I will *not* make her or her kids think that I'm the same as that asshole.

As I look her over while she scrolls through my phone, I'm torn. A part of me wants to make it so that she isn't in pain anymore, but the other part of me agrees with her and wants her to know the truth. She's had so many choices taken from her all these years. I'm not going to push her on this, but if I notice that the pain is getting to be too much, I'll step in.

However, there is something I can do for her eye right now.

Walking over to the cabinets, I pull out one of our medical ice packs and squeeze it. The chain reaction of the chemicals inside starts to lower the temperature, and I hand it to Mary. "Try to hold this to your eye. That should help minimize some of your swelling."

Mary eyes me hesitantly, and then takes the ice pack from me. Her fingers brush mine, and just like in the past, a current zips through me at the contact. Judging by her sharp breath, she felt it too. I have to bite my cheek to keep from reacting when I see that gorgeous blush staining her cheeks. Crap, if this keeps up, the insides of my cheeks are going to be raw as fuck.

I clasp my hands behind my back as the silence stretches so I don't do something stupid like reach out and touch her before she's ready for me to. Instead, I watch Mary as she flicks through each picture. I know when she gets to her past hospital records logs because the blood drains from her face, but I give her credit. She keeps going.

A tug on my pants has me looking down, and I see Cassie standing there looking up at me in confusion. I glance back toward Asher in surprise, but he just smirks at me, a proud little smirk. I hadn't even seen or heard her move.

"Well, aren't you a little ninja?" I say as I crouch down again. "What's your name? I'm Luke, but some of my friends call me 'Patch'," I ask, since I can't very well let on that I already know all three of their names.

"I'm Cassie. Do you really know my mama?"

I glance up at Mary to find her watching me like a hawk, and when I refocus on Cassie, I nod. "Yes, Angel, I do. She's very important to me. Always has been and always will be."

Cassie frowns. "Why do some people call you Patch?"

I honestly thought she'd ask about what I'd just said, but maybe Mary has talked to her about me in the past. Or this is just a reminder of how kids' brains work sometimes.

"I'm part of a motorcycle club here in town, the Steel Archangel's MC. I'm their club medic. When I was prospecting with them, a friend of mine was riding his motorcycle around town when someone clipped him and caused him to wreck his bike. He didn't want to go to the hospital, so I cleaned up his road rash and injuries at our clubhouse. Someone made a joke about me patching him up and it just stuck. When I earned the right to be a Steel Archangel, Patch became my road name."

Isaiah slowly slides down off his chair and takes a tentative step forward. "I'm Isaiah. What's a road name?" he asks me, and I grin when I notice that he has motorcycles on his t-shirt. Guess talking about motorcycles is an ice breaker topic for him.

"It's like a nickname. One that all my brothers and sisters call me rather than Luke."

Cassie's eyes widen in surprise. "How many siblings do you have?"

I can't help but chuckle. "They aren't my brothers and sisters by blood, but brothers and sisters by choice, and there are a lot of them. As for blood relation, I have a little sister, Amanda, but everyone calls her Mandy."

I pause and glance up at Mary, and frown when I notice she's staring at my phone in disbelief. "How you doing there, Siren?"

"You never got them," she whispers as her eyes turn misty.

"Never got what?"

She sniffs and I stand, grabbing the tissues off the counter and hand them to her.

"Ash, Baby, can you please grab my cell phone out of my purse?"

Asher turns around and digs through the purse behind him on the chair before handing Mary her phone.

As she fiddles with something on it, she continues. "I don't know why, but Stephan kept my old phone and has been paying service on it this entire time. When I found it, I sent messages to you and when you didn't respond, I tried Alli, too. I never texted Brady because I figured he wouldn't help me.

"I saved them all on the cloud login that Dad had. He mainly used it for his accounting jobs but he let me use it to. But I saved pictures of everything there so that there'd be no way Stephan would know about the texts. Then I'd delete them off my phone and put it back in its hiding place. Neither of you ever responded," she says with a defeated look on her face as she hands me her phone.

I quickly scroll through the information and my heart breaks at the desperation in her words. She never mentions if Asher is my son, but now isn't really the time to ask with the kids here. Plus, I'm not sure if Mary's ready to have that talk yet. When I get to the last one, I frown when I notice that the messages stop three years ago, almost to the day.

Glancing up at her, she's blinking rapidly as her good hand clenches at the hem of her t-shirt.

"No, I never got them, but I bet that f—jerk blocked all of our numbers."

She bites her lip at my almost curse but then her face pales and she shakes her head in disbelief. "God, I never even thought about that. I'm such an idiot," she says as she buries her head in her hands and then winces. Her hand flies to her ribs and I set the phone down on her lap as I switch into nursing mode again.

Chapter 14

Mary

As soon as I wince, it's as if Luke has changed. Like a switch has been flipped and he's now in nurse mode.

Luke takes off his stethoscope and listens to my heart. While he checks my vitals, my mind whirls with what I've just seen and what he's told me.

Is it all real?

Is it really true that he never stopped looking for me? Not only Luke, but Sam, Alli, and possibly even Brady as well?

That they didn't forget about me?

When Luke's done, he pins me with a look that I recognize all too well. It's the look he'd give me when I would put myself down or if he noticed me comparing myself to others.

"You're not an idiot. You had a lot on your shoulders trying to take care of your kids and yourself while also trying to stay out of the crosshairs of that f—jerk. Based on those messages, you risked yourself by trying to find out more about what he did so that you might be able to escape. You're very brave and you're the strongest woman I know." He pauses and licks his lips.

My gaze tracks the motion, and I bite my own lip at the memories of how soft his lips used to be. Then his words sink in, and I shake my head.

"I'm not strong. He broke me years ago and continues to do so every time I 'mess up'," I say with quotation marks and then bite my lip hard when another flare of pain radiates from my ribs. A motion Luke doesn't miss.

He pins me with a stare before stepping over to the counter to grab the clipboard with my chart. "So, the information you gave us is that you were carrying a laundry basket upstairs. You tripped on some toys and then fell down the stairs.

On the way down, you knocked your broken arm again, your ribs are hurting again, and your eye is already swelling."

He cocks an eyebrow at me, and I feel my face heating as I look down at my hands.

Suddenly, Asher stands and places himself between Luke and me.

"Even if we wanted to, we couldn't tell you everything. That will just make things worse for us. Somehow, Dad always finds out what the nurses and doctors write on those papers and the notes anyone makes in her files."

Luke's eyes flash with rage, but a second later, it's gone, and his face softens as he squats down in front of Asher. "What's your name, son?"

My breath hitches, and I wonder if Ash has made the connection yet.

Or Luke.

Ash knows Stephan isn't his father. He was five when he first asked me about it because he looks so different from Stephan.

Stephan has light blond hair, hazel eyes, pale skin that burns instead of tans, and a bunch of freckles spattering all over his skin. He used to be relatively thin, but over the years, he's let himself go and now sports a beer belly. Not that I'm one to talk, since I'm heavier than I've ever been, but I've always struggled to lose the baby weight after each of my kids were born.

Ash got my black hair that ended up being straight as a board instead of my curly hair. He got Luke's green eyes as well as his strong jaw and cheekbones. Both Isaiah and Cassie have hazel eyes like Stephan, but Isaiah has my black, wavy hair, whereas Cassie has blond curls. All three of them have a light olive skin tone thanks to **πατέρα** (dads) Greek genes. He was one hundred percent Greek, or as close as you can get to one hundred, that is.

After that, and whenever Stephan wasn't around, I would tell Ash bedtime stories of Luke so that he'd know about him, though I never told him his name. I had hoped someday that they could meet. I just never expected it would be like this.

"Asher, but I go by Ash."

"Well, Ash, thank you for protecting your mom and your siblings. That's got to be incredibly hard. Especially for someone so young."

A tremor runs through Ash, but he fists his little hands, trying to hide it. "It is. Especially when she takes his punishment for us," he whispers, and his little body starts to shake.

Luke's gaze snaps to mine and the empathy, love, and determination in his eyes hits me so strongly it's like someone's knocked the wind out of me. And under all of that is anger, but somehow, I can tell it's not directed at me or the kids.

"Ash, I promise I won't put the real reasons in my report, but can you tell me what happened? Why did your dad try to hurt you? I want to help you guys, all of you, but if I don't know what he's doing, then it's harder for me to help."

Ash's body tenses, and I nibble my lip as I debate about asking for help or not. God if I keep this up, my lips are going to be bloodied and raw.

"The club... Are they really like what we heard about as kids?" I ask him, and Luke nods as he looks up at me.

"They are. None of us tolerate women or children being abused. All of them are a good group of guys and my President and Enforcer actually just settled down with someone. I don't know if you remember Levi Wallace at all? She's four years younger than us, I think. Actually, if you heard the news, two of them and one of our Prospects were involved in the shooting yesterday, but all of them pulled through. They'll be getting out later today if all goes well."

I had heard about the shooting, and I bite my lip hard as I remember how Stephan had actually celebrated at them getting injured yesterday. He broke out what he calls his 'good whiskey'. Though he had said he wished they all had died. Same for the woman that was with them. That it was a pity more of the Steel Archangel's hadn't been hit in the crossfire.

Taking a deep breath, I nod as I close my eyes.

Am I really going to do this? If I do, I could put Luke and the club in danger. However, if they really are like how all of our parents talked about in the past, as well as what I'd heard around town and school these past few months, then they might be my last chance to get free from Stephan.

Looking up, I lock eyes with Luke. "You promise it won't go in the reports or beyond these four walls?"

"I give you my word, Siren."

Taking a deep breath, my gaze lowers to Ash.

"Today is Ash's ninth birthday," I tell him, my voice trembling slightly as I think back to earlier this morning. "Like always, I baked a cake for him and decorated it. We sang happy birthday to him in whispers since Stephan was asleep after working a night shift. At the end, we all 'air clapped' and the kids quietly high-fived each other. He was just about to open his presents from Isaiah and Cassie when Stephan came barreling into the kitchen, screaming at us for waking him up, even though I know that wasn't the case."

I pause and swear I can still feel his hands on me. A tear falls down my cheek, but I make no move to wipe it away.

"He grabbed Ash by his shirt and threw him against the wall before I could get in between them. I... I..."

Suddenly, it feels like the air's been stolen from my chest. Stephan's threats throughout the years slam into my brain, one after the other, paralyzing me and silencing my voice.

"Breathe, Siren. I need you to breathe. Can you open those beautiful blue eyes for me?"

His voice cuts through my memories, and it's then that I realize his hands are cupping my face.

"That's it. It's okay, Siren. I'm here and I can help you. All of you."

I shake my head on habit. "He'll hurt you. He'll hurt your parents and sister. He'll go after the club. He already hates the Steel Archangel's. If you or the club help, it'll be like throwing gasoline on a fire."

"Siren, I need you to listen to me and listen good." He pauses as if he's making sure I won't look away. I can't. Not with him touching me again after all these years. I swear it's like a current is running through me with his touch and its awakening feelings that have long since been dormant.

"My club and I are more than capable of taking care of ourselves in dangerous situations. It's you and the kids I'm worried about. He's escalating and you know it. I can help you, but you need to be ready to make that jump. Are you?"

I lick my dry lips and take a shaky breath, already knowing my answer. "Not right this instant."

Disappointment flashes in his eyes and he goes to pull away. My hands automatically come up and hesitantly, I wrap them around his wrists, not wanting him to pull away yet. Taking another shaky breath, I push on.

"Luke, I'm not saying 'no', just 'not yet'. There are things I need to get in order before I make that jump. Personal things. The evidence I've gathered so far that isn't or can't be stored in the cloud account. Once I have that around, I need to somehow get in touch with **παππούς** (grandpa) about a couple of things. Then I can be free to make that jump."

Luke rests his forehead on mine, sighing heavily.

"Okay, Siren. I'll follow your lead on this, even though I don't like it. I kept my phone number the same in case you ever tried to get a hold of me. Alli and Brady did the same, too."

I can't help my flinch at hearing Brady's name and Luke gives me a small, sad smile.

"He's changed, Mary. Not too long after you were kidnapped, he realized how much of an as—, I mean jerk, he was to you. He's one of the good cops on the force. You gotta trust me on this."

Hesitantly, I nod, and he smiles wider. I glance over at my kids, and for once, I see hope in their eyes. I also notice Ash looking at Luke as if he's contemplating something. No doubt he'll have questions for me later, but if he straight out asks if Luke's his father, I won't lie to him. However, I'll need to make sure Isaiah and Cassie aren't around. I don't think they're ready to hear that just yet.

Turning back to Luke, I give him a small smile in return.

"I still remember your phone number, as well as the others, but it'll take some time to get everything lined up. There are a couple of big meetings in the next few months that I need to keep an eye on." Pausing, I give him a stern look. "However, you and the club need to keep an eye out. Sam, Brady, and any of the other good cops, too. They're planning something, but I don't know all the details yet. Once I have that, then I'll make my move."

He frowns, but then nods. "I don't like it, especially since it'll be a few more months that you and the kids will still be in his clutches. But if that's what you want to do, then I'll support you. You've had years of people taking your choices away from you, and I don't want to do that. However, I need you to promise me something."

"What?" I ask, my voice shaky and hesitant.

"That if it gets too dangerous, call me. We can come and get you out. We can always find out what's going on later. It might take longer, but you and the kids are more important. Just... Please promise me that you'll call. It also wouldn't be a bad idea to have Ash memorize my number as well."

Swallowing thickly, I nod, knowing his unspoken words.

To have Ash call if I can't.

"I promise I'll call if I feel like things are getting to that point. So far, I don't think he suspects I know as much as I do. Or if he does know, he might think he's programmed me enough to never talk."

The muscle in his jaw ticks, but he gives me a curt nod. "Good. Now let's get you patched up. I'll look over Ash, too, just in case."

A few hours later, we're home, and thankfully, Stephan is still asleep.

Hanging my purse up, I slip off my flats and look around the kitchen.

Ash's birthday cake is still splattered around everywhere.

On the table.

On the counter.

On the walls.

On the tiles.

Looking up, my shoulders drop. Even on the ceiling. Hopefully, the light blue frosting doesn't stain the walls. They're painted a very light beige.

"Mama?"

I turn, looking at Cassie, who is clutching her gift for Ash to her chest.

"Can I give Ash his birthday present now?" she asks, her voice barely even audible.

My heart clenches at the crumpled and slightly torn wrapping paper. My gaze goes to Isaiah, and he's doing the same. God, I hope Stephan didn't break or ruin the presents during his rage.

I'm not allowed a large budget when it comes to presents. Normally, I take the other two kids to a thrift store or the dollar store for them to get presents for their sibling. As for the main present, I'm capped at fifty dollars, so I'm never able to get them much. Even Christmas presents are capped at fifty dollars per kid. Then again, I should be grateful he didn't say fifty dollars was all I could spend between the three of them.

Forcing a smile, I nod. "Yes, Angel, you guys can give him his presents. We just need to remember to be quiet, though."

Fear creeps into all their eyes, and I wish I would have been able to take Luke up on his offer earlier. To get them away from Stephan sooner rather than later. However, I wasn't lying when I said I'd overheard how important these next couple of meetings are for Stephan, Diego, and Antonio. I have a feeling that Luke, his club, and **παππούς** (grandpa) will need all the information I can give them.

Tucking Cassie and Isaiah into their respective beds, I head into Ash's room to check on him. He's been quiet for the past few hours. Sure, he played with the kids and enjoyed his new toys, books, coloring pencils and sketchbooks, but not like he usually does.

Shutting the door, I walk over to his bed and sit down next to him. He's holding the stuffed cat that Cassie had gotten him as he stares off into space.

Reaching up, I push a lock of his hair out of his eyes. It's actually a little funny now that I think about it. His hair cut is very reminiscent of Luke's, but more like when we were kids than how he styles it now. Ash's hair is cut short on the sides, but the top is kept long. It's styled so that it mostly drapes over his right eye and the right side of his face. Luke's hair is the same but stops right around his left eye, whereas Ash's hair goes down to a little below his jaw.

"What's going through your mind, Hawk?"

My nickname for him gets me a smirk, and he cuddles up against my good side. Ever since he was younger, he's had an eagle eye for things. I swear he has an eidetic memory because he can look at something for a few seconds and be able to recite exactly what he saw, even if it's months later. He's also really good at reading a person and their body language even though he's only nine.

He snuggles his stuffed cat tighter and plays with its tail.

"That nurse from today," he whispers as he shifts to look up at me. "Was he the one you told me about? Is he my dad?"

Smiling softly, I ignore the pain in my ribs and lean down, kissing his forehead. "Yeah, Hawk, he is. You look so much like him. A lot of your personality traits remind me of him, too."

We sit there in silence and after a while I feel him nod against my side. "I'm glad. He seems like a nice man, and I hope he really meant what he said."

Thankfully, he doesn't repeat anything else from our conversations earlier. Even though Stephan's at work, I still don't want to risk talking about it.

"Me, too, Hawk. Me, too."

Chapter 15

Patch

Two Months Later

With a grunt, I sit my ass down on a stool at the bar in our clubhouse and ask our Prospect, Alexei or Lex, as most of us have started calling him, for a beer.

Taking a big swig, I try to force myself to be happy, but it's hard.

Today is a big day for our club.

A double wedding.

Three men, that are some of the best men that I know, are getting married today. Thor, our club President, and his twin brother, Dragon, who is our Enforcer, are both getting married to Levi. Well, technically, she's getting married to Thor, but she's also going to repeat the vows with Dragon. Levi's one hell of a woman, and I admire her greatly. She's perfect for both of them, and honestly, all three of them balance each other out.

Not too long after they tie the knot, Timber, our Treasurer, will be marrying Mae. Timber's a good friend of mine and has actually been a confidant for me for the past few months with what's been going on with Mary. His Old Lady, Mae, is a total sweetheart and is actually the long-lost daughter of Smoke, our resident IT guy, security man, and hacker extraordinaire.

I still can't believe that Mae's bitch of a mom and stepdad told Smoke that Mae was stillborn. It was all a hoax and a way for Preston, Mae's stepdad, to con some money from the insurance company. Not to mention laundering money under Mae's 'dead name'. We still have no idea if her mom was in on any of it, but my gut is telling me that she's not.

Shaking my head, I take another swig of my beer as this week's past events run through my mind. Thankfully, Mae's and Smoke's relationship seems to be on the mend, but it was bad in the beginning when she arrived here a little over a week ago. Really bad.

I was surprised when we found out that Timber had planned to ask Mae to marry him so soon, but the big lug fell hard and fast for sweet little Mae. You only have to spend about five minutes, if that, around the two of them to realize they are the real deal. The other half to each other. Some would say that a week is too soon to marry someone, but again, the two really are perfect for each other.

That thought has me thinking about Mary. The one I wanted, no, want to be my forever.

I've seen her around town, of course, in the last couple of months, however after our conversation when I was examining her back in June, I knew I couldn't approach her in public. Even though it killed me, whenever I saw her, I went in the opposite direction to avoid temptation. I haven't been able to talk to her in person since the day she came to the ER on Ash's birthday.

I did hear that there was another ER visit a few weeks ago, but neither Alli nor I were on shift when that happened. It's probably for the best since her asshole husband was with her. I don't think I could have seen him and not throttled him right then and there for what he's done to her and the kids.

However, I did look over the notes when Uncle Sam sent them to me. Thank God, we have a punching bag in our gym downstairs because I was at it for a long time to burn off the rage of what he'd done to her. I'm honestly surprised her bones aren't dust by now. Especially her ribs. However, he's escalating just like I had known he would. Now he's taken to cutting her, too.

A hand lands on my shoulder, and I look up in surprise, not having noticed anyone approaching me.

"What's going on, man?" Timber asks as he sits down on the stool next to me and Lex slides him a beer.

I sigh, but I know I can trust Timber with this. He already knows some of what's going on, but not everything. "Remember that woman I told you about that's been in and out of the ER multiple times the past six months?"

"Yeah. Her name's Mary, right?"

I nod glumly. "Yeah, well, back in the day, she was my best friend. She, Alli, Brady, and I were close as could be. We were always together, though it helped we all lived next to each other, and our parents were all friends.

"In high school, Mary and I started dating. We were each other's firsts. Then, some months later, she disappeared with no warning and her house was put on the market." I pause, not being able to tell him what else happened that night. At least not yet. Or that I know the reasons behind the house going for sale. And for my choices after that. Out of the corner of my eye, I notice him frowning, but I'm not about to spill that info when we have numerous guests here. Mary would never forgive me.

"I never heard from her the past nine years until I saw her that first time in the ER six months ago. Every time she's in there, her injuries are worse than the last time," I say, my lip curling as I think back to all those hospital logs.

"I know you can't tell me specifics, but I hope like fuck you aren't suggesting her husband is beating her."

I turn toward him and pin him a look. His face pales and then it starts turning red with anger.

"Fuck. Who's the dead man walking?"

This is one reason why I love my brothers. They're there in an instant, supporting you. Thinking back to the asshole, I clench my hands, and am surprised I haven't cracked my phone, which is still in my hand. I had been hoping she'd call, but she hasn't yet.

"Fucking Deputy Chief Stephan Hayes."

"You've got to be fucking shitting me," he snarls. "I always knew I hated that fucker. I don't know how he weaseled his way into our town, but I knew he was crooked from the first time I saw the slimy bastard."

I can't help my sneer. "He always plays the doting husband in public, but at home, it's a fucking shitshow. I know because Mary and one of her kids told me what's been happening. I gave her my number and the club's number. Told her oldest to memorize it as well. That if they're in danger, they can call us and we'd get them all out of there."

He narrows his eyes at me. "What aren't you telling me?"

Not wanting anyone to really hear this, I look around nervously, but thankfully, no one's paying us much attention. I swallow thickly as I stare at my phone, willing it to ring and needing to hear her voice again.

"I'm almost positive her eldest, Asher or Ash as she calls him, is my son. She's been away for a little over nine years and he's nine. I had suspicions she was pregnant before she disappeared, but that's all they were at the time. However, I found out from my uncle that she gave birth ten weeks after she was taken. So unless she was with someone else behind my back, which I doubt is true, he's my son.

"She has two other kids that are younger, Isaiah and Cassie, with Cassie being the youngest. Ash looks just like I did when I was that age, if he were to have my blond hair instead of her black hair. While all three kids have a lot of Mary in them, all of them but Ash have bits of Stephan in their looks," I whisper.

"Fuck..." he hisses.

Large hands land on both of our shoulders, and we both jump as Thor chuckles at our surprise.

"We've got your back, Patch, on whatever needs to be done to get her and her kids away from that fucker. Later, come find me and fill me in on what's all happened so far. Keep me posted."

And with that, he walks off and heads upstairs.

"Fuck, I didn't even hear him walk up behind us," I say, a sad laugh escaping as I shake my head.

"I swear he's been taking stealth lessons from Lex and the others," Timber replies, laughing, and I can't help but join in.

Lex grins from behind the bar, which has us both laughing harder.

"Timber," Kristy, the wedding planner, yells from upstairs. Timber finishes his beer and clasps my shoulder.

"Like Thor said, I've got your back on this. Let me know if you need me for anything."

I give him a chin lift, and he heads upstairs to see what Kristy wants.

Last night should have been a time of happiness and celebration, and it was for a while. Until Drae's asshole dad, Ghost, the ex-VP of Black Plague MC, left us a package that ended up blowing up our front gate. Thankfully, no one was injured.

I had taken yesterday and today off for the weddings, but tomorrow I'll be back to it at the ER. I nurse my drink as I stare down at my phone in my hand. It kills me that I can't reach out to Mary to make sure she's still okay. Not without putting her in danger, anyway.

"Patch," someone calls out, and I look up to see Thor standing in the doorway of his office and he tilts his head, silently telling me to follow him.

Draining the last of my beer, I head up to the bar, grab a fresh one from Ethan, and head into his office.

"Shut the door behind you and have a seat."

My chest tightens, but I do as he says. "I'm surprised to see you here. Thought you three would be holed up all day, tangling in the sheets." I grin at him and he grins in reply.

"Oh, I definitely plan to still be doing that, but I wanted to check in with you to see how you're doing. Tell me what's going on with your woman."

That has my eyebrows raising, but fuck. I do want her as my woman. I want her as my Old Lady. My wife. And if she's willing, the mother of my children.

I fill him in on everything that's been happening the last few months, including what happened that night nine years ago, and what's been going on since then. I'd told him some of this back when I asked if Smoke could help me look for her, but I hadn't filled him in on the new stuff since then.

He stares at me for a few seconds, and worry starts to set in. "We've got to be careful with this. There's no way we'll be able to keep the cops fully out of this. There is a chance you won't be able to dole out justice yourself. Are you going to be okay if that happens?"

My gut churns at that. I've dreamed of making him suffer everything he's put her through, but he's right. I might not be able to do that. Sighing, I nod. "While I'd definitely like to make him suffer, if it comes down to it, I really just want the four of them free of that fucker. To make her mine and adopt her other two kids as my own."

He nods, though he's still staring at me like he's trying to peel back the layers. After a few moments, he clears his throat. "Is there any way to get a burner to her? So you can have some way of keeping in touch with her or checking in to make sure they're okay?"

I shake my head. "I asked her that a couple of months ago, but she said it'd be too risky. While she's had more liberties here than anywhere else, that asshole still keeps a tight leash on her. She's found him going through her things a number of times, searching for other means of communication with other people."

"Did she say what she wanted to find out before leaving the bastard?" he asks, and I frown.

"No, and I asked her about it, but she refused to say anything. Though, I do wonder if it's tied to her grandfather and his dealings."

"Who's her grandfather?"

"Don Antonio Vasquez."

"Fuck," Thor hisses, and I nod in agreement.

While Diego Vasquez has been tied to the human trafficking ring for years, he's never been sentenced for it. Surprisingly, it's only been Diego in the news tied to it. If Antonio was really in on it, I would think his name would have popped up somewhere, but it never has.

Whenever Diego makes the news because of someone else tying him to the trafficking ring or abusing someone, he always gets away with it. The cases are dismissed due to lack of evidence, key witnesses not showing up or retracting their statements. Shit like that.

It also doesn't help that Uncle Sam suspects that almost half of his fellow officers and a couple of judges in town are crooked. He's been on cases where evidence he filed suddenly disappears, and usually, it's key evidence, too.

"Try to convince her to carry a burner phone the next time you see her. Have one with you at all times in case you run into her. Program in your number, mine, and the clubhouse. That way, all she has to do is hit speed dial. Fuck, you can even put Phoenix's number in it if you want as well. Just don't list our names, so if he does find it, it won't look as bad with her having the numbers of so many men.

"Once you have the burner number, give it to me and I'll make sure Phoenix has it, too. If she calls the clubhouse, just have her say who she is, and to ask for you, Phoenix, or me. I'll make sure the others know not to turn her away."

I stiffen at that. There's no way Mary would want everyone to know how fucked up her life's been for the past nine years or the abuse that she's been through.

"Don't worry, I'm not going to tell them the details, just the gist of it. That she's a friend of yours that's trying to escape her abusive husband."

My body relaxes at that. "Thanks, Pres."

He gives me a chin lift. "Keep me posted. We'll get her out of there if she's not able to do it herself."

"I will. Thanks again, Pres."

Chapter 16
Mary

Two Months Later ~ Thanksgiving

Present

Pulling the turkey out of the oven, I pray that tonight goes well. This is the first time that I'll have seen my **παπποὺς και γιαγιά** (grandparents) since I was kidnapped and sold. To say I'm nervous is an understatement. However, also being back home has brought its own troubles, and surprisingly, rewards for the kids and me.

Stephan has had to let up on a lot of constraints and rules now that I'm back home around family and friends that I've known since I was a kid. To keep me out of some social events would have made people suspicious and when I told him that, I could see the wheels turning in his mind. Knowing about that secret conversation with Diego months ago has inadvertently helped me regain some freedom and privileges.

It also helped with **γιαγιά** (grandma) seeing me in the grocery store last week after I had dropped Cassie off at school.

Reaching up, I grab a box of stuffing off the shelf when I hear a startled gasp behind me. Twirling around, my body freezes.

Is it really her?

"**Λουλούδι μου** (My flower)," *she whispers and my eyes fill with tears.*

"**Γιαγιά** (Grandma)."

A strangled cry escapes her lips that she tries to muffle with her hands. Then the next thing I know, her arms are wrapped around me and her signature scent of lilies engulfs me. I'm not sure how long we stand there, wrapped in each other's arms as we cry. When she pulls back, both of us wipe our cheeks, drying our tears.

"**Λουλούδι μου** (My flower), *where—*"

My eyes widen in alarm and I quickly look around before returning my focus to her. "Not here," I hiss quietly at her. "I'm probably being watched. You can't mention any of that or Luke."

I pause when I spot a familiar person entering the same aisle that we're in, and I can feel my muscles tensing in response. **Γιαγιά** (Grandma) *must be able to tell because she gives my arm a soft squeeze.*

"**Λουλούδι μου** (My flower), *it is so good to see you again. We must have Thanksgiving together. After all these years, your* **παππούς** (grandpa) *and I have missed you terribly. I won't take no for an answer," she tells me, and she gives me a look I know all too well.*

She really won't accept no.

"I would like that. However, you should come to our house. You can see the kids," I tell her. Carefully glancing toward the man that's one of Stephan's underlings, I'm relieved when he's still at the end of the aisle. "And to meet my husband, Stephan Hayes," I whisper quietly to **γιαγιά** (grandma), *knowing that she'll tell* **παππούς** (grandpa) *his name. With me suddenly disappearing, he'll look into Stephan. That is, if what Luke and Alli have told me is true.*

Γιαγιάς (Grandmas) *eyes light up in understanding, but I also see excitement there that I'm agreeing to have dinner together and that she'll get to meet her great-grandkids.*

"**Λουλούδι μου** (My flower), *that sounds perfect. Give me your new phone number and we can text as we get all the details lined up for our get together."*

Out of the corner of my eye, I can see Stephan's underling clenching his fists, so I'm guessing he heard her. However, since it's in public, I can't really deny her without making her suspicious. And I think he realizes that because he doesn't step in like he had in the past.

Digging my phone out of my purse, I try to stop my shaky hands but a sharp glance from **γιαγιά** (grandma) *tells me she's noticed my nervousness. Still, we exchange numbers and after another hug, we part ways.*

When I got home that day, I wasn't surprised when I saw Stephan was waiting for me. He went into a long rant that I should have been more careful and as soon as I spotted her, I should have turned and walked away. I tried reasoning with him that if I had walked away, it would have made things worse because then she would have sought me out on her own. That we would eventually have had a surprise visit at the house at some point. I tried to butter him up by saying I suggested our house so that he could better control how things went and that he wouldn't get that if we went to their house. It took the better part of an hour, but he finally relented and agreed that we could host Thanksgiving at our house.

Since then, Stephan has threatened me several times that if he's going to continue to allow me to do these things and have these privileges, like being able to see my family and friends, I have to be the perfect, loving and supportive wife in public. In no way am I to tell anyone about what he does to us behind closed doors. Over the years, I've gotten good at acting like things were fine, but that was around strangers.

Tonight is going to be a major struggle.

I used to be extremely close to my **παππούς και γιαγιά** (grandparents), even though we didn't see each other more than five or six times a year before we moved to Forest Creek. Once we moved, I saw them multiple times a week, if not daily. I'm afraid that they're going to see right through my lies, but I have to try. If they do realize I'm lying, I just hope that they don't say anything around Stephan that will set him off. I have a plan to get some information to **παππούς** (grandpa) tonight and I need it to go off without a hitch.

If everything goes according to plan, this will be my first step toward freedom.

As a just in case, Ash knows where all the important documents are and things we'll need to grab if we're in a rush. That way, we can divide and conquer. Or if need be, he can call Luke.

About a month ago, I ran into Luke at the grocery store. I was moving gingerly thanks to another beating. I was trying to reach a box of cereal on the top shelf when I felt someone step up close behind me.

A hand stretches above me and grabs the box of cereal I'd been trying to reach. Spinning around, I stare in shock at Luke standing right up in my personal space. The smell of his cologne takes me back to when we were in high school. However, now there's the added scent of leather with a tinge of oil mixed in with it, probably from his motorcycle. The combination is heady, and I feel my knees wobble. Though, that could be in part because Luke is most definitely not *dressed in scrubs with a long-sleeve undershirt this time. No, this time he's dressed in blue jeans, boots, a leather cut, and a snug fitting t-shirt that shows off many tattoos on his arms and how muscular he is.*

"Here you go, Ma'am," he says with a wink as he steps back.

"T-Thank you," I reply, grateful that he isn't saying anything too out of the ordinary.

"Mr. Patch!" Cassie calls out as she jumps up and down in the cart, holding her hands out like she wants a hug.

I stare at her in shock. My generally shy, introvert daughter wants a hug from a man she's only met once.

However, what Luke does damn near has my knees buckling.

He pushes his grocery cart to the side so that he's not blocking the aisle and steps forward, hugging my daughter. He says something quietly to her that has her giggling as she clings to him. Then Isaiah, who has stepped closer to Patch, grins and raises his fist like he's seen people on TV do. Luke chuckles and bumps his fist. His gaze cuts to Ash, who's standing at my side protectively, and gives him a chin lift as he ruffles his hair slightly.

Shit, I feel like my ovaries are ready to combust from the heated look he's giving me and how he's interacting with my kids. Holy hell, if I hadn't been in love with Luke all these years, I think this whole scenario might have been my first turning point.

"You doing okay, Siren?" he asks quietly, pitching his voice low.

Licking my dry lips, his gaze follows the action and I have to squeeze my thighs together as his eyes turn even more heated than they were when he sees my reaction.

"I'm doing okay. Thank you for checking on me." My brain is short circuiting, being this close to Luke again, but I still have to try and be careful about my words in case one of Stephan's underlings is around.

He steps close to the cart, and out of the corner of my eye, I see him slip something inside the kids' backpack. I always carry it around when we go out. It's stocked with fresh clothes, toys, snacks, wipes to clean up said snacks, and things like that in case of emergencies. I hadn't noticed that the bag was slightly unzipped before.

"It's been killing me not knowing you were safe, Siren. Keep this someplace safe. I've got four numbers programmed in. The first is mine. The second is Thor, my President. Third is Phoenix, my VP. Last is the clubhouse main line. Just say your

name and you need to talk to one of us. My brothers and sisters know not to turn a phone call from you away."

My face flames at that as I wonder what all he told them about me. His face softens when he notices my alarm and panic.

"Don't worry, only Thor knows what's happened since he's my President. To get his help, he needed to know what we'd be up against, but he would have helped you regardless because of the fact that we don't condone what he's *been doing to you. Phoenix might know a little more than the others, but that's only because he's the VP. Everyone else was only told a very high overview. You call and we'll come running. You have a whole club behind you, Siren."*

Tears prick my eyes and I blink rapidly to keep them from falling. I'm also grateful that he didn't say Stephan's name out loud.

Luke steps back and I hate it when the cold starts to seep in again.

"I'm glad you're doing better." He pauses and looks at the kids again. "What are you all going to be going as for Halloween?"

My smile falters at that, and being as attentive as he is, Luke doesn't miss it. His face darkens, but he quickly masks it for the kids' sake.

"We take turns handing out candy at our house. We dress up like ghosts while watching Halloween movies," Ash tells him and a muscle ticks in Luke's jaw as he clenches it.

"Well, I hope you all have a fun night, but don't eat too much sugar. And don't forget to brush your teeth after having candy. You don't want to end up with cavities."

Surprisingly, all three of my children nod in agreement, almost in sync.

"We will, Mr. Patch," Cassie says and Luke grins at her, though I can tell it's strained.

"Well, I should let you get back to your shopping." He pauses as his gaze comes back to me. "Take care."

Swallowing the emotion clogging my throat, I smile, though I know it's probably weak and shaky. "I will, thank you. You, too."

With that, he says goodbye to my kids, and turns, continuing down the aisle to finish his own shopping.

As soon as we got home, I had Ash hide the burner phone in his closet with instructions to only use it if I tell him to. Then we went on like nothing out of the ordinary had happened.

Even now, I'm still surprised that no beating came that night. I was sure there would be one since we had spent about five minutes talking. That one of Stephan's underlings had seen us and ratted me out. But it never came and nothing was ever mentioned about it.

A small part of me wonders if Luke had his club watching out for Stephan's men, but I shake that thought away. I doubt they'd do that. I mean, they don't even know me.

Thinking about Luke sends my mind spiraling again. The things he showed me and told me back on Ash's birthday when I was in the ER has been tumbling around my mind for the past few months.

Did he really mean everything he said? Was he really looking for me all this time?

Then there's what he whispered to me.

Luke had apologized about bringing it up right then, but that he needed me to know the truth since he didn't know when he'd be able to talk to me again. He told me that Alli had shared with him what she and I had talked about the last time I'd been in the ER and she was my nurse. That the pictures I showed her about him were probably all fake. Thankfully, he didn't say the words outright, but he reiterated that what Alli told me was true. Meaning he'd only been with a handful of people all these years. He also told me that the last time anything had happened, which was just a blow job, was almost a year ago.

At the time, I had just stared at him, trying to find any clue or hint that he was lying to me, but he wasn't. It seems that the connection we'd always had was still strong. We always knew when the other was lying or not telling the whole truth. With just a look, we always knew when something was wrong or off with each other, too.

These last few months have been strange. Now knowing that Stephan somehow has been creating these fake images has had me wondering what else he'd been lying to me about. I'd found my old phone again after moving here and had shaken my head when Stephan didn't hide it as well as he had in years past. I'd fiddled with it and found out that he had blocked all the numbers of my friends and family. Since I didn't remember all of them by heart, I wrote them all down and kept the list in a safe place since I couldn't very well put them into my phone. He still sneaks my phone every now and then and looks through everything on it. He thinks I don't notice when he takes it, but I do.

The doorbell rings, bringing me out of my thoughts, and my nerves instantly skyrocket. While I'd been able to tell **γιαγιά** (grandma) a few things at the grocery store, I don't think she'll say anything about Luke or why I haven't been in contact over the years, but you never know.

I just pray this goes well.

I want to keep being able to see my family.

Chapter 17
Mary

"I'll get it," Cassie yells as she races toward the door.

The kids were beyond ecstatic when I told them that they'd be meeting their **προπαππούδες και γιαγιάδες** (great-grandparents) for the first time today. My heart clenches, wishing my **πατέρας** (dad) could be here to meet them too, but that will never happen, thanks to my so-called family. I shake off my melancholy thoughts at the sound of **γιαγιάς** (grandmas) voice.

"Well, hello, precious. You must be Miss Cassandra," **γιαγιά** (grandma) says, her voice floating down the hall, and I can just see her pinching Cassie's cheeks. Her almost instant giggle confirms it.

"Uh-huh, but you can call me Cassie. That's what Mama calls me."

Wiping my hands off on a towel, I set it down on the counter and head toward the front door as I listen to the kids introduce themselves.

Almost instantly, I'm engulfed in **γιαγιάς** (grandmas) arms.

"**Λουλούδι μου** (My flower), I've missed you," **γιαγιά** (grandma) whispers into my ear.

"Missed you, too, **γιαγιά** (grandma). So much."

I tighten my arms around her and after a few moments, she steps back and then I'm wrapped in **παππού** (grandpas) arms.

"**Έχουμε την πλάτη σου, λουλούδι μου** (We've got your back, my flower)," **παππούς** (grandpa) whispers in my ear, which brings tears to my eyes and I close them to keep Stephan from seeing them.

After the introductions are done, **γιαγιά** (grandma) whisks me into the kitchen. "**Λουλούδι μου** (My flower), what do you still need help with?"

Clearing my throat, I look around my kitchen, wishing we were back in hers instead. Ours is cramped with not nearly enough cabinet or counter space. "Well,

I just pulled the roasted turkey out of the oven. The lamb and potatoes are tented on the stove. We've got mashed garlic potatoes, salad, fruit and veggies, and for dessert, I made some baklava and a pumpkin pie."

Γιαγιάς (Grandmas) eyes turn misty, and she pulls me in for another hug. "**Λουλούδι μου** (My flower), you've done your roots proud. I can tell by the smells that this is going to be a delicious meal."

Emotions bombard me, and I fight not to cry. "Thank you, **γιαγιά**. That means so much to me."

"Now," **γιαγιά** says as she pulls back and dabs at her eyes. "Let's set everything out. I also brought baklava and bougatsa."

My mouth waters as we pull all the food out and set everything out on the counters and island. While Stephan doesn't like me cooking Greek food, I still do it and my kids absolutely love to eat anything Greek. Though, until today, I haven't spoken any Greek since that first time a few months after I'd been kidnapped. That beating had resulted in my first ER visit. Hopefully, I won't endure another beating tonight for speaking Greek, but if I don't speak it, my **παππούς και γιαγιά** (grandparents) will know right away that something's wrong. I just hope Stephan will realize that.

Shaking my head, I refocus on the food. The roasted turkey has a rosemary, garlic, and lemon zest glaze. Thankfully, our kitchen has double ovens, the only upside to this kitchen in my opinion, so I was even able to make honey glazed roast lamb with potatoes at the same time. Lamb is a must for my family. Every single big family gathering I can remember had at least one lamb dish provided. Baklava and bougatsa are traditional Greek desserts and I can't wait to dig into them. I haven't had them in years since Stephan's never allowed us to have a large gathering like this.

Over the years, I've learned to keep our holiday dinners small and not very complicated. It didn't make sense to go all out when half the time the food ended up strewn across the kitchen because he'd find some fault in it. I pray he won't say anything about the food today. I know my **παππούς και γιαγιά** (grandparents) will counter anything he says with their own thoughts, which will end up with me being punished later. He hates it when anyone questions what he says or what he does. Especially in front of other men.

Ten minutes later, everything is set out, and I walk into the living room, pausing at what I see.

Despite turning seventy earlier this summer, **παππούς** (grandpa) is sitting on the floor, playing with ponies and toy motorcycles and cars with all three of my kids. Smiling, I pull out my phone and snap a couple of pictures.

My throat tightens with emotion again as I hug my phone to my chest, hating that my kids had to wait so long to meet their **προπαππούδες και γιαγιάδες** (great-grandparents). I also hate that **πατέρας** (dad) was taken from me because he would have loved them all to pieces.

Spying Stephan enter the room out of the corner of my eye, I shake off my emotions and slip my phone into my pocket. "Time to eat, everyone," I call out and Cassie jumps up in excitement.

"Yay! I've been hungry all day smelling everything as it was cooking. You're going to love it, Grandpa. Mama's a really good cook," she says as she takes **παππού** (grandpas) hand, eagerly leading him into the kitchen.

Not being able to resist it, I smile and chuckle at her excitement and adorable, smiling face as she beams up at **παππούς** (grandpa).

Παππούς (Grandpa) laughs. "**Άγγελοε** (Angel), I'm sure everything is going to be delicious. She had a very good teacher," he says with a smile as he winks at **γιαγιά**, who blushes despite their years together and smiles lovingly back at him.

Cassie pauses as she looks up at **παππούς** (grandpa) in confusion. "What does that mean? **Ά- Ά… γγε… λον**?"

Παππούς (Grandpa) smiles as he looks down at her. "**Άγγελοε**," he repeats for her, but a bit slower. "It means 'Angel'."

The smile that lights up her face is one of pure happiness as she turns to me. "Mama! He calls me Angel, just like you do!"

My smile widens as I lean down, kissing the top of her head.

Stephan grunts, and my smile dims slightly as worry swirls in my gut. He makes a beeline for the plates, and **γιαγιά** goes to chide him, but I catch her eye, slightly shaking my head. She frowns, but says nothing as she steps back, letting him go first.

Normally, guests eat first otherwise we all eat together or the men eat first. But Stephan should have let **παππούς** (grandpa) eat first. However, here, if Stephan's home, he demands that he gets to eat first since he's the one paying for everything.

Once he has his plate, I take Cassie's hand, placing myself closest to Stephan, just in case he decides to lash out for some reason. Something passes over **παππού** (grandpas) eyes when he sees me doing that, but it's gone just as quickly. Clearing my throat, I try to keep things flowing as smoothly as possible.

"Let's get you a plate, Angel."

My **παππούς και γιαγιά** (grandparents) help Isaiah and Ash get their plates, and then, when they are seated at the table with their glasses of water, we all load up our own plates and take a seat as well.

Everyone eats and after the first few bites of food, **γιαγιά** gives me a wink, and my shoulders relax slightly. I'm a little rusty with some of the dishes. I had to go off memory for the recipes since I don't have my beloved cookbooks, and it's a relief that she thinks my food tastes good.

"So, Mary, what have you been up to all these years?" **παππούς** (grandpa) asks and my fork freezes halfway to my mouth. Partially because of his question, and the other that he called me by name instead of **λουλούδι μου** (my flower) like he usually does.

Swallowing, I give him a small smile, hoping what I say won't trigger an outburst from Stephan. I try not to look at him to gauge how he's feeling, but it's hard. It's also hard that I'm going to have to lie to my **παππούς και γιαγιά** (grandparents). I just hope they buy it.

"Well, I was blessed to be able to stay at home to raise my babies. Ash is in fourth grade, Isaiah is in second, and Cassie is now in pre-school."

Γιαγιά (Grandma) gets a far-away look in her eye before reaching over and patting my arm, which is easy since she's seated to my right and Stephan's to my left.

"I remember those days. What will you do when our **άγγελου** (angel) goes to kindergarten next year?"

I lick my lips, dreading that this question came up. "I don't know, honestly, but I've got some time to think about it."

Stephan frowns at that, and I silently beg my **παππούς και γιαγιά** not to push on the topic any further. Thankfully, the conversation moves from me, and **γιαγιά** starts asking the kids questions about what they like to do and their interests.

"I love to color and watch my princess movies," Cassie says around a mouth full of garlic mashed potatoes.

"Cassie, Angel, don't talk with your mouth full. It's rude," I chide, and she gives me an apologetic look before quickly looking at Stephan and then back at me.

She finishes eating her food and swallows, though I can tell her little body has tensed up. "Sorry, Mama."

I give her a nod that she's okay and go to say something myself, but Isaiah speaks up first.

"I like playing with my cars and motorcycles. Mama sometimes lets me watch the car shows where they work on them and restore them."

Παππούς (Grandpa) leans forward, resting his forearms on the table, and his eyes twinkle as he looks at Isaiah. Oh, boy. I know where this conversation is heading, and **γιαγιά** and I share a knowing look.

"You know, I've got an old first-generation convertible Mustang sitting in my garage that I've been restoring over the years. It first came out when I was ten years old. My pops used to have one, and when I saw that same car for sale years later, I knew I had to have it. Even if I did need to restore almost the entire interior and the engine needed some work. There are a few body panels that need some fixing and when it's all done, it'll get a new paint job as well. Maybe you'd like to help me work on it sometime?"

Isaiah's jaw drops as he stares at **παππούς**. "Are you serious?" he whispers, his voice shaking slightly with excitement.

Παππούς nods as he smiles at him. "Dead serious. In my opinion, it's important to know how to fix at least the basics with cars. Same for things around the house." He pauses as he nods his head toward Stephan and me. "As long as it's okay with your parents, you can come and help me. My garage is heated, so we won't be out there freezing or anything."

I quickly look at Stephan. He's watching **παππούς** with a look I can't decipher before his face hardens slightly.

My heart sinks. Shit.

"We'll see," he replies, and Isaiah's shoulders and face fall.

We all know what 'we'll see' means when Stephan says it.

It means it'll never happen.

Γιαγιά (Grandma) clears her throat and I'm thankful for the break in charged silence. "Ash, what things do you like to do, Dear?"

Ash looks at Stephan for a beat before looking down at his plate. "I like playing cars with Isaiah, drawing, and I like animals. Someday I want to be a veterinarian."

Stephan scoffs at that and Ash's little body tenses, not looking up from his plate. Slowly he takes a bite of food and I clear my throat, trying to get Stephan's attention off the kids.

"What have you both been up to? The family?"

Thankfully, the redirection works, but I can tell from the tension rolling off Stephan that he's reaching his limit. However, **γιαγιά** takes my question for what it is and the attention is off all of us. For now, at least.

I learned that **θεία** (aunt) Catherine, who is the eldest of my **παππούς και γιαγιά'** (grandparents') five kids, had her third baby, Rosa, earlier this summer, which was a complete shock to everyone since she's in her early fifties. I had stared at **γιαγιά** in shock as well, but she just smiled, happy to have another grandbaby, and continued talking about the rest of our family. Then again, as long as Catherine and Rosa are okay and healthy, that's all that matters in my opinion.

Θείος (Uncle) Daniil, who is the second oldest, is now married and they have one child. I knew that he had joined the marines after high school. Apparently, when his current tour is up next summer, he's decided not to reenlist and instead retire after thirty-four years of service, wanting to focus more on his family. The two youngest of my **θείες** (aunts), Selena and Sofia, have decided to both stop at two kids each and they've been up at **θεία** (aunt) Catherine's house a lot after the birth to help her settle in.

Πατέρας (Dad) had been the middle child. For years, I had wished for him to find someone that made him happy and maybe have another baby. I'd always wanted a sibling, but unfortunately, he never remarried. I know he'd seen a few women when I was a teenager, but nothing serious had ever happened with their relationships.

When everyone's done eating, I get up and clear the plates away, telling my **παππούς και γιαγιά** that I got it when they get up to help. Both of them eye Stephan for not getting up to help me, which has him clenching his jaw even harder than he was before. His fists curl under the table and ice slides down my spine.

My hands tremble when I set down both of the Baklava dishes, bougatsa, and the pumpkin pie, making sure the pie is near Stephan, as I know that's the only thing he'll touch. I hope no one notices my trembling hands, but when I look up, I know they all did. Even the kids. My **παππούς και γιαγιά** share a quick, concerned look before it disappears.

Out of the corner of my eye, I notice Stephan intently staring at my hands. His lips tick up in one corner as he clocks that he's knocked me off kilter, which has more ice sliding down my spine. Whenever he does that, it doesn't bode well for me. I swallow down my panic as I retake my seat. However, when I take my first bite of the bougatsa, I can't help but moan slightly at the taste, my shaky hands forgotten. I've greatly missed eating Greek food.

We continue chatting about my side of the family. Occasionally, the kids ask questions, but Stephan says nothing else through the remainder of the meal.

When we're all done with dessert, I put everything away and we move into the living room. Thankfully, the rest of the evening is mostly uneventful.

When nine o'clock rolls around, the kids are barely able to keep their eyes open after playing and eating so much. Normally I would have had them in bed earlier, but I made an exception tonight so that they could spend more time with my **παππούς και γιαγιά**.

"We should go so that you can get the little ones to bed. Call me later this weekend and we can set up a time to come and see you and the kids again. One day isn't enough to catch up on so much missed time," **γιαγιά** says as she gives me a hug.

I wince internally, and Stephan gives her a hard look. "Because of the cases and divisions I was assigned to over the years, it was critical that we cut off ties with our families. We had wanted to wait to start our own family until after I was done with my assignments, but then we were surprised by Asher. Since we already had one, we decided not to fight nature, and the others soon followed after."

Παππούς stands, and I'm not able to decipher the look he gives Stephan. "All the same, we'd like to reconnect and get to know our great-grandchildren and our granddaughter again." He pauses and turns to me, giving me his usual soft smile. "Maria is right. Too much time has passed and we miss you."

Ignoring how tense Stephan is, I step forward and give **παππούς** a hug. "I've missed both of you as well. **Σε αγαπώ** (I love you)."

He tightens his arms around me. "**Κι εγώ σ' αγαπώ** (I love you too), **λουλούδι μου** (my flower)."

He lets me go and then kneels on the ground in front of the kids. "Come here," he growls playfully and Cassie giggles as she leads the pack, racing into his arms. Ash steps to the right of Cassie and Isaiah to the left of her as all three of them hug him tightly.

Smiling down at them, I force myself to keep a happy smile on my face when, in fact, I'm anxious beyond belief and praying to every deity right now that this works.

The kids step back and hug **γιαγιά** as she smothers them with kisses. **Παππούς** stands and puts both his hands in his slacks pockets. He smiles down at the kids and when he looks up at me; he gives me a slight nod.

Asher's the first to break away, and he comes to my side, wrapping his arms around my waist. "I'm so happy Grandma ran into you at the store and that they're here now," he says quietly, and I ruffle his hair before resting my hand on his shoulder.

"Me too, Hawk, me too."

He hugs me again, and as he pulls back, I feel his finger lightly tap three times against my back. That, along with the nod **παππούς** gave me, means that he's passed him the scan drive.

I'd fretted about doing it this way for weeks, afraid that by doing it like this, Stephan would hurt Ash if he was caught. But Ash made a good point when he told me about his idea. That Stephan's focus would be mostly on me and making sure I didn't do anything wrong. If I were to give the scan drive to him, I'd most likely be caught and then our chance for escape would be completely blown away. Not to mention Stephan would then have my proof of snooping around.

"Love you, munchkins. We'll see you soon," **γιαγιά** says as she waves before heading out the door. **Παππούς** waves as well and then closes the door behind them.

Stephan walks to the window to watch them leave. I don't miss the increased tension and anger wafting off him now that they're gone. It's even more intense than it was a minute ago. I need to get the kids to bed and out of sight before he snaps.

Quietly, I usher the kids down the hall and upstairs to the bathroom, where they all start brushing their teeth. Taking out Cassie's hair ties, I run a comb through her hair. Their little bodies are all tense, their muscles tight, as they feel the same tension in the air that I do. My gut churns, worried that this time will be the time when Stephan fully snaps. When he does, I just hope the kids will be safe.

Ash gives me a worried look in the mirror before spitting out his toothpaste. I shake my head slightly when I catch his gaze again. I don't want him saying anything and possibly triggering Stephan and I *definitely* don't want his anger directed at them.

Within minutes, I've got them all tucked into bed, and I'm just closing Ash's door when I'm suddenly yanked backwards.

I stumble and then find myself being flung into our room. Stephan shuts the door, but in his anger, he doesn't realize that he's left the door slightly ajar.

Oh, fuck.

With the crazy glint in his eyes, I know I'm about to be punished for something. Did he see Ash slipping **παππούς** the scan drive? Or is it something else?

"Time for your punishments for tonight," he sneers.

"W-What did I do wrong?" I swallow the bile that rises and try to calm my trembling body.

The look on his face turns even more menacing and dangerous. "You didn't get them off our trail fast enough, and now your grandfather is suspicious of me."

Well, that really isn't my fault, I think to myself. If he wasn't the type of man that he is, then he would have behaved like a normal husband. Instead, his inability to do anything but sit there and keep his mouth shut for almost the entire day and sending constant glares will always make people suspicious. Something in me snaps, and I find myself speaking up when I know I should have remained silent.

"That's not my fault. You sat there all afternoon, not speaking and glaring at everyone. Of course, that would make them suspicious. It would make anyone suspicious."

He backhands me and pain explodes around my eye.

"Your job is to make sure nobody suspects anything. I can do whatever the fuck I want. I'm the man of this house. Not only did you fail, but I had to sit through this stupid tradition, choke down your disgusting fucking food that you insisted we have, listen to you all speaking another fucking language, and having those fucking people in my house all fucking day," he yells, and then backhands me again, but this time it's so hard; I stumble, falling to the floor as black dots dance across my vision.

"I had to speak Greek to them. They would have been suspicious if I hadn't," I pant as I try to push up off the floor.

His hand latches around my throat as his face contorts in rage and he pins me back down on the floor. "You had better not told them anything when you were speaking in that fucking stupid language. If I find out you did, you're fucking done."

What little breath I have left in me explodes out of me as he lands a punch to my stomach while still squeezing my neck.

"And most importantly, don't forget that I *own* you. I can do whatever the fuck I want with you. To you. You know better than to ask questions of me like that. To talk back to me like that. That little misstep is going to cost you big time, Mary. That and along with your punishments for everything else you've fucked up today."

He squeezes harder and my vision starts to darken as I claw at his hands, desperate to breathe.

After a few moments, he lets me go, and I fall to the floor, gasping for air.

However, as soon as I get a good breath, it goes whooshing out of me as he kicks me, hard, in the stomach. The next second, his fists rain down on me as he spews threat after threat at me.

Every now and then, he'd stop before spewing more bullshit about how I messed up and then he would start beating me again.

I'm not sure how long the beating goes on for, but I'm barely hanging onto consciousness when I hear an alarm go off on his phone. This is by far the worst beating he's ever given me.

Ever.

My entire body throbs. I swear I hurt from the tips of my hair all the way down to my toes. A metallic taste coats my tongue and I know it's my blood. It's not the first time I've tasted it.

My entire body is probably black and blue by now. Not to mention that at some point, he'd taken out his pocketknife. While I am beyond thankful that he didn't stab me, I have a bunch of cuts all over my body, including one on my face, which surprises me. Then again, I know my face is swelling up, so I'm sure he didn't care about adding another mark.

"Lucky for you, bitch, I have to get ready for my shift."

He grabs a fistful of my hair, and a cry escapes when he yanks my head back, hard.

"You better still be here when I get back home. If I find out you went to the hospital, I'll start killing those fucking leeches, starting with your bastard son. After you've watched all three of them die a horrible death, it'll be your turn. Now, do as I say and stay the fuck inside. We'll be finishing our little discussion tonight. Things will be different from here on out, or I'll make sure no one will find you and those fucking pests."

The menace in his voice sends a shiver of fear through me and he grins darkly when he sees the fear in my eyes. He slams my head against the floor a couple of times and my vision swims again. Instantly, I'm seeing double.

I try to stay conscious while he cleans himself up quickly and washes away my blood. My vision returns back to normal, and I hope that this means I don't have a concussion. When he comes back in our room, he strips, throwing his bloody clothes in the hamper before putting on his uniform. Darkness rims my vision and I hope that **παππούς** is able to get the scan drive to Luke and Sam, because I'm not so sure if I'll survive this beating, let alone the next twelve hours until Stephan comes home again. And when he does return, I'm sure it'll mean more pain.

The last thing I see of him is his dress shoes as he stalks out of our room without another word to me. Then my eyes focus on the boots he had on, which are now sitting by the dresser, the tips covered in blood. Next to that is our hamper and I can see the blood on his jeans from where he had wiped his pocket knife a few times.

My blood.

The slamming of the door leading into the garage tells me that Stephan has left and some of the tension in my muscles bleeds away. I pray the kids didn't hear any of this and are still safely tucked in their beds.

With that thought, I finally give in and let the darkness surround me.

Chapter 18

Patch

WALKING INTO THE CLUBHOUSE, I stalk toward the bar and by the time I've reached it, Ethan already has a beer uncapped and hands it to me.

Giving him a chin lift, I scan the room.

All night I've been jumpy, anxious, and worried about Mary. Stephan has a tendency to beat her enough on the holidays to send her to the hospital. With today being Thanksgiving, I'm afraid of what he'll do to her. Especially with a new factor being thrown in.

I know from talking to Mary's grandparents that they are going over to her house today. To say I was shocked is an understatement when they told me that, but I'm going to bet that the asshole didn't want to appear suspicious by turning them down now that they live in the same town. That said, I'm also worried their appearance will trigger Stephan. That he'll feel threatened by something they say or do and that he'll take out his frustrations and anger on Mary once Harris and Maria leave.

Shaking off those thoughts, I'm about to head to my room when the door opens and Brady walks in. It's not the first time he's been here, but he usually doesn't come here unless he needs to. I'm not saying that he doesn't like the club, he's just trying not to draw attention to the fact that he's close to us since almost half the cops in town are dirty.

Judging by his face, he's here on unofficial business.

"Want a beer?" I ask him, and he shakes his head before turning to Ethan.

"Can I have a water?"

Ethan gives him a chin lift, and a second later, Brady's breaking the seal on a water bottle as he heads toward a secluded corner of the main room. Following him, I take a seat next to him.

"What's up?"

He sighs and rubs the back of his neck. "Nothing good, that's for fucking sure."

Growing frustrated, I take a sip of my beer, but still, he doesn't say anything. "Well, are you going to make me drag it out of you?" I damn near growl, fisting my hand in frustration.

He hangs his head for a moment, shaking it, but when he looks up at me, his face is etched in worry. "Rumor on the street is that something's going on with the Vasquez family. Per one of my informants, the Don is absolutely pissed about something going on in the family. Diego's also been walking around like he's about to explode. I get the feeling something's going to be going down soon. I just don't know what."

Twirling my bottle with my fingers, I debate telling him what Mary told me a few months ago. Taking a swig of my beer, I make my decision and fill him in just in case Uncle Sam hasn't already.

Brady already knows most of what has happened since he's one of the officers on Mary's cold case. Some may say that he's too close to the case to be on it. Even though our town is relatively large, between eleven and twelve thousand residents, most everyone knows each other to some degree. We're a pretty tight-knit community and most of us care about each other and the wellbeing of the town.

That said, I don't know exactly how corrupt the police are here in town. Or how far the corruption has spread. We haven't seen signs of corruption except for the cops, and maybe a few judges, but they could just be good at hiding it. I seriously hope that the town has been spared from all this shit, but time will tell.

"Yeah, Pops told me about that. I hate that she's putting herself in more danger, but if the information she has can help us close down that trafficking ring," he pauses and runs a hand over his face. "Fuck, that'd be beyond fucking fantastic if we could put a stop to it. I—"

My phone rings, interrupting him and I fish it out of my pocket.

Unease swirls throughout me when I see who's calling. *"What's up, Drae?"*

"I've got two people here at the gate who say it's urgent to talk to you. Harris and Maria Catarino. Am I good to let them through?"

My gut tightens, and I motion for Brady to get up along with me. *"Yeah, send them through. They're family."*

I hang up and drain the last of my beer as I set it down on the table. "Mary's grandparents are here, and they say it's urgent."

Brady and I share a look.

"Fuck," he hisses and follows me as I walk across the room and then the door is flung open. Maria almost runs in with Harris hot on her heels.

"Sorry to barge in like this, but we needed to talk to you. It's about Mary," Maria says between gasps. Fuck, she looks like she's about to have a panic attack.

"**Γιαγιά** (Grandma)," I say gently, trying to use Greek to break through her panic, as I lead her over to a chair. "I need you to take a deep breath."

"Here, Patch," Levi says as she comes up beside me and hands me a water bottle. Looking over my shoulder, both of her Old Men, Phoenix, Timber, and a few others have gathered around.

"Thanks," I reply and break the seal before handing it to Maria. She takes a couple of sips and I hand her the cap. I look up at Harris and note the murderous look on his face. "Tell me what happened."

He fills us in about having Thanksgiving over at Mary's house. How Mary seemed to fold in on herself more and more at Stephan's hard looks, words, hell, even grunts. He had her so anxious, nervous, and scared that her whole body was damn near trembling when he hugged her before saying goodbye.

Harris reaches into his pocket. "Ash slipped this in my pocket as we were saying goodbye. I think this is what you told me about. What Mary was sticking around for before she tries to get out and away from him."

I knew it was risky, but Uncle Sam, Brady, and I had looped in Harris and he must have told some things to Maria. We knew Mary would need Harris' help when she got away with the restraining order. And I secretly hope his help includes filing fucking divorce papers.

I'm about to say something when my phone rings again. Looking at the caller ID, my gut churns as my gaze shoots to Thor's. His face goes grim, and I bet he knows who's calling.

Quickly, I look at Brady and notice his phone is out. Well, fuck... Has he been recording what Harris and Maria said just a moment ago? He smirks at me, showing me his phone, and I shake my head. I should have known he would do that. Looking over my shoulder, I whistle to get everyone's attention.

"Everyone shut the fuck up. I have a call I need to put on speaker." Instantly everyone goes quiet, their focus on me.

Swiping, I answer the call.

"Hello?" I purposefully don't say their names in case Stephan somehow found the phone.

"P-Patch?"

The churning in my gut tightens when I hear Asher's scared voice come over the line. *"I'm here, Ash. What's going on? Are you safe?"*

"I-I got Cass and Izzy into the closet and hiding as soon as I heard him go crazy, but Mom... she... M-Mom is... S-She's hurt... really bad, P-Patch." A little sob comes through the phone, and I feel the surrounding tension increasing tenfold. *"He's... he's n-never d-done anything t-this b-bad before,"* he whispers and sniffles. In the background I can hear a moan and the need to get her and the kids out of there intensifies tenfold.

"Ash, I'm coming to you and I'm bringing my friends. We'll help your mom and keep you all safe. Okay?"

"O-Okay, D-Dad. I trust you. Mom said I could always t-trust you to keep your w-word."

Fuck... It's true.

And he knows.

I turn toward my brothers and then to Thor. He nods and I return it, then he gives the signal to prepare to head out. My brothers quickly disperse, checking their weapons and getting more ammo, just in case. Dragon holds his hand out for my gun and after handing it to him, he checks it before going into Thor's office, most likely for another magazine.

"That's right, son. You can trust me, and you can trust my brothers and sisters in the club. Now, I need to know something really quick before we head out. Is Stephan home?"

He sniffles again, and I worry he isn't going to answer me.

"H-He left a few minutes ago for work. He's on a twelve-hour night shift and won't be back until noon tomorrow."

"Alright, I'm going to hang up and we'll be there in a few minutes. Are any of your mom's wounds critical?"

"S-She's bruised almost everywhere. It's hard to tell. B-But she has lots of c-cuts, too. The w-worst cut is on her face. I think. Her leg is b-bent funny." I hear more sniffles across the line and white-hot fury in me rises even more.

Dragon comes back at that point and hands me my gun. Even though he checked it, I still do the same before putting it in my holster and pocketing the extra magazine. I give him a chin lift in thanks.

"Here's what I want you to do, Ash. Tell your brother and sister to start packing some of their clothes and things that they'll need. When you've done that, I want you to find a towel and put pressure on your mom's worst wounds. It will hurt, but it needs to be done so that she doesn't lose too much blood. We'll be there soon, I promise."

"O-Okay. Please hurry. I'm s-scared, Dad."

My heart clenches and I send up a prayer to whoever's listening that Mary will make it through this.

"I know you are, but I need you to be strong right now. I'll see you in a few minutes."

Ending the call, I note Maria's pale face and that her body is shaking slightly, but I can't focus on her right now. We need to get to Mary. Turning to Harris, he gives me a curt nod as he squeezes her shoulder, silently telling me that he'll take care of her.

"Harris, I need you to go home and find out whatever the hell is on that scan drive. We're going to need every advantage we can to keep Stephan away from them." Pausing, I turn to Brady. "Brady, you—"

"I'm going with you. I failed her all those years ago and I'm not doing it again. Plus, it'd be good to have a cop there when you all go in so I can speak to what we see and that everything is how we found it. I'll call my partner to meet us there and to keep it quiet."

Brady turns to Harris and my shoulders relax at that. Dixon, his partner, is one of the good cops and I've always liked the guy.

"Call my dad and have him go to your house. Do not open anything on the scan drive until he gets there. Actually, don't even put it in your computer until he gets there. This needs to be by the books so we can nab the fucker."

"You heard him. Roll out," Thor bellows and then turns to me. "We'll follow your truck there."

I've known where she's lived for a while, thanks to her files that Sam got from Curtis, Alli's father who is one of the department heads at the hospital. Curtis also unofficially slipped me her address so I wouldn't have to spend hours trying to figure out what alias their house was under this time around. I've driven by many times, hoping for a glimpse of her, but never stopped for obvious reasons.

Thor pauses and turns to Levi, Mae, Sasha, and the other Prospects. "Make-up rooms for everyone, Wildcat. Sasha, go with Patch. They might need your help to get the kids around if they get scared of us."

"She's got three kids, right? They can stay with us. We have three bedrooms upstairs as well as a bedroom on the main floor. That way they can still be together, but the kids can be away from the clubhouse most of the time," Mae tells me as she turns to Timber, her Old Man.

Drae and his daughter, Lindsey, stayed with them for a while after we rescued Mae and Lindsey from the Oasis fuckers. But after a while, and Drae being Drae and not wanting to intrude on their newly wedded bliss for too long, he had asked if they could move to a room upstairs in the clubhouse and away from most of the commotion. Thor gave the okay until his house is finished, and we all helped soundproof the room better for the nights when things get a bit wilder in the main room. Luckily, there haven't been any issues so far.

Timber must have filled Mae in about Mary just now, but even if he had told her about Mary before, I wouldn't have cared. I trust them both implicitly. For that matter, the same goes for all my brothers and sisters.

Timber gives me a chin lift. "Agreed. They can stay with us. We can also put a fold-out couch in the main floor bedroom for you, Patch, so you don't have to leave her."

I return his chin lift, grateful that he knows I'll want to be close by her. Also, for opening their home to my Siren and her kids.

"Sunshine, make the Prospects move anything you need to so that you aren't doing it yourself. Same for you, Queen. Don't need either one of you lifting anything heavy since you're both pregnant."

Levi's pregnant with twins and Mae's pregnant with triplets. We definitely don't want anything happening to their babies, so I hope like fuck that they listen. They can be hard-headed at times.

"We know, we know," Levi says, rolling her eyes at him. "Now, go and save your woman and kids, Patch. We'll get everything ready here."

Giving both ladies a quick hug, I stalk out of the clubhouse and head straight for my truck. Brady gets in his cop-issued SUV and follows right behind me.

I make it to Mary's in ten minutes when it should have taken me fifteen or twenty. I sped like a bat out of hell, but thankfully, no cops pulled me over. Though, that could be because Brady's right behind me in his work SUV. At least he didn't turn on his lights. That would have drawn even more attention to us, even though the streets are mostly empty since it's just before midnight.

Slamming my truck in park and turning it off, I jump out and grab my kit out of the backseat before racing to the front door.

Just as I'm about to reach it, the door flies open and Cassie comes running out, Isaiah right behind her. I kneel down and she runs straight into my arms. Brady gives me a nod and leads my brothers inside. Bear takes my kit and gives me a look that says he'll take care of Mary for me until I get in there.

"Mr. Patch!" Cassie cries and then her little body shakes as she wraps her arms around my neck. Almost immediately, I feel her tears against my skin.

"I'm here, Angel. These are my brothers I told you about."

"Ahem," Sasha says as she steps up next to me, cocking an eyebrow at me.

"And sister," I clarify.

Cassie looks up and wipes her eyes. "Mandy?"

My heart clenches that she remembers my sister's name, but I shake my head. "No, this is Sasha. She's a Prospect with the club so that makes her my sister as well. Is it okay if she helps you and your brothers get things packed up? You're going to stay at the compound with us."

Her big eyes turn back to me, and though they're hazel like her asshole father's, I can see Mary shining through them. "We're going to stay with you?"

Nodding, I tighten my arms around her. "Yes, Angel. You're going to stay at my friend's home, and I'll be there too. But right now, I need to get inside to help your mom. Can you go with Sasha?"

She nods and then reaches for Sasha, who takes her into her arms.

Instantly, Isaiah hugs my leg tight, and I look down at him before lifting him and giving him a hug. Timber steps up next to me.

"This is Timber, Isaiah. It's his and his wife's house that you'll be staying at. You can trust him and the others to protect you."

He wraps his arms around my neck and squeezes. "Thank you for coming to help Mom, Mr. Patch."

"Always, Bud. Always." Emotion clogs my throat as I hug him one more time before handing him to Timber. As soon as Timber has a good hold on him, I make a beeline inside.

"Dad?" I hear Ash call from somewhere deep inside the house and my brothers point upstairs and to the left. They all give me a sympathetic look and my gut twists in response.

Taking the steps two at a time, I get to the room and fear slides down my spine when I finally lay my eyes on my Siren.

Out of the corner of my eye, I can see Brady taking pictures of everything and a part of me wonders if he's taken a picture of her on the floor as well. In a way, I hope he has so that it's documented how we found her, but I also don't want anyone looking at pictures of her when she's so vulnerable.

Ash wasn't kidding.

Any visible skin has almost completely turned black and blue. If her arms and face are anything to go by, I'm betting her chest and stomach area will also be black and blue. No doubt her ribs are at least bruised. Hopefully they aren't broken. Since she's wearing pants, I don't know if her legs are also bruised, but I'm guessing they are. And her left leg is definitely broken.

He must have hit her face a few times because her left eye is completely swollen shut already. There's a large laceration on her face from just below her temple to mid-cheek. There are also several other lacerations on her arms, upper body, and a few on her legs.

Bear is already hovering over her, and when he looks up, he gives me a look that reads that none of the wounds he can see are critical. I exhale hard in relief and know she's in good hands because he's had medic training back when he was in the Army.

Seeing Ash hovering over her and looking so worried, I'm thankful for Bear's help, because I'm positive I'll have to take care of Ash before I can get to Mary. Bones steps forward and goes to the other side of Mary to help Bear.

When Bones kneels by Ash, he turns around and his eyes widen when he sees me before they fill with tears. He gets up and almost runs toward me. Kneeling, I wrap my arms around him, finally holding my son for the first time.

Pulling back after a few moments, I wipe his tear-streaked cheeks. "I need you to go with my brothers while I take your mom to the hospital, okay?"

He sniffles and nods. "Where are we going to go until then?"

Relief flows through me. Thank fuck I'm not going to have to fight him on this. "You'll stay with some friends of mine at the clubhouse. When your mom gets out, she'll be staying in the same house as you guys. I'll be there, too."

He stares into my eyes for a bit and then nods and sniffles. He takes a deep breath and then holds himself taller, almost like he's flipped a switch. "Since Mom can't get the things around, I'll get the important things she said we need to take with us. Some of them we need to give to Grandpa Harris. But I'll need help with some things because they're up high."

Dragon kneels down next to me. "How about I help you get everything around while Patch helps your mom?"

Ash looks at me in question, and I can see he's nervous about leaving my side. I nod in encouragement. "This is Dragon. He won't let anything happen to you. He's one of our club Enforcers which means he's really tough. He'll keep you safe."

After a few moments, Ash nods, and hugs me one more time before he takes Dragon's hand, leading him to the closet in here. He reaches into the neck of his shirt and it's then that I see he's wearing a necklace with a key on it, which he hands to Dragon and then points to the upper shelves in the closet.

"This is for the big lock box hidden in the boxes up there. I know which files we need to get out of it. I'll remove the false wall down here to get the other documents Mom said we needed. Then we need to go to Stephan's office, and after that, I need to get some things out of the crawl space downstairs. Also, there are a few other things I hid in my closet."

Dragon shares a look with me and my gut tightens as I wonder what exactly Mary thinks they need, but I push that thought out of my head.

My Siren needs me.

Chapter 19

Patch

KNEELING DOWN BY MARY, I reach out and feel for her pulse. I release a heavy breath when I feel a semi-strong pulse. With her injuries, I was worried it might be weaker.

"Someone get me the hardback stretcher from my truck bed," I call over my shoulder, and then look back at Mary. With her broken leg and not knowing how injured her ribs are, I don't want to lift her into my arms and possibly hurt her worse. The stretcher will be the easiest, and less painful, way of getting her out of here. Quickly, I look over all the knife wounds, but thankfully, none look serious and she's not losing copious amounts of blood.

"Siren, Baby, I'm here." I brush her matted, bloody hair out of her face, and she struggles, but finally cracks her good eye open.

"L-L-Luke?"

"Yeah, Siren. I'm here. We're going to take you to the hospital."

At that, she struggles to fully open her eye, but when she does, it widens and she starts to panic as she tries to scoot away from me. The moment she puts weight on her right arm, she cries out in pain as she grips her shoulder.

"N-No. I can't g-go to the hospital. H-He'll kill me. Stephan will k-kill the k-kids and then k-kill me. He t-told me he would if I l-left the house and w-went to the hospital. He's finally s-snapped. I can't r-risk them. They're why I n-never left before this. I couldn't r-risk it until I knew for s-sure how to g-get out and g-get the information to n-nail that b-bastard once and for all so he c-couldn't c-come after us."

Once again, the anger and rage that's been simmering pulses red hot at what this asshole's done and said to her. Tonight, and over the years. Reaching out, I gently cup her less injured cheek and brush the lock of hair that had fallen down out of her face and behind her ear.

"Siren, I promise I won't let him get to you or the kids. I'm sure by now Harris is gathering information to help with getting a restraining order against him, along with Uncle Sam. Please, Siren. You need to trust us to protect you."

She stares into my eyes for a few moments before tears start to form in her eyes and her body relaxes slightly.

"I do trust you, but it's hard reconciling what he's told me all these years with what you, Alli, and even what my **παπποúς και γιαγιά** (grandparents) told me today. I think that's part of why he snapped. While **γιαγιά** (grandma) and I were cleaning up the kitchen after we ate, she whispered to me how much everyone missed me when I was kidnapped and how much everyone's been looking for me since then. I think Stephan heard her because of some of the things he said while he was beating me."

When she's finished speaking, a wave of exhaustion washes over her and her eye starts to droop. At that moment, panic starts to set in as I worry about a concussion. "Siren, you need to stay awake. You might have a concussion. Talk to me, Mary."

She nods weakly, but then shakes her head. "I don't think I have one. My ears aren't ringing, and there's only one of you. While yes, I have a terrible headache, it's from the beatings, not that. I'm nauseous, but that's most likely because I can taste my own blood."

My fists clench and my jaw clenches at how she *knows* she most likely doesn't have a concussion, but I tamp it down. Seconds later, Gunner comes in with the stretcher.

"We're going to put you on the stretcher now, okay? With not knowing how your ribs are, I'd rather not risk injuring them further by picking you up myself. It's most likely going to hurt, but we've got to get you to the hospital, Siren."

She nods weakly again, but at least her eyes, er eye, is staying open, which is a relief.

Stepping back, I lay the stretcher down and between Bones, Bear, and I, we get her laying down on it, though she does cry out in pain when we touch her broken leg as well as her right shoulder. Shit. Just going off looks alone, it doesn't seem dislocated, but it could be partially dislocated. Carefully, we secure her to the board.

Glancing around, I'm relieved that Ash isn't in the room anymore, but I'm not sure at what point he and Dragon stepped out. I'll just have to trust him and the others to watch over Ash. Not to mention Cassie and Isaiah as well.

Turning toward Thor, we share a grim look.

"If possible, I want everything of theirs out of here. I don't want them coming back here. There's no way he's getting a chance to do what he threatened." Determination fills me. I will protect my Siren and our kids. Even though they aren't mine, I'm claiming them.

He gives me a chin lift, his eyes hard and cold, no doubt at the fact that Stephan threatened her and the kids the way he did. "Was kind of figuring you were going to say that. We'll make sure it's done. Between all of us, it should be pretty quick. I already have the Prospects in route with the vans and those that have trucks have left to switch out vehicles to help get stuff out of here quickly. We don't know if Stephan has this place being watched. Hopefully, we can get them all out before someone comes by. Smoke's working his magic to try and track Stephan's movements. You take care of Mary. We've got your back."

Thor clasps my shoulder and I give him another chin lift in thanks before stepping around to grab the board at Mary's head. Bear takes the spot at her feet and within minutes, we're loaded up in my truck with Mary laying on my lap and Bones' in the backseat. Bear's driving us with Gunner in the front passenger seat as we follow Brady in his SUV. This time, Brady's got his lights on as we race to the hospital. The sound of motorcycles fill the air and I know some of my brothers are following to support us. Not to mention for protection in case that asshole shows up. I know he will at some point—it's just a matter of when.

Reaching into my cut, I pull out my phone and dial Alli. I know she's working tonight, and I want them prepared for us. As I wait for her to pick up, I run my thumb over Mary's forehead, hoping to help her relax some. She's trying to keep her eye open, but it looks like it's getting harder for her.

"Hey, Luke. Is everything alright?"

"Not really. I need you to meet me at the entrance of the ER with a gurney. I'm bringing in Siren."

Instantly, her light-hearted voice switches and is in nurse mode. *"Shit. What are her injuries?"*

"Multiple lacerations, including one on her face. Her left eye is swollen shut. Multiple contusions are all over her face and body, including her ribs, but I don't know if they are bruised or broken. Her left leg is broken and it hurt her when we got her on the backboard. Something's wrong with her right shoulder as well. It hurts her if it's touched or if she puts weight on it. I'm thinking it might be partially dislocated. She doesn't think she has a concussion, but so far, she's trying to stay awake just in case."

"Dr. Rodgers is working tonight and is right next to me. I'll fill her in after we hang up. We'll have a pod and a gurney ready for her. How far out are you?"

Good. Dr. Rodgers is one of the best doctors we've got. *"Five minutes, maybe less. Brady's leading the way."*

"Got it. See you in a few," she says before ending the call.

Tucking my phone back into my cut, I reach back down and rub my thumb across her forehead again. "Almost there, Siren."

She blinks and takes a shaky breath in, though I don't miss the panic in her eyes. "He's g-got connections in the hospital. P-People he pays. He'll f-find me. That's how he always k-knew what was said in the r-reports." A tear rolls down her cheek and I wipe it away.

I keep talking, partly to take her mind off the pain she must be in but also so that she doesn't go to sleep because of the possible risk of a concussion. "That's why I'm going to talk to Curtis as soon as we get there. We'll get guards outside the OR and your room. This isn't the first time we've been allowed to guard a hospital room. He won't get to you, Mary. Or the kids. My brothers and sisters will protect them.

"Once Harris and Uncle Sam have done their thing, I'm going to extend our protection to Harris and Maria as well. You and I both know Harris is set in his way about doing things. He'll want to make sure he gets everything set up for you as soon as possible." I smirk and her lips kick up as a little huff escapes her. Thankfully, she doesn't wince in pain, so maybe her ribs aren't hurt that badly this time.

"Yeah, he is. I just h-hope he took my suggestion to h-heart all those years ago and s-saved his files in the c-cloud or somewhere external. Especially if someone b-breaks into his office or house." She pauses and tears fill her eyes again. Even though her other one is swollen shut, a tear still falls from it. "If S-Stephan can't get to me, he'll go after anyone I c-care about in order to hurt me. Even if it means d-destroying their p-property, if he can't get to them d-directly. I've seen him d-do it before. To innocent p-people. He m-made me watch as part of my p-punishments." More tears spill from her eyes and I wipe them away as I tamp down my rage.

"I'll talk to Brady and Uncle Sam for help. Since Stephan's the Deputy Chief, this can't be a completely club thing and Thor, my President, knows this. I just hope the Chief of Police is clean."

The panic in her eyes intensifies, but then it's replaced by determination. "I know the d-dirty cops and the C-Chief is clean. I've known who the d-dirty ones were in every t-town we've lived in, and I can give S-Sam a list if he wants. For Forest C-Creek, I can either just tell t-them or if they can b-bring the roster lists, I'll mark everyone d-down. Just depends on w-which way they'd r-rather document it. I can also tell you which cops S-Stephan's men have been p-pressuring to give in. They're t-threatening their f-families and jobs. T-Their homes."

A sinking feeling fills my gut and I look up, catching Bear's eyes in the rear-view mirror. This is definitely not good. We had a sneaky suspicion most of the police here were crooked, but to threaten their families? Their livelihoods? Their homes? That's taking things way too far.

The hospital comes into view and I look back down at Mary. "Just a couple of minutes and we'll be there."

Bear pulls into the parking lot and doesn't stop until he's right in front of the ER entrance. Alli and Dr. Rodgers are there waiting for us, as well as two other male nurses, Chris and Jonesy. A groan of frustration escapes when I see Claudia there. I have no problems with Chris and Jonesy, but I do with Claudia. Though from the glare Alli just gave Claudia, she wasn't asked to be out here. Claudia's been a pain in my ass since she's started here a few months back. Ever since then, she's been trying to get me to sleep with her and go out with her. That was never going to happen. Especially not when I finally had my Siren so close.

Alli comes forward and opens Bones' door. Chris and Jonesy step forward, and once Bones is out, Chris takes his end of the stretcher from him. Carefully, I get out and Jonesy takes over for me.

I follow them and when they lay her down on the gurney, I'm right there, pressing my forehead to hers. "I'm not allowed back there in the ER since I'm so close to you, but I'm not leaving you. I'll be there when you get out of OR. **Σε αγαπώ** (I love you), Siren."

She stares at me in shock. She must not have thought I'd continue learning Greek, but I have. Though, I did slack off for a few years. However, at the start of the year, a few months before I saw her for the first time, I had picked it up again. Then, after seeing her at the ER that first time, I started upping my lessons. Her family means everything to her, and I wanted to respect her roots when I won her back. Not to mention, it helped fill the time since I couldn't be with her.

Her eyes turn misty, and she swallows thickly. "**Κι εγώ σ' αγαπώ** (I love you, too)."

My heart feels like it's going to burst at hearing she still loves me. Giving her a quick kiss on her forehead, I step back and watch as they wheel her inside. Claudia frowns at me, a weird, confused look on her face, but I ignore it. Dr. Rodgers gives me a nod and my shoulders relax. Even though I'm not family, she'll make sure I'm kept informed about her. Alli must have filled her in a little about us.

Someone clasps my shoulders, and I turn to see Brady standing next to me. "Come on. Let's go talk to the receptionist and then to Curtis. We need guards on her."

Seeing Mary disappear down the corridor has my chest tightening, but I nod and follow Brady.

It's been a couple of hours and there have been no updates about Mary. I'm about to go out of my mind and storm my way back there when Alli comes speed walking down the corridor, tears running down her face. Worry fills me as she walks straight to me and I wrap her in a hug. Not surprisingly, Ryder steps forward with an irritated look on his face at Alli in my arms, but thankfully, he doesn't say anything. For a while now, I've been wondering if there's something going on between them, but I wasn't going to pry. She'll tell me when she's ready.

I hold her as her shoulders shake, her tears soaking my shirt, but I don't care. After a few moments, she pulls back and wipes her cheeks.

"I'm sorry, Luke. I didn't mean to cry all over your shirt."

Rubbing her arms, I give her a look. "You should know by now that I don't give a shit about that. Are you on break?"

She shakes her head. "I only had a couple hours left, but Tiffany told me to clock out early. I think she could tell I'm a complete mess because of Mary. And before you ask, I haven't heard any updates. I would have told you right away if I had."

Alli sniffles again as more tears threaten to fall, and I'm about to pull her back into my arms when the door opens, and Harris, Maria, and Uncle Sam walk in.

Ryder pulls Alli into his arms and I cock an eyebrow at her when she snuggles into his side. A shy smile crosses her face, but she shakes her head slightly. At some point, she'll tell me, but I hope Ryder treats her right. I'd hate to have to kick his ass if he hurts her.

I motion for Uncle Sam and Harris to step over to an empty corner and they follow me, along with Brady. Looking over my shoulder, Alli has stepped away from Ryder slightly and already has Maria wrapped in a hug as they talk quietly.

"There's no news yet on Mary. What did you guys find out?"

Uncle Sam gives me a smug, satisfied grin, which I see mirrored on Harris' face as well.

"Thanks to Mary, we're going to blow quite a few of our cases out of the water. The information she was able to gather..." Uncle Sam pauses as he stares off into space, a look of shock and disbelief on his face. "I can't begin to thank her for this information, but I fucking hate that she was hurt so much while she gathered it."

Harris nods in agreement. "Between the scan drive and what Ash gave us, there's enough information to clean up a lot of shit that's been happening around here." He turns to me, and a look crosses his face that I can't decipher. "I've talked to a judge friend of mine that I know we can trust. As soon as Mary's out of surgery and awake, we'll be able to process the restraining order against Stephan. Then we'll go from there on other things as she's able to, but we have to get that restraining order in right away."

"It'll be for all of them, right? He won't be able to go near the kids either? Did the guys tell you what Mary said at the house?"

Both Uncle Sam and Harris nod, a furious look crossing both of their faces before they mask it.

"It'll be for all four of them. Ash asked Dragon to talk to me after they got back to the clubhouse." Harris pauses as his eyes turn misty, and he takes a deep breath before continuing. "Apparently, Mary must have known something like this would happen, because Ash told me that Mary told him I'm a lawyer. She told him that when it got to this point, he was to seek me out and tell me everything that Stephan had done to all of them. That he had to do that to keep his siblings away from Stephan."

"*When*, not *if*," I mutter as I run my hand through my hair in frustration, and Harris nods glumly.

"Yeah, I noticed that, too. But the information he was able to rattle off," he pauses, a bewildered look on his face. "He has to have eidetic memory or something, because he was able to provide a ton of details including dates."

I'm about to say something else when the doors to the ER open, and I step forward along with Harris and Maria.

Dr. Rodgers nods at us, a grim look on her face. "Mary's out of surgery and in recovery. They've already weened her off the anesthesia, so it won't be long before she wakes up. She doesn't have a concussion, but we still elected to perform surgery. Reason being that any movement from her while we were working on her could have resulted in permanent damage being done or even nicking or severing an artery. A few of her wounds were close to a couple of arteries.

"Overall, she had twelve wounds that needed stitches. Most of them will unfortunately scar, especially the one on her face. Her left leg was broken in two spots, so she'll be in a cast for a minimum of six weeks. X-rays showed no other broken bones, but that doesn't mean that her ribs aren't bruised which we are worried about due to the amount of bruising she has. We'll be able to find out more about that when she wakes up. Her kidneys are bruised so don't be surprised if she mentions blood in her urine. Her right shoulder was partially dislocated but wasn't broken. There's also heavy bruising around it. We've put her in a sling for now until it's healed a bit more.

"She'll be in recovery for a while before we move her up to TCU, our transitional care unit. She'll stay there for a minimum of twenty-four-hour observation. After twenty-four hours, she'll be moved to a regular room for an additional twenty-four-hour observation. If no issues arise, then she will be able to be released."

Dr. Rodgers pauses as she tucks the chart under her arm. She turns to look behind her before her gaze cuts at me and then Uncle Sam and Brady. She nods when she notices their badges clipped to their belts. She looks around again and steps a little closer to us. "Is my assumption correct that this is an abuse situation and we will need to bring security up to speed?"

Uncle Sam gives her a curt nod, stepping closer and pitching his voice low. "Yes, it is. I'm Captain Sam Morgan. It's already been discussed with Mr. Thatcher that we will need to post guards outside her room rather than using the hospital's security staff. Because of the nature of who the abuser is and adding in the fact that he has people placed in the hospital, the Steel Archangel's will be providing security, not the police. In fact, I'd like to limit which police officers are allowed into her room to myself, Officer Brady, and Officer Dixon for now," he says, pausing as he points to them in turn. "Once she's awake, we'll begin the process for a restraining order."

Dr. Rodgers' eyes blaze in anger, probably at verifying her guess that this is an abuse situation and at the implication that there are people working in the hospital that are corrupt, but thankfully, she doesn't say anything more on the topic. After a few seconds, her shoulders relax slightly.

"Good. I've seen her when she's been in here in the past and knew that it was more than what she was telling us. I'm just relieved you got her out of there before it was too late."

"Can we see her?" Maria asks, her voice trembling.

"Yes, but we can only allow two at a time while she's in the ER. The two men that were posted outside the OR are outside her room now." She pauses before looking over at me, cocking an eyebrow. "I take it you're going to relieve one of them for a while and provide security from inside the room?"

I can't help my relieved grin, even though everything in me is coiled tight and will be until I set eyes on my Siren. Dr. Rodgers has always been able to read me pretty well and right now is no exception. "Yeah, I am."

She returns my grin, and we follow her down the hallway to Mary's room.

Chapter 20

Mary

My head hurts.

Actually, my whole body hurts, and my limbs feel heavy.

The smell of bleach assaults my nose, which makes my already queasy stomach even queasier. Someone, or a few someones maybe, are talking quietly nearby, but I can't make out what they're saying. Their words are fuzzy.

A beeping sound registers, and it's only then that I realize where I'm at.

I'm in a hospital.

I'm in a hospital!

The kids!

Oh, no! Did someone find me and bring me here? Oh God, please don't say Stephan's carried through on his threat toward my children. God, please say my babies are all right!

The beeping sound intensifies as my panic rises and someone curses.

"Shit. Get the lights," someone hisses and then I feel hands on my face. One cupping my cheek and the other brushing my forehead.

The hands feel... familiar in a way.

"Siren, it's okay. You're safe. The kids are safe and they're at my friend's house. It's okay. Stephan's not going to get his hands on you. Not again. You're safe. Can you open your eyes for me?"

Luke? Is he really here? Or is it a dream?

I struggle, but after a few attempts, I'm finally able to open my eyes. Well, eye. One of them must be swollen shut.

"L-Luke?" I all but croak out, wincing at how raw my throat feels. At the same time, relief flows through me at seeing his blurry figure sitting beside my bed.

He turns, grabs my glasses and a cup with a straw off the table. After putting on my glasses, he brings the cup up to my lips. I almost moan when the cool liquid hits my throat.

After a second, he chuckles, and the sound warms my chest. God, how long has it been since I've heard that sound?

"Don't drink too fast. I know it feels good on your throat, but with all your injuries, getting sick from drinking too fast is gonna hurt like a bitch."

I slow my drinking and take a final sip before leaning back. Looking at him, the rest of the pieces start falling into place.

Thanksgiving with my **παππούς και γιαγιά** (grandparents).

Tucking the kids in bed.

Stephan delivering the worst beating he's ever given me.

Stephan threatening to kill the kids and then me if I left and went to the hospital.

Vaguely, I remember talking to Luke at the house and in the back of a truck.

He puts the cup back down and when he faces me again, he slightly tilts his head to his left, a soft smile pulling at his lips. I turn, my eyes watering when I see my **παππούς και γιαγιά** (grandparents) standing at the foot of my bed, smiling down at me with tears in their eyes.

"**Γιαγιά** (Grandma). **Παππούς** (Grandpa)," I barely get out before a sob rips through me, tears spilling down my cheeks.

Luke steps back and at the action, they both rush to my side, one on either side of me.

On my right, **γιαγιά** (grandma) leans forward, wrapping my upper body as best as she can in her arms. Leaning forward a little further, I rest my forehead against her shoulder. **Παππούς** (Grandpa) takes my hand in his calloused one, threading his fingers through mine before raising it and kissing the back of my hand.

"Shhh, **λουλούδι μου** (my flower). It's okay. You're safe now," **γιαγιά** (grandma) says as she soothes me and pats my hair gently.

"I'm s-so s-sorry," I sob and both of them immediately tsk me.

"**Λουλούδι μου** (My flower), none of this is your fault." **Παππούς** (Grandpa) pauses and **γιαγιά** (grandma) leans back slightly as **παππούς** (grandpa) gently grasps my chin, making me look at him. "The fault for all of this lies with Stephan.

Stephan, Diego, and Isaac. I don't know who else in the Vasquez family was involved in this, or anyone else for that matter, but we'll find out and make them pay. None of this is on you, Mary Elizabeth Catarino."

My breath hitches when he uses my full maiden name and fuck do I want to get rid of my married name so I can go back to that name. Back to me. I shake that thought off for now as he continues.

"You did what you had to do to survive that bastard and protect those three precious babies of yours. When you found out they were up to something, you put yourself at risk to get information that will help bring them down. While I hate that you had to endure more of his abuse while you did that, I'm also so fucking proud of you. We all are, and I know our Nikos would be, too. We're all here to help you get back on your feet. To get that spark back. Like I said earlier, '**Έχουμε την πλάτη σου, λουλούδι μου** (We've got your back, my flower)'."

His words unlock something in me and opens the floodgates. Tears pour down my cheeks once again and they both crowd closer, holding me gently as I cry. A gentle caress on my calf lets me know that Luke is still in the room, and I'm thankful that he's here. Well, not to see me completely losing it, but thankful for his presence. I've always felt safe around him.

After a few minutes, I feel much lighter, and I pull back. My ***παππούς και γιαγιά*** (grandparents) step back as I wipe my eyes, but then hiss when I move my right arm and shoulder. Glancing down, I didn't even realize my arm was in a sling.

Luke clears his throat and I look up at him. "Doc said your shoulder was partially dislocated. You'll need to wear the sling until it heals."

I look down again and then notice all the little bandages wrapped around my arms and I can feel a few more on the rest of my body. Not to mention the itchy cast on my leg and something itchy on my cheek. Turning my attention back to Luke, I swallow thickly. "What all did the doctor say? What all did he do to me?" My voice wobbles on that last bit and I blink rapidly to keep my tears from falling again.

Luke steps forward, taking my left hand in his, but instead of looking at me, I notice he's checking my monitors. After a few moments, his gaze returns to me.

"Before I answer that, how are you pain wise? I need to tell the Doc that you're awake so she can go through her checks."

Chewing on my lip, I nod. "Could definitely use something, but I really don't want morphine or anything like that. I'd rather take ibuprofen or something similar. I don't like the way those other drugs make me feel or knock me out..." My voice trails off after that, and as I clear my throat, I swear I see his jaw clench, but then it's gone. His gaze turns worried and I lick my lips, figuring it's probably best if he knows why.

"If I was ever given stronger meds, like hydrocodone, when he broke something, I'd have to painstakingly hide them. No pun intended. If I didn't, he'd find them and take them. I'm pretty sure he was either taking them himself or selling them. Or both. Besides, I didn't like taking a full pill anyway because they'd knock me out. I didn't like being that vulnerable around him. Or leaving the kids vulnerable. It reminded me too much of being drugged at my house and waking up in that cell-like room. Whenever I needed to take the edge off pain-wise, when over the counter pills wouldn't touch the pain, I'd only take a partial pill of the heavier meds."

"Motherfucker," Luke curses as his other hand rakes through his hair roughly. His eyes close for a minute, tension running through his body, but his grip on my hand remains loose. None of his tension bleeding into it or squeezing me too tightly.

When he opens his eyes again, I can still see the tension and anger, but I know it's not directed at me.

"We can talk to Doc about that, but if you do need something stronger, you can accept and take it. You never have to worry about leaving yourself vulnerable around me. I'll make sure nothing happens to you or the kids."

As if he hasn't just tilted my world on its axis, he pushes the nurse button on the bed, letting them know that I'm awake before he turns his attention back to me. All the while, I'm left reeling at his words.

I've practically been 'on' twenty-four-seven for the past nine years. Never able to fully rest or relax. Not to mention having a good night's sleep. I learned quickly to never fall into a deep sleep around Stephan. A shiver works down my spine as memories of those beatings threaten to bring more tears, but I push them down for now.

Other than working, Stephan never did anything to help with things around the house or with the kids. It was all on me. Cook. Clean. Laundry. Groceries. Pay the bills, well, before we were able to set up automatic payments on practically everything. Take care of the lawn. Clear the driveway in winter. Doctor appointments. Take the kids to pre-school. Any school event or bake sale. All of that and everything in between fell on my shoulders while I was also doing my best to stave off Stephan's beatings and protect my children.

Luke clears his throat and I shake my head to clear my thoughts.

"Other than your shoulder, you have twelve wounds that needed stitches. Your leg was broken in two spots, so you'll be in a cast for at least six weeks. Thankfully, your ribs aren't broken, but they could be bruised. Especially with how much your skin is bruised in that area. Your kidneys are bruised, and Doc said that you'll most likely see some blood in your urine. Your eye is swollen shut, but I'm sure you already noticed that. The silver lining in all of this is that you don't have a concussion."

Right as he finishes, a woman in a lab coat enters and smiles at me while also nodding toward Luke.

"Thanks, Luke, and yes, I'm very glad that you don't have a concussion on top of all of that," she says before turning and looking me over from head to toe. "Hello, Mary. I'm Dr. Rodgers. How are you feeling? Need anything for pain?"

I nod. "Yes, please, but I don't like how drugs like morphine make me feel or knock me out. It's too close to..." I bite my lip as I pause, looking down at my hand. "Maybe for just when the pain is too bad? Or a lower dose? If that's not possible, maybe something over the counter?" Tears sting my eyes once again, but I try not to let them fall.

Tension fills the room again, but I don't look up. I continue staring at my lap as I pick at the blanket.

"We'll get you a painkiller prescription when you leave so that you have it for when you need it. And yes, you can use over the counter medicine, but never together. We don't want you overdosing on us. I would like to give you a painkiller for right now though, but I'll lower the dosage. Your body needs to heal and being in pain will hinder that. Is that okay?"

I chew my lip as I think about it, and finally nod. The pain is pretty bad. I just hope Luke means what he said. That he won't let anything happen to me if the meds knock me out. "Okay."

"I'll get the order in after I'm done in here. Luke, how about you help me get her into a sitting position so I can listen to her lungs?"

For the next ten minutes, Dr. Rodgers checks me over and tells me that once a room opens up on TCU, their transitional care unit which is sort of like the ICU but a step down, then I'll be moved up there for a minimum of twenty-four hours. Assuming things go well, I'll spend another twenty-four hours in a regular room before being discharged.

When she leaves, tension fills the room again and I swallow thickly. Looking up at the clock on the wall, it's just after two in the morning. I'm tired, and hurting, but there's something I want to do before I give in and fall back asleep.

Clearing my throat, I look over at Luke. Then at **παππούς** (grandpa). "I want to file a restraining order against Stephan. For the kids and me. Then file divorce papers."

Παππούς (Grandpa) gives me a knowing, sort of smug, smile and then walks over to a bag laying on a table that I hadn't noticed before.

"Funny you should say that, because I already have the paperwork drawn up for both of them, **λουλούδι μου** (my flower). I figured you'd want to take this route. I've already talked to a judge I know I can trust, and as soon as they are signed, he'll process them," he says as he raises the papers.

Panic seizes me, and everyone's faces turn worried.

"What is it, Siren?"

Licking my lips, I take a deep breath. "What's his name? The judge?"

Both Luke's and **παππού** (grandpas) foreheads crease while they share a look. **Γιαγιάς** (Grandma's) gaze bounces between all of us in confusion, but I know from history she won't ask. At least not yet. After a few seconds, it's **παππούς** (grandpa) that speaks.

"Judge Tom Hansen. Why?"

Immediately, the tension in my body leeches away. "I vaguely remember telling Luke this in the truck, but is it possible for Sam, and...," I pause as I clear my throat, nervous about this next part. "If Sam and Brady can come in? I'd rather only say this all once."

Understanding dawns on Luke's face as he nods and pulls out his phone, probably texting Sam and/or Brady.

Once again, my body tenses as I think about Brady. I wonder if he really has changed, or if I'll be on the receiving end of his vitriol once again.

Guess it's time to find out.

Chapter 21

Mary

SOMEONE KNOCKS ON THE door, but instead of waiting for an answer, it's thrown wide open and then Alli's rushing in. She makes a beeline straight for me, but then she pauses by the bed as if she's unsure if I want her to touch me. Taking a chance at what everyone else said was true, I raise my good arm.

Immediately, relief fills her face and I'm engulfed in a gentle hug, my best friend's signature watermelon scent wrapping around me. Seconds later, I can feel her tears dropping onto my hair and hospital gown. Feeling her tears has fresh tears of my own running down my cheeks. God, I've missed my best friend.

"Thank God you're alright," she whispers after a few moments before pulling back and wiping her face. "Since Luke brought you to the hospital, that means you're not going back to that bastard, right?"

I nod as I wipe my own tears. "No, I'm not going back. I'm going to work with Sam and **παππούς** (grandpa) to file the paperwork for me and Luke said we could stay with some friends of his."

Excitement lights her eyes and she turns toward Luke. "Levi's or Mae's house?"

Who's Levi and Mae? And how does Luke know them? Wait, how does Alli know them?

"Mae's. They offered since it's getting close to Levi's due date."

Alli turns back toward me and giggles at my apparent confusion. "Levi is Thor and Dragon's Old Lady. They're twins. Thor's the President of all the chapters in the Steel Archangel's MC. Dragon is their Enforcer. Well, one of them. Levi's an unofficial Enforcer as well, though I think she'll end up taking the position once the twins are born."

My eyes widen in shock, my gaze bouncing between her and Luke as I try to wrap my mind around that. One man is hard enough to handle, but two? And twins at that? "She's with two men? Wait. The club allows women?"

At Alli's, Luke's, and even my grandparents' nods, I shake my head. She must have the patience of a saint. A badass saint, apparently.

Laughter rings out throughout the room and my cheeks heat. "I said that out loud, didn't I?"

Alli nods as she wipes tears from her eyes. "You did, and she has them wrapped around her little knife-wielding fingers. She's also pregnant with twins that are due early February, but since they're twins and adding in the fact that both Thor and Dragon are big men, I'm betting they'll be born shortly after the new year."

I shake my head again, purposefully avoiding the 'knife-wielding' part, and then remember what else she had said earlier. "Who's Mae?"

"She's Smoke's daughter. He helped us with trying to track you down the past couple of years. Before that, it was just me, Uncle Sam, and Brady. Mae is Timber's Old Lady. I should tell you that she's also pregnant but with triplets, though she's not due until early June."

Once again, I feel my eyes widen almost comically. "What's in the water at the clubhouse? Twins and triplets?"

Almost immediately, tension bleeds into Alli and Luke and my gaze pings between them as worry swirls in my gut. "What? Is something wrong? Did I say something wrong?"

Luke clears his throat and threads his fingers through mine on my good hand. "No, Siren, you didn't say anything wrong. It's just there was a lot of shit going down around the time Mae got pregnant and that's her story to tell." He must have seen my panic, because he instantly starts reassuring me. "She wasn't raped or anything like that, but..." he pauses as he sighs. "I don't want to overshare something she might not be comfortable sharing until she's ready."

Swallowing thickly, I nod. "I understand." I think.

Alli pats my leg. "You'll like Mae. She's a total sweetheart, and I swear she's like pure sunshine. Though I will warn you, she has a unique way of cussing that will probably have you laughing and shaking your head most of the time."

I smile at that. "She sounds like a fun person. I'm also thankful for that. Even though I cuss a lot, I try not to in front of the kids."

A yawn escapes me and Alli squeezes my calf. "I'm sorry. Here I am gabbing and you're trying not to fall asleep before you talk to Sam, Brady, and Dixon. Luke had me bring them back, saying you wanted to give your statement."

Nodding, I try to swallow the lump that forms in my throat.

Alli leans down and gives me another hug. "I'm on shift for the next three days, so I'll be checking in on you later. I know it'll be hard with all your injuries and the pain, but try to get some sleep tonight."

Nodding, I give her a little squeeze, thankful that I'll have a familiar face around while I'm here. "Thank you, Alli."

She gives me a smile as she pulls back and leaves the room as Brady comes in.

He nervously looks over at me, a small smile on his face and then, as if coming to a decision, stands taller as he looks over at my grandparents and Luke. "Is it okay if I talk to Mary for a few minutes really quick? I'd like to clear the air a bit before she gives her statement."

My muscles go tight and my chest tightens. Luke must feel the tension running through me because he squeezes my hand. He leans down and kisses my temple, and I feel my body leaning into it. God, I've missed him.

"It's okay, Siren. I promise that he really did change. Hear him out, okay?"

I nod, not able to trust my voice right now. Luke doesn't know everything that Brady said to me those months after the accident my mom caused and before I was kidnapped. I could never bring myself to tell him everything. Especially since before the accident, they were more like brothers rather than cousins.

After a few moments, it's just Brady and me in the room.

He's standing to my left before he sits in the chair next to my bed, resting his elbows on his knees. His hands fidgeting as he twirls his phone absently in his hands.

"I can't even begin to say how sorry I am for how I treated you. For what I said to you. I was angry, so angry, and had no idea how to process that anger. If Eileen had hit the car differently, I'm almost positive my dad wouldn't have made it. I was young, and dumb, and took all my anger out on you since there was no one else to take it out on. I'm so sorry, Mary."

Tears sting my eyes as I try to find the words to express what I felt these past nine years. "You hurt me, Brady. You have no idea how badly or deep your words cut. They reopened wounds that my mom had made years ago. But you were my best friend. Your words and actions cut even deeper than hers because of that."

His face falls and his Adam's apple bobs as he swallows. "What can I do to make it up to you? I want to be your friend again. To go back to the four of us being thick as thieves again."

My answer to him is interrupted when the door opens and a nurse walks in. She's thin and young with blonde hair that's tied up into a bun, and her makeup is overkill, in my opinion. She looks like she's ready to go to a club instead of working the night shift in a hospital ER. Frowning, I glance over her again. There's something about her that puts me on edge.

She gives me a fake smile. One that doesn't reach her eyes and my unease increases. "Hi, I'm Claudia. I've got your pain medicine that Dr. Rodgers ordered for you."

She walks over to the computer to my right, but in the process, I see her dropping a vial into her pocket and then she pulls out a different one. As she types, my gaze swings to Brady in panic. What the hell was that?

His brow furrows and he gives me a slight nod. Did he see it too? He types something out on his phone, his fingers flying, and it dings right as Claudia turns toward me.

"I-I'd really rather wait to be given the pain meds until after I give my statement. Can it be left for Luke to give me when I'm done?"

She scowls at me, but quickly covers it. "I'm sorry. The doctor said I needed to give it to you right away."

My frown deepens at that and my skin prickles. Something's not right. Never has a doctor said something like that before and ignored what I wanted. "I don't want to take it right now," I reply, my voice firmer.

She ignores me and when her scowl deepens, I pull away while also trying to scramble and grab my IV line away from me.

"Help! Luke!"

I hear a shuffle outside the door right as Claudia's scowl turns darker and her face turns red. Brady's already rounded the corner of my bed and trying to grab her hands. Her fake nails scratch my arm and hand a few times as she tries to grab my IV line. I cry out when she puts weight on my right shoulder, and it's then that I catch the scent of something familiar.

Seconds later, Brady gets a hold of her, but Claudia continues to fight him and me before he finally gets a hold of both of her wrists securely right as Luke comes in, followed by my **παππούς και γιαγιά** (grandparents) who seem to be leading a small army.

Brady squeezes her wrists harder and she cries out in pain, dropping my IV and the vial. My fingers are shaking so much, but I still manage to snatch the vial before she can get away from Brady and grab it again. Brady yanks her arms behind her back and I hear an audible click. Did he just handcuff her?

"I don't know what stunt you're trying to pull, but I'll figure it out," he all but growls at her. He turns toward me, and as our gazes lock, guilt shines in his eyes. I'm almost positive he's blaming himself for not getting her away from me quicker.

Sinking back in my bed, I give him a small smile of thanks. "Thank God you were in here, Brady. Though she is pretty fucking stupid for trying to pull that kind of a stunt with a police officer in the room."

Brady's lips roll in as his shoulders shake with his silent laughter. Claudia looks at him over her shoulder in confusion but then pales when Brady unclips his badge from his belt and shows it to her.

"I agree. Pretty fucking stupid," he says with a sneer as he looks down at Claudia.

Despite the roller coaster of emotions running through me, a small laugh escapes at the irony of her pulling that stunt in front of him.

Lifting the vial, it doesn't escape my notice, or everyone else's, that my hands are still shaking. So much so that it takes me a bit to be able to make out the name of the medicine. My blood runs cold when I don't recognize the name. I don't think this is a painkiller. But if it's not a painkiller, then what is it?

My gaze snaps to Luke's. "What's propofol? Did I say that right?"

His gaze turns thunderous. And it's then that I realize who else is in the room besides Luke and my **παππούς και γιαγιά** (grandparents)—Dr. Rodgers, Alli's father Curtis, Sam, and a man in a police uniform whom I'm guessing is Dixon, based on what Alli said earlier. And at the rear of the group is another man in a similar vest as Luke's. His patch says his name is Thor. If memory serves, Luke and Alli said he was the President of the Steel Archangel's. Wait, why is the President of Luke's club in my hospital room? Also, how the heck are all these people fitting in this tiny room?

"Mary, can I see that vial? What happened?" Dr. Rodgers asks and I nod, holding it out to her while Brady and I fill everyone in.

Brady shuffles Claudia around and Dixon steps forward, patting her down. He reaches into her pocket and pulls out another vial before handing it to Dr. Rodgers.

Luke steps closer to Dr. Rodgers and frowns. "When I stopped Claudia before entering, she showed me this vial, hydrocodone. She must have had propofol in her pocket. I didn't check her pockets," he says before turning to me, guilt written all over him. "Propofol is an anesthetic and a sedative. It's also used to put patients in a medically induced coma to let their bodies heal."

Bile rises in my throat. "He tried to silence me."

As that realization slams into me, and how badly things could have gone, more memories and feelings from the past threaten to drown me. Shaking my head, I force them to the back of my mind to unpack later when I'm alone. Refocusing back on Luke, he looks even more guilty than before as he studies my face.

Crap.

I bet he saw all of that play out on my face just now.

Glancing at Brady, the same guilty look is mirrored on his face as well.

Double crap.

I hold out a hand and Luke takes it. If my other arm wasn't in a sling, I would have done the same to Brady. "This is not your fault, Luke. Or yours, Brady. You had no idea that she'd try something like this." I pause and turn toward Brady, Sam, and Dixon. "If I were you, I'd look into who she's been hanging out with. It could just be coincidence; I've had to wash many shirts of Stephan's that reeked of the same perfume Claudia's wearing and had lipstick stains that match that same tacky bubblegum color she's wearing right now. It's been going on since a couple of months after moving here. In fact, I know there's still a shirt in the laundry room that has a lipstick stain on the collar if you need the evidence. I didn't get through all the laundry the other day and I knew I wouldn't have time to finish it yesterday while I was cooking." I pause as I see her eyes flash. The feeling that Stephan is behind this intensifies. "I wouldn't be surprised if he put her up to this. He's manipulative enough that he's probably filled her head with a bunch of lies already."

Worry churns in my gut. Has Stephan already found out I'm here? Or is this tied to someone else?

Claudia struggles in Brady's arms and she scoffs. "If you were a better wife, he wouldn't have sought me out."

I can't help the bitter laugh that bubbles out of me, and Claudia looks at me like I've grown two heads. "Bitch, I didn't want to be his wife in the first place. He paid someone to kidnap me and kept me prisoner for nine years, threatening the lives of my children if I were to leave him. Two of my children were conceived by him forcing himself on me."

She looks at me in confusion before shaking her head. "He said you'd probably say something like that. That you had mental issues and would often mix reality with your delusions. He stays with you because he pities you and knows how crushed the kids would be if he sent you away for treatment."

I shake my head sadly at her. "Can someone please get her out of here? Stephan has her wrapped up so tightly in his manipulations that she'll never see reason."

Dixon starts reading Claudia her rights as he takes her from Brady. Just before they go to leave, I raise my hand and they stop, but my focus is on Claudia.

"If you end up going back to him, I pray you're able to get away from him before my life becomes yours. Beatings for no reason at all. In the ER at least once a month. I hope you're able to eventually see through his 'charming' cHarrisma, his lies, and his manipulations to see the truth before he puts you in an early grave," I tell her, using air quotes around the word charming as I describe Stephan's public front. "I don't know why, but his beatings are always worse on birthdays and holidays. If you're still with him at Christmas, be careful. It could be you in this bed at some point."

She looks at me in confusion and I almost think she's going to take my words seriously. A few moments later, Dixon leads her from the room only to reappear again.

"Jonesy's taking her to the station. He's on call tonight and as soon as it became clear we'd be booking her," Dixon says with a wave of his hand toward the door, "I messaged him, asking if he'd come to book someone for us since you said you wanted me here. Sorry for not introducing myself before, but I'm Officer Dixon Hughes."

I give him a little wave. "Mary Hayes, hopefully soon to be Mary Catarino again."

He tilts his head at me but then I notice Luke looking at him weird, his brow furrowed.

"You mean Max's brother?"

Dixon tips his head, a small smile on his face. "I forgot for a minute that you work with Max, but yeah, his twin brother, Oliver. We call him Jonesy all the time."

Luke chuckles. "That's funny because we call Max 'Jonesy' as well."

Dixon's smile widens as he shakes his head slightly, and then Luke turns to Dr. Rodgers and Curtis.

"Is it possible to limit who administers Mary's medicine going forward to just Alli and me like we did a few months ago? It also needs to be unopened so we can make sure it isn't tampered with. For any medicine that will be given on the regular, we can set up storage in the room and I can keep it in here. I won't be leaving until she's discharged, so if Alli's not on shift, I can administer her meds. Especially since I don't know if the other units would let Alli do it once we leave the ER."

Curtis nods and he and Dr. Rodgers share a look before she nods as well, but it's Curtis who answers him.

"Yes, I will make sure all the units know and when you leave the ER, you and Alli are the only ones to be able to administer her meds. I'm sure a few feathers will be ruffled, but I'll make sure they know this is how it needs to be."

Jaw dropped, my gaze bounces between the three of them like a ping-pong ball. Luke's not leaving my side? He's going to stay?

I shake my head. "Luke, you're going to need to leave at some point. I mean, you're in clothes that are covered with my blood," I say, my hand gesturing the length of him even though my stomach threatens to empty itself at exactly how *much* of my blood is on him.

A throat clears, and I turn to see Thor looking at me. He holds up a duffle bag and I stare at him in shock and disbelief. Well, there goes that argument. I had hoped I'd have some time alone to process all these emotions.

Thor turns toward Luke and tilts his head at him. "Wildcat got your key out of the office and packed you a bag. She wasn't sure how long you'd be here, so she packed enough for a week. A few other things are in here, too." He pauses and then holds up another bag while looking at me. "Asher and Sasha helped pack this for you after you left. If you need anything else, either of you, let me know and I'll get it arranged."

My confusion must have shown because Luke chuckles softly. "Thor's nickname for his Old Lady is Wildcat. Her name's Levi, the one we told you earlier that's pregnant with twins. Sasha is a Prospect with the club and Levi's sister. She's who I had Cassie go with when we got to your house."

Unease swirls throughout me as I realize my children are staying somewhere where I have never met any of the people who are living there. What if Stephan has someone planted there? He could take my children while I'm still stuck in this hospital.

"Hey, where'd you go?" Luke asks as he leans down and rubs the crease in my forehead I hadn't realized was there.

I shake my head, not ready to say the words out loud. Instead, I take a deep breath and settle for the half-truth. "I'm just tired and in pain. Can I give my statement so we can do the restraining order? I feel like I'm going to crash soon."

Luke frowns but nods, no doubt knowing that wasn't what was bothering me, but thankfully he says nothing.

"I'll check in later on you and before my shift ends," Dr. Rodgers says as she taps the end of the bed with her hand and then slips out of the room.

Curtis steps forward, giving me a gentle hug. "I can't tell you how happy I am to finally set eyes on you again, Mary. Luke's been beside himself the entire time, spending almost every free minute he's had searching for you and I know Alli's been missing her best friend and reading buddy. Brady's also been trying to dig up any information that would help lead to finding you."

Even though I'm in shock, I still manage to hug Curtis back. My mind is warring with what everyone's been telling me compared to what Stephan's been saying all these years. Even though I know Stephan's a manipulative asshole, it doesn't immediately erase his words or his so-called proof that everyone had moved on without me. That they'd forgotten me. Abandoned me.

I give him a shaky smile when he pulls back and then steps out of the room.

When he's gone, it's just Luke, my **παππούς και γιαγιά** (grandparents), Sam, Brady, Dixon, and surprisingly, Thor.

"Is it okay if I stay, Mary? I'd like to know what we're up against so that we can prepare accordingly. Patch has given me a bit of information, but I'd like to hear it from you, too. Also, this way you won't have to relive everything again," Thor says with a gentle smile on his face that is at odds with how intimidating he is. The man has to be around six feet tall, muscles for days, and gives off an aura that says 'don't fuck with me or no one will find your body'. However, I get the impression none of this is directed at me and that he'd never hurt me.

Chewing on my lip, I pick at the blanket as I try to swallow around the lump in my throat. What he's saying is true. It would be easier to say everything only once, but why would they help me? I'm nobody to them.

"Oh, Siren, that's not true."

Luke's soft and pained words haves me looking up. Shit... Did I say that out loud?

He laughs. "Yeah, Siren. You said both of those things out loud. Trust me in that you aren't the only woman we've helped. I think it might help if you spoke to Levi and Mae once you're up to it. Maybe Mae first, as your story has a few more similarities to hers than Levi's. They can tell you their stories and it might help ease some of your worries and concerns. I swear to you, Siren, no one will judge you about what you went through. We don't stand for anyone abusing people, but especially women and children. You're safe with us."

Taking a deep breath, I force myself to relax before looking over at Thor. "You can stay."

He tips his head at me. "Thank you. And I just want to emphasize that what Patch said is true. We will protect you and your children from this fucker. You're welcome to stay as long as you want to."

Luke stiffens slightly at that and I frown, wondering what Thor said that could have him worried. Is it because he said I could stay as long as I want? Does Luke not want me there? Or does he want me to stay there with him?

Shaking off those thoughts, I decide to unpack them later after I've gotten some sleep. Sighing, I look up at Sam and then to **παπποὺς** (grandpa).

"How do you want to do this?"

Chapter 22

Mary

SAM HOLDS UP HIS phone. "I'd like to record your statement, if that's okay?"

Chewing my lip, I look over at **παππούς** (grandpa) and he gives me a small nod. "It would be best to have a recording for when this goes to court. I'm also glad that you aren't under the influence of any painkillers right now. No one can say that they are altering your mind."

His words bring Claudia back into my thoughts and I shiver at what she was trying to do. Swallowing thickly, I refocus back on Sam. "Yes, you can record it."

He turns to Dixon. "You take the lead on this, Hughes. That way, no one can say there was a conflict of interest."

Dixon tilts his head in acknowledgement. "Not a problem, Captain."

He pulls his phone out and moves to sit in the chair next to my bed. **Παππούς** (Grandpa) holds out a legal pad and pen for him, which he takes.

"Thank you, Harris."

I look between them. "You two know each other?"

Παππούς (Grandpa), Dixon, Sam, and Brady all chuckle.

"Yeah, we do, **λουλούδι μου** (my flower). We've worked together on a lot of cases over the years. Same for Sam and Brady."

Absently, I nod. Apparently, I have a lot to catch up on.

Once Dixon's all settled in, Luke wheels the table closer to both of us and I reach for the cup, wanting to wet my throat a little before I start talking. After setting the cup back down, Luke refills it for me.

"Okay, Mary. In a moment, I'll start the recording. Everyone else, try to stay quiet. I know you guys already know this, but I'll repeat it anyway. Harris, Sam, Brady, if any of you need to ask for clarification or if a question arises, please identify yourself first, and then ask your question. Thor, I'm going to have to use your real name for this. Same for you, Patch. Is that alright?"

"It's alright with me," Thor says, his voice gruff and deep. I get the feeling he and Luke are going to be the ones to worry about when I get everything out.

"It's alright with me, too," Luke says.

The others nod in agreement and when everyone's settled in a seat, Dixon starts the recording.

"It's half-past two o'clock in the morning on Friday, November 24th, 2023. This is Officer Hughes taking the statement of Mary Hayes. Present are Captain Morgan, Officer Morgan, Harris and Maria Catarino, Luke Morgan, also known as Patch, and Ryan Gilbert, also known as Thor. Mary, can you please tell me what happened tonight?"

Taking a deep breath, I start telling him what happened since waking up this morning, er, yesterday morning, when I started preparing the food.

"After getting myself and the kids ready, I headed to the kitchen to start preparing the food. When Stephan got up and came into the kitchen for his breakfast and coffee, he saw how much food I was preparing and *what* I was preparing when he saw the recipes that I had spread out on the counter. Years ago, I had tried to recall as many recipes as possible of Grandma's that I could since Stephan had told me he had burned or threw out everything of mine from my old house." I pause, shaking off those memories and look down at the blanket, picking at it as I continued.

"He started muttering that all the food was a waste of money and that he never should have agreed to let my family come over. At the time, I had ignored him, which was hard, and went about preparing everything. I was too excited to finally be cooking a large Greek meal again and to see my grandparents to really care if he liked the food or not." It's hard since I've started doing it again, but I try to refrain from using the Greek words for my family members.

Internally, I sigh and my chest aches as my mind goes back to those recipes. I'm just glad I remembered the recipes correctly. However, thoughts of all of my old things and **πατέρας** (dads) things being gone has my eyes stinging with unshed tears, but I will them not to fall. Shaking myself, I refocus back on Dixon.

"Stephan doesn't like you cooking Greek food?" Dixon asks with a look of bewildered confusion on his face and I shake my head.

"No, he doesn't. He doesn't like me speaking Greek, either. Over the years, he's tried to force me to sever any tie I might have to my life before he bought me, thinking it would help increase his control over me. However, I knew if I didn't speak Greek when my grandparents came over, that they'd immediately know something was wrong and then things could have gotten ugly really fast. Despite knowing that I'd most likely be beaten for disobeying his rule, I was determined to speak Greek with them. I needed the day to go off without a hitch so I could give Grandpa the scan drive of information I'd collected about what Stephan has been up to."

"Okay, we'll come back to the 'buying you' part and the scan drive later. For now, keep going about yesterday."

I fill them all in on the rest of yesterday's events with very little interruption from anyone. That he toyed with me in the beginning, taunting and threatening me in between beating me. Then, when I got to the part where Stephan's rage increased and his beatings and threats became worse, my body starts shaking and my breathing becomes more erratic as I relive that nightmare.

Luke scoots closer and takes my hand in his, squeezing it slightly. Instantly, my body relaxes, albeit only slightly, and I give him a silent nod of thanks as I try to block out **γιαγιάς** (grandmas) sniffles. If I focus too much on her right now, I'll be crying along with her and never get out everything I need to say.

With Luke's support, I'm able to get through what Stephan did to me, however, I'm still an anxious wreck at having to relive those memories.

After explaining what happened here at the hospital with Claudia so that it's on record, my hands are shaking even more, despite Luke still holding onto my good one. On top of that, I'm getting really, really tired and my pain is worsening.

"Okay, I think we'll stop here for now. When you're feeling a bit better and you've had a chance to rest some more, please call me. We can get the rest of your statement about the night you were kidnapped," he says as he pockets his phone and notes before handing **παππούς** (grandpa) back his notepad and pen.

I give him a tired smile as I take his business card. Turning toward Luke, I nibble my lip. "Can... Can you hold on to this for me? I'm not exactly wearing something with pockets."

Giving me a small smile and a tilt of his head, Luke takes the card and puts it in his wallet. "Yeah, Siren, I've gotcha."

My cheeks heat at the look in his eye, and I force myself to turn toward **παππούς** (grandpa) and Sam, breaking the connection. "What all do I have to do for the restraining order?"

Παππούς (Grandpa) hands me one of the packets of papers that he's holding. "First, give this a read. If you have any questions, let me know. If there's nothing you want to add or have corrected, then sign next to the arrow sticky notes and I'll get it over to Tom to process."

Dixon says his goodbyes to give us some privacy, but Brady hovers hesitantly as he chews nervously on his lip.

I hold out my arm, and immediately, he leans in for a hug.

"Thank you for earlier," I whisper, and I can feel his head nod against mine.

"I'm sorry I wasn't faster."

Shaking my head, I hug him a bit tighter. "I'd probably be in a coma right now if it weren't for you." He pulls back, and I wipe my cheeks, drying the tears that had escaped. "What you said earlier? Before she came in?"

Brady's brow furrows, but then his cheeks pinken slightly when he realizes I'm referring to him asking what he can do to make it up to me.

"I think we're square now," I say and reach over, squeezing his hand, which is easy because he's still standing at the head of my bed.

He gives me a doubtful look, but I nod.

"I mean it. I'd be in a coma if it weren't for you. God knows if she had anything else planned for after I was under."

Shit.

That thought has me freezing and I can feel my eyes widening as my worry increases. Why hadn't I thought of that earlier?

Brady's body stiffens at my words and out of the corner of my eye, I notice that Luke's body stiffens as well, even though he's talking quietly to Thor. The look Luke gives me in response speaks volumes.

I'm not the only one who hadn't thought of that.

Double shit.

I'm even more thankful that they were all here now, and that I wasn't alone.

Brady clears his throat. "I'll see what I can do to find out what else was her plan. Try to rest, Mary. I know it'll probably be hell getting good sleep because of the pain, but still, please try."

Knowing he's just worried and not trying to boss me around, I nod, but then a yawn escapes.

"I'll get out of your hair so you can review the restraining order before you crash. Take care, Mary and I'll be in touch," he says before he disappears.

Thor clears his throat just as the door closes. "I'll get out of here as well. Thank you for allowing me to stay. I meant what I said. We will protect you and your children." He pauses and then turns toward Luke. "Keep me posted."

Luke gives Thor some sort of a chin lift thing and then he's gone.

Reaching over, I grab my cup off the table and take a drink as Luke settles into the recliner next to me, whereas **γιαγιά** (grandma), **παππούς** (grandpa), and Sam bring their chairs closer to my bed.

For the next few minutes, I read over the restraining order, but then pause as I reach out for the pen.

I'm right-handed and my right arm is in a sling.

Blowing out a breath, I try to position the papers against my torso and I'm about to ask for a notebook or something hard to use as backing when a clip board is gently laid on my lap.

"I'm sorry, **λουλούδι μου** (my flower). I should have thought of this sooner."

Smiling, I shake my head. "No worries, **παππούς**, and thank you. I'm good with everything you wrote in here," I tell him as I clip the papers to the clipboard and start awkwardly signing my name next to the sticky arrows.

In a few minutes, I'm done and hand the clipboard back to **παππούς**. A weight lifts off my shoulders as he takes it and I nibble my lip as I eye the stack of papers he put on the table next to my drink at some point.

I want to break the chains.

All the chains.

Soft chuckles break the silence, and I look up at my **παππούς και γιαγιά** (grandparents) to see them smiling softly down at me. Did I say that out loud again? When **γιαγιά** (grandma) gives me a slight nod, I feel my cheeks heat, but thankfully, no one says anything.

"If you want to do everything now, I can tell you what I put in there and then you can just sign, rather than reading it all through, but it's up to you, **λουλούδι μου** (my flower). Even though your marriage was a complete sham and you never gave consent in the first place, in the eyes of the state, you are still married, since you have the copy of the marriage license."

Relief fills me that Ash was able to find the marriage certificate, even though I hated that it existed. Still, I'm glad that I told Ash that if anything were to happen, that he needed to make sure to grab that certificate when we left Stephan.

"Can you tell me what you wrote up? I trust you completely and know you wouldn't do anything that could potentially hurt me or the kids."

The smiles I get in return makes my chest tighten. God, I've missed them over the years.

"Of course, **λουλούδι μου** (my flower). I figured that you didn't want anything except what I know the club has already taken, which is everything for the kids and your belongings. I put a clause in here that if you find something is missing, that you will be allowed into the house to retrieve said item or items. Also, should you need to go back to the house, I put in there that there will be a police officer present to ensure you're able to retrieve the items without interference."

Nodding, I relax even further into the bed. "You're correct, that's all I wanted. When we get to wherever we're staying, I'll look through things to make sure nothing was missed."

"Dragon, one of my brothers and Thor's twin, texted and said that when the club got everything out of the house, Ash went through each room, double checking that nothing was missed. I know there's still a chance something could have been missed, but he thought he had everything on your list," Luke says as he holds up his phone.

That has me chuckling. "I swear Ash has an eidetic memory. If he thinks he got everything, then he probably did. If anything's missing, it's most likely replaceable. Once I'm healed enough, I want to get a job. I need to be able to support us, though it's going to be rough without a car. I'm sure the one I had years ago is long gone."

Tension fills the room and my gaze bounces between all four of them nervously.

"What am I missing?"

Γιαγιά (Grandma) clears her throat and leans forward, patting my good leg. "**Λουλούδι μου**, your car is in our garage. We've been making sure it gets proper maintenance so it should be ready for you whenever we found you. As for money, everything you got from Nikos was put into a trust for you since you were kidnapped, otherwise it would have gone straight to you. We figured there could be a chance that the kidnappers had your banking information and we didn't want them getting their hands on it. We wanted to make sure you would have it for when we found you. The house... well..." she pauses, looking over at Luke nervously.

I turn to him and frown at how nervous he looks. Even his cheeks and the tips of his ears are a little pink. His eyes nervously flit around, though he mostly fixates on his hands as he picks at a nail.

"I... uh... I... um... Iboughtthehouse," he tells me, his words rushed and said so quickly that it takes a minute for me to realize what he said.

I blink at him in disbelief. "You bought my house?" The words are barely whispered, but he nods his head, the pink on his cheeks and ears darkening even further as his gaze bores into mine.

"I knew you would want your things and memorabilia. I also knew there was a chance you wouldn't want the house after what happened," he pauses as he licks his lips and my stomach clenches at the memory of **πατέρας** (dad) laying on the living room floor in a pool of his own blood. "But still, I wanted you to have the chance to make that decision for yourself. Your grandparents helped, but I didn't want them to have to pay for two mortgages, especially since we didn't know when we would find you again. They took over the mortgage payments in the beginning until I was able to work enough to build up a good nest egg, then I took them over. Other than cleaning things up, nothing's been changed or removed from the house. Twice a month, either **γιαγιά** (grandma) or I go over to clean it so it wouldn't be a mess whenever we found you. I also check in regularly to make sure nothing needs repaired."

Tears stream down my face at that and almost instantly, I'm wrapped in Luke's and **γιαγιάς** (grandmas) arms while **παππούς** and Sam squeeze my calf. Though, I know if I were upright, both of their arms would have also been around me as well.

They hold me until my tears run dry and when she pulls back, **γιαγιά** (grandma) hands me a tissue box which I gratefully take and blow my nose.

"I can't even begin to tell you how much that means to me. All these years, I'd been tortured with Stephan's words. That he'd had the entire house emptied. He told me he'd sold off what he could and trashed or burned the rest. That I would never have a reminder as to who I was before he bought me. That I was his and that I was never going to be free of him. It killed me that I'd lost everything of ours. That I'd lost anything to remember **πατέρας** (dad) by. Thanks to all of you, I have all of that and will hopefully be free of him soon. I know he'll fight the divorce, but I still want to file for it."

Muscles tick in Luke's, Sam's, and **παππού** (grandpas) jaws, but they don't say anything about Stephan's threats. If they're like this after hearing just those couple of threats, I'm not sure how they'll be once I get into more about the last nine years. I repress a shiver, not wanting to worry them any more right now.

Picking up the divorce papers, everyone takes the cue, and for the next ten minutes, **παππούς** goes through them with me. I'm relieved that it's just like he said. I'm not contesting the house or the cars. Even if I wanted to, it would be hard since none of them are in my name and I didn't contribute to any of the payments. The only things I want are our personal belongings, which we have from what Luke said. I don't even want any of his money, which thankfully, **παππούς** put in there that I wasn't asking for any. I just want us to be free of him. Besides, even if it isn't much, whatever money I got from **πατέρας** (dad) will hopefully tide me over until I'm able to work.

Regardless, it's going to be a tough fight, because that's exactly what Stephan will do.

He'll fight.

Well, first he'll blow a gasket and I'm sure more than one room in the house will be trashed. But for once, he'll have to clean it up himself. Not to mention figure out how to take care of himself. The man has no cooking ability whatsoever, so I'm sure his future will include a lot of takeout and frozen meals.

Twenty minutes later, I've signed my name on the last line and sink back into the bed, relieved that this part is over.

"I'll get these to Tom as soon as he's in the office later this morning.

I try to tell him thank you, but a yawn interrupts me. One so deep my jaw pops. They all chuckle.

"**Λουλούδι μου**, we'll let you get some rest. Later today, we'll stop in to check on you," **γιαγιά** says as she gets out of her chair and steps forward, leaning down to kiss my forehead.

"See you later, **λουλούδι μου**. I'll text Luke with updates as I have them," **παππούς** tells me before he also leans down and kisses my forehead.

"I'm glad you're out of there and now safe. We'll get out of your hair. Give us a call when you're feeling more rested," Sam says as pats my calf again.

"Good night and thank you, all of you. For everything." They all wave me off as another yawn strikes, and then it's just Luke and me.

"Let me get you your pain medicine. I wanted to give it to you earlier because it was obvious you were in serious pain, but I knew Harris wanted your mind clear while going over everything." He gets up and logs into the computer before measuring out my dose.

Sleepily, I nod, too tired and in too much pain to really say anything. Now that everything's done, I'm crashing hard and am looking forward to when the meds kick in.

Moments later, Luke gives me my pain meds and I give him a smile in thanks, my eyelids heavy with sleep.

"Sleep, Siren. I've gotcha."

And for the first time in nine years, the last remaining thought that crossed my weary mind was that I was finally safe. With that, I let myself succumb to a deep sleep.

Chapter 23

Patch

It's been about ten minutes since Mary's breathing changed and I know she's finally fallen asleep. My body sags in the recliner as my mind whirls with everything she's told us tonight. Then my gut clenches when I think about the fact that she still needs to tell us about that night and what's happened these past nine years. That thought has my chest tightens as I realize what I know now is probably only a small portion of what's been going on.

The urge to find Stephan and lock him in the sticks is high, but I know I probably won't be able to do that. Not since we have to include the cops in this. Why did the fucker have to be a cop? It would be so much easier to make him disappear if he was just a regular guy off the street.

Pulling out my phone, I check the messages I ignored earlier. I wasn't going to make Mary think I wasn't interested or that I was ignoring her. With how much her body was shaking when she repeated tonight's events, I'm worried about how she'll be when she has to recount everything else when she's ready to give the rest of her statement.

> *Timber: Kids are all settled in. They made a fort, and we had a popcorn and movie night to help them settle down and relax. We let them sleep in the fort because they all wanted to be together.*

Biting my lip, I hesitate to respond. He sent his text a little after one o'clock and it's half-past three now, but I'm not sure if I'll be dozing when he wakes up. He's normally an early riser, but they were also up late. Fuck it. I know Mary will want to know how they are doing once she wakes up.

Patch: Thank you. Mary just now got to sleep after giving tonight's statement and filling out some paperwork. Let me know how they are doing after they wake up. If Mary's feeling better tomorrow, I'll try to line up a video chat. It'll be best to wait until she's in a normal room for them to come visit her in person. They don't limit the number of visitors that much up there.

Not surprisingly, there are a few texts from some of my club brothers and sisters asking how Mary's doing. There are also a few from my parents and sister. I take a few minutes and respond to them all, catching them up on the gist of how she's doing. I wish I had more of Mary's family's numbers, but I'm just going to have to trust that Maria will take care of updating them all. Hopefully, they won't all try to come and see her until she's at least upstairs in a regular hospital room.

I also don't want her to get overwhelmed while she's still healing. The next week is going to be a roller coaster for her as she adjusts and gives the rest of her statements. That and I'm almost positive that fucker is going to fight Mary tooth and nail on everything. I'm glad that whatever Mary inherited went into a trust because now, the fucker can't try to take the kids for lack of income to care for them. Not that she or they would want for anything with me around, but in the eyes of the law, I'm just a concerned friend and a friend of mine is offering their home for them to stay in.

Groaning in frustration, I drop my head back against the headrest.

I wish I had gone with my gut and asked Timber to start the process for building a house a few years ago. Problem is, I had wanted Mary by my side while we planned it. The only thing I really know is that she wants a kitchen like Maria's. Other than that, I'm clueless as to what other features she wants to have. Or what she wants the house to look like, either.

I'm almost positive she doesn't want to keep her old house based on the look she gave earlier when we were talking about it. Granted, she masked it quickly. At least I know she's happy about having the rest of her things again and that they weren't trashed.

I scowl as I remember those few weeks after Mary was kidnapped.

It took a few weeks for the house to be gone through for Mary's case and then my dad, Uncle Sam, Brady, Curtis, and I cleaned up the blood. None of the women could come in without bursting into tears, and even though Harris said he could help, none of us wanted him to have the memory of cleaning up his own son's and granddaughter's blood. I wasn't too far off from the women, and my cheeks were wet more often than not while we cleaned, but I felt I needed to do something for Mary.

After we had everything cleaned, we had all gathered and talked. All of us were worried about what Mary's kidnappers might do with the house. Brady and I volunteered to stay there and watch over things. Since I was then part of the club, well I was a Prospect, I asked Steel Security to install their best security. Multiple people, even Uncle Sam, thought it was overkill, but they quickly changed their tunes.

In two weeks, there were five attempts to get into the house. Unfortunately, the bastards were good, and we never got a picture of their face on the cameras. None of them made it in, because as soon as they tried, an alarm wailed and I was immediately texted about the break in. Three of those times, I was at the house alone and Brady was there alone one other time. The last time, neither of us were home, but I had been visiting my parents, so I was able to quickly get over to the house.

Each time, there were no fingerprints left. Nothing. We have no idea who it really was, but we all suspect it's one of Diego Vasquez's cronies, Mary's so-called uncle. He was responsible for her kidnapping and, most likely, Nikos' death. At the time, it only made sense that it was him who had ordered it.

Knowing what I know now, I'm leaning toward the fact that it was most likely Stephan. Mary had said that he wanted to erase everything about her past, so it wouldn't be a stretch for him to also order everything to either be secured from her house or trashed.

Another thought has ice sliding down my spine.

Was there something in the house that was important to Stephan or Diego? Or maybe someone else? Something they wanted? There have been numerous attempts over the years to break into her house, but each time, they were thwarted. Is there a reason why Nikos and Mary were targeted? That someone had wanted to silence them?

Shaking my head, I file that thought away. I'll talk to Mary about it once she's healed a bit more.

Settling back in the recliner, I grab the nearby blanket and close my eyes. I know either Drae or Lex will wake me whenever a nurse comes in. It's going to be a long night with how frequently Mary will have to be woken up so that the nurses can check on her, and I'm determined to be with her every step of the way.

I can tell Mary's becoming more comfortable around me. She's still hesitant, and I'm going to bet she's wondering how serious I am. I plan to prove it to her. She'll always be able to count on me to have her back and support her. Which, when she's ready, will also include her going to school to be a teacher if she still wants to do that. If she doesn't then, I'll support her in whatever she wants to do.

Thoughts of a life with Mary swirl around my mind, and my determination grows. I'll fight to have her by my side for the rest of my life.

I just hope that's still what she wants as well.

The sound of quiet laughter wakes me up and it takes me a moment to remember where I am.

Cracking open my eyes, I blink a few times to clear my vision, and can't help but smile at the sight before me.

Alli is sitting in a chair close to the head of Mary's bed as they pour over what look to be photo albums.

The fog of sleep clears a little more, and a groan slips out when I realize what's probably happening, which has the girls giggling even more.

"Photo albums, Alli? Really? It wasn't enough to threaten to show my baby pictures to the Old Ladies?"

"Nope," Alli giggles. "Besides, I'm catching Mary up on what's happened the past few years."

I let out a slow breath. Yeah, I can understand that, and I'm also glad she didn't elaborate more on that night or Stephan.

Unfortunately, the happy cloud surrounding Mary seems to dissipate before my eyes and I mentally curse myself for my knee jerk reaction.

Fuck it.

"So what shenanigans were you telling her about?"

Alli laughs again and bites her lip as she tries to keep from laughing harder. However, what has my attention is the small, shy smile that plays across Mary's lips again.

"About the time when you and Brady got drunk and went streaking down the street."

Groaning dramatically, I let my head fall back. "You took pictures of that?"

They start laughing again and out of the corner of my eye, I notice Mary's bright smile again. I'd do anything to keep that smile on her face. Which apparently includes Alli spilling a bunch of embarrassing stories about me. Wait...

"Seriously. You took pictures of that?" I ask her incredulously.

Instead of an answer, I get roaring laughter and the sight of Alli almost falling out of her chair. While I can still see a cloud hanging over Mary, it isn't as bad as before, and she's also laughing along with Alli.

When Alli finally quiets down, well, sort of, she wipes tears from her eyes as she catches her breath. "I-I knew you didn't remember," which starts another round of laughter out of her and she wipes more tears from her eyes. "You guys actually *asked* me to take the pictures."

Frowning, I shake my head. "I don't remember that at all. I just remember racing Brady down the street and then him tripping, scrapping his leg all up. Then you showed up with a first aid kit and our clothes, telling us to get dressed."

"That would be the whiskey drowning out your memories." She flips the book around and I lean forward, taking it from her.

Flipping through the pages, I can feel my cheeks heat as I recall that night. Well, what I can remember of the night, anyway.

We were only eighteen and it was the weekend after Mary had been kidnapped. I had put my name in to become a Prospect and it seemed like the President at the time, Poseidon, thought I'd make a good one, but I knew it had to go to vote. Poseidon was Thor and Dragon's old man. Thor took over for Poseidon a few years after I patched in.

Shaking my head, I hand the photo album back to Alli and take a look at the clock, surprised that it's nine o'clock already. Looking back at Alli, I take in the fact that she's dressed in scrubs and it's then that I remember her saying last night that she was working the next three days.

"When does your shift start, Alli?"

"At 12:30 pm, but I wanted to come in and see how Mary was doing. Plus, I knew you'd get shit for sleep, so I figured I'd give you a bit of a break. I saw your schedule of her meds on the board, so I added to it. She was due for another dose at eight and I gave it to her. Dad talked to me about your request, and I'm happy to help out with administering her meds while she's here."

Nodding, I stretch, and feel my chest puff out at how Mary's eyes track the movement. I'm even more grateful that I'd changed my clothes after the nurse had come in that first time.

Stupid me, I'd fallen asleep in my bloodied clothes. When I had stood to watch what the nurse was doing, I realized my mistake when I had seen Mary's face go deathly pale.

Once the nurse left, I apologized profusely and quickly gathered my things before having Lex come in for a few minutes while I went to the restroom to change. After that Claudia fiasco, I wasn't leaving Mary alone for one second.

"Oh!" Alli says loudly before reaching down and grabbing her purse. "I forgot that Mae texted me, asking me to stop by the clubhouse before coming here. Smoke got you hooked up with a new phone. All of the club members' phone numbers are already programmed in. I added Dixon's number, Brady's number, my number, and all of our parents' numbers into it as well. Same for Maria and Harris. Asher gave Smoke your old phone and he transferred the pictures of your kids onto it. The rest he has on a scan drive for you to decide what to do with. Though, he did tell me that you have to set your password to lock your phone when not in use." She pauses as she hands the phone to Mary. "Mae said there's a little present in there for you in your gallery."

Digging my phone out of my pocket, I see that I've missed a few texts, but I click on Smoke's first.

Smoke: Sending a new phone with Allison for Mary. Her other one had tons of tracking software on it. After leaving their house, I drove around and ended up at a hotel before I disabled everything. Not wanting to lead him straight to us, I didn't go near the clubhouse, so hopefully the fucker doesn't make the connection just yet. Transferred her family pictures, but I moved the rest onto a scan drive. Fucker is messed up sending her those fake pictures of you.

Looking up, Mary tentatively takes the phone from Alli, but I don't miss the tremble in her fingers. Her gaze shoots questioningly to mine. "Why?"

Standing, I grab another chair and scoot closer to the bed, resting my hand on her thigh, right above her knee. I raise my own phone. "Smoke said there was a shit ton of tracking software on it." Her eyes widen in fear, and I quickly continue. "He drove around town with it and when he reached a hotel, he disabled all the software. Only then did he head back to the clubhouse. Hopefully, the jackass won't realize that's where you all will be for a while."

She nibbles her lip, not breaking eye contact with me. "That won't stop him. Or deter him. He knows about you, that you're a part of the Steel Archangel's, and he knows you're Asher's father. That's why he tormented me with all those pictures of you with those women. I'm not sure how he got them or made them, but it still hurt. Especially when I didn't know they were fake." She pauses, nibbling her lip even more as her eyes turn misty. "They were fake... Right?"

"Most likely. I haven't seen them, so I wouldn't be able to tell you one hundred percent for sure. There's only been nine or ten times that happened and that's in total." My cheeks heat in embarrassment as I admit that, and it feels like lead is sitting in my gut. I wish I had been able to be stronger and been able to deny my urges. I only sought one of the bunnies out when I couldn't stand it any longer.

Clearing my throat, I'm about to say something else when there's a knock at the door. Standing, I go to see who it is and am surprised when I see Harris, Uncle Sam, Brady, and Dixon on the other side. Surprisingly, Thor is there as well. All of them wearing grim expressions.

Shit… Now what happened?

Stepping back, I let them into the room.

Alli scoots her chair back from where she had been sitting next to the head of Mary's bed and Harris steps forward toward Mary. He kisses her forehead before whispering something to her that I'm not able to hear. When she nods, he gives her forehead another kiss and steps back. Alli scoots back closer and gently squeezes Mary's thigh in support. I take a seat close to the head of her bed on the other side and clasp her hand, threading her fingers through mine before giving her hand a little squeeze. Whatever they have to say, it can't be good, but I'll be here for her.

"I'm sorry we came by unannounced, but Stephan was just notified of the restraining order at work. He flipped his shit as soon as he realized what he was handed. It got so bad the Chief threatened to throw him into a holding cell if he didn't calm down. It would be best if we got your entire statement before he gets off the clock," Uncle Sam tells Mary and immediately, I can feel my body tensing, but not as much as hers does.

When he pauses, I turn toward Mary and notice that the color has drained from her skin and her hands are trembling. Squeezing her hand again, I bring it up to my lips and press a kiss to her knuckles.

"Mary, look at me."

She turns toward me, and the fear in her eyes would have taken me to my knees if I had been standing.

"I'll be by your side through all of this, Siren."

A hesitant look crosses her face and the vulnerability shining through has my chest tightening, almost painfully. I think I know what's going through her head and I intend to put a stop to it. To show her exactly how far I'm willing to go to make sure she's mine again.

Leaning forward, I place a kiss on her forehead even though I'd rather kiss her plump pink lips instead, but I know she isn't ready for that. Bending down further, I whisper in her ear. "Nothing you say about your past and what that fucker put you through will ever stop me from wanting you, Siren. From loving you. You've always held my heart, and you always will. It beats for you and your three precious babies. One of them, I want to officially claim and change his last name to mine, and the other two I want to adopt as my own once you're free from that fucker. To make you my wife and maybe even grow our family more. **Πάντα σε αγαπούσα και πάντα θα σε αγαπώ** (I've always loved you and always will), Siren."

Pulling back, I use my thumb to wipe the tears that had escaped while Mary stares up at me in surprised shock. Out of the corner of my eye, I notice Alli grinning at us. I had hoped for only Mary to hear that, but I don't really care if the others heard it or not.

"**Φοβάμαι** (I'm scared)," she whispers as tears pool in her eyes again. Not for the first time, I thank fuck that I started learning Greek hard core at the start of the year. Though, it helped having a number of years under my belt already. That, along with Maria and Harris tutoring me, gives me the confidence to say this next part to her.

"**Το ξέρω, αλλά δεν είσαι μόνος πια** (I know, but you're not alone anymore). **Υπόσχομαι ότι θα είμαι δίπλα σας σε κάθε βήμα** (I promise that I'll be by your side every step of the way). **Σε αγαπώ** (I love you), Siren."

Her throat works as she swallows a couple of times before she gives me a slight nod and exhales, her body almost completely relaxing. "**Κι εγώ σ' αγαπώ** (I love you, too)."

I can't help my smile as I lean in and kiss her forehead again.

As I settle back down in my chair, keeping a hold of her hand and my other one on her thigh, she takes another deep breath and opens her beautiful blue eyes. While I can still see her fear and hesitation, it isn't as consuming as before, but there's also determination there.

She turns toward the others and nods. "Okay. I'm ready to give the rest of my statement."

That's my Siren.

Chapter 24
Patch

After everyone settles in, with me on Mary's left and Alli on her right at the head of the bed, Thor clears his throat.

"Is it still okay if I stay for this, Mary?" he asks, and I say a silent thank you that he's purposefully trying to not speak as loud as he normally does since I can still feel slight tremors in her hand.

Mary licks her lips nervously and nods. "Yes. Given that we're going to be staying somewhere on the MC grounds, it's only fair that you hear everything. Just... If you need to tell the others in the MC... Is it okay if you and Luke fill them in on what I said earlier this morning and what I'll say in a bit? I can always clarify things or if you guys have more questions, but..." She pauses as she takes a deep breath. "Some of this I don't think I'll be able to repeat multiple times unless absolutely necessary."

I squeeze her hand and when I glance up at Thor, his eyes have softened, but I can also see the anger thrumming through him.

"Of course, Mary, and I understand. Also, I wanted to let you know that Levi and Mae would like to come and visit you whenever you feel up to that. No pressure or anything—it can happen after you're released if you prefer."

Mary hesitantly squeezes my hand and I turn toward her, nodding in agreement with Thor when I see the question in her eyes. They'll be able to help her feel like she's not an outcast or a burden.

She nods. "Okay."

Relief fills me because I know they'll be able to help her.

Someone clears their throat and we all turn toward Dixon.

"Like earlier this morning, everyone please try to stay quiet, and if you have questions or need clarification, please identify yourselves and then ask your question." He pauses, and his gaze returns to Mary. "Are you ready?"

Mary takes a couple of deep breaths, and then nods. "I'm ready."

Dixon nods in return and then fiddles with something on his phone.

"It's 9:30 am on Friday, November 24th, 2023. This is Officer Hughes taking the statement of Mary Hayes. Present are Captain Morgan, Officer Morgan, Harris Catarino, Luke Morgan also known as Patch, Allison Thatcher, and Ryan Gilbert, also known as Thor. Mary, thank you for your statement earlier today. This morning, you mentioned that you were kidnapped and that Stephan bought you. Can you tell us what happened the night you were kidnapped on April 11, 2014?"

Mary's throat works as she swallows a couple of times.

"I'll back up a little, because part of what happened earlier that day is relevant." She takes a deep breath, but for this next part, her gaze snaps to mine and stays on me. "I hadn't been feeling well for a few months prior to that day. After school, I was supposed to help Luke, Brady, and a few others with the sets for an upcoming play. However, I wasn't feeling well, so I went home and stayed with my friend Alli since I didn't want to be alone and Dad was going to be working for a few more hours. We studied together for an upcoming test. When it was time to head home for supper, she gave me a pregnancy test and listed off a bunch of symptoms that I hadn't noticed. After supper, I took the test and found out I was pregnant.

"I went to lay down and that's when I felt movement in my stomach. Freaked out, I called and made an appointment with a women's clinic in the next town over, Ridgeview, for eight o'clock the next morning. My periods have always been, and still are, sporadic and light, I had no idea how far along I was. But if I was feeling movement, I knew I had to be pretty far along. I don't know how I didn't know I was pregnant, but looking back on my symptoms now, I could see where I should have connected the dots sooner but didn't. Needing to tell Luke, I texted him and asked if he could call me once he got home. After gathering up the courage to tell my dad, I opened my bedroom door and that's when I heard the sound of glass breaking downstairs."

Her eyes turn misty and her grip on my hand tightens.

"Take your time, Mary," Dixon gently tells her.

She nods, swallows thickly and tells us what happened next. About thinking her dad, Nikos, had dropped a glass or something. That the rest of the house was pitch black with no sign of Nikos.

When she gets to the part where Diego tells her it's time to fulfill her duty, blood rushes through my ears, almost drowning everything else out.

"Back up, please. Can you repeat what Nikos said to you?" Dixon asks her.

"H-He told me to run. That D-Diego wanted me, but he died before he could say more," she stutters out and she pulls her hand away from mine for a moment to wipe away her tears. Both Alli and I place a hand on each of her thighs. She squeezes my hand again, resting her hand on mine, as she continues to sniffle. If her other arm wasn't in a sling, I know she'd also be holding Alli's hand.

"That's when Diego spoke up from behind me. H-He told me that they killed him because Dad wouldn't do what he was ordered to do."

"Did either of them say who shot Nikos?"

Mary shakes her head as she blinks rapidly to keep more tears from falling from her misty eyes. "No, but they were the only two people in the house. I did notice that the coffee table was overturned and a couple of the chairs were pushed around, which would have taken effort even though we had hardwood floors. One of the windowpanes in the living room was broken. I'm not sure if it was from a stray bullet from Diego or Isaac or if there was someone outside shooting in."

Uncle Sam clears his throat. "This is Captain Morgan. Based on the analysis of the scene that was done, they suspect that something hit the window from the inside."

"Thank you, Captain. Mary, then what did Diego say?"

"That Dad was supposed to hand me over so that I could fulfill my duty as a Vasquez. That the Don ordered me to be married off since I had recently turned eighteen. Everything was already arranged and by midnight that night, I would be in the hands of my new owner. He even said me being pregnant wouldn't break the deal. In fact, it made him more money. I have no idea how they knew I was pregnant, since I'd only just found out myself, but they did."

She then goes on to explain that Diego ordered Isaac to capture her, the struggle her and Isaac had all throughout the downstairs, Isaac injuring her and then capturing her before restraining her, threatening her friends and their families, and finally, Diego injecting her with something that has her quickly passing out.

Fury runs in my veins at what they did to her. The fact that he not only threatened to kill Mary and my baby, but also to rape my sister and Alli before killing all of her friends and their families, damn near has me launching out of my chair.

Mary tells us about waking up in a room, which was practically a jail cell where she was held for a month. Her only contact was a doctor who didn't even talk to her or respond to her begging for help. When she was moved upstairs, she was told that she was married to Stephan the day she was kidnapped even though it was all fake.

When she had Asher, she said that Stephan had told her she could name him whatever she wanted so long as it wasn't a relative's name and that the child had to have his last name. He was insistent that he wouldn't allow her child to live under his roof or provide for him if she gave him any other last name than his.

My chest had warmed, Brady grinned, and Alli had cried when she said she gave the kids her best friends' names as their middle names as a way to still have a part of them in her life. Asher Lucas, Isaiah Brayden, and Cassandra Allison. It stunned me, but more so Brady than me, that she gave Isaiah Brady's name, even though she had serious doubts about Brady because of how he treated her after his parents' accident.

She then goes into detail about how life had been for her ever since—the restrictions on what she could do or say, where she could go, what happened to her when she 'disobeyed' and then gradually, the punishments becoming more severe and more frequent. How for the past two years, she studied her surroundings, paid attention more, and found out more about what Stephan was doing for her grandfather and Diego.

"So, you overheard a number of phone calls between Stephan and Diego?" Dixon asks her and she nods.

"Yes. I think that as the years went on, Stephan believed he'd trained me enough and wouldn't even think of going against him. Enough so, that he became more lax about things."

"What kind of things?"

"When he would get a call from Diego, he stopped listening to it privately in his office and started putting the phone on speaker phone. Most of the time, he left his office door ajar. That's when I learned that whenever Diego spoke to Stephan that he'd say that 'the Don' wanted Stephan to do something. I don't know if that's really true or not, but that's what Diego would say." She pauses as she tilts her head slightly. "Actually, the more I think about it, the more I think Diego was giving those orders and using the Don as a scapegoat."

"What makes you think what Diego said might not be true?"

Mary bites her lip and I feel a slight tremble run through her. "Out of all the family on my mother's side, it was only my mother, grandmother, Diego, Carlos and his wife and son, Gianna and Isaac, that seemed to have an issue with Dad and me. All of the others never gave me reason to suspect them. And there was only once that they sided against me, which was when I was a kid. Or I should say, didn't stand up for me."

"What happened?"

"We had a family get together at my Aunt Anita's house and there was a playset in the backyard. My cousins and I were all out there playing when one of the adults called out that it was time to eat. My two younger cousins raced inside which left just Isaac and I to come inside from playing. Isaac pushed me off the ladder as I was climbing down, and I fell and broke my arm. He told everyone I was the one picking on him and bullying him. That I was the one that attacked him first and he pushed me off him and that's when I fell. The only adult that saw what happened was Uncle Mateo, and even though he stood up for me and told everyone what really happened, Gianna and Carlos wouldn't listen to him. They yelled at me for attacking their 'precious, innocent, baby boy'. Then, they kicked Dad and me out, even though it wasn't their house, and said that we could come back to pick up my mother later before slamming the door in our faces. That was the year before we moved to Wisconsin.

"Even though I never liked Isaac, I'd never hurt him. It's not who I am. I also know Carlos knew Isaac was in the wrong, because as Dad and I walked to the car, we passed by an open window. I could see Carlos and Diego lecturing Isaac that if he was going to pull a stunt like that, to make sure there were no witnesses around to rat him out. Then they both gave him pointers on what he should have done instead. I could tell Dad wanted to go back inside to set things right, but instead, he turned and ushered me to the car to take me to the ER."

Dixon frowns as he jots something down.

Three hours later, Mary's body sags slightly into the bed and Dixon turns off the recording.

Bringing her hand up to my lips, I press a kiss on the back of her hand. "You did good, Siren. I'm proud of you."

And I am.

However, I thought that she would have freaked out more about having to relive the past nine years. Don't get me wrong—I felt her body trembling a number of times, but it wasn't as bad as it was earlier this morning when she gave her first statement. I don't know if my earlier words helped relieve some of her worries and that she's not alone in this or if there was another reason she didn't freak out as much.

"Mary, can I take a picture of the scar you incurred from when Isaac injured you before you were kidnapped so that we can put it with your file?"

A determined look comes over Mary's face and she releases my hand to raise the bed slightly. Once she's steady, she lowers the bed but stays sitting up.

"Alli, can you help? The scars are on my right shoulder and with this sling, I don't know if it's covering it up."

Knowing both the sling and the gown are going to be in the way, I stand up, sweep Mary's hair over to her left side, and undo the gown ties at the base of her neck. "Mary, we've got to move the gown slightly. Place a hand to your chest to keep it in place."

Crimson snakes up the back of her neck, but she does as I ask. Alli unhooks the strap of her sling and steps back to allow Dixon to step forward. Moving Mary's gown out of the way, my anger once again surges at seeing the jagged three-inch-long scar on her shoulder. I can also see a couple of other smaller scars near the larger one, most likely from the same sconce that Uncle Sam had found broken, and I find myself praying that none of the wounds were deep.

Dixon takes a couple of pictures and I right Mary's gown while Alli helps with the sling.

Right as I sit back down, my phone vibrates in my pocket and I fish it out, instantly pissed when I read the text.

"W-What is it? What's wrong?" Mary's voice is shaky and scared, and I instantly curse myself. She's probably thinking it's about the kids.

Instead of answering her right away, I turn toward Uncle Sam. "Smoke just texted me that he saw Stephan entering the hospital."

Refocusing back on Mary, I notice that her face has paled, but then a determined look comes over her face. Glancing at the time, I realize it's almost 12:30pm.

"My guess is that Stephan went home and found us and all of our things gone. I wouldn't be surprised if he trashed something or a room. What's going to happen when he gets up here?"

Those were my same thoughts, but before I can say anything, Uncle Sam beats me to it.

"We've got enough evidence to arrest him for what he's done to you. I want you to stay in here when he comes up here. Same for you, Alli. Text your boss that you're going to be a little late while we handle this situation. I know you could just slip out right now, but I'd rather you stay where I know you're safe. I don't want you getting caught in the crossfire, so to speak. We'll handle Stephan and get him booked. But we need you both to stay safe during all this. Okay?"

Alli nods and muscles tick in Mary's jaw as her eyes blaze.

"I mean it, Mary. Don't forget that I know you," Uncle Sam teases and just like that, some of the tension running through her releases as she huffs but nods her head.

"I'll stay in here even though I'd like to give him a few choice words. I know he's going to make himself out to be the victim. He might even spew some of that shit that Claudia said earlier. Anything to keep him looking like the dutiful husband and not put a stain on his precious reputation."

Brady chuckles and grins. "Well, then it's a damn good thing we all, with the exception of Thor and Dixon, know you in and out. He isn't going to pull a fast one over on us."

Mary frowns. "But that doesn't take into account the dirty cops or the ones that Stephan's trying to pressure into working for Diego. That reminds me, do you have a roster list, Sam?"

"As a matter of fact, I do. Luke told me what you had said the other day." He reaches into his pocket right as there's a commotion outside the room. Uncle Sam hands her the list and a pen before turning to Brady, Dixon, and Thor. Then he turns toward Harris and me. "You two stay in here with the ladies. Harris, you know what to do. The rest of you, follow me."

Chapter 25

Brady

I'm BEYOND FUCKING PISSED at what this asshole has put sweet Mary through these past nine years, but I've got to rein it in. There's no doubt in my mind that Stephan will say shit to get under our skins and I refuse to lose my cool. I won't do anything to jeopardize helping Mary get free of this shitbag so that she can live her life with Patch. Like she was originally supposed to.

Stepping between Bear and Dragon, who are standing on either side of Mary's door, I'm relieved that Thor brought more men with him since we figured Stephan would be here as soon as he could. I'm also relieved that Thor put two of his biggest men on the door as soon as we arrived. Intimidation factor is a real thing and I know Stephan's not in his prime anymore. Seeing both of these bulky, muscled men protecting Mary is going to both piss him off and scare the piss out of him.

I step forward until I'm standing behind my dad and a little off to the side. A moment later, Dixon is at my side..Movement behind me tells me that Thor is right behind us as well. Even though I know we've got the backing from the Chief to be doing what we're doing, I can't help but be nervous. Based on what Mary has told us, when Stephan feels threatened, there's no telling what he'll do. And he better not hurt any innocents in the process.

As the elevator doors part, Stephan emerges and advances straight toward us. I keep an eye on him, but at the same time, my gaze finds Theresa, the head nurse on this floor. I tilt my head to the side and she nods back before discreetly going around to the other nurses and in seconds, it's just us and a pissed off Stephan in the nurse's station.

"Get the hell out of my way, Morgan. I need to see my wife."

"I'm sorry, but I can't do that," Dad replies. His voice is calm and level, but I see the tension running through his body.

"What?! Why the fuck not? That's my wife in there," he shouts angrily as he points toward Mary's room behind us.

I'm not sure how he knew which room was Mary's, unless he took our presence to mean it was hers.

"And what are these thugs doing here? Maybe they were the ones that hurt my Mary. Get these lowlifes out of here. I'm bringing in my own guards to protect her," he leers as he looks down his nose at Thor, Bear, and Dragon. Behind me, I feel their anger growing and I swear the aura of danger that normally surrounds them drastically intensifies at Stephan's false accusations.

Dad moves forward a step. "You will be doing no such thing. These men are following my orders, which come directly from Chief Cane. You are in no capacity to refute his orders. Not to mention, I know for a fact that you have a restraining order that was served to you this morning. You aren't supposed to be anywhere near Mary or your children."

Stephan swings his arm out, madly gesturing behind us as he spews more nonsense. Worried that he may try to take a swing at one of us, I grab his arm and slap a cuff on his wrist before grabbing his other arm. I take great pleasure in hearing the clicks of the cuffs around his wrists. It takes him a moment to realize what just happened before he starts struggling in my arms, trying to get away from me. We shuffle a little and Dixon steps forward to grasp his other arm. When both of us have a tight hold on his arms, Stephan's anger rises so much his cheeks start turning red.

"Uncuff me, Officer! Instead of going after me, you should find the asshole that broke into my house and did this to her! Mary needs me to take care of her! She has several mental conditions. Whatever she told you is a lie, dreamt up from her delusions."

A humorless laugh escapes me and I shake my head. Dad steps forward and it's then that I realize in the shuffle, we've shifted so that my right shoulder is near Bear and I can see into Mary's room through the crack from the door. Her eyes are wide with panic, but then her face hardens and determination fills her.

There's that spark I remember.

Mary's always been one of the sweetest people I've known, but if you ever crossed someone she loved and cared about, you'd quickly be introduced to her backbone of steel. Dad's voice has me turning my attention back toward the asshole in my grip.

"Actually, we already know who is responsible for Mary's current condition. Not to mention past injuries."

"And you made our search all the easier by coming to us instead of making us look for you," I tell him and smirk internally when I see his eyes go wide with the realization of what he's done.

"Stephan Hayes, you are under arrest on charges of domestic abuse against your wife and your children. You have the right to remain silent..."

I tune out Dad's voice and focus on Stephan. With every word, his face grows redder and I share a concerned look with Dixon.

Unfortunately, Stephan takes that exact moment to lunge at Dad and my grip slips slightly.

In an instant, Bear's hand clasps Stephan's shoulder and helps us halt Stephan's momentum, but not before his forehead makes contact with Dad's nose. Dad had tried to pull back when he realized what Stephan was going to do, but it was too little too late.

"You'll pay for this, Morgan," Stephan hisses, and Dad levels him a hard glare as he takes the handkerchief from Thor and holds it to his bloody nose.

"Looks like I'll be slapping on two other charges on top of your domestic abuse charge. Resisting arrest and assaulting a Police Officer. Also, as stated earlier; by coming here to the hospital, you are in violation of the restraining order that you were served earlier this morning, which will be going on your record."

Stephan struggles in our arms again, and I shake my head at how much of an idiot he's acting like as he tries to lunge for Dad again.

"For being a Deputy Police Officer, you sure are making a lot of stupid mistakes right now. Don't forget that we're in Wisconsin. That little stunt you just pulled by assaulting a Police Officer is considered a Class H felony. You face up to a maximum of six years in prison, $10,000 in fines, or both if you are convicted, plus a three-year confinement, followed by three years of extended supervision.

"On top of that, if for some reason you're released before all of this goes to trial, Wisconsin has a no-contact law. You are required to avoid contacting your victims after being released from police custody. Which means Mary and your three children, who are very much still alive. And on that topic, since we're talking about charges, we'll be tacking on fraud charges for submitting false death certificates for Asher Lucas Hayes, Isaiah Brayden Hayes, and Cassandra Allison Hayes as well as collecting hefty life insurance policies on all three of them."

Out of the corner of my eye, I notice Mary's jaw dropping in shock as her hand goes to her mouth. Seconds later, tears spill down her cheeks as Alli wraps her in a hug.

Stephan stills in our arms before he huffs. "You have no proof of any of that. You'll regret arresting me and bringing these false accusations forward. You'll see."

The elevator nearby dings but I don't take my eyes off Stephan, worried that he'll try to pull another stunt.

"Morgan, I can take it from here with Hughes," someone says, and I immediately relax when I hear my friend's voice, Oliver Jones.

"Thanks, Jones."

As I relinquish my hold on Stephan, worry swirls in my gut as Stephan calls over his shoulder as Jonesy and Dixon lead him to the elevator. "This isn't over! You'll pay for this! You'll all pay for this! Mary's my wife—I have a right to see her! You have the wrong person! Whatever she's told you is a lie due to her mental illnesses!"

Shaking my head, I turn back toward my dad to see Oliver's twin brother, Max, in front of him inspecting his nose.

"Your nose doesn't seem broken, but you'll have a hell of a bruise for a while."

Dad tilts his head toward the room, but I pause when the elevator dings again and groan internally when I see two men step off surrounded by four bodyguards.

Don Antonio Vasquez and one of his sons, Lorenzo.

Standing to my full height, I cross my arms over my chest and plant myself in front of Mary's door.

"We have your back," Thor says quietly behind me, and I ever so slightly tilt my head to indicate I'd heard him.

The Don's bodyguards eye us warily when they stop a few feet in front of us, but none of them say a word. After seeing that we aren't moving, Don Vasquez steps forward.

"If you would kindly move, I would like to see my granddaughter."

I cock an eyebrow at him, but before I can say anything, Patch is at my side, glaring the Don down as he steps forward, almost toe to toe with him.

"Why? So you can whisk her away? Give her back to Stephan, the asshole who bought Mary from you and your fucking son? The asshole who has been beating and abusing her for the last nine years? The man who took away the woman who was carrying my child and who I was going to ask to marry me? Why the fuck should we let you anywhere near her?"

Even though I know Patch is beyond fucking furious, not once does he raise his voice, though it is cold and deadly. Far colder and deadlier than I've ever heard before.

Well, scratch that.

I'd heard it once before.

The night Mary was kidnapped and Nikos was killed. The night where he thought I had had a hand in her disappearance.

Confusion mars the Don's face. "I don't know what you are talking about, son. Mary left to marry the love of her life, Stephan. They've been happily married ever since. We haven't been in contact due to the nature of Stephan's job, but as soon as I'd heard that she'd been hurt, I came straight here."

What the fuck?

"I don't know where you've been getting your information, asshole, but *none* of that is true," Patch damn near spits out.

The lines of confusion etch deeper on the Don's face, and I almost believe he's telling the truth.

"Luke, let him in. There's only one way to settle this, and I'd rather it be in the privacy of a room rather than shouted in a public hospital ER."

Mary's voice and words have Patch tensing before his gaze narrows on the Don.

"You try anything at all, and I will make sure you endure *everything* she has. Every bruise, broken bones, bruised ribs, fractures, concussions, and cuts. *Every-*

thing she's suffered at Stephan's hands these last nine years, you'll experience tenfold."

With that, he turns and stalks into Mary's room.

I don't know if this is a good idea or not, but we also need answers.

Is Don Antonio Vasquez a part of all of this?

Or is Diego Vasquez and Stephan behind everything?

Chapter 26

Mary

I GRIP THE SHEET of paper and pen in my hands as I stare at the door. The door that Sam had left slightly ajar. **Παππούς** (Grandpa) steps closer to the door with his phone in his hand and I realize what's happening.

He's recording what they are saying. Hell, he probably has video going too.

Knowing enough about the law, I know he'll also ask Curtis for the official video of this fiasco, but **παππούς** (grandpa) will use his copy for his notes in the time being. And probably as a back-up.

Tears prick my eyes when I hear Brady saying that Stephan had claimed my children had all died and collected insurance money on them. Is that all he saw them for? A paycheck? And how long ago had he done it? Was he planning to do the same to me?

I'm not sure how long I've been lost in my thoughts when I hear my grandfather's voice and dread fills me. Luke leans forward, kisses my temple, and then he's out the door.

I frown as I take in my grandfather's words. He sounds sincere, but the two images I have of my grandfather are making it hard to determine which one is right—one from when I was younger and another from hearing about his orders for the past nine years. My gut churns with what I'm about to propose, but I don't want everyone and their dog to hear about my messed-up life.

Clearing my throat, I make sure to speak loud enough that the guys can hear me in the hallway. "Luke, let him in. There's only one way to settle this, and I'd rather it be in the privacy of a room rather than shouted in a public hospital ER."

Moments later, Luke comes back in followed by my grandfather, Brady, Sam, and Thor. I'm surprised when another man steps in, in a black suit much like Grandfather's, and my eyes widen when I realize it's my uncle, Lorenzo. A third man, also dressed in a black suit and looking rather intimidating, attempts to follow them in, but Grandfather shakes his head. A conversation seems to happen without words, and the third man ducks his head in acknowledgement before closing the door.

Alli stands and gives me a hug. "I hate to do this, Mary, but I have to go. Theresa needs me for a patient."

"Thank you for being here for me." I squeeze her tight as best as I can, trying to express exactly how much her presence has helped me. And it has. Being surrounded by my best friends again has given me a much-needed boost of confidence.

"Anything for you, girl. I'll be in later to check on you," she replies and then slips out of the room, closing the door behind her.

Grandfather turns, looking at me for the first time, and my chest aches at seeing the shocked and empathetic look on his face.

Luke steps forward, pressing a kiss to my temple and stands by my side. Hoping to help calm him, I reach up, slipping my hand in his. He squeezes back but doesn't take his eyes off Grandfather and Uncle Lorenzo. Movements and actions neither of them misses.

"**Mi precioso capullo de rosa** (My precious rosebud), who did this to you? And who is this man?" he asks, his voice rough and gravely, just like I remember, while gesturing to Luke.

Instead of answering him, I ask him a question of my own. "What do you know about what happened the night of April 11th, 2014? Did you make any edicts when I turned eighteen?"

My chest tightens as memories of that night bombard me again, but I push them aside. I need answers.

Grandfather frowns. "No, I never made any edicts regarding you. Though, I did ask Nikos if he needed help paying for your college. He told me he had saved quite a bit over the years for your tuition, but that if he got in a bind, he would let me know. As for that night, someone broke into your house, killed poor Nikos, but you were nowhere to be seen. We tried looking for you, but we came up empty-handed at every turn. I'd later learned that you had left not too long afterward and had eloped with a man you loved, Stephan, but due to the nature of the cases he was taking on, you had to cut ties with your family and friends for safety's sake and had assumed different identities."

A dry, humorless laugh escapes me as my chest aches even more. "And you believed that? Even though we rarely saw each other after my parents divorced, you still believed that I would do such a thing? You didn't know me better than that?"

Even I can hear the pain and disappointment in my voice, but I'm once again surprised when both Grandfather and Uncle Lorenzo sadly shake their heads.

"No and despite what I said out in the hallway, because it was in public, we never believed that. Not for a second. However, the fact that you think we would have believed that bullshit means that we've also failed you. No matter how much we tried looking for you, we couldn't find you, but we never stopped looking.

"Carmen swore you were fine and happy. Diego, Carlos, and Isaac also spoke up about you, and when we questioned as to why they knew about you and no one else, we were told that they were talking to Carmen when she had received a phone call from you. She told us that the life you chose was the life you wanted, but again, the rest of us never believed it. Family is extremely important to you, and if it was your choice, you'd never have cut us out like you had."

Tears sting my eyes and I swallow thickly. "That's because they were all in on it, is my guess. I know Stephan's working for Diego and Isaac. Occasionally Carlos would be with them, but I don't know how involved he was with everything. I shouldn't be surprised about Carmen since she's always hated me."

Grandfather frowns and shakes his head. "That's not true, **mi precioso capullo de rosa** (my precious rosebud)."

I huff and shake my head in return. "No, you don't understand, Grandfather. I've heard what Carmen has said about me for years as a child and it got even worse when I was a teenager. Everything was either straight from her mouth or when she would talk to Eileen about me on the phone. When we would meet up at your house after the divorce, Carmen made sure to find me whenever I was alone to reiterate that I wasn't wanted there. That I was an embarrassment to the family because I put my own 'selfish' needs before others. That I refused to be the daughter her daughter needed. That I didn't love Eileen enough to consider her needs over mine. The last time I was there was not too long after my sixteenth birthday. Carmen told me I was to never come back or she'd make sure **πατέρας** (dad) wouldn't live another day. That was the last time I ever stepped foot in your house and why I refused your later invitations. I would never have jeopardized **πατέρα** (dads) life. I loved him too much."

Stunned silence descends on the room, but I can see the fires of anger burning in every single set of eyes in the room. Though, what is surprising is that the level of intensity in their eyes burns the same between Grandfather, Uncle Lorenzo, Luke, and Thor. Even more so than **παππού** (grandpas).

Both Grandfather and Uncle Lorenzo share a look before refocusing back on me.

"Mary, did these conversations happen in our house?" Uncle Lorenzo asks.

"For the in-person ones, yes. I don't know if the conversations she had with Eileen on the phone were all from inside your house or not.

Uncle Lorenzo pulls out his phone and texts someone.

Grandfather's fingers drum against the foot of my bed and my gaze moves to him. "Who did this to you, **mi precioso capullo de rosa** (my precious rosebud)?"

"To answer that, I think I should fill you in on the past nine years."

"Do you think that's wise, Siren? How do we know we can trust them? That they aren't in on everything with Diego, Isaac, and Stephan?" Luke looks at me, concern evident on his face.

A sliver of unease runs through me, but in the past, neither of them had ever given me suspicion. I have a feeling that if they were to have been at the party where Isaac had broken my arm, they both would have stood up for me. However, due to some meeting, they and a few other of my uncles hadn't arrived until after I had already left to go to the ER. Uncle Mateo was the only other person who had seen it. My other aunts and uncles that were at the party weren't sure what to make of what had happened or who to believe. Though I think the murderous glares Diego and Carlos were giving them probably helped them stay silent.

My gaze cuts to Sam and he gives me a slight nod of his head, giving me the approval to share if I should so choose. If he's doing that, then he must not have any reason to believe that they are in on it. Or he wants Grandfather's side of the story to flesh out if he really was behind Diego's orders to Stephan or not.

Refocusing back on Grandfather and Uncle Lorenzo, I look for any sign of deception or deceit, but I only find sincerity. Squeezing his hand, I look over at Luke.

"I think they're telling the truth," I pause, but then turn toward the men in question. "However, if I find out that either of you or the others were in on this clusterfuck, heads will roll, and I won't stop anyone from putting a bullet in any of you. Do you understand?"

Once again, I'm surprised when both of them smirk as they share a quick glance and then they nod in unison. Then again, I know *who* they really are and have a pretty good idea about how bloody their hands are.

"Guess you do have a bit of Vasquez in you, **mi precioso capullo de rosa** (my precious rosebud)."

Choosing to ignore the comment, I start from the beginning.

"The night of April 11th, 2014, I had just found out I was pregnant with Luke's baby. Luke, who is *actually* the man I've always loved, not Stephan, whom I despise with every fiber of my being. The only things I'm grateful for from my time with Stephan are Isaiah and Cassie."

At the part where I say I've always loved him, Luke leans over and kisses my temple again as he gently cups my cheek, lingering for a few moments before sitting down and weaving his fingers through mine. While the lies Stephan told me were extremely painful at the time and seeing Luke intimate with other women almost killed me, I never stopped loving him. I couldn't. It's like loving Luke is woven into my very core. I'm not sure if I can ever stop loving him. In all honesty, the day I stop loving Luke will most likely be the day I draw my last breath.

It takes a while, but I finally recap the events of the last nine years and draw on Luke's strength through the really bad parts. God, I hope that this will be the last time I have to recount all of that. I also give them, Sam, and Brady, all of the aliases we've used over the years. Well, at least the ones that I knew about. I'm not sure if Stephan had more. I had debated about giving that information to Grandfather and Uncle Lorenzo, but then I remembered that they mentioned that their accountant, Emilio, was going to check to see if Stephan ever worked for Diego. And I definitely want to know what they find out. I also give Sam back the roster list, noting which policemen are dirty and which are being pressured by Stephan and the others to join them per Diego's orders. On top of that, I give them a list of the crooked judges I know.

When I'm done, silence meets my words and I chance a look up at Grandfather and Uncle Lorenzo. Grief mars both of their faces, but under that is the same undercurrent of anger that I'd seen on Luke and the others earlier this morning.

"I swear to you, **mi precioso capullo de rosa**, on the grave of my true love, Esmeralda, that we had no idea. Or that your relationship with Eileen, and later Stephan, was so abusive and toxic," Grandfather tells me before turning to Lorenzo. "Did you ask Emilio?"

My brain stutters at Grandfather's words. What did he just say?

"Yes, and there is no Stephan Hayes, or any of his aliases, on any of our payrolls. Emilio's going to try and dig into Diego's accounts, but he has a separate accountant for some of his books, which I didn't know about until now. He's going to try not to tip off Diego or the accountant in the process. Hopefully, Diego doesn't have a lot of security measures in place. We'll have to wait and see if Stephan is on his payroll or not."

Grandfather frowns, and when neither of them says anything for a moment, I finally find a voice for my question. "Grandfather, what do you mean, true love? Who is Esmeralda?"

His frown turns into a scowl. "Why am I not surprised that Eileen lied to me? Especially now knowing what else she's done to you." He pauses as he shakes his head. "Eileen told me that she'd told you about Esmeralda, so I hadn't talked to you about her." He pauses again, a look of grief overcoming him and he clears his throat a couple of times before continuing.

"I was in love with Esmeralda for years before we finally got together in college. We'd known each other growing up, but I was afraid to date her in high school, worried it might ruin if we didn't work out.

"I was at a Christmas party my sophomore year in college when Father had asked me why I never had a date with me. In years past, I had always brushed off those questions, but something had me wanting to talk to him. I finally caved, telling him that there was someone special, but that I was worried about ruining our friendship if we ended up breaking up. He gave me the courage to finally ask her out and I couldn't have been more relieved when Esmeralda said yes."

A look of happiness comes over him, similar to the one I'd only seen when he'd looked at his children. Well, most of them.

"After college, we were wed and I thought I couldn't have been happier. That is, until she told me she was pregnant. Not too long later, Mateo and Diego came into the world. Then she blessed me with six more beautiful children—Lorenzo, Anita and Azura, Marco and Miguel and finally Luiza, over the years.

"When Luiza was ten years old, Esmeralda started getting violently sick. I still don't know exactly how it happened, or who did it, but I found out through her autopsy report that she was poisoned over time until her body could no longer fight it and she succumbed to the poison." Grandfather pauses again, the grief surrounding him almost palatable. I blink rapidly to keep my tears from falling.

He clears his throat before continuing. "Five years later, I started seeing Carmen. A few years into our relationship, we were married, and she gave me Carlos and Eileen. Carmen hates when I talk about Esmeralda because she knows that I'll never love her as much as I loved Esmeralda. Looking at things now, I'm not sure how I didn't see it before. Except for Diego, she's never once shown my other children as much love or support as she has for Carlos and Eileen."

Luke huffs and shakes his head. "No wonder the three of them turned out rotten to the core."

Grandfather nods sadly and then tilts his head toward me. "It wasn't until the whole mess with your parents getting a divorce that I started to see their true colors emerging. Carmen and I fought more, and I thought for sure we were heading toward separation since we do not divorce in my family. I was having more fights with Carlos, Eileen and even Diego at the time as well." He pauses, almost as if he wants to say more, but with a brief glance toward Sam and Brady, I can see him deciding not to say what he was going to.

He sighs and shakes his head. "Then, suddenly, they all changed. Especially Carmen. Knowing what I know now, it was around the time of your kidnapping. Maybe a month or so beforehand. Once again, she was the dutiful wife and things between us got better. My relationships with my children improved as well. That is, until earlier this year, when things became strained again. Not as bad as before, but noticeable. It was around the time I heard that you and Stephan had moved back to Forest Creek."

Uncle Lorenzo crosses his arms across his chest, a thoughtful look on his face. "You may be on to something. I've noticed them acting weirder than usual, too, but I've noticed it in Diego more so than the others. Thinking back, it was around mid-February when it started. Usually, Diego has an air of arrogance around him. That he's untouchable. Since February, he's been more on edge. More cautious. Almost afraid, though of what, I don't know."

A dry, humorless chuckle escapes me, but before I can say anything, Grandfather beats me to it, his eyes lighting up with understanding.

"This is because of the human trafficking ring along the Great Lakes, isn't it? Even though he swears to me that he isn't involved, I know he has to be involved to some extent. That many people trying to tie him to it can't be a coincidence."

My gaze cuts to Sam. I'm not sure how much I should be sharing about what I had uncovered of Stephan's meetings, the paper documents and the contents of the scan drive and the cloud account, since I know it's for ongoing cases the cops have built up against Stephan and Diego. Hell, it might even help with other cases they have. Now that I think about it, I have no idea if the FBI is involved, so I should probably tread carefully here. Thankfully, Sam speaks up for me.

"I'm sorry, but that matter is an ongoing investigation. The only thing I can tell you, since you are Diego's parent, is that he is being investigated. I'm sure at some point, we'll need to question you, but seeing as Mary just finished giving her last statement moments before Stephan showed up here, we need to get everything documented in our system and go from there."

That and probably to finish reading through *everything* I'd gathered for them. There's a shit ton of information on the scan drive and the cloud account.

A solemn look comes over Grandfather, but then he nods as he sits straighter, determination and sincerity shining through his eyes. "Whenever you are ready for our statements, let me know and I'll make sure to clear my calendar. Same for my family, since I assume you'll need to question all of them."

"Yes, you are right. We will need to question everyone. Your cooperation in the matter is appreciated."

We're all silent for a few moments when Uncle Lorenzo clears his throat.

"Mary, may I ask you something?"

I turn my attention toward him and nod, though I am hesitant about what he could be asking and if I'll even be able to answer him. Surprisingly, his cheeks heat slightly. Almost as if he's a little embarrassed by what he's about to ask.

"Why do you always say 'Grandfather' and 'Grandmother'? And just a bit ago, you were calling Carmen by her name. You know your other cousins aren't that formal. So why are you?"

I chuckle even though my chest tightens painfully at the memories. "Carmen and Eileen. It's all because of Carmen and Eileen," I reply with a heavy sigh and it doesn't escape me that they frown at me not calling them 'Grandmother' and 'Mom'.

"Eileen always wanted me to call you 'Grandfather' and to call Carmen 'Grandmother'. She absolutely hated when I spoke informally about both of you. So much so that she'd spank or slap me when I misspoke. It didn't take long to learn to go along with what she wanted. Even though the words seemed to create some sort of barrier between us. It never made sense to me why I had to address you so formally and I hated it.

"Then, when I was five, I noticed my cousins never addressing you the same way, so I switched and started calling you the same as them. I wanted to feel closer to you both, well, more so you than Carmen, and had hoped that changing that might be the first step toward becoming closer to you. To have a relationship with you like my cousins have.

"However, for the first half-dozen times or so that I called you 'Grandpa' or '**Abuelo** (Grandpa)' and Carmen 'Grandma' when I visited, I was royally chastised by Carmen. She told me that I had to learn my place in life and address them accordingly. I didn't understand it at the time and asked why I was the only one that had to address them that way. Or why none of my other cousins had to do the same. Those questions earned me a backhand and a beating across my ass with a cane that was nearby. I wasn't able to sit properly for two weeks after that. I'm not sure if **πατέρας** (dad) ever knew about that or not. Mom told me my punishment would be tenfold if I ever told him.

"On the times that you would ask me to call you 'Grandpa' or '**Abuelo** (Grandpa)', Carmen would give me a severe look that promised retribution. Fearing what she'd do, I lied to you and said I preferred to call you Grandfather."

Dark looks come over both Grandfather and Uncle Lorenzo's faces, and I'm wondering what's in store for Carmen when they return home. I'm way past caring what happens to her after dealing with her verbal and physical abuse over the years. Honestly, I kind of hope she gets a dose of her own medicine.

Grandfather glances around the room before his gaze settles on me again. "Can I please speak to my granddaughter alone?"

Chapter 27

Mary

LUKE LOOKS OVER AT me hesitantly, and I silently plead with him to understand that I want to talk to him, too. He sighs, nods, and then leans forward, giving me a kiss on the lips.

Our first kiss in nine years.

All too quickly, he ends it, but the look he's giving me says he'd much rather keep kissing me. My cheeks heat in response to the desire in his eyes.

"I don't like it, but I understand, Siren. I'll be right outside," he tells me, and I understand his unspoken request.

To yell if I need him.

Brady's the last to leave, but he pauses at the door, looking back at me with an eyebrow cocked. A silent question to make sure I really am okay with this. I'd forgotten how protective both of them could be, and right now while I'm at my weakest, I can't begin to express how much I appreciate it. Giving him a small nod, he nods in return and then leaves, closing the door behind him.

Turning my focus back to Grandfather, I'm surprised to see such a crestfallen look on his face.

"I'm so sorry that I failed you, **mi precioso capullo de rosa** (my precious rosebud), but I can't tell you how happy I am to see that you now have men around you that are protective of you. That love you. That will fight for you." He pauses, almost as if he's debating about telling me something. "I swear to you, **mi precioso capullo de rosa** (my precious rosebud), I had no idea Diego and Isaac did that to you. Or Stephan. Or any others. We do many things, but we do not deal in skin. I have made this stance many times with Diego, yet he still thinks we should be involved. Yes, we have strip clubs, but that is as far as it goes. The girls only dance and the men cannot touch. I will get to the bottom of this. Whoever is involved will not get away with what they have done to you. You are family and we do *not* treat our family like this."

He pauses, his face going hard, but I know the anger in his eyes isn't directed at me.

"I hate to speak ill of the dead, but Eileen should be thankful she's already six feet under, otherwise her punishment would be most severe for what she's done to you. I promise, you will get your retribution, and if you want, your revenge. You are **mi precioso capullo de rosa** (my precious rosebud). My family. And I protect my family. I understand that you will be staying with your Luke and the Steel Archangel's MC. If you ever need assistance, please don't hesitate to let me know. I will also let Thor know of my offer."

Once again, he pauses. His face softens and his eyes turn slightly misty, which has my own tears nearing the surface again.

"I would like to visit you again. To rebuild our relationship. I've greatly missed you, **mi precioso capullo de rosa** (my precious rosebud). Since they made you believe otherwise, I wanted you to know that you are always free to call me 'Grandpa' or **Abuelo** (Grandpa), if you so choose. I don't give a rat's ass what Carmen thinks. I also promise you, **mi precioso capullo de rosa**, that I will find out how deep Carmen is in all of this mess. She will already be paying for what she has done to you, but if she is also in this as deep as Diego, nothing will be able to save her. Not even being my wife."

The look on his face hardens again and I completely believe him.

Swallowing, I can't believe the words are about to come out of my mouth, but I need to say it. "I want to be kept informed about what you find out about them. All of them. I understand that you may be hesitant to share things with me because of my relationships with Brady and Sam, but I won't rat any of you out.

"However, if it involves Diego, Carlos, Isaac, and Carmen, then Brady and Sam will be informed. Hell, I wouldn't be surprised if Gianna knows about this clusterfuck. I will do the same and keep you informed as well." Pausing, I rewet my lips as I try to keep my emotions under control. However, as I feel the familiar sting behind my eyes, I'm probably going to fail at some point.

"I would also like to rebuild my relationship with you and the rest of the family. Also, I'd like to start with me getting to know you all again first. Once I feel comfortable with everyone again, then my children can get involved and learn about the family. However, until my children and I are safe, I'm going to bet our conversations will mostly need to be done over the phone or possibly even *Skype* or *Facetime*. I doubt Thor would let all of you onto the clubhouse grounds for safety reasons."

The corner of Grandpa's lips kick up as he nods. "I wouldn't expect anything less. The safety of you and your three precious **bebés** (babies) are the most important thing right now." He pauses as he takes a deep breath and sits down in the chair Luke had been using just moments ago. "I didn't want to say this earlier, but you should know."

I wait as he swallows a few times, and hesitantly, I reach out and am relieved when his giant hand clasps mine. When he looks up, the pain in his eyes would have sent me to my knees if I had been standing.

"There were rumors among some of the lower ranks. The guards that we have posted around the house and the property. Rumors about overhearing Diego, Carmen, and Eileen arguing about needing to have, in their words, 'some bitch taken care of and shown her rightful place'."

My mouth goes dry. "When was that?"

"It was about a month before Eileen killed herself trying to kill Sam Morgan. I don't know the specifics, but the rumor was that they had two plans in place. One to take out a cop that they thought had been sniffing a little too close to home, and the other was taking care of a thorn in Eileen's and Carmen's side. They never said any names, but knowing what I know now, I think you were the 'thorn' they were talking about."

I frown, but then a memory pops up and I can't help but question if they are related. "Grandpa, on my fourteenth birthday, my family and friends threw a big party for me since it was my golden birthday. I know she wasn't invited, but Eileen showed up anyway. She was drunk off her ass as she shouted obscenities at me. That I would never be happy or find love as long as I remained fat and looked like a beached whale. Then she went on, blaming me for not inheriting her rightful place in the family. At the time, I had no idea who you really are. What the family is involved in. **Πατέρας** (Dad) called the cops on her and because of her fighting the arrest, as well as all the hateful things and threats she said, **πατέρας** (dad) took out another restraining order on her. What did she mean by 'I'm the reason she didn't get her rightful place in the family'?"

Grandpa's frown deepens and his eyes go unfocused, almost like he's lost in a memory. He stays like that for a few moments and then he scowls.

"She came to me a few weeks before your fourteenth birthday. I knew Nikos' stance about us not attending the parties because he was trying to protect you from Eileen. While I missed you and Nikos, and wished things could be different, I respected his decision. With how things were with Eileen, it was the right decision.

"That day, I had just finished writing in your birthday card and had sealed it when she stormed into my office. She was ranting on and on about my previous decision to not allow her to work for the family. She hated being a teacher and had gone back to school to be an accountant because she wanted to do our books. I had refused. Multiple times. Mainly because I didn't trust her not to skim money and I didn't think she would be professional enough. She had a habit of trying to bed anyone with money and power ever since the divorce, and I didn't want that to bleed into our businesses. With how many legal businesses we run or have our hands in, there are a lot of people that depend on us for those jobs.

"Also, I suspected she was up to something because I'd frequently seen her talking quietly to Diego and Carmen, but as soon as anyone would approach, they'd switch to talking about something else until they thought they were alone again. I didn't know what they were talking about because they were careful not to do it around any of our cameras that catch audio, but I didn't have a good feeling about whatever it was they were discussing.

"When I explained my reasonings to her, and went more in depth, she got pissed and her ranting continued. It got worse when she saw the envelope addressed to you on my desk. She asked why I was still communicating with you since you weren't part of the family anymore. I told her that you would always be my granddaughter. Divorce or not. I was always going to support you and help you any way I could, just like I do with the rest of my grandchildren."

He pauses and a sorrowful look crosses his face before turning to grief. "The things she said, **mi precioso capullo de rosa**."

My chest tightens and my eyes sting. Taking a deep breath, I close my eyes to steel myself against what he's about to say. When I open them, he gives me a small, sad smile so quick that I almost miss it.

"Tell me."

Grandpa swallows thickly a few times and squeezes my hand.

"She said that you weren't worth the effort. That I was throwing away my time and money. Anything that I was giving you should have gone to her as compensation for having to go through the pain of carrying you, birthing you, and then all the effort and trouble of having to raise you correctly. Said that she should have just gotten an abortion in the beginning like she had wanted to, but Carmen, Diego, and Carlos convinced her not to. And we all know Nikos wanted you, there's no debating that."

My eyes bug out at that. "Do you think they planned to sell me from the get go?"

He shakes his head sadly. "I don't know, **mi precioso capullo de rosa**, but I wouldn't put it past them now that I know the real history."

Swallowing thickly, I hate to ask, but I need to know. "What else did she say?"

He sighs. "It wasn't pretty. She kept saying that you never listened to her and could never follow even the simplest of her rules. She had to fight you tooth and nail on everything. Instead, you insisted on being a fat whale with the fashion sense of a troll, who always shoveled food in your mouth and took after that deadbeat of an ex-husband in almost every aspect. Once you started taking after him, she knew you were a lost cause, but still tried to mold you into an image worthy of the family lineage and business.

"The day that she walked away, she said she was actually grateful to be relieved of the burden of raising you. How happy she was that she didn't have those balls and chains shackled around her neck anymore. Her dismissal of you, a mother saying her child was no longer part of her family, that she had wished she had gotten an abortion... The things she said about you and Nikos made my decision even clearer.

"I told her in no uncertain terms that she would never work for me or for one of my companies. That she would never regain her place in the mafia side of the family. That she didn't and wouldn't understand the meaning of family. You will always be my granddaughter, divorce or not, and she had no right in saying that I couldn't keep in contact with you. That I would not tolerate her saying those things about you and Nikos in my presence ever again. Once again, she got pissed and said even more hurtful things toward you that I won't share. I told her if she kept this behavior up, she would be cut off financially. She balked, saying I was playing favorites. That I would never pull something like this with her brother or stepsiblings.

"What she didn't know is that I had, and I told her that. Diego and Carlos were on thin ice at the time. That was when the first accusations tying them to the human trafficking ring around the Great Lakes came up. Just so you know, in the past, some of my ancestors had a hand in skin, but it stopped when my great-grandfather Antonio, my namesake, came into power. There were a lot of people that disagreed with his decision and there were several attempts on his life as a result. That was the start of our family becoming even more powerful. The amount of blood on his hands would have led one to believe that his heart and soul were as black as night, but that wasn't the case. To his family and the men that served him, he was loyal to a fault.

"His wife, Veronica, came from the wrong side of the tracks as some say. That's why some of our businesses are in some of the poorest areas. To provide steady jobs for low-income families. I know that seems a bit odd. A mafia family wanting to improve people's livelihoods in our backyard, but his decisions were twofold. Yes, he wanted to improve people's living standards, but he also didn't want them joining other gangs that were trying to encroach on our territory. If anyone was going to join an organization, he wanted them to join his."

Shaking his head, he squeezes my hand and continues. "Back to Eileen. After threatening to cut her off, she got so belligerent that I almost did as I threatened. I knew that if I did, there would be hell to pay, but I was about ready to do it, regardless. She's so much like Carmen in that regard that it's a good thing our family has a lot of money since it seems like all they do is shop. Something that got worse ever since she moved back into the family estate. Eileen got so out of hand that I eventually had to call the guard in to escort her out of my office and lock her in her suites after the doc sedated her. At the time, I couldn't understand how she could be so cold and cruel to her own child. Knowing what I know now gives some insight, though it doesn't answer all of my questions.

"The next day, it was like a light switch was flipped. She was cordial, but otherwise seemed like the young woman I used to know. But it was such a change that I was suspicious and watched her closely for a while. Unfortunately, she didn't do anything that raised any red flags, so I pulled back some of the extra guards that I had watching her since her outburst. She was so different that I figured maybe I had finally pounded some sense into her head. I'm so sorry, **mi precioso capullo de rosa**. I should have continued watching her, and then maybe I could have prevented what happened to you."

Shaking my head, I squeeze his hand. "You had no idea that they would stoop so low and do something like that—"

A knock on the door interrupts us, and before I can say anything else, Luke enters with Alli behind him.

"Sorry to interrupt, but it's time for another round of antibiotics. I've also got a low dose pain killer since you said you wanted to save the heavier stuff for at night so that you don't conk out as much during the day. We don't want you getting off your medicine schedule and possibly have problems arise," Alli says as she walks over to the computer and starts typing away. Luke marks the time down on the marker board and then comes over to sit down by me, sitting in the chair that I hadn't even realized Grandpa had vacated.

Reaching over, I slip my hand into his, beyond grateful that I can touch him again. The look he gives me as he picks up my hand to kiss my knuckles has heat curling in my stomach. A feeling I haven't felt in nine years.

Whenever Stephan would decide to have sex with me, not surprisingly, it was all about getting him off. He never cared about my needs. Also, in those nine years, I never once pleasured myself for fear that he had cameras planted that would catch me doing that. I'm positive I would have gotten a severe beating in response. Especially since he tried whatever he could to erase my past and to enforce that I belonged to him in all ways. Anything I did needed his permission.

Shaking away those thoughts, I give Alli a small smile as she finishes giving my shots into my IV. She takes note of my vitals, logs them, and gives me another quick hug before slipping out of the room. Surprisingly, Luke stays seated at my side.

"Mr. Vasquez," he starts, and Grandpa raises his hand, stopping him.

"Please, call me Antonio. With everything that **mi precioso capullo de rosa** has said today so far, I have no doubt in my mind that you will one day be a part of our family. However, if we are ever discussing business with my associates or men, I will need you to address me as Don or Don Vasquez. Though, I guess I need to ask the same for you. Should I be calling you Luke or Patch?"

Luke gives him an understanding nod. "Around the club, it's Patch. If we are alone like this, Luke is good."

Grandpa gives him the same nod in return.

"I just wanted to come in here and say something real quick without an ER audience. I'm not against you two communicating, but we need to keep it secure until everything is handled. We can't be having Diego, Carlos, Isaac, Carmen or anyone else hearing what you talk about. Is that something you can arrange on your end? Making sure there are no bugs wherever you decide to have the conversations? Smoke, our tech guy, can give you a secure line to call, either phone or Skype. Anything sensitive must not be written down, like in a text, in case one of them gets their hands your device."

Grandpa gives him a curt nod. "Yes, that is something we can do. We have regular sweeps to check for cameras and bugs, but I'll be upping that with this news. It will also only be done by myself, Mateo, or Lorenzo. Mateo will eventually take over for me and he has chosen Lorenzo as his second. We will be keeping this close to the chest, as we don't know how far the betrayal goes."

My eyebrows shoot up at that. "That has to be part of this. I bet Diego is beyond fucking pissed that Uncle Mateo was chosen to be your successor and that Uncle Lorenzo was chosen as his right-hand man. Speaking of, why didn't Uncle Mateo come today?"

A sigh escapes Grandpa and I swear I see him age almost ten years in a blink of an eye. "Mateo is handling a meeting which could not be postponed. I left Tomás, my right-hand man, behind in case Mateo needed him for anything." He pauses as he sighs again and shakes his head. "You are correct, **mi precioso capullo de rosa**. He did not take the news well. As you know, Mateo was born just minutes before

Diego. Between the two of them, Mateo has always been the more mature one. The one who thought through situations first and then acted. Diego has always shot from the hip, so to speak, and acts before thinking most of the time. When I spoke with him about the upcoming changes in the organization, he actually threatened me. Told me I would regret passing over him if I didn't change my mind. Not surprisingly, I told him if he tried anything, he was no longer a member of my organization. He would always be my son, but he would not work for me.

"You may know this, **mi precioso capullo de rosa**, but Luke most likely does not. It is a family tradition to have the eldest son succeed the Don, and the second-born son is usually their right-hand man. Only three times has that tradition been side-stepped. When Mateo succeeds me, this will be the fourth time that the second-born son will not be the Don's right-hand man. In those three cases, it was unfortunately due to inside betrayal from the family. We deal with betrayal the same way your club does, I'm sure."

He gives Luke a hard look, which he returns, and a silent conversation seems to pass between the two of them.

After a few moments, Grandpa smirks and gives a head tilt in approval. "Good." He pauses and then turns toward me. "**Mi precioso capullo de rosa**, I will take my leave so that you can rest. Once Smoke gives us the secure line to communicate, I will be in touch."

Grandpa comes around the side of the bed, and I let go of Luke's hand to give him a hug. He kisses my forehead before leaving, and hearing a hushed conversation just outside the door, I'm betting he's letting Thor, or his men, know of his offer.

Looking over at Luke, I figure now is as good of time as any to ask a question I had thought of earlier.

"Is that what I need to do, too, going forward? Call you Patch around the club?"

Luke smiles as he leans forward and gives me a quick kiss. "Siren, you can call me whichever you want."

Frowning, I shake my head. "I believe you said there are two other Old Ladies as you called them. What do they call their men around the club?"

For some reason his cheeks pinken a little as he chuckles. "They call them by their road names or a nickname. Though Levi usually calls Smoke by his name, Jax, since he's one of her brothers. Same for Mae—she calls Punisher by name as well, Kai, though she calls Axe by his road name."

My eyebrows raise at that. How many brothers do these ladies have?

Luke chuckles and I feel my cheeks heat. "I said that out loud, didn't I?"

He nods. "It's a little confusing, but I'll try to explain it. Levi is an only child, but she has a large chosen family. Her father's name is Roy, and she's a few years younger than us. I don't know if you remember the Russian twins that always hung out with her?"

I nod but then frown. "Yeah, but I don't remember their names anymore."

"Sasha and Alexei Petrov. Though, we sometimes call him Lex. They are two of her chosen siblings as well as Ethan Mills. She considers all of them her siblings."

"Wait," I interrupt as I frown. "Wasn't there another guy? Travis something-or-other?"

A vicious look crosses his face which has my frown deepening. "Travis West. He died earlier this summer."

Something tickles at the back of my mind, but I can't place where I've recently heard that name.

"When Thor and Dragon claimed Levi as their woman, and later their Old Lady, she got to know the club members a lot better. Especially because of the shit that was happening to her, but that's her story to tell. Soon, she had two more brothers, Smoke and Reaper. Smoke is our tech guy and he also runs our security business. They are the ones who installed the security system in your house for me. Reaper is the President of our Junction Creek chapter. She calls him 'Andre' sometimes. When Mae came along, we found out she was Smoke's long-lost daughter."

At my confused look, he shakes his head sadly.

"That's her story to tell. She's also an only child. Anyway, during everything that happened with her, two of my brothers claimed her as their sister. One is Axe, who is from our club and runs our tattoo parlor. The other is from the Junction Creek chapter, Punisher. He runs the Harley dealership in Junction Creek and also helps to run the attached garage. Punisher asked her to call him by his real name, Kai."

"Wow." I pause, my gut clenching in worry. "That sounds like a lot of trouble came to the club. Did they help out with what was going on with Levi and Mae?"

Patch nods, but a look crosses his face that I can't decipher. "Yes, we did help them. Same as what we'll do to help you. I meant what I said before. I think talking to Levi and Mae will help you understand a few more things about the club."

Swallowing thickly, I nod. "I'll meet with them, but I'd like to wait until I can have more visitors. Also, I'd rather have the conversations here so that there's no chance for my kids to overhear."

Relief fills him and a little tension bleeds out of him. "Just let me know when. You're doing great so far, so I'm betting later this evening, you'll be transferred up to TCU. I'll arrange a time for them to come once you're ready. For now, Thor brought a tablet for us so we can video call the kids."

My eyes water and the tears threaten to spill over. I've missed my kids so much. "Thank you, Luke." Lifting his hand to my lips, I press a kiss against his knuckles as I chuckle. "Guess I need to start getting used to saying Patch. I'm sure we'll be around the club most of the time. Just please don't be mad if I slip up. All this time, you've been just 'Luke' to me. It'll take some time to get used to calling you Patch."

Leaning forward, he kisses me, and I can't help the moan that escapes. It's like I'm catapulted back in time as his lips caress mine while his fingers gently thread through my hair. Desire curls through my belly, and when he nips at my lip, I swear it's like an inferno blazes through me. I've always had a weakness for when Luke would nip or bite me, and it seems like that's still the case.

I'm not sure how long we kiss when he pulls back slightly and rests his forehead against mine, both of us panting as we catch our breath.

"Still sexy as fuck, Siren, and still able to take my breath away. But as much as I want to keep kissing you, I promised Ash a little bit ago that we'd video call when we were done talking with your grandfather."

Still feeling slightly blissed out, I nod. I want to see my kids. Aside from school, we've never been apart this long, even with all my past injuries. If I had to stay in the hospital, Stephan would go home, get the kids, and come back. Though sometimes he just left them here with me while he went to work. Even if it was a school day.

Shaking off those thoughts, I focus on Luke as he refills my cup with water and hands it to me before propping up the tablet on the table and moving it closer. Once he's satisfied, he dials and not even three rings later, my children's smiling faces fill the screen.

God, I miss my babies.

Chapter 28

Mary

THE NEXT DAY, AROUND eleven in the morning, a knock sounds on the door and Luke gets up to answer it. Murmured voices reach my ears, along with the sound of plastic bags rustling. A moment later, he steps back and two women follow him in.

They both turn slightly as they hug Luke and say their hellos. Both of them are young. Well, younger than me, anyway, not that I'm that old since I'm only twenty-seven. The first woman has long curly red hair that goes down to her waist. Her curvy figure is wrapped in black boots, skinny jeans, and a black long-sleeved henley underneath a vest that looks like... Wait, is her vest just like Luke's? When Luke had said that she was an Old Lady, I thought for sure that her vest would be different, but aside from the patches, it looks exactly the same. Wait. Cuts, not vests. Shaking those thoughts off, my gaze snags on her heavily pregnant belly. I wonder if she's the one that's having twins or triplets?

Movement has my gaze flicking to the other woman. She's even younger than the first woman, but her smile and posture almost oozes sunshine. Like the first woman, this woman's hair is also long, almost reaching her waist, but her blond locks are straight. She's fairly skinny but I can already see a small baby bump resting underneath a dark blue long-sleeve shirt. Her skinny jeans mold to her small figure and she's wearing tennis shoes. Remembering the cut, my gaze cuts to hers and I frown when I realize it's different from the first woman's. Both women's smiles widen as my gaze bounces between them.

"Hi, Mary, I'm Levi," the red-haired woman tells me.

"And I'm Mae. Nice to finally meet you," the blond-haired woman says as she gives a small wave.

Shaking my head, I clear my throat. "Nice to meet you both. I've heard a lot about both of you from Luke and Allison."

They both grin and then Levi holds up her hands, showing multiple bags on each hand, each bag filled with stuff. "If you're anything like us, we figured you're getting really tired of these four walls, so we brought you some stuff to help keep you entertained later."

Chuckling, I nod. "Thank you, I'm definitely going stir crazy. I've never been stationary for this long before, including my prior injuries. I was always expected to continue my 'duties' as soon as we got back to the house." Instantly I bite my tongue, I hadn't meant to let that slip out but thankfully, neither one of them comment on slip.

"And since we all know hospital food is so blah," Mae says as she scrunches up her nose and then holds up a cooler and some other bags. "I made some sandwiches for all of us."

Luke sighs and shakes his head. "If Timber finds out you carried that heavy cooler up here all by yourself, you're going to have a sore ass later on."

Mae gives a saucy grin and winks at him. "I'm looking forward to it." She chuckles and shakes her head. "That man needs to learn that just because I'm pregnant, it doesn't mean I'm made of glass. If what happened before didn't break me, carrying a cooler for a few minutes isn't going to do it. Besides, I set it down when we were waiting for the elevator and while riding it, so it wasn't like I was always carrying it."

A chuckle escapes before I can stop it, and Luke gives me a questioning look. "It seems like you aren't the only protective one in the club." At my words both women start laughing and Luke's cheeks tinge a little.

"They are all very protective of us and all the kids. It can get a little annoying and frustrating at times, but in the end, I think it's worth it," Levi says as she sets her bags down on the little couch in the corner.

"Very true. Now, let me hand out the food and then you've got to scootch that heiny of yours out of here, Patch. It's girl time."

Biting my lip to keep in another chuckle, I take a club sandwich that Mae hands me and my mouth waters as I unwrap it. From smell alone, I know this is going to be better than the bland hospital food I've been forced to eat so far. She also puts a small bowl of fruit salad on the nearby table as well, and then she holds up some bottles.

"I have raspberry, lemonade, and white cherry flavored water as well as regular bottled water. Which would you like, Mary?"

I pause, the sandwich halfway between my lap and my mouth. Anger swirls in my gut, but I swallow down the words threatening to escape. Swallowing a few more times, I finally meet Mae's gaze and she gives me a sympathetic, understanding look.

Fuck, does she know there have only been the 'extras' Stephan deemed 'necessary' in my life? Or is she suspecting based off of her own history? Taking a deep breath, I figure I'll find out soon. Luke's words from the other day come to mind and I wonder exactly how similar Mae's story is to my own. Giving her a small smile, I clear my throat.

"I, uh, I've actually never tried the flavored waters before. I like all of those flavors in general, so surprise me."

Mae gives me another smile, this one brighter than before, as she sets down the raspberry flavored one on the table and opens it for me. Something I'm grateful for since my right arm and shoulder are still rather stiff and sore from being partially dislocated and my left one has the IV and all wires connected to it.

"It's my favorite," she whispers as she slides it closer to me along with a few napkins.

Giving her a smile of thanks, they hand out the rest of the sandwiches to Luke and the guards outside before he also steps out into the hallway, but then he pauses as he ducks his head back in.

"Just a heads up. In about two hours you're due for more antibiotics and pain meds, Siren. Either myself or Alli will be in to give them to you, but we'll leave right after we're done to give you more time with Levi and Mae."

Nodding my head in thanks, since my mouth is full of food, I meant to say something as soon as I swallowed, but instead, a moan escapes as the flavors explode on my tongue. Closing my eyes, I chew, beyond grateful for Mae's consideration to bring us food. I know I haven't eaten out very much over the years, except for when Stephan demanded my presence on a few occasions, and any other food has been made by my hands, but damn. I think this might be the best club sandwich I've ever had.

Opening my eyes, they immediately widen and I feel my cheeks heating. Levi and Mae are trying to stifle their laughter, but Luke... Luke's looking at me with heated eyes that have me wanting to squirm and rub my legs together to relieve some tension. A strangled noise escapes him and he shakes himself, but the look he gives me before he leaves has my face flaming red at how much desire I see in his eyes.

Desire for *me*.

Even in my broken state.

That last thought almost sends my mind into a deep spiral, but I do my best to push those thoughts away for now. I can focus on that later when I'm alone.

As the door latches, both women grin at me and Mae winks.

"I think someone's in for a good time later," she purrs, which has me almost choking on the water I'd just drank in an effort to cool down after that look.

Wiping off my chin, my mind whirls once again. While a part of me wants to believe her, the other part still has trouble letting go of everything Stephan has beaten into me over the years. Even if I know they were manipulative lies, when you're told something repeatedly, it's hard to shake it off or ignore it.

Frowning, I roll my eyes in an effort to distract them from seeing the true depth of my emotions. "I doubt it. Besides, I'm still technically married, even if I don't want to be. Yes, there's been a few times where Luke and I have kissed, but that's as far as it's going to be able to go for a while. Plus, I'm still healing. I know he wouldn't do anything to jeopardize my progress."

My frown deepens when they both give me little saucy and knowing smirks.

"Maybe after you hear our stories, you'll realize you can still have a little fun while you're healing and not by him sinking into your honey pot," Mae says and my cheeks blaze while I simultaneously try not to laugh at her using the phrase 'honey pot' instead of the word vagina or pussy.

Levi hums. "Yes, there are still plenty of ways to have fun while you're healing, but I agree. I have a feeling you won't believe us about that, or about how the club can protect you and those cute kiddos of yours until you hear more about our stories."

Standing, she takes a deep breath as she sets down her drink and sandwich. She slips off her cut and her long-sleeved shirt quickly follows, revealing a tank top underneath.

A gasp escapes me when I see the many pinkish, almost silvery-white scars on her arms and upper chest. Levi rolls up her tank top and my hand flies to my mouth in an almost futile attempt to keep from sobbing out loud. Tons of scars bisect and crisscross across her stomach. Levi pulls her long hair over her shoulder, and when she turns, I can't stop the next sob when I see that her back is even worse than her front.

After a moment, she turns as she smooths her tank top back in place but then I frown when she starts unbuttoning her pants. Tears stream even harder down my cheeks when I see the word 'slut' carved into her thigh. She turns slightly and that's when I notice she has a very large tattoo of roses and what I think are knives that stretch from around her hip down to mid-thigh.

"I got this tattoo after my wound had healed. They had carved 'BP' into my thigh. I was almost sixteen when I was kidnapped the first time. They were responsible for the scars on my back and some of the scars on my torso as well. The rest of them happened earlier this summer. I'll tell you more about both of the attacks in a bit, but I wanted to show you my scars first."

I can only nod in response as Levi rights her clothes, my throat thick with emotion at what she'd been through. Twice.

Movement has my gaze moving to Mae as she stands. After slipping off her cut, she takes off her long-sleeve shirt as well. However, unlike Levi, Mae isn't wearing a tank top, just her bra. Much like Levi, Mae has scars littered across her breasts, her chest, her stomach, and her arms. She unbuttons her jeans and lowers them a little, her scars going down to around her hip bones. Pulling her hair to the side, once again, tears stream down my cheeks when she turns around. Her back is also worse than her front. It looks like she was whipped or something the way they crisscross all over her back, neck, shoulders, and down to her upper buttocks.

Turning back around, Mae starts to get dressed again and Levi hands me some tissues, which I gratefully take. Blowing my nose, I dry my cheeks repeatedly as a few tears refuse to be held back.

They both sit back down, and when I'm finally composed enough, I'm about to ask them a question when my stomach rumbles loudly. My cheeks heat and they both softly chuckle. Levi pushes my sandwich back toward me. In between bites, I'm damn near stunned silent when Levi starts telling me about a rival motorcycle club's attack on her and her mom right before she turned sixteen. An attack that claimed her mother's life.

Of course, she didn't know who they were at first. That was revealed during the lead up to their second attack on her. She goes on telling me about Scott, aka Fang, of Black Plague. About the betrayal of her uncle selling her to Fang, as well as what he did to her when she was a little girl. The threats against the people she considered her brothers and sister as well as her men. Finding out she was pregnant and that same day, both of her men and one of her brothers being shot.

Then, when they were headed back home, Black Plague caused a car accident where they finally got their hands on Levi as well as Reaper, the President of the Junction Creek chapter of the club. My gut clenches so much I thought I might throw up when she tells me about the betrayal from a man who she had considered a brother, Travis. About how her men and the men from both clubs rescued her and Reaper.

Hearing Travis' name has me remembering Luke's words from the other day. Knowing about his betrayal, at least as much as she's willing to share with me that is, I have a feeling I know how Travis met his end. Especially since I know how Grandpa would have handled that kind of betrayal.

An icy sliver runs down my spine as I wonder exactly how far Grandpa would be willing to go since at least one of his sons, his grandson, and his wife have already betrayed me. Well, and Eileen, but she should be thankful she's already dead, otherwise her punishment might be as severe as Diego's. Pushing those thoughts aside, I wipe away the fresh tears that have fallen down my cheeks.

When Levi's done telling her story, Mae tells me about what her stepdad did to her and her mom. About her rocky start with her biological dad, Smoke, when she showed up at the club asking for help and explaining who she really was. That she had found proof of her true identity the night before and that her stepdad was trying to sell her to someone called Bruce. At first, due to some false information Smoke received, he tried to shut out Mae, thinking she was just like her mother,

Lillian. A deceitful, manipulative, druggie whore. Mae gave all the proof that she had and refuted the information Smoke had received, showing him that the woman in the pictures and notes wasn't her, but he still refused to believe her. To give both her and Smoke some space to process the new information, she and Timber went to the Junction Creek chapter for a while.

There, she met a man who tried to take Mae for his own, Carter Johnson. After Mae publicly turned him down, things took a turn for the worse when Carter broke into the clubhouse and kidnapped Mae after drugging her. He caused the scars on her chest, stomach, hips and most of the ones on her arms. Thankfully, Timber and the club rescued her before she could be hurt worse.

Then, not too long after her wedding, Smoke was shot and Mae was subsequently kidnapped from the hospital and unfortunately drugged again. Bruce was responsible for that kidnapping. The guy that had wanted to buy her from her stepdad. When Mae refused to submit to him, he whipped her. Once again, I was thankful that the club rescued her before she was hurt worse. Especially since her own mother, Lillian, and Lindsey's mother, Jane, were killed by those monsters. Not to mention what poor little Lindsey must have seen and heard while in those asshole's clutches. It shocked me when they said that Lindsey is the daughter of one of their Prospects, Drae.

So much trouble came to the club in such a short timeframe. My worry that the club will get sick of helping people out increases and despite what they've said, I still worry that they'll send me on my way to handle my problems on my own. Shaking my head, I push those thoughts away as I let out a shaky breath before blowing my nose and drying my cheeks again. A thought has my hand freezing and my gaze bounces between both of them.

"Please say you both weren't pregnant during all of that? That neither one of you had to wrestle with thoughts that what those assholes did to you might have caused you to lose your baby? Babies I mean?"

Both of them avert their eyes and my heart feels like it's been swallowed up by my stomach.

"I had found out a few weeks prior to the second attack that I was pregnant. The day that both of my men and Ethan were shot was when we'd found out I was having twins. That was the day before I was kidnapped the second time by

Black Plague." Levi's face hardens, but her eyes are slightly unfocused, almost as if she's back in her memories of those two days.

Mae shifts uncomfortably in her chair. "I didn't know that I was pregnant at either times of my kidnapping. It was after I woke up from Doc and Patch stitching up my back that Timber asked me about my period. I took a home test, which was positive, and Patch took in a sample to test so I would know for sure. We still don't know how I didn't miscarry, because of the extent of my injuries, but I can't express how thankful I am that I still have them," she says as she rubs her hand over her baby bump.

Levi's head turns quickly toward Mae, and Mae shrinks back slightly at the action. Though, I'm not sure if it's by surprise or worry.

"I thought you were just pregnant during the second attack."

Mae's face flames red. "Well, it seems Timber's swimmers were very determined. We did the math and he got me pregnant that first time."

A second later, Mae's face falls for some reason, and Levi reaches out, grasping her hand.

"Hey, those babies of yours are going to be just fine. They've got both Timber's and the Witlock's stubbornness. They aren't going to let what those fuckers did to you win."

Dread washes over me, and then I remember Luke's words. That something else happened to Mae around the time that she got pregnant. And I don't think he was alluding to her kidnappings.

"What happened?" Even I can hear the waver in my voice, and I'm beyond worried for Mae and her babies at what she's been put through. "If it's okay that I know, I mean. I don't want to force you."

Mae swallows a few times and Levi gives her hand another squeeze. She looks up and I'm momentarily frozen in place at the pure fury and anger radiating out of her normally cheerful face and eyes.

"I mentioned before that I was drugged." At my nod, her face hardens even further. "Well, we found out later that while yes, the drug had a sedative in it, they also had some sort of drug in them to make me extra fertile. Bruce, and maybe even X's, intent was to use me as a baby making machine for them. We know that I received the drug at least four times, maybe more. My family, the club, and

OB-GYN doctor know about me being drugged, but outside the club, no one else knows. Because of the drugs, my doctor is seeing me more than usual as a precaution. So far, the boys are all healthy and doing well, so I'm hoping the drugs haven't given them any adverse reactions." She pauses, and her face pales as her gaze darts to Levi's. *"Futtenfarter."*

"Wh—" I start to say but then I'm cut off by Levi jumping up from her chair and cheering in excitement as she does a little shimmy. I'm almost positive that if she wasn't so pregnant, she'd be jumping up and down.

"I knew it! I knew it! I picked the right team! I knew it!" She practically sings over and over again.

Mae groans and bends over, cradling her face in her hands right at the moment that Luke pokes his head in.

"Everything okay in here?" he asks, eyeing both of them before his gaze settles on me.

Nodding, I bite my lip at Mae's stricken look. I'm going to guess she didn't want to let the babies' genders slip, so I go out on a limb.

"We're all good. Just some much needed girl talk." At my emphasis of 'girl', he smirks and then nods before stepping into the room and closing the door.

"Well, after I give you your meds, I'll step back out so you can continue your girl talk."

Mae gives me a relieved look behind Patch's back before giving Levi a stern look in warning who mimes zipping her lips shut as she retakes her seat. I think I may have been on the mark about her not wanting to reveal the genders just yet.

A few minutes later, Luke finishes up his notes, and I'm shocked when he leans down, kisses my temple and then leaves without another word. I wonder if he's wanting to reassure himself that I'm really here as much as I want to do the same for him. Adding in the fact that he hasn't seemed to have changed in his level of affection that he used to give me when we were teenagers has my cheeks heating as I realize just how much I want his affection again.

I'm brought out of my thoughts by Mae's voice.

"I mean it, Levi. You can't tell anyone yet and you know why. Not even Sasha or Roxy."

Levi pouts and I can't help the chuckle that bubbles up at the sight. Then I realize that we're alone again and I can ask the question I had wanted to earlier. "Are you planning some sort of reveal party?"

I've heard about those over the years, but I've never been to one or seen one. Hell, I've never even been to a baby shower before and Stephan sure as hell would not have approved of me having one.

Levi rolls her eyes. "So, it started with the twins. Somehow, both our club and Reaper's club managed to keep it a secret from my men that we were all betting on the genders of the babies. We used our old dirt bikes to do the reveal. We had them shoot out a cloud of either pink or blue smoke to show the genders. In my case, the twins are both girls. With Mae, we decided to continue the bet, only this time, Timber knows about it. The only reason why Mae and Timber know the gender this time instead of being surprised is because they were insistent on watching every single ultrasound to make sure the babies were developing normally. Not that I blame them on that one. Her reveal and baby shower are going to happen on New Year's Day."

A smile stretches across my face. "That sounds so cool. I've never been to a baby shower or reveal before. What all did you guys do at yours?"

Both of their smiles slip from their faces as they stare at me.

Oh, shit.

I hadn't meant to reveal that to anyone. To give them a glimpse as to how deprived Stephan has kept me from the outside world.

Mae gives me a small, understanding smile. "There was a bunch of food, cake, and cupcakes. They had timed it so that it was the same day as their first knife throwing contest between the two clubs. So, after they had the gender reveal and doled out the winnings from the bet, it went right into the competition."

"I know other people do a bunch of baby games and such, but I just couldn't see the guys doing that, so I decided to skip that part with them. Besides, I think the bet thing was the guys' version of a baby shower party. That and they gave most of the money to the guys and me to help set up the nursery. A couple of days prior to the reveal party, the girls and I got together and we did the games with just us ladies."

"We're going to do the same thing with mine. Us ladies are going to get together the Saturday before the party at our house to do the games. Oh! You should come, Mary! You can even bring the kids. Levi's sister, Nikki, is bringing her daughter, Sadie. My sister, Susie, is bringing her son, Jordan. Drae's mother-in-law, Elvira, is coming as well and bringing Drae's daughter, Lindsey. Aside from them and us, there will also be Sasha, Levi's sister; my friend, Peggy; our friend Erin, who owns the bakery here in town; and from the club, there will be Roxy, Ashley, Ginger, CJ, Amy, Sarah. Oh, and Alli will be there, too."

I bite my lip. I've never really been good in crowds, but Alli will be there, so that should help calm my nerves. Plus, I think it might be good for the kids to be around the other kids. They were never able to have play dates or slumber parties before.

Swallowing my nerves, I give what I hope is a confident smile. "Sounds like fun. We'll be there." Both women give blinding smiles which helps relax some of my nerves. It gives me hope that my kids and I are on the right track to getting our lives back and truly living.

Levi gives me a mischievous smirk. "So. About the spicy things you can get up to while you're still healing."

My cheeks heat and I'm sure I probably look like a tomato. Even with my olive complexion. My stomach somersaults at the thought of being intimate with Luke again, but a small niggling voice reminds me that even though I don't want to be, I'm still married to someone else.

Levi's smirk deepens and I have a feeling I'm going to be learning *way* more about these two women than I originally thought.

Oh boy...

Chapter 29

Mary

THE LAST COUPLE OF days since being admitted to the hospital have been a whirlwind. Physically, mentally, and emotionally.

Yesterday, while Levi and Mae were here, Dr. Rodgers said that I was doing well and so far, have had no infections and my wounds are healing nicely. Because I was doing so well, she thought I'd be able to be released shortly after lunch today so long as nothing else happened overnight, which thankfully, nothing had.

Since I knew my kids wanted to be here today with me, I'm beyond grateful that Luke lined up for me to see Mae and Levi yesterday. After hearing their stories, I felt more comfortable telling them my own. After our talk, I felt much closer to both Levi and Mae.

To see the strength that both of these women have after undergoing such vicious attacks is completely mind blowing. If I could regain just a smidge of the strength they have, I would be happy. To get some semblance of the young woman that I had been back.

After hearing everything that they'd been through and how the club helped them, what they said eased almost all of my worries. They even put to rest the ones I had about the club being tired of helping someone so soon after Mae's ordeal ended and most likely, especially knowing Stephan so well, being in danger yet again. Now, the only worries I really have are about what Stephan, Diego, and the others will do as well as a few about Luke and me.

As we talked, I had finally had the courage to ask about their different cuts. While Mae's cut is how a normal Old Lady's cut would look like, Levi's cut had surprised me. The reason hers is exactly like Luke's is because she is a patched member in the club and one of their Enforcers. Her sister, Sasha, is a Prospect with them, too.

Apparently, earlier this year, the club voted to allow women into their club. It was on the tip of my tongue to ask what made them change their mind and allow women in, but from what I'd already learned from them about the club, and from knowing things about Grandpa and his family, I'm almost positive I wouldn't get the full truth since I'm not *in* the club.

I'm brought out of my thoughts by a vibrating sound and grab my new phone off the table. It still surprises me that the club got me a new phone and they won't let me repay them for it. When I had asked why, Levi just looked me straight in the eyes and said, *'It's what we do when someone needs help. We don't stand for violence against women and children. You've now got an even bigger family, Mary. One that will have your back, and your children's, no matter what.'*

However, judging by how her face changed and the way she had said 'violence against women and children', it makes me believe there's more to Levi than she's telling me. My earlier thoughts about how the club and Grandpa handle betrayers comes back to me, and I wonder if Levi, and maybe even Sasha too, handle things with any women that bring trouble to the club.

Another vibration brings me back to the present and I smile when I open my texts.

Mae: Just parked in the parking garage. Be up soon.

Levi: Just got some updated pictures from Timber's crew. Here's a look at your soon to be new home :)

Following Levi's texts are a bunch of pictures of the condo. Yesterday Levi dropped another bombshell of a surprise in my lap. She mentioned that a few of Timber's construction crews were working overtime to get a couple of condos finished at the compound. Apparently, the idea was brought up after Timber and Mae came back from visiting the Junction Creek chapter. They have a couple of duplexes on their club grounds for guests or club members who have Old Ladies and families. The club agreed, and Timber put all of his crews toward building the first set of condos. They have plans to build a total of eight condos—two buildings of four condos each. As more of his men became available, he put them on this project in hopes of getting at least the first set's shell done before winter hits. Right now, two condos are close to being finished.

Originally, the first condo was supposed to go to Drae, Lindsay, and Elvira until their house was finished. Levi told me that after hearing about me and my kids, Drae approached her and asked that the first available condo go to us instead of them. That they could continue living at the clubhouse until another one is ready.

Tears had sprung to my eyes, and they are now as I remember his offer. That they had given up their space so that my kids and I could settle in and have privacy while we heal. Something I couldn't be more thankful for. I was originally worried about imposing on Mae and Timber's newly wed bliss. Not to mention that with us there and filling each of their bedrooms, Mae and Timber wouldn't be able to prepare the nursery for their triplets. Now with us getting a condo, we'll stay with Mae and Timber for a few weeks while it's being finished up and then move in.

Shaking my head slightly, I refocus on the pictures and feel my eyes widen when I see how nice it is. A gorgeous and spacious kitchen, hardwood floors, soft plush carpet in the bedrooms, enough rooms for each of my kids to have their own space, and I bite my lip to contain a groan when I see a soaker tub in the master bathroom. I haven't been able to take a bath since I was kidnapped and I can't wait to soak in one until the water cools and my fingers are all pruney.

"What's got you biting that sexy lip, Siren?"

Looking up, I feel my cheeks heat in embarrassment and a second later, feel my teeth clamping down even harder on my lip. He reaches up and cups my cheek. His thumb caresses my lip before he slightly tugs and frees my lip before rubbing his thumb across my lip again. My breath hitches but I know that if we start kissing now, my kids will probably choose that moment to walk in and I'm not ready to explain why I'm kissing a man when I'm married to someone else. Well, trying to divorce him, but still.

"Levi sent me pictures of the condo and one of them was of a soaker tub. I realized I hadn't been able to soak in a tub since before I was kidnapped."

His eyes darken and he licks his lips. "Well, Siren, when your stitches heal, that's the first thing you can do. I'll wrap your leg to keep your cast from getting wet and you can soak as long as you want. I'll take care of the kids so you can just relax and read or whatever. Your *only* focus will be on relaxing and nothing else. You deserve to take some time for yourself."

I know someone else would probably think I'm a weirdo, but the fact that he's saying I can take a simple pleasure and not have to worry about anything but my own relaxation sends my mind reeling. I've been 'on' twenty-four-seven for the last nine years. Not once was I able to take a moment's relaxation for myself. Never. Tears prick my eyes and his calloused thumb brushes one away that escapes.

"What's wrong, Siren? What is it?" His worried gaze makes my chest tighten even more.

Swallowing thickly, I blink back more tears. "Everything. What you're doing for me and the kids. Protecting us. Finding us a place to stay. And then add on insisting I take a relaxing moment for myself while you take care of everything else. I..."

My throat tightens even more as my breath catches and more tears threaten to escape.

"Shhhh, Siren. It's okay. I've got you."

Immediately, I'm encased in his strong arms and he holds me as I fall apart. Just like in the past, a feeling of safety wraps around me while he holds me. The feeling unlocks something in me and tears cascade down my cheeks in a torrent. I ugly cry for everything that has happened. My **πατέρας** (dad). The kidnapping. Family members betraying me. Stephan. The abuse and pain and injuries of the past nine years. The worry about what Stephan, Diego, and any others will do next. About Stephan fighting the restraining order and divorce. For if he tries to take my children away from me. All of that, I cry about as I cling to Luke's shirt and cut.

I have no idea how long we sit like that, but when my tears finally start to fade, Luke pulls back slightly and kisses my forehead. A second later, a box of tissues, the soft kind, is placed in my lap and I gratefully blow my nose and dry my cheeks.

"I'm s—"

"There's nothing to be sorry about letting your emotions out, Siren." He stares me straight in the eye, and eventually, I nod. "I would much rather hold you as you let out your emotions and dry your tears than have you bottling everything up until it becomes too much. I will say it as many times as you need. That I am here for you and you can rely on me for things. I will be there to help balance and support whatever life brings us. That includes taking care of those three precious kids of yours. I'm all in, Siren. I would marry you the second after the divorce is finalized if I could."

My breath hitches, and all I can do is nod as everything he said whirls around my mind. He seriously still wants me? Wants to marry me? *Me?* The woman who is broken? The woman who has a crazy psycho-abuser as a husband?

He hands me another tissue, and I take it, drying my cheeks and blowing my nose again.

"Are you ready for the hoard?"

It takes me a minute and then I glance up at the clock, realizing it's been almost twenty minutes since Mae texted me. Luke must have asked her to wait to come in because of my breakdown. My cheeks heat again, but I nod.

He reaches into his cut and pulls out his phone, probably texting Mae. A second later, the door opens, and a smile breaks out at seeing my kids rush into the room.

"Mama! Mr. Patch!"

A chuckle escapes me as Cassie flings herself into Luke's, I mean Patch's arms. Lord, that's going to take some getting used to.

He kisses her temple and sits her on his hip. Isaiah gives him a fist bump and he and Ash give each other chin lifts. Ash is still watching Patch like a hawk, and I have to bite my lip to keep my smile from growing. Soft words bring me out of my thoughts and I realize I missed whatever Cassie had asked about.

"Yes, you can, Angel, but you have to be careful. Remember what I said about your mom's injuries and all the wires?"

"Yes, and I promise to be careful, Mr. Patch."

He gives her another kiss on her temple and then carefully sets her down on the bed on my left side. She scoots up closer and wraps her little arms around my neck. I breathe in her scent as I hug my baby girl and I have to bite my cheek to keep from crying again.

"Missed you, Angel."

"We missed you, too, Mama. But guess what?" she asks as she pulls back, bouncing slightly on her heels. The sight has me smiling while my heart clenches at the same time. There isn't a speck of the usual dark cloud hanging over her head. She's happy and bubbly, without a care in the world—just like a four-year-old should be.

"What, Angel?"

"MaeMae and Timber let us build a cool pillow and blanket fort in their living room and we've had movie and popcorn nights every night! They even let us sleep in it. Timber's also building a tree fort in his backyard and guess what? Guess what? We get to help!" she cries without waiting for my response.

I can't help my chuckle at her excitement and I look up to see Mae, Timber, Levi, Thor, and Dragon, all with soft smiles on their faces as they watch Cassie bounce on her heels.

"That sounds like quite the adventure that you had, Angel."

We sit there for a few hours, the kids talking about what they've been doing the past couple of days. Mae and Levi fill me in on what's going on at the clubhouse, about Levi's bar and grill that she manages, and Mae telling me about some coursework she's been doing while the guys quietly talk in the corner. Eventually, the kids go over to the little couch and watch a movie on a tablet that Mae gave them.

"What are you studying?" I ask her.

A light blush stains her cheeks. "I want to own and run my own daycare someday. What about you? Patch had mentioned you used to want to be a teacher before. Is that still what you want to do?"

I pause at her question. Once again, the simple choice of choosing what I want to do makes my brain stutter to a stop. For a moment, my anger rises. I should have always had this choice and many others. Why did this have to happen to me? To have my life and choices taken from me these past nine years by someone who thought they could fucking *buy* me. For my fucking family members to have the audacity to *sell* me to a monster. Taking a deep breath, I push those emotions away for now. I can unpack them later when I'm not surrounded by an audience.

Opening my eyes, I give a tight smile. "Yes, I still want to get my teaching degree and license. It will take a while to get it, but that's still what I want to do." However, as I say that, a part of me cringes but I bury that deep inside for now. What I really want to do is not going to be possible on my budget. I'll just have to be happy doing it as a hobby.

"What grade do you want to teach?" Levi asks, and I gnaw on my lip as I think.

"Early childhood, so maybe preschool, kindergarten or even first grade."

"Oh! When I get my center up and going, maybe you could come teach there!"

That gives me pause. From the little time we've spent together, I know I'll get along great with Mae, but do I want to do that? To teach at a daycare versus in a school district? There might be more flexibility with working with Mae than in a school district. It might not be a bad idea.

"You don't have to give an answer now, but I wanted to at least plant the bug for an option for you. Besides, at the rate Levi and I are going, half of the kids will probably be Steel Archangel babies," she says with a chuckle that Levi and I join in on.

"That's true," Levi says as she rubs her stomach. "Plus, I think my men secretly want to keep me knocked up until our house is full," she says, chuckling again.

Thor and Dragon must have heard her, because, damn, the heated look they give her makes even me want to fan my face.

"We can always build onto the house," Thor says with a smirk.

Levi's face heats as she curses and shakes her head. "What about you, Mary? I know you have three already, but do you want more kids?"

This time, it's my face that heats and my gaze instantly goes to Patch. The longing in his eyes makes my face heat even more as desire curls in my belly. I want to rub my legs together for some friction, but I force them to stay still. There's no way I'm doing that in front of all these people, not to mention with my kids in the room who, thankfully, are blissfully unaware of the conversation since they all have headphones on.

"Holy smoke on a snickerdoodle. That look has even me wanting to find a broom closet," Mae says as she fans her face. Timber gives her a heated look to which she winks at him before her gaze returns to me. "So, I take it that's a yes?" she asks with a saucy wink.

I can't help it. A laugh bubbles out of me and soon the three of us are laughing so hard we have tears in our eyes.

"Yes, I'd like to have more. I hated being an only child, so I've always wanted a large family. Now, exactly how many more kids? That I don't know. Time will tell on that one."

As our laughter dies down, Patch rounds my bed and places a kiss at my temple before whispering huskily in my ear. "I'll have as many kids with you as you want, Siren. You want a football team? I'll make sure the house we build will fit them all."

A shiver runs down my spine and when he pulls back slightly, I can't help but stare into his green eyes that almost seem to dance with electricity. Wait. He said he'd *build* a house to fit how many kids I want? "Seriously?"

"As a heart attack, Siren."

"Even though you know... about everything? You still want to be with me?"

"Like I said before, I'd marry you this instant if I could. I want you back by my side like we had originally planned on. As long as that's still what you want."

"It is," I respond, my words barely above a whisper, and the blinding smile I get in return has my own smile forming again.

He turns back toward Levi and Mae before glancing toward my kids. "What are you ladies and kiddos hungry for? It's almost lunchtime. We can have a Prospect go pick it up and bring it back."

Relief flows through me. The hospital food here is definitely not my favorite, and I wasn't sure how I was going to handle another bland and cold meal.

"MaeMae?" Isaiah's hesitant voice comes from the corner of the room, and we all look over at him. Apparently, they had all taken off their headphones and I hope it was just recently and that they hadn't heard any of our conversation. Isaiah hides slightly behind Ash when he realizes all of our attention is focused on him.

"What is it, Izzy?" I ask him, hoping to take his mind off the fact that every single adult gave him their attention as soon as he spoke up. Something that I know he's never had in a positive way outside of me. Whenever Stephan's focus was on him or the others, it was never in a good way.

His shy gaze flicks from Mae's and meets mine. I give him a slight nod in encouragement and he looks back at Mae.

"Can we have the noodles again? Like last night?"

"Oh! Those were really good! What did you call it again, Mr. Timber?" Cassie asks as she perks up on the couch, bouncing a little. I'm not surprised to see that she's full of energy. The only times I've seen her energy dim was whenever Stephan was around. Those times, she'd close herself off and become a shell of her bubbly self.

"Lo mein. It's a Chinese dish," he responds, and I can hear the smile in his voice. Turning toward him, he steps up behind Mae's chair and rubs her slightly rounded stomach. "How about it, Mama? You and the babies up for some more Chinese?"

Mae hums as she tilts her head back and gives him a quick kiss. "Chinese sounds good, Babe. You know what I like, but if you could get some extra crab rangoons, that would be heavenly."

He gives her another kiss. "You got it, Sunshine."

I can hear Levi and her men murmuring quietly, but my focus is on Patch who is crouched low in front of the kids as he reads off the menu to them while Timber takes everyone's orders.

My chest warms at seeing the kids so open with everyone, but especially with Patch. Even Ash is talking a bit more like his usual self. He'd only do that around me or people that he trusted in the past, which means he feels comfortable and safe around Patch.

A small weight releases off my shoulders at seeing them interact together. It gives me hope that what Patch said was true. That he wants a future with me and my children. Then I feel butterflies in my stomach when I remember his husky words about wanting more children with me. Something I'm very much looking forward to when the time is right.

It's nearing four o'clock when Dr. Rodgers comes back in, and when she smiles, my gut tightens in anxiety. I hope I'm able to be released soon. I've always hated staying in hospitals, but at least this time, I had friends who kept me distracted for the duration of my stay. Mae and Levi gather the kids, saying they'll be outside to give us privacy. Thor, Dragon, and Timber follow them out, and soon, it's just Luke, the doctor, and me.

She checks my vitals and takes a peek at my stitches, nodding her head in what I think is approval.

"Okay, let's slip off this sling and run through your exercises to see how your shoulder is doing."

Ten minutes later, Dr. Rodgers gives me a warm smile. "Congratulations, Mary. Everything looks like it's healing correctly. I'd say you are good to be discharged. If any of your wounds become red or angry looking or start seeping, have Luke look at them if he's available. If he's not, then you need to get to a doctor to check for infection. Follow up with your doctor regarding your leg. I know Luke said you don't currently have a doctor, but that once you decide on a new one, make sign to the forms to have your information here faxed over. Usually, I would expect you to be in a cast for six to eight weeks depending on how everything heals, but remember, that's a guideline, not an absolute timetable. As soon as I leave, I'll get your discharge paperwork going. Now, do you have any questions for me?"

Shaking my head, she continues.

"Okay, well, a nurse will be in shortly with your paperwork and information regarding aftercare with your stitches and your cast." She steps forward and squeezes my calf. "I'm glad you're out of that man's clutches, and I know this one here will take good care of you." She winks at me as she points to Luke, whose cheeks pinken slightly. "Take it easy and don't push yourself too hard. Here is a prescription for some pain killers. I'm okay if you keep the same schedule—the pain killers at night and over the counter relief for during the day, just make sure they don't overlap. If you're in too much pain, your recovery won't go as smoothly or as quickly. Let yourself heal; you hear me?"

Nodding, I give her a genuine smile. "Yes, Ma'am."

"Good. We'll get you unhooked from everything, and then you can get dressed. I'm sure the nurse will be in soon with your paperwork."

Excitement flows through me to finally be getting out of here. To be able to breathe fresh air and to snuggle my babies.

Chapter 30

Patch

A KNOCK SOUNDS AT the door. Squeezing Mary's hand before kissing her knuckles, I stand and cross the room to see who it is. Opening it, I'm surprised to see Alli on the other side.

Quirking an eyebrow at her in question, she rolls her eyes and huffs.

"Like I was going to let my bestie escape without saying goodbye to her." She pauses as she gives me a mischievous grin. "Besides, I figured I'd help her get changed. We don't need you going crazy on her when she starts showing skin as she changes. Our girl needs to heal! Which, in Mae's words, means no hanky panky!"

I feel my cheeks heat because I most likely would be kissing every exposed inch of Mary's olive skin as she changed if I could, but even in a lust-filled fog, I know I would have held myself back. Barely. I'd rather shoot myself than cause Mary any pain or harm.

Out of the corner of my eyes, I see both Bear's and Dragon's lips twitch slightly at Alli's teasing. While I'm slightly annoyed they're witnessing this, I'm relieved Thor has two of our biggest brothers on protection duty today. I know when we leave, more of them will join us for the ride home as an extra precaution, something I'm extremely grateful for because I know Stephan or Diego will try to pull something. It's been too quiet from both of their ends.

Stepping back, I cross the room and lean down, kissing Mary's temple. "I'll be right outside while you get ready. Holler if you need me for anything."

She nods, and I can practically feel the excitement pouring out of her. While she's not once complained, I know she's tired of being stuck in the hospital.

Anger wars in me. I'm sure part of that is because that asshole beat her into submission if she so much as thought about complaining. I sure as hell hope to be able to get my hands on that fucker for a little bit before we have to hand him over to the police. He needs to feel some semblance of what she's been put through at his hands.

Taking a calming breath, I kiss her temple again and step out of the room.

As soon as the door latches, Dragon pins me with his gaze. Out of the corner of my eye, I see Timber making his way over to us. After talking with a few other guys, Thor joins him.

"So, what's our plan?" Dragon asks, pitching his voice low in an effort to keep anyone from overhearing.

"We'll get her discharge paperwork soon. On our way home, we'll swing by the pharmacy drive through to get her meds. Doc said she'd call ahead so that they'll have it ready for us. Hopefully, we won't have to be waiting long. I'll feel a lot better having her behind the compound walls. Out here, she's a sitting duck. Timber, I'd like the kids to go back in the same vehicle they came in. I don't want to waste time being out in the open and switching booster seats around."

He gives me a chin lift. "We had already planned that they'd be going back with us. Ash did ask to ride with Mary, but I pulled him aside and explained why we needed to get back as quickly as possible. Kid is smart as a whip. Said that makes sense, because Stephan or the men he worked with will try to get them, especially Cassie and Isaiah, at some point. Then he'd use Ash to get Mary. Kid even asked if Stephan's friends got him out of jail yet. Told him I didn't know on that last one. I figured I'd leave that up to you and Mary to figure out how to tell the kids. Didn't want to step on your toes or anything."

"Fuck," I curse, not liking the idea that Stephan would focus on getting Cassie and Isaiah first. A pit forms in my stomach as my mind goes to dark scenarios for exactly *why* they'd be the first targets.

"Any word from either of the fuckers?" Bear asks and I frown.

"No, and that worries me. I have a feeling one, or even both, of them will try something. If not today, then soon."

Their frowns deepen and then Dragon winces slightly.

"What?"

"Fucker posted bail."

Once again, anger runs through me. "How the fuck did the asshole get out so quickly?" I seethe as I pull my phone out and dial Uncle Sam. He picks up right away.

"It happened when I was off shift," he says before I can get a word out.

His growl coming over the line is the only thing keeping the words at bay that I really want to let fly so badly, but I know it's not his fault. *"What happened?"* I ask instead.

"Chief told him he's on unpaid suspension while this whole thing is investigated and his job depends on the results of the investigation as well as his court charges. His case somehow went to Judge Bradley, who is on Mary's list of those being pressured. I'm going to bet the assholes threatened his family. His wife gave birth to their first baby a couple of months ago."

I bite my tongue to keep from spewing another string of curses that threaten to erupt. I won't be any good to Mary if I get kicked out of here because I end up blowing my top. Not even me working here will save me.

"And let me guess. Your guys haven't seen hide nor hair of him since?"

His heavy sigh is answer enough and I can't help but grind my teeth as my mind reels. The fucker has probably already split town or is hiding in a safe house somewhere. Wait...

"Do you have eyes on the house of your other guest?"

"Claudia lives in an apartment complex, so that one is harder. Fucker could be wearing a disguise."

"Fuck," I curse and make a mental note to ask Smoke about his facial recognition software. We might be needing it. If it'll work for this kind of a scenario. *"Keep me posted and I'll do the same."*

Hanging up, I shove my phone into my pocket and really wish I was already back at the compound. I could really use a session with the punching bag right about now.

"We need to get out here. Like ten minutes ago," Bear says under his breath and I give a chin lift in agreement. I'm guessing they heard all of that since I didn't step away from them.

"Agreed. Let me see how things are going with Mary. Hopefully, the nurse will be by soon with her paperwork. If it were anything other than pain killers, I'd send a Prospect to pick up her script, but we gotta do it in person." I pause, angrily running a hand through my hair. "I hate that she'll be a target while we're there."

"While you were on the phone, I texted Phoenix. He's sending some of our guys to the pharmacy to blend in and be backup if need be. They're on their way."

A little of the tension lessens from my shoulders, but I won't be able to relax until we're back at the clubhouse.

Clasping him on the shoulder, I give a curt nod. "Thanks. I'll go see how close they are to being ready."

Knocking on the door, I hear a faint 'come in'. Taking a deep breath, I push those emotions away for now. I need to keep a clear head for the next hour or so. Then I can process everything.

Entering, I'm relieved to see Mary already dressed and Alli's helping to pack up the rest of her things.

Seeing Mary, my Siren, sitting on the edge of the bed, warms my chest. The last few days, I've pinched myself numerous times to make sure she's really here. That I'm able to put my arms around her and hold her again. Not to mention beyond grateful that she's taking the steps to regain her freedom and independence.

Her face lights up when she realizes it's me, but then it falls as she purses her lips. "Tell me."

Fuck. I must not have been able to mask my emotions well enough.

She smirks, and as she points a finger at me, her smirk widens, but I can see the fear in her eyes that she's trying to hide. "You forget that I've grown up with you. Well, ever since I was ten, that is. I know all your tells. Your eye is twitching, and to make matters worse, so are the muscles in your jaw. Something's wrong. So, spill, Luke. I know from Levi and Mae that there are some things I won't be able to know with the whole 'club business' stuff, but they also told me I'd be allowed to know the cliff notes version if that was the case and if it pertained to me, which I'm guessing is the case right now."

Giving her a small smile, I shake my head as I walk over to her and wrap my arms around her, bringing her close but also being mindful of her shoulder. "It's not 'club business' yet, though, I'm betting we'll be having Church soon." Sighing, I run my hand up and down her back, loving when she leans into me more at the action. I hate that I have to burst her bubble of happiness.

She sighs, and then turns, burying her face in my shirt for a moment before she tilts her head up to look at me expectantly.

"We just found out that Stephan posted bail and no one's seen him since leaving the station."

Her muscles tense and her hands fist my shirt and cut. She bites her lip as she stares at my chest, almost like she's lost in thought. After a few moments, she nods slightly, but I notice her body is still tight with tension.

"If he sticks to his past MO, he's going to dye his hair and possibly even wear colored contacts. He doesn't always wear the contacts each time he changes his appearance, but I'm going to guess he will this time since he knows so many people will be looking for him. Once, he even wore a fake mustache for a while. Then a few weeks later, he'd 'shave it off'. He'd also switch up the style of clothing he'd wear when he wasn't in his uniform. Since moving here, he had been dressing kind of laid back, so he'd have a better chance of blending in. He'll probably switch to more of a preppy look. Like polos and jeans or khakis. Sometimes even button-down shirts. At least, that's what he used to do when we would move."

Frowning, I bite back a groan. I really need to talk to Smoke about his software. I know Stephan has a cleft chin, so that's kind of hard to hide unless he goes full-on Hollywood and uses make-up or molding shit or whatever the fuck that stuff is called to alter his face. Fuck, I hope he doesn't go that far.

Shaking my head, I lean down and kiss the crown of her head. "Thanks, Siren. I'll pass along the information to the guys on lookout and to Uncle Sam. In the meantime, I'll help finish packing so that we can leave as soon as the nurse comes with your paperwork. We'll swing by the pharmacy on the way home, but that'll be the only stop. We'll be using the drive through so you don't have to get out of my truck."

For the next ten minutes, Alli and I finish packing Mary's things and we've managed to condense everything down into three duffle bags and a backpack. Thank God, Levi offered to take home Mary's flowers with them. That'll make things easier.

Right as I'm about to go and get a wheelchair, there's a knock at the door and I breathe a sigh of relief when I see that it's the nurse who has Mary's paperwork in hand as she wheels in the wheelchair.

Walking back over to Mary, I pick her up and set her down in the wheelchair as the nurse goes over the aftercare for her stitches, shoulder, and leg.

A few minutes later, the nurse hands her the paperwork. "That's everything. I hope your recovery goes smoothly. Take care and have a good rest of your day."

"Thank you."

After she leaves, I grab the backpack off the bed. It doesn't escape my notice that both Mary and Alli are silent as they wait to hear how we're going to handle our exit. I'm slightly surprised by Alli's silence, but then again, she's been hanging out a lot with Levi and Mae, as well as at the clubhouse. I'm going to bet she's heard a little about how we handle situations like these.

"Mary, I want you to hold this since it has some of your personal stuff in here and your wallet. You'll need that when we get to the pharmacy. Alli, for now and until my brothers can take them from you, can you grab two of the other bags? I'm going to put the last one on the back of her chair, but I need to keep my arms free in case I need to move quickly. Also, I would really prefer if you didn't leave the hospital with us, Alli. I don't know if the assholes have lumped you in with us and I'd rather not put a target on your back."

She purses her lips, and right as I think she's going to fight me on this, she nods and then walks over to Mary, hugging her tightly while also being mindful of her shoulder. "Text me when you get to the clubhouse, otherwise I'm going to be worrying about you for the rest of my shift. We'll get together soon. I want to spend some time getting to know the kids."

"Can't wait."

The smile that lights up Mary's face warms my chest and I make a mental note to have Alli over as much as possible. As long as it's safe for her to do so, that is. I meant what I said—we're pretty sure they know about Alli's tie to the club and I don't want to paint a larger target on her back.

Chapter 31

Mary

Even though I'm trying to portray calm, I'm anything but calm on the inside. Gripping onto the backpack in my lap with my good hand, I take a deep breath, trying to calm some of my nerves. I'm so focused on calming down that I don't notice Patch squatting down in front of me until he places a hand on my knee and I jump a little.

"Siren, I'm sorry that I made you more nervous by explaining what we were going to do and the precautions that we're taking. I sometimes forget when explaining things that you're new to the club life." He pauses as he sighs before squeezing my knee. "I should have worded that better."

Giving him a small smile, I reach out and squeeze his hand. "It's okay. I knew at some point Stephan would get out and make his first move. Same for Diego. I know too much, which means he'll be coming down on me too, especially if Grandpa confronts him about the trafficking. If he does, then I'm sure he'll connect the dots which will lead back to me. I was just hoping for a little more time before their first move." Taking another deep breath, I squeeze his hand again. "Now, let's get out of here. I'll feel much safer when we get to your clubhouse and I can wrap my babies in my arms."

Patch grins as he stands and then he surprises me when he leans forward and places a chaste kiss on my lips. "That's my Siren. Love you, Mary."

My chest warms and my breath hitches. I shouldn't be so surprised to hear him saying that since he's been telling me he loves me multiple times a day these last few days, but I just can't seem to shut off that small part of my brain that keeps saying he'll change his mind someday and realize I'm not worth the trouble and leave me. Leave me and the kids.

Shaking off those gloomy thoughts, I smile up at him. "I love you too, Luke." Thankfully, he doesn't call me out on using his real name, but I didn't want to use his road name for that. Maybe someday, but not yet.

Alli hoists the two duffle bags over her shoulders. When Patch turns to move behind me, she gives me a saucy grin and a wink when his back is to her. Shaking my head, I feel my smile widening. It's so good to have her back in my life.

Out in the hallway, I wave goodbye to the nurses that helped me and as we near the elevator, I'm surrounded in a sea of leather, denim, and biker boots. Someone named Ryder takes the bags from Alli and I raise an eyebrow in question at her when he leans down and places a quick kiss at her temple. She blushes and mouths the word 'later' as she waves at me and then heads down a different hallway, most likely to head back down to the ER.

Turning, I frown when we reach the elevator and I realize my kids aren't out here anymore. Mae had said they were going to wait in the hallway. Where did they go?

I jump slightly when I feel Patch's breath tickling my ear.

"I texted the guys a bit ago that we were almost ready, so they escorted the ladies and the kids out to their trucks. Some of the guys followed them back to the clubhouse, since we didn't want the kids out in the open while we go and get your meds."

A sigh of relief flows through me and I blink back tears at the emotions surging through me at the lengths Patch's club is taking to ensure our safety. Well, as much as they physically can, that is. I know some things will be out of their hands, but I know they'll do everything they can to minimize those risks.

Turning and looking over my shoulder at him, I give him a grateful smile. "Thank you, all of you."

The man next to me grunts as we all file into the elevator, which is a tight fit with how many men are with us. When he looks down at me, I'm surprised by how soft and gentle his warm brown eyes are. Glancing at his cut, I see his name is Bear, which is fitting. The man is a few inches taller than Patch and he's built like a brick house. I wouldn't want to see the damage he can do with those fists if someone ever crosses him.

"Don't worry, Mary," Bear says. "You're Patch's woman, which makes you family, and we keep our family safe. And if the unthinkable does happen, you can bet your ass that we'll be finding you as quickly as possible."

"Speaking of, here, Mary." Thor, who's standing on the other side of me, hands me a little pouch. "When you're in the truck, put these on. Patch can explain them to you."

Opening the pouch, I peek inside and am puzzled when I see a couple of bracelets inside that are made out of small paracord strands. What's so special about these bracelets?

The elevator door opens and I cinch the pouch closed before tucking it into the front pocket of the backpack. I don't want to risk dropping it.

Once again, the guys surround me as Patch quickly wheels me through the entrance of the doors and out to the drop off/pick up area in front of the hospital. Two more men in cuts are waiting by a truck that's idling and Patch steers me toward them.

As soon as we reach the truck, I'm startled to find myself suddenly in Patch's arms, especially since I'm so heavy, and then in the next second, I'm seated in the truck and the door is shut. Blinking in surprise, I watch Patch jog around the front of the truck before he climbs in behind the wheel. The back doors open and then two men that I haven't met before climb into the backseat.

Turning to look behind us, I note that the two men carrying our duffle bags before are getting into the truck behind us. A few moments later, the roar of multiple bikes starting up fill the air. Five of them pull in front of us and Patch pulls out behind them. Looking behind us again, more bikes pull out behind us, then the second truck. Even though I can't see them, I'm betting there are more motorcycles behind the second truck as well. Some of the tension in my shoulders leaches away from my body at being so surrounded by Patch's club.

Patch clears his throat and I turn toward him.

"Those bracelets are made by Levi and a friend of hers, Gray. Open one of them up."

Reaching into the bag, I pull out the pouch and retrieve one of the bracelets. Undoing the latch, I freeze when I see the little blade at the end. Suddenly, a part of Levi's story comes back to me. About how Reaper and she used these to cut through the ropes that held them. Is this what she meant?

"Are these what Levi and Reaper used to free themselves?" I ask to clarify things for myself.

A grim look passes over his face before he jerks his head in a sharp nod. Then, for some reason, he grins. It doesn't escape my notice that the man seated behind Patch is grinning like a loon and I'm sure the other guy behind me is as well. But why are they suddenly grinning?

"Sure are, Mary. Our Queen has been instrumental in helping to keep all of us safe. There's also a tracking beacon sewn into the band, but they aren't monitored unless we need them to be. Oh, and I'm Gunner, by the way."

I'm actually surprised that I relax more at hearing the bracelets have trackers on them. Especially since I know my ring Stephan had given me had one in it. But then again, I trust the club not to monitor the trackers unless need be. My gaze tracks the thin band imprint on my finger where Stephan's ring used to sit. I had asked what happened to it the morning after Luke rescued me and he told me that they'd given him my jewelry while I was in surgery. He then gave my ring to Smoke for safekeeping. When I pressed on that, worried that the ring was possibly broadcasting from the clubhouse where the kids are, he told me that Smoke put it in a specially made box that prevents the broadcast, or signal, from escaping.

Pushing those thoughts out of my mind, I refocus on Gunner and give him a grateful smile. "Nice to meet you, Gunner." Then I freeze as a thought hits me. "I saw the kids wearing bracelets like these but didn't think anything of it earlier. Are their bracelets kid friendly versions or do they have the blades as well?"

A grunt comes from behind me and I twist a little more in my seat to try and see the guy better.

"I'm Axe, by the way. They're kid friendly, so no blades. Also, Smoke took a few liberties and asked me to tell you that in case the bracelets are removed or cut off, your kids have trackers in the soles of all their shoes as well. With your situation, he wanted to be a step ahead in case anyone got their hands on them. He'd like to put them in your shoes too"

"I think Levi, Mae, and the other ladies and kids are going to get the trackers, too. Smoke had thought of getting trackers that could be injected under the skin, but I don't know if he got them or not," Patch says as he glances at me. "We can talk to him about all that when we get back to the clubhouse. He's our eyes a lot when we're in town."

I frown at that, trying to figure out what he means, and then my eyes widen in surprise. "You mean he can hack into the town's security cameras?"

All the men give me feral grins. "It helps to own the company that installed almost all of the town's security cameras," Gunner says and I feel my jaw dropping in surprise.

"How did I not make the connection that you guys own Steel Security?"

His grin grows bigger. "Smoke is the brains behind everything and the majority owner. The club just has shares in it."

Well, fuck.

The guys all chuckle and I feel my cheeks heat. "I said that out loud, didn't I?"

Patch shakes his head, but judging by his smile, I know I said that out load.

Again.

I groan. That's been happening a lot lately. Thankfully, it's then that I realize we're in the drive-thru for the pharmacy and relief flows through me that it's our turn.

Digging through the backpack, I find my wallet and pass my driver's license over to Patch, knowing he'll need it to get my script. While we wait, I can't help but clutch my wallet tightly as I discreetly look around, trying to see if I spot Stephan or any of his goons. Or any of the so-called family members that betrayed me.

My gaze snags on a beige Honda Civic, and I can't seem to look away. My breathing increases when I realize who I'm staring at.

A hand wraps around mine, and I jump a little, but can't tear my eyes off the man in the car.

"Siren, I think I know which car, but tell us what and who you're staring at," Patch's voice is quiet, and low, most likely so that it doesn't pick up on the speaker that leads into the pharmacy or for the cameras they have littered throughout the drive-thru lane.

Licking my dry lips, I swallow thickly. "Beige Honda Civic. Illinois plates, URM1N3. It's Stephan. I know it is. He's dyed his hair black. He looks exactly how he did when I first met him after Diego and Isaac kidnapped me. I can't tell his eye-color from here, but I bet it's blue."

My hands clutch my wallet even tighter as his license plates meaning dawns on me. "You are mine," I whisper, and Patch's hand tightens in mine.

"He's trying to get in your head, Mary. Don't let him," Gunner says from the back seat, his voice low and so growly that it makes my skin break out in goosebumps.

Taking a deep breath, I try to calm my racing heart and mind. Gunner's right. He's trying to screw with me. Taking another deep breath, I square my shoulders and then casually look away from him, as I admire the flower baskets out front of the neighboring business. Ignoring him is a surefire way of pissing him off, but I'm not willing to be sucked into his mind games anymore. I just need to convince my body and my mind not to panic or tremble every time we see him or any of his 'associates'.

A soft chuckle has me turning toward the backseat to find both Gunner and Axe wearing matching grins.

"Looks like you know how to get under his skin too, Mary. Don't look, but he's—" Axe starts to say and I can't help but grin in response.

"Let me guess. Running his hands through his hair roughly? Drumming his fingers on the steering wheel? Unbuttoning the buttons on the neck of his polo?"

Their grins widen at my words and they both nod. "All of the above."

My grin fades and I swallow nervously. "I just hope I'm not provoking him too much. I don't want him to hurt anyone, but especially my kids."

Patch's hand tightens on mine. "Or you," he growls, and I have to fight to not press my legs together.

Who knew that I'd find a possessive streak sexy, especially after everything with Stephan? But it's incredibly sexy on Patch. Maybe that's some of what Levi meant the other day—that sometimes their protectiveness and possessiveness can be a good thing?

The pharmacist chooses that moment to come back and gives Patch my script. Tucking the medicine into my backpack, I force myself not to look directly at Stephan as we pull out of the parking lot, but I do keep him in my periphery.

"I texted the others about him, so they'll all be on the lookout for him. I also sent the car's info to Smoke. Maybe it'll give us a lead as to where he's staying."

While I'm sure the address tied to the car is bogus, if Smoke can track his car on his cameras, it just might help us fill in some blanks.

Driving through town, I can't help it, but my gaze keeps bouncing to all the cars and people, wondering if anyone is going to do something.

A siren in the distance has me looking behind us and my eyes widen when I see a cop car behind our little caravan. "Fuck."

Axe reaches up and squeezes my shoulder. "Don't worry. Everyone will stay together as we pull over. Even if it is one of that asshole's little pissants, they won't do anything stupid with so many witnesses."

"Also, Smoke fitted out all of our vehicles with cameras for situations like this. If anything does happen, we'll have the footage as proof," Patch says and I feel myself relaxing even further.

My eyes burn with unshed tears as my throat tightens with emotion. Seeing the officer get out of his car, I push those emotions away for now and steel myself.

"It will probably be Wolfe. Or possibly O'Grady. They are Stephan's two closest buddies who will do anything he says because he helps keep their pockets lined with cash from Diego."

Patch tenses and I wonder which part of what I just said caused that reaction, but I don't have time to ask because the cop takes that moment to approach us. I force my body to remain calm as Wolfe's face comes into view. Fuck. Why did it have to be him?

"License and registration," he all but barks at us, his eyes never leaving me. Then again, he'd have to bark or yell to be heard since none of the guys have shut off their engines.

"What seems to be the problem, Officer?"

"License and registration."

With a sigh, Patch pulls out his wallet and gestures to the glove box as his gaze flicks to me. "Can you grab the registration?"

Displaying a calm I definitely don't feel, I do as Patch asks. When I hand him the registration, I'm beyond proud that my hands don't shake in the slightest. But then again, that could be because of the three muscular bikers in the truck with me and the eight bikers flanking our truck.

Patch hands Wolfe the registration and I'm not even surprised when Wolfe barely even gives the documents a glance before returning his gaze to me.

"What seems to be the problem, Officer?" Patch asks again and Wolfe almost snarls as he tears his gaze away from me to look at Patch.

"Failure to give the appropriate advance notice of your indication to turn." He looks behind us, glaring at the bikers who are probably giving as much as they are getting, and then he does the same to those in front of us and finally, to Gunner and Axe in the backseat before his gaze settles icily on me. I barely repress the shiver that runs through me as memories of the last time I saw him threaten to bombard me.

"Seems you've taken in with the wrong crowd, *Mrs.* Hayes. Why are you with these low-life thugs when you have a loving husband that misses you and wants you to return home where you belong?"

Borrowing on the strength of the guys in the truck, I straighten my shoulders. "It's Mary Catarino. I've officially changed back to my maiden name after filing for divorce. I will never be with Stephan again." Biting my lip, I force myself not to say what I really want to say. That there is no love in that man except for his love for himself. Well, himself and his bank account. The only things he's missing are his cook, maid, and punching bag.

"Is that right?" He pauses as he passes Patch a piece of paper along with his license and registration. "A warning. Make sure you're obeying the traffic rules, or next time you'll be getting a ticket." He pauses again as his gaze returns to me. "Have a good day, Mrs. Hayes," he tells me, though his body language and eyes wish me anything but that. "If you know what's good for you and Stephan's children, you'll return home. The children need a positive male role model in their lives, especially your older son. They'll just turn into more thugs if you keep hanging around with this crowd. You wouldn't want that, now would you?"

Gritting my teeth, I force my jaw to unclench. "I have everything handled with *my* children's care. Thank you for your concern, Officer Wolfe."

"Remember what happens when you disobey your husband," he says with an evil glint in his eye before he makes his way back to his cruiser. Moments later, he pulls out and drives by us, sending me one last menacing look before he's gone.

He may be gone, but all my spiraling mind can focus on is his parting words. I know that was his intention, but I can't stop my mind from remembering every scenario where Stephan claimed I 'disobeyed' him and the beatings that followed.

Or who was present during those beatings.

Chapter 32
Patch

Fuck, fuck, fuck.

Something Wolfe said triggered Mary to shut down, and based on the last few days, I'm betting she's trapped in her memories.

Trying to anchor her, I reach over and clutch her hand after pulling back onto the road. "Mary, Siren, I need you to come back to me. You aren't with Stephan anymore. He can't hurt you."

My words don't reach her through the fog, but I don't give up. For the rest of the ride, I keep talking to her, trying to coax her back to reality.

Pulling through the gate, I drive up to the clubhouse and come to a halt. Throwing up the console, I scoot over and cup her cheeks, making her look at me. I'm beyond grateful when Gunner and Axe quietly slip out, giving us some privacy.

"Mary, Baby. Come back to me. Talk to me."

A trembling hand reaches up and touches my hand. "L-Luke?" she says weakly.

"Yeah, Siren, it's me. You aren't with him anymore. You're safe."

She blinks rapidly and her eyes come back into focus. "Luke?" She looks around and a confused look comes across her face. "We're here already?"

"Yeah, Siren, we're here. Do you want to talk about it?"

She takes a couple of deep breaths and then shakes her head. Disappointment fills me until she speaks. "Later we can, but I think what'll help most right now is to be around my kids." She pauses again as she shakes her head. "Fuck, I told myself I wasn't going to let him mess with my mind again, and then it happens anyway at Wolfe's threat and promise."

Anger burns through my veins that the fucker's still causing her pain, but she's right. We need to go inside. Plus, I'm sure Thor will be calling Church sometime today.

"Okay, give me a moment and I'll help you get out."

Reluctantly, I pull away, open my door and round the truck to her door. I smile when I see her kids' faces peering out at us through the window and I find myself giving them a little wave.

Opening her door, I take her backpack and sling it over my shoulder. Then I notice Levi's bracelets are still sitting in her lap, and I'm not really surprised that she forgot about them after seeing Stephan. I put them both on, one on each wrist, to which she gives me a small, weak smile. Kissing her temple, I breathe in her scent, noting it's something floral, as I lift her into my arms, careful not to squeeze her too tight since her injured shoulder is against my chest. She reaches up and places her good arm around my neck, stabilizing herself. However, when she starts running her fingers through my hair, I damn near trip over my feet. It's a sensation I've been dreaming about feeling again for nine years—I've always loved the feeling of her hands in my hair.

Using my hip to shut the truck door, I climb the clubhouse steps and thankfully, the door opens when we get there. Mary lets out a little gasp and I grin when she looks up at me in surprise. My heart clenches when I see unshed tears shimmering in her eyes and I know it's because Stephan never would have given her this kind of attention or care in the past.

"You think I was going to leave you totally dependent on someone in a normal wheelchair, Siren? Only the best for my woman."

As soon as I heard confirmation that her shoulder was partially dislocated, I knew she wouldn't be allowed to use crutches or wheel herself around in a normal wheelchair. I called Doc and he was able to get me a motorized wheelchair for her.

"We even put a ramp at the backdoor so you can come into the clubhouse." I pause and lean in closer to her ear. "But just so you know, at least one of us will be with you and the kids at all times until we catch these assholes."

I press a kiss below her ear and my dick twitches when she shivers in response. A second later, she frowns, and a worried expression flits across her face before she masks it.

Realizing I'm just standing right inside the door, I cross the room and sit her down in her wheelchair. I take a moment to explain the controls to her and then step off to the side. Immediately the kids swarm her, and she reaches down, hugging and kissing each of them. Cassie tries to climb up Mary's good leg. I look at Mary, raising an eyebrow in a silent question, and she nods. Leaning down, I lift Cassie up, giving her a snuggle and pressing a kiss to her temple. My chest tightens and warms when she giggles as I lightly tickle her tummy.

"Remember to be careful, Angel," I tell her and she wraps her little arms around my neck, squeezing me tight.

"I will, Mr. Patch."

Carefully, I sit her down on Mary's lap and am not surprised when she burrows into her side, pressing as close as possible as she leans her head against her chest. Mary leans down and kisses the crown of her head as she blinks away tears.

Mae breaks through the silence as she steps up toward Mary, reaching around Cassie and giving her a hug. "We've got a mini party planned tonight for your homecoming. It'll just be with our club—no hang-arounds or people from town. This next weekend, Reaper's crew is coming up for our combined club Thanksgiving dinner, so you'll be able to meet them all as well. They're also a bunch of great guys."

I step away and head over to the bar which Colt is currently manning. "Can I have a beer and one of those raspberry waters?" Mary had taken to Mae's flavored waters when they visited the other day, and I want to make sure she's getting enough fluids while she's still taking her meds. I know some of them can cause a lot of dry mouth, which I know she'll hate.

He slides my beer over to me after uncapping it and reaches down to the fridge we keep sodas and waters in before passing me the water. Popping the tab, I grab our drinks and walk back over to Mary, flipping out the cup and phone holder attachment. She gives me another surprised look before grinning and shaking her head as she reaches out to take the water from me while being careful not to disturb Cassie, who has fallen asleep against her. How she can sleep in a room full of noise is beyond me. Taking a closer look, all three of the kids have dark circles under their eyes. I wonder if they weren't able to sleep very well with Mary being in the hospital.

I'm brought out of my thoughts by someone tugging on my jeans, and I look down to see Ash at my side.

"What's up, Ash?"

He cocks his head slightly as he looks at me with a gaze that reminds me of a hawk watching someone. "Can we talk?"

Smiling down at him, I nod and point at a table not too far away but still in Mary's eyesight. "Of course." I'm not surprised to see her frequently checking on the boys. Right now, Dragon and Timber are trying to teach Isaiah how to play pool. Ash was over there with them, but I'm not sure when he stepped away.

Taking our seats, I'm surprised when he fidgets a little before speaking, but then I remember what Harris had said about how Stephan was with the kids when they were at their house for Thanksgiving.

"So," he pauses as he licks his lips. "So, you're my dad?"

Grinning, I nod. "Yeah, son, I am. What I said in the hospital on your birthday was true. I've been looking for your mom ever since she was taken. I had suspected she was pregnant, but had no idea she was as far along in her pregnancy as she was." Pausing, I debate exactly how to word this next part before deciding just to throw it out there. "Asher, I want you to know that you can talk to me about anything at any time. Well, later, when I go back to work, it'll need to wait until I'm on break or back home unless it's an emergency. You won't be judged or punished for what you say unless you're being mean to someone."

His little shoulders relax some and he gives me a small smile as he nods.

"So, tell me about yourself. What do you like to do?"

Ash grins fully. "I love to draw and play cars and motorcycles with Isaiah. But my favorite things to do is to read or watch shows about different kinds of animals." He pauses, a sheepish-shy look coming over him. "Someday, I want to be a veterinarian."

Rubbing my chin, I think back to a few months ago when Bastion came to live with Levi, Thor and Dragon. "You know, maybe sometime we can have Carter come here for a visit? Or go into town to see him? He's a vet and he's how Bastion came to be here. You two could talk and see if that really is what you want to do with your future."

Ash's jaw drops in shock and my chest aches at the disbelief in his eyes. After a few moments, he seems to come out of his shock, but he's still staring at me in disbelief. "You really mean it? You aren't going to tell me that it's a waste of time or that I'm not good enough or smart enough to do something like that?"

My chest aches even more at the pain in his voice and at what Stephan's said, and done, to him over the years. Reaching out, I put a hand on his little shoulder, ignoring that it feels skinnier than it should be, and squeeze slightly. "Son, I will never say anything like that to you. Ever. Or to Isaiah and Cassie. I'm here to support you, all of you. To help you learn about things as you grow up and to give you the tools you need to live your life when it's time to start taking your future into your own hands. If you want to be a veterinarian, then we'll take steps for you to learn more about it to make sure it's what you are really interested in. If you find out that it's not for you, then we'll go in a different direction.

"But know this, Asher. You are not worthless. Your interests are not a waste of time or effort. You are smart as a whip and don't think I haven't noticed how you seem to catalogue everything you see or hear." I'm relieved when he smirks a little at that and see hope starting to fill his eyes. "Very few people are able to do that and recall the information months or even years later. I've seen how protective you are of your siblings and your mom, which are great traits to have, and I can't thank you enough for protecting them when I wasn't able to. You are a very special kid who I know is going to grow up into an amazing man one day. Someone that I already am very proud of."

Tears form in his eyes, and for a moment, I think I've said the wrong thing, but then he launches out of his chair and into my arms. Seconds later, I feel my shirt turn damp with his tears and I hold him a little tighter, allowing him to let go of everything.

Glancing up, I notice Mary's wiping her eyes and she mouths 'thank you' to me. Giving her a nod, it seems like I need to have a talk with her, too. I should probably have similar talks with Isaiah and Cassie, too.

She should never have to thank me for doing what I just did.

And when I get my hands on that fucker, on top of everything else he's done to Mary, I'm going to make him pay for what he's done to my kids. They may not be mine yet legally, but they will be.

They will know they can count on me for anything they need. That their ideas and voices are seen and heard. That they are wanted and cherished. That they are protected. For them to know that if anyone messes with them, they'll have an army of steel and leather at their backs, ready to defend them.

After a few minutes, he pulls back and I help dry his cheeks. Cheeks that pinken as he looks down at my shirt.

"Don't you dare say you're sorry. I'll tell you something I told your mom the other day." I wait until he looks back up at me and he bites his lip in worry. A trait he seems to have gotten from his mother. "I'd much rather you let out your emotions like this rather than bottling them up until you feel like you're going to explode. That's not healthy. Even if it's me that you need to rant about. If you feel like your emotions are all over the place and need a safe place to vent, I am that safe person. I will never judge you. I'll listen and support you in any way I can. If I did something wrong, I'll fix it. And if I'm not the right person to help you, I'll find the right person for you. You hear me?"

He wraps his little arms around my neck again and squeezes slightly. "I hear you. Thank you."

Giving him a little squeeze, I blink back my own tears. "Anytime, Ash. Anytime."

"Church!" Thor yells out over the common room, and I give Ash one more squeeze before pulling back.

"I gotta go in for a meeting. Stay in here with your mom, your siblings, the ladies and the Prospects. Don't go outside for anything, okay?"

At the sternness in my voice, it's almost like he changes with the flick of a switch, which makes sense if he was used to altering himself on a dime because of Stephan's mood swings.

"I'll make sure they stay inside and are safe."

The conviction in his voice makes me believe he'll do exactly as he says. Damn, this kid would make a good member when he grows up. "Good man, Ash."

He slides down off my lap and goes over to Isaiah, who is sitting on the couch. Mae's flipping through the channels on the TV trying to find a show for them and Mary wheels over next to them. Cassie slides down off her lap and promptly climbs up on the couch, snuggling in between Isaiah and Ash. The way they crowd around her and shield her with their little bodies is a telling sign that has me frowning, making me wonder how much they've had to shield her before. Or how much Ash has had to shield the both of them because his eyes haven't stopped scanning the room since they sat down. How he positioned himself propped up against the arm of the sofa so he can see almost the entire common room, part of the kitchen, and one of the hallways.

Mary wheels over to me and I tear my gaze away from the kids and focus on her.

"So," she pauses as she licks her lips nervously. "How does this work, exactly?"

Crouching next to her, so that she doesn't have to strain her neck looking up, I place my hand on her thigh and squeeze it reassuringly. "Everyone but Thor and Phoenix will put their phones in the basket on the bar and we head in for a meeting. Prospects will stay out here with you, Mae, and the kids. I really don't want any of you leaving while we're in Church. If there's an emergency, you can have the Prospects come and get us or you can knock on the door. Smoke said he programmed everyone's numbers into your phone, so if you absolutely need to, you can call or text Phoenix or Thor. If there's a situation where you need to go to the panic room, Mae can show you where it is, otherwise I'll show you afterward just so you know where it is and the entrances."

Her eyes widen, and I hate dumping all this on her at once, but I haven't really had the chance to talk about this yet and I didn't want to bring it up in the hospital.

"Everything should be pretty quiet tonight. Mae and some of the bunnies will be cooking something for dinner. I will say, you can see the kids from the pass-through window if you want to join them. All I ask is that you don't tax yourself too much since you just got out of the hospital."

She bites her lips and looks behind me toward the kitchen before nodding. "Um, I'll probably be in the kitchen unless the kids need me. I want to get to know Mae better, but I'm nervous about meeting the bunnies, even though Mae said most of them are actually pretty cool and easy to get along with."

I nod in agreement. "If I remember the rotation correctly, the ones helping tonight, Sarah, Amy, and Ashley, are easy to get along with. Roxy and Sasha also help in the kitchen each weeknight unless we order out. If we didn't have Church,

Levi would have been helping as well. You remember what I said about the other two?"

Her lips thin as she purses them and nods. Crystal still tries to stir up shit occasionally, but not as badly as when Gigi was here. Gemini and Cici are fairly new, and I've purposefully made a point to not spend any time alone with them, so I don't know them as well. Though so far, they haven't tried to raise too much shit. However, time will tell on that as both have tried to corner me since I've never been with them.

"Alright. I've got to get in there."

Standing, I give her a quick kiss and after putting my phone in the basket, I head into Church, shutting the door behind me.

Chapter 33

Patch

INWARDLY, I GROAN WHEN I see everyone is already in their seats and waiting on me as I make my way to my own seat.

"Don't worry, Patch. We get that you didn't have much time to prep her about the meetings. I would have given you a heads up except that I had just gone through the club's mail from yesterday and snagged these before she could potentially see it."

Thor holds up a couple of envelopes and my blood runs cold at seeing Mary's name scribbled on the front of one of them with no return address.

Fuck.

Are they both for Mary?

Shit. I glance at his hand and a breath of relief goes through me when I see he's holding them in a gloved hand.

"Unfortunately, I did touch it before without gloves, but as soon as I realized what it was, I grabbed one," he says, practically reading my mind. "Patch, since she's your woman, I figured you'd want to open them first."

Exhaling heavily, I give him a chin lift before standing and going over to the table behind me in the back where we keep my kit. We also store Ryder's supplies back here that he uses to gather prints as well as some other gadgets of his. Ryder works almost as Smoke's second, or whatever the fuck his title is, at Steel Security. A moment later, Ryder's next to me gathering supplies while I grab some gloves and a sterile letter opener and tweezers.

Retaking my seat, I spread out both envelopes that Thor had set down at my spot and frown when I notice they used Mary's married name on both of them. Both of them are thick and from history, my nerves skyrocket at what I suspect is enclosed. I also note something right off the bat. "These both appear to be written by different people based on the handwriting."

Taking the one on the right, I carefully open the envelope and use the tweezers to pull out the letter before passing the envelope over to Ryder to dust for prints.

Unfolding the letter, a bunch of pictures fall out, and I swallow the bile that rises in my throat.

Almost all of them are of Mary after enduring beatings, most likely by Stephan's hands, and in varying degrees of undress. In some of them, it's obvious the perp beat her while also either having sex or raping her. My gut clenches at that and I remember her telling Claudia that Isaiah and Cassie were both conceived from him forcing himself on her. Fuck. Looking through the rest of the pictures, my gut clenches even further when I see a few pictures of the kids sporting bruises and one that clearly shows Ash with a broken arm.

Anger has my muscles tightening, but I force my hands to stay loose so that I don't tear all of this up right this second. We need to know what's in the letter and maybe Ryder can get some prints off all of these. Exhaling, I force myself to pick up the pictures again and look at each one with a critical eye—trying to spot if there's any evidence in any of them, but there's really only two things that I'm able to see other than Mary and either carpet, tile or hardwood floors.

One is that in some of the pictures, you can see the toes of someone's boots. The other is that you can see the person in the picture being held or held down by someone's hand. Wait...

Squinting, I look closer but then jerk back when a magnifying glass is placed over the picture.

"Here," Ryder tells me as he hands it to me.

Grasping the handle, I examine the pictures again. "There are at least two, maybe three, people holding her down in these pictures." I pause and point them out to Ryder to see if he thinks the same as me. "This guy has something circling his wrist. This guy has maybe a quarter inch or so sunspot on the back of his hand. And then this guy has a bunch of freckles on the back of his hand and arm. All of the pictures capture their right hands."

Ryder hums. "Give me that."

I hand him back the magnifying glass, and he looks at each of the pictures with it before frowning. "You can also see bloody footprints, some full and some partials, in the pictures. They look like they could be from the boots in the pictures, but the boots appear to be the same, so we don't know which perp was wearing them."

"What's the note say?" Thor all but growls. Its then that I notice he was standing off to the side, watching over our shoulders.

Carefully, I unfold the letter and feel a growl of my own growing in my chest. Whoever sent this must have watched a number of crime movies or shows because they've used letters from magazines to write their note. Clearing my throat, I read it out loud.

Return Mary and the kids to their rightful owner or you and your club will pay the consequences. It would be a shame to mar the pretty faces and bodies of the women in your club. Not to mention the price the unborn babies will bring.

You have until Monday night at midnight to return them or you have signed your death certificates.

Curses ring out but my gaze stays locked on the word 'owner'. This note has to be from Stephan. Especially after hearing Mary recount what happened that fateful night and Diego saying that by midnight, Mary would be in her new owner's clutches.

Pushing down my anger, I pass the note over to Ryder and take the other one. This envelope has Mary's name and our clubhouse address printed on it. Using the same care, I open it and pull out a letter, freezing when I see the first picture enclosed in said letter.

It's of Nikos, dead on Mary's living room floor, a pool of blood surrounding him. Next are pictures of Mary, her kids, Mary's grandparents, Levi, Mae, Nikki and Sadie, Susie and Jordan, Alli, Alli's parents, my parents and sister, myself, and all my brothers in our club with targets on our faces. Setting them off to the side for Ryder to do his thing on, I focus back on the letter, which is also printed.

Leaving Stephan was an extremely stupid thing for you to do, Mary. Now, you've painted targets on even more people's backs, including those lovely pregnant women and that woman nurse you've been hanging out with lately. Not to mention the women friends and children of those scumbag bikers you have aligned yourself with.

If you don't return to your owner, you'll experience pain and suffering unlike anything else you have endured so far, as well as bringing the same fate on all the women in your boyfriend's pathetic little club. Not even being given the Kiss will save them.

It would be a shame to submit them to the horrors of my little establishments just so you can have your 'freedom' back. They will pray for a death that doesn't come and have to watch what their children will be subject to once they are of age.

All of this can be avoided if you return to your owner, though I can't promise you will come out unscathed as your owner is quite displeased with your acts of treason and betrayal.

You don't know the scope of what you are messing with, Pet, and it would be wise to heed my warnings. If you and your leeches are not back where you belong when midnight this Monday night comes, you will have signed all your little friend's death and slave certificates.

The letter is pulled out of my hands by Thor, who's still wearing his gloves, and I'm grateful because I was about two seconds from ripping it to shreds. "That one has to be from Diego and the first from Stephan," I grit out. "And based on how the two are phrased, I'm thinking they didn't realize the other was writing a letter to Mary."

"Or they did and wanted Mary to focus on the thought that Stephan 'owns' her and she needs to do whatever the fuck they say," Thor all but growls out, which has my chest rumbling with my own growl.

Mary belongs to herself and no one else.

Ryder hums again. "You're right about Stephan. Since he's a government employee, his prints are in the system. I got a full one that matches his from the corner of the first letter and a partial one from the worst of Mary's pictures from that batch." He pauses and a look of disgust comes over him. "I also found what looks to be him kissing said picture as well."

He holds up the picture he's referencing with tweezers, and I feel my lip curl in a snarl when I see an outline of lips in whatever the fuck he's using to dust the print with.

Thor clears his throat and I look up at him.

"I hate to suggest this, Patch, but do you think Mary would be willing to see if she could identify the other men in these photos?"

Bile rises in my throat at subjecting her to this after she's already been through what's depicted in these pictures, but I know why he's asking.

Frowning, I slowly nod. "I'll go ask her."

He gives me a chin lift in return. "We'll bring the others up to speed while you do that."

Handing the rest of the stuff over to Ryder, I stand, ripping my gloves off and tossing them before heading out into the common room. Ash perks up when I step out, but I raise a hand to stop him. He nods, settles back against the arm of the couch, and turns back to the movie they're watching.

Not seeing Mary with the kids, I head into the kitchen and my chest warms at seeing a bright smile on her face as she laughs and talks with the other women. Since her arm is still in a sling, I hadn't thought there'd be anything she could help with, but here she is peeling brussel sprouts for someone else to cut up.

Mary notices me first and the warmth I just felt turns to ash when I see her body tense up for a moment before it relaxes. She immediately turns toward the other ladies, her smile now strained and small. Picking up the small bow holding scraps from her lap, she places it on the table before wiping her hands on a nearby towel.

"I'll be back in a bit, ladies," she calls over her shoulder as she wheels over to me. "What is it?" she asks me quietly.

I lead her out into the hallway and into an empty room so we can speak in private. Swallowing thickly, I wet my dry lips, once again hating that I have to burst her happy bubble. However, before I can get anything out, she sighs as she simultaneously squares her shoulders.

"Luke, I mean Patch, whatever it is, just tell me—I'll help you any way I can."

The strength and determination in her frame and eyes have me marveling at how strong my Siren truly is. Exhaling heavily, I pull over a chair and take her hand in both of mine, rubbing my thumb across the back of her hand.

"Siren, two letters were sent to the club. Both were addressed to you." I pause when I feel a slight tremble work through her but her gaze hardens.

"Stephan? Diego?"

I nod. "We know Stephan sent one of them and I think Diego sent the other based on the wording. But that's not all..."

"The pictures," she whispers and I see the first crack in her determination.

Slowly, I nod again. "Yeah, they both sent pictures. In the ones Stephan sent, there were some other people's hands, and possibly shoes, also in the pictures. We know it's a long shot, but we didn't know if you would be able to identify them or not."

She swallows nervously a few times but then gives me a curt nod. "I'll do it."

Leaning forward, I give her a quick kiss. "Thank you, Siren."

Standing, I open the door and lead her into Church. I'm surprised when I see Timber's spot vacant and when I glance around, I find him in my seat.

He gives me a chin lift. "Figured it'd be easier because of her chair."

I give him a chin lift in return, noting that Mary's moved her chair next to the open seat and is angled slightly toward the table. Not giving her any warning, I lift her in my arms and set her on my lap once I take my seat. She looks up at me startled, a blush staining her cheeks.

"What are you doing?" she quietly hisses and out of the corner of my eye, I notice a few of the guys trying to hide their smiles, though Levi's full-on grinning as she twirls a pen in her fingers. "I'm fully capable of sitting on my own."

Pressing a kiss to her temple, I try and fail, judging by the look on Mary's face to hide my smile. "Just continuing the tradition Timber started."

She rolls her eyes and shakes her head, but I definitely don't miss the way she leans into me and relaxes even more into my body.

"Mary," Thor starts, as he levels a look at her. "What we say in here, stays in here. I need you to understand that. If someone else needs to know something, one of us will let them know a very high overview—you do not. Do you understand?"

She sits up straighter in my lap and nods. "I understand. I won't put you all in jeopardy, especially since you are risking so much to help my children and me."

Her words have my chest tightening and Thor and I exchange a look.

Clearing my throat, Mary turns back to me. "Siren, I need you to understand that even if those fuckers threaten someone else, that you will not leave and offer yourself up on a platter to save them. We know what we are doing and this isn't our first rodeo. We will protect you. Please tell me you understand that?"

Her brow dips but she nods. "I understand," she all but whispers and it's then that I feel the little tremors running through her body.

Thor motions to Smoke and after a few clicks, the screen behind Thor lights up. "This is the first letter that we were able to determine through prints that Stephan was most likely the sender."

I shift Mary slightly on my lap so that she doesn't have to crane her neck to read Stephan's letter. I can feel her muscles tremble as she leans into me more. Then her worried gaze jumps to Levi's.

"Do not doubt the men and women in the club, Mary," Levi states. "Even those related to the club members. We will do everything that we can to protect everyone involved in this as well as our own. You are Patch's woman, which means you are family. We rally around our family. Anyone who dares to mess with us will regret it."

The hardness in her voice has Mary tensing even further. "But I'm still married to someone else. I can't be L—Patch's woman yet."

Levi waves a hand nonchalantly in the air as she shakes her head, but her grin gives her away. "Semantics. You are Patch's woman in every way that counts, and if what I heard was right about way back when, you would have already been Patch's woman after you graduated."

Mary's surprised gaze whips around to me and while I hadn't wanted to tell her like this, I guess now's as good of time as any.

"She's right, Siren," I say as I reach up and cup her jaw. "I had a ring picked out and everything. I was going to propose the night we graduated."

Her eyes turn misty and she bites her lip as she reaches up and clasps my wrist. "I would have said yes," she whispers and I give her a quick kiss.

"I know," I whisper back. "But we can talk more about this later."

Her lips kick up a bit and she nods, blinking rapidly to keep her tears from falling. Taking a deep breath, she turns back toward Thor. "Patch mentioned he sent pictures with the note as well? Even though I could probably already tell you who was present, I'm not sure which ones he sent you. There were eight others, sometimes nine, that Stephan would bring in to beat me as well. After each beating, he'd take a picture. He had a thing for always taking pictures after hurting me, but especially after a group beating. Kept a polaroid camera just for that purpose."

Silence meets her words and I can feel the anger rising in the room.

After a few moments, Thor gives Smoke a chin lift and the screen changes to the first picture, which is the guy with the sunspots on his hand. Mary squints and then frowns. "That's Leonardo Adams, I think. Goes by Leo. See his crooked pinky? He broke it a few times while beating me. That was when we were living in Rock Ridge."

Smoke makes some notes and then, when he flips to the next picture, a shiver visibly runs through her.

"Officer Zachary Wolfe. I'd know that pattern of freckles anywhere. Besides Stephan and my so called 'family', his beatings were up there among the next worst."

Frowning, I turn my attention away from her and back toward the picture. It takes me a moment, but then I see the pattern similar to the big dipper on his arm. Then I remember Wolfe's parting words from earlier about remembering what happens when she disobeys her husband. He knew what happened to her because he was there and a part of it. The fact that he's a fucking Police Officer just makes this even worse. Fuck, I haven't told Thor about that yet.

Turning toward Thor, he nods his head toward Axe. "They filled us in on the confrontation with Wolfe while you were talking to Mary."

Giving them a chin lift in thanks, I turn back toward Mary only to notice that her body's frozen as she stares at the screen, and I can feel that all her muscles have pulled tight. She's white as a sheet, which is saying something with her light olive skin. Looking up, I notice it's the picture of the hand with the tattoo on it. Turning back toward Mary, I rub my hand up and down her back, trying to help calm her, but it doesn't work.

"Siren?"

Nothing. No response at all.

"Mary?"

Finally, she blinks and looks over at me. When our gazes lock, the pain in them would have brought me to my knees if I hadn't been already sitting down.

"That man is a monster. He relishes in beating others and gets off on it. Not only women, but men and children, too. He never hurt my kids, just me, but he did threaten to hurt them," she whispers, and I reach up, wiping away a tear that escapes.

"Who is he?"

She shakes her head slightly. "I'm not a hundred percent sure. I never heard his last name. Some of the guys that Stephan would bring around would call him 'Kristoff'. Others called him 'X'. That tattoo around his wrist? It's actually the tail end of a huge cobra tattoo that winds up his arm. It's mirrored on his other arm, too. He has another, even larger snake, that circles around his torso and goes up his neck. The snake's mouth is open, fangs barred, and little drops of green poison dripping from the fangs. The head of the snake is about here," she says as she points to an area below her ear.

I freeze, the dread I was feeling before increases. My gaze going to Timber only to see him staring intently at the image, his hands fisted tightly on the table. Mary's muscles tighten even more as she looks around the room.

She licks her lips nervously. "I... I'm going to take a guess that you guys know who I'm talking about?"

"Yeah, Siren, we know of him," I tell her, and she follows my line of sight. I know she's put two and two together when she gasps, her hand flying to cover her mouth.

Timber shakes his head. "He never hurt Mae, physically that is, but he wants her."

Thor clears his throat. "Smoke, show the other letter."

Seconds later, the letter I suspect is from Diego appears on the screen. I didn't think it was possible, but Mary's muscles tighten even further before she starts frantically looking around after reading it. Tripp, who's to my right, figures out what's wrong at the same time I do, jumps up and grabs the trash can. Pushing back from the table, I gather Mary's hair just in time for her to throw up into the bin.

Taking the bin from Tripp, I nod toward the back of the room. "Can you grab her a water?"

Seconds later, a water bottle is set down next to us, along with some tissues. Grabbing some, I hand them to Mary when it looks like she's done. She takes them, wipes her mouth, and grabs the water bottle before struggling to break the seal. Setting down the bin, I take the bottle from her, break the seal and hand it back to her. After taking a few sips, she looks over at Timber, her face crestfallen and tears in her eyes.

"I'm sorry I didn't make the connection sooner."

What connection? What's she talking about? Looking up, I notice everyone else is just as confused as I am.

Chapter 34

Mary

I SERIOUSLY CAN'T BELIEVE I didn't connect the dots sooner. I should have after Mae told me her story.

"What do you mean, Mary?" Thor asks me and I turn toward him before turning to Smoke.

"Did you copy the scan drive I gave to my grandfather?"

"Yeah, I made a copy."

"Open it and find the file named 'AK'." I pause and turn back to Timber. "It stands for Aphrodite's Kiss. I'm almost positive it's what Mae said she was given. I don't know what all it's composed of though."

Timber's hands fist in anger and I don't blame him one bit. Mae and his children were put at risk from that damn drug.

Still tasting the bile on my tongue, and knowing my dry throat is going to need the water for this, I take another couple of sips before capping it. I pick at the label on the bottle, a nervous tick of mine, as I debate where to start.

"A little backstory real quick regarding Stephan's business meetings. Whenever we had company and Stephan needed to talk business, the kids were ordered to their room and could only leave to go to the bathroom. My orders fluctuated. If he didn't need me, I was ordered to our room. If I needed to clean, do laundry, or prepare a meal for them, then I had to wear earbuds and listen to music during those meetings. It was one of the things he insisted on 'training' me to do. However, I had stopped doing that and just wore the headphones about a year prior to those conversations when I'd started gathering evidence against him and trying to figure out a way to escape.

"A little over a year ago, I overheard two conversations. One of the conversations was a phone call between Stephan, Diego, Kristoff, and a man I've never met, but they said his name was Andrew. The other conversation was in person at our last house in Credence between the same people, but Andrew was on speakerphone. I was in the kitchen preparing supper during both meetings. Stephan's office was just down the hallway off the kitchen, so I heard everything since he kept his door slightly ajar.

"Andrew said that he had the supplies all lined up for Aphrodite's Kiss so that he'd be getting steady shipments for the organization's teams. He didn't say what the organization's name was, but he did mention that there was one leg of the operation here in Wisconsin. The others were out of state. And before you ask, I don't know where the others are—they mainly focused on the one that is, now that I think about it, probably not too far from here. Or at least it was at the time of that conversation. I'm not sure if that's changed since then."

I pause when I hear Smoke sigh and scrub a hand over his face. "It's Oasis."

I can't help but perk up at that, even though the fact that they apparently know about Oasis makes my nerves even worse. That is *not* a group I want anyone, especially someone I know, to have ever crossed paths with. Smoke must have looked in the other folders while I was talking, because I know that Oasis wasn't mentioned, by name at least, in the AK files.

Licking my dry lips, I nod. "I know a little about them and it's in those files, too. Stephan and Diego have had a lot of conversations with Kristoff about them, especially in the past couple of years. They were renting out some land north of here, but they also had a couple of locations nearby where they were housing what they called 'their product'. I'm assuming that meant the people they abducted or tricked."

Pausing, I clench my hands as I grit my teeth. "I even heard Kristoff saying that every product sample brought in went through a physical to see how healthy and 'intact' they were, as well as noting their temperament. Those deemed viable would be given Aphrodite's Kiss and quarantined from the rest of the product.

"The rest were to have their tickets immediately put up on a website. Depending on how 'used' they were, some were held aside for Kristoff's men's use. They kept them drugged up so that they'd be compliant for anything they wanted to do to them. Unless the men wanted them to struggle, that is. Stephan often bragged about how he 'saved' me from that fate. He would often threaten that if I didn't 'behave' or listen to him, that he'd toss me to them for their use and then work with Kristoff to get rid of the 'leeches'. That's what he called my kids whenever they weren't around. Leeches that were sucking him dry.

"I also found evidence of Stephan funneling people from Kristoff to Diego and vice versa. That's part of why they employ cops. They use their profession as a cover to get close to people and when they realize the truth, it's too late. Some of it's in code, but while doing some digging through Stephan's office, I found a couple versions of the translations."

"Mary, you said eight, sometimes nine, people would take part. You mentioned Leonardo, Wolfe and X. Who were the others?"

A shiver works its way down my spine as I try to suppress the memories. Leaning more into Patch, I try to take comfort from his warmth and his arms around me.

"Derrick Rodriguez, Donnavan O'Malley, Officer Finn O'Grady, and not surprisingly, Diego, Carlos, and Isaac. Isaac wasn't brought around near as much as the others, but when he was, he made sure to hurt me, both with pain and with his lies."

Patch's arms tighten around me and he buries his face in the crook of my neck. Smoke clears his throat and I look up at him.

"Mary..." Smoke pauses and I feel Patch lifting his head at his tone and looking up as well. Smoke's gaze bounces between the two of us and a pit forms in my stomach at the tormented look on his face.

Sucking in a shuddery breath, I reach for Patch, and he entwines his fingers with mine. "Yes?"

The sorrow, anger, and some other emotion I can't describe flit across his face. He types something on his keyboard and out of the corner of my eye, I notice the screen changing images. Turning, I hear a strangled cry and it takes a moment before I realize it came from me. My vision turns blurry as I stare at the screen. Blinking rapidly, I can't believe what I'm seeing, but then again, I can believe it.

He's made good on his threat.

Curses ring out throughout the room and Patch's arms once again wind around me, pulling me in close to his chest. Turning, I bury my face in his shirt and cut, wanting to believe this is some sort of prank even though I know it isn't.

Stephan has listed all of us for sale on the website they use to move around their 'product'. Even his own children, Isaiah and Cassie.

Thor bangs his hammer on the table a few times to quiet everyone down, and I wipe my eyes as I look up at him.

"Smoke—keep an eye on the website for any changes. Also, comb through the rest of the documents Mary gave us for anything that might help. We're on semi-lockdown and no one rides alone. Timber, if possible, put a rush on the unit Mary will be taking." He pauses and turns toward me. "Guards will be posted around the clock as a precaution. While you're home, I won't post anyone inside the condo unless we get new information. However, if you leave the house for any reason, even if it's to come to the clubhouse, to our house, or Timber and Mae's house, you need at least two guards with you, and not the ones that are posted at your unit. Your unit will always be under surveillance in case those bastards find a way in here. I know it'll be hard, but I want you exposed as little as possible. Those fuckers will not get their hands on you or your kids."

"What about school for the kids? Or doctor appointments?"

"Maybe we can talk to Uncle Sam and then talk to the school? We might be able to arrange for the kids to either go virtual like they did when COVID hit or if their assignments could be emailed and then emailed back once they are completed."

Thor nods. "See if Sam can come here and then Smoke can set up a secure link with the principal of the school to see if it can be done. If not, then each of your kids will have a guard with them. As for doctor visits, there isn't much we can do about that unless we can get the doctor to come to the compound. If not, then you'll have guards with you. Patch shared the list Dr. Rodgers gave for possible doctors you could see here in town. Smoke can check out them out and then you can make a decision for which one to use going forward."

My nerves are almost shot, but I force myself to take a few deep breaths as I nod numbly in response. Once I feel a little calmer, I can't help but look over at Levi, worried about what I'm bringing to their doorstep and the fact that I've put a target on their backs as well as on their unborn babies.

She gives me an understanding smile and mouths the word 'later' to me. I'm not really sure what all I'll say to her later, or ask, so all I can really do right now is nod in return before turning to Patch and then to Thor.

"Is there anything else you need me for? Or need of me? I'm going to assume you don't want me around for everything you need to talk about."

Thor shakes his head, the corner of his lips kicking up into a knowing smirk. "Not right now, but if any questions come up, we'll let you know."

Nodding, I feel Patch shift and I wind my good arm around his neck to steady myself. He sits me down in my awesome chair that I've already fallen in love with, and I miss his heat when he steps back to get the door. As I wheel past him, he leans down and kisses my temple.

"We'll be out later. If the food's done before we're finished, make sure the kids and you ladies eat. The other bunnies not cooking will be out to eat, but other than that, they were told to stick to their rooms since it's family night."

"But what about you guys? Won't the food get cold?"

He shakes his head. "We have warmers that Mae and the others know to use if we end up taking a while."

Frowning, I nod even though I'm not happy that the food might not be warm enough for them to enjoy. I'd much rather they took a break, grabbed food, and went back in if that was the case.

Wheeling out into the common room, tears spring to my eyes when I look over and see my kids cuddled on the couch. Ash sits up in concern, but I give him a small wave and force a smile on my face. There's no way I can tell him what's bothering me.

Arms wind around me from behind and I jolt before I realize it's Mae.

"I think I can take a guess as to what's running through your head, but we can talk more about that later, after supper. How about you come in the kitchen with the girls and me and we can try to take your mind off it for a little while?"

I sink back into the chair and rest my hand on her arm, grateful beyond words to be surrounded by people that care about me again. "I'd like that."

After dinner, I set my plate on my lap to take it into the kitchen when it's suddenly picked up. Looking up, Patch smirks at me.

"I've got it, Siren. Besides, I think a few people would like to talk to you." He tilts his head behind me and I turn, seeing Sasha, Mae, and Levi walking toward me. Mae's got a couple of backpacks in her hands, and I frown, wondering what's in them. Then I see that the others have a backpack with them as well.

As Patch leaves, he guides the kids away and between him, Ash, and Timber, they clean the empty dishes off the table. When the ladies take a seat, Mae pulls out some baby wipes and quickly wipes off the table, and I can't help but smirk.

"Those things will be your best friend for the rest of your life," I tell them.

All three of them laugh and nod.

"We learned about this trick from Smoke's sister, Nikki, and how useful they are. Now, I always carry some in my purse," Mae replies.

Levi clears her throat and Mae places one of the backpacks she was carrying on the table and lays it down on the center of the table.

"Mary, after my first attack, my therapist suggested that I keep a journal. I took it one step further." Levi reaches into the bag and pulls out two journals, one blue and one black, as well as a pack of multi-colored pens. She then reaches into her backpack as she continues. "The blue one is my everyday journal to chart how I'm feeling. I use whichever colored pen strikes my fancy at that time, but I never use the black or red ones for the lengthy daily journal entries. On days that are exceptionally hard, or my thoughts are extremely dark, I make a note in my journal like this one."

She pauses as she points to an entry in her own blue journal. In black ink she's written the date and then in red ink, she wrote 'used the black journal today'.

"The times when I feel like I'm in a really dark place, I put all of those thoughts in my black journal. Times where it seems like I'm caught in the clutches of darkness and trying to claw my way out. Every single dark, and often torturous thought, I write down. Later, when I'm feeling like I'm crawling out of that dark hole, I'd go out back to a firepit and light a fire. Then, I'd rip out the pages, tear them up, roll the pieces into little balls, and throw them one by one into the fire, letting the fire burn away my hateful and gruesome thoughts.

"After each incident, as I call them, the time periods between needing to write in the black journals were pretty frequent. My dad had heard a saying that some therapists use with their patients to gauge how they are doing. He'd ask me 'how long'? Only for me, he meant it as 'how long has it been since I felt the urge to write in the black journal' and I'd always answer truthfully.

"Eventually, the time periods between using the black journal and burning the pages lengthened and I found myself being able to process my emotions better and not needing to use the journals as much. When I felt like I was in a good place, I'd then burn the blue journal pages as well."

I stare at her, stunned, at what she just shared. How did she know I was struggling so much? I thought I had been masking my emotions regarding what I'm going through and have gone through at the hands of Stephan and my family. It appears I didn't do a good enough job. Sasha clears her throat and I turn toward her.

"I started using the journals with Levi after her first attack, and it really does help you process everything."

"After my first attack, Levi and Sasha gave me the journals as well. They helped me tremendously the last couple of months with processing the attacks and the fears of what that drug may do to my babies or me," Mae tells me.

Reaching forward, I run my finger along the spine of the journals before looking up at Levi. "How did you know?"

She reaches forward and places a hand on top of my own. "Because I struggled with the same thing that I think you are struggling with right now. I wanted to turn myself into Fang to save my men, family, and friends, but my men wouldn't hear of it. Or my friends and family. Later I realized that even if I had turned myself in, Black Plague still would have gone after my men and anyone I cared about. Yes, I got taken a second time, but that time, I knew help was coming. And fast. Yes, I got hurt, but it could have been a lot worse. I could have been raped, sold to some sick fuck and seen my babies sold into that life before probably being killed after I'd 'served my purpose'.

"What's different with these men and women, this club, is that they will do whatever it takes to save the people they love and care about. You were kidnapped, drugged, sold, and forced into a marriage that you had absolutely no say in and didn't want. Patch looked tirelessly for you all this time, spending almost every free waking moment following the leads, only to have to start all over again when you moved. After a few years, he asked Thor if Jax could help in his free time as well, and he did.

"They came really close to finding you many times, but when they got to the address you'd been staying at, you were already gone. That man will move heaven and earth to make sure you're safe, and if the unthinkable happens and those fuckers get their hands on you or your kids, we'll find you as quickly as we can. That's one reason why we use the trackers. Besides our bracelets, our phones can be tracked and our cuts have them in them, too. Jax is toying with other ideas to get trackers on us, especially the children and women, but I don't know where he is on all that." She pauses and squeezes my hand. "The point is, you can place your trust in us to protect you, to support you, to lean on. We're your family now. And don't even think of bringing up that sham of a marriage. You are Patch's woman in every way that counts. That last bit will get resolved after we nab those fuckers and you're finally set free."

My eyes burn with unshed tears, and I blink rapidly to keep them from falling. I've cried way too much the last couple of days. Probably more than I have since I was eighteen, but part of that is because if Stephan ever saw me crying, he would then give me a reason to really cry.

"Thank you," I tell them, making sure I look all three of them in the eye to show them how sincere I am and to express exactly *how* thankful I am for them, for their help, and for their support. They each smile back at me and Mae winks at me.

"Now, how about we all spend a little time exorcising some demons by putting our thoughts on paper?"

A soft chuckle slips past my lips before I can stop it. This isn't really a laughing matter, but I do love how these women are somehow able to make even these dark times just a little less dark. "Sounds like a plan. Can one of you help me unclip the sling? I won't be able to write for very long, but I would definitely like to put some of these emotions down on paper."

Sasha stands to help me slide off the sling. I'm sure at some point I'll be able to handle taking the sling off on my own, but my entire body is still pretty stiff from Stephan's beating and then being stuck in a bed for a few days.

As I gather the journals and pens, I can't help but glance up at Levi and we both share a small smile. Feeling someone's gaze on me, I look around, only to find Patch watching me closely. I smile, but I'm sure it's pretty shaky, and mouth 'thank you' to him. Once again, I have to blink rapidly to keep tears from falling when he rests his hand on his heart and mouths back to me 'always'.

My chest aches with all the emotions swirling through me. I can't even begin to express how thankful I am that Patch was able to save me when he did. Not to mention finally being able to be with him again, well, sort of. I can't wait to be free of Stephan and start building my life with Patch.

Chapter 35
Patch

Knowing my Siren needs me and to not be able to help her right now is killing me as I retake my seat in Church. Thor bangs his hammer on the table and I reluctantly tear my thoughts away from her to focus on what else he has to say.

"Listen up. We don't know when or where these fuckers will pop up. Smoke, work to get pictures for everyone Mary mentioned and pass them around so that we all know who to watch out for. Hopefully, we can get it arranged so the kids can do school virtually, otherwise that's going to spread us a little thin. We'll also meet again once you've gone through the information."

"If they can't do it virtually, maybe we can ask Reaper or some of the other clubs if they could spare a few guys?" Phoenix asks, and almost all of us nod in agreement.

It's been a few years since we've had to request help from a club other than Reaper's, but I'll do whatever it takes to protect my kids. Even though they aren't mine by blood, I already see Isaiah and Cassie as mine. Mine to love and protect.

Thor gives Phoenix a chin lift. "If we need to take that route, we will. In the meantime, no one goes out alone. We don't want anyone trying to pull a fast one on us like Wolfe tried to do earlier today. The last thing we need is fake charges on top of this. Make sure your cameras are on whenever you're riding."

Smoke lifts his hand, and Thor gestures for him to talk. "I've been working on some more cameras that we can wear that'll feed into a server. It's a pin and I've got enough for everyone to have two since we're going into the winter season—one for a coat and one for your clothes. I'll get them passed out later tonight, but I would suggest always wearing them. That way, if something happens, we can grab the feed and either have it to figure out what happened or have it as evidence."

"I agree. Wear them at all times and at night, have them right by your phone for those of us that don't wear cuts," Thor replies. "Right now, we can use all the help we can get and something tells me these fuckers are going to try to sneak up on us whenever they can."

"What's the camera's battery life?" Bear asks him.

"About three days, however, you can recharge it and record at the same time. Think of those external battery packs you can hook up to your phones to charge them on long road trips and such. I've created a pack like that for each camera, but much smaller. You can either charge up the battery pack at night or while you're working. I've also got it set up where you will get notifications to your phone for both the camera and the battery pack for charge levels, so you'll get a message when the battery gets down to forty percent and then a ten percent warning. The pack can fit in your pocket, which will be easier for those of us wearing cuts and you connect the cable around the back of the pin that'll be hidden behind your cut or clothes."

The rest of the meeting we talk about Reaper's club coming up this next weekend as well as the little surprise we have planned. For the most part, I tune them all out, and when Thor bangs his hammer to dismiss us, I make a beeline for the door, needing to put my eyes on my kids and Mary. The tension in my shoulders slightly relaxes when I see that the kids are still watching a movie and I can spot Mary through the pass-through.

Someone clasps me on my shoulder and when I turn, I'm not surprised to see its Timber.

"I'd like to say it gets easier, but during situations like this, it'll keep being a constant need to put eyes on them. Only yours is probably worse since you have four people whereas I only had Sunshine."

Exhaling heavily, I can only nod in agreement. That's exactly how I feel. Turning toward him, I frown."Are we okay?"

He cocks his eyebrow at me and shakes his head as he grins. "Of course, man. You didn't know anything about it. If you had, I know you would have told us. When Mary did find out about it, along with everything else, she literally risked her life over and over to get us and the cops this information. If anything, we owe her for what she's found out. That said, I think these next few months are going to be pretty busy as we deal with all the angles and tie up loose ends."

My frown deepens when I realize he's most likely right. We got lucky that we were able to mostly tie things up fairly quickly with the men that were after Mae. It took about half the time wrap everything up than it did when Black Plague started going after Levi again earlier this year. With all the people involved in this, I want to hope we can tie everything up within a couple of months, but it'll probably take longer.

Shaking my head, I follow Timber over to the bar, grab my phone from the basket and take the beer Colt hands me. I don't miss the hopeful and cautious looks he's trying to hide as he gets us all fresh drinks. Colt just finished his year of Prospecting today, so I know he's going to be wondering if he made the cut and will earn his patches. Unfortunately, he's going to have to wait a bit. We never make a decision the day of—we always make them wait a few days to sweat it out a bit.

With another glance over at the kids to make sure they're still good, I head over to the sofas and sit down with Timber, Thor, Dragon, and Bear.

"How's it feel to have her back?" Bear asks and my gaze automatically goes to Mary as I take a pull from my beer.

"Fucking fantastic, though I wish she wouldn't have been hurt so badly."

They all grin at me, having known how long I've been searching for her, and I can't help but grin in return at the thought of her being at my side again.

I'll never admit this to anyone, but with each passing year, more of my hope of finding my Siren faded. Especially the few months before I first saw Mary at the ER. Reports were high about a bunch of women going missing within four counties surrounding us, and I knew their abductions had to be connected to the trafficking ring and Oasis. I just didn't have proof. Hopefully, there's something in the information Mary gathered that will shine a light on their locations.

As the ladies finish up cooking, I can't help but notice Bear casually sneaking glances toward the kitchen as we talk. I have to bite my cheek to keep from grinning when I realize he's watching Elvira, Drae's... mother-in-law, I guess, for lack of a better term. He and Jane weren't married but they did have a daughter,

Lindsey, together. I hate that we were too late to save Jane and Mae's mother, Lillian, but at least we were able to save Lindsey when we rescued Mae.

I'm brought out of my thoughts by a tug on my pant leg, and I look down to see Cassie shyly looking up at me. Smiling down at her, I put my beer between my legs and hook my hands under her arms, lifting her up onto my lap. Wrapping my arm around her, she curls into my chest and I kiss the top of her head.

"What's up, Angel?"

I barely hear her muffled 'nothing' as she partially buries her face in my chest and clings to my cut.

My throat tightens, and I exhale slowly to keep my body from tensing up. Once again, my hatred toward Stephan rises. I'm almost positive he's never done anything like this with any of the kids. Any attention he gave them was most likely negative and probably hurtful. Aside from Mary's attention, I'm betting these three kids are probably starved for positive interaction with men.

Leaning down, I whisper to her. "Whenever you need a hug or a snuggle, you'll always get one from me."

Cassie looks up at me, and my heart breaks at the tears in her eyes. "You mean it?"

"Yes, Angel, I mean it."

She gets to her knees and I have to fight not to wince when she comes close to kneeing me. She wraps her little arms around my neck and I tighten my arms around her. Opening my eyes, I notice Isaiah and Ash standing nearby and I shift Cassie so that I'm only holding her with one arm. Gesturing to them, I can't help but smile when they both rush into my arms, and I hug all three of them tight. Cassie giggles as she kisses my cheek and I look at her in question.

"You give the bestest hugs, Mr. Patch."

I can't help but chuckle at her, and I'm not surprised when I hear Bear scoff.

"I think you might be missing out, little Miss Cassie. When Levi was a little girl, she used to say I gave the best bear hugs ever," Bear says as he winks at me, teasing me.

"Nope. I give the best hugs according to Sadie," Gunner tells her.

"Hmm." Thor hums as he crosses his arms and taps his chin. "I think you're going to have to get hugs from everyone to see who gives the best ones. Especially

Timber, Dragon, and me. We need to make sure our hugs are up to snuff for when our babies come."

Cassie and Isaiah giggle as they practically launch out of my arms and into my brothers' waiting arms. What comes next reminds me of how lucky I am to have found this club and my brothers and sisters. They all take turns hugging my kids and a few of them get creative and start tossing them in the air a little before catching them.

Feeling Ash shift in my arms, I look down at him. "You can join them if you want."

He shakes his head and leans into me even more. "I'm good right here."

I hug him tighter and every now and then, we both laugh at the antics my brothers are getting up to as they try and keep the smiles on Isaiah and Cassie's little faces. Out of the corner of my eye, I notice Sasha, and when I turn toward her, she tips her head at me. I can't help but smile when I notice she's recording this. I'm going to have her send me that later.

"I wish you could be their dad, too. That way we wouldn't have to leave," I hear Ash say quietly, so quietly I almost didn't hear him.

"If I have my way, you won't have to leave. I want to adopt them and treat them as my own as well."

His little body jerks and I wonder if I said something wrong. When he looks up at me, I realize I didn't when I see the hope in his eyes.

"Seriously?" he whispers, and I nod.

"Seriously, Asher," purposefully using his full name so he knows I'm serious. "I love your mom. I love you. I love your siblings. When spring rolls around, I want to build us a house here where there will be plenty of room for all of you to play, both inside and outside. I want us to be a family once your mom is free from Stephan. Is that something you want?"

He launches forward, wrapping his arms tightly around my neck and when I feel his tears on my skin, I hug him tighter.

"More than anything," he whispers in between his little sobs.

Right then, someone whistles loudly and shouts that dinner is ready. Ash pulls back and I help dry his tears. "Then that's what we'll do."

He grins and hugs me once more before climbing off my lap. I walk with him up to the pass through and give a chin lift in thanks when Bear helps Cassie with her plate and Dragon helps Isaiah with his. Grabbing a plate, I help Asher with his, and then carry it over to a table. Setting the plate down, I turn toward the kids.

"I'm going to go help your mom and then grab some drinks for you."

They all nod, already diving into their food with enthusiasm. I grit my teeth at the familiar anger rising. Hopefully, with a few more weeks of eating as much as they'd like, their little frames will fill out more.

While we were in the hospital, Mary had told me that Stephan liked to torture the kids in ways that wouldn't be very easily noticeable to an outsider since he knew he couldn't hurt them physically as much as he did Mary. One of those ways was limiting their food intake. While they don't look starved, they are noticeably skinnier than they should be for their ages. Previously, their hair was dull and lacked a healthy shine. They'd been with the club and getting good meals and nutrients for only three days, but already their hair is looking better than it was on Thanksgiving. Within the next few months, you probably wouldn't be able to tell them apart from someone who'd always had access to a steady food supply.

Walking up to Siren, I grab a plate for her and one for me. As we move down the line, I make a note of the things she points out that she wants. Once we're able to move into the condo, and yes I'll be moving in with them too, I plan to make sure she has everything she wants to cook whatever she wants. I still remember how much she loved cooking with her dad, grandma, and aunts, and I plan to make sure the house we build has everything she needs to continue that tradition with the kids.

"What's got you thinking so hard?" she asks as she nudges my leg.

Smiling, I lean down and kiss her. "Just remembering you cooking with your family. I think when we start planning a house, the kitchen needs to be a focal point."

She stares at me in shock, her jaw dropped. I have to bite back a groan as memories of when she sucked my cock years ago flood back.

Probably knowing what's running through her pretty little head, I once again mentally strangle Stephan at instilling these insecurities in my Siren. I'll do whatever it takes to help her rebuild her trust and faith in me, as well as helping her regain her confidence.

Stepping closer to her, I pitch my voice low, since I bet she doesn't want anyone to overhear how she's struggling. "I'm serious, Siren, and I'll tell you as many times as you need to hear it. I'm all in, Baby. If it's still what you want, I'll marry you as soon as the divorce is final, but I want to start planning our house here soon. It'll take time to finalize the plans. I know Timber won't be able to start on it until the spring, but I want him to have everything he needs so he can order materials to be here in time for when the weather changes and the ground thaws."

Mary nods, though I can still tell she's in shock. I guide her back to the table and when I set down our plates, I make my way back into the kitchen to get drinks for all of us. However, once in the kitchen, I'm surprised to see Levi finishing putting three little glasses of milk on a tray along with Mary's favorite flavored water, raspberry. I know she's tried the others in the hospital thanks to Mae, but so far, raspberry is the clear winner in Mary's eyes.

Levi smiles when she sees me. "Mae said that Cassie let it slip the other night that she really wanted milk with their Chinese, but that it wasn't allowed. Of course, our sweet little Mae swore up a storm as she got all three of them glasses of milk and told them they could have milk whenever they wanted."

I cock an eyebrow at her in surprise and question. "Mae swore? She actually swore? And in front of kids?"

Levi laughs and shakes her head. "She swore in her own usual way. I think Timber said she called Stephan a 'duckin clusterfluff of a fudgernut knuckle sucker'."

Laughter spills out of me and it only intensifies when Mae comes in and shrugs, apparently having heard Levi.

"Well, it's all true. He's a spineless lump of donkey doo doo that doesn't know his head from a hole in the ground."

Shaking my head as I continue to laugh, I grab a water bottle for myself out of the fridge. Putting it on the tray, I pick it up and head back to our table.

Mary freezes when I set the tray down on the table, a look of panic in her eyes before she quickly masks it and shakes her head slightly. When she sees how much the kids' eyes light up as they grab their cups of milk, a pained look crosses her face and she ducks her head. Her shoulders shake slightly and I wrap an arm around her shoulders.

"Hey, you okay?"

She shakes her head slightly and wipes her eyes. "Only Stephan was allowed to drink something other than water when we had meals. Well, except for cereal, but even then, they got minimal milk that was watered down to save money. If they asked for something different, he'd slap or spank them before sending them to their rooms without another bite. As for me, the only other thing I was allowed to drink besides water was whatever coffee he left in the pot, and if there wasn't any, I wouldn't be allowed to have any. Somehow, he knew when I brewed another pot because whenever he got home, I'd get a beating. He'd also limit what they could have for meals unless it was salad or in season veggies or fruit. He purposefully kept them below the normal weight ranges for their ages so they'd be weaker."

Kissing her temple, I swallow down another bout of anger. I'm definitely going to have to hit the gym at some point. Reaching out, I tuck a lock of hair behind her ear that had fallen into her face. "Well, here, you'll always have the basic necessities. You don't have to ask to buy said basic necessities either. You want a cup of coffee? You can have a cup of coffee. They want milk? They can have milk. You want to make one of your Greek meals, which I always loved by the way, then make it. You aren't under that f—I mean, that twatwaffle's thumb anymore," I say with a sheepish look toward the kids. I'm going to have work on curbing my swearing around them. Mary bites her lip as she tries to keep from smiling at my slip up.

"What I'm trying to say, Siren, is that you're free to do what you want. Well, within reason, for your safety right now. All I ask is that you let me know when you're going somewhere and if you or the kids need something, then we'll get it. Okay?"

She melts against me and when she leans up to kiss my jaw, a shiver of need snakes down my spine, but I push it down. This isn't the time or place.

Giving her a kiss, I settle back into my chair and dig in.

Chapter 36

Patch

SEEING MARY GETTING ALONG so well with the ladies cements the fact that I made the right decision to bring them here. However, as I shift a sleepy Cassie in my arms, I think it's time to call it a night. Even though Mary's having fun, I can tell she's crashing as well. I'm sure she's in pain, too, as it's about time she'd take a pain pill if we were still in the hospital.

Carefully standing, I soothe Cassie when she whimpers slightly and I weave through the tables until I come to the one Mary and the ladies are sitting at. As I approach, Mary looks up and gives me a bright smile.

"Looks like someone conked out pretty good," she says and then the little minx bites her lip.

I have to bite my cheek to keep back the growl that threatens to break loose at the gesture. She knows what that does to me, and it's only intensified since seeing her again and seeing the gorgeous woman she's turned into. She winks at me, and I narrow my eyes at her. The little minx is purposefully taunting me, but she'll have to wait. There's no way I'm jeopardizing her recovery.

Clearing my throat, I smirk knowing it has the same effect on her as biting her lip does to me, playing the game right back at her. "Yeah, she did. Ready to head out, Siren?"

She nods, and it's only then that she slightly drops her mask and I see the tightening around her eyes. I think I'm going to have to have a conversation with her later about hiding how she's feeling. She puts her things back into her backpack, and I take it from her, hooking it on the handlebars behind her back. I made sure the model I got her had them for this very purpose. I knew with taking the kids anywhere on the compound, she'd most likely bring a bag everywhere she went, and when I saw the one Ash had been constantly lugging around, I knew I was right in my thinking.

"Good night, ladies. See you tomorrow," she calls out and I call out my own good night as well, not surprised when Timber steps up behind Mae and she says her good nights, too. With both of us leaving, I'm going to bet that Thor and Dragon will be ushering Levi home before long. Especially since it's only a month or so before she's at thirty-six weeks, which is when the doctor thinks she'll most likely go into labor.

We head over to the pool tables where the boys are, and as soon as Ash sees us, he taps Isaiah on the shoulder and they both put their pool cues back into the holder on the wall. I give a chin lift in thanks to Smoke, Axe, Ryder, and Gunner for teaching them how to play. They give me chin lifts in return, and my chest warms when they all say good night to the boys. Judging by the looks on my brothers' faces, I don't think the boys will have any problems hanging out with them in the future.

It's a juggle since I have Cassie asleep in one arm, but I help bundle up the boys in their coats. Then I help Mary put hers on backwards and hold Cassie's over her as we head out into the cool night air. Isaiah and Asher chat excitedly with Mary and Mae about tonight's festivities and when we reach their house, I hear Mary's surprised gasp. I had asked Timber if it was possible to put a temporary ramp on their deck, and at the time, he had just grinned at me. Apparently, he had already installed it the day after Thanksgiving and even went one step further.

Mary looks up at me and I tilt my head toward Timber. "I had asked him to do it, but Timber had already installed the ramp on their deck and Levi's, just in case you ladies met up there."

Her throat bobs as she swallows thickly and I'm almost positive she's still wondering, and probably worried, about why everyone is helping so much. It'll take time, but I'm hoping she'll soon see that we'd do this for any one of our brothers or sisters brought here and needing help.

"Thank you," she says quietly as she wipes her eyes. "Your house is absolutely gorgeous."

Both Timber and Mae beam at her words. "Wait till you see the inside. Timber did an absolutely fantastic job designing this house," Mae says, her eyes lighting up as she goes up on her toes and presses a kiss to his jaw.

I look up at their house and try to see it through her eyes. I've always loved the craftsman design—I'm a sucker for exposed wood beams and other wooden features. My mind starts to whirl with possibilities for the house I'll build for us and as soon as I hear another gasp from Mary when we enter the house, I know we'll have an open layout similar to theirs. In fact, it's extremely close to how her dad's house is laid out, now that I think about it. From the kitchen, you can see the entire living room and almost all of the dining room. You can also see the door to Timber's office and door to the spare bedroom down here that they saved for Mary.

I can't hide my smile when I see Mary's gaze repeatedly going back to their kitchen, not that I'm surprised. It's a cook's heaven with tons of counter space, double ovens, and a gas stove. The island has its own deep sink, I think it's called a farmer's sink. I know having two sinks in the kitchen will be a plus from having to watch Mary and Maria trying to cook using only one sink in the past. And I know she'll be drooling over the walk-in pantry when she sees how big it is.

"Holy sh-crap. You weren't kidding, Mae. This is absolutely gorgeous and I am in total kitchen envy," Mary gushes.

Us adults laugh and I instantly regret it when I hear Cassie whimper. She lifts her little head off my shoulder and rubs her eye with her little fist.

"Sorry for waking you, Angel." I kiss her temple and shift her so that she can see better when she lays her head back down on my shoulder.

"I think it's time to get you kiddos off to bed. Cassie, can I carry you upstairs so Patch can help your mama? I bet she'd love to see your rooms and give you all goodnight kisses and hugs," Timber asks her as he holds out his hands in anticipation.

Instead of saying anything, Cassie sits up in my arms and holds her arms out to Timber.

I'm honestly surprised at how much and how quickly the kids, especially Cassie, have taken to my brothers because of Stephan. I was worried that it would take a while for them to open up to us until they realized that we aren't anything like Stephan. It also hasn't escaped my notice that from listening to all three of them talk about their time here, that they all seem to quickly absorb details about a person that most others wouldn't notice for a while.

Timber takes Cassie from me and I bend down and lift Mary into my arms, following after them as they head upstairs.

"I can't wait to show you my room, Mama! MaeMae and Timber even took us to the store to get some things to decorate our rooms! Timber said that we should be able to remove them and put them up in our rooms when we move into the codo," Cassie chitters excitedly as she bounces in Timber's arms, sleep seemingly forgotten, and we all chuckle at her attempt to say 'condo'.

"It's condo, Angel," Mary says as she continues chuckling.

Turning the corner into Cassie's room, Mary once again gasps in surprise and I can see why as I set Mary down on Cassie's bed. The walls are painted a blue-ish gray color and there are floral and butterfly decals decorating them. On the opposite wall under the window is a twin bed decked out with a purple bedspread that has flowers on it and a couple of small pillows in pink and blue, along with a couple of stuffed animals. There's a little desk in the corner that's set up with coloring books, notebooks, pencils, crayons, colored pencils, and even markers. In the middle of the room is a colorful plush circular rug laid over the hardwood floors and nearby is a toy chest that looks like it's stuffed with toys. I don't know if all of the toys are new or if they are what she brought from their old house.

"Flowers and butterflies, Mama! I finally got flowers and butterflies!" Cassie cheers excitedly as she twirls around the room, pointing them out on the wall to Mary.

Tears well in Mary's eyes, and I rest my hand on her good shoulder, squeezing it slightly. Her good hand comes up and clasps my hand, squeezing back hard.

"It's absolutely beautiful, Angel."

Cassie beams up at Mary before rushing forward and hugging her. Mary looks up at Timber and Mae, mouthing 'thank you' over and over to them. Both of them smile back, and as Mae snuggles into Timber's side, she gives Mary an understanding smile. Mae, like the kids, was deprived of a lot of things growing up. If anyone understands what they went through, even a portion of it, it's Mae.

"My room next, Mom!" Isaiah says as he excitedly points to his room.

He opens a door I hadn't noticed before and it's then that I realize he and Cassie have a Jack-and-Jill bathroom attached to both of their bedrooms.

Picking Mary back up, we head through the bathroom, noting that they decorated in here too, and I let out a chuckle when we enter Isaiah's room. On the far wall, a large motorcycle decorates the wall and on the other is a classic old car. Multiple books sit on his little desk, some of which look pretty advanced for a seven-year-old. His bedspread is decorated with classic cars and like Cassie, he also has a toy chest, but his rug is one of those that has highways on it that you can drive little toy cars on.

"Judge helped me pick out a bunch of books at the bookstore about cars, engines, and motorcycles, Mom!" he says excitedly as I set Mary down on his bed and he brings over a stack of books. "He even said that if it's okay with you, I could go over to the garage with him and help the guys sometimes. After everything's done with Stephan and we don't have to see him again, that is."

All of us adults freeze at his words, and I squat down next to Mary, resting my hand on her leg in support.

"What?" he asks as he looks around at us in confusion. Then he seems to shrink in on himself. "Did I say or do something wrong?" he asks in a quiet, almost defeated voice.

"No, Isaiah, you didn't do anything wrong," I reassure him.

He looks up at me and stares at my face for a few moments, almost like he's trying to decide if I'm lying to him or not. He nods and the tension in his body bleeds away.

"You said 'Stephan' not 'Dad'," Mary replies quietly and Isaiah looks over at her, shrugging his shoulders like it's no big deal. Cassie and Asher both come over and each of them takes one of his hands in theirs.

"Because he wasn't a 'Dad'. When I began preschool, I started noticing the difference between Stephan and the other dads. How they interact with their kids at school when they drop them off or pick them up. I noticed it at the grocery store, the doctor's office, and the playground, too. Stephan never acted like that with us. Instead, he was mean to us. He hurt us, and especially you. That's not what a dad or husband is supposed to do. He's supposed to be like Patch, Timber, and the others."

Cassie and Ash both nod their heads.

"Me too, Mama. The other daddies hugged the kids and kissed them goodbye and when they came to pick them up after preschool. The only time he came to get us was when he'd hurt you," Cassie tells us.

"You know I started questioning things when I was five. I hated calling him 'Dad' but I knew if I didn't that, he'd just hurt me," Ash says, his voice quiet but with a current of anger underneath. "Dads are supposed to love you, protect you, provide for you, and play with you. I want Patch to be our dad, Mom. He stayed with you when you were in the hospital. Stephan never did that except for the time it took to make sure they believed his lies.

"Today, Patch has always been at your side or if he wasn't, he was either watching over you or us. He played with us, held Cassie as she slept, and listened to us. *Really* listened to us. He even told Ash that they could talk to the vet in town to see if that's really what he wanted to be when he grows up. Please, Mom. I heard him tell you he loves you. Please, can Patch be our dad, Mom?" Isaiah begs and damn does it feel like my heart's beating out of my chest.

Mary sniffles and a few tears of my own escape at Isaiah's words. All three of them are staring hopefully up at Mary and it feels like all the air has been stolen from the room as I wait for her response. I want nothing more than to take all four of them in my arms, but I need to wait for her to make that decision.

She tries to slip off her sling, but struggles with the clasp, so I reach up and help her slip off the sling. I watch her careful movements, making sure she isn't pushing herself too much, as she pulls each of them into her arms, hugging them tight and kissing them. Cupping Isaiah's cheek, she gives him a watery smile. Glancing around, I'm relieved to see that Mae and Timber stepped out for this to give us some privacy.

"I love Patch, too, and I'll be forever grateful for what he and the club have done for us. However, we have to do things in order before I can be with Patch. The first thing is that I have to divorce Stephan, which I've already submitted the paperwork to start the process."

"What's di-divorce mean?" Cassie asks as she carefully climbs up into Mary's lap.

"It means that once it's signed, Stephan and I won't be married anymore. I'll be free from him and be able to choose who I want to be with."

Mary's gaze comes up to mine and the love radiating in them cements everything. The previous hesitation I'd seen in her eyes toward me is completely gone.

I've got my Siren back.

Now to just get Stephan to sign the papers and either make sure he's taking a dirt nap or locked up for the rest of his life. Though, I'd prefer the first one so that there's no chance of him getting out again to come after them. Cassie's voice brings me out of my thoughts, and I look down at her.

"But why did you marry him? He's a bad man and you've told us we have to stay away from bad men," she asks, confusion apparent on her face.

Worried, I look up at Mary and can practically feel the wheels turning in her head on how to explain what happened nine years ago.

"Come here, kiddos," I tell them as I hold open my arms. Cassie slides down off Mary's lap and then all three of them hug me tight as I wrap my arms around them. Looking up at Mary, I cock my eyebrow in question, and thankfully, she gives me a slight nod. I'm not going to make her go through this alone.

"Your mom and I have been friends since we were in fifth grade. When we were in high school, we started dating and I had even planned to ask her to marry me after we graduated high school. But then, she was kidnapped and taken away a little over a month before graduation. She was forced to marry Stephan; it wasn't her choice. I looked for her for all these years and some of my friends and family helped me look for her as well. I never stopped looking. Almost every spare moment I had I spent chasing leads. I got close, really close, three times, but by the time I got to your house, you were all gone. I love your mom and I love all three of you."

All three of their eyes mist over and Cassie's little lip starts quivering. The sight breaks my heart. I wish I was able to get them away from him sooner, but I can't change the past.

"Honest?" she asks, and I nod.

"Completely honest, Angel."

"Do you know who kidnapped her?" Ash asks and I pause trying to figure out how much to say.

"We know the identity of some of them, but the cops and us are still trying to find them. They've gone into hiding, so it's hard for us to track them down."

All three of them are silent for a bit and I pray they don't ask more questions on the identities of who kidnapped Mary. I don't want to have to get into that can of worms right now if I don't have to.

After a few moments, Cassie's little hand fists my shirt as she looks up at me hesitantly. "Can we call you 'Dad', too? Like Ash does?"

My breath hitches and I turn toward Mary. "That's up to your mom, Angel. But if it's okay with her, it's more than okay with me."

Cassie turns in my arms and the boys mirror the movement. "Mama?"

Mary wipes her cheeks and reaches for me. I entwine my fingers with hers and she gives the kids a wide but watery smile. "It's more than okay with me. The only two things I don't regret about being with Stephan are you two. I just wish Patch was your dad from the beginning."

So do I, Siren. So do I.

After a few moments, Ash tugs on my cut. "Can I show you my room now?"

Smiling, I nod. "You betcha."

The kids slide off my lap and I move to lift Mary, grabbing her sling as well. When she's in my arms, she winds her arm around my neck and buries her head in it.

"Thank you," she whispers before kissing my neck.

Goosebumps erupt on my skin as a shiver of need skates down my spine. "Always, Siren. Like I said before, I'm here for the long haul and will help support you in any way I can."

Kissing the crown of her head, I follow the kids as they giggle happily, the previous dark cloud that was over them when we were talking about Stephan seeming to have dissipated completely. Setting Mary down on Ash's bed, I look around at all the animals that are on the wall. Puppies, cats, and a few zoo animals as well decorate half the room. The other half is decorated in cars and motorcycles. His room has its own attached bathroom.

Looking at his bed closer, emotion clogs my throat when I see his bedspread decked out in medical gear.

"I think I get it from you, Dad. Only instead of helping people, I want to help animals," Ash says as he leans against my side and wraps his arms around my waist.

Not trusting my voice, I wrap my arm around his shoulders, hugging him into my side.

Chapter 37
Patch

TEN MINUTES LATER, THE kids are tucked in and more than a few tears fell when all three of them kissed my cheek and called me 'dad' as they wished us good night.

Carrying Mary downstairs, I head into her bedroom and set her down on the bed. Cupping her cheek, I kneel in front of her and notice her unfocused eyes. "How are you feeling, Mary? Where's your head at?"

She blinks a few times and tears pool in her eyes. "I tried so hard to shield them from his darkness, but they still saw it. Saw more of it than I ever wanted them to see. I don't want what he did to taint them for the rest of their lives."

Tears roll down her cheeks and I stand, scooping her up in my arms before sitting down with her in my lap. She turns, burying her face in my shirt as she sobs. Holding her tightly, I run a hand up and down her back, trying to give her as much comfort as I can.

After a few minutes, I feel her body sag and I kiss the top of her head.

"Feel a little better?"

She nods as she sniffles before pulling back to look at me. "Yeah, surprisingly, I do."

Tucking a lock of hair behind her ear, I kiss her forehead. "Let's get you ready for bed. I bet you're probably drained and needing a pain pill."

She nods and I kiss her one more time before setting her back down on the bed. Walking over to the sofa, I pick up her duffle bag and bring it over to her. "Do you need help changing? I could help you or I can see if Mae is still up? Or I can step out if you'd prefer."

A gorgeous blush stains her cheeks and she shakes her head. "You can stay. I might need help with my pants and getting them over my cast, but," she pauses and her blush darkens as a shy look comes over her face before gesturing to her body. "I'm not the same as I was when I was eighteen. My body, I mean. I'm heavier and have stretch marks. For some reason, I had a hard time losing the baby weight after each of the kids' births. I—"

I cut her off by placing a finger against her lips and capture her good hand in mine, which is still gesturing to her body. "No more of that. I don't want to hear any more about you putting yourself down. If you haven't noticed, the extra weight doesn't bother me. In fact, it's a turn on for me."

Taking a chance, I take her hand and place it over me. Her eyes widen when she feels how hard I am for her through my jeans.

"And your stretch marks are proof of you bringing three babies that I love into the world. I could never hate them. I love everything about you, Mary Elizabeth Catarino. Every freckle, your gorgeous curves, your stretch marks, your eyes, but most importantly, I love your heart."

Her hands fist in my shirt, pulling me down, and she crashes her lips on mine.

Instantly, the kiss turns heated and desperate. Emotions from nine years of not having my Siren in my arms come pouring out. Mary whimpers as she tugs on my hair and I growl into her mouth, needing her taste like I need my next breath.

A sharp hiss breaks through my lust filled fog and I back off, softening the kiss before pulling back. Mary whimpers again, and fuck do I wish we could keep going, but I won't hurt her.

"You're still recovering, Mary, and I refuse to cause you pain."

She licks her lips and her eyes glint mischievously. "There are some things that we can do that won't cause any pain."

Groaning, I rest my forehead against hers. "Siren..."

"Make me cum, Luke. Please. You were the last person that made me cum, and I desperately need it."

Well, *fuck.* I can't really say no to that. However, a part of me is secretly in love with the fact that no other man has brought her that pleasure but me.

"Then you best be getting undressed, Siren. Grab a pillow because I'm going to make you scream and I don't want the kids to hear you."

Her blue eyes darken and she bites her lip. Reaching up, I rub my thumb across her bottom lip, caressing it and her pupils dilate even more.

"You know what nibbling on your lip does to me, Siren."

She nods and then the little minx darts her tongue out, licking my thumb. A shiver works its way down me and I pull back, slipping off my cut and laying it over the arm of the sofa. Reaching behind me, I grab the back of my shirt and yank it over my head. Her hands, which were starting to lift her shirt, pause as she stares at me.

Smirking, I shake my head slightly. "Eyes up here, Siren, and keep undressing."

My fingers itch to rip her shirt off myself, but I just barely resist, knowing she needs to figure out her limits with her shoulder while it's still healing. She struggles a little, but right as I'm about to step in, she gets it off.

I lick my lips as her olive skin is exposed, but I can't bite back my groan when she slowly slides the straps of her bra down her arms. She holds the cups of her bra, keeping it in place and denying me access to her breasts. Fuck, I wonder if they are still as pink as they used to be.

"You're killing me here, Siren," I grit out, just barely keeping my body from launching myself at her. As much as she needs this, I do, too. I can't even begin to describe how much I've longed to have her sweet body under mine again.

With a coy smile, she unclasps the front of her bra, and fuck if the sight doesn't make my mouth water as she slowly reveals her gorgeous breasts. I groan when I notice her nipples are still pink, though they are a bit of a darker shade than they used to be.

Not being able to stand it anymore, I step forward and cup her heavy breasts in my hands before taking a nipple in my mouth. Her back arches as she pushes her chest forward and I take her cue, licking and nibbling her breast while tweaking the other with my fingers.

After a few moments, I switch breasts, and she gasps when I nibble on her nipple. Her hands tighten in my hair as they tug slightly. Her body trembles, and I moan, loving that her breasts are still as sensitive as they used to be. Making up my mind to wring a few orgasms out of her tonight, I softly bite down and instantly she shatters in my arms. Her hands fly up to her mouth, muffling her moans and cries.

When the aftershocks subside, I pull back and hook my fingers in the waistband of her leggings. Well, I'm not sure they're called leggings exactly. They're stretchy black pants, but instead of hugging her legs the entire way down to her ankle, they're sort of loose, which is perfect for getting her legs in and out of the cast a bit easier.

Blinking through her post orgasm haze, it takes Mary a moment before she realizes what I'm doing and she shifts, allowing me to lower her pants and underwear at the same time before sliding off her socks and slip on shoe.

Having my Siren laid out bare in front of me has my cock hardening even further in my jeans, and I rearrange myself, groaning when she licks her lips at the sight.

"Come here," she tells me, her voice husky with need.

I shake my head. "This is about you, Siren. I can wait."

This time it's her that shakes her head. "Nope, get your sexy ass over here so I can put my mouth on you. I've been dreaming of having you come down my throat for years and I will not be denied, Sexy."

"Sexy, huh?"

She smirks saucily at me and makes a come-hither gesture at me. I walk forward but make no move to undo my jeans. At least not yet.

"Yes, Sexy." Her hands go to my belt, but I capture them.

"Siren, I don't want to come just yet. I want to milk a few more out of you and then, and only then, can you put your hands and mouth on my dick. Are we clear?"

She pouts, sticking out her bottom lip, and I take the opportunity to lean down, nip it and suck it into my mouth. She moans and I swallow the rest of her moans as my fingers trace down her delicate neck, teasing along her collarbone before sneaking down and tweaking her nipple. She arches into me as she winds her arm around my neck, and I gently guide her back on the bed. Pulling back, I snag a pillow and put it under her head and move between her legs.

"Snag another pillow, Siren."

That's the only warning I give her before I lean down and suck her clit into my mouth as I spread her lips with my fingers. I'm honestly surprised that she's shaved except for a small patch above her pussy. As soon as that thought enters my mind, I force it from my mind, not wanting to think about *why* she kept up this level of grooming. I seriously hope that it was because of her own choice and not anything else.

Redoubling my efforts, I flatten my tongue, licking from practically ass to clit before spearing it and fucking her with my tongue. Her hands slide into my hair and she tugs on the strands.

"Oh, fuck! Yes, Luke, yes!" she whisper cries as her hips buck up.

Withdrawing, I replace my tongue with my fingers as I tease her clit. Curling my fingers, I instinctively tilt them slightly and like a rocket, she goes off again, gushing over my fingers. Moaning, I remove my fingers, lapping up her juices. When her tremors have mostly subsided, I slip in my fingers again.

"Fuck, yes, right here," she pants as she tries to catch her breath.

Her hips jerk and she pulls harder on my hair as she grinds on my face.

She's so tight, I don't dare add another finger yet. Continuing to finger fuck her, I redouble my onslaught on her clit with my tongue, needing to bring her at least two more times before I let her anywhere close to my dick. With how hard I am, and feeling the wet spot in my boxers, I have no doubt I won't last long once she puts her mouth on me.

"Harder, please Luke, harder. I'm so close," she cries.

Sucking on her clit, I lightly nibble on it and her pussy clamps down on my fingers as she cries out into the pillow. The trembling in her legs lessens, but it's still there slightly. Using my other hand, I take some of the juices on my finger and snake my hand under her ass and press against her hole. She moans deeply, a low, guttural sound as she pushes against my finger, increasing the pressure against her hole. She grinds against both of my hands, the motions almost like she's not sure which one she wants more pleasure from—the hand that's pleasuring her pussy and clit or the one that's teasing her ass.

"Sometime, I'm going to take this sweet, juicy ass and redden these cheeks with my handprints as I take you. Would you like that, Siren? Maybe I'll take you while also fucking your pussy with a dildo. Make you come so hard you see stars."

"Yes, I want that, oh fuck," she hisses out as her hips grind into my hands harder and my finger slips past the ring of muscle. The trembling in her thighs increases, and I speed up, thrusting into her pussy and her ass in unison.

Her hand tightens in my hair as she cries out once again into the pillow. Her legs lay limp on the bed as she pants and then hisses as I lick her pussy, making sure to get the last of her juices.

"Too sensitive," she says between pants.

Kissing my way up her body, we both moan when I finally get my lips on hers and she pulls me flush onto her body. Using my elbows, I try to keep my weight off her because of her injuries. After a few moments. I roll us so that she's laying on her left side.

"Please, Luke. Let me have you."

Her hands snake down my torso leaving goosebumps in her wake. She pouts when I pull back and slide off the bed until she sees me undoing my belt. Her eyes darken and she licks her lips. Toeing off my boots, I shed the rest of my clothes. Squeezing the base of my cock hard, I groan when she licks her lips again.

"Sit on the side of the bed, Siren," I tell her before grabbing the shirt I wore earlier. Walking over to the couch, I lay the shirt down on the cushion before crossing the short distance back to Mary. Lifting her up, I walk back over to the couch and set her down. The position puts her about the right height as my waist.

Grasping my cock, I line it up with her pouty lips that she parts and groan when her lips wrap around me.

"Fuck, Siren," I hiss as she grasps my hips, and takes as much of me into her mouth as she can.

My hands sink into her hair, holding it back and away from her face as she sucks me. Feeling her hand massaging my balls, I widen my stance a little and moan when she tugs slightly. The tingles that were at the base of my spine earlier increase and I know I'm not going to last much longer, especially since it's been so long since my Siren's touched me like this.

"That's it, Siren. Suck my cock and massage my balls."

She redoubles her efforts, bobbing on my cock faster as she hollows her cheeks. Her other hand comes up, grasping onto the base of my shaft and pumps as she continues to swallow my cock. A moment later, she once again takes me as far as she can and then my little minx swallows, triggering my orgasm, and I shoot ropes down her throat. Mary swallows it all and then licks my shaft to make sure she got it all.

Cupping her jaw, I pull out of her mouth and lean down, kissing her, not caring that I can taste myself on her tongue.

After a few moments, I pull back. "I love you, Siren."

She smiles up at me as she places her hand against mine, which is still cupping her jaw. “I love you, too, Luke.”

Giving her one more quick kiss, I pull back. “Be right back.”

Heading into her bathroom, I rummage through the cupboards until I find a couple of wash cloths. Wetting them both, I clean myself off, and then head into the bedroom to clean Mary up.

“Do you need to use the bathroom at all before we head to bed?”

She shakes her head, her eyes already drooping.

Tossing the washcloths in the hamper, I pull on my boxers and rummage around in Mary’s bag for her pills. Thankfully someone, probably Mae, had left some water bottles on the nightstand so I don’t need to head out to the kitchen. Grabbing one, I crack the seal and then hand it to Mary along with her pill.

“What do you want to wear to bed?”

She scrunches up her nose as she thinks and she looks so fucking adorable that I have to fight to not lean down and kiss her again.

“Mae said she bought me a sleep shirt and some shorts that she put in the bag.”

Rummaging in her bag, I find the items and help her into them before pulling back the covers on the bed. Lifting her from the couch, I lay her down in bed, but she grabs my arm as I pull away.

“Sleep next to me?”

Indecision wars in me. What if her kids barge in here? What will they think if they see me sleeping with her?

“The kids won’t care. They asked you to be their dad, Luke. If they see us lying in bed together, that will probably only cement the fact that we want to be together after everything with *him* is done.”

Pressing a quick kiss to her lips, I nod. Pulling back, I pick up our clothes off the floor before putting them in the hamper. Shutting off the light, I crawl under the covers next to her. Pulling her close, she snuggles into my arms and I inhale her scent. It hits me then that it’s similar to the scent that she used to wear back in high school. Some sort of cherry blossom scent.

As Mary settles in my arms, I close my eyes, thanking every deity that my Siren is back in my arms again.

Chapter 38
Mary

A WEEK LATER, I still can't believe the changes my life has taken.

I'm no longer under Stephan's thumb.

The kids' attitudes, moods, and even their grades have improved since coming to live here on the compound. With the help of Sam, we got the school principal to agree, though it was more of a begrudging agreement, to let Ash and Isaiah attend school virtually. For Cassie, since she's in preschool, her teachers are just emailing me her assignments daily and then giving me things to work on with her throughout the day. Luke and the club made sure we had everything we needed to ensure the kids were able to do their assignments which had started a whole 'nother round of waterworks when they surprised me everything.

The kids are also thriving beyond just school with having positive male role models around them all the time. They all started calling Luke 'Dad' or 'Daddy' that first night after our heavy conversation. I know he told me he loved all three of them, but I won't lie, a part of me worried he'd treat Cassie and Isaiah differently than Asher. I should have known better. He treats all three of them like they're his own flesh and blood, and they love spending time with him, especially Cassie. I often find her curled up in his arms, and it's pretty obvious that she has him wrapped around her little pinky.

The kids were beyond happy when they found out Luke had taken three weeks of vacation time to help us while we were getting settled in. I know they'll be bummed when he has to go back to work next week Monday, but Ash was the one that was finally able to get through to Cassie. *'Dad's a nurse in the ER, Cassie. People need him there so that he can help them get better. Maybe even save their lives.'* To say I was proud of him is an understatement, and while I know Cassie was still disappointed, she said she understood.

Yesterday, which was Saturday, the Junction Creek chapter arrived for the joint club Thanksgiving celebration. The kids were in heaven being able to play with more people and, in turn, to have them fawn over and pay attention to the three of them.

Isaiah got more than a few looks of approval as he, Judge, Drae, Punisher, and Devil all talked about engines, motorcycles, and cars for a few hours. I do believe he'll end up as a mechanic in one of their garages the way things are looking and by overhearing snippets of their conversations. Ash was pretty reserved, but he did talk with Doc and Luke a lot, and when Brady and Sam stopped out for a bit, he talked to them as well. When Cassie had overheard that Mama Astrid and Odin hadn't come over because she was sick, she was bummed. Apparently, when the kids were staying with Mae and Timber while I was in the hospital, Mae had told her a lot about Mama Astrid, and she was excited to meet her in person.

Thankfully, Mae pulled out her phone and let Cassie do a video chat with Mama Astrid. From their familiarity, I almost asked if they'd done this before, but I bit my tongue, not wanting to ask the question while Cassie was excitedly chattering away. Instead, I held the phone for her so Cassie could show Mama Astrid her new dress and shoes. She twirled, her little curls dancing with every move, and I swear Mama Astrid fell in love with my little girl.

And, judging by a lot of looks, I'd say if anyone ever messed with my baby, the ladies and men of both clubs will be getting their guns and knives out to be at her back. Which will make dating very interesting when she's older.

While I knew Levi and Mae told me they had brothers in the club, it was still surprising to see the guys dote on them so much. Though, when Levi had had enough and threatened to put a blade into the next one that treated her like she was made of glass, I barely suppressed my laughter at seeing all of the guys' faces pale momentarily. Even now, the memory has a laugh threatening to escape, but I bite it down because today isn't really a laughing sort of day.

Yesterday, the guys also surprised me by offering to help move any furniture or things I wanted from **πατέρα** (dads) house to the condo. The rest I decided I'll put into storage for now. Some we'll use later when we build a house, and other pieces, I'll donate to whoever needs them in the club.

Then this morning after breakfast, guys from both clubs helped us move our things from Mae and Timber's house into the condo they are letting us use. The kids were beyond ecstatic when Luke moved some of his things into the condo as well.

The club's, both clubs', support for my kids and me still surprises me, and I go to bed each night, thankful for Luke coming back into my life.

Right now, though, we're on our way over to **πατέρα** (dads) house, and nerves are swirling in my stomach. While they haven't said anything, to me at least, I know everyone in the club is on edge, not knowing if Stephan or his cop buddies will try anything like before. Luke is driving me in his truck, and Levi's sister Sasha, who is one of the club's Prospects, is driving Levi's SUV with Levi and Mae safely secured in the back seat. Three of the other Prospects, Alexei, Ethan, and Colt, are driving large rental vans to move everything. Men from both clubs are in front and behind each of the vehicles as we caravan through town.

I haven't even seen our house since that fateful night, and even though we've been living in Forest Creek since March, I've purposefully never driven by it, even if it meant taking a longer route. My chest tightens as I remember the conversation Luke, **γιαγιά** (grandma), **παππούς** (grandpa), and I had two days after we arrived at the clubhouse.

*"***Λουλούδι μου** (My flower)*, we would like to discuss something with you and Luke,"* **γιαγιά** (grandma) *tells me as she sits down at the table in Mae and Timber's house.* **Παππούς** (Grandpa) *sits down beside her a moment later.*

My breath catches in my chest, and I just know this is it.

This is the decision I'd been dreading to say aloud but had already known my answer when Luke told me what he'd done. I just don't know if I'll be able to vocalize my thoughts without breaking down. Arms snake around my upper body from behind, and I'm wrapped in Luke's familiar cedarwood and leather scent. I lean back, resting my head on his shoulder as I try to calm my racing heart.

"It'll be alright, Siren. If you aren't ready, you aren't ready. I'll support you whichever way you choose."

Some of my panic eases at his words and I lean down slightly, placing a kiss on his arm. "Thank you."

Luke releases me and I wheel over to the table. He walks further into the kitchen and returns with water bottles for all of us.

"With the condo almost done, we were wondering if you wanted to use any of the furniture at your old house? After... that night," **γιαγιά** (grandma) *says as she pauses, blinking rapidly to keep her tears from falling.*

Emotion clogs my throat as I do the same thing. If I start crying now, I don't know when I'll stop. **Παππούς** (Grandpa) *takes her hand in his, squeezing tightly.*

Γιαγιά (Grandma) *clears her throat. "After that night, we took some family heirloom pieces to store at our house just in case someone did manage to break in. We can bring them after you move in if you'd like. I also took the photo albums and your cookbooks to store as well as anything else I knew would crush you if it was damaged or destroyed."*

I swallow thickly, and despite my best efforts, a couple of tears escape. "Thank you," I whisper hoarsely as I wipe away the tears. "I would definitely like the photo albums and cookbooks back. But without knowing what all else you took for safekeeping; I don't know if it's something we should take back or not."

I chew on my lip as my mind races. Looking down, I pick at my nails as I try to sort out my jumbled thoughts and emotions. I don't know if I'm the best person for the family heirlooms to go to with everything that's going on. Also, I haven't heard from any of my other family members. Do they even consider me part of their family anymore?

Γιαγιά (Grandma) *tsks, and I look up at her. "Why shouldn't you take them back? You're our* **εγγονή** (granddaughter). *Those family heirlooms are as much yours as they were our Nikos'."*

"But what would the others think if I took them? Wouldn't they be mad?"

Γιαγιά (Grandma) *reaches over and takes my hand in hers. "***Λουλούδι μου** (My flower), *you needn't worry about that. They all care for you and are chomping at the bit to descend on you en masse. The only reason they haven't yet is because the three of us asked them not to so that you would have time to adjust, process, and heal after everything you've been through. You know as much as I do that when* everyone *gets together, it can be overwhelming. In fact, a lot of times 'overwhelming' is an understatement," she says with a chuckle, which I can't help but chuckle in agreement.*

"I'm sorry, Siren. I didn't realize you'd take the fact that they hadn't reached out as a sign that they didn't want you in their family anymore. Like **γιαγιά** (grandma) *said, we were trying not to overwhelm you with a lot of things and changes at once." Luke's dejected face and tone has even more tension bleeding out of me.*

My family didn't abandon me.

Sighing, my shoulders slump and I pick at my nails again as I berate myself internally. I should have known better, but Stephan's voice won out in my head, even though I shouldn't have let him. When will I stop hearing his voice? When will I stop hearing the lies he whispers in my ear whenever someone says or does something, or hell, doesn't do something? When will it stop? Will it always be like this for the rest of my life?

Rough hands encase mine, and I blink as I come out of my thoughts and look up.

"Hey, what went through your head just now, Siren?"

Swallowing, I shake my head as I look away and lower my gaze. I don't want him to know what I was really thinking. I don't want to give voice to those thoughts, fears, and pain.

*"Maria and Harris, can you please give us a few minutes?" Luke asks, and I look up sharply at the hardness in his voice. Not to mention that he said their real names instead of '***γιαγιά και παππούς** (grandma and grandpa)' *like he normally does. They both get up without a word, and despite knowing that he'd never hurt me, I can't stop sinking in on myself.*

"Siren, please talk to me. I can't help you if I don't know what's going through your head, though I have a pretty good idea based on how you shrunk in on yourself and the sparkle in your eyes disappeared. Please, Siren. Let me help you. You don't have to carry that burden alone anymore."

Tears prick my eyes and I swallow the lump in my throat as I shake my head and lower my gaze, staring at his chest. If I looked into his eyes, I might crack. "No. I don't want to give voice to those thoughts. If I do, then it'll be even worse." My voice is barely a whisper, but I know he heard me because of how his muscles tense at my words.

He reaches out, grasping my chin and makes me look up at him. I try to advert my eyes, but they snap back to his as a growl emanates from his chest. "I will never judge you for your thoughts. You matter. Your thoughts matter. Your voice matters.

You are safe with me, Mary. Now, please. Tell me what went through your head a moment ago."

Tears well in my eyes and I bite back a sob that tries to escape. Taking a shuddery breath, I prepare myself for his reaction. Once he realizes how messed up in the head I am because of Stephan, this might be what pushes him over the edge and away from us.

"You don't know the depths of what he did and said to shatter me and beat me down as much as possible. I never fully broke or submitted to him, but I came close too many times to count. As much as I don't want to, I keep hearing all the lies he's spewed over the years. I try not to listen to them, I really do try, but sometimes I can't help it. I don't know how to stop his voice from invading my thoughts. I knew my family would never abandon me, but I let his lies make me think they did. How do I make them stop? How long will I be hearing his voice whispering in my ear about every little thing someone says, does, or doesn't do? How do I make them stop? Why won't they stop?"

A sob rips out of my throat and this time, I can't stop the tears from falling. Immediately, I'm wrapped in his arms. A moment later, he shifts and I feel his arm sliding under my knees as he picks me up and sets me down on his lap. Once again, shame rolls through me at my weight, even though he seems to not have any problem lifting or carrying me despite the number on the scale. His *voice slithers through my mind that I might be crushing him because of my fat ass, but I force them back. Turning slightly, I bury my face in the crook of his neck as another sob breaks free and more fat tears roll down my cheeks like a current.*

After a few minutes, my tears ease, though a few still escape. God, all it seems like I do lately is cry. Why is that?

"I think that's a good thing, Siren. You haven't been allowed to grieve, to decompress, and let things go before now. Honestly, I'd be more concerned if you didn't cry."

A groan escapes. I hadn't meant to say that aloud.

"I'm sorry."

He kisses my shoulder and hugs me tighter. "You have no reason to be sorry. The one that should be sorry is that jackass. Together we'll beat his lies back, but you gotta let me in so I can help you. It will take a while, maybe even years, but you'll get there someday. And if you want to see someone to help you through this, we'll find someone for you to talk to."

My chest warms at his words and I shove my previous worry of Luke walking away from us to the back of my mind. I need to relearn to trust him. To trust that someone else is there to help and support me. Maybe later, I should use the journals the ladies gave me. I don't quite feel like I want to tell someone else everything *that Stephan's done to me, plus, I'm not sure how that would all work with so many cases being brought against him.*

After a few moments, I pull back and wipe my face. He hands me a napkin, which I happily take and blow my nose.

"While we're alone, there's something else I want to talk to you about and it's along these lines." He pauses, grasps my chin and makes sure I'm looking at him. "Siren, you need to get rid of that mask you wear to hide your pain. If you aren't ready to fully let it go, then at least don't hide your pain with me. Please, Siren. Let me in and let me help you. You are not alone anymore. I'm here. Lean on me."

My breath hitches and tears prick my eyes again at the amount of love shining out of his eyes. Directed at me. Me. *The woman who has been beaten down more times than I can count. That he loves me, despite what I've been through because of Stephan, and that he loves my children as if they were his own. Is this finally my happily ever after? Like in all the books I used to read as a kid and teenager? That I found someone who loves me for me despite being cracked and bent because of my past?*

Shaking myself internally and refocusing on what he'd just said, I nod as I swallow thickly. "I'll try, but please understand that it'll take some time to get used to it. Please don't get mad if I don't even realize I'm wearing the mask. After nine years, it's become my default, so to speak."

He reaches up, running a thumb under my eye and wiping away another tear that had escaped. He cups my cheek and I close my eyes as I lean into his touch.

"Of course. And if I ever do get mad, please know it isn't directed at you, Siren. It's at that fucker that did this to you."

He leans forward, pressing a chaste kiss to my lips before resting his forehead against mine. We sit like that for a few minutes and the more I relax against him, the more I feel the weight that was usually on my shoulders lifting.

Someone clears their throat and I jump slightly, looking over my shoulder. Both of my grandparents are standing at the other edge of the kitchen and living room, wrapped in each other's arms, their eyes misty with unshed tears. A sliver of worry runs through me, and I really hope they didn't hear all of that.

"Is it alright to come back in? There's one other thing we'd like to discuss," **παπποὺς** (grandpa) *says and my stomach tightens.*

"Yeah, you can come back in," Luke replies. He presses a kiss to my forehead and as they retake their seats, he repositions me slightly on his lap so I don't have to strain my neck so much to look at them.

*"***Λουλούδι μου** (My flower), *I know this is hard and it's okay if you haven't decided yet, but we were wondering if you wanted to keep your old house or sell it?"*

My breath hitches again and my stomach tightens. Black dots dance across my vision as the memory of **πατέρα** (dads) *body splayed out on our living room floor, lying in a growing pool of blood. Diego's words circle through my mind.*

My body shifts and then hands grasp my cheeks.

"Mary, Babe, I need you to take a deep breath, hold it, and then release it. You need to slow down your breathing, otherwise you might hyperventilate and pass out. Focus on my chest. Breathe with me, Mary."

Sucking in a large breath, I do as he says, even though it's hard as hell to concentrate with my mind going a million miles a second and my body tingling from the memories. After a few moments of breathing with Luke, my body sags against his.

"Sell," I whisper as I close my eyes, my heart breaking that I'll lose this last connection to **πατέρας** (dad). *"I want to sell our house." I don't think I'd ever be able to sleep a night there without nightmares plaguing me. Nor do I think I'd ever be able to be alone in the house without having a panic attack.*

Things shifted between Luke and me after that conversation. While I still struggle from time to time, I do my best to not hide anything from him. It's hard, *really hard*, after wearing a mask for nine years. A mask that hid all the emotions, hate, anger, pain, everything. I had to shut myself down in order to survive living with Stephan. The only times I had let that mask slightly slip was when he wasn't home, and it was just the kids and me. Granted, I kept most things masked around them, but those were the only times I was able to be a sliver of my true self.

A rough hand grasps mine, bringing me out of my thoughts, and I look over at Luke. "It'll be okay, Siren. We'll be with you the entire time and your grandma and a few of your aunts as well as Sasha and the Old Ladies came today to help pack and wrap everything up. I'm sure you'd rather not have a bunch of bikers trying to be gentle with all those tchotchkes, trinkets, and knickknacks you used to collect."

His distraction works and a chuckle escapes at the image of Bear, who I think has the largest hands I've ever seen, trying to delicately handle some of the more intricate figurines I'd bought at the fair the summer before my senior year. "No, I really don't want them to handle those items."

Taking a deep breath, I think about meeting my **θείες** (aunts)—Catherine, Selena, and Sofia—again after so long. Knowing them, we're all going to be in a hug pile for a few minutes as they cry and then they'll fuss over me. Or at least that's what happened in the past whenever anyone was injured, had surgery, or had a baby.

"What's got you gnawing on that lip so badly it looks like it might bleed?"

At his words, I release my lip, not realizing I'd been biting it. Flipping down the visor, I wince when I see how badly it looks. "I didn't even realize I was doing it," I tell him as I reach into my pocket and put on some lip balm. Sighing, I shake my head. "I'm just worried about seeing my **θείες** (aunts) again. What they'll think when they learn what happened. If they'll really treat me the same as before or if I'll be on the sidelines looking in."

Luke lifts my hand and kisses the back of it. "Trust me on this, Siren. They still love you and have missed you dearly. In fact, I think they may even be with us in wanting to make Stephan and anyone else that hurt you pay for what they did to you and the kids. Hell, I could see **θεία** (aunt) Catherine brandishing her kitchen blades and going after him herself."

Another chuckle slips out at the mental image, and soon, laughter pours out of me. I can totally see her doing that, but she wouldn't be alone. My other **θείες και θείοι** (aunts and uncles) would be right behind her. Though, my **θείο** (uncles) would have their guns rather than kitchen knives.

My gaze snags on the bikes in front of me as we round another corner, and I nervously lick my lips. "I'm sorry."

Luke shoots me a confused look before focusing back on the road. "What for?"

"If it weren't for my injuries, you'd be out there riding with them. Who knows when we're gonna get snow and then you'll have to wait for spring."

His hand tightens on mine and I sheepishly look over at him. He pins me with a hard look before looking back at the road.

"Mary, I would take riding in a cage the rest of my life if it meant always riding with you. Could I have had a Prospect drive you? Yeah, I could have, but I wanted to be the one driving you. I will always choose you, Mary. Always."

My heart beats frantically at the amount of love I see in his eyes, and I smile as my worries melt away.

Turning forward, my smile slips as we round the corner to the street I used to live on. My gaze automatically zeros in on my old house and stays there. In particular, the living room window. Luke parks in the driveway, but I make no move to unbuckle as I stare at our living room window. Memories threaten to bombard me, but I need to do this.

Taking a deep breath, I nod, more to myself than anything. "I can do this. I can do this," I whisper to myself as I unbuckle the seat belt. Luke squeezes my hand and then he climbs out before rounding the hood and opening my door. He tosses the keys to someone behind us, and I look over my shoulder to see Alexei and Ethan unloading my chair out of the back of the truck.

"Park my truck on the street and then you guys can back in two of the vans."

Alexei catches his keys and when they have my chair unloaded, Luke picks me up and sets me inside it. Alexei shuts my door and moments later, he slides in behind the wheel, waiting till we're out of the way before doing as Luke said. Shit, I need to remember to call him Patch now that we're around the club again. That's another thing I'm struggling to remember, but it's getting better.

"How about we go in through the garage?" he suggests, and I nod silently as I wheel into the garage, only taking my gaze off the living room window when I can no longer see it.

My chest warms when I notice a ramp has already been set up for me and I ride up it into our old mudroom. Then, my breath hitches when the space which normally held **πατέρα** (dads) shoes and coats is empty.

"We packed up some things when Brady and I stayed here when the house was released back to us from the cops in case anyone tried to break in. Neither of us stayed in your dad's room, but we put his things that were down here in his room. Brady took the spare room, and I took your room."

Continuing down the hallway, the ball of nerves in my stomach grows when I can hear my **θείες** (aunts) and **γιαγιά** talking in Greek and then my stomach grumbles when I smell the delicious scents coming from the kitchen. Chuckling softly, I shake my head. I should have known they'd have food made up for today.

As I round the corner, their talking stops when they see me. Wheeling further into the room, I stop about halfway between the table and the kitchen counter. I purposefully don't look toward the living room for fear that I'll have another panic attack.

Patch rests his hand on my shoulder, giving me a slight squeeze. My **θεία** (aunt) Catherine is the first to break out of her shock and tears well in her eyes as she wipes her hands on a towel that's hanging from the string of her apron that's wrapped around her waist.

"Oh, Mary, **το γλυκό λουλούδι του τίτλου μας** (our sweet little flower)," she says as she rushes forward and wraps her arms around me.

Seconds later, I feel the rest of their arms wrap around us, and their murmured words of love and support have the dam, once again, breaking in me.

It feels like hours pass, but has probably only been a couple of minutes, when they pull back and we all dry our eyes. Looking around, I'm relieved when I see Patch standing back in the hallway, and I know he's kept the others out to allow us these few minutes alone.

Once again, my heart warms at his gesture, knowing what I needed without me even having to say anything. I know I probably sound like a million broken records by now, but God, I'm so lucky to have found him again.

Chapter 39

Mary

I FOLLOW MY ΘΕΊΕΣ (aunts) and **γιαγιά** (grandma) into the kitchen, my mouth watering from all of the amazing smells.

"Luke, **εγγονός** (grandson), go tell the others to get their heinies in here. Lunch is ready and I want them to have full bellies so they have the energy to move everything. There are extra tables and chairs in the garage that they can bring in with them and set up. And remind those men that there will be no boots on in this house," **γιαγιά** (grandma) calls over her shoulder and I can't hold in my chuckle at the shocked look on his face at her calling him her grandson.

Though the heated look he gives me when he turns my way has me trying not to squirm and rub my legs together. While we haven't had sex yet, we have had plenty of make out sessions every night since that first night we arrived at the compound.

"Will do, **γιαγιά** (grandma)," he says and then he spears me with one more heated look before turning and walking down the hallway. I quickly look away and will my cheeks to cool down. Women in my family aren't very sexual, especially around groups of people. I don't always agree with that myself, but that could be because I didn't grow up in as close knit of a community like the rest of my family. That and **πατέρας** (dad) really tried to let me express myself how I wanted to, for the most part anyway.

Patch isn't even gone a minute when I hear the heavy thud of motorcycle boots clomping into the mudroom, and then I hear the sounds of their boots being placed on the hardwood floor like they were asked to do. Wanting to feel useful, I grab the mismatched plates, cutlery, napkins and cups, balancing everything on my lap and wheel around to the end of the island closest to the hallway.

"Fuck, that smells good," I hear Bear say from behind me as I finish setting everything out, and I bite my lip as I hear the rest saying similar murmurs of appreciation as they set up the tables and chairs.

Γιαγιά (Grandma) and my **θείες** (aunts) wince, most likely because he swore, before quickly masking it and smiling brightly back at them as they pull the dishes out of the ovens. I know the club swears a lot, but I might need to see if they can curb the cussing around my family next time. I mean, I swear a lot myself, but I try to limit it around my family.

"We've got moussaka, pastitsio, and pastourmadopita. For sides there are a variety of cheeses, bread, and salad. We have lemonade and water to drink," **θεία** (aunt) Selena tells them.

"I don't know what the fuck those three dishes are, but I'm trying all three," Reaper darn near growls and I, along with **γιαγιά** (grandma) and my **θείες** (aunts), smile back at him. He looks like he could start drooling at any moment.

"Moussaka is a casserole with eggplant, potatoes, a tomato meat sauce and is topped with a béchamel or a white sauce. Pastitsio is a pasta bake casserole with ground lamb, onions, meat sauce, béchamel, and penne. Pastourmadopita is a Greek pasturma or air cured, seasoned beef and cheese pie," I explain as I point to each of the dishes.

I'm half expecting them to get right in line, but instead, they usher Levi, Mae, Sasha, **γιαγιά**, my **θείες** (aunts) and me to go first.

"Our rule is women, kids, and those that cook eat first. I know that isn't normally the Greek way, but that's our way. Women and children first," Gunner explains to them before stepping into line behind us.

My family stare at them in shock for a moment, because that's not how it is for us. Everyone either eats together or the men eat first. But then, to my surprise, my family beams back at the guys. I think they're already half in love with them and I know they had some reservations years ago when Patch mentioned he wanted to Prospect with them after turning eighteen.

Patch steps up beside me and takes my plate out of my hands. He dishes me up a little bit of everything before bringing it over to the table. I head over to the drinks and pour myself some lemonade and then head over to the table.

As everyone digs into the food, moans and grunts of appreciation sound throughout our dining room, it feels good to be surrounded by so many people again.

"Fuck, please say you can cook like this, Mary," someone says, and it takes me a moment to realize it was Bones that spoke. The look he's giving me is a mix between pleading and begging.

Smiling, I nod. "Yes, I can. Especially once I get back my recipe books that **γιαγιά** took for safekeeping." His brow furrows at the word safekeeping, but it's **γιαγιά** that explains before I can. As she squares her shoulders, I can't help but smile. I've missed listening to her explain about our family's love of cooking and about our treasured recipes to others.

"In our family, cooking is extremely important to us. It's one way that we show our love, appreciation, and thanks to those around us. That's why after... that night, I took **του λουλουδιού μου** (my flower's) cookbooks and a few other items for safekeeping since the boys were worried about if the people that kidnapped **λουλούδι μου** (my flower) would come back and trash the house.

"The collecting and creating of new recipes is a tradition in our family that we still carry on today. The eldest matriarch of the family is the gatekeeper, so to speak, of our ancestor's original recipe books. Over the years, that position has morphed slightly to be the eldest matriarch that also has a passion for cooking, as throughout the years, more and more women were working outside the house and wanted to make simpler dishes since they had less time to allocate toward cooking. Especially the large family meals.

"Any children that show an interest in cooking are given copies of our family's recipes to start their own cookbooks with. As their skills grow, so do their collections of recipes. Once the children turn eighteen, they are gifted another cookbook that also has copies of the original on the back of handwritten or typed recipes. When they get married, they are gifted another cookbook, which is usually the final one they receive unless a family member creates a new recipe that they want to share with the family."

"That's so cool," Mae says, her eyes lighting up at the thought. I know she loves to cook as well, and she's shared with me how her friend Peggy and her husband

Glen taught her how to make all the dishes they served at their diner, so I'm sure she's excited about the thought of all of those old recipes.

Each of my **θείες** chuckle at her excitement and I have a feeling Mae will be asking to see my recipe books in the near future. As if she's thinking the same thing I am, she looks over at me with a hopeful look in her eyes. At my slight nod, she does a little shimmy in her chair as she softly chants 'yay' over and over again, which has even more of us chuckling.

Γιαγιά (Grandma) smiles softly at me and with her nod of approval, I feel my own smile growing even more. I've told her about Mae and Levi, so she knows both of them like to cook, but especially Mae.

"**Λουλούδι μου** (My flower) started putting some of us to shame before she was even twelve years old. She's added her own little twists to almost every recipe we've given her, more often than not improving the dishes, and she's added many of her own recipes to our collection. On top of that, she wanted to pay homage to her Spanish heritage. She's gathered many recipes and treated us to many fabulous meals over the years. This next part, not even you know, my dear Mary."

She pauses again and dabs at her eyes as everyone quiets down, sensing the somberness that's fallen over her. I straighten in my seat, trying to keep my emotions at bay.

"Your dedication to knowing your heritage through your love of food is unmatched in our family. I reached out to Antonio shortly before your eighteenth birthday and asked if there were any family recipes that he might be willing to share with you. When he learned of your deep love for cooking and how you had taken it upon yourself to learn how to cook real Spanish food, he told me he had something even better in mind for you. He had planned to give you them when you graduated, but unfortunately, you were taken before he could give them to you."

My eyes burn with unshed tears, and I blink rapidly in an attempt to keep them from falling. Murmurs behind me have me looking over my shoulder, and my jaw drops in surprise when I see Grandpa Antonio and one of my aunts, Luiza, standing behind us with a couple of their bodyguards. I notice a few of the guys, especially the ones from the Junction Creek chapter, shifting in their seats and I know they're making it easier to grab their guns if need be. I had hoped Thor and Patch would have filled them in by now, but maybe they hadn't.

Luiza ignores the guys and fixes her gaze on me as she gives me a warm smile and a small wave, which I return. Grandpa eyes the men from both clubs warily, but they soften when he settles his gaze on me.

"**Hola** (Hello), **mi precioso capullo de rosa** (my precious rosebud). It is good to see you looking so much like your previous self." He pauses as he tilts his head toward **γιαγιά**. "Your grandmother invited us today so that we could finally give you your present. Luiza, **mi niña** (my girl)?"

Aunt Luiza takes a box from one of the bodyguards, and steps forward. She's about to place the large box that she's carrying on my lap when she pauses. Biting her lip nervously and her gaze bounces around to the people seated around me until it settles on Patch.

"Patch, from what **Padre** (Father) has said, you are with our Mary, **sí** (yes)?"

He gives her a curt nod. "Yes, Ma'am."

She scoffs, shaking her head slightly. "None of that ma'am stuff with me. You're **familia** (family) now. However, this box is a little heavy and with Mary's broken leg, I don't want to hurt her. Can you—," before she can even finish her sentence, he takes the box from her, sits back down in his seat, and sets it on his lap.

Both Aunt Luiza and Grandpa give me encouraging smiles, so I start unwrapping the box. Lifting the lid, my hand flies to my mouth in shock. Hesitantly, I reach out, running my finger along the edge of the beautiful cover.

"It was **el libro de recetas de mi madre** (my mother's cookbook)," Luiza says quietly before pausing and blinks away the tears in her eyes. "She also had a love of cooking and baking. Out of all of my siblings, I'm the only one that liked to cook, and I did, countless times, with her before she died. However, my skills never even came close to hers. I copied all of her recipes into my own books, and held onto her original books, hoping that someone in **nuestra familia** (our family) would pick up her torch, so to speak. Then **Padre** (Father) got the call from Maria. He set up an appointment between the three of us and Harris. When she told us even more about your passion, I knew these were meant to be yours and **Padre** (Father) agreed."

I look up sharply at that as I quickly pull back my hand, staring at her in shock, then to Grandpa and then back to Aunt Luiza. "B-But this was your mother's. Shouldn't you keep the originals?"

Both her and Grandpa shake their heads, warm smiles on their faces. Well, as much as Grandpa is willing to smile in a room full of armed bikers, that is.

"**Nuestras familias** (Our families) are very much alike in this regard. The original cookbooks are always handed down to the woman who loves cooking the most." He pauses and shakes his head slightly. "Well, I should say it would go to whoever loves cooking the most. It has just always happened to be women in the past in **nuestra familia** (our family)."

He steps closer, putting an arm around Aunt Luiza's shoulders and then resting a hand lightly on my shoulder.

"You are meant to be the keeper of these recipes, **mi precioso capullo de rosa** (my precious rosebud). I know you will do my Esmeralda's memory justice and I look forward to when we can break bread together. Perhaps when we are able to meet your little **bebés** (babies) in person and I bring a few of **tus tías y tíos** (your aunts and uncles) to visit along with me."

Swallowing thickly, I nod. "I would love that as well."

Both of them smile brightly at me, and I move to pick up the book out of the box, but Patch beats me to it. He lifts out the first book and sets it down gently on my lap.

Opening it, another gasp escapes as I look through the first couple of pages. "These are almost as old, if not as old, as some of our family's recipes," I say in awe as I continue looking through them, the excitement in me growing with each turn of the page.

I know Esmeralda had to have loved her family's history and their recipes, because all of the old recipes are protected. She laminated each one and the holes in the pages have little rings around them to prevent them from tearing, sort of like grommets, but thinner than the ones I'm used to seeing. Or at least, I think she's the one that protected it like this, but then I see a handwritten message in beautiful script at the back of the book and know it was her.

To the next keeper of our family's recipes:

Please treat these cookbooks with the same care and love as I have done. To protect our family's recipes for future generations, I created these binder books, which are separated out by cooking, smoking, and baking. There is room in each binder to add more recipes as your own skills develop and grow. Should you need or want more binders made, I have placed my contact's information below. Clarissa knows to never get rid of this pattern, so it will always be available to be made again, even if she is no longer the one that will craft it.

I hope you will enjoy these recipes. Good food is meant to be shared with loved ones and friends alike. Continue to grow our family's recipes and spread your love of good food to our future generations.

With all my love,
Esmeralda Vasquez

Closing the book, my fingers trace the intricate patterns crafted into the leather encasing both the front and the back and then over the scripted 'Vasquez' on the front. Clutching it to my chest, I look up at them as I blink rapidly to try and hold back my tears.

"I'll treasure them and will do the family proud."

"There is also more in there than just my Esmeralda's recipe books, **mi precioso capullo de rosa** (my precious rosebud)," Grandpa says with a mysterious glint in his eye.

Confused, I turn back toward the box and Patch pulls out all the books inside. Two are the ones Esmeralda mentioned, the smoking and baking recipe books. However, there are three other ones that steal my breath when I see them. My gaze flicks to **γιαγιάς** (grandmas) in shock before turning to each of my **θείες**.

"But..." I start, and then **γιαγιά** shakes her head softly and I snap my mouth shut.

"Mary, **λουλούδι μου** (my flower), it's time. You know how much we all love to cook our people's food, but no one has your passion, not even me. I think you should follow your *true* calling, **λουλούδι μου** (my flower). I know you've always wanted to teach kids and help them as they grow into young adults, but I do not think that is what you are truly meant to do, Mary."

I stare at her dumbfounded.

How did she know?

I never told *anyone* about my secret dream, not even Patch or my **πατέρας** (dad).

"How did you know?" I ask quietly, and all four of them share a knowing look before turning back toward me.

"It was little things you said throughout the years. You gave hints without even realizing you were doing it, it seems," **θεία** (aunt) Sofia tells me and my cheeks heat in embarrassment.

"What was your dream, Siren?"

My cheeks heat even more when I realize everyone, and I do mean *everyone*, is staring at me, waiting for me to answer him. A part of me shies back at so much attention focused on me. Patch squeezes his hand that's on my thigh, and I bring my attention back to him.

"I wanted to open a restaurant. To cook our family's food for everyone to enjoy." My voice is quiet, but as soon as the words are out, everyone's faces break out into grins and I feel a little spark ignite in me again.

A spark I haven't felt since before I was kidnapped.

"If what Maria is saying is true, and that you cook better than the four of them, then I can't fucking wait to have your cooking," someone says and soon everyone's voicing similar agreements.

Someone squeezes my shoulder, and I look up, realizing it's Grandpa.

"Follow your heart's true desire, **mi precioso capullo de rosa** (my precious rosebud). Do what you were meant to do."

Tears fill my eyes that spark fans with everyone's encouraging words.

"I will. Thank you, all of you," I whisper, and they both beam at me. Turning toward the rest of my family, I see their beaming smiles shining right back at me.

"Looks like you have some more motivation to get back into the groove of things, Siren," Patch says with a huge smile on his face, and I can't help but nod in agreement.

With their approval, I feel myself shifting yet again. Especially since Patch is looking at me with so much pride and not hurt that I hadn't told him about my secret dream. Excitement fills me as I run my hands over the leather binding of my grandmother's cookbook.

I can't wait to get back in the kitchen and try out both old and new recipes.

Aunt Luiza wraps me in a hug, squeezing me tightly, but not enough to hurt me. "Thank you. I know you'll do justice to **las recetas de mi madre** (my mother's recipes)," she whispers, and fuck if that isn't what causes a few of my tears to escape.

"You're welcome and thank you. I look forward to when we can get together and get to know each other again. I'd love to hear more about Grandma, too. Maybe we can even cook together as well."

She pulls back and wipes her cheeks, but I know I chose my words correctly when I see her smiling even brighter. "I'd like that very much. I'm sure the others would love to get in on the stories as well. We never knew why Carmen forbid us from getting too close to you, but fuck her and her stupid jealousy. She always hated it when anyone outshone Carlos and Eileen or went against her word. I'm still shocked she took to Diego so much, but knowing what I know now, a lot of things from over the years make sense now."

I stare at her in shock. "She forbid you guys from getting to know me better?" Suddenly, even more things are clicking into place, and I'm not liking where my train of thought is going.

Aunt Luiza pales slightly but nods. She looks over at Grandpa, and at his nod, she continues.

"**Sí** (Yes). While your parents were still married, Carmen's excuse was because you weren't raised in the right culture, so we had to distance ourselves to not bring shame down on **nuestra familia** (our family). After your parents divorced, she started saying you were beneath us because of what you'd done to Eileen and what you'd put her through. That you didn't deserve your tie to the Vasquez name. None of us believed her, but we also knew the hell she would rain down on us if we went against her word.

"After **Padre** (Father) came back from visiting you at the hospital last week, I overheard a conversation between Carmen and Diego. They both said that you would have been better off dead after the beating Stephan had given you so that they could get what they thought was theirs to take. I'm pretty sure they didn't know I was there, so I stayed put and listened until they left the room. After that, I went straight to **Padre** and told him everything about what I'd just witnessed, plus what Carmen had said about you being beneath our family years ago. I had already been getting suspicious of what Diego's been doing and saying recently, but I'd never thought he'd do something so heinous to his own family. **Padre** told me that they would soon be paying for their actions and that he'd share everything I'd told him with you, Patch, and Thor."

She pauses as Thor stands and walks over to us, her eyes widening slightly as she sees him at his full height. All of these guys are intimidating on a good day, but when someone they love is threatened, that intimidation factor skyrockets, and right now—he's pretty fucking intimidating. Surprisingly, Thor squeezes my good shoulder, but I don't know if it's in support or warning me not to say too much.

"Let's set up a time, and we'll discuss everything over a secure line. We have information we need to share with you as well, but here is not the best time."

Ah, warning it is. Fuck, is he mad that Aunt Luiza shared as much as she did?

Grandpa tilts his head in acknowledgement. "Agreed. Let me know the time and date and I'll arrange everything on my end." He pauses and then leans down to kiss my cheek. "We'll let you get back to everything here, **mi precioso capullo de rosa**, and we'll be in touch. Please take care and stay safe. You may call on my assistance, if you ever need it."

Aunt Luiza gives me one more hug and then they leave just as quietly as they came in.

Turning back toward Patch, I gently place the recipe books back in the box and close it. My mind reels with this new information, but I shake myself internally. I can deal and process those emotions later. Right now, I need to pack and direct what goes where. Tonight though, tonight I'll journal and then dive into these recipe books.

At the thought of all of those old recipes, that spark inside me flares even brighter than before.

I'll focus on my recovery and when I'm able to regain my strength in my arm and shoulder, my ass is going to be parked in the kitchen as I cook, cast or no cast.

Chapter 40

Patch

After Mary's family's surprise, the rest of the afternoon seemed to fly by. It's nearing four in the afternoon and we really only have Mary's and Nikos' bedrooms left to pack up. Once the house is empty, I'll hire a cleaning service to clean, refinish the hardwood floors, and shampoo the carpets. Then, her house will get listed. We had toyed with the idea of keeping it as a rental, and if we have trouble selling it, we'll take that route.

I'm helping Judge carry out Nikos' desk when Thor calls out my name. He's got his phone to his ear and his lips are pressed in a thin line.

Fuck...

What's happened?

He gestures me to follow him and we head back into the house and into Nikos' old office, closing the door behind us.

"I've got Drae on the line." He pulls his phone away from his ear and puts it on speakerphone.

"*What's up, Drae?*" I ask, keeping my voice low so it doesn't carry.

"I was just telling Thor that I think you need to get the ladies back here and tell her family to head home. We've had a couple of drive-bys in the last half hour that match the description she gave of that fucker. There was also a package addressed to her that was delivered by courier today. I haven't opened it, but it's in the safe box. At first, I just texted Thor about the package when it arrived, but coupled with the recent drive-bys, I think you need to be wrapping things up soon."

"Good job, Drae. We'll finish what we absolutely have to and head back. The rest we can get another time. Call me if anything else changes."

"You got it, Pres," he says before disconnecting the call.

"Fuck," I hiss as I run my hands through my hair angrily. "I knew he'd do something soon, but I had hoped we could at least finish this trip without any interruptions."

Thor clasps my shoulder, and I take a deep breath, trying to calm my anger.

"Come on, we need to spread the word. I don't want it looking like we're rushing out of here, but I also don't want to give them a heads up about what we're planning. We'll load up the rest of anything important to Mary as carefully as we can and get the hell out of dodge. Later, we can send some guys to get the rest of the stuff and Mary can sort through it at the compound."

Nodding, I prepare myself to give the bad news to Mary.

Thor follows me upstairs and to Mary's room, where we find the rest of the women. Mary's sitting on the bed as she helps wrap her things. They're halfway done with packing her collection of crystal figurines and other trinkets. Mary looks up as I come in, and the smile instantly fades from her face.

"Time to move?" she asks, and at her tone, Levi, Mae, and Sasha also look up sharply.

In an instant, all four of them change like a switch has been flipped inside them. I shouldn't be surprised at how quickly Mary can switch gears, but I still am. I know part of it's her past, but it's also incredibly convenient for being a biker's Old Lady. Which she will be once I can get rid of her fucking husband. Maria and Mary's aunts are eyeing our ladies with a look I can't quite decipher, but I'm thankful that they aren't freaking out.

"Yeah, we gotta roll, Siren."

"Keep acting as normal as possible, but pack everything that's irreplaceable to you, Mary, and do it quickly. The rest we'll send a few guys to get after whatever the fuck this is cools down." Thor pauses as he shares a look with Levi, and then me. Occasionally, it still baffles me that we're able to communicate without words, to read each other's looks and body language, but it fucking comes in handy way too many times. "Church as soon as we're back. Patch, bring Mary. Mae, can you watch the kids with Elvira?"

"Of course, Thor. We'll do popcorn and a movie in the common room so that we are all in one place."

Fuck, Mae still surprises me with how far she's come since she's been here, and it's only been a few months. Still, I hardly ever see a glimpse of the woman who came here at the beginning of September—the shy girl who would flinch away from any male's touch except for Timber and her brothers, and would do anything not to make waves. The only times that I get a glimpse of that shy girl is if everyone's attention is on her, but not in situations like these. Here, she's ready to kick some ass if need be, and I know she's been training with Levi on how to throw knives and she's been taking shooting lessons from Gunner, who before Sasha and Lex came here, was the best shot in the club.

"Good. We roll as soon as possible." He pauses and looks over at Mary's family. They've all paled slightly, but they're all standing proud. "It'll possibly draw attention if we follow you to your homes, but we'll do drive-bys periodically to make sure you're safe, if that's alright with you?"

They all nod, but it's Maria that answers. "We'd appreciate it. Is it okay if I give them your number and have them text their addresses?"

The corner of Thor's mouth ticks up slightly and I already know what he's going to say. Hopefully, they won't be too mad.

"Don't take offense, but I wasn't going to allow anyone here that I didn't know about. Especially since two of our Old Ladies are pregnant, one of them being mine. We ran all three of your ladies' information as we already had Harris and Maria's information. Maria, you can give them my number along with Phoenix's and Patch's. Mary, you can give them your new number as well. Call us if anything happens, but we'll drive-by occasionally. Especially tonight and the next couple of days."

"We will," they each respond, and though I can tell they are a little ticked off at us having done a background check on them, I think they all understand why Thor had Smoke do it.

"Also, until we know the scope of what's going on, I think you guys should follow Antonio's lead and communicate only via a secure line going forward. Hopefully, it won't be for too long and then, when it's safe, you can all get together in person again."

Once again, they aren't happy, especially with just getting Mary back, but they seem like they understand.

"All right, let's hustle."

He leaves the room, but Mary gestures for me to stay.

"Ladies, besides what I already told you, please pack the rest of the figurines, and if there's time, my books. Patch, please take me to **πατέρα** (dads) room."

I pick her up off the bed but am surprised she wants to go in there since she was extremely hesitant to before. After crossing the threshold, she points to a chair in the corner.

"Set me down over there. Then can you close the curtains and shut the door?"

Frowning, I do as she says.

"Okay, I can't believe I forgot about this for all these years," she says more to herself as she studies the hardwood floor.

I'm about to ask if she's okay when she points to a spot on the floor that's in front of the middle of the bed.

"See that board there, with the slight chip in the corner facing me?"

"Yeah," I reply as I kneel and run my fingers around the corners of the board. Does she want me to pry it up?

"Okay, this is the part where I don't know if you'll be able to do it by yourself or not, but if you follow that board underneath **πατέρα** (dads) bed, close to his headboard, you'll see another slightly chipped board. You need to pry that board up."

Worries from years past come rushing to the front of my mind as I try to lift the bed, but of course, Nikos had chosen a nice, heavy, wooden bedframe, headboard, and footboard. I can't do it by myself without possibly scratching his hardwood floors.

Walking back to the door, I open it and spot Thor, Reaper, and Dragon in the hallway outside of Mary's old room.

"Hey, guys, can you give me a hand with something quick? This fucker's heavy and I don't want to scratch the floors all to shit."

They all give me a chin lift and follow me back into the bedroom.

"Shut the door, will ya?" I ask and Reaper shuts it after him. "Okay, we need to lift and move the bed back that way so I can get at something hidden under the floor," I tell them as I point to my right.

All of their eyebrows shoot up as they give Mary a curious look. She tries not to squirm under the weight of their gazes but isn't quite successful.

We manage to move the bed as far as we can to the other side of the room. Grabbing my pocketknife, I find the chipped board Mary mentioned and pry the board up. Three boards on either side of the chipped one lift in unison and when I flip them all up, I realize Nikos had hidden a floor safe in here.

"What's the code, Siren?"

She clears her throat and I can almost feel her pain without even having to look at her, not that I could since the headboard is blocking my view of her.

"8-25-20-06."

I reach for the lock but pause. "The day we met."

"And also the day that Eileen's poison was first exposed to πατέρας (dad)."

My hand pauses again at her quiet words after entering the twenty-five, but I continue, even as my worries worsen. Was I right before all those years ago? Was there a reason why Mary and Nikos were targeted?

The lock unlatches and I open the door, revealing some papers and a couple of books that I grab.

"Grab everything that's in there, please. He never showed or told me what he stored in there, and I didn't even know about it until about a month after the accident Eileen caused. He said that if anything should ever happen to him, to look in the safe. I thought it was just a copy of his will or something since she'd just recently died, but now I'm starting to think there might be something more to everything that's happened."

Closing the safe, I lower the floorboards and stand before walking over to Mary and give her the stack of papers and books.

"Is there anything else you want us to grab of your dad's? Otherwise, we'll just move the bed back in place and get ready to head out."

She looks around the room and nods. "I'll ask one of the ladies to come in and help me grab a few things, and then that will be it."

We move the bed back in place and Thor turns back toward Mary.

"Just tell us what you want, Mary, and we'll put them on the bed. If it's something we can pack, we will so that the ladies can finish up with your room."

She asks us to grab all of the picture frames, some books, and a few trinkets, some of which I remember being with her when she bought them.

"I think we can manage these things. I'll go get a box, tape, and some of that bubble shit," Reaper says as he opens the door, heads out into the hallway, and returns a moment later.

Since my hands are the smallest out of all four of us guys, I grab the bubble wrap and start ripping off sections before quickly wrapping everything to pack up. A few minutes later, Dragon tapes the box shut.

"I'll get this down to the van," he says as he picks up the box and leaves.

I walk over to Mary and pick her up. "Let's go see how the ladies are doing. We need to get out of here."

The guys follow us and seeing quite a few boxes already sitting in the hallway, they start carrying them downstairs. Stepping just inside the room, I'm surprised to see quite a few boxes in just the short time that we were gone and all of them ready to go as well.

"How's it going, ladies? Need any more help?"

Levi and Maria shake their heads as they gesture to the two boxes they're currently filling.

"These are the last two boxes, I think. Let's get these out in the hallway and then Mary can take another look around to make sure we didn't miss anything," Levi tells me and I sit Mary down on her bed before I start carrying the boxes out and into the hallway.

Mary points out a couple of small things that they pack into the last couple of boxes, but other than that, I think we're done for the day.

"Okay, I'll start taking these down and let the guys know that this is the last of things for today. Ladies, how about you gather up all of your stuff and start getting around?"

Hoisting up a box, I head down and out to one of the trucks in the driveway. "We have just a handful of boxes and then we're done," I quietly tell Thor and the few guys that I can see right now. The others must be watching the perimeter or something. Thor gives me a chin lift.

"Here's how we're going to roll out. Prospects will lead in one of the vans, then Sasha, Wildcat and Mae, a van, then you two, then the last van. Like before, those on bikes will be pairing off to ride in front of and behind each vehicle. Make sure you all get through the intersections and traffic lights together. I wouldn't put it past that bastard to make a move on your woman to separate her from us. Keep an eye out."

"You got it, Pres. Was already planning on it."

Heading back inside, I pause at the base of the stairs as Smoke carries my woman down and sets her down in her chair. It bugs me that someone else other than me is holding my woman, but I know Smoke wouldn't try anything on her.

"Ready to go, Siren?"

Her face hardens and her lips thin. "Yes. I just hope that those assholes will know what's good for them and they leave us the fuck alone."

Smoke and I share a look. I'd love to agree with her, but everything in me is saying that someone's going to make a move. And I don't think the box that was delivered and the drive-by's are going to be the last of what they do today.

After saying goodbye to her family, I carry Mary to the truck while the guys secure her chair in the bed of my truck. Once she's buckled in, I realize she's clutching her backpack but is making sure it's not visible from any of the windows. I'm gonna take a stab that it contains whatever was in her dad's safe. I flip up the center console, revealing the stowaway area I had custom created when I got my truck.

"Here, Siren. Put that in here for now."

She does as I ask and I lean in, giving her a quick kiss.

"I'll go lock up, set the alarm, and be right back."

She nibbles on her lip nervously but nods and then looks around at the guys as they finish securing the other three vans.

Heading inside, I make sure no one is still here and that we didn't leave anything out before setting the alarm and locking the doors. Walking back to my truck, I notice everyone else is either on their bikes or in one of the vehicles.

Climbing in, I buckle up and start my truck, waiting for the others to pull out and for our turn.

Chapter 41
Patch

We're already more than halfway back to the clubhouse and I'm seriously on edge. I've seen three blacked out SUVs driving around and I swear that one followed us for a while. My body automatically tenses even further as we roll through the intersection where those fucking Black Plague assholes plowed into us and kidnapped Levi and Reaper earlier this summer.

We clear the edge of town and ten minutes later, when we turn onto the road that leads to our clubhouse, the hairs on the back of my neck rise and I look around, but I don't see anyone.

"Something's not right," Mary says quietly as she looks around.

"Got the same feeling, Siren. But what the fuck is it?"

I'm about to say something else when I hear a tire blow out and my truck swerves.

"Fuck, hang on, Siren."

Gritting my teeth, I grip the steering wheel tighter as I try to keep my truck under control, but then I hear a second tire blowing out, and I swear under my breath. Where are those fuckers hiding?

A phone rings and Mary digs in her purse for it. "It's Thor."

"Put it on speakerphone," I grit out.

"Patch, see if you can limp along to the gate and don't stop until you get to the back of the clubhouse. Some of our guys are fanning out, trying to locate these fuckers."

"You got it, P—"

I'm interrupted by an explosion of some sort, and then we're rolling. Mary screams and I pray like fuck that she isn't seriously injured by this shit. Her injuries have been healing nicely since she isn't constantly getting beat up all the time. My head slams against the window, and for a few moments, black dots dance across my vision, but I fight it. I will not leave my Siren vulnerable.

As soon as we stop rolling, we land on our side, my side to be exact. I rip off my seat belt, hissing through the pain in my shoulder, and climb toward Mary who's frantically clawing at her seat belt.

"It won't unlatch, Luke!"

Reaching into my pocket for my knife, I once again hiss in pain and out of the corner of my eye, see my shirt starting to turn red with blood. Fuck, I hope it isn't anywhere near the major arteries in my shoulder area.

I'm almost done cutting her free when her window explodes above us, sending glass raining down on us. Fire licks at my forearms and a couple of spots on my forehead as I try to shield Mary as best as I can from the glass.

She cries out as someone tries to drag her out by her hair. A moment later, a second hand latches onto her arm as he tries to hoist her out, but the seat belt prevents him from yanking her out of the truck.

"Hurry the fuck up and grab the bitch, Bren," someone hisses right as I grab the fucker's arm that's wrapped around her bad arm, twisting it forcefully, making him to let go of Mary.

"Quickly, cut through the rest and stay down and out of sight," I tell her as I hand her the knife.

The asshole tries to reach out for her again, but I grab him and land a punch to his temple, dazing him enough that I can push him off and then climb out through the busted window. My palms flare in pain and I'm sure I cut them up by getting out of the truck so quickly. I hadn't bothered to make sure all the broken glass was cleared, not wanting to send more cascading down on Mary.

A different guy is helping up the one that I'd punched, though a sick satisfaction courses through me that the fucker is royally dazed and probably has a nasty concussion. He can barely get his hands under him and he's struggling to get to his feet. I launch myself at the newcomer, tackling him to the ground and raining my fists down on him. Out of the corner of my eye, I notice a third guy trying to beat in the windshield to get to Mary.

Shit!

The fucker uses my distraction against me and lands a blow to my chin that has my vision dancing again, but I refuse to succumb to it.

Three more figures appear through the smoke and dust, and I breathe a sigh of relief when I recognize Axe, Loki and Colt charging in to help.

"Colt, Beast, help Mary!" I yell as Axe helps me with the other fucker who still can't get his feet under him. We need these assholes alive to question them.

Bullets whiz by us and I curse as one narrowly misses me, but the guy I'm holding screams out as it buries itself into his arm. Fuck, I hope the others can find where those fuckers are and take them out. Landing a hard right hook to the fucker's face, I'm thankful when he passes out.

A hiss pulls my attention toward my truck and my eyes widen at the growing pool of gas on the ground.

"Axe, take this fucker," I yell out as I shove the guy's limp weight toward him.

The guy who initially grabbed Mary is gone and I hope like fuck our guys have him and that he didn't get away. Beast disappears into the smoke with the body of the guy who had been trying to kick in my windshield slung unconscious over his shoulder. Colt's almost got Mary out of the truck and I rush forward to help her before those assholes decide to hit my tank or their bullets create a spark that ignites the spilled gas.

As we help her to the ground and she leans on Colt, I quickly look her over, thankful that she doesn't seem to be seriously injured.

"Wait! My bag and purse," Mary cries as she moves to try and get back in the truck.

"I'll get them, Siren. Colt, get her to safety."

His face hardens, knowing I'm trusting him with my woman and also, how fucked he'll be if anything happens to her. He gives me a chin lift before picking up Mary and running off through the smoke and dust from the explosion.

Hopping up, I open the truck door, snagging Mary's purse and just as I flip open the center console, I hear it. A barrage of bullets bounces off the asphalt and I can hear the pings of them hitting the bed and the roof of my truck. I bite through a hiss as I feel a sharp pain sear through my thigh, and I hope it's just a graze. Though, I should be thankful it's just that one since I'm ass up in the air right now.

Grabbing the backpack, I hop back down and as I stuff Mary's purse inside the backpack, I pause for a moment, using the truck as a cover until the bullets die down a bit. When they taper off, I run in the direction Colt took off in.

As I clear the smoke and dust, I realize the explosion hit us maybe a few hundred feet or so from the gate. Some of my brothers are using some old bulletproof shields the club got their hands on way back in the day before we turned fully legit. They're fanned out in a circle around the entrance to the gate as they rain down bullets on whoever they see in the woods on the opposite side of the road. Not to mention I'm sure our Russian duo are picking off anyone that tries to step foot on the asphalt from their eagle's nest atop the clubhouse. But with being this close to the gate, there's unfortunately nothing really for me to hide behind as I race toward the compound. As I run, I notice a few motorcycles that were caught in the explosion, their mangled bodies lying on the ground, but none of them look like I'd be able to grab them and ride the short distance back.

More bullets whiz by as someone shouts from the forest. "Get that fucking biker scum! I want his head on a platter for what he's done!"

I don't recognize the voice but with how loud he's yelling, I know our security system will have caught it so long as it hasn't been destroyed yet. I grin darkly when I see a few of my brothers changing their aim and shooting toward where the voice came from. Hopefully, we can nab some of the assholes hiding in the woods.

Relief flows through me when I see Bear and Dragon heading my way with an extended bullet proof shield. It's like three normal shields put together, but it requires two people to carry it, one on each end, since it's so much heavier than the others. As soon as I'm close enough, Dragon's arm reaches out and pulls me in between them, his shield taking a bullet that would have most likely have hurt like hell or possibly even put an end to me.

I must have been the last one that needed to get to the clubhouse, because as soon as the three of us make it back to the rest of the group, everyone starts inching their way back behind the gate. We stay in place as the bullet and bombproof reinforced gate closes and I breathe another sigh of relief.

Someone runs over to us, and I turn, relieved to see it's Colt. He must have gotten Mary to safety.

"She's inside and safe. But instead of going down into the panic room with the others like I wanted her to, she flat out insisted she's going to help Doc while he digs a couple of bullets and some shrapnel out of Phoenix's shoulder and side. He got caught in the explosion while trying to get to you guys."

"Fuck," I hiss out. I'd really prefer she was down with the others, but right now, being at Doc's side might be the next best place for her.

He hands me a couple of extra clips, and after double checking my gun, I pocket extra clips as we wait to see what the assholes will do.

We back up further from the gate but don't lower the shields. Their bullets bounce off the gate and after a few moments, several curses come from the forest.

"This isn't over yet, you fucking biker scum! We will get what belongs to us! *Everything* that belongs to us! Even if that means we kill every single one of you to get what's rightfully ours!"

I growl, along with several of my brothers, at their words. Mary and her children are not *things.* They don't belong to anyone. While I claim them as mine, that doesn't mean I own them like these assholes think they do. They are mine to protect and love.

The assholes make a whole fucking lot of noise as they walk through the forest for people who are theoretically wanting to sneak around to get the drop on us. Either that or since we already know they're there, they don't give a fuck anymore.

A few moments later, the sound of car doors closing reach us and then multiple engines starting up before driving off. It's then that I remember that we weren't the end of our caravan.

"The guys with the last van. Did they make it through?" I ask Colt, and my chest tightens when he shakes his head.

"They were about to turn onto the road when they saw your first tire blew out and changed course. Thor called Ethan and told him to hide out in town until he was told otherwise. Bones, Razor, and Smithy were ordered to go with him. The rest of the guys rode in to help you and Mary. If there's anything else in Mary's belongings that could give us tips on what the fuck is going on, he didn't want the cargo falling into these fucker's hands."

Fuck, he's right.

If whatever was in that floor safe is why Nikos and Mary were targeted, they could try to hit that van thinking it could be in one of the boxes inside.

This is turning into a major clusterfuck.

Chapter 42

Mary

My arms burn like fire from where the shards of glass ripped through my shirt and skin when the asshole broke the window and then tried to pull me out without making sure all the glass was cleared. I don't think any are deep though, because I can only see small little dribbles of blood coming out of the wounds. Not to mention my scalp stings from him trying to pull me out by my hair.

Thank God I wasn't alone, because if I had been, I'm sure I would have been taken and who knows what would have happened then.

I cling to Colt as he runs toward the gate. Bullets bounce off the cinderblock wall and I duck my head.

"Just hang on tight, Mary. I've got ya and won't let them get you," he says and surprisingly, I believe him.

Footsteps approach and I can't stop praying that it's our guys and not anyone who's attacking us. A shadow falls over us and I take the risk, glancing up. Bear and Dragon are holding up some sort of shield and I wince as I hear the bullets hitting it, just waiting for them to tear through the metal of the shield.

"It's bulletproof, Mary, you're safe," Colt says between his ragged breathing and a part of me is, once again, ashamed of my weight and the extra burden I'm giving him.

They follow us as we clear the gate and then around to the back of the building.

"Get her inside and with the others," Dragon grits out and then they're gone.

Since Colt's hands are busy holding me, I reach out and open the door, wincing as the action pulls on my bad arm and shoulder that's wrapped around Colt's neck. He heads into the kitchen right as the door down the hallway opens up and Doc comes out, his hands bloody. He riffles through the kitchen and then heads back into the hallway.

"Colt, take me to Doc," I say as I push on his shoulder.

"No, I have to get you into the panic room with the others."

Conflict is apparent on his face, as I'm sure he's guessing what my intentions are.

Narrowing my eyes, I grip his chin as I do my best to stare him down, even though I'm looking up at him because of the positioning, and put all the steel I can into my spine and my voice.

"If you don't set my ass down on a chair in the room Doc's in so I can help him, I will beat your ass even though I'm crippled. Whoever is in there got hurt because of me and I will not let them suffer more when I could have helped. The women are in the shelter and the only other one that has medical knowledge is still out there. *Take. Me. In. There.*" I force myself not to focus too much on Patch still being out in the open and possibly hurt. If I dwell on it too much, I'm probably going to break down.

His lips thin and for a moment, I think he's going to dump me in the panic room and ignore me, but then he turns on his heel and heads down the hallway after Doc. We find the room easily since Doc didn't close the door all the way, and I can't contain my startled gasp when I see Phoenix lying on the bed with a couple of gunshot wounds and what I think are little pieces of metal in his arm and thigh.

"Take me to the sink," I order Colt and it's then that they both notice us in the room.

"Get her to the panic room, Prospect," Phoenix grits out.

I turn my glare on him as I soap up and wash my hands and arms. Doc's holding... whatever they call those tweezer-like things to pull out bullets. He stares at me in shock, like he can't believe I'm back here offering to help him, his hand holding the tweezer-things is hovering over one of Phoenix's wounds.

"Can it, Phoenix. I'm helping Doc patch you up. Colt is doing what I ordered him to do. You got hurt because of me, so don't you dare think of punishing him for this. I'm going to be Doc's second set of hands whether you like it or not, so just sit back and try not to move so you don't fuck up Doc's work or injure yourself further."

Once my hands are dry, I grab some nitrile gloves, slip them on, and then point to the doctor's chair. "Sit me down on that and then help me slip that gown hanging on the wall on over my clothes," I tell Colt and after he does as I ask, I grab his cut. "Make sure my man makes it back inside the compound safely. Please," I half ask, half tell him.

His eyes soften and he gives me a chin lift, then his gaze lifts to Doc.

"Make sure to check her arm later. Fucker was yanking hard on it," he tells him and then he's gone.

"Before you say anything Doc, my arm is just slightly sore, but in comparison to what's going on out there, it's pretty fucking small. So, tell me what to do, Doc."

Instead of telling me what to do, they both just stare at me with a weird look on their faces.

"What? Why are you looking at me like that? We've got work to do and we need to get Phoenix patched up. I'm betting he isn't the only one that's going to need your attention today, so let's get to it."

Both of them blink a few times and then seem to shake themselves.

"Fuck, you fit right in, Mary," Phoenix says softly as he leans his head back down on the pillow and I breathe a small breath of relief when I see some of the tension in his body relaxing. It'll make things easier for Doc if his body's relaxed and not strung tight. "But Doc is looking you over after me, whether you like it or not," he says, using my own words against me. "Our women and children come first, you know that, and I won't be having Patch cussing our asses out because we didn't take care of you right away." His lips kick up slightly in the corner and I can't help but huff slightly and shake my head.

These men.

Then again, I wouldn't have them any other way.

Doc gives me a nod of what I think is approval before tilting his head to the cabinets behind me. "Second drawer right behind you, grab the suture kit. Drawer above it, grab the gauze, tape, and scissors. Try to use mainly your left arm until I can take a look at your other arm."

Spying a second tray already set up that has other sanitized utensils on it, I snag it and use it to set everything on and then wheel back to Phoenix's other side.

All in all, Phoenix and Devil were the only two that were seriously injured, though Patch's injuries are right behind theirs. Both of them had multiple bullet wounds, both direct and grazes, as well as shrapnel injuries. Patch had several bullet grazes, all on his right side—two in his bicep, his side right under the ribs, and two on his thigh; the palms of his hands have several gashes, a couple of them deep, from the glass when he got out of the truck; and several other gashes on his forearms that we think are from when he protected me when the window was busted out. Drae, Ryder, Beast, and Punisher each had to have a bullet dug out and a few grazes stitched up. A handful of other guys had grazes, but other than that, we got lucky.

The assholes that shot at us? They weren't as lucky, I think to myself as I help Doc as he finishes up bandaging the last of Patch's injuries. Thor, Phoenix, Smoke, Reaper, Devil, and Python have crowded in the room with us.

"Bear said they found two guys trying to crawl to the highway due to their injuries. Fuckers didn't even bother to take them with them when they hauled ass out of here," Thor grunts out. "They found five others dead. They scouted around and found spots where they'd been camping and watching the gate, but they couldn't tell how long they were there."

"Did we get the three that tried to grab Mary?" Patch asks and Phoenix gives him a curt nod before turning to Smoke.

"Any word that the cops got wind of this?"

Smoke shakes his head. "Nothing so far on the scanner."

I frown at that. "Should we be preemptive and talk to Sam and Brady? If Stephan was behind this, he could send some of his goonies out here and try to nail this on us. Or they could try to nail us for some other asinine reason."

They're all silent and I worry that I've overstepped. I could kick myself for speaking up out of turn. Fuck, are they going to be pissed at me now? I'm berating myself silently when Patch's fingers lift my chin to make me look up at him.

"Whatever the fuck just went through your pretty head, throw it out the window, Siren. We're just trying to figure out if we should contact them or not. With Stephan being a cop, this complicates things. Normally, we try to handle as much shit like this by ourselves."

Swallowing, I nod.

"And don't you dare say 'I'm sorry'. This is on him, Siren. Not on you."

I stare at him in shock because I *was* about to say that very thing. Smiling softly, I shake my head. "I just don't want you guys to be wrongfully accused is all. I've seen Stephan pull that kind of shit on people who have tried to help me and the kids before, and he's literally destroyed them and then went even further by destroying their families. After the first time, I never asked for help again, but still, I had to witness it two other times because nurses have contacted the authorities before on my behalf. Of course, they didn't realize at the time that the police were corrupt, but they soon found out."

All of the guys curse and I notice more than one muscle ticking in their jaws as their eyes blaze with anger. Thank fuck that anger isn't directed at me, because I don't know what I'd do if it were.

When their curses die down, I lick my lips, and take a deep breath. "If you guys want, I can look at them. Both the ones you captured and the ones that died and see if I recognize any of them. It wouldn't surprise me if Stephan pulled some of his friends in from previous towns we lived in to help him out. Especially if Diego decides he's more trouble than he's worth."

All of them frown at my words.

"I don't want you to see that, Siren. It's not pretty."

I scoff and shake my head, even as my stomach rolls. "I know it won't be pretty, but let me just tell you that it wouldn't be the first dead body I've seen and I'm not talking about **πατέρας** (dad). Stupid ass that he is, one of the ways he liked to make sure I 'stayed in line' is that he'd take me with him when he had to 'take care of business' for Diego. I've watched brains splatter around abandoned warehouses more times than I can count. Of course, that was after having to watch him torture them for hours. Seeing a few more dead bodies isn't going to make a lick of difference. If it could help us figure out who was behind this, then yes, I'd like to help you any way that I can." Frowning, I look up at Smoke. "But if we did go to the cops, wouldn't they want to look at your security footage? They'd see you taking those guys… wherever it is that you took them."

Smoke gets a mischievous look in his eye. "They won't see jack shit. I know how to make things not come back at us. Those five never made it to our clubhouse." He gives me a pointed look and I grin. "For that matter, I already know four of the five guys. I ran their faces through my program, but I think it would be a good idea to have Mary take a look at their pictures. Who knows if these fuckers have more than one alias?"

Patch sighs and reaches for my hand. "Pictures only." He pauses and makes sure I'm looking at him. "Even if you have seen them, I don't want you to see more."

Giving him a small smile, I turn back toward the others when I hear a rustling sound. Smoke moves the trash I hadn't thrown away yet off the little tray I'd been using and sets down his laptop. His fingers fly over the keyboard and after a few moments, he turns the laptop toward me.

"These assholes are the ones Bear found dead."

Nodding, I look through all five pictures. My chest tightens as I recognize all five of them and the memories threaten to bombard me. Some of them were my abusers, and others are guys that Stephan and Diego worked with.

"I know all of them. On the right is John Hart. Then it's Aiden Anderson, Logan Reyes, Matt Finch and Scott Pierce. Aiden, Logan, and Matt were part of the last crew Stephan used back in Credence when he had to do work for Diego. John and Scott were street thugs, also from Credence, that Stephan used to intimidate people into doing what he wanted them to do, which was usually to cough up money for protection or some other BS."

Smoke makes note of everything and then flicks to a different set of pictures. One of the pictures has me squeezing Patch's hand so hard that he cups my cheek and turns me away from the screen. His eyes are filled with worry as he rubs his thumb across my cheek.

"What is it, Siren?"

"One of them was in the pictures sent with those letters. Leonardo Adams." Pausing, I turn back to the pictures. "He's the one in the middle. Jack Huxley is on the right, then it's Brendan Creed, Leo, Liam Gray, and Daniel Cassidy. When we were in Credence, if Kristoff, Wolfe, or O'Malley weren't available, he'd call in Leonardo and his crew to beat me when he thought I'd 'misbehaved' or had done some other grievance he'd thought up. Sometimes Leo was there with Kristoff and the others, like that time in the picture, but not always. Brendan and Daniel are part of Leo's crew. I recognized their voices when they were trying to pull me out of the truck. Jack and Liam are new guys under Lawrence, Stephan's main street thug in Credence. If they were here, then Lawrence most likely was too, but it looks like he got away."

Once again, Smoke makes note of everything I say, and then he frowns.

"Mary, I'd like to see if you recognize this voice."

Confused, I nod and he clicks play.

My blood runs cold as I hear the voice that comes through the speakers.

"Get that fucking biker scum! I want his head on a platter for what he's done!"

He was *here.*

Outside the compound.

Shooting at the building *my kids were in* just so he could try to get us back.

White-hot anger fills me at what he could have done.

"Stephan," I grit out as I ball my hands into fists. "He could have hurt or killed my kids or Patch or any of you with this stunt! Not to mention he could have hurt one of the ladies. Oh my God, if he hurt Mae or Levi or the babies, I'm going to skin him alive," I seethed.

Patch hisses in pain as he sits up and I spin toward him, trying to stop him from moving.

"Luke Morgan, don't you dare move another muscle! You don't want to rip a stitch, ruin all of Doc's hard work, and make him redo everything," I hiss at him, but the jerk just chuckles and cups my cheeks in response.

"Knew you were perfect for me, Siren."

Frowning, I'm about to ask what he means when his thumb traces my lower lip and I feel myself melting into his touch.

"You're perfect for me and you fit in so well with everyone here. Hell, you're still injured yourself and you're about to go to war to protect our family and the club."

My eyes burn, but thankfully, they don't spill out this time. I'm really tired of crying. I never used to cry this much, but I do think Patch is right that I'm finally working through all of my emotions now that I'm free of Stephan's grasp. "Of course I would. I've come to love everyone here. They're my family just as much as they are yours."

Patch's hands tighten on me and heat flares in his eyes. I'm vaguely aware of the others leaving, but I can't pay attention to that when Patch touches me like this. His eyes rake down my body. When desire flares in his eyes, I realize I'm leaning toward him while still sitting on Doc's rolly-doctor-chair and am probably flashing him since I'm wearing a v-neck shirt.

"Fuck, I'm trying really hard to be a gentleman, Siren, but I'm hanging by a thread here."

"Maybe I don't want you to be a gentleman."

"Fuck," he growls before his lips slam down on mine. I know I should be scolding him since he practically launched himself off the bed and is now kneeling in front of me, kissing me like he's trying to devour me, but I can't. Not when he's touching me like this and kissing me like his life depends on it.

I'm not sure how long we kissed for when we're interrupted by a knock on the door.

"Necking time is over, cops are on their way," someone's muffled voice comes through the door and Patch curses as he rests his forehead on mine.

A second later, the door opens and I pull back, looking over my shoulder to find Smoke at the door.

"Right as I was going to make the call, Thor's phone rang. Sam, Brady, and Dixon are on their way. Not sure if any others are coming with them or not."

I frown. "Did someone hear the shots or explosion and call it in?"

Smoke frowns in return. "They didn't say, but there's not a lot of people around us—it's mainly forest, farmland, and wild fields. The land we don't own, the owners know not to come anywhere close if they hear that shit. They also don't run their mouths on anything they happen to see or hear and they are compensated for that."

Sighing, my body slumps and on instinct, I lean into Patch, but at the last second, I pull back a bit so that I don't put too much weight on him. "If I'm honest, I'm going to bet Stephan had someone anonymously call this in to try and pin you guys with those guys' deaths."

"Don't worry, we'll take care of everything, Mary. Come on, since Patch can't lift you right now and the fact that your chair is riddled with bullets, I'll carry you out to the main room."

Patch hisses as he gets to his feet and I glare at him, silently telling him to be careful. His lips kick up, but then his face darkens when Smoke picks me up and I roll my eyes. Though, I'm still surprised that these guys can carry me around so easily. While a part of me is ashamed, another part of me revels at how strong they all are, and while I'm in love with Patch and wouldn't do anything with anyone else, it's definitely nice to have so much eye candy around.

Smoke sets me down on the couch, and then I hear a stampede coming down the hallway. I spin around, wincing slightly as I accidentally bump my broken leg on the coffee table, worried something else is wrong. My body sags in relief when my kids come barreling into the room, their little heads frantically look around, and when they see me and Patch, they all race toward us. Not surprisingly, Bastion's right on their heels. The kids have fallen head over heels in love with Bastion and I'm sure we'll be getting a dog at some point as a result.

"Wait," I call out as I put my hands out, hoping to stop them before they throw themselves at us. "Patch got hurt today, so you have to be careful." Thankfully, they all skid to a halt.

Cassie's little chin wobbles as she looks over Patch, the trembling worsening when she sees the blood and bandages. "Daddy got hurt? Where all are you hurt?"

Carefully, Patch lowers himself to the couch. "Most of the injuries are from when the window on my truck was busted and I tried to shield your mom. Also, some are from when I had to climb out the window," he says as he shows them his forearms and hands.

Ash frowns. "But what about this?" he asks as he gently runs his finger over the bandage peeking out from under the arm of Patch's shirt. Patch hesitates, and I get why he might not want to tell them the truth, but I hope he still does.

"A few bullets grazed me. Two of them hit here," he says as he points to his right arm, "another got my side, and there are two more on my right thigh."

Isaiah's and Cassie's eyes fill with tears, whereas Ash's face darkens as he clenches his fist. His gaze cuts to mine and I know he has questions, but he won't voice them in front of Isaiah and Cassie. He never does.

"We can talk later, Hawk," Patch tells Ash, "but right now, I just want you three in my arms." His voice is rough and thick with emotion. All three of them go willingly to him and he kisses their heads as he whispers to them. My heart feels like it's going to burst at seeing them like this.

Movement has me looking up, and my body sags in relief when I see Levi and Mae unharmed, their men surrounding them.

"You're both alright," I say right before a sob rips out of me. They both come round the corner of the couch and Levi sits down next to me while Mae sits down on the coffee table after scooting it closer. We all embrace as we cry, though Levi's trying really hard to hide that she's crying.

After a few moments, a phone buzzes and I look up as I wipe my eyes.

"Drae says the cops are here and it's not just Sam, Brady, and Dixon. There are some guys by the names of Shyvers and Wilson as well," Thor says, his voice hard and icy, though I don't know why. Then the names register and I groan.

"Shyvers and Wilson are as crooked as can be. Like Stephan, they both hate the club with a passion, but I don't know why."

Someone chuckles darkly as they walk up to us and I look up at Bear in question when he stops next to Thor.

"Probably because they're still pissed they never made the cut back in the day. Both of their granddads and old men were in a club that we took over years ago. They were some of the very few that we let stay and the rest, who didn't want to go clean, were told to get the fuck out. Shyvers and Wilson thought that since they had family in the club, they could do whatever the fuck they wanted. That they were a shoe in. Well, they took it too far by trying to force themselves on a couple of hangarounds and Poseidon, the previous president and Thor and Dragon's old man, tossed them out on their asses. They've held a grudge to this day, especially since they were practically disowned by their families because of what they did."

"They've been trying to bring us down ever since," Dragon grits out.

"Come on, let's go meet them and see what they say," Thor says and Patch kisses each of the kids before having them slide off his lap.

"Stay in here, Siren."

Clutching his hand, I tug on his cut. He carefully bends down and kisses me.

"Be careful and be safe. They'll try any trick they can think of to make you incriminate yourselves."

"Don't worry, Siren. We'll handle this."

He gives me one more quick kiss and follows the guys outside.

"How about we get you all set up in the game room with a movie?" Mae asks as Elvira comes forward with Lindsey, but the kids all but cling to me instead.

Cupping Cassie's cheek, I kiss her forehead. "I don't know what those men will try to do, but I'd rather you three not be out here for that. Can you please go with Mae and Elvira? We'll come get you when we're done, I promise."

"Pinky promise?" Cassie asks with tears in her eyes. I'd really rather cuddle them all close after what's happened today, but I don't want them to witness whatever lies those two will spew. I already know just me being here will be like throwing gasoline on a flame, but I have no idea what seeing the kids will make them say or do.

Hooking my finger around hers, I smile. "Pinky promise, Angel."

My chest tightens as all three of them hug me and place a kiss on my cheek before going with Mae and Elvira, Bastion trailing behind them like the protector that he is. I watch them disappear down the hallway and release a shaky breath.

I can do this, I tell myself as I follow Levi over to a table, hobbling on the crutches one of the guys gave me. I can deal with these assholes and not let them get under my skin.

The clubhouse doors open and my stomach plummets at the smug looks on Shyvers and Wilson's faces, and they do nothing to hide their lecherous looks as they practically eye fuck Levi and me. After a moment, recognition dawns in their eyes as they stare at me, and I repress a shiver at the dark looks that cross their faces.

Fuck, what are they going to try to do or say?

Chapter 43
Patch

Walking out of the clubhouse, I will my pain to the back of my mind as I try not to limp. Everyone's on edge, not that I blame them. Three police cars are lined up outside our gate and I know for a fact that my truck and the mangled motorcycles are still out on the road for them to see. Normally, we would have already had them loaded on a flatbed and taken to the garage, but since we were trying to figure out if we should call the cops in or not, we'd left them there until the decision was made.

Uncle Sam is in the lead car and he gives me a head tilt, along with a sympathetic smile, as he walks back to his car, climbs in behind the wheel and shuts the door while he waits for Drae to open the gate. I know if he had his say, those two slimy assholes wouldn't be with him, Brady, and Dixon. I'd never met them in person, but I'd heard plenty about them. And not just what Bear told the women.

All three cars pull up in front of the clubhouse, but none of us move from our spots on the steps or porch. Shyvers and Wilson get out of their car, and I bite back a scoff. They're puffing up their chests and adjusting their gun belts, acting like they're the top dog when they're lower than dirt. Not to mention, neither of them would last if they tried to take one of us on, and I don't mean that in a bad way. Both of them prefer to drink their coffee and eat their donuts rather than get out on the streets to help people. Their ample waistlines are proof of that.

Uncle Sam, Brady, and Dixon roll their eyes at their antics, all of them looking extremely pissed to have them here.

"Well, seems you boys are in a heap of trouble," Shyvers sneers, as he glares daggers at Thor and Dragon. Wilson's also glaring at them but, thankfully, stays silent. Seems like nothing's changed then. Even though Thor and Dragon weren't the ones that tossed them out, they're the ones they are focusing the most on bringing down.

Thor cocks an eyebrow at him. "Now, what makes you say that, Billy 'ol boy?"

Shivers' eyes narrow on him. "It's Officer Shyvers, *Ryan*. Show some respect for the law."

More than one of us chuckles at that.

"We would show you respect, but you and your partner are crookeder than your busted nose. Just like half the fucking officers in town. Though, I could always break your nose again for you. Maybe then it'd heal straight," Thor throws back at him which just has Shyvers' face turning red in anger.

I grin at that. I'd witness a few of their fights, but they were all before Shyvers became a police officer. Shyvers never stood a chance. The dumbass thinks that just because he used to play football, not that he was that good—he was just your average joe in high school, and clings to his parents' coattails that he's still the big man on campus, so to speak.

"Maybe we should take you downtown for that threat, boy," Wilson says, finally finding his balls enough to speak up, but I'm not surprised that he's backing Shyvers. It's always seemed like Wilson followed Shyvers and did whatever he said, but if he had half a brain cell, he should have known that Shyvers was just going to get his ass in trouble if he kept following him. Or dead.

Thor shrugs. "It wasn't a threat; it was just a friendly offer."

Uncle Sam steps forward, and he pins Shyvers and Wilson with a hard look. "Shut the fuck up, you two. It's no wonder you guys are on thin ice if you treat every citizen like this."

Both of them look like they want to say something, but for once, they wisely keep their mouths shut. Uncle Sam turns toward us. "Now, you called in that you were attacked on the road, but that none of you know who it was. How about you back up and tell us what happened from the beginning?"

"Why don't we go inside? It's fucking December," Wilson whines. "Unless you have something to hide?"

The way he says that last part has ice sliding down my spine, and it has nothing to do with the December chill. Judging by the looks on my brothers' faces, I'm not the only one that feels that way.

"Sure, we need to show you the security footage, anyway." Thor tilts his head toward the clubhouse, ignoring Shyvers and Wilson's scoffs, and some of my brothers head inside. However, me and a few others wait to follow after them, wanting to keep an eye on these fuckers.

Once we're all inside, my gaze flicks to the couch, and for a moment I panic until I see that Mary is now sitting at a table next to Levi. She must have asked someone to help her move while we were outside. I hope like fuck these assholes don't focus on her, and I hope the others won't draw attention to her.

"So," Wilson starts, but Uncle Sam cuts him off with a hard glare.

"Start from the beginning, and tell us what happened," Uncle Sam says as he pulls out a notepad and pen.

Wanting to keep the focus off Mary, I step forward. "We were on our way back to the clubhouse and shortly after turning onto this road, someone shot out one of the tires on my truck. A few moments later, another one was shot out before an explosion caused the truck to roll. Once we stopped rolling, I unbuckled and tried to help Mary out, but her buckle was stuck. By then, bullets were flying around, but thankfully, none had made it through the truck yet. As I was trying to cut the belt, someone busted in the front passenger window and tried to start pulling her out and another one hollered for him to hurry up, but they weren't any of our guys."

"How do you know?" Wilson asks, his eyes narrowed on me.

"Because I didn't recognize their voices." Turning back to Uncle Sam, I continue. "One of my brothers must have pulled him off because the next thing I know, Colt's face fills the window and he helps me get Mary out. I told him to get her safely to the clubhouse, since I still needed to get out myself. He took off with her and after a few moments, I was able to crawl out, but because of a new wave of bullets, I had to stay ducked behind the truck for a bit. When the bullets died down some, I made my move and ran for the gate. As I did, I heard someone call out that they wanted my head, but thanks to Bear and Dragon, I got here with only minor injuries."

"What all did that person say?" Brady asked and I motion to Smoke.

"How about we just show you—we already know who was speaking, and it was Stephan Hayes."

"What makes you say that? It could have been any number of people," Shyvers sneers and I'm about to speak up when someone else does.

"I know my soon-to-be ex-husband's voice and it was him," Mary tells him with an edge to her voice.

His and Wilson's eyes light up and I move closer to her, not liking how they're now solely focusing on her. Or I should say leering at her—both of their gazes are glued on her breasts.

I'm about to say something when Uncle Sam raises his hands, halting my words in my throat.

"Let's watch the feed."

Turning to Smoke, I give him a chin lift and he hits play.

You can clearly see the truck swerve both times the tires are shot out and all five of them flinch when the explosion happens and I frown when I notice it came from the street below. I didn't drive over the bomb with the tires because you can clearly see the explosion happening from under the middle of the truck, so it must have been triggered by someone when we drove over it. I gotta give Smoke credit—I can't even tell where he cut out the assholes after they tried to grab Mary. Through the dust, you can see Colt, and only Colt, approaching my truck. Thank fuck Smoke verified my suspicions on our way out front that the video only showed Colt approaching me. Since he was the one helping Mary get out, I figured he'd cut out the others.

Uncle Sam's, Brady's, and Dixon's eyes harden when they hear Stephan's voice come over the speakers loud and clear, but Shyvers and Wilson share a look that has me worried. What angle are they going to try now?

I get my answer when the video stops and Shyvers pins me with a hard, narrowed-eye look. "This seems like it could be retaliation. So, what exactly did you do, Luke? Cause where I'm sitting, it looks like you kidnapped Hayes' wife and are keeping her and his children here, away from a loving husband and father."

"Bull-fucking-shit," Mary hisses out and uses a crutch that I hadn't noticed was by her to stand up, pinning the assholes with a glare that rivals a few I'd seen Levi dole out in the past. "All Stephan cares about is that his punching bag, maid, and cook has left him. I took my kids because I was *not* going to leave them there with that abusive asshole. I've got the injuries, health records, and other proof to prove he was abusing me for years. All Patch did was find me after Stephan gave me the worst beating of my life, took me to the hospital and brought me here when I was discharged. I am not being held against my will. My kids and I are here because we choose to be," she grinds out.

"And how did he find you? Was he casing your house?" Wilson asks, but his look seems to be more curious than before. Or maybe it's just my imagination?

"I got a call from my son, telling me what Stephan had done to Mary," I tell him and they both frown.

"Who's your son?" Wilson asks.

"Asher."

Shyvers scoffs. "Yeah right, kid's last name is Hayes. Stephan is his father, not you."

Stepping closer to him, I stop about a foot in front of him, and disappointment flashes through Shyvers eyes. What the fuck is that about?

"Mary was kidnapped two months before graduation when we were eighteen. She was pregnant with my son when she was kidnapped. Asher is my son, not Stephan's."

A growl reaches my ears and I step back, looking over my shoulder to see Bastion sitting by Mary who, thankfully, has sat back down.

"Bastion, **suchen** (search)," Mary commands Bastion and everyone freezes, though quite a few give her questioning looks.

How does she know Bastion's commands? Wait, does she know German, too? How many languages does she know?

Bastion steps forward, a low growl still rumbling from him. He circles Wilson and barks once before sitting down. I notice a slight tremor in Wilson's hands that he tries to hide by moving them to rest them on his belt. Then, after a few seconds, Bastion gets up and walks over to Shyvers, a low growl emanating from him again. After circling him, he sits and barks once, but doesn't stop looking at Shyvers.

"Bastion, **bleiben** (stay)," Mary tells him. "Captain Morgan, I think Officer Shyvers needs to be searched. Possibly even Officer Wilson, but I'm going to guess by Bastion's actions that he's only getting a trace scent from Wilson."

Chapter 44

Patch

"WHAT THE HELL IS going on? Why the fuck is this mutt growling and staring at me?" Shyvers grits out as he stares down at Bastion.

"That is Bastion," Levi tells him, her voice smug as fuck. "He's a pitbull and he's a retired police dog who used to help his partner search out drugs, bombs, and things like that. I'd remain still if I were you," she tells him when Shyvers shifts to step back, causing him to halt. "You wouldn't want him attacking you by thinking you're trying to hide something by running away now, would you?"

"This is bullshit. If there was a retired police dog here, why isn't there a record of it?"

Levi scoffs and shakes her head. "There is, you just obviously didn't look in the right spot, or you didn't care to look." She stands, flipping her pen in the air, before walking over to her men, both of them placing an arm around her when she's close enough. "Bastion is my dog and is registered to myself and my husbands, Thor and Dragon."

"Want me to search him, Captain?" Brady asks as he crosses his arms across his chest, waiting for Uncle Sam's orders.

"What makes you think we should just trust this mutt? They could have trained him for anything."

Uncle Sam shrugs. "Alright then. Dixon, call in Richards and Charlie," he calls over his shoulder and Shyvers face pales slightly. "We'll see if there really is anything on you when our own K9 unit gets a good sniff around."

I can't stop the dark grin that forms at Shyvers' reddened face. Richards hates Shyvers with a passion because one of the women Shyvers tried to force himself on years ago was Richards' little sister. Charlie is the German Shepherd K9 assigned to Richards.

"You're going to believe these low-life thugs over me?" Shyvers yells as he points angrily in our direction and Wilson wisely steps away from him.

Uncle Sam grabs his arm, spins him, and cuffs him before taking off his utility belt. He holds it out to Brady, who's wearing a smug smile as he takes it. Uncle Sam spins him again and gets right in his face.

"Bet your ass I'm going to believe them over you two. You're both only here because you're on thin ice with the Chief. I was ordered to take you with me so I could report back to Chief on your performance. Let's just say my report isn't going to look good on your records," he grits out as Dixon's radio crackles again.

"Captain, Richards is currently responding to a call and will be here as soon as he can."

Uncle Sam nods and turns to Thor. "Any chance we can get some coffee while we wait?"

Levi nods. "I put on a fresh pot earlier. Let me get you guys some mugs."

Dragon snags her wrist, pulling her back in between him and Thor and kisses her forehead as he caresses her stomach. "We'll handle it, Spitfire. Today was an emotional day, and with you so close to your due date, I'd prefer if you'd rest right now."

Levi glares at him and Thor wraps his arm around her waist, tucking her into his side.

"I'm not made of glass. Women have been giving birth for years. Walking into the kitchen to get mugs and coffee isn't going to make me go into labor," she protests and fuck am I glad she hasn't pulled a knife on either of them with the cops here.

Thor grabs her chin and makes her look at him. "Please, Wildcat, humor us for a bit. The accident is dredging up bad memories for both of us."

He gives her a chaste kiss and she gives a reluctant nod, her glare softening a touch.

"Fine, I'll give you this pass for now," she replies before kissing them both and then goes and sits down next to Mary as she calls over her shoulder. "Can you bring Mary and I back some waters while you're in there?"

"Sure thing, Queen." Timber follows Dragon into the kitchen, no doubt also wanting to check in on Mae while he's at it.

Remembering Wilson, I turn back to him to find him frowning as he takes in the scene. His gaze finds Mary's and then mine as his frown deepens. I quirk an eyebrow at him, but he doesn't say anything. What was that about?

"You mentioned earlier that you were heading home when the attack happened. Where were you before then?" Wilson pins Mary with a look I can't decipher.

"We were at my dad's house, packing up his and my old belongings."

His frown deepens and he looks back at Mary. "The house doesn't belong to you. How did you get in?"

Mary's worried gaze finds mine, but she doesn't need to be worried.

I clear my throat and Wilson's gaze snaps to mine. "I bought it from her grandparents years ago."

Wilson gives me a disbelieving look.

"Look it up if you don't believe me. It's listed under my name, Luke Morgan. Or did you not connect the dots that it was me? I bought it from her grandparents once I'd built up some savings so that they wouldn't have to have two mortgages. At the time, I figured that when I found Mary, she would then have the choice of keeping her childhood home or not, rather than having the decision made for her."

He scoffs and I'm getting really fucking tired of his attitude.

"Why would you do something like that? You barely know her. She could be trying to fleece you for everything you have."

A dry, humorless laugh escapes me as I plant my hands on my hips, ignoring the pain from the tightening of my skin around the stitches in my arm and hands. "You need to do your fucking homework before accusing people of doing things, Wilson. Do you not remember me saying that Mary and I had been going out when she was kidnapped and that she was pregnant with my son? I've known Mary since we were in the fifth grade. I knew as soon as I saw her that she was someone special and would always be. We already knew we wanted to get married after we graduated. I had an engagement ring picked out and everything. I planned to ask her after the graduation ceremony. But then, she was kidnapped. I looked for her and my son all this time and finally saw her for the first time in nine years when they moved back to Forest Creek. So yeah, I know my Mary isn't the woman you're describing."

He grins and worry churns in my gut.

"Is that so? Well, for one, she can't be 'your Mary' because she's still married to Stephan. Besides, are you sure you want to tie yourself to someone like her? She brings trouble everywhere she goes. It's why her mom left her. It's why her father shot himself. It's why the rest of her family abandoned her. Hell, Stephan had to deal with all sorts of shit since she tricked him into marrying him. So yeah, I'm questioning your story because if she really did love you, she would have married you and not run away to marry Stephan. Hell, even when she was with him, she wasn't loyal to him. How do you know your son is really your son?"

Mary sighs as my blood boils. How dare he say that shit about her?

"You two really are just lost little puppies, doing whatever your master tells you to do. Not to mention naively believing everything they tell you without using your own brain. Nothing we say will make you realize the truth, and quite frankly, it's none of your damn business. If I had to guess, Stephan ordered you both to try and stir up shit to get the club to kick us out of here so that it'd be easier for him to get his hands on us. He's worried about what will happen when I testify against him, and I will be testifying against him. So, go ahead and tell your master that his day is coming and he can pound sand for all I care."

Wilson steps forward menacingly, and Bastion lets rip another low growl. Moving in front of Mary, in case this asshole doesn't take Bastion's warning, my muscles tense, ready to throw down if need be despite my injuries.

Uncle Sam pushes himself between us as he gives Wilson an icy glare. "Wilson, you will stand down. You don't know what the hell you're talking about, and you will cease badgering Mary, or else you will be under further investigation. We have new evidence on several current as well as old cases that are being reopened because of this new evidence. If you do not stand down, I have orders to bring you in for harassment. Among other things."

Wilson clenches his jaw as he glares at Mary. He's not going to let this drop. Why are they so insistent on driving a wedge between Mary and me? Is it just to get the club to drop our protection of her and the kids and kick her out? Or is it something else? What are we missing?

Thankfully, the doors open and I'm relieved to see that it's Richards with his K9, Charlie, at his side. Another police officer is with him, but I don't recognize him.

"Apologies on not being able to get here when you needed us, Captain. What's going on?" he asks right as Charlie starts growling low. Both Richards and the unknown police officer glance down at Charlie, frowning.

"Bastion, the Gilberts' retired police dog, picked up a scent and we want you to see if Charlie also picks it up, but based on how Charlie's already reacting, I think Bastion was right."

Richards' nods and looks down at Charlie. "Charlie, **suchen** (search)."

Charlie walks over to Wilson, circles him, and barks once as he sits. Then he gets up and walks over to Shyvers, barks once, sits down and stays sitting down in front of him.

"Charlie, **bleiben** (stay)," Richards commands.

"This is fucking ridiculous. I'm a fucking police officer for fuck's sake. They should be the ones you're searching, not me," Shyvers growls, his jaw clenched, but the beads of sweat on his forehead betray his nervousness.

"Well, like Wilson said earlier, if you've got nothing to hide, you won't mind Richards and Daniels searching you then." Uncle Sam crosses his arms and waits to see if Shyvers will respond. When he says nothing, he nods to Richards and Daniels, who step forward.

Shyvers stupidly takes that moment to throw himself at Richards, trying to fight him even though his hands are handcuffed behind his back. Brady and Dixon step forward and after a few moments, are able to get Shyvers back on his feet, both of them gripping his arms tightly.

Richards makes quick work of his search and pulls out a baggie filled with white powder. Fuck. Daniel's searches Wilson but shakes his head.

"That asshole planted it on me," Shyvers hisses as he glares at me.

Uncle Sam chuckles lowly. "You really are a stupid fucker. You just saw that they have security footage of the attack from multiple angles. Do you really think they wouldn't have security cameras inside as well? If I was a betting man, I'd wager it was you that was hoping to plant the fucking drugs on Patch or one of the other members." He pauses as he looks over his shoulder at Smoke. "Can you pull up the feed since we arrived?"

Instead of answering him right away, Smoke gestures to the big screen. "I think it'll be easier to see it on the other screen. I've got multiple camera angles we can look at."

He hits play and after a few moments, I grit my teeth at the sight of Wilson passing the bag to Shyvers when they walk up the stairs and into the clubhouse. Maybe Wilson wasn't always following Shyvers' lead. Later, Shyvers palms the baggie as we argue, but when I stopped about a foot in front of him, he slipped the bag back into his pocket.

Uncle Sam smirks. "Smoke, can I get a copy of both this footage and the accident?"

"You got it." Smoke's fingers fly across his keyboard as he gets to work.

"Officer Bill Shyvers and Officer Ray Wilson, you both are under arrest for possession of illegal drugs, intent to falsely incriminate the innocent as well as harassment."

Shyvers takes that moment to try and break free of Brady's and Dixon's grasp at the same time that Wilson tries to make a break for the door, slipping out of Daniels grasp before he's able to cuff him.

I grin as Wilson comes to a halt when he sees Bear, Ryder, Punisher, and Beast already blocking the door.

"Going somewhere?" Bear growls menacingly and Wilson pales, but he doesn't fight Richards when he cuffs him and unhooks his utility belt.

Uncle Sam steps forward, not stopping until he's nose to nose with Shyvers. "Looks like we'll be adding resisting arrest to those charges. And who knows? Maybe more charges will be added on as we continue to comb through the copious amounts of new evidence."

Shyvers bares his teeth at him. "You'll all pay for this. You're arresting the wrong people, *Captain*."

"We'll see about that. Richards, Daniels, if you'd be so kind as to escort these gentlemen to the squad cars? Daniels, you can drive back Shyvers and Wilson's car for now. Morgan and Dixon, let's start on the claims for the truck, motorcycles, and make sure there's no damage to the property that needs to be reported."

Richards whistles for Charlie to follow after him as he leads Shyvers toward the front door with Daniels and Wilson right behind him.

A couple hours later, I'm sitting next to Mary with the kids on both of our laps as they watch a movie in the main room. Mary snuggles into my side and I pull her tighter against me as I lean over and kiss her forehead. A small smile plays at her lips and after everything that's happened today, I'm fucking glad to see her smiling.

"What's got you smiling over there, Siren?" I give her a little squeeze with the arm that's draped over her shoulders and she giggles.

She shakes her head, but her smile grows. "I was just thinking back to when I was helping Doc with your wounds. Then I remembered earlier this year when you told the kids how you earned your road name. Was just thinking of the irony that I was helping patch up Patch."

I chuckle and kiss her forehead again, beyond thankful that she wasn't injured worse than she already was. Doc checked her shoulder, but other than being a bit sorer than before, he doesn't think it was injured further. However, I did notice that she took some over-the-counter pain medicine right before we all headed out to look at the vehicles so we could report our claims. Not that it really matters. I could have easily paid for another truck without putting much of a dent in my savings.

The clubhouse doors swing open and Judge walks in with the rest of the guys that rode around to scout and make sure no more of those assholes were hiding nearby. Ethan, Bones, Razor, and Smithy are right behind them and Ethan makes his way over to us.

"I parked the van over by the others, which are in front of your condo. Keys are in the usual hiding place."

"Thank you, Ethan." He looks down at Mary's voice and dips his head before heading over to help Colt behind the bar.

"Church", Thor bellows, and reluctantly, I give Mary one more squeeze before removing my arm from her shoulders.

"Stay inside, all of you," I tell each of the kids as I hug and kiss their foreheads. Cassie clings a little tighter and longer than the boys, but eventually she lets me go. "Don't worry, Angel. There are lots more cuddles you can have after we're done meeting."

"Okay, Daddy," she says as she rises up on her knees and I just barely catch her in time before she nails my dick. I'm going to have to talk to her about this later. She places a kiss on my cheek and whispers in my ear, though it's not much of a whisper, "Love you, Daddy."

My eyes burn with unshed tears and I wrap her little body in my arms one more time. "Love you, too, Angel."

When she slides off my lap, I gingerly get up, trying not to show how much my thigh and side burn by the action. However, by the look Mary shoots me, I wasn't very successful in hiding my wince.

Leaning down, I carefully brace my hand against the back of the couch as I cup her cheek and give her a quick kiss. "Stay in here and don't go outside for anything. If the kids get tired, you have the key to my room here."

She nods and points at the ground toward the bag that's at her feet, and I realize it's the backpack we stowed in the truck. "I'll start reading through this stuff to see what's all in there. If there's anything important, I'll let you guys know."

Giving her one more quick kiss, I'm about to stand up when Phoenix walks up to the sofa and places a hand on Mary's shoulder. She jumps a bit but relaxes instantly when she sees who it is.

"Thanks for what you did earlier, Mary. Like I said, you're gonna fit in perfectly around here," he says in his normal growly and gravelly voice.

Reaching up, she squeezes his hand. "I'll always help if I'm able to and I'm glad you and the others weren't hurt worse. I just ask that you guys don't treat me like I'm made of spun glass and will break at any moment."

His lips kick up slightly, and Devil comes up, clasping him on the shoulder before turning toward Mary and giving her a chin lift as well.

"Welcome to the family, Mary. Thanks for helping patch me up."

They both lean down and kiss the crown of her head before walking across the room and into Church. Mary stares at their retreating backs in shock and I chuckle, shaking my head. No doubt she's wondering what the hell just happened. I don't know if those two will end up claiming her as their sister, but if not, then I'm sure they're going to be looking out for her just like an older brother would for their sister.

She blinks rapidly and looks up at me again. "What just happened?"

Chuckling again, I can't help but give her another kiss, though I don't voice my suspicions in case they take the silent protector route. "Not quite sure, Siren. Time will tell."

Shaking her head, she tries to hide her smile as she shoos me away. "Head on into Church. I've got reading to do."

Smiling, I push off the back of the couch and make my way across the room, but then my smile fades as I think of those fuckers down in the sticks. They are going to pay when I get my hands on them. But first, they'll be sitting on ice for the night.

Chapter 45
Patch

GRITTING MY TEETH, I ignore the throbbing of pain in my hands. Not to mention the throbbing that's been getting worse from the rest of my wounds. Doc had given me some light painkillers after he was done stitching me up, but I might have to break out the heavy meds tonight, otherwise I know I won't be able to sleep much.

Grabbing my phone, I'm about to drop it into the basket when someone gently clasps my shoulder. Looking over my shoulder, I notice Thor shaking his head.

"Keep it on you just in case she needs you or finds something we need to know."

We both turn slightly and my chest tightens when I see her going through some documents, a frown marring her beautiful face and her brows drawn in the more she reads.

What will she find? Is it just Nikos' will? Or is there more? Then I remember what she had said as I was opening the safe. Did Nikos think someone was after him and has proof of something his murderer did?

Shaking myself internally, I slip my phone back into my pocket and follow Thor into Church. The Junction Creek guys are all standing or leaning against the back wall. It's then that I realize how crowded it is in here with both clubs in here. If the clubs get much bigger, we're going to need a bigger meeting room. Once everyone else has taken their seat, Thor bangs his hammer.

"Just to recap, Drae called me shortly before we left Mary's old house. Not too long after we'd left, a package arrived for Mary," he gestures over at Ryder, who's currently dusting for fingerprints on a small box. "He set it aside in the safe box, figuring he'd give it to Mary when she got back. Then there were two drive-bys and one of the men in the car matched the description Mary gave us when Stephan changed his appearance. After the second one, he called me, which prompted us to wrap things up quickly at Mary's old house. We all know what happened once we got back to the clubhouse."

He pauses again as he looks around the room at all of us. "But before that begins, I think we need to take care of some overdue business."

Phoenix goes to get up and Thor turns his icy glare on him. "Sit the fuck back down, Phoenix. Doc had to dig two bullets out of you and a shitload of shrapnel. Dragon, go get Colt."

Phoenix grumbles but sits back in his chair as Dragon does as he asks. After a few moments, Colt steps in and shuts the door behind him. He's trying to hide his nerves, and it can't be easy with this many men staring him down. And woman. Fuck, Levi would have my ass if she realized I'd accidentally left her off that list. Though to be fair, our Queen can be downright as terrifying as some of us men.

"You asked for me, Pres?"

"Yeah, strip out of your cut and hand it over."

His face pales and his fingers shake slightly as he takes off his cut. As he does, he winces slightly and it's only then that I realize he's got a bandage peeking out from under the arm of his sleeve. Fuck, did he get that protecting my Siren? Or before?

I'm brought out of my thoughts as he hands his cut over to him. Thor takes it and stares at him. His icy glare is one that has made men piss themselves before, but Colt holds his ground under the weight of his stare, head up and shoulders back. He's so focused on Thor that he doesn't notice Tripp handing Dragon something, who is still standing behind Colt.

"Get out of here," Thor says, his voice clipped.

Disbelief and shock crosses Colt's face for a moment before he masks it. With a curt nod, he turns on his heel but stops when he sees Dragon standing in front of the door, his arms crossed, as he gives his own terrifying icy stare that rivals Thor's.

After a few moments, Dragon smirks. "You know Prospects aren't allowed in Church except for dire circumstances. Put this on and grab a seat, Cowboy."

Dragon tosses him a cut, which Colt thankfully catches. He stares for a moment at Dragon before looking down at the cut in his hand. A grin spreads across his face before he slips on his new cut, his new road name, Cowboy, stitched across the front.

Colt, though his real name is Troy, earned his nickname in school because his family farms and raises horses. His family's land actually butts up against ours. His dad and his uncle, who are brothers, run the farm together. Every now and then Colt helps them out with the horses, especially if they take in a horse that needs a lot of work. I've heard he's a fucking horse whisperer, but his passion has always been art, and he has grown so much as a tattoo artist under Axe's tutelage. Thankfully, his parents understood and didn't force him into staying on the farm. So, yeah, we kept the horse theme with his road name since horses are still a love of his, just not his passion.

Cowboy takes a seat as those nearby him clasp him on his shoulder in congratulations.

Thor bangs his hammer and everyone settles down.

"Ryder, what'd you get?"

Ryder frowns as he stares at his computer. "The prints don't match anyone in the system. Did it come snail mail or by courier?" It's then that I see he'd already dusted the outside of the box, which I'm assuming, is the one that was sent to Mary that Drae mentioned.

"Courier."

"Fuck, maybe something inside will give us a hint as to who sent it then. Last time, they weren't so careful. Maybe this will be the same."

Thor frowns and looks over at me, giving me a chin lift.

Standing, I grab some gloves out of my kit and dig my knife out of my pocket. While a part of me doesn't want to be the one to open this box, the other part needs to know what the fuck they sent Mary.

Right as I'm about to start cutting, I pull back and look up at Ryder. "Did you take pictures of the outside?"

He gives me a chin lift. "I'll also take pictures as you open it."

Carefully, I start cutting, but as soon as I make the first cut, I know whatever is inside isn't going to be good.

The stench is awful.

Glancing up, Thor's and Ryder's faces harden before my eyes, no doubt smelling the same thing I am since they are both standing right beside me.

Breathing through my mouth, I finish cutting open the box, and open the flaps to find a bloody note inside. Taking a deep breath, I read it aloud.

You took what's mine. What belongs to me. Things do not go well for those who steal my belongings. I'm going to ruin you. Take everyone you love from you and enjoy watching them suffer before snuffing out their pathetic, worthless lives. Times a ticking. Can you save them all?

There is a way to prevent all of this pain and suffering. Return what's rightfully mine and drop all the charges.

My hand shakes with anger as I re-read the note. Ryder sets down his phone and I pass him the note.

"Don't test it just yet. I have a feeling this is going to be bigger than us."

He frowns but nods as he puts the note into a plastic baggie to protect it.

Looking back down in the box, I move the newspaper out of the way and my stomach rolls when I see a dead mama robin and three little babies.

"What the fuck?" Thor growls.

"What is it?" Reaper all but demands as he pushes off slightly from the wall.

"A dead mama robin and three dead little babies."

Everyone curses and I can almost taste the anger in the room.

"I hate to ask this, but is there anything else in there besides them?" Ryder asks and I frown.

"Can someone grab a couple of tongue depressors out of my kit?"

A moment later, someone hands me the depressors, and I do my best to not disturb the birds as much as possible.

I shake my head. "I don't think so. But this fucker just threatened everyone I know. I need to warn them. Shit, Mandy's at college. It'd be so easy to get to her." Not everyone knows I have a sister, and quite frankly, I was hoping to keep her away from this life as much as possible. It's not that I don't trust my brothers with her, it's that she's too sweet, too pure. I don't want to taint her with our darkness.

"Where's she going?" Timber asks.

"She's at the Wisconsin UNI branch on the outskirts of town."

"Depending on her classes, I can help keep an eye on her. Sunshine's starting next semester and I can help out for the rest of this semester too. If I can't make it, I'll send Ethan in my place."

I give him a nod of thanks before looking back at the note on the table.

"To properly warn your family, and Mary's, we need to call this into Sam. Not sure if he can keep this on the down low, but we'll see," Thor says as he tilts his chin in my direction. "Call him, Patch."

Ripping off my gloves, I pull out my phone and dial Uncle Sam, putting him on speakerphone.

"Patch, everything okay?"

"Not really. A package was delivered to Mary earlier today, but we forgot about it with all the commotion. Any chance you and Brady can head back this way?"

He grunts over the line. *"He's here at the house, so we'll be there in a few. See you in a bit, nephew."*

I smile as I end the call and look up at Thor. "They're on their way, and they're coming as family, not the law."

Thor frowns. "What makes you so sure?"

"He used a familial term. It's their code, so to speak, to let whoever called them know that they're showing up as family rather than as the law. We haven't had to use it very many times in the past, but it's useful for when we do need it."

"Who's on gate duty right now?" Ryder asks.

"Drae's still out there," Cowboy answers.

Thor grabs his phone and taps out a text. After a moment he nods. "Drae knows to let them in and to let us know when they get here."

"Alright, you guys take your seat for now." Thor pauses as we throw our gloves away but instead of taking my seat right away, I walk back to my stash. Grabbing some more tools, as well as a box of gloves, I cross the room again and set them down on the table by Thor before retaking my seat.

"Smoke, I want you to reach out to Antonio and set up a time as soon as possible so that we can talk on a secure line. See if you can loop Harris in on it as well. In the meantime, is there anything we need to discuss business-wise?" Thor asks, but I can't focus on what they're discussing.

My mind whirls as the scope of who all is affected by this threat sinks in. There're so many people on both sides of Mary's families. My own is fairly small, but nonetheless, they are just as important to me as Mary's family is. Then there's my brothers and sisters in the club. I hope like fuck they don't try to do anything to Mae and Levi. If either of them, or their babies, are hurt, it would kill their men. Hell, it would kill all of us. I've seen, along with the rest of my brothers, how the lives of those three men have changed, and how they themselves have changed. We all would lay down our lives for Mae, Levi, and the babies, but especially their men. I sure as fuck hope it never comes to that, because I think that in turn would destroy Mae and Levi. Sure, they'd keep going for their kids, but they'd never be the same.

I'm brought out of my thoughts by someone pounding on the door. Looking down at my watch, I'm surprised ten minutes have already passed. Fuck, I hope I didn't miss anything important.

Timber gets up and lets Uncle Sam and Brady in, and their faces instantly scrunch up at the smell.

"Well, fuck, this isn't a good sign," Brady mutters as he walks straight to the table and puts on a pair of gloves.

"I found a couple of prints on the outside of the box, but they don't match anyone in the system. We haven't dusted the note, but you can see partials in the blood," Ryder tells them.

"Fuck," Uncle Sam hisses out as he reads the note as he puts on his own gloves.

He peels back the newspaper, and they both curse. Uncle Sam looks over at Ryder. "Get me your kit."

Ryder grabs his kit and together, they dust the note and do whatever the fuck it is to get copies of the fingerprints left on the card. Whoever this is, even though I'm fairly certain it's Stephan, is stupid as fuck to be leaving evidence for us. Either that or he doesn't think he'll be caught.

Another knock on the door has all of us looking up as Timber goes to find out who it is. My stomach drops as I hear Sasha's voice mentioning that something happened with Mary.

"Just a second, let me tell Thor," Timber says before shutting the door and partially turning around. "Mary's pretty shaken up about a voicemail and some stuff she just read. Sasha thinks it might be related to everything else."

I freeze at that and then I'm on my feet, stalking toward the door. Opening it, I take Mary from Ethan, holding her tight in my arms. She's shaking like a leaf. What the fuck is going on now? Don't we have enough to worry about?

Chapter 46

Mary

My hands shake as I read through the book that was in πατέρα (dads) safe. Well, more like journal. There are years of entries dating back ten years ago. Sometimes, they are days apart. Others are months and even years apart. At first, they are about my late grandma Esmeralda, but then it switches, and the rest of the entries all have two things in common.

Or I should say two someone's in common.

Carmen and Eileen Vasquez.

My stomach is in knots and I'm nauseous. Grandpa is going to be so devastated when he reads this.

When I finally get to the end, there's a name scrawled on the back.

Lucia Delgado.

Was this Lucia's journal? Who was she? How did she know Esmeralda, Carmen, and Eileen?

And how, or why, did her journal end up in πατέρα (dads) safe?

I'm brought out of my thoughts when my phone vibrates next to me on the couch. Flipping it over, I frown when I realize it's an unknown number.

That's strange.

No one other than the club, my family, or the kids' school and daycare should have this number. Setting my phone back down, I let it go to voicemail. If someone really wants me, they'll leave a message.

Putting down the book, I look through the rest of the papers. There's a copy of πατέρα (dads) will and power of attorney, which I set aside to go through in more detail later.

As I reach down to put them back into my backpack, the pages shift on my lap and a letter slips off the stack, falling to the ground. Picking it up, my stomach tightens when I recognize the Vasquez family crest in wax on the back of the envelope.

I also recognize the stationery.

Eileen had sets of stationary identical to this and I remember her using them many times while my parents were still married, but in the year before they divorced, I swear she used that stationery at least once a week, if not more. I always assumed she was writing to her family given that we were in Iowa at the time, and they were in Wisconsin. Then again, I very well could have been wrong. Whenever I asked if she was writing them, since I had wanted to write to my grandfather numerous times, she always told me it was none of my business in a clipped tone. If she was feeling particularly cruel, she would sometimes slap me as well. After a while, I stopped asking her and stopped writing those letters because I'd lost hope that she'd let me send them.

Shaking my head, I turn the envelope over in my fingers and frown when I realize it isn't addressed to anyone. No markings. Nothing except the wax crest. Noticing that someone opened the letter at the top, I take it out, but pause as I recognize the handwriting. Or at least, I'm almost positive I know whose it is. It could be that someone else's writing is extremely similar to her style, but I highly doubt it.

No, it's hers.

I'd recognize that script anywhere.

My phone rings again, but when I look, it's the same unknown number. Worry gnaws at me that it could be someone important trying to get a hold of me, but I don't recognize the number. Once again, I let it ring and after a few moments, I hear a beep letting me know a voicemail was left.

But I don't pick my phone up to check. My gaze goes back to the letter, and I stare at the familiar cursive handwriting.

Eileen's handwriting.

However, the message has both confusion and nerves swirling throughout me.

> *You can try to keep me away from her, but you won't be around forever to protect her. That worthless brat ruined everything for me, stole everything from me. It should have been mine, not hers. It was meant for me, not her.*
>
> *I will get what's mine.*
>
> *No matter the cost.*

What is Eileen talking about? Is she talking about me? Or someone else?

If she means me, I never took anything from her. Unless she wanted **πατέρας** (dad) all to herself and to never have kids, which, after hearing some of the things Grandpa told me she'd said, it may very well could be that.

Was she talking to **πατέρας** (dad) in this letter? Or someone else and **πατέρας** (dad) just happened to find the letter? Did she write it to this Lucia person?

Ugh, this is so frustrating!

As I plop my hands down in my lap, the letter starts to fold around in my hands but as it does, my gaze snags on some numbers in black ink at the bottom of the letter. Fully opening it to get a better look, I pause.

This isn't possible.

Eileen died a little over ten years ago. There's no way she could have written the letter this past January, almost a year ago. And if she really has been alive all this time... How did this letter get into **πατέρα** (dads) safe?

Maybe someone else really does have handwriting similar to hers. But then, who could have written this?

My phone vibrates again and I set down the papers to check it, but it's just reminding me of the voicemail. Hitting play, I frown as I hear heavy breathing come over the line. I'm about to delete it when the person finally speaks, but the voice is slightly distorted.

As the person continues to speak, my muscles tighten and my body starts to shake at the vile things the woman rants about. What she says she's going to do to me if I don't give her back what's rightfully hers. My gaze snaps to the letter that's sticking out of the book I was reading.

It can't be.

But there are too many coincidences and the things she's saying, it has to be. Too many—

A hand lands on my shoulder, making me jump, but it's only Sasha.

"Hey, are you okay, Mary? You're clutching the phone so hard your knuckles are white. You're also really pale and shaking like a leaf."

I open my mouth to speak but nothing comes out. Swallowing a few times, I try again. "While reading through some of πατέρα things, I found some stuff that I think I need to show the guys and my grandpa. I also," I pause as I lick my dry lips and stare down at the phone in my hand. "I also just got a voicemail." Opening my mouth, I'm about to repeat what she said, but then I snap it shut. I can't bring myself to repeat what the person said.

Sasha's face hardens as she nods. "Okay, wait here for a moment."

She walks over to the bar and talks quietly with Ethan. After a few moments, he gives her a chin lift, and she turns on her heel before walking over and knocking on the door to Church. I'm so focused on her, while also trying not to break down, that I don't notice Ethan approaching me until he takes the papers and book out of my hands causing me to jump. He gives me a small smile.

"Let's get you into Church."

I nod because right now, I really need Patch.

I vaguely hear Sasha and Timber talking, and the next thing I know, I'm in Patch's arms. They tighten around me as he walks and then he settles me on his lap.

"What's going on, Siren?"

Still not trusting my voice, I clutch the bag in my lap and hand him my phone. He presses play, and as soon as I realize he's put it on speakerphone, I shrink in on myself. I hadn't wanted *everyone* to hear what she'd said about me.

Listen, you fat fucking bitch! You need to return what you've stolen from me. I know you have it because that fat fuck never gave it back to me when he sent me my things. It was given to me when I came of age. It should have never *of been in his possession, let alone yours. Without it, I can't take what's rightfully mine. Not to mention YOU should not have inherited everything, it's all rightfully MINE! You have until the end of the week to return everything to me. If you don't, you and your precious leeches will pay.*

Patch tosses the phone down on the table and wraps me in his arms.

"It's her, Patch. I don't know how, but it's *her*."

"How do you know it's her, Siren? She died over ten years ago."

I shake my head as I pull back and reach into the bag, pulling everything out except for **πατέρα** will and power of attorney paperwork. I pull out the letter that I believe she wrote and hand it to him.

"Partially because of this and what's in here," I say as I first hold up a letter and then also gesture to the journal.

He opens the letter and his jaw ticks as he reads it.

"I know her handwriting. It's her. But the confusing part is the date at the bottom. She wrote this in January of this year. And if it really is her, I have no idea how it got into **πατέρα** safe."

"Can I see the letter, Mary?"

I startle at hearing Brady's voice, but then I remember them getting here not too long ago along with Sam, but I was so engrossed in reading the journal that I barely paid them any mind.

I hand him the letter and frown as he takes it over by Sam and Ryder. My frown deepens when he puts some dust over the letter. What is he doing?

"Seems stupidity is a continuing trait," Ryder mutters.

"They're looking for fingerprints," Patch whispers in my ear.

"Oh."

Patch chuckles and leans in closer. "Close that mouth, Siren, this isn't the time for me to be thinking those kind of thoughts."

I feel my cheeks heat and I snap my mouth closed. Then I notice the box on the table.

"Is that the package Drae mentioned arrived today?" I ask as I point at it.

Patch's fingers tighten around my waist and thigh. "Yeah, but you aren't looking inside, Mary. We'll tell you the message and what it is, but I don't want you to see that."

Swallowing thickly, I look between Patch and the box a few times before I sit up straighter.

"Tell me."

Patch motions to Brady and he picks up a piece of paper that's in a plastic baggie. Walking over toward us, I can tell by the look in Brady's eyes that he's pissed and is probably a hair trigger from going on a rampage.

"What was in the box?"

The muscle in his jaw ticks as he holds out the baggie. "A dead mama bird and three dead babies."

My anger rises at what that asshole sent, because I'd bet it was Stephan who did it. I take the baggie from him and feel my anger rising even more as I read it again to make sure I didn't misread anything the first time.

You took what's mine. What belongs to me. Things do not go well for those who steal my belongings. I'm going to ruin you. Take everyone you love from you and enjoy watching them suffer before snuffing out their pathetic, worthless lives. Times a ticking. Can you save them all?

There is a way to prevent all of this pain and suffering. Return what's rightfully mine and drop all the charges.

"That fucking piece of shit!" Raising my head, I force my body to remain still even though my anger has me wanting to inflict serious pain on Stephan for this and so much more. My gaze goes to Sam, then Brady, and then to Patch. "We need to warn everyone. He's hurt innocents before; he won't hesitate to do it again."

"Got a hit," Ryder calls out and gaze snaps up his. Brady walks back over to him, as do Sam and Thor.

"Who?"

Thor, Brady, Sam, and Ryder all share a look.

"It's her, isn't it?" Fuck, even I can hear my voice shaking. But it's not from fear, it's from anger.

Brady comes over and squats down in front of me. "I'm sorry, Mary, but it's her."

Lightheadedness instantly hits me as I stare at him. Then, a different anger lights inside me. Why did she do it? What was she trying to accomplish by doing that? What does she want? And what does she think I have? Why does she hate me so much?

"If she didn't die, then who did we bury?"

Brady frowns and shares a look with Sam. "We'll look into who was in that casket, and I'm sure you and possibly Antonio, will have to approve us to dig up the casket but it's starting to look like she faked her death."

Taking a few deep breaths, I try to calm my racing heart.

"Was there anything else you found, Mary?" Patch asks and I nod.

"I think we need to get Grandpa here, because this," I say as I hold up the journal, "has information he needs to know about. I also need to talk to you about some stuff, Patch, but I don't know who all it will affect."

"I can arrange to get Antonio here," someone says, and I look up, trying to figure out who spoke when Smoke tilts his head toward me. "I was already trying to get a secure line with him, but if you think he needs to be here, then we can get him here. The problem will be that we don't want to draw attention to the fact that a Don and his goon squad are coming to our clubhouse. If anyone's watching us, they'll know."

Chewing on my lip, I look down at the journal in my hands and my fingers tighten around the edges. "I don't trust sending it to him because it'll probably get snatched and be lost forever. I also don't want to scan the information and email it to him. This needs to stay as is. He's going to want to deal with this person himself, and I will not provide breadcrumbs that will incriminate him if anyone else catches wind of what he's done after reading this."

I'm not sure what it was I said, but the air in the room changes after I'm done with my little rant, and every single club member gives me a chin lift. There's a look in their eyes that I can't quite identify. Even in Patch's eyes. I'm going to have to ask him what's going on, but I'll wait until we're alone. Hopefully, they aren't mad at anything I've said.

A phone rings and everyone quiets down.

"Smoke."

I gnaw on my lip as I watch Smoke. Every now and then, he nods at whatever's being said over the phone. Wait, I thought only Thor and Phoenix could have their phones in here? Or did Smoke get his back when he was trying to set up the secure call? Then I nod as Patch whispers in my ear, confirming my suspicions about his phone.

"I'll let Drae at the gate know. Keep it as low-key as possible and don't bring a fucking army. We don't want to wave a fucking red flag at these assholes."

He nods again and then hangs up. "Antonio will be here as soon as he can. Let's fucking hope he listens and doesn't bring a fucking army with him. I'll arrange for Harris to come here too, so we don't have to repeat everything."

I take a couple of deep breaths as I try to calm down. Patch pulls me closer to him and, once again, I thank my lucky stars that he's by my side again.

Especially with everything going to hell in a handbasket.

Chapter 47

Mary

Thor bangs his hammer and everyone quiets down. "Patch, Mary, keep us posted if you learn anything new or if something gets sent to you. We'll reconvene when we have more information. We're still on semi-lockdown, though Mary, I'd prefer if you had others get anything you need for you for the foreseeable future and you stay on the compound. When you have doctor's appointments, you'll have a fleet with you."

After today I am all for that, so it's no hardship to nod in agreement.

"Alright then, Wildcat already called in catering for tonight, so we'll be having a party to celebrate Cowboy patching in. Patch and Mary, if you could stay behind, the rest of you, dismissed."

My gaze roams the room, and I smile when Colt, I mean, Cowboy comes over when I wave him over. I reach out to hug him, and when he hesitates and looks at Patch, I narrow my eyes at him.

"I'm allowed to decide who the fuck I hug or not. Now come here, Cowboy."

They both chuckle, but I can tell Patch's is strained. I don't know if it's because I'm touching another man, or if it's *everything* that's happened today.

Tightening my arms around Cowboy, I give a little squeeze. "Thank you so much for getting me to safety earlier and going back to help Patch."

He pulls back and smiles down at me. "Don't mention it, Mary. You're family. It's what we do."

Tugging on his cut, my smile widens. "Congratulations. Though don't be mad if I slip up and call you 'Colt' sometimes. It's gonna take a bit to get used to the new name."

This time, it's his grin that widens. "I'm sure you won't be the only one. Now, if you excuse me, I need to go find my woman."

Chuckling, I shake my head as I watch him leave and shut the door behind him. Then, I turn my focus back to Thor and notice Phoenix, Reaper, Devil, Brady, and Sam have stayed behind as well.

"Mary, we'd like to be there when you talk to Antonio and Harris tonight, to get a better feel for what we're gonna be up against and figure out the best way to protect everyone. If that's okay with you that is?" Sam asks.

"Same here, if that's okay?" Thor asks as he tilts his head toward the others.

Immediately, I nod my agreement. "Of course. I was going to talk to Patch first about some things, because I don't know what they mean, but I do have theories."

"Can we take a look at them?" Reaper asks.

Grabbing my bag, I thumb through the papers until I find the ones that I need and then grab the journal.

"This has a bunch of random towns with numbers next to them. I recognize some of the towns, they're along the coast of Lake Michigan. You don't think this could be tied to the trafficking ring, do you?"

I put the sheets of papers down on the table and immediately feel a shift in the air. Shit... Am I right?

"Mary, how were the papers all laid out in the safe?" Sam asks, and my brow dips in confusion as to why he's asking, but instead of questioning him, I dig the rest of the papers and the ribbons out of the bag before arranging them just like how Patch gave them to me.

"On top of the pile was a copy of **πατέρα** (dads) will and power of attorney. To be honest, I had put that aside to look through in more detail later. Below that, papers, including the two you guys have, the journal, and the envelope with the scan drives were like this in the safe." Pausing, I look over at the table holding everything Ryder and the guys dusted. "I'm not sure where Eileen's note fits into this though. It fell out of the stack as I was moving things around. The ribbon tied things together," I tell them as I gesture to the stack of papers and journal.

"Is there a name or anything in all of this?"

"I haven't been able to go through everything yet—just the journal, those two pages and the letter you guys dusted earlier, but yes, there are a few names I've come across." Undoing the ribbons, I flip to the back of the journal. "Lucia Delgado, and so far, that's the only time it's shown up, but I don't know who that is. However, in the book, there are three names that are mentioned frequently. Well, my grandma, Esmeralda Vasquez, is mentioned a few times in the beginning, but then for the rest of the entries, it's mostly just about Carmen and Eileen Vasquez."

My hands shake and Patch intertwines his fingers with mine on my good hand, giving me a squeeze. I turn toward him, with tears in my eyes. "I'm pretty sure I know who killed Grandma and what the reasonings, or at least some of them, were behind it."

His eyes harden as he looks from me to the journal and then back to me. "Who?"

Gnawing on my lip, I replay everything in my head, but it has to be. I don't know who else it could be. Plus, Lucia mentioned overhearing a conversation at the lawyer's office after Grandma's death.

"I'm almost positive it's Carmen."

His eyes blaze with anger, and I feel his muscles shaking under my. These last few weeks, we've all grown closer to Grandpa and some of my aunts and uncles. I've even introduced them to the kids—via video, not in person. We aren't quite ready for in person visits just yet, that and I didn't want to draw attention to us while this fiasco was going on. Though, we're careful not to say anything about why Carmen, Diego, Carlos or his wife, Gianna, aren't included in the video chats, but I think my other aunts and uncles know.

There's a knock at the door and Thor goes to see who it is. After a moment, Grandpa, Uncle Lorenzo, and **παππούς** (grandpa) follow him into the room.

"**Λουλούδι μου** (My flower), are you alright? We saw the crater in the road." **Παππούς** (Grandpa) rushes forward and looks me over. I know he worries a lot about us, especially with just getting me back, but to see the lengths the club went through to protect me was extremely eye opening.

"It's okay, **παππούς** (grandpa), I'm fine. The guys protected me, but unfortunately, a few of them were injured in the process. Patch was one of them. Oh, shit! Your leg!"

Oh, my God! How could I forget he had two grazes on this thigh, and here I'm sitting my heavy ass on his lap. I shift to get up but his hands tighten around him.

"Not a chance, Siren. After this shit, I need to hold you close."

I scoff and shake my head at him. "You could do that while I sit next to you and not cause you additional pain."

"Siren, I'm okay. Does it hurt? Yes, it does, but you sitting on my lap isn't making it worse."

I still at his words and look into his eyes for any hint that he's lying to me and that I am, in fact, making his pain worse. Not seeing any hint of a lie, I settle back against his chest.

"Okay, but if your pain increases, you need to tell me. I'll sit next to you so you can still have me close." I don't say it aloud, but I hope he's okay with having a shadow, because I don't want him to be away from me either for the foreseeable future.

Turning back to my family, I hug them all and they fuss over me for a few moments until Sam clears his throat.

"How about we back up? Mary, tell us what you found."

Before we begin, **παππούς** (grandpa) steps forward. "I just want to clarify for everyone, even though I don't think it needs to be said, I'm not here on official duty tonight. I'm here because Mary is my **εγγονή**, my granddaughter. Whatever is said, will not be repeated. Unless of course, something does come up in what Mary's found that she would need a lawyer for, and even then, I'll be selective in a court of law."

Παππούς (Grandpa) gives Thor, Grandpa, and Sam meaningful looks, to which they all tilt their head in acknowledgment.

"We are here as family tonight as well. In fact, we left our badges back at my house," Sam tells everyone. When he turns his gaze back to me, I nod. Taking his signal, I start again.

That when we were at the house, I remembered **πατέρας** (dad) telling me that if something ever happened to him, to look at what was in his floor safe. I show them the will and power of attorney, the package that was delivered today, and then I move onto the papers. However, I leave out the letter the guys dusted for right now. I'm not sure how Grandpa and Uncle Lorenzo are going to take the news.

"I was just telling the guys that I'm not positive what this is, but I have theories as to what it is. I recognize some of those towns along the coast. Stephan had taken me to a few of them before to 'watch him work' when it really was his tactic to try and keep me in line. I think it might be tied to the trafficking ring. I heard women crying and screaming in one of the warehouses, but I wasn't able to help them. That was when Stephan said what those women were going through would be my fate if I ever pushed him too far."

Tears threaten to pool at the memories of their screams and cries, but I shake my head, trying to clear them away. Patch's arm tightens around me and I soak in his strength.

The men scour over the papers, and then Grandpa's frown deepens. "A few of these towns we have warehouses in. I'll send some people to scout around and see what I can dig up."

"Do you remember anything about the warehouses he took you to?"

Gnawing on my lip, I nod at Uncle Lorenzo's question. "In each of the three locations," I tell them as I point out the names of the three towns, "the warehouses were practically on the coast. There were other warehouses around the ones we went into, but they looked abandoned. Well, more abandoned than the ones they were using. There was also dried blood splattered around in each of them, or at least in the areas of the warehouse they took me into, anyway. The last one is where I heard the women crying and screaming."

"How long ago was it that he took you to one of these warehouses, Siren?" Patch asks me, his voice lethal.

"A few months ago, in September. That was when I heard the women at that third location. With everything going on, I'd forgotten about the warehouses." Once again, the air in the room turns thick with tension. Sam's and Brady's eyes are practically ping ponging between Patch, Thor, and Phoenix, which has me looking between them as well. Turning toward Thor, he gives me the slightest shake of his head. Something tells me that they know more than what they're saying, but for some reason, they don't want Sam or Brady knowing. Or either of my grandpas. Taking my cue from Thor, I continue.

"While Stephan never took me to any of the other locations, I have heard him talking in code plenty of times but I'm not sure if the code I found, which is on the scan drive, is the one he was using during those conversations. I don't know how many different codes they might have, but I only found a copy of that one."

"Can you think of anything else, **mi precioso capullo de rosa** (my precious rosebud), that could help us narrow this down?"

Frowning, I rack my brain for any other clue, but nothing comes up about the locations. "No, he didn't really say anything else about the other locations, only referring to them by the town names or code. He mainly talked about the product they moved or the jobs Diego had him doing. Or at least I think they were talking about moving products since it was mostly in codes."

Grandpa's frown deepens. "I'll dig into this further on my side to see if I can dig anything up."

Glancing down at the journal, I bite my lip as I try to think about how to ask this next question, but there's really no way to dance around the topic.

"Grandpa, who is Lucia Delgado?"

He inhales sharply and his gaze follows mine, going to the journal that's clutched in my hands.

"Esmeralda's younger sister. Why do you ask, **mi precioso capullo de rosa** (my precious rosebud)?"

"Because I think this was hers, but I don't know how her journal ended up in **πατέρα** (dads) safe." My knuckles whiten as I clutch the journal. "Did Lucia know that **πατέρας** (dad) was applying to work at her company? Did you know?"

His shoulders fall slightly and he nods his head. "Yes, **mi precioso capullo de rosa** (my precious rosebud), I knew and he knew as well. When I heard that your parents wanted to move because of how things were at the company your father previously worked for, I told him I knew of a few places who were looking for a new accountant. Nikos took the information but was adamant that he be treated like the rest of the applicants. He didn't want any special treatment; however, I knew that wouldn't happen. Lucia wasn't, well isn't, like that. Nikos earned his job fair and square and he earned each promotion after the fact. And I'm willing to bet, I know how we can find out how this ended up in Nikos' possession."

Grandpa holds a hand out to me for the journal, and my hand shakes as I hand it to him, but thankfully, no one calls me out on it. He flips to the back and removes a knife from a sheath around his ankle. Carefully, he cuts in a straight line along the edge of the decorative paper lining and lifts it slightly. Uncle Lorenzo reaches over his shoulder, and using the tip of his own blade, starts to slide a piece of paper out which Grandpa takes. Pocketing his knife, he unfolds the paper and reads it aloud.

Antonio,

Should this reach you, I am so sorry that I was unable to bring this to your attention myself. Carmen knows that I know she killed my sister and is blackmailing and threatening me to keep me silent. She's threatened the lives of my children and grandchildren, and as much as I want to avenge my sister's death, I cannot risk their lives. I'm sorry. There is proof within these pages and the rest of the documents of her treachery and treason to both of our family's ways of living in our world.

Even though he's married into your family and that he didn't realize who you all were until after the divorce, I know Nikos Catarino is a man that I can trust implicitly. Therefore, I am trusting him with the safekeeping of this journal because I fear my time may be coming to an end and one of the reasons why I'm giving this journal to Nikos is that I don't want Carmen's secrets to die with me. I just pray my actions don't put a target on his head or his sweet daughter's head.

Carmen thought she could take my sister's company, among other things, when she married you. The company Es built from the ground up. I refuse to let Carmen ruin my sister's memory and make it a cover for their laundering and other underhanded things I'm almost positive Carmen, Diego, and Eileen are involved in. And yes, Eileen is very much alive, however, I don't think that they know that I know she's alive. They thought her cover was good enough to allow her to slip through the cracks, but I only hired her to keep her close. I've kept her under surveillance, and her actions are being recorded. She's tried multiple times to create shell accounts, but each one is shut down immediately. They are hellbent on destroying everything of Es' and I will not let them.

As a result of all of this, I've altered my will. Should anything happen to me or my children, Nikos' daughter, Mary, inherits everything since my grandchildren are all still underage and none of them have Es' drive or desire. From the stories I've heard from Nikos, she's the next one I'd trust to keep Es' dreams alive. I had considered listing Luiza as my beneficiary, but Carmen would have had an easier time of getting her hands on Es' company if I had done that. Also, I know Luiza is much happier in her current role within the company than she would be if she were to inherit the company as a whole.

The other reason why I'm giving this journal to Nikos, along with some other information, is that Carmen, Diego, and Eileen are up to something. Something that has to do with Mary, but I don't know what. I was able to copy some of their documents, but they are careful not to discuss their plans very much in the offices here. They don't realize how much security I have throughout the company, and the few conversations my cameras have recorded are on the scan drive that's with the information. I don't know if Carmen, Diego, and Eileen are going after Mary because I changed my will and they somehow found out about it, or if there is another reason. I'm sorry that I don't know more about their intentions. I also seriously hope that my actions haven't painted a target on Nikos or Mary. Please protect them if I have.

Sincerely,
Lucia Delgado

I blink as I stare up at Grandpa in shock. I know a few of the things I read in her journal were definitely about me, but are they really after me because they thought I knew Carmen killed Esmeralda nine years ago and that I'm supposedly a beneficiary in Lucia's will? Or are they after me for a different reason? Then there's that other letter and the voicemail. What do I have that Eileen wants?

I shake my head and pick up the other papers I hadn't gotten to yet. Maybe there's a clue in them.

Scanning the documents, a pit forms in my stomach and tears sting my eyes, but I desperately try not to let them fall. While Grandpa had told me she had wished she'd gotten an abortion as soon as she found out about me, I never thought she would have gone to these extremes.

"How could she?" I whisper. "I mean, she's my mom. How can someone hate their child so much? So, when I started to take after **πατέρας** (dad) more and couldn't keep the weight off, she started looking into ways to get rid of me in a way that'd give her the most profit?"

Patch takes the papers out of my shaking hands and I clutch my hands together in my lap, trying to minimize the shaking. A few moments later, he curses and looks up at the others.

"They are copies of some want ads. We should have Smoke look into it. It lists what the fuckers are looking for in a person and there's handwritten notes by each one. Money reduced if they'd do certain things. If the buyer continued doing what she wanted, they'd also get a hefty yearly bonus. She also highlighted and circled some of what the ads listed they were wanting or wanting to do to the person they bought. It looks like Eileen's handwriting."

Grandpa holds his hand out for the papers and the others read it over his shoulder.

"It is," I whisper as my mind replays what she'd written.

The worst was that she actually wanted the buyer to physically, sexually, and mentally abuse me as much as possible throughout the time period that I was in my buyer's possession. How can a mother wish for that to happen to her child?

I'm brought out of my thoughts by Grandpa's voice. Looking up, both his and Uncle Lorenzo's faces redden in anger and the deadly look they share sends a shiver down my spine, but surprisingly, it's not fear I feel. No, I want in on whatever they are planning for Eileen.

"Lucia said Eileen is still alive. Was there anything else in here that collaborates with Lucia's note?" Grandpa asks me.

Swallowing thickly, I nod.

"Show us," he demands.

I pull out the envelope from the stack of papers and hand it to him. "They dusted it for prints and it's hers. It's also dated January of this year, but I have no idea how it got into **πατέρα** (dads) safe. Earlier, I got a voicemail as well. While she did distort her voice, I know it's her from the things she said."

Once they are done reading, Patch takes my phone and plays the voicemail for them.

"I'll contact Lucia and get the alias that Eileen is using. I'll pass it along to all of you when I have it. I swear to you, **mi precioso capullo de rosa** (my precious rosebud), I will find her and revenge will be yours."

"Thank you."

For another ten minutes or so, they all go through the rest of the documents and I listen, hoping that there's more information that will help untangle the threads and show who all is behind what's going on.

"I think that's all that we can do tonight. Sam, Brady, Antonio, Lorenzo, and Harris, be discreet when you warn the others. Have them be aware of their surroundings, don't travel alone, if at all possible, text their whereabouts to another person, things like that. We don't want this fucker getting a window and him abducting anyone."

As they all say goodbye, I hug Grandpa tight as I gnaw on my lip.

"Grandpa?" I ask as he pulls away and he nods as he looks down at me.

"Can I... I mean, you know how much I like to speak Greek with my family and use Greek when talking to them or about them. I like doing that because I feel even more connected to my roots when I do that and also as a sign of respect to them." My cheeks heat and I lick my dry lips. "What I'm trying to say, or ask I mean, is if it's alright that I call you **Abuelo** (Grandpa)? And **Tío** (Uncle) Lorenzo? Would the others be okay if I spoke Spanish with them, too? I want to recognize and give respect to both sides of my family and our heritage. Unfortunately, I've forgotten almost all the Spanish I learned in high school, but I downloaded an app after I got out of the hospital and have been relearning it. I know you said I could earlier, at the hospital, but at the time, I was dealing with a lot of things left over from Stephan's abuse. I'm better now, but still, I wanted to ask and to make sure it was still okay with everything that's happened."

The beaming smiles both of them give me warm my heart and I feel some of the anxiety I've been holding onto bleed out of me.

"It would be an honor if you called me **Abuelo** (Grandpa) and spoke Spanish with me, **mi precioso capullo de rosa** (my precious rosebud)."

"Same, **mi sobrina** (my niece), and I'm sure the rest of our family would absolutely love it as well."

They both hug me tight and say that they'll be in touch.

Παππούς (Grandpa) beams down at me, a proud look on his face.

As everyone heads to the door, Patch lifts me in his arms and I freeze.

"If you so much as pop a stitch with this stunt, Luke Morgan, you are going to be in so much trouble, Mister," I hiss at him but then my breath catches in my throat at the heated look in his eyes.

"I'm not going to pop a stitch, Siren. Not by just doing this. Now, let's head out to the party because I'm not sure how long I'll last before I need to get my hands on your gorgeous olive skin again."

My face heats and I quickly glance around, making sure none of my family heard him, and I release a shaky breath when I see them across the room. Biting my lip, I feel my legs clench in anticipation and his nostrils flare.

"I can't wait. I need you, too."

He sets me down on a chair at a table and slips behind me slightly. I chuckle when I notice him adjusting himself.

God, I really hope he means what I think he means. After almost losing him today, I really need him.

Chapter 48

Patch

Carrying Mary out into the common room, I do my best to not show how fucking hard I am for her, since her grandfathers and uncle are still mingling by the door before they say goodbye to Thor and Reaper. I felt her clenching her legs moments ago and fuck did that have my semi going to full mast so fast I was dizzy for a moment.

Setting her down at a table, I step behind her to adjust myself, but then I hear her soft chuckle and I know she caught me. Glancing toward the door, I breathe a sigh of relief when her family says goodbye one last time before leaving. Leaning down, I brush her hair off her shoulder and place a kiss right where her neck meets her shoulder. My cock leaks when I feel her shudder in response and I smile. I hope she's ready because tonight, I'm not holding back. Not even our injuries will stop me tonight, but they do mean we'll have to be creative.

Pushing those thoughts out of my head, I kiss her again. "I'll go and get you something to drink and some food. I'm sure the kids are around here somewhere."

As if thinking about them summoned them, I hear their footsteps stampeding down the hall and turn, grinning when they come running straight for us. Crouching, I fight back my wince as my stitches pull and hold open my arms. All three of them run into my arms as they shriek 'Dad' and 'Daddy'. As I hug them, I thank my lucky stars that none of them were hurt today.

Giving them each a kiss on their heads, I pull back slightly. "How about we get some grub?"

Ash looks up at me, a curious look on his face. "I heard there's a party tonight. What's it for?"

I point over at Cowboy, who is standing across the room with his arm around Sasha as they talk to Axe and Gunner. "Colt is no longer a Prospect. He got his patches today and his new road name is Cowboy."

A few days after Mary was discharged, all three of them had asked about the difference between the roles in the club, so when all three of their faces light up with smiles, I'm not surprised when they run over to him, Cassie latching onto his leg as they shout 'congratulations' at him. He smiles and picks her up as he bumps fists with the boys.

Chuckling, I give Mary a chaste kiss. "I'll get your food and then wrangle the munchkins to get theirs."

The smile lighting up her face as she watches the kids brightens even more when she turns toward me. "Thank you."

Heading to the food line, I grab a little bit of everything I think Mary would like, as well as one of the flavored waters out of the fridge that she's come to love.

"How's she doing?" Mae asks as she comes up next to me to grab her own flavored water.

My gaze lands on Mary again and I nod. "I think she's doing okay. Time will tell, though." I make no mention of what we'd just found out, as I'm not sure if Mary wants that spread around.

"Tomorrow, after the kids are done with school, we're planning a little mini-spa day over at my house to kind of help us all relax after all of this. Nikki and Sadie are also coming, and I think Susie and Jordan are as well. Timber said he'd help watch the boys while we did our thing. Do you think Mary and the kids will be up for it?"

Smiling down at her, I nod. If my hands weren't full, I'd give her a hug for how much her and Levi have been including Mary and the kids in things. "I think she'd love that. I'm probably not going back to the hospital for a while due to my hands, so I'll help Timber out with the boys." Fuck, I really need to call my boss and let her know, but I'll wait to do that until after supper. I still have some vacation time left since I don't go back until next week Monday, but if my wounds don't heal before then, I might need some more time off.

"Great! I'll talk to her about it while we eat." Grinning, she heads to the food line to get her own plate and I head back to Mary.

Handing Mary her drink, I almost spill her plate when someone crashes into my legs. Looking down, I grin at Cassie's face, smiling up at me. Mary laughs as she takes the plate from me.

"You have to be careful, Angel, Patch almost spilled."

Carefully, I pick up Cassie. She wraps her arms around my neck and kisses my check. "Sorry, Daddy."

God damn, my heart tightens at hearing them all calling me their dad and I clear my throat, swallowing my emotions. "It's okay, Angel, just be careful next time. Now that your mom has her food, let's get you three your plates."

Heading back to the line again, I set Cassie down and help all three of them fill their plates.

"I've got their milk," Mae calls over her shoulder at me as she walks by us right as I'm finishing up plating the rest of their food.

"Thanks, Auntie MaeMae," Isaiah replies, jumping up and down on his toes, his eyes bright with excitement as he watches her. Ash and Cassie both call out their thanks as well. I'm not sure when they started adding on the 'Auntie' like the other kids, but judging by Mae's beaming face, she loves that they think of her like that. However, it still wrecks me how much they get excited over having milk to drink at a meal.

"Okay, Ash, you carry your plate. Isaiah and Cassie, I've got yours. Let's all follow Mae to the table."

Setting down their plates, I scoot all of their chairs in and then head back to the line to get my own food.

Minutes later, we're all seated and Mae's already excitedly explaining their plans for tomorrow.

Mary bites her lips and looks shyly at me before turning back to Mae. "That sounds like fun. It's been forever since I've done anything like that. What will the boys do, though?"

Timber catches my eye and I'm sure he's feeling the same as I am, neither one of us missing what she's really saying. He clears his throat before turning back to Mary.

"I figured we'd either hang out in the backyard playing games or watching them has they play in the treehouse. I finished it a few days ago, so it's ready to be broken in." The smile he and Mae share has me grinning like a loon. Both of them are excited for their kids to be born, and I'm hoping I'm right in that they are all boys. With how many girl kids and babies we have right now, we need some more boys to help look out for them.

Isaiah's eyes light up as he looks between Timber and me. "Can we play with the nerf guns again? That was so much fun last time."

Chuckling, I nod. "As long as it's okay with Timber, then yeah you guys can play with them."

Seeing both his and Ash's eyes light up even more, I pull my phone out and text Timber.

Patch: Let me know which ones they really liked of yours. I want to get some for our house, too.

Timber: Already got you covered. After Sunshine surprised them with the nerf guns back when Mary was in the hospital, I bought extras of the ones they really liked as well as a shit ton of darts. Prospects should have brought them over and put them in the garage for you.

Shaking my head, I give him a chin lift in thanks. I shouldn't be surprised that he did that, especially after seeing how close the kids got to him and Mae, but I still am. Putting my phone away, I dig into my supper.

After supper, Mary excuses herself to the bathroom, which she insists on being able to do herself in the wheelchair Doc brought up from downstairs, even though it's a regular wheelchair. The kids run off to the playroom and I head to the bar to grab a drink. Leaning against the bar, I scan the room.

A few minutes later, arms encircle me, and I smile, but as I turn around, the smile vanishes in an instant.

"I've told you multiple times not to touch me, Cici. What do you want?"

She pouts as she flicks her hair over her shoulder and sticks out her chest. I know she thinks she's being sexy, but it isn't coming across that way. God, why did I ever sleep with her? Granted, it was before she became a bunny, but as soon as she tried to hit on me once she came here, I put a stop to it fucking quick.

"You look so tense and stressed. Why don't you let me ease some of that tension, Baby? We used to have so much fun together, why not repeat it?"

Bile rises in my throat at the thought of touching her like that again. And it isn't because she isn't pretty, she is, but her kind of pretty is only skin deep. I quickly found out she's a jealous, hateful, spiteful bitch wrapped in a pretty package. That and the only way I could get off was to picture she was Mary.

"Why the fuck would I ever tap you again? That was a mistake I never should have made. Especially with how you turned into a stage ten clinger afterward."

Anger flares in her eyes, but it's quickly snuffed out. "Ah, you don't mean that, Patch. You're just too stressed. Let me help you." She reaches forward, running her hand down the length of my cock before I can grab her hand and yank it off me.

"I told you never to touch me," I growl and hear the room go silent behind me.

She smiles slyly and I know Mary's in the room without even having to turn around. I've always been able to feel when she's in the room. "See, Baby. You're hard for me. Let's get out of here and I can rock your world again."

"For the last time, I will never have sex with you again, Cici. You are never to touch me again, either. I hate to break it to you, but the only way I could get off before was thinking that you were Mary. What we had was a one-night stand that was supposed to stay in the past, but you just refuse to let it stay there. The woman I want is Mary. She will be my Old Lady and she will be my wife someday as well as mother of my children. Get lost, Cici."

Her face turns in disgust and she wrenches her hand out of mine. "How the fuck can you continue to reject me?" She pauses and waves her hand behind me. "How the fuck can you want that fucking cow with those three little brats over all of this?" she asks as she gestures to her scantily clad body.

Smirking, I shrug. "Easy. Mary is beautiful inside and out. She's been my soulmate since we met when we were ten years old. I love and worship every single one of her curves. She's also given me the greatest thing ever—my children. And yes, they all are mine even if two of them don't share any blood with me. She is my ride or die.

"I hate to be this fucking blunt, but you seem to not be able to get it through your thick, stubborn skull. You were just a release. I needed to scratch an itch and you were willing. That's all it was. If you came here and signed up as a bunny hoping I'd take you as my Old Lady, you were sadly mistaken. It's always been Mary for me, and it always will be."

I hear Mary come up next to me and she puts an arm around my waist.

"And you've always been mine," she says as she tugs on my cut.

Bending carefully, I kiss her passionately, and when I hear her sweet moans, I get even fucking harder. However, this is not the time or place for that. Also, I know the kids are still playing with Lindsey and I know Mary wants to talk to the ladies some more.

Turning my back on a sputtering Cici, I wheel Mary over to the ladies and go to sit with the guys nearby. My gut churns when I see Cici staring at Mary with a look of hatred and anger, and I really hope that she doesn't end up causing problems for us like we've had in the past with other bunnies.

Chapter 49

Patch

A COUPLE HOURS LATER, I can tell the kids are lagging and with tomorrow being a school day, I think it's time to call it a night. Not to mention, I have plans of my own for tonight.

Getting up and walking over to the table that they're sitting at, I lean on the backs of their chairs and then pull back, biting back my hiss of pain as I look down at my bandaged palms. Fuck, this is going to take some getting used to. Looking down, I smile as I take in the pictures they've been drawing.

"Hey, munchkins, those are some amazing pictures, but I think it's time to call it a night. If you want, we can take the ones you've finished home and put them up on the fridge."

At my voice, they look up from the coloring books someone got for them and then quietly start gathering everything up. Ash puts them all back in the bin that's on the table and then runs down the hallway with it. I make it a mental note to check out the room Mae said they'd set aside as a play area for the kids tomorrow.

Isaiah puts their pictures in a pile right as Ash comes back and is carrying their coats and Mary's. I help them get into them before walking over to Mary, who is talking to Elvira, Levi, and Mae. Placing my hand on her shoulder, she looks up and smiles at me before turning back to the women.

"I think this is my cue. It's time to head out, but I'll see you all tomorrow."

"Have a good night," Levi says with a wink, which has a beautiful blush staining Mary's cheeks.

After helping Mary into her coat, I pick her up off the couch and set her in the wheelchair we had stashed downstairs. I've already put in for a new powered one for her. Unfortunately, it won't be here for a few more days, so this one will have to do for now.

As we walk back to the house, the kids tell us about how much fun they had today and my heart squeezes when they get to the part where they had to go down into the panic room.

"It was so cool, Mama! Levi opened a secret door in the playroom and we got to play with new toys! There were a bunch of movies, games, coloring books and so many toys!"

Ash's lips thin as he looks from Cassie to me and he holds my gaze for a few moments, questions filling his eyes. In this moment, he seems so much older than his nine years, and I hate that he's had to grow up so fast. He knows they weren't down there to play, but how much do I really tell him?

Once we reach our front door, I unlock it and we all file in.

"Make sure to hang up your coats and put your shoes on the mat in the mudroom," Mary calls out and the kids run through the house to do as she says. While we do have a closet by the front door for coats and shoes, we've already decided that the kids' stuff will be in the mudroom by the garage door to make it easier for when we go places or for when they go back to school.

After hanging up Mary's coat and slipping off her shoes, I do the same. Shutting the closet door, I lean against it and take another look around our new home. Well, our home until we can build a house.

There are hardwood floors throughout the main floor, which is a major bonus for Mary right now. The living room is spacious, with two large couches facing the TV in sort of a 'V' shape. Off the living room and down a short hallway is a full bathroom that also connects to the office, which we're using as Mary's room, and hopefully, my room as well. The kitchen is extremely spacious, and I love that you can see most of the living room from the island. I know that once Mary has enough strength, she'll be cooking up a storm in here.

Upstairs, there are three bedrooms and another full bathroom. They're a little small for my taste, but from what I've gleamed from a few conversations with Mary, these rooms are bigger than anything they'd ever had before. I will say though, when we build our own house, there will be more bedrooms, spacious ones, because I plan on having more kids with Mary. If she agrees that is. I'd never force that on her. And I can't forget to make sure there's a big enough space for her garden. That is one Greek trait I knew she liked doing—growing her own food.

Pushing off the wall, I walk toward them.

"Okay, kiddos. Give mom hugs and kisses and then I'll tuck you all in."

The beaming smile Mary gives me as she looks at me over the top of their heads warms my chest and simultaneously makes my pants even tighter than they were.

Cassie whines a little. "But why can't you come tuck us in too, Mama?" she asks but Mary shakes her head.

"Remember, Daddy got hurt today and he's already carried me around a lot. Probably more than he should have, and I don't want to make him hurt worse."

Fuck, I would have totally carried her upstairs if she wanted to, but the look she gives me has me biting my tongue. I know she's holding herself responsible for everyone that got hurt, but it's not her fault. It'll take some time, but I'll make sure she eventually understands that she's not at fault for what someone else did.

Taking her lead, I lean down, pick Cassie up, and set her on Mary's lap. After doing this with all of them, I lead them upstairs, but Ash hesitates. He looks between us a couple of times, almost like he wants to say or ask us something.

Squeezing his shoulder, I turn toward Cassie and Isaiah. "How about you two head upstairs, brush your teeth, and start getting ready for bed? I'll be up there in a moment."

They both clamor up the stairs, giggling as they go and talking about how much they like their new rooms.

I wheel Mary further into the living room so that she's next to a couch, grateful that we don't have snow right now, otherwise I would have had to dry off the wheels of her chair. Sitting down in the middle of the couch, I pat the space between us.

"Come sit and tell us what's on your mind, Ash."

He chews his lip for a moment, his gaze nervously going between me and the cushion next to me. Frowning, I don't like where his mind immediately went, but I know it'll take time for all of them to overcome their demons.

"Asher, look at me, son," I tell him gently before pausing as I rest my elbows on my knees and wait until his gaze meets mine. "I will never hurt you, Ash. I know it'll take some time for your mind to realize I'm not like him or any of his friends.

None of the men and women here are like them. But, until you're at that point, it's okay to tell us if you need more space or if you want me to sit across from you rather than next to you. I won't be mad at you for that. Well, I will be mad, but my anger isn't directed at you—it's directed at him for doing this to you. You will never be punished for telling us how you feel. And while I'm sure you'll have questions about things while we live here on the compound, I will do my best to tell you as much as I can."

"But not everything?" he asks and his face falls a little when I shake my head.

"Ash, there will be some things that I won't tell you because I'm trying to protect you. Others may be because it's something us grownups need to handle, and while you're a very bright and smart kid, you are still a kid. Now, I'm not saying this to be mean, but I don't think you and your brother and sister were allowed to really be kids unless you were home alone with your mom. Even then, you weren't really free to be kids because there was always that part of you that was alert and waiting for him to come home unexpectedly. Am I right?"

He nods and his eyes mist a little, but just as quickly as the tears appear, they're gone.

"Well, now, you three get to be the kids that you are. Let your mom and I worry about the adult things for now. We'll protect you, keep you fed and clothed, keep a roof over your head and make sure you have an education. As you get older, we'll give you more responsibilities, but for now, we just want you to focus on being you. On being a kid. We'll protect you so that you don't always have to be looking over your shoulder, okay?"

This time when his eyes mist over, one escapes and I slowly reach forward, giving him time to step back, but he leans into my hand and I wipe away the tear.

"Now, tell us, Ash. What's got you worried?"

"The panic room."

I nod for him to continue. I'd wondered if that was what was bugging him. Or at least a part of it, anyway.

"I overheard Aunt Levi telling Auntie MaeMae and Granny Elvira that we needed to get to the panic room. Then they quickly moved us and Lindsey down into the secret rooms. But, Dad, why do you guys even need a panic room? I thought you weren't the bad guys? There's a kitchen down there with a huge pantry stocked full, a couple of rooms full of bunk beds and cots, two bathrooms, and I saw Aunt Levi getting a gun out of a secret panel in the wall. There were lots of guns in there. I even saw all the knives she keeps under her jacket. Why do you need all of that if you're the good guys?"

"Oh, Sweetie," Mary starts and then wheels forward a bit to take his hand. "Your dad and the club are good men and women. They fight for what's right. But sometimes, like today, bad guys attack them in an attempt to get back someone that they're protecting. I will tell you this, but you have to promise that you don't breathe a word about what we say to your brother and sister. Is that understood?"

He nods and I swear he stands taller.

"Stephan was behind today's attack. He tried to take me and he wanted to... He wanted to hurt Patch. And I can't thank Levi and the others enough for getting you kids to safety so quickly."

Ash's face pales slightly but his jaw clenches. "We're not going back with him."

"I know," Mary replies as she nods and squeezes his hand. "He refuses to take no for an answer. In his mind, us leaving him is an embarrassment. A stain on his reputation. He thinks he owns us because he bought me from my kidnappers years ago. To him, we're possessions. Not people. Your dad, the rest of the club, and our families are trying to stop him and prevent him from ever hurting us again."

He frowns and shakes his head. "You can't buy people."

Mary's eyes mist, but she stays strong. "You're not supposed to be able to, but he did, and he kept me a prisoner these past nine years. Thanks to your dad and the club, we were finally able to get free of him."

Ash nods a few times as he thinks over everything we've just told him, and probably the cliff note version we'd told them a few weeks ago.

"Okay, I think I understand, but I still have a question about the panic room."

"What's that?"

"Is there only the one? Do we need to know about any others in case this happens again?"

"We used to have a couple of them, but shortly after Levi came here, she suggested we combine them to make a bigger panic room setup for when the club grows. The new, larger panic room is the one that you all were in. We have a couple of secret entrances throughout the clubhouse that all of us club members and Old Ladies know about. Well, and Elvira, since she's taken to helping watch over the kids. After combining the panic rooms, we made sure there were a couple of really thick steel doors you have to pass through before you are allowed into the room. That's to help keep out anyone outside of the club should they find the entrances. Or slow them down if they manage to get through them.

"Now, as for your earlier question as to what all was down there, it's for if we need you kids and the women down here for an extended period of time while we fight off the bad guys. Think of Levi and Mae for a moment. Soon, they'll be having their babies, and they're going to need the kitchen area to prepare food and bottles, and an area for the babies to nap. For the older kids, we made sure there were things like movies and games to keep you all entertained while you're down there. We wanted it to be a safe place but also homey and comfortable, for instances like today. Did you feel safe down there?"

Instantly, he nods. "Yeah, Gunner, Tripp, and Smithy were down there with us as well and they stayed near three doors and watched something on a tablet. When Auntie MaeMae put on a movie for us, Cassie kept getting worried about you and Mom at first. She only calmed down when Tripp offered to hold her while she watched the movie and promised he'd let her know as soon as you guys were safe. He kept his promise and told us when Colt, I mean Cowboy, carried Mom into the clubhouse and then when you safely made it behind the gates. It was only then that she started playing again with Izzy and Lindsey."

Relief flows through me at my brothers' actions. I'll need to make sure to thank them later for helping them calm down, especially Cassie.

"Good. We want you to feel safe down there and we will always do whatever we can to come back to you. Understand?"

He nods and steps forward, wrapping his arms around me. "I'm so glad we moved back here and you and Mom found each other again."

My chest tightens and my eyes burn. Fuck, this kid. Kissing his head, I tighten my arms around him slightly. "So am I, Ash. So am I."

After a few moments, he pulls back and then goes over to Mary, hugging her as well.

"Is there anything else you wanted to talk about tonight?" I ask him when he steps back from her and he shakes his head.

"I think I understand things better now. In my head, I kept hearing the lies he'd tell us about the club." He pauses as he shakes his head, looking down shyly. "I shouldn't have let them get to me. I'm sorry."

"It's okay. It'll take time, but eventually you'll stop hearing his voice in your head. If that ever happens again, you can come and ask me about whatever's bothering you and I'll tell you as much as I'm able to. However, just know that I might not be able to tell you everything so that I can protect you. Okay?"

Once again, he comes over and hugs me tight as he whispers, "Thank you," in my ear.

After a few moments, I pull back and stand up. "Head on upstairs and start getting ready for bed. I'm just going to help your mom get into the bedroom."

He heads upstairs and I turn toward Mary, cupping her cheek and kissing her. "Let's get you in the bedroom," I all but growl and when I see the shiver that runs through her, my dick hardens almost painfully.

She bites her lip as she looks up at me, and thank fuck, I see the same desire reflecting back in her gorgeous green eyes.

Wheeling her into the bedroom, I stop at the entrance to the bathroom and lock the wheels. Helping her undo her sling, I hold my hand out, help her stand, and support her as she hobbles to the bathroom sink. I'm always nervous when she does this, afraid that she'll fall and hurt herself. She's been healing so well now that she isn't getting beaten every other day and has been getting better and more nutritious meals.

"Are you going to be okay with me leaving you here to tuck in the kids?"

She rolls her eyes and nods. "Yes, Luke, but thank you for worrying. Besides, we left the crutches in here earlier to help with instances like this. I'll be fine. Go tuck the kids in and I'll do my thing."

The blush that stains her cheeks and how she's nibbling on her lip has me thinking her thoughts are probably as dirty as mine. Not being able to resist, my fingers thread through her curls and I kiss her like my life depends on it.

"Fuck, Mary. The things I want to do to you and your fucking gorgeous body." A growl escapes and I feel a shiver run through her.

She looks up at me with a saucy look. "Well, then, you better get out of here and take care of our kids."

Taking a deep breath, I grind my palm on the base of my cock. I need it to go down before I head upstairs. Sometimes I'm still surprised that she's come so far these past few weeks, not to mention letting me touch her so soon after everything.

Kissing her forehead, because if I kiss her on the lips, I'd never make it upstairs, I step back. "Be back in a bit. Yell if you need me for anything."

She rolls her eyes as she waves me off and I head upstairs.

Chapter 50
Patch

TWENTY MINUTES LATER, THE kids are all tucked in after I read them a couple of short stories and I go around to each of their rooms, making sure all the windows are locked before shutting off their lights and closing their doors.

As I head down the stairs, my pulse kicks up with every step I take toward Mary, but first, I do a walk around and do the same thing down here, making sure everything is locked up. Satisfied, I head to our bedroom and open the door, only to stop in my tracks.

Mary is laying on the bed wearing a sexy as fuck black nighty. My blood boils at seeing all of her olive skin on display and how the nighty hugs her curves.

"Fuck, Siren." I close the door behind me and lock it so that if one of the kids wakes up, they can't just barge in.

Quickly crossing the room, I slide her hand down her thigh and almost groan aloud, but then I see it. A slight tremble in her hand. I don't know if it's just being nervous since this is the first time she's done this for me, or if it's something more.

"You like what you see?"

I crawl over her, causing her to shift onto her back, and lean down on my forearms to keep the pressure off my hands as I settle in between her thighs.

"Very much so, Siren. I always think you're sexy, but when you're like this, or even naked and laid out in front of me, you're even sexier."

Her gaze lowers at my words and she turns slightly off to the side, a look I know all too well on her. I'm going to beat his ass black and blue when I finally get my hands on that fucker, but I push those thoughts away. I will not let him take any more of our night away. Or Cici. I should have warned Mary about her, but I had hoped that Cici would have seen she never had a chance of getting with me permanently.

Grasping her chin, I turn her so that she has to look at me.

"Don't let them win, Siren. I've always loved your curves, and I'm willing to prove that over and over again until you believe it. While yes, I've found many skinny women beautiful, not one of them compares to you. How aroused I get when I see your gorgeous olive skin and every single curve. Is that what I need to do? To prove it to you again? To prove how much you mean to me and how you make me feel?"

Her pupils dilate and when she licks her lips, I bite back a groan. I am not rushing this tonight. This is too important.

I kiss her gently before I start kissing down her jaw, and when I get to the spot right by her ear, I feel her shudder under me.

"To kiss and lick every inch of your body?"

I continue down her neck, my teeth scraping the skin of her collarbone slightly and my cock twitches when I feel another shiver run through her.

"To repeatedly worship your gorgeous body over and over again until you believe that your body is heaven for me. Honestly, you're even sexier now than you were in high school with this even curvier body." I pause, leaning into her more so she can feel how hard I am. "This is all for you, Siren. No one else. You are the only one that has ever gotten me this hard."

Kissing down her chest, I run my tongue through her cleavage and her breathing picks up as I get closer to her nipples. Finally reaching my goal, I run my tongue in circles a few times around her nipple, leaving a wet mark on the silk. Her fingers thread through my hair, tugging slightly on the strands. After a few moments, I switch to the other nipple, giving it the same treatment while I slide a strap down her arm and free the breast I'd just been teasing in my hands and start teasing the nipple with my fingers. Taking more of her breast in my mouth, I groan at feeling the weight of her breast in my other hand. Fuck, I love her breasts, and I love how sensitive they are.

"L-Luke," she pants and when I gently bite down, she cries out as she shudders. She grinds her hips against me, trying to get the friction she so desperately wants.

Pulling back, she whimpers at the loss and I smirk as I cross the room, slipping out of my cut and placing it on the dresser. I open the nightstand and put my gun away in the gun safe and then toe off my boots.

Her hands trail down her stomach and I narrow my gaze at her. "Don't you dare touch my pussy, Siren. That's mine to pleasure and trust me, by the time I'm through with you, you will be thoroughly pleasured."

Her eyes blaze with lust which only deepens when I reach over my head and pull my shirt off. I unbutton my jeans to give me some relief, but I keep them on as I approach the bed again. If I were to take them off now, I'd be sinking into that sweet pussy and I'm not entirely sure if she's ready for that just yet.

Grabbing her hips, I pull her toward the edge of the bed and a growl escapes when I see her black thong is already drenched with her juices. Hooking a finger under the fabric, I pull and smirk when she moans at the sound of the fabric tearing away from her body.

Carefully kneeling down, I lick her from practically ass to clit, humming as her taste hits my tongue, before pulling back and kissing her thigh.

"Luke," she grits out as she glares at me and I look up at her before biting her thigh. She cries out and wiggles as I lick the sting away. She's always loved when I bite her like this, and it seems that's still the case.

I kiss and lick my way down her leg to her ankle and then make my way back up to her thigh, but I purposefully skip over where she wants my mouth the most and repeat the process on the other leg.

"Luke, please," she whimpers as her hips tilt up, looking for friction that isn't there.

"What do you need, Siren?"

Smiling, I bite her thigh again and lick her harder before leaning up a bit and kissing my way up to her stomach, kissing and nibbling along the way. She shakes her head as her fingers tug even harder on my hair.

Grabbing her breasts, I release the other one from behind it's silky confines and push them together; teasing, biting, and licking them until I feel her body quivering beneath me.

"Tell me, Siren. What is it that you need?"

Her face and neck flushes and I know I'm pushing her outside of her comfort zone, but I think this is what she needs to get out of her head.

She pushes on my head. "Lick my pussy, Luke."

"As you wish."

Kissing down her stomach, I grin when I feel her body's response to my words. Growing up, Mary was a huge *Princess Bride* fanatic, and I can't tell you how many times I've seen that movie in my life. Or seen her re-reading the book. It started out as just a little fun, but then she started craving hearing the words whenever we would be intimate.

Flattening my tongue, I lick through her folds, and when I get to her clit, I start sucking on it.

"Oh, my God!"

Reaching up, I run a finger through her juices before pumping it into her, and after a few moments, I add another one. Her thighs tighten around my head, and I feel the slight tremble in her thighs. Sucking harder, I curl my fingers which has her juices exploding out of her as her orgasm crests. Releasing her clit, I lick her juices up, not wanting to waste a drop. Her body twitches with aftershocks, but I don't let up. I keep licking and pumping my fingers in and out of her, prolonging the aftereffects of the orgasm.

Mary tugs on my arms, and I kiss my way back up to her plump lips. She kisses me hard, and I gather her in my arms, pulling her tight against me as I grind against her center.

"I need you," she pants and I pull back, tucking a few damp strands behind her ear. Her eyes mist and I kiss her again. She cups my jaw, running her thumb across my cheek. "I'm serious, Luke. I could have lost you today. I need you."

"You have me, Mary," I tell her as I peck her lips. "You had me since that first day I saw you. I always knew that you were someone special, but at the time, I never knew that you'd come to mean this much to me. If we do this, there's no going back. You're mine, Mary."

"I've always been yours, Luke. Even when everything surrounding *him* happened, it's always been you. Now, get undressed and fuck me."

"As you wish."

Kissing her one more time, I pull back and taking her hand, I help her sit up. Sliding her nighty up her torso, I let my fingers trail just after the silky material, leaving a wake of goosebumps as I go. Tossing it to the floor, I step back and hook my thumbs in the waistband of my jeans and boxers and drop them both to the floor. Reaching over and into the nightstand, I grab a condom, but she reaches over, placing her hand on my arm.

"No, you don't have to use one unless you want to."

My heart rate kicks up as my head whips around to look at her. Is she serious?

Dropping the condom, I cup her cheek as I study her. "Are you sure, Mary? I know you aren't on anything."

She nods and licks her lips. "I'm sure. They ran tests when I was in the hospital as a just in case and I'm clean." She pauses and licks her lips again. "I want you to take me bare. I want to have another baby with you, Luke. Well, babies. If you want to, that is."

The words are barely out of her mouth when my lips slam down on hers. Fuck, this woman is going to be my undoing. Breaking the kiss, I pull her back down to the edge of the bed. I'd much rather be fully on top of her, but with my injuries and hers, this is going to have to do for now.

Grabbing a pillow off the bed, I tap her thigh. "Up, gorgeous."

She lifts her hips and I settle the pillow under her ass. Pumping my cock a few times, I damn near burst when she licks her lips as she watches me. Fuck, I need to get a handle on myself, otherwise I'm going to blow as soon as I'm inside her. Grasping the base of my cock, I hold it tightly for a few moments until I feel myself coming back from the edge.

Lining myself up, I ask once again. "Last chance. Are you sure you want me to take you bare?"

She hums as she wraps her legs around my hips and grasps her breasts, playing with her nipples. Her pupils are so blown there's hardly any green in her eyes anymore. "I'm sure, Luke. Now fuck me already and put a baby in me."

Notching myself at her entrance, I enter her slowly, even though I'd much rather thrust into her in one pump. Leaning forward, I rest my weight on my left forearm as I kiss her and play with her breast with my free hand. Her body tenses around me and I slow down, allowing her time to adjust to my size.

Once I'm fully seated, I take a deep breath.

"Give me a sec, Siren. You feel so fucking good. This first time is going to be fast, but I'll for damn sure make it up to you tonight."

She moans as I tweak her nipple, her body arching up off the bed and pressing into mine.

"I definitely like the sound of multiple rounds, but if you don't move, Luke, I'm going to take matters into my own hands."

A growl rumbles in my chest and I pull out before slamming back into her. She cries out and I kiss her to swallow her screams. Fuck, she feels so good. I can feel every quiver of her pussy as her orgasm climbs while I piston in and out of her.

Pulling back, I grasp her hips, lifting her higher.

"Grab a pillow, Siren."

She does right as I change my angle and drive deeper into her. Her mouth opens in a silent scream as her eyes roll up. Her perfect breasts bounce with each move, and I swear that sometime tonight I'm going to cum pressed between those beauties. Fuck, that thought has the base of my spine tingling, but I can't finish before she does.

Swiping a finger through her juices, I reach around and put pressure on her ass. Unlike last time, she freezes and shoots me an uneasy look, and I wonder if she thinks I'll take her there tonight. I won't, she needs to be prepped if that's something she wants.

"Trust me, Siren. This will feel good, and it'll only be my finger. But if you say stop, I'll stop. You know I'll never hurt you."

She nods and takes a deep breath before pushing back against me. I take that as my cue to start moving again and as I put more pressure on her ass, I feel it.

Her body coils tight as she presses a pillow to her face, muffling her scream as she cums. Taking advantage of her orgasm, I push my finger in all the way as I pump in time with my thrusts. I don't stop as her body spasms, instead picking up speed and soon I feel her tightening around me again.

"Cum for me, Siren. Soak my cock with your juices."

She cums immediately for me and her orgasm triggers my own, causing me to shoot ropes and ropes of my cum inside her. Fuck, I don't think I've ever come that much before.

We both pant as we catch our breath, and I lean back over her, kissing her. Her hands roam over my body and feeling her hands on me again after all of these years has me already half hard again.

"Mmmm. I think someone's up for playing some more," she sasses as I feel her clamp down on me again, drawing a moan out of me.

"Siren, I'm going to fuck you so much, I'll wear your pussy out. But first, there's something I've been dying to do again."

Nipping her lip, I regretfully pull out of her. A groan escapes at seeing my cum leaking out of her and it cracks something open in me. Scooping it up, I push it back into her pussy. She gasps when she feels what I'm doing. I re-angle her hips so they're tilted up more, and I finish putting all my cum back inside of her.

"You said you wanted me to put a baby in you tonight, Siren. I'm not letting any of this go to waste."

Her eyes blaze as she reaches for me, pulling me up, wraps her hand around the back of my neck, and pulls us together so hard our teeth clash as we kiss. The kiss quickly turns even more heated, and I moan into her mouth when her hand grasps my cock. Fuck, I'm almost ready to explode again after not having my Siren for so long. Breaking the kiss, I kiss down her neck and grab both of her breasts in my hands.

Licking her cleavage, a low groan slips past her plump lips and she arches her back into me. I spend a few moments licking and nipping her breasts, while I try to get myself back under control enough so that I won't cum right away. Shifting, I straddle her waist and give the base of my cock a hard squeeze at seeing her laid out like this underneath me. Her inky hair splayed out over the white pillows and sheets, which also makes her olive skin stand out even more. She licks her lips; her gaze focused on my cock as I come closer, no doubt knowing what I'm going to do.

Cradling her breasts in my hands, I slide my cock in between them, and we both moan. She surprises me further by licking my tip when I push forward.

"Fuck, I've missed your taste, Luke. Missed you. Missed this."

A shiver runs down my spine at her throaty voice. The fact that she's not shying away from the taste of our combined juices has my pace increasing.

"I've fucking missed you too, Siren. Missed you and your gorgeous body."

Readjusting my grip slightly, I run my thumbs over her nipples.

"Yes," she hisses, and I feel her body trembling between my thighs.

After a few moments, another tingling in my spine has my body tightening. My fingers pinch and tweak her nipples, needing her to cum with me.

"I'm gonna paint your beautiful titties with my cum and then I'm going to fuck your pussy so hard, you're going to feel me with every move you make tomorrow." I pinch both of her nipples, praying this will set her over the edge because I can't hold back any longer.

"Fuck, Luke!" she cries out right as the first rope of cum paints her breasts.

Throwing my head back, I moan as I continue to thrust, emptying my cum all over her. Looking down at Mary, something carnal in me calms at seeing her marked by me. Fuck, I've always loved fucking her tits, but this feels different somehow. The sight of her like this already has me semi hard for her again.

Mary smirks at me as she swipes at some cum that had hit her chin. "I think I need a little more protein," she purrs before licking her finger clean. She hums as she continues, swiping up more of my cum and licking her fingers clean again. I go from semi to fully hard so fast that it leaves me slightly lightheaded.

Smirking at her, I shift back as I grasp her thighs and line up with her pussy. "You need more protein, Siren? I've got your protein injection right here."

Chapter 51

Patch

My phone buzzes right as I finish getting ready, and I'm not surprised when I see that Thor has called for Church at 8 am. Since it's only a little past seven now, I should be able to get the kids fed and clothed before I have to head to the clubhouse. I know it's about the fuckers that thought they could get their hands on Mary. We let those assholes sit overnight in the sticks to mess with their heads, making them wonder when we'll be coming down to deal with them. Well, they won't have to wait much longer.

Mary's still asleep, which I'm not surprised by since I kept her up so late last night. My dick twitches at the memories and I adjust myself as my jeans grow tight. Sex with Mary had always been great before, but now it's even better. I don't know if it's just time and that we're older and more mature, or if it's something else. But now that she's fully let me in, I'm never going to let her go again. Her words from last night come back to me and fuck do I hope I was able to get her pregnant last night. Doing the math, I know somewhere in those first few weeks we started having sex when we were teenagers was when I think Asher was conceived.

Footsteps on the stairs has me turning to see three smiling faces beaming down at me. As soon as her feet hit the floor, Cassie runs to me and I grin as she hugs my good leg. I'm actually kind of surprised by how fast they've accepted me, but especially little Cassie. I don't know if it's because she's the youngest and up until they arrived here, she hadn't had a good male role model or what. Whatever the reason may be, she's already got me wrapped around her little finger.

"Did you guys have a good night's sleep?"

"Uh-huh," Cassie says as she nods along with the others and I reach out, ruffling their hair in turn. They both grin up at me and they take turns giving me a hug.

"What do you guys want for breakfast? I have to go to Church at eight, but I have time to whip something up."

"Can we have pancakes?" Isaiah asks and I nod, stepping over to the pantry when Cassie lets go of my leg.

"With bacon and eggs too?" Ash asks.

"Absolutely. You guys can watch some cartoons until breakfast is ready if you want."

Both Isaiah and Cassie race into the living room and soon I can hear a certain mouse's voice filling the air. I shake my head as my grin grows even though my chest tightens. They both love the show and it kills me that they were kept so sheltered when they were with Stephan. Cassie had innocently let it slip that they had only a handful of movies that they were allowed to watch, and most of the time, they could only watch them when he'd already left for work.

That was when Mary had told me she scavenged all the sale and clearance bins as well as thrift stores to get them the things they needed or wanted. Only clothes, shoes, and school supplies were things he allowed her to buy full price because it would have looked poorly on his reputation if his wife and kids went around dressed in rags or if they didn't have all the school supplies they needed.

For birthdays and Christmas, she was only allowed to spend fifty dollars per kid. For any other holiday, since he didn't think they needed anything, she went without to save money so the kids could have something for Easter or to take candy for their classmates when Valentine's Day came around. For Halloween, they weren't allowed to go out and trick-or-treat because he didn't want them sneaking away. They were forced to stay home and hand out candy instead. Since she wasn't allowed to buy them costumes, Mary had found some white sheets in the clearance bins that she cut up and made ghost costumes for them. Those were the only costumes they'd ever had.

Never again.

I'll make sure they never want for anything again and I'll personally be taking the kids trick-or-treating next year. As for Christmas, Mary doesn't know it yet, but I've got stuff on order for all four of them. I won't be going overboard every year, but I'll be damn sure doing it this year. I hate that I missed so much of Ash's life, and I plan to be there for all his, as well as Cassie and Isaiah's, big moments in life. While I wish more than anything that Mary was with me these past nine years, I wouldn't trade Cassie or Isaiah for anything. I've come to love both of them just as much as Ash and as soon as I can, I'm going to adopt both of them and give them my last name.

The refrigerator door opening pulls me from my thoughts, and I shake off the melancholy feeling of everything I've missed. Asher pulls out eggs and bacon from the fridge and I pull out the pancake mix and syrup from the pantry.

"Can I help make breakfast, Dad? I used to help Mom all the time, and sometimes I even made her breakfast."

My heart clenches at the meaning behind his words and I have to take a deep breath to keep my anger from showing on my face. Exhaling slowly, I nod.

"Of course. Which parts do you want to do?"

"I've done bacon in the microwave before since Mom says she doesn't want me doing the bacon on the griddle by myself just yet and I can also make scrambled eggs."

"Alright, then you can do both of those, but holler if you need help with something."

"Okay."

We get to work side by side and as I pour some batter into the skillet, I watch him out of the corner of my eye as he expertly prepares the bacon before cracking enough eggs for scrambled eggs for everyone into a couple of bowls.

After taking the first batch of pancakes off the griddle, Ash pulls out a stepstool that Maria gave us and puts the bacon in the microwave. At first, I was curious as to why she gave it to us, but now knowing that Ash has helped Mary cook before, I'm glad she got it for us. Hell, I wouldn't be surprised if she'd done the same thing with Mary in the past now that I think about it.

About halfway through making breakfast, I hear the shower turn on, and even though I know she'll yell if she needs help with something, I still worry that she'll fall and injure herself further. However, whenever it's time to wash her hair, I still insist on helping her since it's easier if she stands differently under the water. Overall, though, her body's been healing nicely.

Just as Ash and I finish putting the food on the table, our bedroom door opens and she carefully wheels herself out and into the hallway, her sling sitting on her lap. With how well Mary's been doing, I figured she could wheel herself around the house in short bursts, but any longer could cause her to re-injure herself. I'm still a little nervous because of that asshole yanking on her arm, but there's still a couple more days until her new chair will arrive. Hopefully, she doesn't push herself too hard in the meantime.

"Breakfast is ready," I call out before walking back into the kitchen and grabbing plates and utensils for everyone. Checking the clock, I grimace when I realize I only have about a half an hour before I have to be at the clubhouse.

"Did Thor call a meeting?" Mary asks me and I realize she must have been watching me just now.

I nod. "Yeah, I have to be over there at eight and I'm not sure how long we'll be."

She nods in return. "Okay. Do you want to dish out your plate first then?"

"Nah. I'll get you all situated and then eat." Turning toward the kids, I pick up the pancakes and place one on each of their plates before putting a dollop of butter on each one. They smear it around until it melts and then I start cutting up Cassie's pancake, since she's right next to me while Mary starts cutting up Isaiah's. Once that's done, I pour syrup on Cassie's pancake and pass the syrup over to Mary before dishing out eggs and bacon for everyone.

Breakfast passes quickly as I listen to the kids' chatter as I practically inhale my food. I just took some over-the-counter pain medicine and I hate doing it on an empty stomach.

After taking the last bite of my food, I stand and head to the sink, quickly rinsing off my plate before putting it in the dishwasher. Grabbing my phone off the counter, I pat my pockets, making sure I have everything I need.

"Wait," Mary calls out as she wheels over to me and I'm surprised she has some plastic wrap and tape in her lap. "Let me help you wrap your arm, at least. I figure you'll be wearing gloves, but I don't want anything possibly infecting your arm," she whispers as she tugs on my hand.

I automatically kneel on the ground in front of her, the pain forgotten in my shock. I hadn't uttered a word about what we were going to be doing today, and yet she knew.

She looks up at me and her lips turn up slightly, even though she has a worried expression on her face. "I figured you were going to deal with our visitors today," she whispers even quieter than before, so quiet that I have to strain to hear her. She pushes up my sleeve and starts wrapping the plastic wrap around my bicep.

"And are you okay with that?" My gut clenches, worry filling me that she'll look at me differently after this. I mean, that fucker *made* her watch him torment and torture others, some were probably innocents too, before he killed them. I don't want her to *ever* compare me to that fucker and I don't ever want to give her a reason to do so.

She looks up at me briefly, determination filling her eyes, before going back to securing the plastic wrap. "More than okay. If I wasn't crippled, I would love to get in a chance to make them hurt, but I can't. I never wanted to leave you in the first place, and I sure as hell am not leaving you this time.

"I'm not sure if you'll be allowed to share anything with me, but I would love to know if *he* was behind their orders to kidnap me or if it was someone else. They often talked about another group, but all they called them was 'O'. I'm not sure if it's the one group you guys already know about, or if it' a different one," she says and I'm glad she didn't say Oasis' name just now for the kids' sake. "Well, I should say, Kristoff would often talk about them, especially with Diego. Much like *him*, as the years went on, the others started dropping their guard around me and talking more freely. I overheard a lot of conversations, but without always hearing both sides, I don't really know what or who they were talking about."

Relief fills me and hearing that she'd love to get in on the action has a sense of pride filling me that she'd be willing to do that. To stand up to her tormentors and be willing to inflict pain on them. Her declaration almost has me hoping that we don't get our hands on Stephan until after Mary gets her cast off and she's able to move around freely just so she can dole out some vengeance herself. That said, I'd prefer the fucker be caught yesterday so that Mary and the kids can stop looking over their shoulders in fear. Also, I want that fucker caught so I can officially claim them as mine and marry Mary once and for all.

She rips off one more piece of tape and then lowers my shirt. "Do you need me to do your thigh, too?"

I shake my head. "No, I'm going to mainly let Dragon, and most likely Levi, take the lead on this because of my injuries, but I'll still get in on some of the action." I probably shouldn't be saying this out loud, but I decide to at least let her know my intentions. Thor, Dragon, and Timber have shared cliff note versions with their wives, well, before Levi became a member that is, so I know I'm not going to get in trouble with any of them over this.

She nods and bites her lip as her gaze drops to her hands in her lap. Gripping her chin, I make her look up at me.

"I'll tell you what I can, but I won't be able to tell you everything. Please know that when I say something like that, it's meant to protect you. Not to isolate you or push you away or demean you in any way."

She gives me a soft smile. "Club business." At my nod, her smile softens even more, though it's sort of reserved at the same time. "Levi, and especially Mae, told me more about that. I was surprised that they pushed so much to make sure I understood, but then Levi told me about how she almost left her guys because they cut her out of everything, even though it was her safety at risk.

"Levi said she didn't want any other woman, or partner, the guys brought here to feel like she had felt that day. When she phrased it like that, I was extremely grateful they took that extra step to help me settle in here." She pauses and an almost guilty look crosses her face. "Their welcomeness makes me feel especially guilty when I first heard about Thor, Dragon, and Timber's wives. I will admit, I had no idea what a biker's woman, or Old Lady I should say, would be like when you all said Levi and Mae wanted to meet back when I was in the hospital. At first, I thought they would be catty or were the type to try and backstab you at any chance. But they're not. I know Stephan's words colored my thoughts a lot that first week and I've worked, am working, really hard to silence his voice whenever it creeps in."

She licks her lips nervously and while my fingers itch to pull her into my arms and comfort her, I don't move as I wait for her to continue.

"What I'm trying to say is, I love it here and those two women are a huge part of why I love it here. They made me feel at home and part of the club family almost instantly. Even when I was in the hospital. While I know I'm really *not* much help right now because of my damn leg and shoulder, I'll do whatever I can to help you guys catch Diego, Stephan, and anyone else working with them. Once I'm better, I can help defend us, other women and the kids. I know how to shoot even though Stephan didn't want me to learn. His chief in Addams, which was the first town we lived in after I was kidnapped, he pressured Stephan into having me learn since there were going to be guns in the house and he was getting assigned a K9 dog. Also, I'm still trying to wrack my brain to see if I can remember anything else that might be helpful to you guys, but again a lot of the conversations I heard were one sided, which makes it harder. But if anything suddenly makes sense after hearing something from you guys, I'll let you know."

I nod in thanks but then freeze. A few things suddenly clicking into place in my mind. "That's how you knew Bastion's commands."

She nods, her eyes misting slightly. "We didn't have Daisy for too long, unfortunately. After my first brutal beating, Daisy got in between us to protect me. Without even thinking, I gave the command for her to attack, and she did." She huffs as she wipes her eyes. "Of course, Stephan turned everything around saying that Daisy had snapped and attacked us. That he stepped in between us to save me and that's how he got the scars from her teeth on his arm. That the only way to get her to stop was to shoot her. He was never assigned another K9, but for a long time, he was wary around me while we still lived in Addams. However, as soon as we moved to Elmdale after that, he went back to his normal self. That's actually one other way that you can verify that it's him if he changes his looks again." She reaches forward and pulls my left arm toward her, her fingers softly tracing my skin. "This is around where it is. A few are just puncture scars, but most of the others are more elongated because she tore through his skin so much. Still, even with them elongated, you're able to tell that he was bitten badly by a dog."

I pull her into my arms but then grimace when I see the clock over her head. Shit.

"I hate to do this, Siren, but I need to leave. I'm already pushing it as it is."

Mary sits up suddenly, twisting around to see the clock. "Oh, my gosh, I'm so sorry. I didn't mean to make you wait while I rambled on."

Shaking my head, I grin as I press a kiss to her forehead before standing, doing my best to hide my wince at the pain that shoots through my leg.

"It'll be okay, Siren. If you need anything, ask Mae or one of the Prospects. If it's an emergency, reach out to Thor or Phoenix, but copy me in case they let me keep my phone."

She nods and makes a shooing motion with her hands. "I promise, but you better hurry before I get you into even more trouble than you might already be in."

Leaning down, I give her one more kiss. "I'll be back as soon as I'm able to, but we might have to meet again afterward depending on what we learn."

She nods and looks over her shoulder at the kids. "As soon as they are done and cleaned up, I'll start them on their schoolwork. If you still aren't home by the time they are done, we'll probably go to Mae's to help her get ready for tonight."

That's right. The ladies are having a spa night tonight and I said I'd help Timber watch the boys.

"Sounds good. Be safe. I love you."

With a final kiss, I walk over to the table and kiss each of the kids' foreheads before telling them I'll see them later today and head outside. Checking my phone, I curse and send a quick text to Thor telling him I'm on my way. There's still five minutes, but I know I won't be able to walk as fast as I normally can. While I told Mary that it'll be okay, I've always hated being late for anything.

As quick as I'm able to, I stalk to the clubhouse and straight into Church.

My cheeks heat as I walk to my chair. Even though I'm right on time, everyone else is already seated and the weight of their gazes is heavy on my shoulders.

"Everything alright?" Thor asks, and I can tell he's annoyed that I came in at the last minute, but he doesn't look pissed thankfully.

"Yeah, Mary wanted to wrap my arm before I left."

His eyebrows go up at that and I shake my head. "I didn't mention anything other than you had called Church, but she told me that she figured we were going to be dealing with those five and didn't want my wounds getting infected."

Levi smirks. "Knew she was a good egg."

A few others chuckle at her words and Thor shakes his head before slamming his hammer on the table.

"Alright, let's recap and then Smoke has some information for us. Then we'll go down and give a Steel Archangel's welcome to our guests."

Chapter 52

Patch

As I walk down the stairs, following my brothers and sister down to the sticks, my blood is boiling from what Smoke was able to uncover about our guests. Not only are these fuckers working with Stephan, but they also have ties to Diego and Kristoff, the man we believe to be X and who was trying to get his hands on Mae. However, it's not only their connections that have me seeing red. It's what they've done and I'm assuming what would have eventually been Mary's fate. Probably Cassie's, too.

Thor unlocks the door and we all pile into the room. The stench of urine is strong, and I fight not to scrunch up my nose in disgust. I spare a glance at Levi, who fails at hiding her disgust, but at least she doesn't turn green or look like she might throw up. I saw Thor passing her a bandana as we left Church, but I doubt she'll use it. Even though we wouldn't look at her differently, I know she tries hard not to show any weakness around us. However, strong smells still sometimes hit her weirdly because of her pregnancy and I make a note to keep an eye on her. She's nine weeks from her due date, but we all know she'll probably go into labor in about a month or so because of the twins. That and Thor and Dragon are not exactly little by any means.

At Thor's chin lift, Dragon steps forward and heads to his toy chest as he calls it. After putting on some gloves, he pulls out a wicked-looking knife with sharp serrations along both the bottom and top of the blade. Surprisingly, he sheaths that knife and also pulls out another knife that looks extremely sharp. So sharp, I know it'll cut through skin like butter. Silently, he walks in front of the men, staring them down. A few swallow thickly and avert their eyes, and I'm almost certain they'll be the ones to cave first.

"Who do you work for?" he asks and when no one speaks up, he starts cutting off the clothes off the man in the middle, the one who had a hand in many of Mary's beatings.

Leonardo Adams.

As Dragon works, the two to Leo's left, Jack Huxley and Brendan Creed, start squirming and can't take their eyes off Dragon's knife. When Leo is naked, Dragon continues until they are all hanging naked by their arms, which are holding almost all of their weight, since their toes barely touch the floor.

"I'm sure your arms must be awfully tired by now, so I'll make things easier. I can make your end painless, or I can make your pain endless. Right now, that is the only control you have. How much pain you endure before you die. Those that tell us what we want to know will earn a less painful death. Refuse, however," he pauses and places his blade against Leo's chest, right by his nipple, "and we will make it *extremely* painful until we get the information we need." Dragon pauses again and slices Leo's nipple clean off. Leo's body and face tighten in pain, but he clenches his mouth shut, refusing to scream. Or talk.

Dragon looks at the other four, and then he smirks darkly when he refocuses on Leo. "I was hoping you would choose the hard path. My little babies have been thirsty for some blood."

Methodically, Dragon cuts into Leo's flesh as he hums. The fucker actually hums as he works.

After about five minutes or so, Leo's body is covered in cuts of varying depths. He's pale, sweating, and there is blood dribbling down his chin from how hard he's biting his lip to stay quiet. Dragon steps back slightly, grips Leo's hair, pulling his head back and exposing his neck. From where I'm standing, I can see Leo's eyes widen as Dragon lightly runs the tip of his blade across his neck. As he swallows, his Adam's apple catches the blade, and a small trail of blood soon appears on his neck.

"Feel like talking now, Leo? Your pain will be greatly reduced if you do, though my babies will definitely be saddened that they won't be able to make you bleed even more for me."

Surprisingly, Leo just glares at Dragon in response. Or at least, as well as he can with the position that he's in. Something that makes me extremely happy.

Dragon smirks. "Well, let's see if working on your friends will loosen your lips. Or theirs."

He takes a few steps over to Brendan, who is to Leo's left, the man who tried to pull Mary out of my truck. Brendan's face is pale and he swallows thickly when Dragon stops in front of him, eying him warily. However, his gaze also darts around periodically, like he's trying to make sure he keeps all of us in his sights.

"Who do you work for, Brendan?"

He swallows thickly again, and even though he pales further, he doesn't answer.

"Cat got your tongue? Well, let's see if we can loosen those lips."

Dragon looks over his shoulder at me and a few others, giving us a slight nod. We'd already talked about this and how to play it out. Ryder, Timber, Gunner, and I stalk to the closet and pick out our choice of instruments. They would take care of Daniel, Liam, and Jack while I took Leo and Dragon took Brendan. While I also want to get in a little action on Brendan for trying to steal my woman, Leo will get most of my attention for the pain he'd caused Siren in the past. As I pass Smoke, he tilts his head slightly and I know he'll be capturing everything that everyone says while we work to see who will crack first and give us information.

Even though Dragon already took a knife to Leo, I pick up a bowie knife, but then I spot some end cutting pliers and I can't stop the grin that forms. I also see that Dragon has a gut hook in the back that I make a mental note of for if I really need to take things that far. Pocketing the sheathed bowie knife, I take the pliers and pinch them a few times in front of Leo's face. He glares and spits at me, but I easily step back before it makes contact.

I tsk at Leo while simultaneously tuning out my brothers as I solely focus on him. "Didn't think you'd stoop that low, Leo. Not someone of your rank." His eyes widen slightly and I smirk. Smoke was able to find out quite a bit on him. Including shit the fuckers tried to keep buried for years. "Now, why were you trying to kidnap my woman?"

He bares his teeth at me and at the action, I bet he's also been biting his cheeks judging by the amount blood in his mouth. "She isn't yours. That bitch and those brats belong to Stephan," his voice is strained, giving away how much he's hurting. However, for the amount of damage Dragon has already done, I'm surprised he isn't showing even more pain.

Rage explodes in my veins and before I even realize what I'm doing, my fist lands on his cheek, whipping his head to the side.

"Mary doesn't belong to anyone but herself. Yes, I call her mine, but that doesn't mean I own her. And as for the kids, they belong with Mary, not Stephan. Especially my son.

Leo spits out some blood, which I avoid again, and he snarls at me. "Stephan paid for her outright and he will get what belongs to him, which includes the leech you think is yours. Even if he has to kill every single one of you biker scum to get to them." He pauses and leers at me. "He paid extra to get her while she was pregnant because that meant she'd be bringing in more profit later."

Well, that confirms one theory we had. Grinning darkly, I step forward and close the pliers around his remaining nipple, pinching as hard as I can go. His face and jaw tighten, but other than that, he doesn't react.

"Stephan can try and get them, but he won't succeed. Besides, I'm looking forward to getting my hands on the fucker who thought he could steal my woman and children from me." Even though they aren't my blood, I've claimed them as my own and will do whatever it takes to protect them.

Before he can say anything else, I pull hard and his nipple, along with some skin, instantly tear from his body. Leo cries out and I drop the skin into the trophy bins as Levi calls them.

"What's the real reason why Stephan tried to kidnap Mary? Not that bullshit you just spewed. What does he want with her?"

Leo refuses to talk, so I move to a section by his ribs and repeat the process. Over and over, I pull sections of his skin off until he passes out from the pain. Stepping back, my gaze roams over the damage we've done so far. There are a few dozen patches where I've torn his skin off and they are littered in between his cuts. Some of them, I even pulled skin from the edge of where his skin was already flayed open.

Looking over my shoulder, Cowboy gives me a chin lift and the rest of us step back as he dumps the ice-cold water over Leo's head. He sputters and shakes his head as he blinks repeatedly, his body immediately shivering from the cold.

Stepping forward, I repeat my question as my brothers get back to work on the others. "What's the real reason you were trying to kidnap Mary?"

Leo's still trying to catch his breath, but he glares at me and purses his lips.

Setting down the pliers, I pull out my knife and jam it into his thigh, making sure I avoid the femoral artery but also making sure it's hard enough to hit bone. I wiggle and twist the blade, making sure it continues cutting into his flesh, before I ask him again.

"Why were you trying to kidnap Mary?"

"Because they need her."

Instead of the answer coming from Leo, it comes from Brendan who's hanging to my right. He's extremely pale, sweating and his body is well on its way to mirroring Leo's thanks to Dragon's handiwork.

Dragon steps back to give me room and hands me his knife since mine is still impaled in Leo's leg. I step up to Brendan, placing the flat side of my knife under his jaw, making sure he keeps looking at me.

"Why do they need Mary? Who needs her?"

I hear a click behind me and then a small whoosh. Judging by the smell, I'm guessing Dragon grabbed his acetylene torch. Brendan's eyes widen and without looking, I know Dragon's messing with the flame to intimidate him.

"Shut the fuck up! Don't tell him anything!" Leo yells at Brendan as he tries to move his body enough to hit Brendan, but he can only move a couple of inches thanks to how Timber rigged everything in here.

"Fuck you, Leo! We're going to die no matter what. No one is coming for us."

"Maybe not for you," he mutters under his breath as he glares at Brendan.

I narrow my eyes at him before shooting a look over at Smoke, who frowns. His fingers start flying over his keyboard, no doubt messaging the others to be on the lookout and to check our security footage.

Dragon moves closer and hands me the torch, which I take and hold it close enough to Brendan's face but not actually touching his skin.

Yet.

He winces from the heat, and I scowl. "Don't make me repeat myself."

"He needs her to finish a deal."

"Who needs her?"

"D-Diego. Diego Vasquez."

Shit. Hasn't he made her life terrible enough as it is?

"Why? What's the deal?"

Brendan shakes his head. "I don't know exactly. All I know is that Diego needs Mary to finalize a deal with his partner, X."

Out of the corner of my eye, I can see Timber's body coiling tight at the mention of X. He looks like he's barely keeping himself in check and not storming up to Brendan looking for more answers.

I narrow my eyes at Brendan. "Continue."

"From what I heard, the exchange was supposed to happen a few years ago, but Stephan wouldn't let her, or the kids, go. Not even with Diego pressuring him to do it. In exchange for not giving up Mary or the kids, Stephan's been supplying X with women for the cause. Mary also has something Diego needs. That's why he ordered them back to Forest Creek. He never said what exactly it was he needed from her, just that it was family business."

A chill runs down my spine. I'll need to talk to Antonio later. He might have some insight on what Diego thinks he might need.

"Where's Stephan been getting the women from?"

"I don't know about all of them, but some of the women and kids he found on the streets as runaways or homeless. He used his badge as cover for telling them that he was taking them someplace safe. That they'd be cared for. He also used that same line on some other women or kids who'd called into the stations to report abusive partners or parents. He told them he'd get them to a safe house, but then hand them over to X instead."

My vision almost turns red from the amount of anger coursing through me at Stephan abusing his badge in such a way. I barely keep myself from burning Brendan, and while I know he's had some sort of hand in things, we don't know the specifics. And since he's started talking and answering our questions, I don't want to jeopardize getting more information out of him. But when or if he stops talking… that's a different story.

"What is your cause?" Thor asks as he comes right up beside me.

Brendan swallows thickly but he doesn't answer right away.

A dark smile comes over me as I'm finally able to get out a bit of this rage and I lower the torch, burning a trail across his thigh as I inch my way closer to his dick.

"Fuck! I'll talk! I'll t-talk!" he yells when I'm a few inches from his dick.

"Don't betray our cause, Brendan. You're dead if you talk," Leo seethes as he struggles even more in his chains.

"Fuck you, Leo! We're already dead. And despite what you think, no one is going to come for us. You know as well as I do that if we get caught, X will wipe any trace of us. I'm not getting my dick burned off for this shit, even if we are going to die in here." He pauses and turns back to us.

"Who do you work for? What is your cause?" Thor asks him again.

"A f-few people, but ultimately, we r-report to X."

"What is X's real name?"

"K-Kristoff. Kristoff D-Davenport."

Well, that at least confirms what we previously had thought, but that means we're neck deep in the Oasis mess again.

"What's your cause?"

He swallows and a look crosses his face that I can't decipher. "Oasis, or we s-sometimes just c-called it 'O' to keep others from k-knowing what we were t-talking about. It's the f-founders' and members' m-mission to revert humanity b-back to how it used to be. Men should be in c-charge of everything and w-women are only here for b-breeding and keeping the homestead. That w-women of this day and age need to be b-broken to revert back to that s-stage and way of living. Or t-taken before they develop their independent s-streak and forced into the life. That women s-should be a s-submissive to their husband and m-master, doing whatever is ordered of t-them."

Growls vibrate through the air from almost every one of us and I chance a look over at Levi who looks like she'd love to come over and carve these fuckers to pieces.

We had suspected that this was Oasis' cause, but now it's confirmed. We have to stop these fuckers. But to do that, we need to know how far their reach is.

Bringing the torch closer to his dick, but also minding that I don't burn myself in the process, I place my other hand around his throat, squeezing slightly. "Who else do you work for?"

"D-Diego. Diego Vasquez. Also, s-sometimes, if either Diego or X ordered it, w-we worked with Stephan Hayes."

"Who ordered you to come after us and attack us today?"

He looks down and to the left, and it's only my hand around his throat that stops him from moving his head. Thor immediately pulls back, slamming his fist into Brendan's stomach. He gasps and sputters for a moment, which I don't make any easier since I don't relinquish my grip on his throat before he starts talking again.

"S-Stephan. Stephan ordered it. Both X and Diego b-backed the orders. Stephan needs M-Mary back with him so that she can't t-testify against him since she's his w-wife and so that she'll d-drop all the charges. That's one of the r-reasons he really wants her back. Also to p-punish her for leaving and w-what she did. Her leaving him put a w-wrench in all of our plans, and as soon as everything q-quiets down, he's going to finally s-ship her and the kids off to X and Diego to d-deal with."

Now that he's talking a bit more freely, I step back slightly. "Why did Diego kill Nikos and kidnap Mary to begin with?"

"Because they w-were getting to be a p-problem for the family, and he n-needed them both handled and out of the w-way. He knew what your p-plans were, to m-marry Mary after graduation, and he also knew she was p-pregnant. He was n-never going to let her be happy b-because of what she'd done t-to and taken from Eileen. Because of w-what she'd already d-done to the family, he w-wanted to knock her d-down a few pegs and then s-shatter her. He thought Stephan w-would be able to break her, but as the years w-went on, he knew more was n-needed to do that. That's w-why he was pushing the d-deal with X and Stephan. He knew X w-would be able to completely b-break her because he'd done it already w-with so many others."

"What problems were Mary and Nikos causing for the family?"

Brendan shakes his head. "I d-don't know. All he w-would say was it was f-family business if anyone asked."

My frustration grows at not being able to get more information about Diego and X's plans for Mary. Pushing it down as best as I can, I refocus.

"Where's Stephan hiding out?"

"He b-bounces around different locations. His n-new chick, Claudia's, apartment; an old s-seedy motel on the edge of t-town; a nearby homestead; and a c-cabin that isn't too far from the homestead. Though, they've already p-probably changed up things b-because we were caught."

Since he already said he didn't know the specifics of the deal or what Diego wanted from Mary, I turn my focus toward Oasis.

"Who is in charge of Oasis?"

"X is our G-Grandmaster. There are now six M-Master's under him. After three of his Masters were killed a few m-months ago, he changed things up. Moved p-people around and ordered more homesteads to be d-developed for them to move between easier. I don't know where the Masters were m-moved to, or the new people's names. The only ones I k-know of are Phillip Cole and Diego. X made Diego a Master w-when Diego partnered with him earlier this year."

It takes me a moment and then I realize where I'd heard that name before. Phillip was Preston's brother and Preston was Mae's stepfather.

"What homesteads do Phillip and Diego control?"

"I don't k-know. That information w-was always kept from us and a-anyone else in the l-lower levels that w-worked under X's other b-branches. The only one of us t-that might know is Leo." He pauses as he tilts his head toward Leo, but he can't really see him much since his right eye is mostly swollen shut from Dragon. "Us f-four report to Leo and then to X."

I look over to Thor, needing to know if we push Leo further now or make him sit a bit more. He turns to Leo and I know he's cataloguing all of his wounds. Then he turns and cocks an eyebrow at me. Stepping toward Leo, I cauterize the worst of his wounds, not giving a shit as he screams out in pain each time. When I'm done, I turn back toward Thor and give him a curt nod.

Thor gestures to Dragon who walks over to Daniel at the end. He grabs his hair, yanks his head back, and holds his knife to Daniel's throat.

"What else do you know about Oasis?"

Daniel shakes his head, but then winces when the blade digs into his flesh. "The only other thing I know is that Phillip took over a homestead a bit north of here, but I don't know where."

Dragon lowers his knife and hovers it over Daniel's dick.

"Anything else you want to add? Your death will be less painful if you give us useful information."

He frantically nods. "I overheard him ordering Claudia to get him money. That's how he's staying off the cops' radar. Using her accounts to fund him until he can get his hands on his accounts again. He was pissed when he found out his offshore accounts were frozen as well. Took those frustrations out on her, which convinced her to give in to him."

My chest tightens. I never liked Claudia, but I never wanted her hurt. After she said she was with Stephan the night Mary was admitted to the hospital, I knew her attempts to seduce me earlier this summer were part of Stephan's plans to try and drive a wedge between Mary and me. I don't know if he knew we talked on Asher's birthday or not, and I hope he didn't. It would have killed me if they were hurt because of me.

Dragon moves to Liam and asks him the same questions but he doesn't have anything new to add and neither does Jack.

Dragon looks over his shoulder at Thor and they have a silent conversation. Since we've all been around each other for years, and been through a lot of shit together, we're all able to read each other pretty well. And that's before you add in our silent cues or hand signals we use, which come in especially handy when we're riding. However, Dragon and Thor take that to a whole new level with their twin thing.

Without a word, Dragon steps behind Jack and slits his throat. He does the same to Brendan, Liam, and finally Daniel. Leo's eyes are wide with fear as he eyes Dragon warily, who comes to stop in front of him.

"Enjoy your extended stay in our lovely accommodations." He pauses as he drags his knife lightly down Leo's cheek, leaving a thin red line in its wake. "We'll give you a bit to say your goodbyes to your underlings and to give you time to think about telling us the information we need."

Turning off the torch, I hand it to Dragon who sets it on a nearby table and we all file out of the room, Leo's curses ringing through the air as the door seals shut, cutting them off.

"Judge, gather volunteers in teams of two to scout each of the locations where Stephan could be. Until we know otherwise, we need to assume that the cabins and homestead that are on Mae's land are the ones Brendan and Daniel were talking about." Thor pauses and turns to Smoke. "Do you have extra cameras with audio that we can plant in the other two locations? Maybe add to the ones at Mae's cabin and the homestead?"

Smoke gives him a chin lift. "I always have some ready for situations like these. I'll get them together and give them to Judge."

"Perfect. Keep digging into Phillip, Diego, Kristoff, Stephan and now this Claudia chick a bit more."

"Can we freeze her accounts too?" I ask. "That could make Stephan act out and give us some more clues as to where he's at. Or trigger him to make his next move."

Smoke frowns and shakes his head. "I already checked that when he mentioned her name. Her accounts were cleaned out yesterday morning."

Muffled curses ring out, mine included. Without knowing how much money he has at his disposal, we don't know when he'll start to run out. I was really hoping to be able to give him a reason to poke his head out of the sand so we could sniff him out.

"Alright, those that were in on the action, get cleaned up. Cowboy, you're on first watch duty, so help Dragon clean up the tools. Grab whoever you need to help you take out the trash." Thor pauses and turns to Smoke and then me. "You two meet me in my office when you're ready. We need to talk to Antonio."

"Give me your boots and I'll clean them with mine," Timber says as he comes over to me and holds his hand out for them.

Quickly, I undo my laces and slip out of my boots. Handing them to him, I give him a chin lift in thanks and head to the locker room down here, along with the rest of the others that took part. Instead of stripping right away, I walk over to the sinks and scrub my hands as best as I can before walking over to the supply bin I keep down here. After Levi and Reaper ended things with her uncle and a few members of the Black Plague earlier this summer, I started keeping a kit of supplies down here for those that need to keep any wounds clean and dry while taking care of business and then while cleaning up from said business.

Inspecting my clothes, I'm pleased to see that I didn't get much blood on them and that I should be able to salvage them. Stripping, I place my clothes in a bag and inspect my wounds. The wrap Mary put on my arm is still holding strong, as is the wrap I put on my hands while we were in Church. Putting my foot on the bench, I inspect my thigh, but everything looks normal. I probably should have wrapped it, but at least I didn't get too bloody. Even though the wounds look okay, I dig out some alcohol wipes as a precaution and clean the area. Wrapping it, I tape it off and grab a nearby towel before heading to one of the empty shower stalls.

Knowing I need to be quick since Thor and Smoke are waiting on me, I wash in record time and dress in some spare clothes I always keep down here. My boots are laying on the drying mat near the door and I put them on before lacing them up.

Heading upstairs, I make sure the secret door fully closes before walking down the hallway and into the main common room. Ethan's working the bar and I walk over to him. He sees me coming and reaches into the cooler under the counter and pops the top off the beer.

"Grab me one for Thor and Smoke as well."

He reaches under the counter for the drinks, and I wince internally when I check the clock behind the bar. We were down there longer than I realized, as it's already almost noon. Granted, we were in Church for a few hours this morning before going downstairs, but still, I hadn't realized how much time had passed. Beers in hand, I walk across the room and knock on Thor's door.

"Come in."

Chapter 53

Mary

After Patch leaves, I put the supplies I used to wrap his arm on the counter, and I wheel myself back to the table. I'm so nervous, I can barely taste the breakfast that Patch and Ash made together. My mind keeps going back to that awful night nine years ago. I hope they're able to find out information that will help us track down Stephan and Diego. I'm tired of looking over my shoulder all the time, worried they, or one of their goons, have snuck past the club's defenses and have found us.

Shaking my head, I sigh. I have to trust that the club will keep us safe. If I keep worrying, the kids will pick up on it and I don't want that. This is the first time that they've really been able to be the kids that they are. To enjoy the things that they like in life.

"Mama, I'm all done," Cassie calls as she holds her hands up, fingers spread wide.

Smiling, I can't help but shake my head again at her messy and sticky face and fingers. She's a little monster whenever syrup, or anything sticky for that matter, is involved and knows she's not to touch anything until we wipe off her hands and face.

Ash gets up and grabs the wipes off the counter for me, and seeing my plate is empty, he picks it up along the way with my glass and takes it to the counter for me.

"Thank you, Hawk." Seeing his plate is also empty, I nod at it. "How about you take your plate to the sink too and I'll take care of it in a minute? Then wash your hands and head on upstairs to get ready."

Both he and Isaiah put their plates on the counter, and they're about to help pick up the leftovers when I shake my head. "Head on up. Get changed, brush your teeth, comb your hair, and come back down. I'll take care of the leftovers as well."

Isaiah heads upstairs, but Ash hesitates. Out of the three of them, he's the one that's having the most trouble letting go and just being a kid. Then again, he's been at my side helping me with whatever I needed since he was old enough to understand Stephan was *not* a good man and never lifted a finger unless it was to hurt us. I tilt my head toward the stairs and smile at him, hoping to convey that I'm alright and that he could go. He hesitates a beat more, but then finally heads upstairs. Turning back to Cassie, I continue to clean up her hands and then wipe around her face.

"Your turn, Angel. Can you put your plate and cup on the counter for me? When you come down after getting ready, I'll do your hair for you."

She leans forward, kisses my cheek, slides off the chair and does as I asked before running to the stairs. I'm just about to warn her not to run on the stairs when she comes to an abrupt halt at the base of the stairs, grabs the railing and walks briskly up the stairs.

Taking a deep breath, I force my nerves to calm down as I wipe up the table and then wheel over to the sink. Carefully, I lean forward and lock the wheels of my chair before using the counter to stand. Rinsing all the dishes and putting them in the dishwasher only takes a few minutes, but it must have been enough time for the boys to have gotten ready and changed, as I can hear their steps on the stairs as I start the dishwasher. Cassie is right behind them and I smile when I see she has her baggie of hair ties, a brush, and a rat-tail comb in her hands.

"Okay. You boys can watch cartoons while I do Cassie's hair, and then it's time for schoolwork."

It's already after three and Patch still isn't back yet. The kids are getting restless and they're begging to be able to go to Mae's to play in the treehouse in their backyard while it's still light out and good weather. Pulling out my phone, I text Mae and am relieved when she says it's okay to head over. However, what makes me pause is that she says Timber will be over to help me. If Timber's home, then why isn't Patch?

Unease unfurls throughout me, but I do my best not to let it show again, and instead look up at the kids and smile. "Mae said we could head over, so grab anything you want to take over and let's get ready."

They cheer and quickly start getting their things around. We'd already decided that tonight would be a pizza night so that none of us ladies would have to cook. Heading to my bedroom, I grab a sweatshirt since it's not too cold out right now. I'll still take my coat for later, though.

In the privacy of our room, I once again dig out my phone, but there's no message from Patch. Is he still doing something or talking to someone? My mind instantly goes to a few nights ago when I got an eyeful of things I definitely didn't want to see.

Levi had instituted a rule that the bunnies couldn't come out until after nine o'clock at night for entertainment for the single guys, and I hadn't realized it'd gotten that late. I was shocked to see how little the bunnies wore and that they had sex right out in the open. However, at least they had the decency to bend over the back of the furniture, so I don't have to worry about someone's body fluids soaking into the couch cushions or something like that. A shudder runs through me as I seriously hope there are no bodily fluids on those couches. Needless to say, we quickly left out the back door that night with the kids.

Then there was what happened last night as well. On top of having to witness Cici trying to seduce Patch, it had stung what she'd said about me. While Patch tried to get me to forget about it by worshipping every curve of mine, multiple times I might add, those words still live rent free in the back of my mind, even if I don't want them too.

I shake my head. No. Patch wouldn't do that to me. Not after what he said to Cici. Not after saying he wants to marry me and have more kids with me. Bringing my mind back to the matter at hand, I send him a quick text saying that we're headed over to Mae's house, just so he knows. Surprisingly, he answers me back right away, saying he should be there soon and that he's been on the phone with **Abuelo** (Grandpa), Thor, and Smoke for the past couple of hours. He also apologized for not messaging sooner, but he didn't think the phone call would take that long.

The knot of worry loosens in my chest before it instantly tightens again. Wait, what are they talking about with **Abuelo** (Grandpa)? And why did they have to reach out to him in the first place? Gah! I wish I could have been with them... wherever it is that they're holding those assholes, so that I knew what the hell was going on.

"We're ready, Mom," Isaiah calls out from the living room, and I take a few deep breaths to try and shake off my frustrations.

"Okay, I'll be out in a moment."

I carefully slip on my sweatshirt and then grab the backpack I'd prepared earlier, twisting in my chair to secure it to the handlebars. I know Mae and Levi said I didn't need to bring anything, but I wasn't sure what colors they all had for nail polish, so I decided to bring mine and Cassie's along with, just in case. Cassie's extremely excited about tonight. As soon as Mae explained what a spa night entailed, Cassie begged to have her nails painted. It hadn't dawned on me until that she'd never had that experience before, and my chest had ached when I thought about even more things that the kids have never experienced because of Stephan's control.

Right as I'm wheeling out of my room, the doorbell rings. All three of the kids run excitedly to the door and panic grips me.

"Wait! We need to see who it is before opening the door," I call out and they instantly screech to a halt, their sneakers squeaking against the floor. Ash steps forward and pulls out a stepstool that Patch had put by the door for instances like this or when he isn't home. Climbing up, he peers through the peephole.

"It's Timber!" he calls out excitedly as he crawls back down and puts away the stepstool before opening the door.

"High fives, kiddos, for remembering to see who's at the door," Timber says as he comes in and my cheeks heat that I had probably shouted loud enough that he could hear me through the shut door. However, I'm extremely thankful that he's helping to instill the importance of checking who is at the door before opening it.

"Thank you," I mouth to him and he tilts his head in acknowledgement before turning his focus back to the kids and leaning down, resting his hands on his knees. He gives them a hard look and all three of them straighten in front of him, almost like they're little soldiers in formation. He frowns, but thankfully, he doesn't mention anything about it.

"Your mom has a very good point. Do you know why it's so important to see who's at the door before unlocking it and opening it?"

Ash nods, but Timber cuts him off with a small shake of his head. He looks at Isaiah and then to Cassie.

"Cassie? Do you know why?"

She nods, her little curls bouncing at the movement. "To make sure we know who it is and so we don't open it for a stranger."

Timber nods in response. "Yes, that's right, but it's also okay to not unlock or open the door, even if it's someone you know."

"Like Stephan, Diego, Kristoff, or the others," Ash says in a quiet voice and Cassie and Isaiah's mouths drop open into an 'o' at Timber's nod.

"That's right. It's your choice who you let into your house and who you don't. Do you remember what you're supposed to do if you see any of them? Even if we're in town?"

Isaiah nods. "We're to find Mom or Dad or one of the club members. If we can't, we find an adult and call Dad's phone number."

"And all three of you have it memorized, right?" Timber grins at their confirmation, and as he straightens, he ruffles Isaiah and Ash's hair. "Good job, kiddos. Now, who's ready to have some fun?"

All three of them hop up and down in excitement, raising their hands and running to grab their backpacks and jackets. Ash grabs my jacket from the closet, but Timber takes it from him and crosses the room to me, helping me slip it on.

"I kind of figured your shoulder might be a little tired after being here alone all morning. I won't make you wear your sling once we get to the house, because of your guys' plans, but you have to promise me that you won't overdo anything. Patch would have my ass if I messed up your recovery."

Smiling, I shake my head. "I promise, and the kids helped me move around today as well. They like steering the chair." I pause, questions buzzing in my skull, but then I frown when he slightly shakes his head.

"Not around the kids," he whispers. "Patch will tell you what he can when you guys are alone. I'm not sure how much longer they'll be, but I know he, Thor, and Smoke went into Thor's office to call Antonio after we were done with our meeting, which was around noon."

Swallowing thickly, I nod. "I texted him a few minutes ago, letting him know what our plans were and where we'll be. He thought they wouldn't be too much longer."

Timber dips his head in acknowledgement and steps behind me, wheeling me toward the door. I dig my keys out of my pocket and hand them over my shoulder to him. He locks up, returns my keys, and I can't help my smile at seeing him listening and participating in the kids' conversations as we walk along the path toward his house. And it's not just him and Patch who do it. Whenever the kids go up to anyone in the club, they all stop what they're doing and listen to and talk with them.

I know to anyone else, their actions probably wouldn't even be noticed, but to me and the kids, it's huge. Stephan never listened to or interacted like this with them before. The kids have flourished so much with the help of the club and for that alone, I'll be forever grateful to them.

I'm brought out of my thoughts as we arrive at Timber's house and he guides my chair up the ramp.

Isaiah opens their front door and I chuckle at his excited voice as he calls inside. "Auntie MaeMae! We're here!"

A grunt sounds from my right and I turn in time to see Mae getting up off the couch.

"I swear, Timber, every time I sit on this behemoth of a couch, it wants to swallow me up whole. And it's only gotten worse since becoming pregnant," she grumbles before coming over and hugging the kids. As the kids head further into house, Timber steps up behind her, wrapping his arm around her waist and whispers something in her ear. Her cheeks turn pink and I bite my lip as I look away, knowing whatever it was, it was something intimate and most definitely not for my ears.

Mae clears her throat and her blush deepens when I turn back toward her. “I’ve got us set up downstairs. Timber moved things around down there, so the kids still have somewhere to play when they come in from outside. Oh! And Levi said she’d be over after a little while. She’s just finishing up some paperwork for the bar and grill.”

I paused and look at them in shock. “How did I not know you guys have a basement? I thought this far north, it would be too rocky to be worth the effort.”

Both Mae and Timber grin.

“We got really lucky with the ground we’re on,” Timber tells me. “When we were building, we only had to move a handful of big rocks at each site, but the rest were pretty easy to remove with the excavator. Sure, it took a bit longer, but in the end, it was worth it. All of the houses have basements so far, and even the clubhouse has one.”

That’s right. The panic room is probably there from what the kids had said the other day.

Mae claps her hands as she grins. “Okay, let’s head down because I’m pretty sure a cute little chickadee isn’t going to be able to wait much longer.”

I return her grin and nod knowingly in agreement. “Very true. She kept begging to come over here earlier, but I made her finish her schoolwork and then settle down for a nap first.”

I follow behind them, but right as we get to the stairs, there’s a knock on the door and when it opens, I smile at Levi as she slips off her coat and boots.

“Sorry! I needed to finish some paperwork really quick. If I don’t keep up on it, it will be a nightmare to dig out of and I’m trying to get as much done before these two come and derail everything,” she says as she rubs her tummy.

There’s another knock on the door and my shoulders fall in relief at seeing Patch there with Levi’s men right behind him. He quickly unlaces his boots and slips them off before stalking my way. He leans down and places a searing kiss on my lips.

The world falls away at his touch and I lean into him. Unfortunately, he pulls away all too soon and my cheeks heat as I remember we're not alone. God, I hope I didn't get too carried away and moan or anything.

"Everything's okay, I'll tell you what I can later," he whispers in my ear and I nod, my shoulders falling even more in relief that he confirmed what Timber had told me earlier. He stands and then bends down, lifting me out of the chair. "Now, let's get you downstairs so you ladies can have a relaxing afternoon and evening."

I give him a stern look and he huffs. "I know, if I pop a stitch, you'll have my ass, but I'm carrying my woman. Yes, they pull slightly, but I'm still good."

Shaking my head, I keep my mouth shut. I'll just have to trust him to know his own limits.

Later, after doing facials, pedicures, and manicures, we're sitting around on the couches downstairs talking. Nikki and Sadie each have a cocktail, whereas the rest of us are sipping on mocktails as the kids play on the other side of the room and warm up from being outside for the past few hours. Surprisingly, I found new friends rather quickly in Nikki and Susie, and their kids, Sadie and Jordan, get along splendidly with mine. Elvira and Lindsey are here as well, and it's been great getting to know them better.

I shake my head at something Mae just said. "Okay, wait. This has been confusing me ever since we first talked. Did you ever find out what happened? How did your mom and Preston end up being able to convince Smoke that you were stillborn?"

She gives a sad smile as she twirls the stem of the glass in her hand.

"Patch started looking into it as soon as he found out the truth. It took him awhile, since he was using his down time when he was on shift, but he finally found the truth about a month before you came here.

"There was another family that had delivered a baby girl a few days before I was born, but their baby was stillborn. What Dad remembers Preston and Mom saying was true. The little girl's umbilical cord got wrapped around her neck and ended up suffocating her. The day I was born, the head mortician discovered the girl's body was missing when the people from the funeral home came to pick up her body to prepare her for her funeral. Everyone, especially the parents, were in a frenzy trying to figure out what had happened."

I stared at her in shock, dread filling me at what mostly likely had happened. Both Levi and Nikki reach over to comfort her, which is pretty easy since Mae is sitting between them. Levi takes Mae's free hand, squeezing it slightly, while Nikki lays her hand on Mae's thigh, also squeezing it slightly in support. Turning, I realize it must be just family that knew the truth because Sadie's and Elvira's faces mirror my own shock.

"Dad and Patch did some digging into who was working in the morgue at that time and found out that one of the guys working there had racked up some pretty big debts playing poker, but then miraculously, they were wiped clean the day Mom was discharged from the hospital. Preston's brother, Phillip, and another guy everyone called Creeper ran the underground poker games. We think this guy's debt was wiped clean by doing a few favors for the three of them, which included swiping that little girl's body and presenting her to Dad as me. There was also a nurse and a doctor who were fired not too long after I was born and per the paperwork, they helped deliver me. We think they were the ones that helped switch us babies around and for someone to watch me until the coast was clear."

My mouth opens and closes several times before finally getting my voice to work. "That's terrible! Did the parents ever get their little girl back?"

"We think so. I mean, they had a burial for her. I even went to the cemetery to see her grave for myself, just to make sure. According to some notes the head mortician had written into the system, a dead baby was found in a box outside the hospital one night. There was a note inside the box that gave a last name, Robertson, which was the little girl's family's last name. Since they already had the little girl's handprint and footprint from her birth, they compared it to the dead baby's, and it was a perfect match. I don't think they did any digging into if the hand and footprints matched other records, because if they did, they would have realized they matched the ones with my real name on it. As for the fake birth certificate, Dad thinks it's really my handprint and footprint since they look different. Unfortunately, everything happened so long ago that Dad couldn't find any security footage still around so we have no idea who returned the little girl."

I shake my head. "That's insane," I mutter, not even able to wrap my mind around why someone would even try to pull a stunt like that on someone.

"Yeah, the whole ordeal fudged with Dad's head big time back then. Which repeated when I suddenly showed up a few months ago looking for help. I'm just thankful that we both got past things and now have a good relationship. I'll be including him in on a ton of things with the kids since he missed everything with me," she says as she rubs her tummy.

"When are you due again, Mae?" Susie asks, her brow furrowed in thought.

"Well, that's the tricky thing with multiples. I'm due June 9th, but the doc thinks I'll deliver a few months before then, so probably sometime in April is my guess," she says as she shrugs and lifts her hands in the air.

"I'm glad my girls are going to have their cousins so close in age and be able to play with them when they're older," Levi says with a warm smile on her face as she rubs her stomach with one hand and places her other one on Mae's stomach.

Mae hums and rubs her hand on the other side of her stomach. "Agreed. I always hated being an only child and not having anyone else to really play with, either friend or cousin, so I'm very much looking forward to it as well."

Levi turns toward Nikki and then Susie, cocking her eyebrow. "Any updates on your guys' fronts? Any yummy men in your lives? Maybe you guys will be next?"

Both of them shake their heads, but I do notice both of their cheeks tinge pink a little.

"Nope! I am a-okay with my battery-operated boyfriend for the foreseeable future."

Nikki wrinkles her nose. "Same. I'm not ready to have another kid or jump back in the dating pool just yet." She pauses and gets a mischievous look in her eye. "Besides, I think Mary might be the next one with the way Patch is always looking at her and following her around."

My cheeks heat with the memories from last night and all four of their jaws drop.

"No way," Susie says, drawing out the words a bit. "Already?"

Biting my lip, I shake my head as my cheeks flame even hotter. God, I'm thankful for my olive complexion and hope that it helps hide some of the redness. "I doubt it. I mean, last night was the first time we'd, uh, done it," I stutter out when I remember there were little ears nearby, but thankfully they're all consumed with their playing and aren't paying attention to us. "So yeah. Maybe at some point we'll have another baby, but we're just going to let nature take its course. Besides, I'm not exactly free of my chains just yet." I pause as I look down at my glass, swirling the liquid in the glass slightly.

"I'm still struggling with a lot of things from what all Stephan had said and done to me over the years, but I think, no I know I wouldn't be as far along in getting passed them if it weren't for Patch's help. It's still shocking that I was able to let him in physically so soon, but under everything, he's still the same boy I fell in love with all those years ago. Yes, he's changed, but at the core, he's the same."

Sadie reaches over and place a hand on my arm, squeezing it slightly as she gives me a soft smile.

"And that's completely okay. Everyone handles their trauma differently. What works for one person might not work for another. Are the journals helping?" Mae asks me and immediately, I nod.

"Very much so, thank you. I'm sure at some point I'll feel comfortable talking about all of this," I say as I gesture circularly toward my head, "with a therapist, but I'm not at that point just yet. And with the trial, I'm honestly not even sure if I can talk to someone about all this until it's over."

The others frown.

"I don't know, but I'm sure your grandpa or Sam would be able to tell you," Nikki says. "Have you heard anything about when the trial will take place?"

I let out a big breath. "Yeah, I just got a letter on Friday saying that it'll start on January 15th. I'm nervous though. With finally getting the trial date, I don't know if that will trigger Stephan into doing something haphazardly or not. I really don't want anyone else hurt because of me."

I swallow hard as I remember *exactly* how much my friends were hurt yesterday since I helped Doc stitch up all of them.

Levi frowns harshly. "What those assholes did yesterday is not on you, Mary. *They* decided to stake out in our woods and spy on us. *They* were the ones trying to kidnap you. *They* were the ones that set off the bomb and were pulling the triggers on their guns in order to try and hurt or even kill us. You didn't do any of that. You weren't the cause of anything." Her face softens and she gives me a soft smile. "Like working through your trauma, it will take you time to be able to come to terms with the fact that those assholes are responsible for their own decisions and actions. Not you. And if you need help along the way, we're all here for you and those gorgeous kiddos of yours. If you need help, just ask. We've got your back, Babe."

My chest warms as I smile. I have no idea how I got this lucky, but after the hell that I've lived through, I'm definitely going to enjoy the luck while it lasts.

Chapter 54

Patch

AFTER SETTING MARY DOWN at the table, I give her another kiss that ends way too fucking quickly. By the look in her eyes, I can tell she's dying to find out what happened today, but it'll need to wait for now. There's no way I'll allow the kids to overhear what we found out or about what we've done.

Straightening, I grin at the excited looks on my kids' faces.

"Cassie, have fun with the ladies, and when you're done, if we're still outside, you can come out and play as well. Isaiah, Ash, are you ready to head outside?"

"Yeah," they both cry out, dropping the small bricks they were playing with, and I make a mental note to get some for our house.

They run upstairs and I follow after them with Timber on our heels. Right as we are about to head out the sliding door onto the back deck, there's a knock on the door before it opens up. Tripp steps inside with Jordan and Susie right behind him. I cock an eyebrow at him because I hadn't known he was going to be here today, but I should have guessed he'd be here. He's had a thing for Susie for years but was always afraid to make a move since she's Axe's little sister.

"Hey, guys. Heard you were getting together and thought I'd give you a hand with the kiddos," he says as he wipes his boots on the rug and follows behind Jordan, who is waving around what looks to be a new Nerf gun.

"Guys! Look what Uncle Tripp got me!" Jordan cries as he runs out the door and toward Ash and Isaiah who both look at the toy excitedly.

My gaze goes to Susie to see her reaction to Jordan, only to find her watching Tripp's back as he walks toward us with an almost curious look before she frowns. I wonder if she realizes what she and Jordan mean to Tripp. Or if she's only starting to realize it now that she's moved back to Forest Creek and is around the club more.

"Come on!" Ash cries out as he runs toward a plastic box that's on the deck and nestled against the side of the house and I quickly find out that that's where Timber stores the other toy guns and darts, as well as some other outside toys. Hell, there are even a few targets in there for the kids to hang up.

Turning, I take in the changes to Timber's backyard. There are two old, mature trees that are semi close together that he's built a large treehouse in and it spans both trees. There're even bridges from the first two trees out to a nearby third tree that has a platform all around the tree. Thankfully, he installed a net under everything for if the kids somehow end up falling since the treehouse, bridges, and platforms are fairly high off the ground. However, with how Timber did all the railings, there's no way they'd be able to fit through. Sure, one of the kids could sit and stick their legs through the gap as they looked out toward the house or forest, but they wouldn't be able to squeeze through them. Though, if they happen to climb on top of the railings or somehow fall over them, I'm glad the net is there as a precaution.

I clap Timber on the shoulder. "Damn, you've really gone all out."

He grins at me. "With having Jordan, Sadie, and Lindsey here, I figured we could watch them sometimes and I could get some practice in before our trio arrives. Then, when Mary and her kids came here, I knew I'd made the right decision to build it, which spurred me to finish it quicker so that they'd have a place to play as well. Hopefully, when my kids get older, they'll like to play up there, too."

"I'm sure they will. Especially since they all look like they're having a blast," Tripp says and the three of us watch the kids play.

After a few minutes, Timber turns toward me. "How's Mary adjusting to everything?"

I frown. "She still has some nightmares, but not nearly as many as when she was in the hospital or those first few days here. I can tell she struggles with some things, like always having the house clean before going to bed or expressing herself in certain situations. There's been a few times where she's had to stop in the middle of conversations to pause and process things. She still hears his voice in her head about every little thing, but she's been working really hard at trying to silence it and to enjoy things again.

"The kids are adjusting pretty well, but Ash is having the hardest time letting go and just being a kid." I pause as this morning's conversation comes to mind and my hands fist at my side as I tell them what Ash let slip.

Both of their jaws tighten and almost in unison, they look over toward Ash and Isaiah.

"I don't know how someone could be so cruel to all of them. The kids are so sweet and innocent, and yet, they have that fucker hanging over their heads like an executioner. It amazes me how resilient they are. And at the same time, I can't wait to get my hands on that fucker for what he's done to all of them, especially Mary," Tripp seethes.

Timber walks over to a fridge near the toy chest and comes back with beers for all of us and I tilt my head in thanks before taking a seat.

"How'd Antonio take the news?" Timber asks and my jaw clenches.

"Let's just say I can't wait to see what Antonio and his son, Mateo, are going to do to Diego after finding out this new information. He completely went against their family's beliefs and wishes with what he's done. However, like Stephan, Diego's now in the wind. So are a few other family members. Antonio and Mateo have frozen their accounts but they don't know if they have any other accounts. Smoke's helping him look into that.

"Also, Antonio did verify that their accountant found Stephan was on Diego's secret payroll. Apparently, Diego's second accountant handles all the books for Diego's side businesses, so they are going to look into it further to see if they can find any other leads." I pause as I debate about telling them more, but then decide not to. Mary deserves to hear the rest of the news first since it directly impacts her. In more than one way. "Thor's going to call for Church tomorrow to fill everyone in and so we can make a plan."

Both of them give me a chin lift and we sip our beers, watching the kids run around and play while it's still warm out.

Mary holds a sleepy Cassie in her arms as she hugs and kisses her good night. With all the kids over playing at Mae's and Timber's, they asked if they could have a sleepover, and Timber and Mae graciously said they could all stay there for the night. Something that I'm extremely grateful for because I know Mary will be wanting to know what happened today.

After saying good night to all the kids, I push Mary back to our house, and I'm honestly surprised that she doesn't ask me as soon as the front door closes. We go through our nighttime routine and after verifying that the house is locked up; I lay down next to her in bed and pull her into my arms. Yet, still, she doesn't ask.

Then it hits me.

Gently grasping her chin, I tilt her head up so she can see me and I can see the questions running through her mind.

"You can always ask, Mary. At worst, I'll tell you that I can't tell you anything, but there's a lot I can tell you this time."

She sighs and her body relaxes against me. "I know, but I wasn't sure if it was something you wanted to talk about tonight or not, so I hesitated."

Letting her chin go, I lace my fingers through hers and with my other hand, I run it up and down her back. She settles her head back against my chest and her fingers play with my chest hair.

"Like you had said, the four of them worked for Leo, who ultimately worked for X, or Kristoff Davenport. He's the sick mastermind behind Oasis and the reason why kids, women, and hell, even some men have been going missing across the country."

"So is Oasis the 'O' I've heard them talk about occasionally?"

"It is." I pause and then fill her in on what Brendan had told us, as well as how Stephan had helped them.

By the time I'm done, she's sitting upright in bed, her body tight, her hand over her mouth in shock, and anger blazing in her eyes. Then her face turns a little green and I bolt out of bed, rushing to the bathroom for a bin and quickly getting back to her side just in time to catch the contents of her stomach as she throws up. I gather her hair in my hands and hold it back out of her face. When she's done, I get her a tissue and grab the bottle of water off the nightstand for her to rinse her mouth out. Flushing the contents of the bin, I crawl back into bed, sitting against the headboard and pull her back into my arms.

"I'm sorry. It's just that even though I didn't want to be, I was married to a man who is even more of a monster than I thought him to be. I had no idea." She cries as she clutches my arm and sobs against my chest.

"We know, Mary, we know. This is bigger than anything we've ever done before, and after we handle Stephan and Diego, we'll be calling our fed contact and giving him the information on Oasis. They're stretched all across the US and into Mexico."

"How many chapters are there for the club?"

"We've got twelve chapters spread across six states—Michigan, Indiana, Illinois, Iowa, Minnesota, and of course, Wisconsin. That's not counting our allies, either."

"What if X and Oasis try to target the other clubs because of what we're doing? We should warn them."

I kiss her forehead, loving that she's thinking about everyone. "Thor sent out a message today to the Presidents of each chapter. Through Smoke and all of the IT guys, they'll line up a time for all of them to talk on a secure line so that Thor can bring them up to speed."

Taking a deep breath, I ready myself to tell her more bad news. "Mary... That night," I pause as Nikos' dead body flashes in my mind and I blink, shaking my head to clear the image. "Stephan had plans to sell you and any kids you guys had to Diego and X. Apparently, he paid extra when he found out you were pregnant because it would mean more profit for him later."

She sighs heavily. "I know. Diego told me that night that I made him extra money since I was pregnant, but it wasn't until a few years ago when I overheard a conversation between him, Diego, and X where I learned why and what his plans were for the kids. That's when I started trying even harder to find a way out for us. At first, I couldn't believe he would sell his own children, but then after I thought about it more, I realized he really didn't care about them at all. Especially when I heard him say how he was going to cover up us being suddenly gone. He was going to find people who were similar to us and then rig the car I usually used to run off a steep hill and explode on impact. They were going to make sure it burned enough so no one would be able to recognize or identify the bodies inside."

Mary pauses as a shudder runs through her. "I know what a possible fate would have been if Diego kept me, and my kids' too. I'd seen the back rooms of Diego's 'clubs' that he runs—I'd become one of his whores that he either sells me off to another horrible person, or he keeps me there to sell my body over and over again. My children would have been sold into slavery to be someone's sex toy, but not before he'd make me watch as it happened. Whenever he got a mother and child pair, that's almost always what he did. The mother had to watch her child being sold off to their new owner. I know, because they've made me watch a couple of times so that I'd know my fate if I pressed Stephan too far."

Her body shudders even more and I pull her closer to me, holding her as more of her tears fall onto my chest. I had no idea that she knew the extent of Diego's dealings, and I wish I could take away those memories for her. After a few minutes, her tears mostly subside and her breathing returns closer to normal.

"I take it **Abuelo** (Grandpa) now knows about how far Diego's treachery and betrayal runs?"

Kissing her head, I sigh. "Yeah, he does. To say he was pissed is an understatement." Pausing, I debate how to say this next part, but then realize no matter how I say it, it's going to stir up painful memories regardless. And possibly gut her.

"Mary, do you remember your father and Antonio giving you anything after your parents divorced?"

She frowns as she thinks and then slowly nods. "Yeah. When we were packing up Mom's things to send back to her, **πατέρας** (dad) came across two of... some sort of knives. Each one was stored in ornate boxes. I don't know what the knives were really called.

"When we went to visit **Abuelo** (Grandpa), he said that one of them was supposed to be mine, but seeing as I had never seen them before, he was confused. He said that he didn't know why Mom never gave mine to me. Knowing what I know now, I don't think she ever intended to give it to me because she never considered me her part of her family." Mary pauses as she shakes her head sadly.

"Anyway, that was when he told us that they were reproductions of a family heirloom. Only the head of the family gets to inherit the original, and everyone else in the family receives a reproduction. Keep in mind, this is before we knew Mom's family was the mafia. **Abuelo** (Grandpa) asked **πατέρας** (dad) to keep both of them. He said he was disgraced by what his daughter had done to me and that she would need to earn the heirloom back, and if she did, then he would get in touch with **πατέρας** (dad) to give it back to her. Since **πατέρας** (dad) didn't trust Mom not to try and get them back from us, he put them in a safe deposit box."

I nod, taking in the new information. "That makes a few things Antonio said make more sense. He had wanted to be the one to tell you this himself, but with everything going on and what we had found out tonight, he said I could share it with you." I pause when she shifts so that she's sitting upright and can look at me better. When she's situated, I take her hand in mine.

"Those knives are actually called eared daggers, which are a type of Spanish knife. The one Antonio has in his possession used to belong to his great-great-great-great-great grandfather. It is a symbol of the Vasquez family and it's what the family crest is based on. The dagger also has another meaning within the family. You cannot work in any aspect of the family business if you don't have possession of your dagger. You see, if a family member loses face with the Don, he can order the dagger to be returned until said person has earned their rightful place back in the mafia side of the family. Antonio's men actually stormed Diego's and Carlos' estates and he took back their daggers, which includes Isaac's since he was still living in his family's estate. They did that a couple of days after we met Antonio at your old house. Unfortunately, that also tipped his hand that he was onto them, and all three of them are in the wind now, along with Stephan and Eileen."

Mary's eyes widen and her jaw drops in surprise. "What about Carmen?"

"Antonio has her down in what he called their cells. She was taken before they breeched the estates so that she couldn't tip them off."

She nods and then pauses. "So that's why Eileen's mad. She can't work for the family because I have her dagger." Then she frowns as she stares down at her free hand as it picks at the edge of the sheet. "However, women aren't really allowed to work for the family, except for in one of their businesses, so I'm not sure what she was hoping to accomplish. As sexist as it is, **Abuelo** (Grandpa) said that the mafia is very much still a man's world. There are a few families that employ women, but they are usually assistants to the women of the house. Though, a few are trained to be assassins or to have the women use their womanly wiles to seduce information from their enemies. Willingly of course." She rolls her eyes and I shake my head and instead choose to focus on her comment about Eileen.

"Antonio believes the same thing about Eileen—that she was trying to worm her way into either his or Diego's side of things, but can't without that dagger. We think that's another part of why she's working at Lucia's company. Antonio, Mateo, and Lorenzo rewatched some security footage and found some conversations where Eileen suspected that Nikos may have given it to Lucia for safekeeping. Though, I'm not sure why it wouldn't be safest with Antonio. With being the Don, you would think he'd be able to have a secure place to put it."

Mary frowns. "I don't know. He could have been worried about someone somehow learning how to access his safes and taking it back. Especially since she lived there. But what I don't understand is, why is she going to all of this trouble for it? She's practically a ghost right now. She could do whatever the hell she wants. Why..." She pauses mid-sentence, a thoughtful look coming over her face. "Do you think she needs it to be married off into another mafia family? I mean, Eileen was never one to put much of an effort into anything other than her appearance, clothes, and shoes. She was always about status, which didn't make sense because **πατέρας** was never wealthy. I mean, he had a lot more money after divorcing Mom and when he started rising in Lucia's company, but he was never rich rich."

I tilt my head as I think about it. "That could be her motive. Trying to set herself up for a free ride. We're supposed to talk with Antonio some more tomorrow, so I can ask him to find out." I squirm as I contemplate the last thing that I need to ask her. "Mary... I need to ask you something. It was posed as a last-ditch effort to get Stephan and Diego. Before I say this, I want you to know that I completely don't agree with this, and I would much rather you stay behind the compound walls as much as possible while we search for these fuckers—"

She reaches forward, presses a finger against my lips and gives me a sad smile. "If it's our last option, yes, I'll be the bait to draw them out. But I really, really don't want to go anywhere alone. I would prefer it if people were staked out at whatever location we decide on and be ready to wound them enough so you guys can grab them." She bites her lip as uncertainty flashes in her eyes before it turns to determination. "I don't like it, same as you, but if it's what needs to be done to bring them down? Then I'll do it. However, under no circumstances are my kids being bait."

Immediately, I shake my head and gather her back into my arms. "Never." I sigh and kiss her. "We'll do whatever we can to prevent using you as bait, but I was asked to ask you about your thoughts on it. Even if I hate it with every fiber of my being."

Mary shifts slightly, laying back down and I do the same. She cuddles into me again and kisses my chest. "I know, and I get it. I don't like it, but I get it. However, this has become home for me and everyone in the club is my family. I don't want anyone else to get hurt, so if that's the best course of action, then I'll do it."

Fuck, I really hope it doesn't come down to using her as bait. Reaching over, I turn off the light on the nightstand and wrap my arms around Mary, holding her close. As I lay my head back on my pillow, I do something I haven't done in years.

Prayed.

Prayed that we're able to find Stephan, Diego, and the others quickly so that Mary doesn't ever have to put herself in the line of fire again.

Chapter 55

Mary

It's been a week since Patch and the rest of the club, uh, 'talked' to some of the guys that attacked us on Sunday and I'm nervously buckling my seatbelt in Luke's new truck for my first trip outside of the club compound since the attack. To say my nerves are frazzled is an understatement.

Patch closes my door once I'm situated and rounds the front of the truck before climbing in behind the steering wheel. Our eyes lock for a few seconds and after starting the truck, he reaches over, squeezing my hand in his.

"We'll be okay, Mary. Worst-case scenario, we're drawing them out and we have more than enough guys to help deal with them."

Taking a deep breath, I nod silently. The Junction Creek guys headed home on Monday after they were done with their 'talk'. Then on Tuesday when Mae had come over to visit us, Mama Astrid had video called her and I got to 'meet' her for the first time. She's a hoot of a woman and I honestly can't wait to get in a kitchen with her, but what was surprising is that she asked how my arm and leg where healing.

"That's wonderful, Dear! My Mae has been telling me so much about you and I can't wait to pick your brains about some recipes. I've always loved trying new things, and I'm sure the boys could use a bit of a mix-up around here. However, that isn't why I was calling. How are you feeling, Dear? Mae and some of my boys told me that there was an attack on Sunday. Your arm and leg weren't re-injured, were they?"

I cock an eyebrow at Mae, and a sheepish look crosses her face, but I smile and shake it off, not really caring that she told her about my injuries since she's part of the club.

"My shoulder got a little wrenched again when they tried to kidnap me, but Doc looked at it and doesn't think it will set me back any and as for my leg, I think I

must have knocked it a couple of times but after taking some meds that night, the excess pain went away. Again, since it didn't hurt worse after the meds were out of my system, Doc and Patch figured I was most likely fine."

"When do you get your cast off?"

"January 4th, I go in for my six-week check-up. They'll cut it off and x-ray it. If it needs more time, then I'll get another cast. I hope that I can actually get it off then. I'm sick of this itchy cast!"

She laughs and nods knowingly. "That's fantastic news, and yes, they really are itchy things. Hopefully, that wonker didn't mess your leg up too badly and that you won't need it to be re-cast."

Laughing, I shake my head at her.

"So other than Sunday's misfortune, how have you been holding up, Dear? Is my boy, Patch, treating you right?"

A chuckle escapes me at that. "Yes, Mama Astrid, he's treating me right. Things have been pretty good other than what happened on Sunday. This next Monday, the eleventh, I have to go into the doctor's office for a check-up on my arm. It was a previously set up appointment and nothing to do with Sunday," I quickly reassure her when I hear a concerned noise come over the line. "In all honesty, I'm a little nervous about going out after what happened, but I know it can't be avoided. I don't want anyone else getting injured further, so yeah, I'm pretty nervous."

Pausing, I take a breath and when Mae reaches over and squeezes my hand; I squeeze right back and try to push down my nerves as much as possible. "Aside from that, we're all moved into the condo that the club is letting us use and the rest of my dad's belongings are in a storage unit here, since the house is now on the market. I took some pictures of the items we're not going to use, and my grandparents are asking the family if they want or need any of it. If not, then I'll let the club use the items in the other condos. They've helped us out so much that I'd like to pay it back some."

Her warm chuckle that comes through the line wraps around me like a balm. Mae had told me before that Mama Astrid has always been like a second mother to the club members. Is this what having a mother is like? A real mother? Someone who checks in to see how you are? Someone who worries about you and wants you to get better when you've been injured? In all actuality, I'm a little shocked that this is surprising me and affecting me so much. I mean, I knew Eileen had a change of heart about me around the time I turned four or so when she started treating me like shit and more like a thorn in her side. I had always imagined that a real mother's love would be similar to how **γιαγιά** (grandma) *always treated me, but to experience it is another thing. And I haven't even met her in person yet!*

"That's good, and I'm glad you're all settled in. I've been telling those boys they needed something like our setup of apartments for years, and I'm happy that they're finally listening and built those condos. Have you and Patch decided if you are you going to build a house on the compound next spring?"

My cheeks heat as I bite my lip and I hope that this mess with Stephan will be cleared up before then.

"Yeah, we're planning to. We actually fell in love with the spot right on the other side of Mae's house, and the kids love that we'll be next door to them."

I bite my lip again as I remember exactly how *excited they all were after Patch and I had looked around the property before deciding. However, in all honesty, the site is absolutely perfect for us.*

The forest butts up to the back of the property and there's a river that is a bit further into the forest that Patch said they fish from occasionally. There's a spacious area for a backyard which has a few mature trees that the boys are already asking if they can build a treehouse in.

Mama Astrid's voice brings me out of my thoughts and I shake my head slightly to clear it.

"I bet the kids are going to love being so close to Mae and Timber. I had a video call with Mae the weekend you were in the hospital, not knowing that was the case of course, and I was surprised when I heard your kids' voices in the background. They had never video chatted with anyone before and were shocked it was possible. Your kids are absolutely adorable and I can't wait to meet them in person! You can bet your patootie that I'll be there the next time the club comes down."

We all laugh and I couldn't help my smile widening at hearing her cursing like Mae does. I guess Mae's habits are rubbing off on a lot of the ladies in the club.

"You okay, Siren?"

I shake my head slightly to clear my thoughts. "Sorry, was just lost in thought. I was thinking about the phone call with Mama Astrid a couple of days ago."

Apparently, my worries spurred Mama Astrid, her husband Odin, Reaper, and four other members of the Junction Creek club into coming down yesterday afternoon. They were planning on coming over on this upcoming Friday, but when they learned about my appointment, they came down sooner to help provide extra manpower. They'll be here for a couple of weeks, but I did overhear that the guys will rotate out because of their businesses back home.

I inhale sharply as we leave the compound and head down the road, nerves instantly bombarding me even more at facing the spot that could have very well taken our lives a few days ago.

But this time, we've got an even bigger army at our backs, which helps ease some of my worries. Besides two other trucks, which also hold more club members, there are eight bikes in front of and behind us. We look like a caravan even though it's the middle of December. Since we've had very little snow so far this year, which is rather uncommon, the guys can still ride since there isn't a layer of salt lining the roads yet.

However, the large number of our group is also part of a two-sided point that the club is trying to make. One, that the club is committed to protecting us, and two, they are hoping to either draw out or anger Stephan and the others. God, I hope we can find those assholes soon! I'm tired of all this worry and stress. I just want to get on with our lives and move forward.

Patch huffs and shakes his head, but his smile gives him away. "Mama Astrid is a force to be reckoned with. I'm glad you two get along so well."

He lifts my hand, pressing kisses to my knuckles, and I squeeze my legs together. This is *not* the time to be feeling horny. Of course, the ever-observant nurse doesn't miss a thing. I don't know if it's because of all of our time apart, but ever since we crossed the line and finally had sex, I've been needing him a lot since then. It's not uncommon for us to sneak off a couple of times a day, especially with him still home on vacation. He has four more days left of his time off, and I'm worried his wounds won't fully close before then, but time will tell.

"Is my Siren feeling a little neglected? Are you feeling a little needy?" His deep, smooth voice sends a shiver down my spine that also has goosebumps rising on my skin.

Taking a deep breath, I exhale heavily. "While I normally love it when you get like this, please don't get me all wired before we head into the doctor's office. You know I'm not patient and don't like waiting," I practically beg.

He hums and lifts my hand again to his lips. A moan escapes when he runs his tongue seductively along my fingers, almost like he's picturing them as my lower lips.

"I wasn't able to have my favorite breakfast this morning, so I'm feeling a little needy myself. I'll have to make sure to steal you away this afternoon to get my fix."

We were interrupted by the kids this morning and had to quickly get ready instead of having sexy times. My cheeks heat even more as he winks at me and lowers my hand.

Holy fudgenuggets, this man is going to be the death of me. But, oh, what a way to go.

Shakily, I take a few breaths, trying to calm myself down. Thankfully, by the time we reach the doctor's office ten minutes later, I feel like I've mostly got myself back under control.

Undoing my seatbelt, I wait for Patch to get my wheelchair out of the back of the truck. After last weekend, we decided I'd just use the regular wheelchair today in case Stephan or my so-called family decided to try anything. I don't want to have to replace another electric wheelchair if I don't have to.

After a few moments, he opens the door and lifts me out before stepping back slightly so Odin has room to close the door and then Patch walks the few steps to the sidewalk and sets me down in the chair. The guys surround me as we walk less than a block down the street to the doctor's office. Peering over my shoulder, I note that a couple of guys are now sitting in Patch's truck, most likely to keep an eye on it while we're inside. I go to face forward when another roar of a bike comes down the street and parks on the other side of the street, opposite of Patch's truck.

Frowning, I wonder what he's doing but when he gets off his bike, leans against it so that he's facing the truck, and pulls out his phone, my jaw drops in surprise when I realize he's keeping watch from behind, to make sure no one messes with anything on the back end of the truck. He sees me looking at him and gives me a slight tilt of his head in acknowledgement before looking back at the truck and then down at his phone. My chest warms once again at the show of support the club has for us. At the same time, something cements in my heart and mind.

I'm finally where I'm supposed to be.

With Patch.

With the club.

A renewed sense of determination flows throughout me. I'll do whatever I need to do in order to help the club bring down Stephan and the rogue members of my family.

I'm brought out of my thoughts when I'm turned and realize that we're at the doctor's office. Patch wheels me inside and up to the check-in desk.

The lady, whose nametag reads Lana, looks up as we approach and frowns when she sees the guys all at my back.

"I'm sorry, but there is no loitering in here. This is a doctor's office. If you don't have an appointment, then you'll need to leave," she tells us as she looks down her nose at us.

Thor walks up and braces his hands on either side of the counter in front of her. Not in a threatening manner, but definitely intimidating as he hovers over her.

"Well, then maybe you should have a chat with your boss, Dr. McGregor, Lana. You'll find that we are, in fact, allowed to be here for Miss Catarino today."

Lana huffs, still trying to look down her nose at us before turning to me, addressing me coldly. "Name?"

"Mary Catarino."

"Have one of your goons wheel you over to a corner so you're out of the way." She says as she waves in a shooing motion like I'm a nuisance before pausing, and then she turns back to Thor. "And make sure that the rest of you don't bother the other patients with your hooligan ways. We are professionals here, and we won't tolerate any unholy shenanigans of yours."

Scoffing, I turn my chair, about to purposefully *not* wait in a corner when I swear I can hear Lana mumbling under her breath that McGregor never should have been the one in charge of the practice, which has me frowning. What does she mean by that?

Turning fully, I look closer at the layout of the waiting area. The room is set up with chairs along three walls and then some more chairs down the middle of them but on the opposite side of the room from Lana, there is a space to walk between the two halves of the room. Instead of going to a corner, which really would have put me in front of the coat rack area since it's the only available corner—the rest all have end tables or the entrance in them, I head toward the end of the room and park my chair at the end of the middle row of chairs. Once again Lana scoffs at me, to which I politely smile in return before turning to find Smoke while, at the same time, pulling my phone out of my purse. Spotting him, I'm grateful he turns toward me at that same moment, and I slightly wiggle my phone. He gives me a barely there chin lift and pulls out his own phone. Opening my chats, I create one with him and Patch just so he knows my concerns as well.

Mary: Do either of you know if there is any back history or bad blood between Lana's family and Dr. McGregor?

Smoke: What makes you ask? Did she say something?

Mary: As I was turning away, I heard her muttering that McGregor should never have been the one in charge of the practice.

Patch: I heard my dad talking about them not too long ago. Dr. Paul Olsen was Lana's grandfather and used to run this practice. He also had his son, Julian, and Mark McGregor working with him, but ultimately, it was Paul's practice.

Patch: Julian is a shit doctor, always doing the bare minimum. Also, there are rumors where he brushes off his patients' concerns or symptoms, especially if the patient is a woman. Dad thinks those reasons and rumors are why Paul decided to leave the practice to Mark instead of his own son. Mark has been my doctor for years, which was why I suggested him for you, Mary. However, I hadn't known how bad the blood was between Mark and Julian. Lana's never said anything or acted like this in the past. I don't know if anything new has happened between their dynamic. I could always ask Dad if he's heard anything.

Smoke: Do that just in case. I'll dig into them more when I get back to the compound and let you both know.

Mary: Thank you

My throat tightens as I reread Patch's texts. Suddenly, images of what Claudia did to me at the hospital bombard me, and I wonder how easily it would be for Stephan and his lackeys to get to me here, too.

"What a bitch," Gunner mutters before sitting in a chair beside me. "Watch your back with that one, Mary. She's been glaring at us since you came over here," he whispers.

I try to swallow the lump in my throat as I nod my acknowledgment.

I'm about to ask him something when a woman calls out my name. Looking over my shoulder, there's a young, blond nurse with a bubbly smile on her face holding open the door that leads further into the clinic.

Patch stands and pushes me toward her, and I'm thankful that Smoke and Gunner both get up and follow us.

"We've got your back, Mary," Gunner says quietly as he walks to my left, slightly behind Patch.

Not wanting to draw any attention, I subtly dip my head to indicate that I heard him.

After the nurse checks my vitals, I'm left in the room with Patch and Smoke while Gunner stands outside the door.

Patch helps me sit on the examination table and when he sits on the chair nearby, he frowns but concern is written all over his face.

"What's going through your head, Siren?"

My throat works as I continue to try and swallow around the lump in my throat. "I'm nervous and a little scared. What if someone pulls a Claudia here? Or tampers with my records? Or..." I struggle to bring in breath and my chest feels like it's on fire.

The next thing I know, Patch's hands clasp mine before moving them to his chest, and then he cups my cheeks as he tilts my head up, making me look up at him.

"Breathe with me, Siren. That's it. Keep breathing in sync with me."

Even though I struggle, my breathing finally evens out some and I lean forward, resting my head on his chest.

"And here I thought being out and about was going to give me a panic attack, not wondering if Stephan or Diego has ties to anyone that works here. I hate how he's made me start questioning everyone's intentions."

"From what I could find, they don't. I did a background check on everyone that works here, even the janitors. However, that doesn't mean something hasn't happened recently that isn't on anything I could dig up." He pauses as he comes over and lightly squeezes my good shoulder. "And it's not your fault that you're questioning everything. It's those fuckers' fault because of what they did to you.

"Besides, there is a plus side to this. It's making you more observant. More cautious. Listen to your instincts, like how you did with Lana a few minutes ago. We never knew there was bad blood here, so now we'll be more cautious." He pauses again before grinning darkly. "And if anyone does try anything, we'll fuck them up, Steel Archangel style."

Even though I know he's dead serious, I can't help but chuckle at that. "Thank you, Smoke. You're going to make some woman very happy one day."

His cheeks tinge just the slightest bit of pink and I briefly wonder if he's been seeing someone, but I shake off the thought. It's not my business to pry. I just hope that when he does find a woman, she's nice and treats him and Mae with respect. I've grown very close to Mae during my time here, and by extension,

Smoke as well. Hell, he's decided to build his house on the other side of ours once our house is completed next spring.

He's about to say something when the door opens, and a man in a white coat, who I'm assuming is Dr. McGregor, enters. He walks forward and does that bro hug thing with Patch and then Smoke.

"Gentlemen, good to see you today, and you must be Mary Catarino. Nice to meet you. I'm Dr. McGregor, but you can call me Mark if you want."

Since that's what Patch keeps calling him, I decide to follow suit. "Hello, Mark."

He sets my file down on the counter, washes his hands and then sits on the little doctor's stool. He gives me a soft smile that immediately puts me at ease.

"I've read through your files that the hospital sent over, but I'd like to hear what happened from you and your perspective."

Taking a deep breath, I squeeze Patch's hand, who's still standing beside me and launch into it, telling him what happened Thanksgiving night. Of course, I give him the cliff-notes version and I purposefully leave out some details. The more I talk, the darker Mark's face gets. When I'm done, he shares a look with Patch and then Smoke.

"Well, Mary, you are definitely in good hands with the club. I've known quite a few of the members for years and they're all good men. They'll help you take care of those scum."

I wonder briefly exactly *how* close he is to some of the club members. Does he know that's exactly what the club intends to do? To *take care* of Stephan, Diego, and the others?

Suddenly, Mark switches modes and any darkness that was there a moment ago is now gone.

"Now, let's see how you're healing."

Fifteen minutes later, I release a breath of relief that Mark thinks all of my wounds are healing the way they should be and he's extremely pleased about my progress with regaining my strength in my shoulder.

"Keep doing the exercises that the physical therapist gave you in the hospital, but remember not to push yourself too far too fast. That will only result in you setting back your progress and possibly even re-injuring it. I'll see you again on January 4th. We'll take a look at your shoulder again as well as get your cast off. Then we'll do an x-ray to see if you graduate into a walking boot or if we'll need to recast it again. Of course, if any problems arise that Patch can't handle between now and then, please call and make an appointment."

Smiling, I nod. "Thank you, Mark, and yes, I will."

"Have a good day," he says before tilting his head at Patch and then Smoke.

"Thank you, you too," I respond and then he leaves the room.

Patch lifts me off the table and sets me down in my chair. As we leave the room and head down the hallway, I can hear two people whispering harshly at each other. As we pass another hallway, I look down it only to see Lana and another doctor in a white coat, who I'm assuming is her father. Both of them scowl at us as we pass. Frowning, I wonder if they're mad because of all the club members that are here or if it's about something else. Shaking my head, I try to push them out of my mind as we leave the clinic, but when Patch stops my chair along the sidewalk and kneels in front of me, my body freezes as I stare at the passenger door.

"Patch."

He looks up at me from where he's hunched. He locks the wheels on my chair and follows my line of sight. His body tenses when he sees what I see.

A note tied to the handle of the passenger door.

I look around, confusion and fear gripping me. How could someone get past Tripp and Razor who are sitting in Patch's truck? Plus get past the guy across the street that was watching the truck? And that's not even mentioning the other guys that came with us today. How were they able to sneak past everyone?

"It's okay, Mary, we'll handle this," Smoke says as he pats my shoulder and both he and Patch walk over to Tripp and Razor in the truck. The guys that were with us in the clinic all close ranks around me, but they leave a slight gap so that I can see Patch.

Tripp, who's in the passenger seat looks surprised as they talk and he peers over the end of the truck, looking at the handle.

"How in the fuck did someone manage to do that? No one walked between us on either side of the truck."

The guys nearby that can hear the conversation all curse.

"Reach into my glove box and give me a set of gloves. There should also be a baggie that we can use to put the note in."

Once Patch puts on the gloves, he carefully unties the note and I frown when I see a little white substance poof when the tie is finally undone. "It's coated in something. Did you see that?"

All three of their faces all tighten in anger. Patch looks up at Smoke and then Tripp before nodding slightly.

"Yeah, we saw it. We'll have to get it tested."

He works quickly, and I can faintly hear a couple of growls as Patch and Smoke read the note. Smoke takes a picture of it and then Patch secures it in the bag. Tripp hands him some wipes, which he uses to wipe down the handle. Patch talks quietly to Tripp, who soon produces another bag that Patch puts the wipe as well as his gloves into.

Patch comes back to me, picks me up, and then walks back toward the door. Tripp steps out and once Tripp squeezes past the door, without touching the handle, Patch sets me down on the seat. Moments later, he and Razor switch spots, again making sure not to touch the outer handle as a just in case. Thor appears at Patch's window and they talk quietly for a few moments, but I can barely make out what they're saying over the sound of the truck engine and the bikes in the background.

Finally, Patch nods and then turns back to me, frowning. "The rest of today's plans are off. Sorry, Siren."

A twinge of disappointment goes through me at that. I had hoped to be able to get a few Christmas things in person for the kids as well as some decorations.

"We need to get back to the clubhouse to examine what was on that note. Smoke's gonna look at his cameras too, to see who the fuck it was and how they did it."

A chill runs down my spine. "What did the note say?"

A dark look comes over his face as he hesitates and then his shoulders slump slightly before he pulls his phone out and hands it to me.

"3-1-4-6-2-4. Check the text messages. Smoke sent it to me."

Emotion swells in me as Patch reverses out of the parking spot and drives through town. He used my birthday, March 14th, and Ash's, June 24th, as his passcode.

Taking a deep breath, I enter the code and find the text message chain. I also see that he has a club text chain with new messages and as tempting as it is to look and learn more, I click on the thread with Smoke instead.

What I read chills me down to the bone.

> *You didn't return what was rightfully mine. Now all your loved ones will pay and their blood will be on your hands. But don't worry, your punishment will be ten times more severe than theirs will ever be. You know how to stop this and you know where to go to find me. The more you stall, the more they'll hurt. The clock is ticking, Pet.*

My mind whirls at who all could be behind this note. The first part makes me think it was Eileen or possibly Stephan. The punishment part sounds more like Diego or Kristoff. As for the 'pet' comment, all four of them have called me that at some point. Some more than others.

Tears burn my eyes. Why can't they just leave us alone?

Chapter 56

Mary

Emotions roll through me as I stare blankly out the window, but my mind is a whirlwind. However, it doesn't escape my notice that Patch's body is tense as hell and I can feel the anger rolling off him in waves.

I keep trying to figure out how someone was able to get past all the guys. The only way I can even think of is if they shimmied under the cars, but wouldn't someone have seen that?

"Siren, I need you to call Thor for me."

Blinking rapidly, it takes me a second, but then Patch's words sink in and I quickly find Thor's number. The phone rings and the call connects via Bluetooth.

"Patch."

"Got a tail. Black SUV. Minnesota 927 URM."

My body freezes and I carefully turn to look out the side-view mirror to see if I can see them. When Patch changes lanes and turns off the normal route to the clubhouse, the SUV follows suit.

"Just got off the phone with Axe. A few have broken off to swing around and follow them. Keep going to the clubhouse. I'm calling Church as soon as we get there. Everyone else should already still be at the clubhouse."

"Got it."

The line goes dead and my guess is that Thor's calling someone, probably Levi, at the clubhouse to let them know about what's going on.

My gaze goes back to the mirror and stays glued to it as Patch drives through town, but the SUV continues to follow us. It isn't until we turn onto the road leading to the clubhouse that the SUV peels off and goes in a different direction.

Minutes later, Patch parks in front of the clubhouse and barely has the engine turned off before he bolts out of the truck and runs over to my door. My fingers fumble with the seatbelt, but I finally get it off and open the door so that he won't have to touch the handle in case they missed anything when they wiped it down earlier. He immediately picks me up and carries me inside. My hands begin to shake as he goes to pull away and he curses.

"I-It's okay. I think the adrenaline is just wearing off," I tell him, knowing he needs to go into Church even though I'd much rather be wrapped in his arms.

He frowns, his gaze roaming over me as he checks me over. "Are you sure?"

"Go on into Church, Patch. We'll help Mary. Like she said, it's probably the adrenaline crash," Elvira says as she and Mae walk up toward us.

Patch hesitates, but I wrap my hand around his neck, pulling him forward and kissing him.

"It's okay, really. I'm sure after a bit, it'll pass. They need you," I tell him as I tilt my head toward Church.

His lips thin and I can see the war raging within him in his eyes. Finally, he gives me a curt nod and kisses me. "Stay inside. Don't go out for anything." With one last quick kiss pressed to my forehead, he stalks to the bar and takes the beer Ethan holds out to them and heads into Church.

Sighing, I look down at my hands and will them to stop shaking.

Elvira pats my shoulder. "Come, let's go into the kitchen and get your mind off things. We've already started preparing supper."

"Okay," I reply weakly. Fuck, even my voice is a little shaky. Looking around, I start to panic. "Where are the kids?"

"In the playroom watching a movie. Drae is with them since I was also helping in the kitchen," she says.

My shoulders sag in relief at her words and I give her a grateful smile that she returns.

Following them into the kitchen, my mouth waters at the combination of smells from whatever they are cooking.

"We're making a beef stew, cornbread, biscuits, garlic mashed potatoes and regular mashed potatoes with gravy, and a salad."

Lord, I can't stop the moan that leaves my mouth. "That sounds amazing. What do you need help with yet?" Pulling up close to the counter, I undo my sling and carefully stand. Elvira brings over the tall stool that Patch got for me, and I get settled in.

Mae passes me a peeler and I glance down at my hands. They're still slightly shaky, but as long as I'm careful, I shouldn't hurt myself.

As we prep and cook, conversation easily flows between the four of us. Watching Mae and Mama Astrid interacting, and even seeing how close Mae and Elvira are, makes my chest hurt with longing. Out of all of us ladies, Elvira seems to be closest to Mae, which is probably in part because of what happened when Mae was kidnapped earlier this year. Still, seeing how close they are and the bond they share makes me wish I could have something similar while growing up with my own mother. But then again, would I have turned out like her as well if I had?

Hours pass and I start to worry that supper's going to get cold if the guys don't get out of Church before long. It's already six o'clock.

"Granny, when's supper going to be ready?" Lindsey asks as she peeks into the kitchen, hanging onto the doorframe. Behind her are my kids with Drae behind them.

I turn back toward Mae and Elvira for direction. They share a look and then nod.

"You guys can come in and we'll get you some food," Mae tells them before turning to get them bowls and plates down from the cupboard.

Out of the corner of my eye, I notice Drae's body going rigid and when I turn to look at him better, he's scowling at his phone. "Ladies, I need to help Sasha with something. All of you stay in the kitchen."

Frowning, I watch him rush out of the room and outside. Dread pools in my stomach and I wonder what's happened this time.

I jump slightly, thankfully not falling off my chair, when a door slams open and the guys file out of Church before heading straight outside after Drae.

Turning toward Mae, intent on asking what's going on, she gives me a wide-eyed look and then purses her lips while slightly tilting her head and looking down at the kids.

Exhaling, I can only sit and wring my hands while we wait. Within minutes, the kids are eating at a small table that's back here while quietly talking amongst themselves. Wringing my hands again, the ladies and I all share a concerned look.

Suddenly, the front door opens up and I frown when the guys all crowd together as they make their way back into Church. A small gasp escapes me when I can see bare flesh peeking out from in between their bodies and I know it's not one of them since the body is bruised, cut, and bloodied.

My gaze darts around the room until I find Patch, who apparently is one of the guys holding the person, but he must have had his head lowered before since I couldn't see him. Briefly he looks up and for a second, our gazes lock, but nothing in his eyes gives anything away as to who they are carrying.

But then I see it.

"**Tío** (Uncle) Mateo!"

Someone curses and I hastily climb down from the stool and into my chair. The ladies thankfully don't stop me, but the men sure do. Either that or the ladies knew the guys would try to stop me.

"Please move! I need to get to my **tío** (uncle). He's hurt," I beg repeatedly, but none of them let me pass. Why won't they let me through?

"Please, Mary, you're going to hurt yourself if you keep struggling," Odin says as he tries to get me to sit back down in my chair and I frantically wipe at the tears streaming down my cheeks.

Wait, when did I stand up?

"Mary, if it really is Mateo, do you think he'd want you to see him as he is now?"

That has me pausing. No, he'd hate to cause me any sort of pain, but also, not being able to see him is causing my anxiety to ratchet up like no other. I need to see him and see that he's alright. I've already lost too many people in my life.

"I know," he replies sadly, and I realize I must have said that aloud, "but give the guys a chance to get him looked at and fixed up. We're going to figure out who he is for sure, but if you could tell me any identifying marks that would be able to help us verify if it really is Mateo or if it's Diego, it would be appreciated."

"Besides their eye color, the biggest difference is their birthmarks and tattoos."

Odin nods for me to continue as he squats down in front of me. My gaze goes toward Church, but the door is already shut.

"Focus, Mary."

My gaze goes back to him and I blink as I nod. "Mateo has kind of bright, silver-gray eyes, whereas Diego has dark, inky-silver eyes. Mateo's birthmark is on his right side and is brown. Overall, it's in the shape of an oval, and the last time I saw it, it wasn't raised at all. Diego's is on his left side and is brownish-red. His is in the shape of a circle and is slightly raised and bumpy."

Odin nods and it's only then that I realize he's been recording me. "What about the tattoos you mentioned?"

"Keep in mind that the last time I saw them together was when I was fifteen and at **la casa de mi abuelo** (my grandpa's house) house. We were out on the deck because they were swimming, but I wasn't allowed to."

I shut my eyes at the onslaught of Eileen's voice in my head, not able to block it out or the residual stinging of my cheeks, which she had slapped repeatedly after being told to head back inside to change out of my swimsuit.

"You're too fat to go swimming. No one wants to see a beached whale when they're trying to relax and have fun. Besides, no one here wants to play with you or get to know you better. You have no place in this family, and I don't even know why you're here or why we're throwing you a party. All of this is a waste of money that's once again *being spent on someone who doesn't deserve it."*

The reason *why* I was there is that **Abuelo** (Grandpa) wanted to throw me a quinceañera, but neither Eileen nor Carmen would let him do things how he wanted. Or at least, that's what I had overheard. They had told him that I wanted a simple party with just family. Nothing extravagant. No extra frills. Hell, the fanciest thing there was the sheet cake with all the pretty roses on it. And because Eileen and Carmen would never allow me to get close to him, he didn't know that I'd been secretly hoping for a nice quinceañera where I could celebrate with my friends and both sides of my family.

Blinking, I shake off those thoughts.

"Both of them have the family crest tattooed on them, but **Tío** (Uncle) Mateo has his over his heart and Diego has his on his back. On **Tío** (Uncle) Mateo's left arm, there are a bunch of roses and some script in Spanish dedicated to **la memoria de mi abuela** (my grandma's memory). Last I knew, he had no tattoos of skulls, but Diego has a full sleeve on his right arm with various skulls on it. Those are the big ones that I remember."

Odin clicks off the recording and I slump back in my chair.

"Thank you, Mary. This will most definitely help. We'll find out what happened, and if he really is Mateo and not Diego, then I'm sure you'll be allowed to see him."

"Thank you." My throat tightens as my vision once again turns a little blurry with my tears.

He gets up and heads toward Church, and Punisher and Beast follow him. It's only then that I realize the three of them must have been the ones to keep me from going to Mateo, but in my panic, I hadn't recognized who they were at first.

Punisher stops before going into Church and he talks quietly with Mae for a few moments before he heads inside. Mae comes over to me and gives me a hug that my body slouches into. I feel like I'm drained and completely wrung out.

"How about we eat and then head to the playroom with the kids? We can curl up with them on the mats and bean bags and cuddle the heck out of them while we watch a movie?"

Not having any energy to argue, I agree and follow her back down the hallway.

Please let **Tío** Mateo be okay. **Abuelo** (Grandpa) would be so devastated if something happened to him and I don't know how I'll take losing someone else.

Chapter 57

Patch

Leaving Mary when she's going through an adrenaline crash tears me apart, but she's right. We need to figure out what the fuck is going on. Giving her one last kiss, I stand and head straight to the bar. I'm going to need a drink for this shit, that's for damn sure.

Beer in hand, I head into Church and take my seat, but seeing the note on the table has me standing back up and heading to my kit at the back of the room. Grabbing a sterile mat, and a box of gloves, I put them on the table by Thor and retake my seat. I'm not sure if Ryder will want my help in taking samples of whatever is on the note or not. With Alli's dad as one of the hospital's department heads, he gives us a lot of leeway in the hospital, but one of the things I'm not sure if he knows about is a friend of mine, Tim Meyers, doing discrete testing in the lab for us.

Thor bangs his hammer and I take a pull off my beer as I wait for my brothers to settle down. Odin, Punisher, Beast, and Reaper stand against the back wall, since we don't have enough seats for them. However, I notice that Python does take a seat before booting up his laptop. They came down yesterday to help us with some more manpower.

"What I want to know is how the fuck did these assholes get by us?" Thor bellows and as I look around the room, everyone's face is hardened in anger, wanting to know the same thing.

"I couldn't get much off the cameras, but there's some shadow movement, a big shadow, underneath a couple of cars that were nearby Patch's truck." Smoke hits a couple of keys and then he replays the video. Afterward, he switches to a couple of stills that he took.

Frowning, I lean forward in my seat, trying to see it clearer, but whoever it is keeps themselves mostly out of sight. However, my eye catches on something.

"Smoke, can you zoom in on that hand?"

He gives me a chin lift and when he zooms in, curses ring out.

"Oasis fuckers," someone growls, and I nod in agreement.

You can visibly see a hand and a part of their forearm for a few seconds, but it's enough to see a tattoo of a snake winding down his arm and around his wrist.

"Fuck," Thor curses as he shakes his head. He looks up at Levi, then Timber, and finally me. He's tore up as much as we are that these assholes are still lurking out there, hurting God knows how many people. "Ryder, get your kit and take samples off the note. We can send a Prospect over to the hospital to meet with Patch's friend."

Ryder gets up and silently starts to do his thing. A heavy sigh has my gaze going back to Thor.

"Smoke, Python, did either of you find out anything more on these fuckers?"

"It wasn't easy, but we were able to hack into Phillip Cole's computers at the homestead. I don't know who is controlling their systems, but it sure as fuck *cannot* be Phillip with how complicated their system was. A fucking ostrich has more brains than him.

"We've got information on all the masters, the locations of their main homesteads as well as their main residences. Same for X. There were a few locations for where they are making this Aphrodite's Kiss drug, but they are heavily guarded. Apparently, after we stopped the operation both the Johnson assholes were doing, they upped their security in all locations." Smoke pauses and he and Python share an uneasy look.

Python clears his throat. "With our combined manpower, we can take care of business here in Wisconsin and the other states our chapters are in, maybe even our allies as well, but we'll probably be facing retaliation from them at some point. Thing is though, there are at least two homesteads in every state. I don't know how X managed to spread his reach this far or if he took over other people's territories to do so." He pauses, a grim look on his face. "Question is, how far do we go with this? Do we still only take care of Stephan and Diego, and then turn the rest of the information over to the feds? Or do we turn it all over at once and let them take care of everyone?"

"Personally, if we can, I'd love to get my hands on Stephan and Diego, but I know my vote isn't the only one that matters," I tell them and several of them nod in agreement.

The room is silent as we absorb the enormity of how far X's reach is. I knew Oasis' operation was big… but I didn't think it was that big. How has he managed to evade the cops or feds for this long?

After a few moments, murmurs start to fill the air as one after another throws out an idea or a question. Soon, it's hard to hear anyone.

Thor bangs his hammer on the table. "Shut the fuck up." He pauses as he glares around the room. "Talking over each other isn't going to solve a God damn thing. Smoke, Python, fill us in on what you know. Then we'll vote."

They both start typing on their laptops and soon a picture of a homestead appears on the wall. If memory serves, this is the one North of town on Mae's land.

"Here's what we got."

A few hours later, a buzz fills the air and all eyes go to Thor as he digs his phone out of his pocket.

"Sasha," he says.

Cowboy tenses at her name and I hope like fuck nothing's happened to her while she was on gate duty. My gaze goes back to Thor's and a sinking feeling in my gut forms at seeing how rigid his body is. The muscle in his jaw is ticking like crazy.

"Both of you stay there. We'll be out in a second."

He hangs up and looks at me. "A body was dumped at the gate. Fuckers hardly slowed down at all before opening a door and tossing a man out of it. He's been beaten, badly. Sasha and Drae got him inside the gate. His pulse is weak and he's unconscious." He pauses, and my jaw clenches as his jaw hardens further. So much so that I'm not sure how he's not cracked his teeth yet. "There's a note taped to his chest identifying him as Diego Vasquez and if Mary and the kids aren't turned over to X before the end of the weekend, then we'll all suffer his fate before having a bullet put through our skulls."

What? Why the fuck would X drop Diego here? I would think he'd be dropping Stephan, not Diego.

"My thoughts exactly," Thor drawls out, and I realize I said that out loud. "Let's head out, but keep your guns within easy reach in case this is a fucking trap."

As we file out of Church, I grab a pair of gloves since Sasha said the guy was bloodied up. It's hard to turn off your training and the nurse in me won't let me touch him without gloves. Walking through the main room, I resist looking toward the kitchen, where I'm almost positive Mary is. My gut is telling me they're trying to pull a fast one on us.

Shit.

What if it's Mateo and not Diego? I wouldn't put it past them to do a switcheroo in the hopes that we'll put him in a shallow dirt grave. I know without a doubt that Diego has been scheming to take their family's business out from under Mateo. Is this part of his plan?

Once we're outside, the nurse in me takes over and my stomach drops at the sight of all the cuts and wounds on his body. Not to mention all the bruising and swelling.

Taking a quick look around, I don't see anyone besides us, so I kneel at the guy's side, feeling for his pulse myself. It's weak like Sasha said, but thankfully not as weak as I had feared.

The guy slurs something unintelligible as I move him slightly to get a better look at his wounds, seeing if any are life threatening. "There's heavy bruising around his ribs. We need to be careful bringing him in. Someone get the backboard out of the back of my truck." As I look over his body, I shake my head in frustration. "I wish I'd asked Mary before if there are any specific identifiers to tell the difference between Diego and Mateo." At a glance, I can't tell the difference.

As I turn him over more, I note that there's a birthmark on his right side and there are multiple tattoos on his arms, torso, and back. However, I don't know if he got these before or after Mary was kidnapped.

"Let's get him inside so that we aren't sitting ducks. Try to keep him from the women's view, especially Mary's," Thor says and I grunt in acknowledgement.

If this *is* Mateo, it would kill her to see him like this.

We work quickly, but as we're walking through the main room, I feel myself tensing when I hear Mary calling out Mateo's name. Not being able to resist, I look up at her, but I do my damndest not to give away anything. A sliver of doubt has me wondering how she can tell it's him when she can hardly see him due to how the guys are carrying him.

I sigh in relief when I hear Odin trying to calm her down. However, my attention immediately diverts to the man on the stretcher, who groans as someone shifts their hold. Fuck, I hope his ribs aren't broken. We don't have an x-ray machine here.

We head into Church and then through an adjoining door since it's easier this way with the stretcher. When Mae set us up with a medical room like Doc's, we put it in the room next to where we hold Church. Before, the room had just been for storage, but thanks to Timber's help, now it's kitted up perfectly for what we need. And as a bonus, I can still hear what's going on in Church while I work. However, since we don't know if this is Diego or Mateo yet, I close the door and put in an earbud that Smoke supplied for instances like this which will let me continue hearing whatever is said in Church.

After washing my hands and putting on fresh gloves, I drop a cloth over his manhood. Then I grab a few vials and take some blood to see if he's been drugged. I also write a note for Tim, my friend in the lab at the hospital. Behind me, Bear washes and gloves up to help me.

"Here." I hand Bear the vials along with the note. "Can you have Thor send a Prospect with these to the hospital?"

He takes them and leaves the room while I get to work cleaning his wounds and inspecting which ones will need stitches or skin glue and which ones are fine to heal on their own. Thanks to the earbud, I can hear Thor telling Ethan to take the blood in and then the others start talking about a plan and our options.

"Do you really think this is Diego?" Bear asks quietly as he comes back and gets to work on the other side of the table.

I look up, but the man doesn't stir at his deep voice, even if it was a whisper. Shaking my head, I frown. "No, not with the way Mary reacted. My guess is she saw something that told her immediately which twin he is. Part of me wants him to be Diego, so we can put at least some of her problems behind us. The other part of me wants this to be Mateo. Who knows? If it is Mateo, maybe when he wakes up he'll be able to tell us more about what the fuck is going on."

Bear grunts, but other than that, neither of us speaks as we work.

As I'm cleaning a particularly nasty wound, the man grunts and winces. "Stop," he mutters and his hand flails out. I drop my tools and catch both of his wrists while Bear works to get him strapped down to the table.

"Fuck, guess we should have done that right away," he curses as the guy's elbow catches him to the right of his eye.

"Calm down, we're not going to hurt you." So long as you're Mateo, I mentally tack on. "You're at the Steel Archangel's clubhouse."

The guy stops fighting at that and barely cracks open his eyes. "Mary's... safe?" he asks, his voice gravelly, and it looks like it took him a great amount of effort just to say those two words.

I give a curt nod and walk over to the sink. Tossing my contaminated gloves, I put fresh ones on after washing up again, and fill a cup with some cold water. Grabbing a straw, I walk back over to him and help him take a drink.

"Yes, Mary's safe. What's your name?"

He leans back and I set down the cup.

"M-Mateo. Mateo Vasquez," he replies and I notice his voice is a little bit stronger than before. Maybe the drugs are starting to wear off?

"Don't take this the wrong way, but we're going to verify if you really are Mateo. We don't know if you were drugged so I can't give you anesthesia or pain medicine yet."

He nods weakly at my words. "I'd do the same. They injected me with something, but I don't know what was in it."

Giving him a sympathetic smile, I nod. "Blood is already on its way to get tested. Once I know for sure, we'll handle your wounds that need stitching.

However, just know that we might need to do it without anesthesia depending on what they injected you with.

He nods again. “That’s fine... I can take it. No cracked ribs. Definitely bruised, though. They wanted me to still be able to talk to some degree.”

Bear and I share a glance at that.

“Did they say why?”

“Diego drugged me at my own fucking house. I don’t know how he got in, but I’ll be going over the tapes the first chance I get. He’s blaming me for his lot in life. That I was chosen over him by **Padre** (Father) to take over for him. For cutting his allowances since I knew what he was funneling them into. For ordering the freezing of his accounts. And for taking out six of his most loyal soldiers. He said he was going to make me pay for taking everything from him and the best way to do that was to hand me over to you as him.”

I huff at that. “And he didn’t think that Mary would be able to tell you two apart?”

He gives me a small, sad smile as he shakes his head, and I notice his eyes are becoming more clouded and droopy.

“He thinks you won’t believe her because she’s a woman. In his eyes, women are meant to serve men. Though, with how he wooes women around him, it’s easy to see how he takes control over them without them realizing most of the time. Hell, Carmen, Eileen, and Gianna will do whatever he says. Even kill their own children for him if he were to ask.”

I pause at that, and Bear and I share another look.

Fuck.

A knock on the door has me looking up. “Come in.”

The door opens and I tilt my head, inviting Ryder in.

Silently, he starts painting Mateo’s fingers with ink and positions his fingers on the card before doing the same to his thumb, and then repeating the process on his left hand. When he’s done, he gets up to leave, but pauses at the door and looks back at me. “Check your phone.”

Stripping off my gloves, I dig out my phone to see a text from Odin, but then I realize it’s a voice clip. Connecting my phone to the earbud, I press play. Mary’s voice filters through the line and as she describes Mateo’s eye color, birthmark and tattoos, I find myself nodding as I check and verify that everything is where she says it is and his eyes, while clouded, are a bright silver-gray color. I look closer and can tell he isn't wearing contacts, so that checks out as well. However, I know Ryder will still verify by his prints if this man really is Mateo Vasquez. Putting my phone back in my pocket, I grab new gloves and continue examining his wounds.

After a few moments, Mateo speaks again.

"You're... her man? Luke?"

His voice is getting quieter, and I go on alert, just in case. "Yes."

"Good. Keep her safe." His voice trails off and as his eyes close again, his body goes even more lax.

Bear presses his hand to his pulse and after a few moments, he nods. "No change. Must have just passed out again. Hopefully Tim can get us what the fuck he was injected with fast so we can get these worse wounds stitched up. Do you think he's telling the truth?"

"Strangely, yes, I do. And that was before I got Odin's message. His eyes are the right color, the birthmark is in the right place as well as shape and color, and the tattoos line up."

Bear's shoulders relax some at that, and once again, we fall into silence as we continue our work stitching and patching him up.

Chapter 58
Patch

About an hour later, Bear and I clean up our tools and the room. We had to stitch Mateo up without anesthesia due to the cocktail of date rape drugs that he'd been injected with, but thankfully, all he did was grunt a few times on the worst ones. In twenty-four hours, most if not all, the drugs should be out of his system. Also, since I didn't know how long he'd be out of it due to all the drugs, I opted to put in a catheter.

Once more, I double check his vitals and that his IV is still in a good position, pumping him full of antibiotics and fluids. Who knows what Diego used to inflict all these wounds with? Or what they could have been coated with.

Knowing the guys got out of Church a while ago, Bear and I head out into the main room. I clap Drae on the shoulder, who's standing outside the door. Now that we're done, he heads inside to keep watch over Mateo.

Turning on my heel, I call out to him before he shuts the door. "Let me know when he wakes up. I'll be down periodically to check his vitals and switch out his IV bags as needed."

He gives me a chin lift and shuts the door.

Spotting Ryder over by Thor and Reaper, I walk over to them.

"Did he say anything?" Thor asks and I fill him in as well as what Odin had sent me, even though I figured Odin told him in Church what Mary had said.

"What'd you find out?" I ask, and not surprisingly, it's Ryder that answers me.

"He was telling you the truth, like you suspected. He's Mateo Vasquez."

Tension bleeds out of my shoulders at hearing it confirmed. "Does Mary know yet?"

Ryder shakes his head. "No. I knew she'd also want to know how he was doing and since I didn't know, I didn't want to cause her more worries or stress."

Frowning, I give my thanks before heading to the bar for a drink. The fact that Ryder *didn't* tell Mary anything, or anyone else for that matter, probably gave her even more worries and stress. I know how her mind wanders and I hope like fuck she hasn't worked herself up into a tizzy.

Since she's not out here and I don't see her in the kitchen, I'm guessing they're in the playroom. Heading down the hallway, I note that the door is closed, so I input my code. Once inside, I give Sasha a chin lift before turning to take everything in. The kids are sprawled out as they watch a movie. However, with the way Cassie's laying, I'm betting she's passed out, which will make tonight interesting.

Mary's the first to notice someone else in here and when she looks up, both hope and worry are written all over her face.

Closing the door, I walk over to her and lean over the couch, giving her a kiss.

"Is he okay?" she whispers and when I nod, relief sags throughout her. "Can I see him?"

I hesitate. "He's asleep right now. When he wakes up, then you can see him."

Tears pool in her eyes. "Please? I just need to put eyes on him, see for myself that he's alive and breathing."

Once again I hesitate, but then pause. "Just a second. I'll do the next best thing." Standing, I walk back toward Sasha.

"Sasha, can I see the tablet?"

She reaches into a cabinet behind her and pulls out one of the few tablets we have secretly concealed around the clubhouse. When Levi became pregnant, Smoke started thinking of additional ways to add extra layers of security to the clubhouse as well as looking at things on the flip side, ways for letting people know they need help. That last bit he added on after Mae was kidnapped out of the Junction Creek clubhouse. If there had been some sort of a panic button, she might have not been kidnapped in the first place. There's also an additional feature that I requested. Access to be able to tap into the feed of the medical room.

Pulling up the program, I input my code and walk back over to Mary. There are four cameras in the room. Three from various vantage points around the room but the fourth one is directly pointed at the monitors that are mounted on the walls, letting me read the patient's stats in an instant.

Sitting down next to her, I wrap my arm around her shoulders and pull her close. "I don't want to disturb him, but at least this way, you can see him. Drae knows to let me know when he wakes up, and I'll be checking in periodically to check his vitals and change out his medicine."

Her body relaxes against mine even more. "Thank you. Can we stay here tonight? I want to be close to him." Mary wipes her eyes and I kiss the top of her head.

"Of course."

She stares at the screen, and I make no move to take it from her. She needs this to put her mind at ease.

I settle in and watch the movie along with the kids, but before long, my stomach rumbles reminding me that I haven't eaten since lunch.

"Oh my gosh," Mary mutters as she sits up. "We put a plate in the oven for you and Bear. The others ate once they came out of Church."

Chuckling, I let her fuss over me, knowing it'll help keep her mind busy. Glancing over at Mae, she gives me a smirk and waves her hands in a shooing motion, letting me know she has the kids. Getting up, I pick her up and put her back in her chair before following her into the kitchen. I know she can shuffle from the couch to the chair, but I still like to help her where I can.

She parks close to the stove, stands, puts on some oven mitts and then carefully pulls out the containers out of the oven. Shutting the door, she then turns it off.

Taking the dishes to the counter, I sit down and watch out of the corner of my eye as she maneuvers to sit on the stool on the other side of the counter. It makes me nervous when she does all of this because of her cast and shoulder, but the nurse in me knows she needs to move around to keep her strength up and to get stronger. Still, it doesn't stop the worry and I do my best not to hover.

A groan escapes when I take the first bite of the stew and Mary grins, though I can tell it's strained as fuck.

"I had the same reaction when I smelled and heard what the ladies were making. It's good, isn't it?"

"It's delicious," I mumble around a bite of meat and then I grab some cornbread, sopping up some of the broth. Another groan escapes and I dig in, devouring the food in record time. I hadn't realized I was that hungry before.

When I'm done, Mary tries to take the bowl and plate from me, but I pull them back out of her reach. "I'll rinse them and put them in the dishwasher."

She retakes her seat, but I can see she's swallowing repeatedly and twiddling her fingers as she watches me.

Once the dishes are in the dishwasher, I start it and retake my seat. Reaching across the counter, I take her hands in mine.

"Mateo will be okay, Mary. Only a couple of his wounds were deep, but most of the others won't take long to heal. He does have significant bruising over most of his body, but again, time will heal them."

She blinks rapidly to keep her tears from falling. "Diego tried to pass Mateo off as him, didn't he?"

I look at her in surprise but then shake my head, grinning. Damn, my woman is smart. "Nothing gets past you, does it?"

The corner of her mouth ticks up, but she waits for me to continue.

"Yeah, he did. Apparently, Diego doesn't think we'll believe you when you said it was Mateo."

Mary rolls her eyes hard and huffs. "Of course he thinks that. Whenever he came over, he acted like I was a servant to him and if I rebuked anything, both he and Stephan would take turns beating me."

Rounding the table, I wrap her in my arms, needing to hold her after hearing that.

My dick perks up at feeling her pressed against me, and since it's most definitely *not* the time to be sporting a boner, I start reciting some of the nastiest infections a person can contract.

Mary hums and presses closer to me. "Feels like someone's excited."

"I'm always aroused by you, but especially when you're in my arms."

She presses harder against me and I feel her hand snake down and moan when she rubs me through my jeans. My half chub goes to fully erect so fast, I'm light-headed for a few moments.

"Fuck, Siren."

The break of a rack of cue balls brings me back to the present and I remember that we're in the kitchen, but thankfully, my back is to the main room.

"Let's head upstairs, Siren."

I lead her back down the hallway and to the lift we had installed when we expanded the clubhouse years ago. Riding up to my floor, I dig my keys out, but then pause outside my door.

"What the fuck?" I curse as I take in the fact that it's slightly ajar.

"What's wro—... Oh," Mary says quietly when she notices it as well.

Pushing the door open, I'm pissed beyond belief.

"What the fuck are you doing in here?" I roar.

Both Cici and Gemini, who were making out naked on my bed, startle but then start trailing their hands down their bodies.

"Waiting for you, of course," Gemini purrs right as she sinks her fingers into her pussy and with the other hand, grabs her breast.

"You worked so hard today, we wanted to give you some relief," Cici replies as she starts to finger herself as well.

"Get the fuck out of my room," I growl as I stalk toward them. At the same time, I hear boots on the stairs heading our way.

They both smirk as I approach them and when I grab them, they try to pull me into bed with them, but I'm stronger than them. Yanking them up, I drag them out of my room and toss them into the hallway, right into the waiting arms of Thor and Phoenix, with Levi right behind them.

"What's going on here?" Thor demands.

"These bitches broke into my room, which was locked by the way, and were fucking each other on my bed."

Thor's eyes harden and his hand tightens slightly on Cici's arm, not enough to hurt her, but enough to show her he's pissed.

"I think we need to have a little chat with you two. Get dressed. Now," Thor barks and both Cici and Gemini jump before hurriedly throwing on their clothes, though both of them keep sending me flirty looks, and I know I have to nip this shit in the bud.

"I'd like to recommend a second strike for Cici and Gemini's first strike," I tell Levi and both of the women baulk.

"What? What for?" Cici shrieks before turning on her heel toward me. "You know you want me, Patch. I don't even mind if Gemini joins us as a trio. I'm way prettier and sexier than that fat wench that keeps clinging to you."

In an instant, I have her by the throat and against the wall. I don't squeeze, even though I'd like to, to show that I mean fucking business. Her eyes widen in surprise and my scowl deepens. I hope like fuck these two haven't screwed things up between Mary and I, but I know I'm going to have to reassure her that I want only her. No matter what her size is.

"Get this through your fucking thick skull. I will *never* be with you. I will *never* fuck you again. I will *never* let you suck my cock again. I will never, *ever*, claim you as my Old Lady. Also, know this. I will *never* tolerate you speaking to my Old Lady like that again."

Cici smirks. "She can't be your Old Lady because the whore is still married to someone else."

We all freeze at that and I narrow my eyes at her. A sliver of fear works its way into her eyes but then she lifts her chin, pressing into my hand that's still around her throat. I release her immediately.

She's about to say something else when Thor grabs her arm, keeping her from throwing herself on me. "You're coming with us and we're going to have a nice, long chat. Patch, Mary, meet us downstairs. Phoenix, find someone to watch Gemini, not fuck, while we talk to Cici."

Thor turns and drags Cici down the hall as she shrieks for me, but I ignore her. Turning toward Mary, I curse when I see that her eyes are blank. Kneeling in front of her, I cup her cheek.

She looks down at me, a tired look in her eyes. "How many more are like her here? Will I always have to hear the bunnies tell me about how much better they can please you and how fat and unwanted I am?"

Hanging my head, I could beat my own ass for being weak and succumbing to needing that itch scratched. Looking her in the eyes, I stroke her cheek.

"I hooked up with Cici two years ago. She wasn't a bunny at the time and I seriously think she followed me here. She became a bunny a few months ago. As for others, yes, I have been with almost all of them in some way," I pause when a pained look crosses her face. "However, I don't think they'll treat you like Cici and Gemini have. CJ, Ashley, and Ginger were the three that I went to when the urge got too strong, and even then, it was only a handful of times."

Some of the tension in her bleeds away at that. She's actually gotten close to who a few of us started calling 'the good bunnies', which are Roxy, CJ, Ginger, Ashley, Amy, and Sara. However, Roxy has never serviced the guys and CJ stopped after realizing her brother was in the club, even though he was, and still is, a Prospect.

"Okay," she replies quietly.

"Come on, let's head back to the lift."

Once we're downstairs, I spot Ethan leaving the bar as Drae takes his place and flag him down. "Here," I say as I pass him my keys to my room. "Get rid of the bed in my room. Pillows, sheets, comforter, all of them. Burn them for all I care. Get me new everything, too." I will not have anything those sluts touched in my room when I bring Mary back to it.

Mary stares at me in shock, but then her face softens and she gives me a little smile.

"Have Drae go with you. We can get our own drinks while you guys are gone," Phoenix says as he comes up to us.

"You guys want something before we head out?" Drae asks and I nod.

"Give me one." I turn to Mary. "Do you want anything, Siren?"

"Can I have a beer, too? I kind of need one right now. And before you ask, Patch, no I haven't had any pain killers today and, no I am not in need of any either."

Smiling, I shake my head. Read my thoughts, like usual. I take the beers from Drae and hand her hers before turning to Phoenix.

"Are we in Thor's office?"

Phoenix nods, a tight look on his face. "Yup. Let's go deal with those bitches. Thor and Levi are already in with her. Bear and Beast are making sure Gemini stays put."

He tilts his head and I follow his line of sight. A dark grin spreads across my face as I realize they've handcuffed her to a chair and she is most definitely not happy that they aren't doing anything kinky.

"Come on," he says before taking a pull of his beer and turning toward Thor's office. Mary and I follow him, shutting the door behind us.

Chapter 59
Mary

I SIP MY BEER and keep my face as blank as possible—I will not show them how much rage is built up in me at what they've said and done. I've heard what's happened before to Levi and Mae with the bunnies and I won't let them walk all over me. Though, I wish I wasn't a fucking crippled so I could handle this myself.

Patch pulls up a chair next to me and slides his hand into mine, squeezing it. Looking down, I notice that I have almost a white-knuckle grip on the beer bottle, and I loosen my grip.

Thor digs out his phone and scowls at whatever he sees before he texts someone back.

A few minutes later, a knock on the door has me turning and I'm relieved when Smoke comes in with his laptop. However, when Gemini comes in behind him, I'm confused. Beast shuts the door once she's through, though not before giving the two women a disgusted look. I'm surprised Thor wants to talk to them together because he'd originally wanted to do it separately, but maybe Smoke found something that changed his mind. Or maybe it was whatever he was texted.

Once they take their seats my gaze goes to Thor, who I find is watching me. My jaw tightens as the memory of those two fucking on Patch's bed flashes in my mind, and I must let something show because he ever so slightly dips his head in my direction.

Turning toward Cici and Gemini, Thor's face hardens and his eyes turn almost ice-hard.

"What the fuck were you two doing in Patch's room?"

Cici gives him a sugary-sweet smile before batting her eyes at Patch. "We just wanted to help him loosen up after working so much today."

Somehow, Thor's face and eyes harden even more.

"Is that right?" He turns to Gemini. "And you?"

Gemini at least has the decency to look a little guilty, but she's also busy sending flirty glances at Patch. My lip starts to curl and I bite my tongue to keep the slew of words I want to say from escaping.

"He always works so hard and we wanted to take care of him like we do the other guys."

"Even though he's taken?" Phoenix growls and both girls wave him off.

"He doesn't have an Old Lady, and besides, the wench is married to someone else. She shouldn't be stepping out on her husband with Patch. Patch deserves a woman who won't cheat on him."

On hell no, she did not!

Patch grips my shoulder and pushes me back in my chair. When I turn my furious gaze on him, he slightly shakes his head before turning toward them.

"So, you think you know everything about Mary's life, do you?"

Cici gives him a smug look. "You deserve better than a cheater, Patch. Gem and I can take care of your needs much better than she can."

Leaning closer to me, Patch winds his arm around mine and grasps my hand again. "Well, since you think you know everything about what's going on between Mary and I, please tell us what you know."

Fuck, I have to bite my cheek to keep my smirk off my face. Out of the corner of my eye, I barely see Thor's lips kick up at the corner of his mouth at Patch's taunt. Time to see what they think they know.

Cici sits up straighter, practically pushing her chest out as she demurely crosses her legs and clasps her hands on her knee. Well, it would be demure if she were wearing more than a couple of scraps of cloth and that she hadn't flashed the room, showing everyone her red thong in the process.

"Well, for starters, that she left her husband, a *loving* husband, and took their kids with her. That she has no money to her name and is mooching off of the club." She looks down her nose at me and curls her lip. "You've fed them a shitload of lies and are keeping a loving father from his children. He never hurt you or the kids. Disciplined, sure, but never hurt. You should be ashamed of yourself for what you've done. Fuck, if you were my partner, I'd force you to sign over your rights and hand over the kids. You'd never have contact with them ever again."

I stare at her, dumbfounded. How the fuck is she this stupid? It's almost like déjà vu with Claudia for some of this shit.

Thor's fist bangs down on his desk and my eyes widen when I swear I hear a crack in the thick wood.

"You are talking about things you know nothing about," he growls in a voice that sends a shiver down my spine. It's even deeper and darker than Phoenix's a moment ago. "Mary is here because she is trying to divorce a man who kidnapped her nine years ago and in those nine years, abused her almost daily. Patch and Mary were together before she was kidnapped. When she was kidnapped, she was pregnant with his son."

He waits a bit, but still Cici looks convinced that she knows my life better than I do.

"Patch?" Thor asks and I look at him before turning to Patch.

"Yup, pull them out."

I blink at them, confused as to what's going on and what they're talking about.

Thor digs into his pocket and pulls out some keys before bending down and unlocking the bottom drawer in his desk.

I feel my stomach flip when I catch a glimpse of the top of one of the stacks. I know exactly what they are.

Thor keeps pulling out stack after stack of papers. The smallest being only an inch or so thick, but the largest stack, which is from when we lived in Credence just before moving here to Forest Creek, is probably about four inches high. At least. Each stack is wrapped with thick rubber bands. When he's done, there are six stacks of papers on his desk and my eyes burn with tears at seeing it all combined in front of me.

Cici frowns at the paperwork, confused as to what Thor's trying to tell her. Thor looks over at me and cocks an eyebrow.

Letting go of Patch's hand, I stand and hobble closer to the desk so I can lean against it for extra support. Setting my beer down, I pick up the smallest packet and stare at her while I thumb the edges of it.

"So, you think you know everything about me, huh? That you know my own life better than me? You think I was in a loving relationship? How's this for a *loving* relationship?" I sneer at her and toss her the stack, smirking when it hits her smack in the face because she wasn't paying attention. "Granted, one of those visits was for delivering my son, who like Thor said, Patch is the father of. However, the rest of those visits in that stack were because my fucking 'loving'," I say with air quotes, "husband put me in the hospital due to his beatings. Those weren't fucking 'disciplines' as you called them. And those summaries? They are only the times that I was beaten so severe that I *had* to go to a hospital. There are thousands of other times where I took care of my injuries myself."

She gives me a look of disbelief which turns into a frown when she looks down and starts reading the summary on top of the stack.

"That stack was when we lived in Addams, the first place we lived after I was kidnapped." Picking up the next stack. I toss it at her. "Elmdale." I toss another packet. "Rock Ridge. Glenbrook. Credence, and finally Forest Creek."

She stumbles to catch them all, but when she finally has them all stacked on her lap, a look of horror crosses her face as she stares at them and realizes that what I said was true. That they are printouts from every single hospital visit or stay. A look of horror is mirrored on Gemini's face, who I notice has scooted closer and is looking over Cici's shoulder and reading the top page.

Bile riles in my throat, but I push it down. "That top visit summary is from when he put me in the hospital on Thanksgiving. The night Patch and the club rescued me and my children from Stephan's abuse. Whatever information you've been fed is complete and utter lies. I have this proof and more of what Stephan's done and is doing." I pause and tilt my head, studying her. "So, which one are you fucking? Stephan? Diego? Kristoff? Or maybe it's one of their underlings?"

She blanches and shakes her head. "God, no! My brother, well, foster brother told me what you'd done. But I don't understand. Why would he lie to me? We've always looked out for each other." As she thumbs through the papers, her increased confusion shows on her face.

I was not expecting that. Turning, I cock an eyebrow at Thor, letting him take the lead on this one. Shuffling back to my chair, I retake my seat and take a drink of my beer as Thor leans forward.

"Who is your foster brother?"

"Leon. Leon Davenport."

Tension immediately fills the air and all four men go stock still whereas I stare at her in shock. There has to be some sort of mistake.

"When did Leon tell you all this about Mary and Stephan?" Smoke asks, but his voice sounds different. Darker. Harder. And with an edge to it.

Cici looks between all four of them, but thankfully, she still answers them. "Just last weekend at our family dinner. We get together every other Saturday. He was upset, extremely upset, because his friend really misses his wife and kids, and he didn't know how or why she could do such a thing to such a great guy. And a cop to boot." She pauses as her gaze returns to Smoke. "Why? Do you know Leon?"

Smoke and Thor share a glance and it seems like some sort of silent communication takes place.

"I think we do. Do you have a picture you can show us of him so we can be sure?"

Gone is the hesitation and confusion from before. She smiles widely as she digs her phone out from between her boobs. Holy hell, that's where she was keeping it? A shudder runs through me, but apparently her preferred storage area for her phone doesn't phase the guys in the least.

She hands the phone to Smoke, who passes it around the room. When it gets to me, I touch as little of it as possible as both Patch and I look at the picture. Boob sweat is a real thing, and even skinny minis like her, though I'm not sure if her boobs are natural as they seem a little too perky, have boob sweat.

I go to hand the picture back to Thor, but then pause.

I know this guy.

Bringing the phone closer, I study him, trying to make sure it really is him. After a few moments, I give the phone back to Thor, more confused than ever as various rants of Kristoff's filter through my mind.

Phoenix's voice has me blinking out of my thoughts. "What all did you tell Leon about Mary?"

"That she and her kids were staying here and she was hooking up with the guy I've been in a relationship with. He was pissed that she's continuing her cheating ways and hurting me in the process."

The scathing look she gives me cuts deep, even though nothing she's saying is true, and I do my best not to let her see exactly how hurt I am that she's still in denial that Patch wants nothing to do with her.

"How did you two break into Patch's room?"

Both of the women hesitate as they look at each other, but neither respond to Thor's question.

Silently, Smoke opens his laptop and hits play.

On the screen, there are two videos playing side by side—one from what looks like further down the hall, and the other is a little to the left of them, but we can clearly see their faces.

After verifying that no one was coming down the hallway, Gemini crouches in front of Patch's door and removes something from her pocket before she starts picking the lock. After a minute or so, Cici's voice comes over the line. He must have one of the videos muted because there's no feedback or echo.

"Hurry up, Gem. We're gonna get caught."

"Calm your tits. This isn't as easy as it looks. I swear they must have picked some of the most complicated locks on purpose."

A few moments later, Gemini gives a little squeal of delight as the door unlocks and she opens it. They slip inside and mostly close it, which is probably why the cameras were able to still pick up their voices.

"Are you sure about this, Cici? He seems like he only has eyes for Mary."

"Oh, please. He's just with her out of obligation, not because he really wants her. He can't seriously want all of her disgusting curves and fat rolls over what I've got to offer him. Seeing us together will remind him of what he can have, and as a bonus, we'll get to keep each other as well."

The sounds of them kissing and the shuffling of clothes fill the air. Smoke reaches around, fast forwards a little, and then stops as soon as he sees us rounding the corner.

I look away when the Patch on the screen opens his door. I don't want to see them fucking again. It's bad enough I have to hear it again.

When Thor and Phoenix come up on the screen, Smoke stops the video and turns it back around toward him. I thought that was the end of it, but when Smoke twists the computer toward Cici and Gemini again, I'm confused.

"While I was looking at the security footage, I found something else," he says before hitting play.

The video starts out shortly after Sam, Brady, and the other cops leave after the explosion yesterday. I see Patch picking me up and after talking with the kids, he leaves carrying me. It's then that I realize that must have been when I needed to use the restroom and he'd asked Ash to watch my bag, which was sitting on the floor by the edge of the couch. A moment later, Ash scoots over and sits where I had been. A minute or so later, my jaw clenches when I see Cici approach and bends down to check on the strap of her stilettos. I see red when the video shows her slipping something into my backpack before straightening and sauntering off.

Eileen's letter.

Smoke stops the video and shuts his computer, everyone turning their attention to Cici who has gone ghostly pale.

"Before we get to whatever the fuck that was, I want to know what the fuck you two were doing in Patch's room," Thor seethes.

Chapter 60

Mary

Neither Cici nor Gemini answers Thor right away as they share a nervous look. Thor's jaw works back and forth as he watches the women.

"Patch, how many times have you told Cici that you weren't interested in being with her?" Levi asks.

"That was probably the sixth or seventh time. Before Mary came here, I'd told her four or five times. This was the second time since Mary has been here."

"And Gemini?"

"Four times. Each time, she seemed to think she had a right to my dick since I've never taken her."

Levi gets up and walks in front of the women, leaning against Thor's desk. "Do neither of you remember the lengthy conversations we had when you came here to be a bunny as well as the paperwork I gave you to sign? We covered that shit for a reason and why I had you initial next to each paragraph stating you agreed to what was said."

She pauses and points a knife at them. Wait, where did she get a knife from? And when did she pull it out?

"Regardless of what you think, you are not the ones who get to decide who a member takes as an Old Lady. If they tell you they don't want sex, to get lost, to never touch them, or whatever, you do as they say. How would you like it if the roles were reversed, and you repeatedly told a man to not touch you or that you didn't want to have sex and yet he still keeps pushing?"

At that, both women look a little sheepish and guilty.

"Exactly. This is why we had those talks. You *must* respect the guys' requests if they rebuke your advances. And if one of them brings a woman or a partner here that they are serious about, you do not interfere in their relationship. How would you feel if some scantily clad woman was constantly worming her way into a relationship of yours?"

Gemini looks down and nods, however Cici's face turns angry.

"That's exactly what's happening here!" Cici rants as she angrily points at me. "I've been pursuing Patch for a long time and yet she's worming her way into *our* relationship. He's only with her out of obligation, not love, since he thinks one of her brats is his."

Exhaling heavily, I shake my head. "You are wrong on so many levels," I mutter under my breath to which she glares at me.

Patch puts his other hand on my arm, stopping me from continuing and gives Cici a scathing look.

"Let's get something perfectly straight here once and for all. *There is no relationship with you, Cici.* Period. I have never been in a relationship with you, regardless of what you think. What we had was a one-night stand, which I made abundantly clear at the time and that it was all it would ever be. I have not pursued you since and I have been repeatedly telling you that I have no intention of pursuing a romantic interest with you."

She's sputters and is about to say something when Patch raises his hand, silencing her.

"Please, just fucking stop. Why can't you accept that I don't want you that way? I hate to be fucking blunt, *again*, but nothing seems to get through to you. I love Mary and always have loved her. Despite your ill-conceived notions on beauty, I've always had a thing for Mary's curves. I prefer curvy women versus someone who barely eats anything because that's what society tells her is beautiful. Well, society is wrong in my opinion. Mary will be my Old Lady and wife someday. You need to learn to accept that. If you can't accept that, then maybe you should leave the club."

Silence meets Patch's words as we all watch Cici. Her eyes well with tears, but no one says anything.

"But I love you. I've loved you since I first saw you in high school. Why isn't that enough?" she whispers and Patch sighs, shaking his head.

"I don't and never have loved you. It's always been Mary for me. I don't remember you from high school, but if you hadn't noticed, I was with Mary since we were sixteen. Before that, we were practically inseparable. When we got together at the bar, all it was was a one-night stand. I needed a release. I just needed to scratch an itch. That's all. I wasn't looking for a relationship with you. If I had wanted a relationship with you, which I don't just to clarify again, it would have happened not too long after that night.

"If you followed me here and thought I'd take you as my Old Lady, you're sadly mistaken because you were never who I wanted to spend the rest of my life with. If that was what you were hoping for, you need to pack your shit and leave. On top of all of that, a brother doesn't want an Old Lady who's been fucked by all his brothers."

She recoils as if she's been slapped and I honestly feel a little sorry for her, but if Patch has told her this six or seven times already, she should have gotten the hint by now that he wants nothing to do with her.

Her gaze lowers and she nods her head glumly.

Thor growls slightly and Cici's head pops back up, paling once again at the icy glare Thor is giving her. "Now onto the other matter—what the fuck did you put in Mary's bag?"

Cici turns her attention back to me, and once again, looks down her nose at me. "Leon had asked me to pass on a note from Mary's mom. He said her mom had been trying to reach her for some time, but Mary kept refusing to answer the calls. She's really concerned about her and the kids. She wanted to offer to help them." Cici shakes her head and her lip curls in disgust. "I don't know how you can be so cruel to your own mother. All she wants to do is help."

Patch's arms wrap around me, and he gently pulls me back down into my chair, which I hadn't realized I'd stood up from.

Cici blanches at the fury I know is etched on my face and when she looks around the room, she turns white as a ghost as she licks her lips nervously.

"Do you have any idea what the fuck that bitch has put me through? Having her for a mother has been a fucking nightmare, and on top of that, she was the fucking instigator in everything I've endured these last nine years," I seethe.

She looks at me in confusion. "What are you talking about? She's a very nice old lady and she was genuinely concerned and hurt that you wouldn't answer her calls."

I bark out a humorless laugh. "The only person that bitch cares about is herself. Like I said, she has made my life a living nightmare since I was three or four years old. Do you know what would have happened if I had gone to her?" I pause and tilt my head, watching her, as her brow dips in confusion. "I would have been sold off to the highest bidder, most likely to be someone's sex slave. Same for my children. You have no idea who the fuck you're dealing with. Both Leon and my so-called mother have more blood on their hands than you can imagine. I'm not going to tell you everything they've done, but if you knew what was good for you, you wouldn't go near either one of them again, otherwise you very well could end up on that lifestyle yourself."

Her brows crease even further when she realizes I mean every word I'm saying. After a moment, she looks down at the sack of papers that are still on her lap. When she looks back up, she looks damn near broken as her eyes glisten slightly. I almost feel sorry for her, but my anger wipes that thought away as soon as it's formed.

"He lied to me again, didn't he? Why would he do that? We've been the only real family each other's had since we were sixteen. He watched out for me, kept me clothed, fed, and warm. Why would he lie to me?"

Some of my anger dissipates when I realize she really doesn't have any idea about what's going on or the danger she could have brought down on me. My gut tightens as I realize what's been happening. So many more conversations I've overheard make so much more sense now.

"He was preparing you."

Her confused gaze snaps up to me again from the stack of papers in her lap.

"He was using you, Cici. Using you to try and lure people into his circle so he can take them and sell them in his trafficking ring. He might even have plans to do that to you after you are no longer useful to him."

Her throat works as she shakes her head. "I don't believe you. Leon would never betray me like that."

I shrug. "Believe what you want to believe, but Leon is nothing like the man you think he is. I've seen the evil he's wrought on people and you really, really don't want to be the one on the receiving end."

The steel in my voice at that last part has her looking back sharply at me, and her hands start to shake slightly before she clasps her hands tightly in her lap.

Levi moves to stand beside Thor, who pulls her down so that she's sitting on his leg. "Cici, this is your second strike and Gemini, your first. I'm not going to reprimand you, Cici, for delivering the letter since it's clear you were taken advantage of. I am going to make this clear though, if Leon, Eileen, or anyone else asks you to do something, you come to us and let us know about it. Mary's right. These are not people you want to be mixed up with. Do you understand?"

Yes," they both reply.

"However, if either of you interfere with Patch and Mary's relationship, or with any club member's relationship again, you will get another strike Gemini, and Cici?" Levi pauses until Cici looks up at her. "You will be kicked out of the club and will be barred from entering any of our businesses. You also won't be allowed to rent an apartment or house from us. Do you understand?"

"Yes," they both reply again, though Cici's is barely audible.

"Thor?"

"Patch, Mary, is there anything else you'd like to add?"

"I've said everything I need to say and I hope like fuck I never have to repeat it again," Patch growls.

Thor turns to me and I hesitate as I figure out how to word this. "You both are very beautiful women in your own way. However, there isn't a cookie-cutter pattern that states beauty has to look only one way. You will find your other half one day, or if you were serious about being together, finding your third. However, I'm going to take a stab that your third is not here, otherwise he or she would have approached you already. Also, please take what I've said about Leon to heart. I know it's hard because you've looked up to him your whole life, but I don't want to see you being thrust into that sort of life or ending up in a ditch."

I pause and look over my shoulder at the bookshelf where Levi keeps spare journals and then turn toward Levi, raising my eyebrow in question.

She tilts her head slightly in a nod before turning to Thor and having another sort of silent communication. Levi turns to the girls, her face softer, but still stern. "So, ladies, do you still want to stay in the club as bunnies?"

They look at each other and nod.

"Okay, please go out to the main room and wait for me there. I'll be out in a few minutes. If the guys approach you for sex, tell them they'll have to wait until later," she tells them.

They murmur their thanks and quietly get up. Cici pauses at the door and glances back at the stack of hospital summaries on the couch, a confused look on her face, before she shakes her head slightly and closes the door behind them.

As soon as they do, Patch gets up and locks the door before sitting back down. The air is instantly heavier and I turn toward Thor, only to find him watching me already.

"What we say next does not get repeated outside of these walls. Is that understood, Mary?"

Instantly, I nod. "Of course. You guys know that man, right? But how can that be? Kristoff has been raving mad for the last few months that Leon's gone missing. He thinks you guys killed him."

"Because we did," Thor growls. "Or at least we thought his name was Leon. Fuck, if he wasn't Leon, then who the fuck was he?"

Smoke frowns. "Ryder took their fingerprints while they were on ice. The only hit they got for him was Leon Davenport. However, I'm wondering if that was their plan all along? To create an alias for him and have him tell us he was Leon so that afterward, the real Leon would be a ghost and could do whatever the fuck he wanted?"

"But if Leon really was Kristoff's son, then how did he get into foster care since Cici said he was her foster brother?"

Smoke's frown deepens at my question. "I'll need to do some digging. I knew Cici grew up in the system, but I didn't look into the families she was placed with. I'll let you know when I find something," he tells Thor.

"Okay, we'll call Church as soon as you know more. Wildcat, you go do your thing, but make sure those bitches understand this shit needs to stop. It wouldn't be a bad idea to reinforce everything with the other bunnies as well. Might be a good time to tell Roxy and CJ that their roles on the books are changing as well per our last vote."

At my confused look, Levi turns toward me. "We have a couple of books we keep here, and no, I don't mean that in an illegal way. When I became Thor and

Dragon's Old Lady, the bunnies' roles switched to reporting to me instead of Thor. At that point, I took over the records for all the bunnies we have in the club, not just our chapter, but all chapters. Jax and I work closely when a new bunny puts in their application to verify if they are related to anyone in the club or in the history of the club.

"The other books are the business ones. On record, the bunnies are hired as housekeepers because that's what we pay them to do. Cook, clean, do laundry, things like that. They have the option of living here or they can live in one of our apartments. What Thor meant a moment ago, is that Roxy and CJ are going to be promoted into more of a management role. I won't be able to do as many of the extra duties once the kids are born and they are going to help me out with those duties.

"Now, the sexual part of being a bunny is their choice and isn't paid. It's not a prostitute situation or holding them here under duress or anything. Some, like Roxy, just came here for protection, so she has never had sex with the guys. In exchange for our protection, she does other duties around the clubhouse as well. CJ, or Trixie as she used to go by, did have sex with the guys before she learned her brother, Drae, was here. I'm going to take a stab that you've heard her story?" Levi asks and at my nod, she continues.

"A lot of these women like the biker lifestyle and like having multiple sexual partners. A few girls have been given shit before they came here because they have high sex drives, which the guys absolutely love. When someone comes here wanting to be a bunny, I have several meetings with them to make sure they know the rules—both their housekeeping duties and the sexual ones, if they decide to do that. For those that have sex, regular testing is required and they are not to have sexual relations with people outside of the club. If they were to do that, they could unknowingly contract something and put someone's life or lives at risk here by passing it along. If a club member says 'no', they are to move on and find someone else to have sex with. They are never to go after someone a member brings in as their partner—like what Cici was trying to do with you, Luscious and Gigi tried to do with Mae and what Monica and Tiffany tried to do with me. All of them were let go as bunnies and told to keep away from the club." She pauses again and looks at Thor, who grunts.

He gives me a hard look and I get that this is another thing that needs to be kept mum.

"In reality, those four bunnies ended up handing over Mae and Wildcat to the guys that were trying to hurt them. They wanted Mae and Wildcat out of the picture so they could stake their claim on Timber, Dragon, and me. Because of what they'd done, they were taken care of, but only the club, Mae, and now you know the truth behind what really happened to them. However, if anyone asks, you tell the story Wildcat just said. They were kicked out for their actions, and we haven't seen them since."

"A lot more of your ladies' stories make sense now, and of course, I'll use the cover if anyone ever brings them up."

Patch squeezes my hand and raises it to his lips, kissing my fingers. "Knew you were perfect for me and the club."

The knot that had been in my chest loosens some at his words, and I once again count my lucky stars for bringing me back into Patch's life and that we're together again. Even if I did have to endure all of Stephan's abuse to get here.

A phone vibrates and Patch pulls his phone out of his pocket. He grunts as he reads a text message. "Mateo is up and asking to see Mary. Then he'd like to talk to us."

Thor pats Levi's thigh. "You should talk to the bunnies and Smoke can get you video of anything you miss. We need to stop this shit with them pronto. I really don't want another brother having to go through this shit and have them fucking with their Old Ladies." He pauses and turns to me. "Maybe after you talk to Mateo, you should join Wildcat along with Mae. You three need to present a united front. If you didn't know, the bunnies are the lowest on the totem pole in an MC, and they need to be showing you the respect you deserve as an Old Lady, even though your title isn't fully finalized. Once we take care of Stephan, then Patch is already cleared to give you your property cut."

My skin bristles on instinct at the word property, even though my mind knows I'm not really 'property'. It's just a sign in the MC world for who my Old Man is. Patch.

At that reminder, my body relaxes and I smile up at Patch. Turning back to Levi, I point to the bookcase behind me.

"I really think we should encourage the girls to use these books. I'm guessing some of them might have come from shitty backgrounds or have had shitty experiences. That could be part of why there are problems. Part of—not completely, because I realize some women can be royal bitches and only thinking of themselves when they decide a biker is 'theirs'," I say with air quotes. "However, we might be able to nip some of that in the bud if we show them we're willing to help them deal with their demons. We don't have to be the enemy or competition."

Levi smiles widely at me. "Knew you were a good egg. Meet me out in the main room after you're done talking to your uncle. I'll message Mae to come meet me out there."

Chapter 61

Patch

WALKING BEHIND MARY, I pause at the bar to get a fresh beer since we'll be going into Church right after talking to Mateo. At the door, Mary's practically vibrating in her seat to see Mateo, and I quickly put in my access codes, making sure no one can see the numerical one.

"Oh," Mary cries as she wheels over to his side and slipping a hand into his. "**Tío** (Uncle) Mateo." She covers one hand over her mouth as she tries desperately to silence her sobs.

Drae gives me a slight nod and quietly slips out, shutting the door behind him.

"Shhh, now Mary. I'm alright now thanks to your man and the club." As gently as he can, he pulls her into his side as much as he's able to since he's still laying on the bed and hugs her as she continues to cry.

After a few minutes, she pulls back, drying her eyes. "Did that **bastardo** (bastard) do this to you?"

Mateo smirks. "Your Spanish is coming along well, but I hope you're learning more than just curse words."

Mary levels him with a glare that could shrivel balls and he immediately sobers.

"**Sí** (Yes), he did, and I will take great pleasure in getting my pound of flesh back. However, I do not know if I can give you more information than that, as I know from working with other MCs that they protect their women at all costs."

Her shoulders slump as she sighs. "Plausible deniability. Fuck, I think the ladies might be right in their idea to get a commiserating tattoo of that fucking line along with 'club business'." She sighs again but nods. "However, I do understand." She looks up at me and I shrug.

"It all depends on what Mateo has to tell us. You know I'll give you the cliff notes version if I'm able to."

Mary gives me a small smile before bolting upright in her chair. "**Mierda** (Shit)! Did anyone tell **Abuelo** (Grandpa) that you're here and safe?"

Mateo turns to me, though I don't miss the corner of his lips kicking up in amusement at Mary swearing again in Spanish, and I wince. "I don't know if Thor did or not. I didn't and I apologize for that. However, I'm sure we will soon because I'm going to bet that we'll be calling Antonio after hearing what Mateo has to say."

She nods as she chews on her lip. "Okay, then I won't say anything to him. However, I don't know if I'll be able to lie if he texts me."

"If he texts you, just tell him he needs to talk to me." Leaning down, I give her a kiss and feel even more tension leaving her now that she knows Mateo is safe.

They spend a few more minutes talking before Mary gives him as much of a hug as she's able to.

"I'll leave you gents to do your thing in Church and go help Levi and Mae. If you're still up for it after Church, come find me. I'd love to fully introduce you to your grandniece and grandnephews."

He squeezes her hand, smiling widely. "I'd very much like that."

Giving Mary a kiss, I watch her as she wheels out to the main room and joins Mae right as Levi calls for the bunnies to quiet down. Shutting the door, I turn back to Mateo.

"Let me just check your vitals, your worst wounds, and remove your IV and catheter, then we'll get you into Church. I've got a t-shirt and sweatpants here that I think will be about your size. How are you on a pain scale? Don't bullshit me."

Mateo huffs. "I'm about an eight, but I don't want to take anything until after I talk to you and the other club members. I don't want to pass out before telling you what I know. Shit, and if possible, not until I see the kids. I've been looking forward to meeting them in person for a long time now."

After taking his vitals and recording them, I look over his wounds, happy that none of them are looking infected or inflamed. There were a few that I was worried about since they were caked with dirt, grime, and who knows what else. Then I get to work removing his IV and catheter.

He shudders when the catheter is finally out. "Fuck, I hope I never have to have one of those again."

"With your line of work, I hope so, too." Tossing my gloves, I wash up and pull out some spare clothes out of the closet. "Let's get you up and see if these fit."

Carefully, I help him sit up, and I'm surprised when he doesn't even grunt in pain, though I do notice that he's clenching his jaw fucking hard enough to rival what I've seen Thor do. But then again, I know these wounds aren't his first with him being the heir to a mafia family.

Nor will they be his last.

Once he's dressed, I press my hand against the scanner and input my code. The door to Church opens, and I lead Mateo to Levi's nearby vacant seat since I don't want him to overexert himself. Then I take my seat.

Thor bangs his hammer on the table and everyone quiets down. He turns toward Mateo, and they seem to mentally size each other up.

"Mateo, welcome to the Steel Archangel's clubhouse. However, I was hoping it would have been on better terms."

Mateo huffs slightly as he shakes his head, and his eyes tighten as he tries to hide his wince. "**Gracias** (Thank you), and that would have been much preferred over how I arrived here." He stops and frowns. "I am assuming you want me to get straight to the point, **sí** (yes)?"

At Thor's chin lift, Mateo continues.

"I was drugged in my own home. Somehow, Diego managed to break into my estate, or paid off or threatened one of my men, and drugged me. It was either in the wine or the food. I am not sure which one it was. I remember getting drowsy after eating and then I woke up in a rustic out building."

"How many men do you keep at your estate at all times? I'm assuming you aren't saying that you were at your family's estate."

Mateo shakes his head again at Thor's question. "No, it was not **la casa de mis padres** (my parent's house). I have at least sixteen men around the perimeter, gate, and outside every entrance. Inside, there are another fifteen. More when Lorenzo and his men are there." He shakes his head, his eyes blazing angrily. "If you have not already, if I could have someone reach out to **mi padre** (my father) and Lorenzo to start combing for how many traitors are in our midst, I would be forever grateful. If they haven't already started, that is."

Smoke gives him a chin lift. "As soon as we had your identity verified, both from your prints as well as from Mary in regards to your tattoos, eye color and birthmark, I called him to let him know. Though, I'll have you know that it was not fucking easy to convince him to stay the fuck where he is. At least, not until we're ready for him to come here."

Mateo smirks. "Let me guess, have him show up with a few of his guards and demanding to either hand 'Diego' over to him for justice or demanding to be taken to him? I'm sure Diego has men watching your clubhouse to see how you react to finding 'Diego' dropped on your doorstep. They'll then report back to Diego that you fell for their hat trick."

"Fuck, he's good," Judge mutters and Bear bumps his shoulder, grinning. "Well, he should be, since he's gonna be the next Don."

A few guys chuckle and even Mateo has a hint of a smile as he shakes his head.

"Yeah, that's what we were thinking of pulling. However, we were leaning more toward the demanding to be taken to him one. Now, what else can you tell us about what happened when they had you?"

Instantly, all smiles disappear as Thor turns the conversation.

"Well, like I said, it was a rustic out building. Once I came to and got my bearings, I realized they'd tied me to a chair and had stripped me down to my underwear. It was still daylight, but I wasn't sure if it was the same day or not. I could hear other people talking through the gaps in the boards, however, it was mostly women's voices. For a while anyway. Going off of how the sun moved through the gaps, I'd say I was in there for a few hours before the women were suddenly quiet and Diego and Phillip Cole came into the room with a few men that Diego had turned from our family over to him. Diego is hell bent on taking over from **Padre** (Father) in my stead. Once he's Don, his plan is to kill **Padre** (Father) and slowly steal power from the other Spanish families. Of course, he plans to use the network of **nuestra familia** (our family) to further his fucking trafficking ring, whore houses, and the Oasis homesteads," he says, curling his lip as bites out the words.

Bones frowns as he leans forward. "Is he really that fucking dense that he doesn't think we're gonna figure out that you're Mateo rather than Diego? Or your father?"

Mateo hesitates. "Back when we were kids, we pulled the stereotypical twin prank of switching places. We both know each other's mannerisms and quirks. The only downside was our eyes, so we could only do it in places where we could wear glasses. I'm sure you two pulled stunts like that as well, **sí** (yes)?" he asks as he looks from Dragon to Thor, both of whom share a knowing smirk and Mateo's lips kick up a little in the corner of his mouth.

"Well, when he came into the room I was being held in, he looked just like I would in a suit. He styled his hair like mine and was wearing colored contacts. He either had his tattoos removed or he used makeup to cover them up. Now, as for how much more he's changed of his body, I don't know the answer to that because Phillip was the one that did all of this to me, while Diego just leaned back and watched," he says as he gestures to his body. "However, Diego was the one who directed where Phillip would cut into me."

Pausing, he rubs his throat and I curse myself for not thinking about that as I get up and walk over to the mini-fridge we keep in here. "Fuck, man, sorry. I should have given this to you right away." I hand it to him and he tips his head gratefully at me.

"**Gracias** (Thank you), and no worries."

He takes a few sips, and then caps the bottle.

Gunner taps the table. "If Diego was so pissed at you, then why didn't he have a more active role in your torture?"

Mateo's brows dip heavily and he frowns. "Honestly, I'm not sure, as I fully expected him to have taken control as well. I do know I was supposed to have a meeting with **Padre** (Father) today and he might not have wanted to ruin his suit if he had planned on taking my stead. Especially if he only bought a few of the style that I prefer to wear."

Thor turns to Smoke. "Did Antonio say anything when you talked to him?"

Smoke gives a chin lift. "Yeah, after describing what all had happened to him, he asked when Mateo showed up and I told him. Then he muttered that he knew it wasn't Mateo in the meeting with the other Dons. At first, Diego-in-disguise acted mostly like how he expected Mateo to act, but then he suddenly started talking more and more like Diego would have. That's when he sent a message to Miguel, who is currently the head of security under Antonio's second, Tomás, to look at the security footage. He said that they found a few moles and were taking care of them, however he did not give me names."

Mateo grunts in frustration. "Diego has always criticized the other Dons, as well as **Padre** (Father) and myself, when it came to our business investments. We look at ways to better our cities as well as our family's stance and power. Not to mention keeping gangs out that hope to encroach on our territory or businesses. By improving our territory and showing that we protect it, **mi abuelo** (my grandpa) hoped that if anyone is going to join a gang or the mafia, they would join our ranks instead. And for the most part, it seems to be working.

"Diego wants to be a dictator, lording over everyone with an iron fist that he uses to threaten people into submission. He wants to bring back how things were done in our ancestors' days. The Dons of the older ages. I'm not saying we don't get our hands bloody with our way of doing things, because we most certainly do, but he wants to take it to the extreme. To reign with absolute terror and brutality. I will not allow him to bring those dreams to fruition."

Sensing we need to bring things back around to Stephan and Diego's plans; I rap my fingers on the table.

"Did they torture you in one setting or multiple settings?"

"Multiple. The first go around, I believe it lasted about a half hour or so before they left for the meeting. Diego ordered some guards to stay outside the door. However, they must have been either incredibly **estúpido** (stupid) or they were dropping false information on purpose.

"If we assume that the information is true, then Stephan is planning an attack that will happen before the weekend is up if Mary and the kids are not turned over to him. Diego is apparently getting tired of Stephan not delivering them and is giving him one last chance to redeem himself. If he doesn't, he's going to kill Stephan himself. I'm not sure what Stephan is planning, as they didn't allude to that. I just know it's coming.

"After a couple of hours or so of sitting there in that shack, Diego came back and tried to get out of me where **mi daga de oreja** was hidden. I am assuming you know about the **daga de oreja**? My family's eared daggers?"

"A little," Thor says, and Mateo takes another sip of water before continuing.

"Diego cannot succeed **Padre** without it. Each **daga de oreja** (eared dagger) is engraved with our names and the dates we are born. The original **daga de oreja** (eared dagger) that the first Don of our family owned is passed on to each successor to show that they are worthy of leading our family. However, in addition to that, the Dons also receive a replica **daga de oreja** (eared dagger). When someone in our family dies, that date is then engraved on their **daga de oreja**. Our family keeps a wall of remembrance of our ancestors, which is currently in **la casa de mis padres** (my parent's house), pictures of those of **nuestra familia** (our family) that have or are working in the mafia side of things. Not everyone wishes to have their **daga de oreja** hung under their picture when they pass, choosing instead to leave it to **su familia** (their family), but most do.

"The Dons are remembered differently. While, yes, our pictures are on display in the **muro ancestral de nuestra familia,** our family's wall of ancestors, they are also on a wall in the Don's office. It is under those pictures where our **daga de oreja** will hang once we have died. However, when we have legal business, the wall of our family's Dons is hidden behind a secret wall.

"Now, the reason why I told you all of that is because Diego must present **mi daga de oreja** (my eared dagger) if he wishes to continue the ruse and succeed **Padre** in my stead. My guess is he's scoured my house and couldn't find it, nor would he have. He also cannot take my place as himself, should I be killed, since **Padre** and I took back his, Carlos, Isaac, and Gianna's daggers by force. He is running out of options and the other Spanish Dons will not recognize Diego's claim as the Don of our family without a **daga de oreja**."

"No wonder he's been acting desperate," Dragon mutters under his breath and Mateo nods in agreement.

"**Sí** (Yes)." He pauses and turns to me. "If his plans fail, his last ditch effort is to eliminate Lorenzo, Marco, and Miguel as they would be in line after me. Reason being that he would only go after them is that, to date, no woman has been allowed to become the Don of our family. Not in a sexist way, at least as of late, but because none have had any interest nor have had what it takes to be the Don. Then, regardless that she is his half-sister's daughter, Diego's plan is to take Mary by force, marry her, and earn the title of Don that way."

"What the fuck," someone mutters, but I don't turn to see who spoke.

What the fuck, indeed.

And there is no fucking way that I'm letting Diego implement any of his plans.

"Then we need to up our fucking game plan to make sure none of that happens. We're on lockdown. Smoke, you said you had more stuff for us. You're up," Thor says, his voice hard and razor sharp.

Smoke grins darkly as he gives Thor a chin lift. "This is what I found out."

Chapter 62

Mary

THE GUYS ARE TENSE as fuck as they come out of Church, and I instantly know that I'm not learning anything else from Patch when I see his face. I turn toward Mae and Levi, and we all share a grim look.

Something is coming.

And it's coming for me.

Levi gets up and heads straight to Smoke. They talk quietly for a few moments before they both head to Thor's office. My guess is to let her watch the footage Thor told Smoke to record for her from their meeting.

Taking a deep breath, I try to steady my racing heart. Looking around the room, I feel both relieved and scared to shit when those that I make eye contact with all give me a subtle nod or chin lift. Fuck, I don't want any of them getting hurt protecting me and my kids, but if I leave, I'll be right back in Stephan and Diego's clutches and my fate will be even worse than it was before. Same for my children.

Patch and **Tío** (Uncle) Mateo walk toward me, and I force a smile on my face. "Are you hungry at all, **Tío** (Uncle) Mateo? I know it's late, but I can warm you up some leftover stew we made earlier. We also have biscuits, cornbread, and potatoes."

He gives me a tight but grateful smile. "**Gracias** (Thank you). Food definitely sounds good, Mary. Lead the way."

Backing away from the table, I lead them into the kitchen and when I get to the fridge, I carefully stand and open it, passing the dishes to Patch to put on the island. **Tío** (Uncle) Mateo dishes out what he wants, and while it's warming up, I put the rest of the food away.

We're silent as he eats, practically inhaling his food, and I wonder how long Diego had him? When he's done, I lead them to the playroom. Opening the door, I smile when I see the boys and Lindsey playing with the bricks, building a giant castle.

"Did Cassie pass out?" I ask Elvira, who nods and points to the blanket fort the kids made in a corner.

"About an hour ago. Since you said you guys were staying here tonight, I figured I'd keep the kids in here and use the hide-a-bed. Levi said one of the Prospects would guard the door, but we'll also secure it when we go to sleep."

I nod. Besides the panic room, this is the best place for the kids to stay while they are at the clubhouse. The windows are bulletproof, the door is made out of reinforced steel, and of course, the room is connected to the panic room down below.

Turning, I point behind me. "Elvira, this is my uncle Mateo."

Mateo steps forward and they both shake hands. "Nice to meet you, Miss Elvira."

She waves him off. "It's either just Elvira, Granny Elvira, or Granny. None of this 'Miss' stuff," she says with a smile as she beams down at the kids.

My heart still hurts for her. Losing not only her husband, but also her daughter a few months ago. She only has Lindsey and Drae left now, but I've seen her opening up the more she's around my kids. And they all absolutely love her as well.

"Ash, Isaiah, come here, please."

They both look up and when they see **Tío** (Uncle) Mateo behind me, both of their jaws drop in surprise.

"**Tío** Mateo," they both cry out as they storm him, but at the last moment, Patch scoops them up in his arms.

I release a small breath, happy that they recognized him correctly. We've had a lot of video conference calls with my family, but after that first one were the kids accidentally confused **Tío** Mateo with Diego, I told them how to tell both of them apart. It also doesn't hurt that **Tío** Mateo is smiling and you can see that he's excited to see them, whereas Diego always told them to scram before he beat them for not moving fast enough. Thankfully, he never beat them, but the threat was enough to get the kids moving quickly to their rooms.

"Hold up there, kiddos. You need to hug **Tío** Mateo gently because he's hurt, okay?"

"Okay, Dad," they both reply in unison before squirming to be let down.

Patch lets them down and they both go over to **Tío** Mateo, hugging his legs. After a moment, **Tío** Mateo walks over to the couch, sits down and holds his arms out. Both boys carefully climb up next to him, one on either side, and cuddle into him as they start talking to him.

Patch tilts his head and I follow him into a corner on the opposite side of the room.

"We're on lockdown, Siren. We need to stay here. No going out unless it's an emergency."

Even though I knew it, hearing it is another thing. "They're coming, aren't they?"

His only answer is his jaw tightening.

"Be cautious, be careful, and even if you're just going to the bathroom, don't go alone. Do you remember where all the triggers are and the entrances?"

Blinking rapidly, I nod. On Monday, Levi and Smoke had taken me around the clubhouse, showing me the entrances to the panic room as well as the concealed buttons around the clubhouse that I could push, almost like a panic button, and the guys would come running.

This is the first time I've been in real lockdown, and I hope that we'll be able to keep the kids entertained enough.

Shit.

"Patch, we don't have much stuff here for the kids. Or us."

"I'll head over to the condo and get anything we need tomorrow, as well as their schoolwork just in case. Make a list, and I'll get it. I just don't want you or the kids going out until we get the all clear."

"Okay."

"Have you given any thought to Smoke's idea of inserting a tracker under your skin?"

My breath catches in my throat as the reality crashes down on me even harder at that thought.

That I, or my kids, could be taken and stripped of the other trackers in my phone, our bracelets, and their shoes that would let the club know where we are.

Eyes stinging with tears, which I refuse to let fall, I steel my spine. Determined to do whatever I need to do to protect us. Even though I still have my doubts about the technology. But then again, I trust Smoke. He wouldn't let us get them if he didn't think they'd work.

"We'll get the trackers. All of us."

Patch exhales heavily and I wonder if he thought I'd continue to object. He pulls out his phone, most likely to text Smoke. After a few moments, his phone chimes and he nods.

"He'll be down here in a few minutes. He and I would much rather we do it now, since we don't know when they'll strike. Especially after what Mateo just told us."

I blanch at that. I was right. Something's going to happen and soon. "You'll need to get Cassie out of the fort, then."

He grins. "I'll never pass up a chance to hold my little girl."

His words have a two-fold effect on me, partially lifting the dark cloud hanging over my head while at the same time, my heart feels like it could burst at his words. He crosses the room, crawling into the fort, almost bringing it down on top of him since he's so much larger than the kids.

A few moments later, he emerges with Cassie in his arms, and when he stands, he runs a hand through his hair before smoothing her hair down as well. She sleepily rubs her eyes as she snuggles into Patch's chest, and I swear my ovaries go into overdrive at the sight.

"Angel, do you want to meet your **Tío** Mateo?" he asks her and her head pops up immediately, sleep apparently forgotten.

"**Tío** Mateo's here? But I thought we weren't going to meet him until after he was gone."

None of the kids call Stephan 'dad' anymore, nor do they mention his name unless they have to. They just say 'he'. Not that I blame them in the least. I just think this is how they're dealing with getting past their trauma.

"Well, that was the plan, but then **Tío** Mateo got hurt and came here. Would you like to give him a hug? I bet that would help him feel better."

Cassie eagerly nods her head and holds out her hands toward **Tío** Mateo. Patch lowers her onto his lap and she carefully wraps her little arms around him.

They continue talking quietly and I can't help but smile as I see the kids excitedly telling **Tío** Mateo about their day and their rooms at the condo.

He looks up and smiles widely at me over the kids' heads. The smile takes me back to when I was a kid, and despite Carmen and Eileen's best efforts, he always made time for me when he saw me.

"I know I said this on our calls, but Mary, your **niños** (kids) are the most adorable and best behaved **niños** (kids) I have seen in a long time," he tells me after the kids clamor down off his lap and go back to building their brick castle.

"**Gracias** (Thank you)," I whisper in return, once again getting choked up with emotions. I tried damn hard to instill good manners in them despite what Stephan would order them to do or not do.

He leans against me, wrapping his arm over my shoulder, and I rest my head on his side as we watch the kids play.

A few minutes later, the door opens and Smoke comes in with Mae and Timber behind him. "I know this was a big decision, Mary, but I think it's the right way to go. Actually, with everything going on, and you deciding to do it, Mae has decided to do it as well."

She comes over to me and gives me a hug.

"Mae, this is my **Tío** Mateo. **Tío** Mateo, this is Mae, she's Timber's Old Lady. I know you guys were just in Church, but if you weren't introduced, this is Timber and Smoke, Mae's dad."

Tío Mateo gives her a small smile as the guys shake hands. "Very nice to meet you, though I wish it was under different circumstances. I've heard a lot about you and your husband from the children."

Turning to Smoke, I rub my sweaty hands on my leggings. "So, how do we do this?"

He cocks his eyebrow at me and tilts his head toward the kids in question.

I shake my head. "I wasn't sure how to broach the subject with them. Or how to explain the technology properly," I whisper and he nods in understanding.

"Kids, can you come over here for a moment?" he asks and they drop their toys before coming over. He gestures to the couch and they sit down, but he keeps Lindsey near him.

"Kids, your mom has decided something that will help keep her and all of you safe. Do you know what a tracking device is?"

Ash nods, but Isaiah and Cassie look confused, so Smoke explains.

"It's a device that will let us know where you are if someone takes you. That way, we can come find and rescue you quicker."

"Is it something you wear?" Isaiah asks and Smoke waffles his hand a little is a so-so gesture.

"Sort of. It's a device that looks like this," he says as he holds up a chip that's still in its packaging, "and it goes under your skin."

All three sets of eyes widen with worry.

"It's okay guys. Uncle Smoke gave me one after they rescued me. There was a pinch and then it was all done. And I got a cool band aid after that," Lindsey says as she points to a spot on her hip.

"Is the hip the only location it can go?" I ask and Smoke shakes his head.

"No, it can also go in your arm, but it's better in your hip. At least with this particular chip. It's my friend's design and isn't even released into the civilian world yet, but in exchange for doing his company some favors, I can get as many of these babies as I want or need. What's special about these is that to help with the battery life, they only start tracking you once they are triggered. They can be triggered and deactivated two ways—you press it three times in a row or I activate and deactivate them on my system. It needs to go below the waistband of your jeans and away from where the seam in the side of your jeans will be so that it doesn't accidentally trigger it."

"How long is the battery life?"

"Ten years depending on use. However, if something does happen and it dies before then, I will get a warning on my computer. I'll also be doing random checks to verify they are still working, but then immediately shutting them off again. When a battery does die, it's just a small incision to remove and then I'd replace it with a new one."

"But why do we need them?" Cassie asks, and I'm about to explain when Lindsey speaks up.

"Do you remember me telling you I was kidnapped before?"

All three of them nod.

"I was missing for almost two months. Some bad men who wanted my mom kidnapped us. If I had Uncle Smoke's tracker back then, they would have been able to find us much faster. But since I didn't, it took them a while to find clues as to where we were hidden." She pauses as she fingers her bracelet, which mirrors mine that Levi gave me. However, hers and my kids' bracelets don't have the hidden blades in them. "These bracelets were what helped them find us because Auntie MaeMae was also kidnapped and brought to the same place I was. If someone takes these bracelets off us, they'd have no way to track us except for the last location of the bracelet."

Smoke gives her a little side hug. "That's right, Sweetie. These are a backup to your bracelets and your shoes. The bracelets and your shoes could be taken and tossed."

"But he had a tracker on Mom. I know because I heard him talking about it when she went to a store he said she wasn't allowed to go into, even though it was just to get us shoes," Ash says.

Patch crouches down by the couch next to them. "This is different. He was using it as a way to control your mom. That's not what we're using it for. We're not trying to scare you or constantly monitor where you go, we're just trying to keep you safe." He pauses and looks over to me, holding out a hand, which I take and squeeze. "You four are my heart. It would kill me if something happened to any one of you. That's why I'd like you all to get the tracker. I'm going to get one, too. So are Mae and Timber."

Ash looks up at me and I give him an encouraging nod. "I'm getting it, too. It's an extra precaution. Worst case, us or Smoke never has to activate the trackers. But if something does happen, I'd rather have the tracker than not."

His little head bobs as he thinks before finally nodding. "Okay, I'll get it too. But how do we get it?"

Damn, I'm so proud of my little boy.

Chapter 63

Mary

SMOKE HOLDS UP A device that's a little like a gun, and once again, worry fills the kids' eyes. "I know this looks a little scary, but all I do is hold it up to your hip, push the trigger, and you'll feel a little pinch as it goes under the skin. Then, you'll get to pick out a band-aid to put over it."

"I'll go first so you guys can see, okay?" Mae asks as she scoots a chair closer to Smoke.

She takes a band-aid that Smoke holds out to her. Then pulls down her leggings and her underwear just enough to expose the side of her hip. I know this must be awkward for her to do this, but I'm extremely grateful she offered to show them how it gets inserted in us.

Smoke holds the gun to Mae's hip and when Cassie whimpers, Smoke stops when Mae whispers to him. Mae holds out her hand to Cassie.

"Come here, Sweetie. It's just going to be a little pinch. It's okay."

Mae hugs Cassie to her and at her nod, Smoke pulls the trigger. Cassie jumps a little at the sound, but Mae doesn't react at all, though her eyebrows raise a little in shock.

"A vaccine hurts worse than that does," she says before Smoke puts the band-aid over the injection spot.

Her comment has most of the kids' worry easing. None of them like getting shots. Not that I blame them. The regular doctor that we use was dictated by Stephan and he never cared for the kids' comfort when doing something like vaccines.

Wait a minute.

"Smoke?" My voice shakes and I try to level it out so that I don't scare the kids. "Um, how small can those trackers be made?"

He frowns at my question and then when he nods as he grits his teeth, I think he's figured out my train of thought.

"Give me one moment and I'll be back." He picks up his little case of tools and the trackers, sets it on a shelf up high and then leaves the room.

"Kids, you can go ahead and play until Smoke comes back. Then we'll finish, okay?" They give me weird looks, but thankfully, they do as I ask.

Turning around, I do my best to keep my frustrations from bubbling up out of me, but I'm almost positive that I'm right. Patch crouches down in front of me and cups my cheek. I'm vaguely aware of Mae, Timber, **Tío** (Uncle) Mateo, and Elvira going to the other side of the room to give us a bit of privacy.

"Talk to me, Siren."

"What if there's one small enough to be put in us with a needle? For regular checkups and vaccines, Stephan made us go to a certain doctor even though he was creepy as fuck. He was never gentle and didn't care if he hurt the kids or me when doing vaccines or exams. What if Stephan had that doctor put trackers on us? What if that's how they keep finding me when we go into town?"

Before today, I had gone into town a couple of times with Levi, Mae, Patch, and a handful of club members for grocery and supply runs. Each time, we spotted someone from Stephan and Diego's circle watching us.

A murderous look crosses Patches face before he masks it and cups both of my cheeks. "If that's the case, then we'll get them out before putting Smoke's tracking in its place. Maybe we can use theirs to lure them into a trap or something. I lost you once, and I'm not losing you again. You are my heart, Mary. You, Asher, Isaiah, Cassie, and any other kids we might have. All of you are my heart. I lost nine years with you. I'm not losing any more."

His words break through the dam, and despite tears falling down my cheeks, I pull him forward, crashing my lips to his.

"Ewwww," Isaiah cries, and we both laugh as we break apart. Turning, I chuckle again when I see his little face squished up.

Smoke comes back with a small bag and comes over to me. "Let's start with you, but I'll need you to take off your bracelets and shoes, then you'll need to stand for this.

I unhook my bracelets and hand them to Patch before slipping out of my flats and standing. Smoke waves the wand over me and when I hear a little ping, I close my eyes and bite my lip to keep from breaking down or screaming out in anger.

He actually did it.

The fucker's been tracking me this entire time.

"Why am I surprised that he did this? I shouldn't be with everything else he's done."

A guilty look crosses Smoke's face. "I'm sorry, Mary. I didn't think to check when you guys came." He pauses and looks up at Patch. "We're gonna need to do hers in the med room."

He grits his teeth. "Check the kids. If they aren't tagged, then you can give them their trackers. We'll do Mary's last."

"Okay, kids. Can you guys come over here?" Smoke asks them. He produces a key out of his pocket, the master key, and unlocks their bracelets. Unlike mine, since mine has mini-blades and theirs don't, theirs are secured and can only be cut off if someone doesn't have a key. To some, it may seem like overkill, but to me, it was a grateful extra layer of protection.

When Smoke is finally done checking all three of them, I release the breath I'd been holding.

Stephan wasn't tracking them.

Just me.

"He probably thought the kids would be wherever you were, with the exception of school," **Tío** (Uncle) Mateo says quietly, which makes sense, but I'm relieved nonetheless.

One by one, Smoke inserts the trackers starting with Patch and Timber.

"I'll go first," Ash offers and both Cassie and Isaiah crowd around him to watch. Cassie takes his hand and he gives it a little squeeze. "It's okay, Cass. It didn't hurt Auntie MaeMae, Dad, or Uncle Timber, so it'll be okay."

My heart squeezes as I watch him reassure her. Damn, he's going to make someone extremely happy when he's an adult.

"Ready?" Smoke asks him.

"Ready."

Smoke pulls the little trigger, and Ash doesn't flinch at all. Instead, surprise floods his face.

"See? I told you it didn't hurt," Lindsey says as she comes around the couch where she was hiding to give him a bit of privacy and gives him a hug.

He looks down at Cassie and Isaiah. "She's right. They were all right. It doesn't hurt at all."

I chuckle when both Cassie and Isaiah move to lower their pants enough for the tracker. Smoke gives Cassie hers first, since she's wearing leggings, and then he gives Isaiah his.

"Thank you, kids. I really appreciate you doing that for us," I tell them and open my arms to give them all hugs.

"What about you, Mom?"

"I'm going to get mine, but because of everything, I need to go to the med room to get mine put in. But come here and give us kisses for the night. Granny is going to watch you in here so you all can sleep in the fort."

"Even me?" Lindsey asks as she hops on her toes as she stares up at Elvira, who smiles down at her.

"Even you, Pumpkin. Your daddy's outside, but he was waiting till we were all done in here. Let's go see him so he can give you hugs and kisses goodnight."

Five minutes later, I follow the others out into the hall, including Drae. I'm sure it will be a bit before the kids settle down, but I can't even begin to describe how happy I am that they're able to play so much with another kid so frequently, especially since Lindsey is right in between Ash and Isaiah age-wise at eight years old. I'm guessing, that when all this mess is over, we'll be seeing more of Sadie and Jordan here as well.

Once in the medical room, my nerves return as Patch pulls out some pills for Mateo.

"Take one of these every six hours or so as needed. Let me know if any of your wounds start to look inflamed or are itchy while you're here. I pumped you full of a bunch of antibiotics, which were these, as well as fluids while you were out of it," he says as he passes him a piece of paper with the medication and times on it as well as a water bottle. "Drae, since I need to help Smoke with Mary, can you show Mateo where his room is?"

Drae gives Patch a chin lift and then Patch turns toward Mateo.

"Our room is two doors down from yours on the same side, if you need anything."

Mateo gives me a questioning look and when I give him a small smile, the corner of his lips ticks up slightly. "**Gracias** (Thank you). **Buenas noches** (Good night), and I'll see you in the morning."

"**Buenas noches** (Good night), **Tío** (Uncle) Mateo," I call out and get a wider smile from him in return.

God, it feels good to connect with him again, and then my stomach sours as I realize that this is it. Time to get Stephan's tracker taken care of.

Wiping my hands on my leggings, I take a steady breath. "How should we do this?"

"Let me see if I can feel it," Patch says as he snaps on some gloves and starts feeling around on my arm, a few inches below my shoulder. "Got it. I can give you local anesthesia for the incision if you want. Once the area is numb, we should be able to use tweezers to get it out and then, depending on if I need to lengthen the incision, I either use glue or stitches to close it up or just a band-aid. If we're lucky, you'll only need a band-aid because it'll be the size of a paper cut."

He gets up, looks through his cabinets and pulls out a headband with a light attached to it. Standing, I hobble over to the table, and with Smoke steadying me, I get situated.

"Do you want the local anesthesia?"

I bite my lip as I look at my shoulder. Patch puts his finger over the tracker, and then I feel around to get an idea of how big it really is.

"With my history, I don't think I'll have any problems going without for this. Do you want me to lay down or stay sitting up?"

He gives me a sad, small smile, but it's the truth. This won't be anywhere close to the worst that Stephan's done to me.

"If you could lay down, that would be better. Then you're not as subconscious about not moving your body and possibly tensing up as a result."

By the time I lay down and am semi comfy, Patch has everything out that he needs and is rolling the table over to me. Smoke has also washed up and is putting on gloves as a just in case.

After cleaning the area, he grabs a scalpel and I stare up at the ceiling for a moment before turning slightly to watch as Patch makes a small incision in my arm. The urge to lay eyes on the tracker is intense. In all honesty, I wish I could crush it, but then the guys wouldn't be able to possibly use it.

"Do you think there's anything in it that can tell it won't be in my body anymore?"

Out of the corner of my eye, Smoke shakes his head. "No, they aren't that sensitive yet. At some point, maybe, but not yet. And especially not with this one because I'm betting he did this not too long after getting a hold of you. Or hell, Diego could have had it done before he handed you over to Stephan as well. Trackers have improved immensely since then."

"Fuck," I curse. I hadn't thought of that. Which one is tracking me? "Is there a way to tell who's been tracking me?"

"It depends on the location it sends its signal to. Since both Stephan and Diego are in the wind, we might not be able to know."

Patch puts down the scalpel and Smoke hands him some tweezers. It feels weird as he digs around inside of my arm, but he does it as carefully as possible. After a few moments, he pulls out a small circular device. Smoke holds out a plastic bag and Patch drops it inside.

"You won't need any stitches since I was able to get it pretty easily," he says as he wipes away a little blood and I take over putting pressure on it with a cotton ball while he gets me a band-aid.

"Okay. Let's stand you up and do a double check that there aren't any other trackers before I put mine in."

Patch helps steady me as I stand, and thankfully, no other beeps emit from the scanner.

"Perfect, and I really am sorry for not thinking about that when you first came here."

Shaking my head, I retake my seat on the table. "It's not your fault, Smoke. I knew he had one in the ring, which you took, but I didn't think he'd go that far, either."

Patch and Smoke switch places and I lower my leggings, trying not to flash Smoke in the process. A few seconds later, I hear him pulling the trigger, and a small sting lets me know that it worked.

Setting the gun down, Smoke pulls out a tablet and opens a program, which is pretty impressive. On the screen that he's on now, he can click to different areas of the compound or look at it as a whole. He picks the clubhouse, since we're all here and on lockdown, and I can see eleven dots light up on the screen. He then goes by floor and I grin when I see four little red dots close to each other in the playroom. He moves the screen slightly and then I see our three blue dots in the medical room.

"So kids are red and adults are blue?" I ask and he nods.

"Yes, and if I click on one, it shows me which code number it's assigned to and then the picture of who it is appears in the bottom right-hand corner, like this."

My eyebrows raise in surprise at how much information he can store and access with this program.

"What if someone goes missing? Can it easily tell you who is not here?" Patch asks and I grimace. Yeah, that would be a nice feature to have to immediately realize who is missing.

"Yes, but not all the guys are chipped yet. I'm still working on syncing it with the trackers in all of our cuts and bracelets, so it's not a hundred-percent complete yet. However, this is at least a start and with the shit that's going on right now, you five are the most likely targets, so it'll definitely help that you're all now chipped."

I lean against Patch's side as I look at the program on Smoke's tablet. A niggling of worry worms its way into my mind. I really hope that Smoke won't have to use his program, but deep in my gut, I know he's going to have to use it.

It's just a question for who Stephan or Diego will try to grab next.

Chapter 64

Mary

"MARY! MARY! YOU GOTTA wake up," I hear someone saying urgently as they shake my shoulder.

"Wha? What is it?" I ask as I sleepily lift my head off my pillow, blinking as I squint to try and see Luke. Then I hear a stampede of boots running down the hallway and bolt right up in bed. "What's going on?"

"There's a fire," he says urgently as he hands me my glasses.

Shoving them on my face, I quickly scoot to the edge of bed and grab the hoodie jacket off the back of Patch's chair, quickly throwing it on before stuffing my phone in the pocket and zipping it up. Thank God I went to bed in my leggings and socks due to lack of pajama options, otherwise I'd probably have been in shorts or very thin pajama pants.

I slip on my flats and Patch scoops me up in his arms and starts running down the hall. "No time for the chair. The guys are working on containing the fire but I don't know how fast they'll have it handled."

"The kids?"

"Prospects got them out along with Elvira. It was along that back outer wall and Elvira raised the alarm when she woke up from the smoke."

Panic grips me. Oh, my God! The pull-out murphy bed was along that wall. The bed Elvira was sleeping in. "But no one was hurt, right?"

"I don't think so, but I'll look them all over once we're out of here."

Since the fire is at the back of the clubhouse, we head out the front and wrap around the side.

"Oh, my God!" I cry when I see the orange flames licking up the side of the clubhouse. It hasn't reached the roof yet, but it won't be long unless they can get it under control soon. In the distance, I hear sirens and I pray the firefighters get here quickly, because I don't know how long those little fire extinguishers will last.

Just as I think that, both Dragon and Ryder toss two down on the ground. Ethan, Timber, Sasha, and Cowboy all race up from the direction of the condos, each carrying a few fire extinguishers.

"Raided the condos until the fire department can get here," Timber says as they start handing them out.

Patch sets me down, and I wobble slightly before finding my balance. Then, with a kiss, he strides forward and takes one of the fire extinguishers. Cowboy takes Sasha's from her, kisses her and points over to the kids and me. She huffs at him but does as he asks.

She comes over to me and lets me use her shoulder to steady myself further.

"Are you okay?" she asks and I nod.

"You?"

"Yeah." She peers around me toward the kids and kind of nods to herself when she sees Elvira and Drae over by the kids.

After a few moments, her phone rings and she digs it out of her pocket before answering it. She covers her other ear, but with the guys shouting at each other, she must still not be able to hear very well because she turns a little away from them and talks louder.

A couple seconds later, my entire body freezes and ice slides down my spine when I feel something round and metal poking into my back.

"Don't fucking move or say anything."

I close my eyes and then open them again, willing Patch, Sasha, or someone to turn around, because I'd know that voice anywhere.

Stephan.

"Look over to your right, but don't say a fucking word."

I do, and my eyes widen when I can barely make out the glint of a metal barrel pointing at the back of Cassie's head thanks to the flames. However, it's too dark to see who it is holding the gun. Not to mention they're wearing a hoodie with the hood pulled down low over their head.

"You either come with me, or I take the brat and sell her. She'll make me a mint since she's so young and at the perfect age to be molded into what we need her to be."

He wouldn't!

But as soon as I think that, I know he would.

He'd sell any of them just to save his own neck. Me included. Fuck, I forgot about him listing us on that fucking website. I need to talk to Smoke about that. Well, after I get out of this somehow.

"Don't hurt her," I hiss and then wince when the barrel of the gun digs into me further.

"Not so loud, you stupid bitch. Now slowly step backwards."

"I can't or did you forget that you broke my leg!" I hiss again, although, I do it as quietly as I can so I don't aggravate him more.

He curses and then mumbles something.

The next thing I know, he's got my arm wrapped around his shoulder and lets me lean on him as I hobble. At first I try to be a little noisy, but then he digs his gun into my side, and even though it's his non-dominant hand, I don't want to test him. Not yet anyway. I go for placating him instead.

"I'm sorry, I'm trying to be quiet, but this is not exactly easy."

"Well, try harder. This would have been a lot easier if you'd have lost some fucking weight like I've told you to countless times already," he growls into my ear as we continue to back away from the property. I have to bite my tongue when he makes comments about my weight. I've come a long way in accepting my curves again—I'm not fully back to completely accepting them, but I'm pretty damn close.

When we're about five feet back from Sasha, someone comes up on the other side of me. I hear a whistling sound and my head jerks toward the new person and when I see a metal cylinder in a large hand, I turn back toward the clubhouse in fear.

Sasha cries out a muffled sound and then drops.

"What did you do?" I hiss at him.

"Tranq dart, now shut the fuck up, bitch, and keep moving."

Fuck! Please let Sasha be okay and that they find her soon. Who knows if they made the shit in that dart too powerful for her.

I stumble when Stephan suddenly steps away from me and the guy that darted Sasha scoops me up into his arms and starts walking toward the condos. When they reach them, they check to make sure no one is following them and then they run toward the tree line.

My mind whirls with what I could do to leave hints for the guys as to where we went. I mean, the snow might help. I'm not sure when it started snowing, but we've already got a few inches on the ground. Unfortunately, it's also still snowing. With not knowing how much we're supposed to get, I don't know if our tracks will be covered by the time they notice me missing or not.

Then I remember the tracker.

Thank God both Patch and Smoke pushed me to get it tonight! Otherwise, I'd only have my phone and bracelets, and I have no idea how much longer I'll have those on me.

Thankfully, Stephan's buddy has my right side toward his chest, and I lower my hand, acting like I'm going to itch my leg, but he shifts and his hand latches onto my wrist, preventing me from activating it.

"What are you doing?" he growls and I wince, thinking up a lie real quick since he noticed.

"Sorry, just have a bad muscle twinge. It's happened ever since he broke my leg."

He pauses as he looks around and then drops me to the ground.

I hiss in pain as I land hard on the frozen ground, the fresh snow easily soaking through my clothes even worse than before.

My eyes widen in surprise when the man pulls rope from a bag he was carrying and starts tying me up.

"Hurry up," Stephan orders him and the man grunts.

"Take it up with your bitch. She was trying to signal them somehow."

Pain explodes on my cheek as Stephan hits me before he grabs my jacket, yanking me closer to him before hitting me again.

Immediately I can tell that our time apart has not been good for him. He's greasy, unkept, and he stinks to high heaven.

"I wasn't doing anything!" I lie right to his face. "My leg has been giving me problems ever since you broke it and meathead over here was making it worse. Because of your threat, I knew I had to stay quiet, so I was trying to put pressure on it, hoping to get it to go away."

He sneers down at me. "Why am I not surprised? Anything that you're involved with always goes to hell in a handbasket. I'll be glad to finally be rid of your pathetic ass."

I bite my tongue as curses threaten to escape. Back talking now would only mean more pain for me. If he could have just let me go, he would have been rid of me, but no. He had to keep coming after me.

He stares at me for a few moments while meathead finishes tying me up. Before he can pick me up, Stephan pulls back his foot and kicks me right in my stomach. Air whooshes out of me and I groan in pain, not able to hold the noise in.

The other guy pulls out a hanky out of his pocket and even though I resist, he still winds up gagging me, which makes catching my breath even harder. Then he hoists me up over his shoulder and I groan again as his shoulder makes contact with the spot that Stephan had just kicked.

To help keep my mind off the pain, I look down to see how I'm tied up. My hands are tied in front of me and then there's a few loops keeping my arms tucked against my torso. I can feel the rope circling down my hips and legs, down to my ankles. At least he didn't tighten the ones around my ankles too tight because of my cast.

Meathead continues onward through the forest. The further he walks, the more the coldness creeps in as the snowflakes get bigger and start falling even harder. However, it seems like the trees are blocking a lot of them from falling on us, since there doesn't seem to be much on the ground. I try to lift my head to look behind us, but I can't really see through my curtain of hair.

I'm not sure how long we continue through the forest before we come to a junker of a side-by-side ATV. Meathead lowers me roughly onto the passenger seat and I'm surprised when he buckles me up, but it's something I'm extremely grateful for. I know how shitty of a driver Stephan is on a good day. Add in the fact that we're going to be driving through the forest in the dark, I'll take all the protection I can get. Especially since I can't even hold the 'oh shit' handle with the way I'm tressed up.

Meathead climbs onto a bench behind us, but instead of facing forward, he faces behind us. Stephan starts up the ATV and when he looks at me, fear spreads throughout my body. I know that look, and I know it means I'm going to be hurting big time in the near future. He presses on the accelerator and as the weak beam of headlights light up the path in front of us, I realize they've cut a path through the underbrush and forest. How long have they been out here prepping this? How were they not noticed?

Turning, I look over my shoulder, but I can't see anything through the trees or darkness. Not even an orange haze of the fire.

Have they noticed that I'm gone yet?

God, I hope Patch and the club find me soon. If they don't, I don't know if I'll survive the punishment Stephan will dole out this time.

Chapter 65

Patch

Making sure Mary's stable, I glance over toward the kids, but both Elvira and Drae give me a nod. They've got the kids and will keep them safe. I press a kiss to Mary's forehead and then run over to Timber, taking a fire extinguisher from them and get to work with the others.

After a few minutes, a commotion has me looking over my shoulder and I realize that Timber has ran some hose from inside the clubhouse and out a nearby window. Running forward, I grab on it and start pulling, helping him untangle it as we go.

Soon, we've got a stream of water hitting further up the wall where we can't reach with our fire extinguishers.

Sirens blare in the distance and I turn, checking on Mary and the kids again, but freeze.

Where's Mary?

My gaze goes over to Elvira and Drae, but she's not over by them. Frantically, I look around, but I can't see her.

"Mary?" I yell, and after a few times of yelling, my brothers notice she's missing and start looking as well.

Bastion's barking has me running toward him and I curse when I come to a stop by Sasha's body, laying in the snow. Behind me, someone runs up and with the light from his phone, I curse as I feel for her pulse. It's weak, but it's there. That's when I see a tranq dart sticking out of her arm. Plucking it out, I hand it over to Thor.

"Smoke!" he bellows and a beat behind him, I'm yelling out as well.

"Cowboy!"

I turn Sasha over and scan her for any other injuries. Not seeing any, I lift her in my arms and turn just as Cowboy runs over to us. "They tranq'd her but I don't see any other injuries. Call Allison and have her come here. They took Mary. I'm going hunting."

A murderous look crosses Cowboy's face, and he gives me a curt nod. After transferring Sasha into his arms, I'm about to head into the woods when Thor grasps my shoulder. Turning, he nods toward the gate and I curse when I see the fire trucks are here.

"Find Smoke and go. Take two others with you. We'll do our best to keep them out of the woods."

Giving him a chin lift, I look through the crowd and spot Smoke. As I walk toward him, he spots me and heads my way, Punisher and Dragon following close behind him. It's then that I notice Smoke has a backpack and I hope like fuck his tablet or computer's in it. A moment later, Ethan is at my side with a gun bag slung over his shoulder.

"Patch, there are footsteps heading southeast toward the forest," he says and I pause, blinking at him. How did he find the tracks so quickly?

"Perfect," Dragon says as he clutches Ethan's shoulder. "Lead the way, Tracker," he says with a grin as he presses a flashlight into my hands.

Taking off at a jog at first, so as not to raise alarm to the firefighters and fuck knows who else that just showed up, we follow Ethan as he heads toward the forest. Then he surprises me when he starts weaving almost effortlessly through the forest. Coming up next to Smoke, I realize he's got a small screen in his hand and is also following the dot of Mary's tracker, but Ethan has yet to look at the screen.

I give Dragon a questioning look, to which his grin darkens as well as widens. "He hunts and tracks with his dad and Roy."

A flicker of hope flares in my chest.

We're coming, Mary.

Hold on tight.

We've been following Mary's trail for ten minutes when we come to a little clearing with the snow freshly stomped and anger blooms in my chest when I see a few red dots on the snow.

"He hurt her," I seethe.

Ethan bends down and picks up something brown and examines it. "They tied her up. These are rope fibers.

Noise in the underbrush behind us has me turning and I let out a harsh breath of relief when Bastion comes into view.

"Good boy," Ethan says as he pets his head. "Bastion, **suchen** (search)," he commands as he lets Bastion sniff the few rope fibers and then he starts sniffing around the ground.

I raise my eyebrow in question at him.

"Levi's been teaching me his commands and she's been letting me work with him." He turns toward Bastion and gives a low whistle. "Let's go, boy."

They both take off into the forest and I look at Smoke as we follow.

"We're on the right trail, but—"

Smoke's cut off by the sound of an engine starting up and we all take off at a run toward the sound.

When we get to another clearing, I pause as I see Ethan scaling a tree with his gun slung over his shoulder, the bag discarded on the ground next to the tree. Bastion is sitting at the base of the tree and I know Ethan has commanded him to stay. Probably so that he doesn't accidentally shoot him.

After a few moments, Ethan settles himself on a thick limb and looks out into the night before quickly raising his gun, which I realize is similar to the twins' sniper rifles. I hadn't realized he'd been training with them, but this might be our best bet to stop the assholes before they break free of the forest.

Ethan fires two shots in quick succession and I grin darkly when we hear curses soon filling the air. He looks down at us and I realize he also has a pair of night vision goggles on.

"Go, I'll keep an eye on them from here," he says as he points a bit to the west.

I give a low whistle for Bastion, and he takes off with us as we run in the direction Ethan pointed in, careful not to make too much noise that will alert whoever took Mary to our presence.

As we get closer, I pull out my gun and creep through the darkness, making sure to keep out of their line of sight as two men argue.

"What the fuck did you do this time, Hayes? Can't you do anything right?" the larger one snarls as he reaches in around Mary and unbuckles her before throwing her over his shoulder.

A 'ooof' sound escapes her and I barely bite back my own snarl. Her clothes are mostly soaked through, especially her thin leggings and socks, and I know she has to be freezing. At least she threw on my hoodie, so that part of her body was warmer, but even that looks like it's pretty wet. Probably from when they tied her up.

"I didn't do a God damn thing, Derrick. Both the tires are flat. That's not my fucking fault. It was your boss that supplied this derelict rig. Maybe he wanted us to fucking fail. Did you ever think of that?"

Dragon gives a hand signal and we creep forward. Dragon moves toward Stephan since he's closer to him while Punisher and I move toward Derrick.

Punisher and I share a glance and at the same time that Punisher pushes his gun into Derrick's back, I rip Mary off of his shoulder.

She squirms in my grasp, and I realize she can't see me through her thick blanket of hair. In the distance, I can hear Dragon and Stephan shuffling around.

"It's me, Siren. Calm down," I whisper in her ear and she immediately stops struggling.

I push her hair out of her face, and the relief in her eyes when she sees me damn near has my knees buckling. Pulling out my knife, I get to work cutting her free.

I hear a shuffle, and I glance up just in time to see Derrick swinging his fist at Punisher. He ducks, and Derrick doesn't even see the punch coming that lands him on his ass. Punisher puts the barrel of the gun right on Derrick's forehead, and he finally stops trying to get up.

"Who the fuck are you?" Derrick seethes.

Punisher chuckles darkly as he digs his gun harder into Derrick's forehead. "You are in no position to be asking the questions. Just know, you tried to steal someone that didn't belong to you."

I lean Mary against a tree as I continue untying her. Slicing off a portion of the rope, I'm about to toss it to him when Ethan comes up behind us and instead, I toss it to him. He wrestles Derrick onto his back and then wrenches his arms behind him, tying his hands together while Punisher keeps his gun trained on Derrick.

Cutting off another portion, I guide Mary over toward Dragon and Smoke just in time to see Dragon punching Stephan in the face, sending him barreling face first into the snow. Dragon yanks his arms behind his back and Smoke takes the rope I toss him, tying his hands together.

Punisher and Dragon force both of them to sit side by side on the wet ground and Smoke and I use the remaining rope to tie them up further.

Stepping back, I frown as I look over at Mary, seeing her shivering violently as she and Stephan stare at each other. Walking over to her, I turn her into my chest. She doesn't need to see him ever again. I'll make sure of it.

Smoke walks over to us, frowning as he takes in the state she's in.

"We need to get out of here and back to the clubhouse," I say as I clutch Mary closer to me, trying to warm her with my body heat, which unfortunately isn't much since I'm only in a t-shirt and jeans. I wish I would have grabbed my other hoodie, but I was focused on getting Mary and the kids out.

"I already sent Thor a message and he's got a couple of guys heading our way with some ATVs. They've got blankets for her. The fire's out and there isn't much damage thanks to Elvira quickly raising the alarm. They found a smoldering pile of rags that were drenched in accelerant outside of where Elvira was sleeping.

"Fuck, she's lucky as fuck she woke up when she did."

"Agreed," he growls through gritted teeth. "Lex accessed our security footage, but you couldn't see who it was that started the fire. Since there were no identifying features, Thor gave him permission to show the firefighters and cops."

He pauses as he looks at me. "Your uncle was there, but I don't know if he's still there."

Digging out my phone, I check to see if there are any messages, but there are none.

Mary's shivering increases and I turn, guiding her to the ATV. Dragon, Punisher, and Smoke all take off their hoodies and give them to her. I help her get out of her drenched zipped hoodie, frowning when I see that her thin t-shirt is also drenched.

"Form a line, will ya?" I ask as I jerk my head toward Derrick and Stephan who are glaring at us but thankfully can't say anything due to their gags.

My brothers form a line with their backs to us, effectively blocking the assholes view of Mary.

She shivers even more as I help her peel her t-shirt off and my cock twitches when her bare skin comes into view before rage fills me at seeing the shoe-print bruises already forming on her stomach.

Tossing her wet shirt on the floor of the ATV, I slip a dry hoodie over her head and then drape the other two over her legs. It's the best I can do until we get her back to the clubhouse and I can get her in a warm shower.

"Thank you." Her voice is small and weak, and I curse myself for not watching over her better.

"I'm so sorry, Siren," I tell her as I cup her cheeks and she shakes her head.

"It was my decision. Derrick, well, I didn't know that's who it was at the time since his face was obscured by a hood, but he had a gun to the back of Cassie's head. Stephan said I either went with him willingly or he was going to take Cassie, mold her and then sell her off. I couldn't let that happen. Then they darted Sasha and I don't know what was in it. Please say they're all okay?" Tears fall down her cheeks and I wipe them with my thumb.

"The kids are safe. I found Sasha and told Cowboy to call Alli in to look at her. I think they just gave her a sedative, but Alli will get the tranq and her blood tested to be sure."

The sound of engines reaches us and Mary's body tenses even more. "It's probably the club, Siren," I tell her, but as a precaution, I slip my gun out of my cut and click off the safety as I stand in front of her.

A minute or so later, my body relaxes when I see Timber approaching in the lead in one of our ATVs with two others behind him.

"It's the club, Siren. You're okay."

Her body slumps against the seat, but her shaking worsens.

"Fuck," I curse as I scoop her up and her discarded shirt, making my way toward Timber. I sit in the backseat with Mary on my lap and Timber helps me cover her with blankets. Warm blankets. Mae or Alli must have used the blanket warmer in the medical room before sending the guys out for us.

"Go," Dragon calls out to us. "We'll handle these fuckers. Get her warm and safe."

Timber climbs back behind the wheel and I hold Mary tight against me and hang onto the 'oh shit' bar to steady us. Mary buries her head in the crook of my neck, and I hold her tighter when I feel her tears against my skin.

"I've got you, Siren. You're okay now," I tell her repeatedly as Timber drives as fast as he safely can with these conditions.

His worried gaze meets mine in the mirror, and I know he's thinking the same thing I am.

How hurt is she and how is this going to set her back? I'd witnessed a lot of Mae's battles after each time she was kidnapped and did my best to help her, along with the others. I worry if Mary's nightmares will return and how she'll fare both physically and mentally after all this bullshit.

About five minutes later, we pull up to the back of the clubhouse, and thanks to the lights from the ATV, I'm shocked to see the fire damage isn't worse.

Timber sees me looking as he gets out and gestures toward the clubhouse. "It shouldn't be too bad, but I'll know more about the extent when daylight hits. Firefighters advised against staying in the clubhouse till we can air out all the smoke and clean everything up.

Standing, I keep as many blankets as I can around Mary as I carry her inside.

My chest warms when I see the rest of the club waiting for us in the main room and there seems to be a collective sigh of relief when they see her with their own eyes. I'd already texted Thor that we'd found her and that the guys were coming back with two "guests".

Giving them a chin lift, I head straight to the med room and am thankful that Alli's there.

"How's Sasha? Is she okay?" Mary blurts out and Alli nods.

"She's sleeping off the sedative and I found no other injuries. I put her and Cowboy in the condo next to you guys' so that it'd be easier for you to check on her tomorrow. I took blood and Thor had someone drive it to the hospital for Tim to test. He'll text us the results as usual. Now," she says as she pauses. "Let's get you looked over, missy."

"There's already bruising on her stomach and the cut on her face, which is also starting to bruise. Are you hurt anywhere else, Mary? Did they drug you at all?" I ask and she nods.

"They didn't drug me, but there are a few other things. Besides freezing, my wrists really hurt from the ropes and I think my tailbone could be bruised from when Derrick dropped me on the ground like a sack of potatoes before he started tying me up."

We work quickly, checking her over, but thankfully we don't find anything else concerning. Rummaging through the cupboards, I find some sweatpants, a t-shirt, and new hoodie for her and help her into them. I wrap some more warm blankets around her and put some fresh ones in the warmer just in case she needs more.

Alli slips out to give us some privacy and Mary's eyes fill with tears. Stepping closer to the table, I hold her in my arms as she sobs.

"I was so scared and I'm sorry. I worried they'd still end up taking Cassie, even if I went with them. And the look Stephan gave me promised that he was going to dole out one of his worst punishments if you hadn't gotten to me when you did."

Kissing the top of her head, I tighten my arms around her. "I'm so sorry that I didn't stay with you." I'll forever be kicking myself for that and vow to be a better protector for her and the kids.

She shakes her head. "Then you would probably have ended up being darted as well. I don't know if the phone call Sasha had was real or if it was a distraction."

Frowning, I make a mental note to talk to Smoke and Cowboy about that when I see them next.

"How are you feeling? Warmer?" I ask her as I rub my hands up and down her back.

She nods and then pulls back, wiping her cheeks. I reach for the tissues nearby and she blows her nose. "I hope I don't get a cold from being out there soaking wet for so long."

"Come on, Siren. Let's get you home, into a bath and then bed. I can help you take another bath in the morning as well."

Her body sags. "God, that sounds like heaven. I haven't had a bath in years."

Suddenly, I remember a promise I made to her a few weeks ago. "Then that's what we'll do. You're going to rest and relax while you recover, and if you get sick from this, don't worry. I'll take care of the kids. You just focus on feeling better."

She looks up at me with such love in her eyes that it's almost overwhelming. Cupping her cheek, I dip my head and kiss her. My cock thickens in my jeans, but I don't press for more. I need to get her home and finish taking care of her. Her health is more important than my needs.

Pulling back, I kiss her forehead. "Come on, Siren. Let's get you home."

Chapter 66

Patch

As soon as I get through the door to our condo, the kids bombard us.

"Mama!" and "Mom!" are repeatedly shouted until I help them all get settled on her lap with Mary's permission. Little Cassie has to sit on both her brothers' laps, but I could tell Mary needed this.

Mateo carefully stands up from the couch and I walk over to him.

"Which one?" he quietly asks, and I look over my shoulder, making sure none of them are paying attention.

"Stephan and someone called Derrick Rodriguez."

Mateo's eyes darken as his face hardens.

I arch an eyebrow at him. "You know him?"

His lips purse in a fine line and he gives a curt nod as his lips curl. "Yes. One of our men that Diego turned against us." He hesitates for a moment and then nods to himself. "I know this is a stretch, but can I be in on the questioning? I want to know why Derrick decided to betray **mi familia** (my family)."

"That's not something I alone can answer, but I'll ask Thor and pull for you." Turning toward the kids, I notice Mary is barely able to keep her eyes open. "Okay, kiddos. Give Mom a goodnight kiss. It's time we all head back to bed."

All three of them hesitate as they cling to Mary, and I make a gut decision, hoping she won't be mad at me for it. "Go upstairs and change into clean pajamas. You can sleep with us tonight, but I need to help your mom wrap her cast so she can get cleaned up as well." All three of them rush forward, hugging me and thanking me before quickly heading upstairs. I turn toward Mateo. "Can you watch them while I help Mary?"

He gives me a small grin as he tilts his head toward the stairs and clasps my shoulder. "Go, I've got them. It's definitely not a hardship to spend time with **mis sobrinos y sobrina** (my nephews and niece)."

Clapping him on the shoulder, I turn and walk over to Mary, once again thankful that I started learning Spanish again when Mary had a few weeks ago. Kneeling in front of Mary, I slide off her shoe and nudge her slightly. Sleepily, she blinks awake and gives me a small smile.

"Let's get you clean. I think we'll save the bath for tomorrow when you have more energy to enjoy it."

She hums and I wheel her into her room, shutting the bedroom door behind us. Mary heads to the bathroom, locking her wheelchair in place just outside the door. Walking over to the dresser, I shuffle through her drawers, looking for her favorite pajamas. Grabbing them as well as some fresh panties and socks, I follow her into the bathroom, stopping when I see her stripping and revealing her mouthwatering olive skin.

Then my lip curls when I see her fresh bruises again and I make a silent promise to her that if we're able to handle Stephan ourselves, that I'll make sure he endures as much pain as I'm able to deliver without killing him.

A dark satisfaction flows through me as I think about keeping him alive for a while and giving him a dose of his own 'punishments' day after day until he finally succumbs. While a part of my brain protests that my decision goes against the oath I took to help and take care of people, I also know that this needs to be done for Mary and the kids' sake. He needs to either die or be kept in a dark hole, never to see the light of day again for them to be able to move on. Though, I'd much rather prefer the first one, just so the threat is completely eliminated.

"Are you just going to stand there and stare?" she asks, her voice while tired, is also teasing me.

"Sorry, Siren. You're just too sexy."

She bites her lip as her gaze lowers to my dick and I groan.

"Siren, I'm trying to be a gentleman here, and you are making it extremely difficult."

She pouts and then gets a twinkle in her eye. "Can you help me wrap my cast?"

She sits back down in her wheelchair and I squeeze past her, turning on the water in the shower so it can warm up before digging under the sink for the plastic and tape. Turning back to her, my muscles go taut as my gaze immediately goes to the apex of her thighs, which are spread and giving me a perfect view of her glistening pussy lips.

"Siren," I growl as I grit my teeth before adverting my eyes and quickly wrapping her cast. Taping it off, I breathe deeply to get myself back under control.

When I look back up at her, she bites her lip again as her hands cup her breasts, tweaking her nipples.

"You're tired, Siren. You could barely keep your eyes open just a moment ago."

"Well, seeing you staring at me like that got me all hot and bothered. Besides, I almost lost you again tonight. I need you, Luke."

"Fuck," I hiss before reaching forward and gripping her hips, pulling her ass to the edge of the chair and diving in between her legs, licking her pussy lips before latching onto her clit.

She cries out and slaps a hand over her mouth to muffle her cry.

I alternate between sucking on her clit and licking her before fucking her with my tongue. Her legs tremble and I gently nibble on her clit, which has her body tightening as her orgasm crests. I lower myself, and lick up her juices, humming as I do so, which has her body jerking as the vibrations prolong her orgasm.

When her body goes slack, I strip out of my clothes and help her stand, guiding her into the shower. She props her leg up on the stool I got for her and she's at just the right position, that I grab her hips and thrust into her in one motion.

She bites my shoulder to keep from screaming as I piston in and out of her, making sure to bottom out on each thrust. Her eyes roll back into her head as I feel her body spasming around me. Reaching behind her, I grab the lube that I put in here a few days ago and dribble some down her ass. Her body tenses and she looks at me hesitantly.

"Trust me, Siren. Like I said before, I won't hurt you. I'll make it feel good. If you ever want me to stop, just say the word and it stops."

She bites her lip before pulling my head down and I kiss her hard as I massage her hole while still thrusting inside of her. After a little bit, I feel her body melting against me and I push harder against her hole as I pick up my pace, thrusting hard into her pussy.

Finally, the resistance gives way and I'm able to push my finger inside to the knuckle. Her moans deepen when I start thrusting my finger in time with my cock and soon she's cuming again. Her walls clamp down hard on me, triggering my own orgasm as I flood her pussy with ropes and ropes of my cum.

After her tremors subside, she reaches up and pulls me down for another kiss. "I think that's something I'm definitely going to look forward to exploring more in the future with you."

It takes me a moment before realizing she means anal, and my dick twitches and I kiss her again. Her body relaxes even further into me and when I pull back from the kiss, I carefully turn her into the water.

Reaching behind her, I grab her body wash and carefully wash her body. As I kneel in front of her, I look up and notice her gaze has turned hooded again, but I can tell she's not going to act on it.

Every time that we've showered together, I always wash her—hair and body. And each time, it's like I'm healing a part of both of us by taking care of her like this.

With her body washed, I move her to rinse all the suds off and then turn her back to the water, running my hands through her hair to make sure it's all wet. Frowning, I pick out the few twigs and leaves that I come across, and when I've gotten the remnants of the forest out of her hair, I rinse her hair one more time.

Then we switch positions and I grab her shampoo, lathering it up and rubbing my fingers against her scalp. Her eyes close as she hums and fuck if that doesn't make me go from half a chub to full mast at the sound. However, I'm not acting on it this time.

Turning, I rinse her hair and then we repeat the process with her conditioner.

When she's clean, she leans back against the wall and I quickly wash myself. Her eyes are glued to my cock which is pointing straight up at her, but other than the cursory cleaning, I don't give into my desires again.

She pouts when I rinse off one last time and shut off the water, and I shake my head.

"Later, Siren. You need your rest and we've got three kiddos who are probably anxious as all hell since you're not in their direct line of sight."

She sobers at that, lowering her gaze immediately, and I shake my head, grasping her chin gently.

"I didn't mean that as a bad thing, Mary. We were all panicking when we couldn't find you. They just need some reassurance that you're here and that you're safe."

"I'm sorry," she whispers, almost choking on the words, and I silence her with a kiss.

"You have nothing to be sorry about, Mary. As much as I hate that the asshole got his hands on you again, I completely get it as well. I would die if anything happened to any of you and I would have done the same if I were in your shoes." I pause and give her another chaste kiss. She takes a deep breath and nods. "Let's dry off and get dressed."

Five minutes later, I've got Mary situated in bed after taking a pain pill and I head out into the living room but stop in the doorway as I take in the scene in front of me.

The kids are piled around Mateo much like they were earlier and he's reading a story to them.

Ash is the first to spot me and the others quickly take notice of my presence as well.

"Is Mom okay?"

"Yeah, Ash, she is. If you guys want to give **Tío** (Uncle) Mateo a hug, we can get him situated, and then we can all head back to bed."

The kids help me take off the couch cushions and I pull out the mattress since Mateo is still recovering himself. I had thought about letting him use one of the kids' beds, but they are all twin beds and much too small for his six-foot-something frame. At least we were able to find a decent hide-a-bed and Mary and I bought a good mattress for it for situations like this. Ash goes over to the trunk in the corner of the room and pulls out extra sheets and blankets.

In a matter of minutes, the bed is made and I get a bottle of water for Mateo in case he'll need to take another pain pill later, which I confirmed he grabbed when they were allowed to go back into the clubhouse. We bid each other good night and I herd the kids into our room.

Mary is laying back on her pillow, barely able to keep her eyes open, but she smiles as soon as she sees us and opens her arms. The kids scramble up on the bed, lying in between us and I slip under the sheets on the other side of the bed. It's a good thing we got a king-sized bed, otherwise this would have been tight.

"Is everyone comfy?" I ask and a chorus of 'yeses' answer me.

Shutting off the light, I get comfortable and reach over the kids. Mary does the same, holding my hand as we stare at each other over the top of our kids' heads.

A resounding peace finally settles over me at having her back home and the kids all safe. I'll do whatever it takes to make sure they stay safe and her so-called-family won't ever hurt her again.

With that thought, I finally drift off to sleep.

The next morning, I let Mary sleep in after everything that happened last night, but when it gets close to noon, I decide to make her a special brunch of finger foods. Cheese, crackers, grapes, sausage, with juice, coffee, and water.

Once that's ready, I carry it into our room and start a bath for her, putting in a bath bomb that Levi said will help her relax more and help sooth her sore muscles.

When the water's ready, I head back into our room and pause for a moment, just watching her sleep peacefully. She'd woken up several times during the night from nightmares, but thankfully, I was able to calm her down each time. I wished I could just hold her myself, but I think having the kids, especially Cassie with us, helped ease her nightmares a lot better.

Shaking myself, I walk over to her and lean over, kissing her forehead as I gently nudge her.

"Mary, Baby. Time to get up. You need to eat something and take some medicine. I also drew you a warm bath."

"Hmmm. That's something I could get used to." Her voice is heavy with sleep, but she smiles up at me, then she tugs my cut and I lean down, kissing her lips.

"Come on, I'll help you up. I want to take a look at your ribs, wrists, and cheek again."

She nods and I start to help her up, but when she winces, I slow down.

"Fuck, I've almost forgotten how much my ribs hurt after being kicked like that."

I bite my tongue, knowing she doesn't really want a response to that, but fuck does that make me want to hurt Stephan even more than I did last night.

Her bruising has spread even worse than it was to where her entire left side and the front middle of her stomach is black and blue. I never looked at what type of shoes Stephan was wearing, but from the size of the bruising, I'm going to guess some sort of a boot. Maybe even the same steel toes he used the night we rescued her and the kids.

After she uses the bathroom and brushes her teeth, she puts her hair up into a messy bun. Then I wrap her cast and lift her into the tub, making sure her cast rests on the towel I'd already set out. Turning on the faucet, I top off the water, making sure she's able to comfortably soak and not have to maneuver around to do it herself.

"Now, you relax, read, or whatever. I've got the kids and if for some reason Thor calls Church, Mae has already said she, Mama Astrid, and Elvira would come here. Here's your phone and your kindle. Towels are right here, along with extra ones if you need more propped under your leg or your neck. If the water gets cold, send me a text and I'll come in and top you off so you don't have to. Take as long as you like."

Kissing her forehead, I ignore the stunned and shocked look on her face. Secretly, I make a promise to myself to frequently do this, or something similar, for her. To show her she can rely on me and that she's allowed to take time for herself as well.

I shut the bathroom door behind me as well as the one leading into our room before making my way to the living room to check on the kids. Instead, I'm surprised to find my brothers, Mateo, Antonio, and Lorenzo, filling the room.

And my kids are nowhere in sight.

"The other ladies took them upstairs and they're watching a movie in Ash's room since it's the furthest down the hall," Levi says as she gives me a knowing smile.

"Thank you."

"She resting?" Antonio asks.

I nod. "I got her up, gave her some medicine and food, and she's now soaking in the tub. She's sore and stiff, but her abrasions on her wrists are healing nicely, and it looks like her cheek is as well. Her bruising on her ribs spread significantly, but other than that, they're just sore."

Everyone's face hardens and I decide just to ask the question that's been burning in my mind all morning.

"Are we keeping Stephan here and doling out justice our way, or are we handing him over?"

"I talked to Sam, and right now, I think we're going to dole out justice. Stephan is pebbles in the grand scheme of things and if he or the feds get anyone, he'd rather it be X or one of his men." Thor pauses and glances at Antonio and Mateo before turning back toward me. "I think he realizes he won't see hide nor hair of Diego, either. I talked to the others after getting your text this morning, and I think from here on out, we work jointly with Antonio and Mateo. We'll do our thing with Stephan and Derrick, but keep them alive. Ol' Leo is still hanging on as well, and maybe he'll cough up some new information when he sees us work them over, or he will when he sees us deal with Diego. Either way, we need to plan how to lure Diego to a location of our choosing."

"We could use the chip I dug out of her last night to lure him to wherever we decide as the location," I said as I tilted my head toward Smoke. "Smoke has it and he's been allowing it to continue to transmit. The thing I don't know is if they both could see where Mary was at any given time or if it was only one of them."

The others think before Mateo looks at his father. "Or we lure him out by letting the word out that you are planning to retire early. Since he thinks you think he is me, he'll come around the estate more. The only problem is he doesn't have **mi daga de oreja** (eared dagger) that's needed in order to succeed you."

Antonio looks between his sons, before settling his gaze back on Mateo. "Lorenzo and I could place ourselves strategically and let him overhear where it is. The truth is that will actually help our plan, since I am in possession of it. It is time anyway. I have been training you your entire life, especially these last few years to take over for me. I also think that when this is done, you should take your rightful place in our family as our Don."

Mateo straightens and inclines his head slightly. "**Padre** (Father), it would be my honor to lead our family forward."

"There is only one thing that I request," Antonio says as he looks around the room. "I deal the killing blow to my wife, children, and grandson." He pauses and a look of regret crosses his face. "I should have seen the man Diego was turning out to be and yet, I did not, which in turn allowed him to hurt countless victims. Plus leading his stepmother, siblings, and nephew down that path as well. Taking their lives will be my final act as Don."

Mateo and Lorenzo step forward, but it's Mateo who speaks. "**Padre** (Father), you do not need to be the one to strike the blows. I can do it. You should not have to kill your own wife, sons, and grandson."

Antonio gives them both a sad smile. "And you should not have to kill your own stepmother, brother, twin, and nephew."

I note that neither say anything about Eileen, but I don't say anything. Then I remember Antonio saying that Mary will have her retribution. My gut churns at what he could be planning, but I keep my mouth shut for now.

A hard look comes over Mateo's face. "Diego and Isaac ceased to be my blood the day they killed Nikos and kidnapped Mary. Eileen was already dead to me long before her faked death. Carmen and Carlos signed their own death warrants when they followed the others down this path and started dealing in skin. We had a sibling meeting, and we all agree. Diego, Carlos, Eileen, Isaac, and Carmen are not our blood or our family. Not anymore."

"You have always had a strong bond with Mary, which is something I have always admired. Be that as it may, it will be by my hand. No other," Antonio replies and for the first time, I see a measure of the Don coming out in him.

Both Mateo and Lorenzo dip their heads, and they turn back toward us.

"Time to plan," Mateo says.

Chapter 67

Patch

After checking on Mary and Sasha, we leave them, the kids, and the other ladies topside with a skeleton crew before heading into the clubhouse. The rest of us follow Thor down into the sticks along with Mateo. He stays silent through our checkpoints, but I do notice his look of appreciation at each step.

As I walk, I lock away the part of me that screams at me that what I'm about to do goes against my nurse's oath. However, I justify my motives by getting revenge for Mary as well as finding out more information to save more unsuspecting victims from Diego's and Oasis' reach.

Once inside, my lip curls in disgust. Like I had suspected, I can smell the growing infection in Leo's wounds. I keep giving him antibiotic shots each day and flushing out the wounds, but other than that, I don't try to stop the inevitable.

Leo's still hanging from his arms, but now, he's positioned along the longer wall and facing our new guests. Opposite of him hangs Stephan and Derrick from their wrists, their toes barely touching the ground and they've been stripped naked. Dragon and I walk over to the toy chest in silence, both picking up our weapons of choice.

"Ah, looks like the vagrants have decided to grace us with their presence," Stephan sneers and I shake my head at his antics.

He might not think it, but I can see him shaking from here, and it isn't from the cold, though we are equipped to use that technique if we wanted to. His high and mighty view of himself isn't going to gain him anything down here.

Dragon steps forward and Leo whimpers slightly when he passes behind him as he tries desperately to keep Dragon in his line of sight. His whimper makes Dragon's dark smirk deepen.

"Don't worry, Leo, ol' buddy. Today's focus is on these two scumbags, unless of course new information comes up that damns you into enduring some more time with my more treasured toys."

My lip curls again as Leo pisses himself, and for the first time, Stephan's and Derrick's armor cracks a bit as they both pale slightly.

Dragon gives me a chin lift. I walk over to him and we each take out the serrated knives that we picked out. Silently, we each walk toward the men—me to Stephan and him to Derrick.

Stephan smirks smugly at me. "So, you're the lowlife that got my wife pregnant before I could take her cherry like I was promised."

Even though it kills me and takes most of my restraint, I don't react to his taunts, knowing that's what he wants.

He hums, a semi-blissful look on his face despite what I'm doing to him. "Yes, she was always a satisfying lay because she fought me so much, especially at first."

I almost crack at that and I force myself to tune him out, otherwise I'll end up killing him before we get answers out of him.

Instead, I focus on inflicting a fair amount of pain for what he's done to Mary. With how many times I've worshipped her body by now, I know every single scar he's given her.

It takes me ten minutes of meticulous cutting, but when I step back, a sick part of me is pleased at seeing his pale face sweating. His head drops and I scoff.

"What's the matter there, Stephan? Can't take what you dish out?"

With great effort, he lifts his head to look at me better, and I'm kind of surprised he's this weak.

"Every cut I just gave you mirrors the scars you left on my Mary's body."

You could have heard a pin drop in the room at my words and even Dragon stops what he's doing and looks at me, rage filling his eyes. When he takes in all of the cuts on Stephan's body, his eyes darken even further.

And he hasn't even seen the back of his body yet.

Stephan's lip curls before he leers at me. "That fat bitch was worth taking off Diego's hands. I got to have a regular side piece to breed and do whatever the fuck I wanted to her. The more she fought, the more enjoyable it was for me. The more I hurt her, the more I got back. Not to mention, I rose in his ranks once they saw how well I made her bleed. How I broke her." The sadistic grin he gives me has my hackles rising, but he's talking so I don't hurt him further.

Yet anyway.

"Why did Diego want her taken off his hands to begin with?"

"Because E ordered him to get rid of Mary. She was getting in E's way of regaining what was hers to begin with. When Diego approached me, we discussed the contract for Mary and E laid out specific clauses that if I were to do certain things and make her bleed regularly, with proof, that she'd dish out even more to me."

Instantly, I think of the polaroids Mary mentioned.

"And what exactly did you get back for what you did to Mary?"

He looks at me like I'm crazy for asking. "Money. Power. Status. The more I did to her and to the others, the better I was taken care of by E. They made sure my bank accounts never went dry so long as I made that cunt bleed and hurt."

I'm pretty sure I know who this E character is, but I need to verify. "And who is this E person?"

He shrugs like he isn't hanging here, naked and carved up. Like he doesn't have a care in the world. Honestly, I'm surprised I haven't had to do more to get him to loosen up and talk.

"I never met them," he says. "We only talked via secure email or a secure line, and they spoke with a voice scrambler."

I frown at that. It sounds a lot like that voicemail Mary got. Deciding to play devil's advocate, I cross my arms across my chest. "So, who's to say that you really are getting the power that you wanted if you never met this E person? They could be selling you an illusion to use as a scapegoat. Kind of like what's happening here."

Stephan gives me a confused look, as if he's never thought of that before. From what Mary's told me before, he really isn't that smart, so it wouldn't be a hard stretch to think he'd never be double crossed.

Then he gives me an incredulous look. "You're lying. I know I got power because I kept getting better positions. Diego kept giving me more and more jobs. Jobs that he'd usually have his trusted men do in the past, which meant he trusted me."

I decide to play along. Maybe we'll get something useful out of him. "So, what jobs did Diego give you?"

A sick gleam sparks in his eyes and it makes my stomach churn.

"Most recently, it was fulfilling orders for X to send to his team of Masters who break and train the product. In exchange, I got to take part in some of their sessions, both at the homesteads and in Diego's clubs."

"And before that?"

"Taking care of people that got in Diego's or E's way. Those that crossed them. Those who wouldn't bend to them. I also helped them move their product around. Brought them people that no one would miss."

He shrugs again like it's no big deal. No doubt there were many innocents in that lot who just didn't want to give up everything they've worked for their entire lives. Or just happened to be in the wrong place at the wrong time.

"Who ordered you to come here last night?"

He smirks but doesn't say anything.

"Suit yourself."

Walking back over to the toy chest, I make a show of pulling out various tools and setting them on a table for him to see.

Crowbar. Pliers. Acetylene torch. Barbed whip. Boards filled with rusty nails with the pointy sides up. A couple of leather bondage cuffs, which are not of the fun variety. No, Dragon modified these so that the cuffs have barbs and pointy metal spikes that will bite into your skin with every movement.

However, first, I grab the pliers and walk back to Stephan. Giving Dragon a signal, he lowers Stephan's arms but then immediately spreads them out so they are straight out at the shoulder. Gripping one of his hands, I clamp the pliers down on his nail and yank hard. Once again, Stephan's cries fill the air as I rip each of his nails out, one by one.

When I'm done, I switch out the pliers for a different sort of punishment. Picking up the boards, a spreader bar, and two of the cuffs, I walk back over to Stephan but stop in front of him. Dragon goes over to the controls and lowers Stephan to the ground so that his feet are flat on it. Then Ryder steps forward and he and Dragon each take hold of one of Stephan's calves, preventing him from kicking one of us or moving too much.

Ignoring Stephan's protests, I lay the boards on the ground. Kneeling down, Dragon lifts his leg and I slide the first board under Stephan's foot, making sure the straps securing the board to his toes and feet and are just a smidge too tight. Then I do the same to the other foot. Around each ankle, I strap the modified cuffs, but unlike with the boards, I don't strap them in too tight. I don't want them to dig in so deep that we risk nicking an artery.

Once the cuffs are secure, I connect a spreader bar to each cuff so that he can't close his legs. Standing, I walk over to a contraption that Smithy had made for us and wheel it over to Stephan. I stop it right in front of him, locking the wheels in place. So that it won't tip with movement, I secure it to the floor, attaching metal chains that connect to eyebolts that are drilled into the cement. When I have the table secure, Ryder comes up to me and I look over my shoulder, seeing Dragon at the controls. Giving him a nod, both Ryder and I grab one of Stephan's arms.

As soon as there's slack in the chains, Stephan tries to wrestle his arms out of our hands. Giving him a dark look, I lift my foot, settling my boot on the top of one of Stephan's feet before applying pressure, pushing his feet into the rusty nails. He cries out in pain, momentarily stopping his fight against us which allows us to secure his arms in the metal bracelets as Levi calls them. Half of the bracelets are welded secure to the table. The other half, clamps down onto the station section, securing someone firmly to the table by their wrists and a portion forearms.

Stepping back, I grab the crowbar off the other table and circle around Stephan while the others step back. He's whimpering even more than before from the pressure his body is putting on the rusty nails that are biting into his feet and the barbs biting into his ankles.

"Last chance, Stephan, who ordered you to come here last night and kidnap Mary."

Sweat drips down his temple as his face tightens with pain, yet still, he says nothing.

Without warning, I bring the crowbar down on his right forearm, twice, breaking it in the same spots that he broke Mary's arm. The injury that sent her to the ER for the first time here in Forest Creek. That day was the first time I'd seen my Siren in person in nine years.

I steer clear of his ribs, not wanting to take the chance that I could puncture a lung if I hit him just right. Then I go to his left leg, breaking it where he'd done the same to her on Thanksgiving night.

For a moment, my mind wanders, and I wish I had the ability to heal him so I could keep breaking his bones over and over again. But that's the stuff of fairytales, so this will have to do.

The howls he cries out have Leo and Derrick wincing in pain, but my brothers and sister don't even flinch as I hit him a few more times.

Setting down the crowbar, I grab the acetylene torch and make a show of adjusting the flame before bringing the flame to Stephan's chest and slowly drag it over his body. He cries out as it passes over his sensitive nipples, but since he isn't giving us any information, I continue, burning sections of his chest and arms. Then, I move on, circling him and burning sections of his back, legs, ass, before moving to his front again. This time, I move even slower as I burn a trail over his thigh as I head toward his dick.

When I'm an inch from his dick, he finally talks.

"D-Diego. Diego ordered us. I h-had to get Mary back o-otherwise he was going to k-kill me."

"See, that wasn't so hard." I grin darkly when he looks up at me, tears are spilling out of his eyes.

"Why does he need her back?"

"H-He's got another buyer all lined up for her. I was limited w-with what I could do to Mary because she'd have to go to a regular h-hospital when I fulfilled the clauses of my a-agreement with E. But this g-guy is a whole new level. He has his own d-doctors on call and won't be l-limited like I was. Though, to f-fulfill Diego's own agreement with X, X gets one m-month with M-Mary before Diego ships her off to her new owner."

Rage fills me and my vision narrows. Its only Thor's hand on my shoulder that stops me from beating Stephan to a bloody pulp right then and there.

"Who's her new owner?" Thor asks, but Stephan shakes his head back and forth.

"I-I don't know. I swear—I d-don't know. A-After she was shipped off, we were going to s-stage an accident to ensure Mary would become a g-ghost. Then,

I was s-supposed to play the d-dutiful widow before taking a new wife, another w-woman who E said needed to be b-broken in for her upcoming role."

"What else can you tell us about this E person?"

"J-Just that they are insanely p-powerful in this region. Even D-Diego answers to them. And rich. Filthy rich. They've got c-clubs all along the G-Great Lakes for their legit and illegal activities."

Thor and I share an uneasy glance at that.

Shit.

Diego's not the one really pulling the strings? I thought Diego owned those clubs. Or are these clubs in addition to the ones that Diego owns?

A grunt has us looking over at Derrick and at some point, Dragon had gone back to cutting into him.

"And where do you fit into all this?" I ask him as I stop in front of him.

His face is pale but he gives me nothing. No reaction at all.

"Dragon, I think you can have a little fun with both of them before Mateo takes over with this one."

Derrick's eyes widen a fraction as Dragon's dark grin turns almost feral as his beast nears the surface even more than it had been before.

Without a word, Dragon walks over to the wall and grabs his go-to weapon when he's allowed to fully unleash. A barbed whip that he made himself.

He walks in front of all three men, and Leo and Stephan both let out whimpers when they see it. Derrick, on the other hand, doesn't look at it. He keeps staring ahead.

Dragon walks behind them, and all three flinch when they hear the barbs hit the floor. One after the other, Dragon whips Stephan's back, and then Derrick's back before repeating the process.

After nine strikes each, he coils his whip and walks around them, letting them see their blood dripping off the barbs.

Mateo grabs a knife from the toy chest before walking over to Derrick.

As he walks, the air in the room starts to feel stifling, and I realize Mateo's changing into Don Mateo with each step. Well, he hasn't been named the Don yet, but he will be soon.

For a moment, he just stares into Derrick's eyes and finally, Derrick lowers his gaze, swallowing thickly. With the tip of the knife, Mateo makes Derrick look up at him.

"Why did you betray **mi familia** (my family)? Go against the orders of **mi familia** (mi family)? You know why we don't deal in skin."

"Because I'm in love with her. I love her and I'd do anything she asked."

We all freeze at that and for a second, a look of shock crosses Mateo's face before his Don persona is back. He lowers the knife and draws it across the Vasquez family crest that Derrick has tattooed on his chest. He had asked Dragon ahead of time not to touch the tattoo so that he could handle his family business. A whimper escapes Derrick, but he quickly covers it.

"Who?"

"Carmen."

Bile rises in my throat at the thought of their relationship and what she's putting Antonio through. A murderous look comes over Mateo before he makes another slice across the tattoo.

"So, you disgrace your Don by bedding his wife?" he grits out through clenched teeth, even though I know he has never liked Carmen.

"He knew I was in love with her and still he pursued a relationship with her, eventually marrying her. She was having his babies when she should have been having mine," he snarls.

Mateo scoffs before drawing another line across Derrick's chest. "And yet still you love her?"

"Always. A few years ago, after Eileen had disappeared and turned into a ghost, Carmen came to me and said she realized what an awful mistake she'd made in choosing Antonio over me. However, the Vasquez family does not divorce. So, we started seeing each other on the side, spending as much time together as we possibly could."

"So why were you with Stephan the other night?"

"Because Carmen asked me to make sure Stephan got the job done right this time. Her and E were tired of Mary causing a shit ton of problems for the family and for not giving into their demands to return what she'd stolen."

"Who is E?"

He shrugs. "I've only ever heard them over the phone, and like Stephan said, they used a voice scrambler. "

"What do they think Mary stole from my family?"

"Eileen's eared dagger and being the heiress to Heritage Roots. Also, Eileen doesn't consider Mary her child because of what she's done, so she wants Mary's eared dagger as well. She wants to destroy it. As for her dagger, Eileen needs it to prove her connection to the Vasquez family, otherwise she's not able to marry her intended."

I frown at that. Well, at least that's one part confirmed. But what's Heritage Roots?

Mateo's nostrils flare, the only sign that he's getting even more pissed off. "Who is Eileen's intended? And why does Eileen think that she deserves to be the heiress to Heritage Roots? Heiress to la **compañía de mi madre** (my mother's company)?"

Oh, so that's the company Lucia had meant in her note. Fuck, I knew there was something I was forgetting to follow up on. Looking over my shoulder, Smoke inclines his head toward me. I'll talk to him later about the company.

"I don't know who her intended is. As for the company, it's because she's the only one in the family who hasn't been allowed to work for the family. Her and Carmen both think Lucia wormed her way into Antonio's graces and that's why he gave it to her after Esmeralda's death. It should have been offered to Eileen. Carmen's been trying to convince Antonio to give Eileen another chance, but he isn't budging."

Mateo growls as he digs the blade deeper into Derrick's shoulder. "That's because Eileen lost her place in the family for what she'd done to Mary and Nikos. Her own daughter and husband. She disgraced our family and was told she needed to earn her place back. So far, she has not. You don't know the depths of what Eileen did to them both, but I do. Her punishment was justified. She starved and beat her own child repeatedly. She sold her child to a known womanizer and abuser who beat her to a bloody pulp multiple times. Forced himself on her countless times. Eileen should have been thankful that she wasn't banished to the old country and forced to live in a hut and sustain herself instead, with no contact to the outside world. Forced to live out her years in poverty."

Derrick curls his lip. "And I know what Eileen has been through. Shunned by your family since birth because she wasn't the perfect and precious Esmeralda's daughter. She wasn't seen as worth knowing. She had to prove over and over again that she belonged in the family and you, your father, and your siblings ignored her. Each and every time. When she tried to follow in your family's true footsteps, she was shamed even more and was forced to marry a man she loathed instead of the one she loved. Forced to have a child, even though she hated children. You and your siblings should have been the ones shunned for what you've done to her."

Mato scowls at him. "Seems **mi hermanita** (my younger sister) has been continuing her manipulating ways. Doing everything she can to worm her way into the family by any means necessary. Contrary to what you think, I know **mi hermana** (my sister) very well, and the garbage you just spewed is just that. Garbage.

"But don't worry. We'll keep you on ice and you can see for yourself how much she's lied to you and everyone throughout her pitiful life. However, you're done. You signed your death warrant when you first bedded my stepmother, your Don's wife. He will take great pleasure in dealing the final blow, but for now, I'll take care of the rest."

With that, Mateo slices through Derrick's skin, ignoring his cries and pleas as he shaves off the family crest tattoo and drops it, bit by bit, onto the plastic covering the floor underneath all three of them.

Mateo steps back as he and Thor share a look. Thor gives me the signal and I go to my bag that I brought with me and pull out two sets of three syringes as well as one more. I give each of the men a shot of antibiotics and then a sedative. The last one is tetanus shot for Stephan.

Those of us that had a hand with things shuck off our boots and head to the locker room to shower and clean up.

Ten minutes later, Dragon, Ryder, Mateo, and I emerge from the locker room and slip into our boots that someone cleaned up for us before trudging upstairs to Church. As we take our seats, Thor bangs his hammer on the table.

"What the fuck is this Heritage Roots thing?"

Even though Thor's looking at Smoke, Mateo's the one who raps his knuckles on the table and answers. "It is a cooking and cookware company that **mi madre** (my mother) started not long after marrying **mi padre** (my father). I think what they want, besides the money, is the distribution network that comes along with it. Products made at the company are shipped around the US as well as to some international locations."

"Fuck," I groan, as I scrub my face and Mateo nods.

"They haven't succeeded in using the rest of the distribution networks of **nuestra familia** (our family), so they're trying to gain the next best thing. Heritage Roots."

Thor frowns. "Do you think this E person could be Eileen?"

Mateo shrugs. "That's my guess. The things they kept saying is similar to the notes, letters, and voicemails you've been receiving. It also makes sense. If Eileen is trying to wed another within the other mafia families, she will need her **daga de oreja** (eared dagger) for the ceremony, otherwise they will not accept her."

"So, is there some special thing that this dagger is used for besides showing you're worthy of representing the family?" Phoenix asks, and Mateo nods.

"The main purpose of the **daga de oreja** (eared dagger) is to show that the family deems you as worthy of representing the Vasquez family name. That the family deems you as trustworthy, backs your decisions, that they believe you are capable of acting on the family's behalf and that you are loyal. While those deemed worthy also wear our family's crest on a ring as an easier show of our place in the family, the **daga de oreja** (eared dagger) is used in special ceremonies, and weddings are one of them.

"Since you may not know, I will give you an overview seeing how we are now **familia** (family). If the wedding is between two mafia families, then first there are meetings between the heads of the families to tie them together, regardless of if it is an arranged marriage or not. Sometimes the exchange happens in private, and others are during a public wedding.

"Presenting our **daga de oreja** (eared dagger), which is part of our family's crest, to the head of our intended's family is a sign of respect. It shows the head of the family that the person presenting the dagger is giving them their loyalty as well. They are swearing to uphold their family's ways as well as carrying on their own family ways. Then, as a sign of them accepting you, they tie silk ribbons of their family's colors onto the hilt of the **daga de oreja** and pass it back to the owner. If Eileen is trying to marry into another mafia family, they will not deem her trustworthy without the **daga de oreja**. Even more so because she also is no longer allowed to wear the family ring either. When **Padre** (Father) took back her **daga de oreja**, he also took back her ring."

I shake my head. All this hurt and hatred toward Mary could have been avoided if Eileen could have acted like a decent human being in the first place and not lost her place in the family.

"Alright, Patch, Mary and the kids are on partial lockdown still. We don't know who this other buyer is that Stephan mentioned. We also need to keep tabs on whether X comes sniffing back around since he also wants Mary," Thor says before turning toward Timber. "Might not be a bad idea to limit Mae going into town either, since X could also still want to get his hands on Mae."

Timber and I share a look that promises no one will hurt our women.

Thor straightens and levels a hard look to everyone. "Stay alert. No one rides alone. We'll get back together when we know more about what the fuck's going on."

He bangs his hammer on the table and everyone stands. I'm slow to rise as I mull over everything, trying to figure out what we're missing.

There has to be a clue somewhere in all this mess to give us a leg up on who wants Mary.

Chapter 68

Mary

I've been a nervous wreck for the past week.

Patch has been somewhat distant, but I think, or at least I hope, it's because something is coming. I can feel it and I'm scared of what might happen.

We got lucky last week and in the light of day we saw the fire didn't damage too much of the clubhouse. Unfortunately, Timber did have to wait a few days for the snow to stop falling before he could start in on the repairs. The help from the extra guys from Junction Creek definitely sped up the repairs. Two days ago, Reaper, Razor, Punisher, Odin, and Mama Astrid went back home, but Beast and Python stayed. Later that afternoon, Devil, Loki, Smithy, Cannon, Atlas, and Doc came down to continue offering support.

I was saddened when Mama Astrid announced that she and Odin had to head back home, but I also got it. They'd been away from home for a while, and Odin needed to get back in the garage to help finish up some orders. The others needed to get back to their jobs as well, but now that I think about it, Reaper was rather distracted the last few days he was here. However, I don't know if it was because of what's going on here or something else.

On top of all of that, I've read snippets the past couple of days in the news and gossip websites that people are speculating that **Abuelo** (Grandpa) is retiring, and I'm wondering if this is their plan to lure Diego out. There's been no word from him, at least that I've heard anyway, since the note last week after my doctor's appointment.

Shaking my head, I look back down at my kindle, trying to focus on the words in front of me, but I can't. Something is strung tight in me and it feels like it's about to snap.

"You look like you're deep in thought."

I jump in surprise, not having heard anyone approaching and when Mae sits down on the couch next to me, I can't help my sigh.

"Did you feel like this before they found you know who?" I ask quietly, not wanting to name any names, but she nods, knowing who I'm referring to.

"Yeah, I did. I hated the fact that Levi was privy to those details, but after I thought on it more, I also realized I could never do what she does and be a full member. I don't have what it takes to do that. It was a sobering moment when I realized that, and it helped me step back a bit and look at things from a different light. They'll tell you more when they can, but ultimately, they're trying to protect you, too."

"But did Timber ever become distant with you?"

Understanding lights in her eyes and she nods. "Yeah, and it almost cost me him as well. Don't do what I did and wait. Talk to him instead and let him know how you are feeling. He might not even realize he's pulling away from you. My guess is it's because they're planning something big, which is taking up most of his time and energy. And use your journals. It helps to get it all out, even if it's just on paper."

Gnawing on my lip, I nod and my gaze goes over her to the closed Church door. Resolve fills me, and I decide that tonight, I'm confronting him.

Snapping my kindle case shut, I nudge her shoulder. "Come on. I'm finally feeling good enough that I think I can manage sitting on the kitchen barstools. Let's break out my cookbooks and plan a meal."

Mae's face lights up and she helps me get up off the couch. We've both been pouring over my cookbooks ever since I got them and trying to figure out which ones we want to try first.

I follow behind Mae in my chair to the kitchen. In two-and-a-half weeks, I have my next doctor's appointment and I hope like hell that I can get this cast off and graduate to a walking boot. I'm tired of having my ass in this chair. Not to mention, I also miss running around after my kids and playing with them. I can't even go out and build a snowman with them. Well, if we were allowed to play outside, that is. We're still on semi-lockdown and have been since they caught Stephan.

"Okay, Spanish or Greek?" Mae asks and I shake my head to clear my thoughts as I refocus.

"I need some comfort food, so Greek." I'm still learning the Spanish recipes in **de mi abuela** (my grandma's) cookbook, so today, I'd like to just get lost in the familiar food that I know.

We end up choosing to make some Greek chicken gyros with yogurt sauce, a moussaka, and a salad so that there's a couple of options for the guys. Another plus is that we have all the ingredients on hand. It takes a lot to feed all of these large men, and we often go three or four times a week to the grocery stores around town. I swear the local businesses are racking in big bucks from us food-wise with how much we buy. Especially when I hit up the mom-and-pop specialty stores where I get most of my Greek and unique Spanish ingredients from.

We get to work prepping everything and the first is to marinade the chicken for the gyros since that needs to sit for a while. I prefer to do a marinade overnight, but we've got enough time to do a three-hour marinade, which is the bare minimum that I would do.

Time passes as Mae and I work, and as my hands work through the familiar steps, my mind wanders to Patch. I really hope the distance between us is about them planning everything and that it's nothing to be worried or concerned about.

Right as we finish prepping the other ingredients and are about to start cooking, the door to Church opens and the guys all file out. My brows dip in confusion when they start to head outside. Mae and I share a look and we head out into the main room.

Patch spots us and a guilty look crosses his face that immediately has my eyes narrowing at him. Next to him Timber and a few others stop as well, and Timber has a similar, though not as guilty look on his face.

"Where are you guys all going? We were just about to start cooking dinner."

Gone is any light heartedness in my voice. Something's up and I'm pissed we weren't told what's going on.

"They didn't tell you?" Levi asks and my eyes narrow even more at Patch.

"No."

Levi gives them a look that has both Patch's and Timber's faces paling.

"We're going out tonight. We're not going to be here for supper."

"That would have been nice to know so that we wouldn't have just wasted two hours prepping dinner for everyone."

"I'm sorry, Mary. I forgot to tell you." He gives me a small smile, but it does nothing to ease how I'm feeling, and I can't help the huff that escapes.

"Forgot or just conveniently ignored me like you have been for the past week?" I seethe and at least he has the decency to look guilty.

"I'm sorry, Mary. We've been planning a huge takedown that needs to happen tonight before Mateo's brought on as the next Don."

I rear back like I've been slapped. "And who all is invited to the ceremony?" Or at least I'm assuming it's some sort of ceremony. I have no idea how a succession is done in our family.

Somehow, Patch's face pales even further and Levi gives me a sympathetic look but all that does is fuel my anger.

"Is the rest of my family going to be there except for me? Am I the only one who doesn't get to witness my own uncle stepping up and becoming the next leader of the family? You all are going to be there and I can't be there to support my own family?"

Silence meets my words, and it's more than I can take.

Backing up my chair, I turn around and head to the lift. Mae can put the food away and we'll cook it tomorrow. Maybe we'll just order a pizza tonight or something. Right now, I just need to get away from Patch and the others before I say something I'm going to regret.

I thought they cared.

That they saw me as family, like I did them, but maybe it was all an act.

My mind is whirling as I press the button on the lift for the third floor. Swallowing down my tears, I try to box up my emotions. To appear calm and in control, but then I catch my reflection in the lift walls. I look like shit and I doubt I'll fool anyone.

When the door opens, I head down the hallway toward the room we're using as the playroom until the repairs on the other one are finished.

The sound of engines starting has my chest tightening and my eyes burn as the emotions roll over me again. Opening the door to the playroom, Elvira gives me a startled look, but I wave her off, plastering a smile on my face that I hope the kids won't see through.

It doesn't work.

All four of them, Lindsey included, look up at me with worry, but I wave it off, saying it's just the stress of everything that's getting to me.

A few minutes later, Mae comes up and joins me, but I can't look at her. I feel like I'm a fake. That I'm an outsider. That when they come back, they'll tell me to get out and take my kids with me.

Biting back another sob, I force myself to take comfort in the feeling of my kids cuddled up next to me and watch the movie with them.

As the night wears on, the men don't return and I start to get nervous.

Despite how they left, I'm still worried about them and I don't want them to get hurt. Patch mentioned they were planning something big. Did something go wrong?

Suddenly I feel like I'm being watched and I look out the window, but I don't see anything.

When bedtime rolls around, the kids ask to do another sleepover with Elvira and Lindsey, and since I don't know if we'll still be here tomorrow, I allow it even though I'd rather be snuggled up in bed with them.

Heading to Patch's room here in the clubhouse, I go about my nightly routine to get ready and slip under the covers. I had thought about finding an empty room to sleep in, but I want to talk to him when he comes back. To find out why he cut me out like he has.

I close my eyes, but sleep doesn't come to me and I toss and turn all night.

For the umpteenth time, I look at the clock on the nightstand. It's 2 am. Only ten minutes from when I last checked it.

I huff out a breath and rub my grainy eyes. I can't believe how used to sleeping in Patch's arms I've become. The clubhouse is quiet tonight since there's only a skeleton crew here and the bunnies were told to stay in their rooms. Every creak of the clubhouse or the hoot of an owl has me jerking back awake thinking that the guys are coming back.

Another creak outside the door has me pausing, but when I don't hear any other noises, I realize it must have just been the building settling as the night grows colder. With another huff, I snag Patch's pillow and bury my face in it, hoping his scent will help me relax.

That thought has me biting back another sob. I'll probably need to start getting used to sleeping alone again, but tonight I'm going to take the comfort. With my face buried in the pillow, I ignore another creek somewhere in the clubhouse and groan as I will myself to sleep.

The sound of voices has me slowly blinking out of my sleep. My head pounds and I groan. What happened? My eyes are crusty from falling asleep as I was crying, and I move to wipe them, but I realize I can't move my arms and my eyes fly open.

I'm not in Luke's bed.

Or the bed at our condo.

In front of me are cinderblock walls and I can feel the rough texture of cement chaffing my bare skin and my body through Luke's shirt that I'd slipped on last night.

Slamming my eyes shut again, I try to slow down my breathing as I listen, but the voices are too muted to be able to tell who it is.

Even though it makes the pounding worse, I try to remember what happened. The fight with Luke, which I don't think I'll ever be able to forget. Watching movies with the kids. Then trying to fall asleep, but not being able to. That I kept hearing numerous creaks last night, which I thought was just like the sounds an old house makes when it settles with age.

Shit.

What if all that creaking was Diego's men creeping around the clubhouse?

Voices once again draw closer and black dots dance behind my eyes as I try to force my body to calm down.

A door opens and I cry out when a pointy boot nails me in the side. The same side that's still healing from when Stephan kicked me.

I roll away, trying to protect my sore side and belly, but I don't get too far because something metal is attached to my ankle. I squint as I try to see better since I don't have my glasses, and I swallow down bile when I realized I'm chained to a wall.

The sound of boots on the concrete has me looking toward the sound, but without my glasses, it's all a blur. However, I think they're women's boots since they kind of sound like high heels. The person crouches down and my eyes widen when I can finally see who's in front of me.

"Hello, Pet."

Oh, shit.

Chapter 69

Patch

MARY'S DEVASTATED FACE CUTS me clean through before she turns and heads further into the clubhouse. I stare after her and I can feel my heart being squeezed like a vice.

"How dare you keep Mary from her family like this!" Mae damn near yells as she glares at me and pokes me hard in the chest.

Quickly, I glance around, but there's no one else out here but us. At least that I can see.

"Mae, you don't know what we're planning or the decisions that were made," I tell her but that just seems to make her angrier.

"Futtenfarter! You have no idea what you just implied, do you?"

I go to answer her, but she just continues her rant, cutting me off.

"You just insinuated that you had more right to her family than she did. Her own flesh and blood. How could you?"

"Sunshine, there are things at play here that you don't understand," Timber starts but the glare she shoots him stops him short.

"Don't you 'Sunshine' me. You guys promised you wouldn't do what you did to Levi with the whole mess with Dragon's ex to anyone else, but here you are doing it again. And this time, Levi's in on it, too!"

Shame rolls through me at her words because she's right. Several of us, myself and Levi included, voiced that today as well. Ultimately, it came down to the fact that Antonio and her uncles didn't want to put more on Mary and would rather risk her wrath by keeping her safe.

"You all should be ashamed of yourself for how you're treating that poor girl." She pauses, her chest heaving as she levels her glare at me again. "And you best hope that when you come back, she's even willing to listen to whatever excuses you've all come up with to keep her away from her family."

Ice slides down my spine as my worry intensifies.

"I get you're trying to protect her from whatever your plan entails, but the way you're going about it is wrong and you know it. You've kept her at arm's length all week and she's feeling the pain of it. Do you have any idea how much it hurts to be cut out by the person you love and the family you've come to love?"

I freeze and I wonder if Timber's said anything to Mae about our plans, but his confused look has me thinking either Mae's somehow guessed what our plan was regarding Mary or if she's thinking this is some male macho protector bullshit we're pulling.

She spins on her heel and stalks back into the kitchen, fuming and muttering curses the entire way.

At the main door, I once again look back, hoping to see Mary, but Mae is the only one in the kitchen, angrily putting all their supplies away.

As the door shuts behind me, I can't help but thinking, yet again, that we're making a major mistake.

It's after midnight and we've been sitting here for hours overlooking the abandoned warehouse from our perch up by the control room, but there's no movement whatsoever.

I don't have a good feeling about this.

Again.

On top of that, I'm still torn up about how things went with Mary earlier. Her devastated face when she thought we were keeping her from her family downright killed me. Not to mention what Mae said right afterward.

I only said that last part about Mateo becoming the next Don for the ears we thought were listening in on us. Since last week, we've been having people walking the perimeter more in hopes of preventing a repeat, and Ethan had come to us earlier today saying he'd seen someone's footprints. Smaller footprints that he thought were most likely a woman's.

The information spurred us into changing our plan a bit, and Smoke ran through the security footage again with a fine-tooth comb, looking for any clues, but he came up dry. Either the person is like a fucking ghost, or they're messing with our cameras.

Shaking my head, I look around the warehouse with another sigh.

Down below, Antonio and Lorenzo are standing close to each other, where if someone was looking in on them, it would look like they were just quietly conversing as they waited for someone to show up. Antonio's even got his jacket pulled back to show a bit of Mateo's eared dagger he's carrying. Something we know Diego is desperately wanting. Around the room, their guards are standing in position like they normally would in a similar scenario.

A few feet away from me, Mateo catches my eye and frowns as he shakes his head, pointing to his watch, and I nod.

For some reason, Diego isn't taking our bait, even though we'd left enough clues that it should have enticed him to come here.

A phone pings, and I look back toward Antonio and Lorenzo. The rest of our phones are on silent, so it's either one of theirs or their guards.

Antonio curses and when his gaze meets mine, my blood runs cold.

Mary.

Instantly I'm on my feet and hurrying as fast as I can down the stairs to him. "What's happened? What's wrong?" I bark as I cross the room to him.

Instead of answering me, he turns his phone toward me.

> *You think you're so clever with your little trap, but you don't realize that I was already ten steps ahead of you. If you want her back, you'll give me back what's rightfully mine and step down to make way for a new leader of the family. Me. Once I have what should have been mine, then you can have your pathetic Rosebud back.*

The phone pings again and this time it's a picture of Mary unconscious and her good ankle is chained to a wall.

My chest heaves as I take in Mary's prone figure, sprawled on the cement floor. She's wearing my t-shirt and some shorts, which has a bit of hope spurring in my chest that I haven't royally fucked things up with her.

I look up at the sound of someone crossing the room to see Thor and Smoke approaching us. "What's happened?"

Antonio shows them his phone and Smoke pulls out his laptop, getting to work.

"How the fuck did they get into the clubhouse? And get her out?" Thor grits out.

My stomach churns the more Smoke's frown deepens.

"Whoever it is, is dressed entirely in black with a mask and everything. Seems they've been watching our patrols carefully. They slipped in the back and used the lift. I can't see if they did anything or drugged her when they got into your room," he pauses as he looks up at me, "which they somehow knew exactly which one was yours. They're only in there for a matter of minutes before they come out with Mary slung over their shoulder and leaves the way they came in. From the outside cameras, they headed south this time toward the edge of our property and disappeared."

"The kids. Are they safe?"

He nods as his fingers fly over the keyboard. "Yes, they are." After a few moments, his brow furrows in confusion. "Uh, Antonio and Mateo, you aren't going to believe this."

He turns his laptop around and on one side of the screen is an aerial shot with a red dot in the middle of a grouping of trees. On the other is a street map.

Wait.

I turn toward Antonio and Mateo and see anger etched on both their faces.

"They took her to my house," Antonio growls, which is immediately followed by a stream of Spanish curses.

Ten minutes away.

That said, how long have they had Mary?

And what have they done to her since getting their hands on her?

"Then we have to assume they took control or neutralized your men," Thor says.

Antonio's face hardens. "Most likely. Or at least some of them, anyway. By the location of her tracker, I believe she's in one of the cells. Smoke, use the access I gave you and tap into our cameras. I think I know what he did."

Smoke takes back his computer as he gets to work, and Antonio shares a look with Mateo before looking at each of us.

"My guess is that Diego somehow snuck into his section of the estate. That shouldn't have been possible, though, unless he got to more of my guards. The tunnels that lead to the cells are linked to our panic rooms. I say rooms, but they are more like multiple control areas, and they are linked to the other panic areas as well as a storage area and the cells. All of it is underground. In his section of the estate, there are two ways to get inside. If I'm not mistaken, that location her tracker is pinging from is by the northern entrance."

Smoke nods. "Correct. Either your man watching your cameras is just an unlucky SOB who is just barely missing seeing them, or he's being paid off by Diego. He darted six of your men and he's got them all locked up not too far from Mary.

"Bad news is that Cici and Claudia are bound and gagged in the cell next to Mary's. Even worse is that I can also see Eileen and Carmen down there with him. Leon's there as well. There's also another person with them, but they are sticking to the shadows. I can't see his or her face."

"Are Carlos and Isaac with them?"

Smoke scans the screens. "I don't think so unless they are hiding somewhere or in a room that doesn't have cameras."

"What about their men? Anyone guarding the exits?"

"As of right now, there's two men outside of the rear entrance, which is where Diego broke in. Four are guarding the entrance into the tunnels. Then there are three outside of where Diego and the others are, however I think one of them isn't one of Diego's men."

I frown. "What makes you say that?"

"Well, for one, this guy is actually paying attention. Two, he's dressed differently and carries himself differently. More refined. And three, he's not waving a gun around like a fucking toddler."

Antonio and Mateo, almost in unison, step around behind Smoke and they both shake their heads.

"He is not one of ours, but I think I know whose he is. And if he's who I think he is, then we've got a wild card on our hands that could help us."

"Do you think she's still helping the feds?" Mateo asks and Antonio's lips purse in a tight line before giving a curt nod.

"Last I heard, she was, but I do not know how much longer she will be able to last the way she's going without her father realizing what she's doing."

"Will you two stop talking in fucking riddles?!" I growl, getting extremely frustrated that we aren't planning on how to get Mary back from them without the three of them slipping away again. "Who is this mysterious person? And who is their father?"

Antonio gives me a sharp look as he straightens, but I'm not on his fucking payroll. What matters is Mary, and after a moment, I think he realizes that as well as he gives me a curt, sharp nod.

"Alexis Sanchez. The daughter of the infamous Alejandro Sanchez."

I stumble back as bile rises in my throat at what CJ mentioned he liked to do to his new 'pets'. "Is he Mary's new owner that Stephan mentioned?" I ask no one in particular, but so far, that's all I can think of.

Mateo clasps my shoulder. "He may very well be, but if Alexis is still working against Alejandro, that can turn in our favor. Especially since I'm sure you already know of Carolina's true whereabouts when her brothers sold her."

I narrow my eyes at him. We never told him any of that shit.

"What? Do you think I'm not going to look into the club that my favorite niece will be tying herself to in the near future? Relax. Other than Cici not knowing her foster brother's true intentions and accidentally spilling some of your secrets when she confronted him, you have no moles."

"And when the fuck were you going to tell us about this shit with Cici?" Thor roars as he gets up in Mateo's face.

For his credit, Mateo doesn't even blink or flinch as Thor stares him down.

"Relax, Thor. I found out an hour ago when my man who I had trailing her texted me. However, since we were here and waiting, I couldn't very well tell you all, now, could I? My man tried following this Leon character, but he lost him in traffic."

Exhaling slowly, I try to focus my mind like I would before starting a shift at the hospital. After a few moments, I feel a bit more in control of my emotions. I cannot go off half-cocked right now. If I do, I could put Mary in even greater danger.

Looking up at Thor, Phoenix, Devil, Smoke, Mateo, and then Antonio, I nod.

"Let's make a plan. I am not losing my woman again."

Chapter 70

Mary

Coming face to face with Eileen after all these years is a shock I wasn't expecting.

Especially since it doesn't look like time has done her many favors, though I can tell she's trying desperately to hide it under her fancy clothes and layers of makeup. She still bleaches her hair too much, and I'm pretty sure I can see some of her shapewear peaking out from under her low-cut blouse when she bends over. She also looks like she's been on the run for a while and hasn't coped very well without her expensive health care regime. Regimes I've had to suffer through hearing about over and over in the past before she'd try to push them on me to try out in an attempt to help me lose weight.

"What? No hello for Mummy?" she fake pouts and then fucking cackles.

"Nope, but it definitely looks like you need to soak in a shit ton of those seaweed wraps you love so much. I'd much rather handle dealing with a real mummy than you any day of the week," I sneer.

God, how I hate this woman!

I was perfectly content with never seeing her again, and yet here we are and she's still making my life a living hell. Just like she used to. All because I know where her precious dagger is and **Tía** (Aunt) Lucia named me as her beneficiary for Heritage Roots, which still boggles my mind.

Eileen huffs and I can see her breath in the air. Do they not heat this area? I knew it was cold, but I didn't realize it was that cold. With how I'm dressed, I'll be freezing in no time. Though, at least this time I'm not wet. At least not yet, anyway.

I was expecting the slap, but I hadn't realized how much fucking hardware she was wearing on her hand. Fuck, I think she just tore my cheek to shreds with all the rings she's wearing.

"I see you still haven't learned any fucking manners, but what was I to expect when you went to stay with those pathetic excuses of human beings?"

I cock my eyebrow at her. "Huh, and yet here you are, my own fucking mother, and you're treating me worse than they ever have." *Except for tonight,* I can't help but think, but I push that thought away. I can't show her weakness. "Hell, you've always had it out for me and I never understood why."

It's something I've always wondered, and since I need to keep her talking as much as possible to hopefully allow the club to realize I'm missing, I might as well ask.

She scoffs as she waves a perfectly manicured hand in the air. "Because I never wanted to marry your father or even have you. I had everything planned out! And because of *you*, I lost everything and the life I was building came crashing down around me! I was working on my side hustles with Diego and Carlos, who were trying to help me get into the family business. I was engaged to the son of another Spanish mafia family, but then when I found out that a one-night stand with Nikos weeks before I met Raul resulted in me being pregnant, they broke everything off. Because of *you*, I lost the love of my life and had to fucking marry Nikos!"

By now, she's pacing in front of me in my small cell as she fumes, her hands gesturing wildly.

"Of course, Nikos was the perfect gentleman when he found out about you. He bought me a ring right away and proposed, even though it wasn't good enough for a Don's daughter, but I couldn't tell him that. I couldn't tell him anything about my family's true nature. He swore that in time, I'd learn to love him and you, but I knew I never could. Not when I hated you both to my very core.

"Then Daddy found out about my side hustles and kicked me out right before college graduation. He couldn't understand my vison of bringing back the true way of the Dons of old. Well, bringing back almost all of their aspects. We could have been billionaires a hundred times over, if not more, if we had stuck to the old ways. But no. Daddy was adamant that the family would never work in skin again and he cut me off. I had no choice but to accept Nikos' proposal. By then, Nikos knew my stance on kids and was determined that I would not abort you, even though I desperately wanted to."

Nausea slams into me at hearing her so casually talk about killing me when she was pregnant. I could never have done that to any of my kids. Even with them having Stephan as a father.

"At first, though, you seemed to take after me and I figured you could be my ticket back into the family, so I faked being a loving wife and mother. And it worked for a while. But then you had to go and start taking after your father. After college, he too started to change when we moved to Forest Creek so that his family could help with you after you were born. He started putting on weight the more and more time he spent around his family and I couldn't stand their cooking or the smell of it," she pauses as she gags, as if she could actually smell it. "Thanks to Mother, she created a secret account for me that I dipped into whenever I needed it. One of the times was to pay an old contact of mine to get us the fuck out of there and we moved to western Iowa.

"For a while, Nikos also seemed to improve until you fucking insisted on learning about your heritage. Of course, being the man that he is, he told his family how proud he was of you. Then both he and his fucking family doted on you like crazy, sending you recipe after recipe, care package after care package of meals to cook up with Nikos. I had to put an end to it and used the account again to bribe a doctor to tell Nikos we needed to get your health under control. I just knew that somewhere in there were my genes, and if I could mold you into the perfect daughter, then Mother would have convinced Daddy to let me come back home and work for the family."

She pauses in her rant as she curls her lip at me in disgust. "But no, you had to go ignore my warnings and spill the beans to Nikos about everything! You ruined everything I was working for! Took everything away from me, *again*, and everyone was siding with you!" She points angrily at me. "I should have just sold you straight away to Alejandro, but Diego insisted that selling you to his new business partner would open more doors since he was a cop. A cop we had on our payroll."

I swear my blood freezes at Alejandro's name.

Stephan talked about him many times. Mainly regarding how much he looked up to Alejandro and how he handled his businesses. Of course, on the nights when Stephan would get himself all riled up, thinking about what Alejandro does to his victims, it always ended up with me bruised and bloody before he'd fuck me. And it didn't matter if I was conscious or not when he did that. Or how much pain I was in.

"But Stephan never made you hurt enough. Never made you bleed enough." She pauses and a chill runs down my spine at the sinister grin on her face. "But this time, this time, you will. After X gets his fill of you, you'll be solely turned over to Alejandro and you'll never see outside of your new gilded cage again. Though, I'm sure with their tendencies, you'll be shared by them since they have quite a few similar interests and preferences." She looks down at me and sneers. "Not even being a fucking fat, beached whale will stop the sale. Unlike Stephan, Alejandro has his own doctors that live on his estate. You'll never need to go to a hospital again. Not even if you become pregnant. And those little brats of yours, we'll get our hands on them eventually, and I'll sell them off to the highest bidder who will ensure they endure as much pain as possible."

I struggle against my restraints and a second later; I feel something slip between the ropes, sliding against my wrist.

The dagger bracelets.

This time, I purposefully wiggle, making Eileen think I'm struggling when I'm really trying to dig out one of the bracelets from under the rope as I glare at Eileen.

"Luke won't let you touch a hair on their heads! And neither will the club," I snarl to which she cackles again.

"So fucking naïve. Still so fucking naïve and stupid. As soon as those two cunts have their babies, we're moving in and storming that fucking whorehouse. When everyone except your precious Luke is dead, we'll make him watch as we take the brats, handing them over to their new owners before slicing his thr—"

"Eileen!" Someone yells as they throw the door of my cell open and I swallow thickly when Diego's hate-filled eyes fall on me before they narrow. "What the fuck, Eileen! There was an agreement that she would be handed over without any more injuries. You know he wants to break her himself."

For a moment, my hopes that they aren't going to hurt me rise. Well, at least not yet. That gives time for the club to find me. I'm sure by now they've noticed I'm missing. But then again, I don't know what time it is. There are no windows in the cells either.

"Don't worry, Diego," she purrs and I fight to not roll my eyes as she switches into her sickly sweet and fake voice. "This, and anything else I deem necessary as a punishment, is already written into a clause in fine print at the end of the contract. If he didn't read it, it's his own damn fault."

Well, fuck. There goes that hope.

"Now, what did you really need?"

"We have a situation."

She scowls and after glaring at me, leaves the room with Diego after locking up my cell.

I wait for a few moments before I glance around better at my cell, but there aren't any cameras. That I can see, at least. I really wish I had my glasses. Shaking my head, I force myself to look around as best as I can in the meantime.

To my right, there are two women laying down that are also tied up, but they're both facing away from me, so I can't tell who they are. To my left, there are at least six, maybe more, men stuffed inside, but they're all knocked out. Or drugged. However, for some reason, the men don't appear to be restrained.

Shuffling to my right has me looking that way again, and I squint, trying to see better. I gasp when I realize who's staring back at me. Her face is hollow and gaunt, and there are yellow-ish green bruises along her jawline that are almost healed. She's wearing some sort of white dress that does little to keep her warm in this cold cell. She gives me a small smile.

"Claudia?"

"Yeah, it's me. I should have listened to you. You were right. When he posted bail for me and we got back to my apartment, he went ballistic on me that I had failed in giving you that drug. He tricked me. Everything you said would happen, happened. That's when I realized he lied to me about you." A tear slides down her cheek and she blinks rapidly to keep more from falling. "I thought he was a good bet because he was a police officer, but I was wrong. So wrong."

A shudder runs through her and despite what she attempted to do to me, I feel sorry for her. No one should be subjected to any sort of abuse in my opinion.

"How long have we been here? Or were you in here before? Or did they bring us together?"

"Just a few hours, I think, but I don't know if we came here at the same time. Before they brought me here, they kept me locked up at some homestead. He made me wear chains as I worked with the other women. I was there for about a week. I went to bed in my cot and woke up here. At least, that was my fate once Stephan burned through all the money he stole from me. I had some privileges then, but when he took me to the homestead, he showed me what exactly I meant to him by selling me to some Phillip guy."

Hatred once again simmers in my gut at Stephan, and I use it to channel my resolve to get the fuck out of here.

"Do you know if they drugged me?"

Nodding her head, she gives me a sympathetic look. "When I woke up, they were in here talking and said that you should be out for about another hour because of it, but they didn't mention what they gave you. They usually drug us before transporting us anywhere. I think it's just a sedative so that we won't fight back against them, but I'm not sure."

Fuck. I tilt my head toward the other woman. "Do you know who that is?"

"No, she was in here when I woke up and she hasn't woken up yet."

"What about those men?"

"I overheard Diego mentioning that they were his father's men who had been patrolling his section of the estate."

That gives me an idea.

We fall silent and I go back to my task, wiggling my arms to try and get enough space to where I can slip my bracelet out. It takes a while, but I'm finally able to get it out.

Carefully, I untwist the clasp and unhook it before starting to cut into the thick ropes.

I'm almost through the last tight section of ropes when I hear shouts coming from somewhere nearby and work faster. Finally, I'm able to get it just loose enough to where I can slip my wrist out. Quickly, I re-hook the bracelet around my wrist and carefully stand, but then I realized I forgot a vital flaw in my plan.

The fucking metal chain attached to my ankle.

"Fuck," I hiss as I sit back down.

I examine the lock closer and what I thought was a chain and shackle, is actually just a metal chain and a bike lock.

Chuckling, I shake my head and grin. "I can work with a bike lock," I mutter.

Last night before bed, I'd been so out of it because of what happened with Luke and the club that I never took down my hair. And right now, I'm grateful for it because I had it half up and had bobby pins helping to keep everything in place.

Taking out a couple of them, I do my best to remember how to bend them correctly, and when I hear the first pin of the lock disengage, I have to bite my lip to keep my giddy squeal from escaping. One by one, I repeat the process until all the pins are disengaged and the lock finally unlocks. Undoing the lock, I rotate my sore ankle a bit before standing again and hobbling over to the main door of my cell. There's another large metal chain holding my door as well as the door holding all the men shut, who I'm assuming are **de mi abuelo** (Grandpa's) guards. It's almost like whoever locked us in here didn't have the actual gate keys to the cells. Unfortunately, my bobby pins aren't going to get this massive lock picked, I don't think, but I'm willing to give it a shot.

Kneeling in front of it, I'm about to start picking the lock when groaning to my left has me looking that way. One of the men in the suits sits up as he holds his head and squints before looking around. When he sees me, his gaze narrows. "Who are you?"

Seeing as I have no point in lying to him, I tell him the truth. "Mary Catarino. Antonio Vasquez is **mi abuelo** (my grandpa)."

Recognition dawns in his eyes and his shoulders slump slightly. "Thank fuck you're okay. Boss would have gone on a rampage if you were hurt again."

I cock an eyebrow at him in question.

"I heard from the Boss that Diego and Eileen were trying to get their hands on you. I feared the worst when I saw you hanging over Leon's shoulder right after they darted me." He frowns when he sees my bobby pins and shakes his head. "Those won't work against a heavy-duty lock like that."

"Yeah, I kind of figured, but it's either this or sit and wait for them to come back for me, and I'd rather take my chances on these."

His frown deepens as he pats his pockets, and then it's my turn to frown when he takes off his shoes. He pulls out his insert and my jaw drops in surprise when he lifts a small box out of the base of his shoe.

"Doesn't that hurt to be standing on that box all day?" Internally, I roll my eyes. That's the question I lead with? Seriously?

He grins but shakes his head. "Nah, with the insole, I can't even feel it. I gotta tell you though, I always thought your uncle was paranoid when I saw him making storage compartments in his shoes and belts. He recommended we do the same, which I did just to satisfy him, but I'll be fucking thanking him after this. Let's see if there's something in here that will help. It's been a while since I did this, so I don't remember everything that's in here. I'm Jorge, by the way."

Jorge didn't end up having a lock picking kit, but he did have something that he thought would work. We both share a nervous look when we hear more shouting getting closer to us. He kneels at the door and starts picking the locks.

"See if you can wake any of the others while I do this, Mary," he says over his shoulder, and I'm about to do as he says when I think about Claudia.

"Claudia, can you see if you can wake the other woman?"

"Yeah," she replies weakly, and then shuffles across the floor as best as she can since she's tied up. Turning around, I get to work trying to wake Jorge's coworkers while at the same time, wondering exactly how weak she is. Did Stephan or Phillip starve her? I wouldn't be surprised if either one did. Both are royally fucked in the head.

"Hey, come on, whoever you are. Time to wake up." I push on the shoulder of the guy nearest me and almost cry out in alarm when his arm suddenly flies out and his hand clamps down hard on my wrist.

"Fuck! Louis, let her go! That's Mary, Boss' granddaughter."

Louis drops my wrist like I burned him and he gives me a sheepish look. "Apologies, Miss Mary."

I wave him off. "I should have expected it since you're **de mi abuelo** (grandpa's) guards. And none of this 'Miss' shit, either. It's just Mary."

He huffs and shakes his head. "Chip off the old block of Mateo's, that's for fucking sure."

I can't help but grin at that. I've heard lots of stories of a younger **Tío** (Uncle) Mateo, and we are a lot alike.

"What the fuck do you think you're doing?" someone snarls, and I spin, falling on my ass as I lose my balance.

My eyes widen as I stare down the barrel of the gun Isaac is aiming at my head.

Oh, fuck. This is so not good.

When did he get in here and how the hell did none of us hear him?

Chapter 71

Patch

THERE WAS NO TIME to go back to the clubhouse for more gear, so we had to use what we had on us and with us in the vans.

Double checking my guns, extra magazines, and knives one more time, I get out of the van and close the door. Antonio said a service trail on his property would get us close to the north side of Diego's wing of the estate. He and Mateo decided to go around the front. They had called Lorenzo when we were still at the warehouse, and everything was business as usual in the main section of the house. The plan is that we enter the tunnels through the entrance in Diego's study, which is in the northern section of the estate. Then, Antonio and Mateo are going to lock all the exits to the tunnels and panic rooms except for the ones we want to be open. Locks that when triggered, only he or Mateo can unlock. They are going to meet up with some of their most trusted men and work from the south toward us. No one will be able to slip by us.

This shit ends tonight.

As we sneak through the property, I give a silent thanks, yet again, to Levi for having bought our fancy ass communication devices. They've come in handy in so many fucking times that they've already paid for themselves in my mind. Which is a sobering thought.

For the first wave, we had already decided that Ryder, Bear, Bones, Beast, and I would go first. The others will have our back just in case. Once we have the main door secured, the rest will come out from where they're hiding and join us.

My group makes a break for some shrubs a bit behind where Diego's goons are guarding the door. I know Smoke is watching with his drone overhead, but it does little to ease my worry about sneaking up on two men from one side. It would have been preferable if we could have been on both sides, but that's not possible with this layout. Though, hopefully the fact that we're using dart guns will help in this instance. It's the quietest and quickest way to take these assholes down. Mateo gave Doc and me as much information as he could about their men, and we think the doses that we came up with will knock Diego's men out for at least a couple of hours. Of course, we always have our guns with silencers attached to help with noise, but they're for when push comes to shove. However, a couple of hours should be enough time for us to get them wherever the hell it is that we're going to question them, though my guess is it'll be somewhere here in Antonio's house.

Bear and Beast go first. If the darts don't knock them out right away, they'll be able to finish the job the fastest, since they are the biggest of us five.

Thankfully, the darts do the trick without them making a single sound, and we quickly disarm them. I pull out some zip ties, securing the wrists and ankles of goon one while Beast does the same to goon two.

Smoke's voice filters through our earpieces. *"Hallway's clear. You can lock them in the bathroom. Two doors down and on your left."*

Standing, I drag my guy inside and when we get in the bathroom, we pat them down, pocketing their weapons before taking off their own earpieces, watches, belts, and shoes. Mateo had warned us that their men often hid tools on themselves to get out of situations like these, and we really don't want them getting away. Grabbing some more zip ties, I loop their wrists together around the base of the toilet and then I hook their ankles together. Tight.

Bones stays behind to guard the assholes as well as to be our backup as he watches us on the monitor. The rest of my brothers that aren't on perimeter watch enter the now guard-free door to Diego's wing and meet up with us.

We follow the quickest path that Antonio said would lead us to the tunnels. The entrance is in Diego's study, and unfortunately, the doors are shut. I press my ear to the door, but I can't hear anything.

"Move," Smoke whispers and I back away as he tests the door, but finds it locked.

He slips off his backpack and pulls out a small metal case. My eyebrows go up when he pulls out something that looks like a lock picking kit... but different. He slides the lever into the keyhole, followed by the tricked out-looking pick.

Normally, you'd hear each of the pins disengaging, but I can't hear anything. It's only when I step a little closer that I hear a very soft little 'click' of one of the pins disengaging. I cock an eyebrow at him, but he just smirks and shakes his head. I wonder if this is his invention, one of his buddies from the government, or if this is another Levi surprise?

Smoke puts the kit away and pulls out his tablet. He checks the cameras and there are still four men lazily standing around the room. Lex and Gunner both step forward to look at the men closer on the screen. While all of us are a damn good shot, they are our best marksmen that we brought with us. Since we knew there were four men in this room, our hope is that they'll be quick enough to dart them and that no one can shout, raising an alarm. Especially since none of us are particularly small and it'd be near impossible to have four large men crowding a doorway without sounding an alarm even sooner. We just wouldn't fit.

Lex and Gunner step close together and after a beat, they open the door enough that they both can see in and quickly fire.

"Ahh!" one of them cries out and I silently curse, but we knew this was a possibility.

When all four are down, we file into Diego's study and lock the door behind us. Lex and Gunner are already getting to work securing and disarming the men and I can tell both of them look guilty as fuck that they weren't quicker.

I walk over and give them chin lifts as I work on securing another guy.

"It's alright. If any of the rest of us would have done it, I'm betting there would have been more noise."

While I can tell my words help a little, it doesn't erase their guilt because they know the men coming for us won't be packing dart guns.

This just got a whole lot more complicated a little sooner than we would have liked.

"The next three are aware that something is amiss, though our mystery guy is actually trying to persuade the other two that it was nothing," Bones says through our earpieces.

Well, that's surprising, but how does he know we're coming? Is this a trap of some sort?

Shaking off that thought, we finish securing the men, but since there really isn't much in here to tie them to, we just zip tie their hands to their ankles and move to the entrance. I feel around for the pressure plate Antonio mentioned and then I push in the code he and Smoke created for the club.

The door slides open and I'm once again surprised that the tunnel is actually more like a hallway. Judge stays behind with Loki to guard the men in case they wake up or someone happens upon them. Or if more of Diego's men come looking for the others.

"As a reminder, go straight, right, left, right, and then you'll find the assholes. The mystery man is in a fancier suit than Diego's goons. Use your discretion with him."

"Any sign of Isaac or Carlos?" I ask.

"Not yet, but they could be in one of the few rooms that don't have much camera coverage. Antonio said there were a couple of storage rooms where the cameras were outside the doors, but not inside. Something he said will be changing after this."

Looking up at a camera, I nod silently to acknowledge that we heard him and then we creep through the hallways. All too soon, we come up to the junction that will lead us to Diego's men. Gunner peeks around the corner before whipping back.

"Fuck," he mouths and then looks around for a camera, raising an eyebrow in question.

"It was mystery man that noticed you. He got the attention of the other two. So far, I think he's on our side. When I tell you to, Gunner and Lex, you reach around the corner and dart the two, but I think we should wait and see what mystery man says."

Lex crouches on the ground at Gunner's feet as they get into position.

"Now!"

Both of them lean around the corner and shoot.

"Ahh! Diego! Car—" one of them cries out before I hear the sound of flesh hitting flesh.

We all round the corner just in time to see one of the goons falling from being hit by our mystery man. He sees us and straightens before holding his hands up.

"I assume you are the Steel Archangel's MC?"

I narrow my eyes at him and Thor comes up to stand in front of us.

"Who's asking?"

"Matthew Baker, bodyguard for Miss Alexis Sanchez. I am on your side, as is Miss Sanchez."

I step forward. "How did you know we'd be here? What are you two doing here?"

"We are here because Mary's mother has sold her to Alejandro," he says as he curls his lip. "We are here to 'escort' Mary, but we were never going to deliver her to Alejandro. Though Miss Alexis figured you'd show up at some point."

I thought Eileen's plan was for X to get Mary before selling her off? Something isn't right here.

Shouts from down the hall reach us and we immediately slink back so we're out of sight, guns at the ready.

"Shit! Carlos and Isaac were hiding somewhere down there. Carlos is on his way toward you, but Isaac split off from him and I've lost sight of him again."

"Is Carlos alone?" Thor whispers from behind me. Matthew raises an eyebrow in question, but instead of answering, I just point to my earpiece. He gives me a curt nod as he double checks his weapon.

"No, he has one other man with him and they are both armed. However, Antonio and his men are closer to them and might get to them first. If he comes your way, Patch, you're in position to be able to dart him when I tell you to."

"All other hallways are clear?"

"Yes. And it looks like you're in the clear for now as well. Antonio and his men have confronted Carlos. Ah, it looks like he had Phillip Cole with him."

I turn toward Matthew, and then to Thor, waiting for his decision.

"Fine, but if you are lying, I'm putting a bullet through you." Thor pauses as he checks his weapons. "Bones, how does it look in there?"

"Leon, Carmen, Eileen, and Diego are arguing over something, and Alexis is slowly inching her way toward the door that leads to the cells. I still haven't found Isaac yet."

Thor repeats the information for Matthew's sake before he turns toward us. "Lead with the darts, but use your guns if you need to. Just fucking try not to make a kill shot," he grits out through clenched teeth. "Matthew, do you have another weapon?"

Matthew pulls back the side of his suit coat to reveal another glock holstered at his side. "I also have extra ammo."

"Since we're trying to use just darts, you open the door for us on my command." He looks over his shoulder and continues. "Same formation and don't get fucking shot."

We get in place. Thor, Ryder, Bear, Beast, and I ease forward and get into position.

At Thor's command, Matthew opens the door and we rush in and come to a halt at the same time Bone's voice comes over the earpiece.

"Fuck..."

And I agree. Fucking Isaac has Mary tied up on the ground in front of us with a gun to the back of her head and Leon, Carmen, Eileen, Diego, and the person who I'm assuming is Alexis Sanchez, all have guns trained on us.

Eileen snarls. "Well, well, well. Look what the cat dragged in. You're too late. The transaction has been finalized." She pauses and smiles smugly. "I guess one positive is that you get to see her fat ass one last time before I ship her off to her new owner." Eileen runs a manicured nail down Mary's cheek but Mary jerks away from her touch, glaring at her.

Eileen sneers and backhands her hard enough that the slap echoes in the room. My body goes tight at the sight, but I force myself to not move. I don't want them to hurt her further.

She looks up to Alexis. "Plans have changed. Get her out of here and deliver her. X will have to come to you for his allotted time with her."

Aside from a muscle ticking in Alexis' jaw, you wouldn't even be able to tell that she has emotions underneath the hard mask that she's wearing.

I look down at Mary to find her staring up at me, eyes pleading for me to do something. I decide to do the only thing I can right now. Here's praying I remember the words correctly.

"**Είναι εντάξει** (It's okay). **Είναι στο πλευρό μας** (She's on our side). **Παίξτε μαζί, εντάξει** (Play along, okay)? **Σε αγαπώ** (I love you)."

Tears mist in her eyes as she gives a slight nod. "**Κι εγώ σ' αγαπώ** (I love you, too)." Then she cries out as Eileen hits her yet again.

My chest tightens as I'm forced to watch Eileen hurt Mary.

"I told you, Bitch, you are to only speak English! English! Can't you learn anything?"

Alexis steps forward and catches Eileen's hand as she goes in for another strike.

"She is not to be harmed anymore," Alexis snarls at her and Eileen rips her hand from her grasp before smiling that smug fucking smile at her.

"Then you should have read your contract closer. In the fine print at the end, it says I can punish her however I want to before she's delivered. I'm the one that shat her out, so I control her pain and blood."

"Not anymore," Alexis replies in a rather sweet voice, but then my gaze is drawn down to her hand as she gives a signal.

Matthew is immediately at her side with a gun to Eileen's temple as he yanks Eileen's head back by her hair, whereas at the same time, Alexis jams the handle of her gun into Isaac's temple with enough force to send him crumpling to the ground.

Well, shit.

Warily, I eye Leon, Diego, and Carmen, who seem... pleased with this development?

I shoot an alarmed look at Thor, who ever so slightly nods. He noticed it as well.

What the fuck is going on here?

"Why aren't you three doing anything?" Eileen screeches. "Why are you just standing there?"

Carmen shrugs. "We let you believe you were in charge, but you weren't, Eileen. If you weren't so focused on your own revenge plans, you might have noticed. And maybe you should have taken your own advice and read the fine print of your own contracts." She saunters forward, a fake, smug smile on her lips. "I have funded you since the very beginning. Everything you have done belongs to me. Every contract you signed, every deal you made, every club you created, every sale you've made. All of it leads back to me. If you had read the fine print of every single contract you've finalized, you would have realized that you were given authority to act on *my behalf*, and that was the only authority you were given. The empire that you thought you created for yourself? It's mine and mine alone. You only get percentages of what's made."

Eileen's eyes blaze with anger as she struggles in Matthew's hold, who is now restraining her arms behind her back while Alexis holds the gun on Eileen.

"And you?" Eileen spits out at Diego, who just shrugs.

"If you were a man, I would have made you my business partner. You grew my business tenfold, but you're just a woman."

Alarm sparks in Carmen's eyes and before she fully turns, Diego pistol whips her against the cheek and she goes down in a heap.

At the action, my brothers and I all aim at Diego. Even Alexis aims at him, apparently trusting that Matthew has Eileen restrained well enough.

Eileen stares at him in shock and starts sputtering nonsense, but Diego cuts her off.

"Again, you both are woman. Neither of you thought you'd ever be double-crossed. You should have realized who you were dealing with when I aligned us with Oasis. A woman's place is beneath the men around her," he sneers at her, which just has her fighting Matthew's hold even more.

He and Leon share a condescending look. Fuckers think they're still going to be able to walk out of here.

Diego turns and smirks at me. "So, you're the pathetic gearhead who has been disrupting our plans all along. You think you have what it takes to take down the next Don of the Vasquez family? You don't have the guts.

"If he doesn't, I do."

Slowly, the smile fades from Diego's face as it changes to a look of shock as Mateo steps out from behind us, gun raised at him. In an instant, Diego changes as his eyes blaze in anger as he glares at his twin.

Mateo smirks. "What? Didn't expect that I'd still be alive?"

"You should be dead by now. These imbeciles should have put a bullet in you as soon as we dumped you at their gates. I knew I should have killed you when I had the chance," he seethes.

Mateo shrugs. "But you didn't, and here we are." He pulls the trigger and fires a dart at Diego. Leon's eyes widen and as he watches the dart fly through the air, he raises his gun, but I fire first, shooting him with a dart as well. He stares dumbly at it for a moment, gun half raised in the air, before crumpling to the floor.

Diego looks down at the dart sticking out of his arm in confusion before groggily looking back up. "Guess you didn't have the guts after all."

The look Mateo gives Diego sends chills down my spine as Mateo reveals a side of him I've yet to see. Diego's face pales.

"Your fun is only just beginning."

Diego's eyes roll back as he crumples to the floor.

Ryder, Bear, and Beast step forward and start securing the others with zip ties.

Striding toward Mary, I pull out my knife and start cutting her ropes around her ankles and then her hands.

"You came. You actually came," she cries and when her arms are free, she wraps them around my neck. Instantly, I can tell she's freezing as I can feel her hard nipples and since I know she doesn't wear a bra to bed, I pull back. Taking off my cut, I shirk out of my hoodie before pulling it down over her head.

'Thank you,' she mouths as she makes sure it's down all the way and then pulls her hair through. I cup her cheek and her eyes mist over.

"Of course, I came for you, Siren. I love you, you're my Old Lady."

"But..."

I put my finger to her lips, silencing her. "We thought we had a mole in the clubhouse. You know I'd never keep you from your family."

Tears roll down her face as relief fills her eyes, and I wipe her tears away with my thumb.

"I thought you were distancing yourself to get rid of me and the kids after this was done. You all were so distant. It was so weird."

"Siren, I'm so sorry. I guess we were all just so stressed about pulling this off right that we kind of ignored everyone else. I'm so sorry, Mary. And I never want you or the kids to leave—you're my heart. I can't live without you."

Leaning down, I kiss her and fuck do I wish we were somewhere else because I need to do a whole lot more than kiss her right now. If she was doubting me, I need to remind her what she means to me.

Suddenly, she pulls away, pointing behind her. "Claudia and Cici are in one of the cells. Cici was just waking up when Isaac came through a secret walkway and

I think Claudia needs help. It was hard to tell for sure without my glasses, but I think they starved her or something. She sounded so weak. Also, six of **de mi abuelo** (my grandpa's) men are in a cell, too."

"We know, Siren. Antonio gave Smoke access to his cameras. It's how we knew who all was here and where they were. We'll get them the care they need."

I help her up and she leans against me.

"So, what now?" she asks before looking over at Alexis and frowns.

Alexis steps forward. "As you've probably heard, I am Alexis Sanchez and yes, my father is, unfortunately, Alejandro Sanchez." Mary's body tenses in my arms and when Alexis notices, she gives Mary a soft smile. "Don't worry, the plan was never to deliver you to my father. We were going to get you out and then call the club to have them 'intercept' us. However, now, I think I will need to take my FBI contact up on his offer for WITSEC. I know my father has his suspicions already, but after this, he'll know for sure."

Matthew steps forward. "You know the men and I will follow you wherever to ensure your safety."

She smiles affectionately at him. "I know, Matty. Don't worry, it'll all work out."

Smoke steps forward, frowning. "Who is your FBI contact?"

"Weber. Agent Creed Weber."

"Well, it just so happens I've got a shit ton of information to talk to him about. Come, we can tell him about your situation first. I'm sure he'll want to know about how we ended up at the same place anyway." He turns to Antonio, who just walked in. "Can we use the control room to the east of here?"

Antonio tips his head. "**Sí** (Yes), of course."

Alexis pauses and turns toward me, then Mary, and finally to Thor. "Just so you know, beware of Dr. Olsen in town. Oasis has brought him and his daughter on as new suppliers for their drug, Aphrodite's Kiss. My father also utilizes him from time to time to get certain drugs to make his victims more compliant." With that, she turns and leaves the room as if she hasn't just dropped another bomb on us. Smoke shakes himself out of his shock and follows after her.

Rage fills me at what these assholes have been doing and how close Mary came to them not that long ago. Over her head, Thor and I share a look. We'll definitely be taking care of those two Olsen's.

After Smoke leaves, Antonio comes over to us, and Mary leans away from me to hug him.

"I'm so glad you are safe, **mi precioso capullo de rosa** (my precious rosebud). I'm so sorry that this happened to you and in my own home."

She shakes her head as she pulls back. "It's okay, **Abuelo** (Grandpa). None of this is your fault. It's theirs," she says as she gestures to the prone figures of her ex-family and Leon.

Antonio nods, but I can tell he's going to be blaming himself for a long time.

Stepping back, he turns to Thor. "It's late, or I should say early since it's just after dawn, and I figured you would all like to be present for our little talk with everyone. Would tonight work for you? Let them sit and stew for a while?"

Thor smirks and after we both share a look, he nods.

"Tonight will be perfect. I take it you want to handle things here?"

Antonio's lips purse. "Yes. We need to handle the final blow family style as well as the handling of the bodies."

"Then we'll bring our guests to you. I'm sure you have further questions for them."

My chest aches for Antonio and when Mary leans further into me, I know she's feeling it as well.

Two of his children, his grandson, and his wife, will not live to see another sunrise.

Chapter 72

Mary

BY THE TIME THE van pulls through the clubhouse gates, I can barely keep my eyes open. Earlier, I was grateful Patch had given me his hoodie because I would have been even colder than I already was if he hadn't. Apparently, sometime after I was taken, it had started to snow again. Hard. There were a few times during the drive that I worried if we should have just stayed at **la casa de mi abuelo** (my grandpa's house).

The van comes to a stop and I rub my eyes. I got shit for sleep last night, and I'm not even sure how long I was out before Leon snuck into the clubhouse and took me.

"Raise the arm of your sweatshirt, Siren. I'll take some blood and send someone to get it tested," Patch asks me as he digs in a medical bag on the bench next to him.

Sleepily, I do as he asks, shivering when the disinfectant wipe chills my skin. Patch draws a couple of vials before writing something on them. He talks quietly with Doc and hands him the vials before turning back toward me.

"Come on, Siren. I'll carry you inside."

I slide across the bench toward the door. When he gets out, he turns around and picks me up, which I'm grateful for since I don't have shoes on or have my crutches with me.

Patch heads up the stairs and someone opens the door for him.

"Mama!"

"Mom!"

Patch takes me over to the couches and as soon as he sets me down, the kids are instantly on top of me. I wrap my arms around them tightly. Cassie sobs quietly against my shirt and I kiss her head, soothing her as best as I can.

"Mary," Patch calls softly and when I look up, I'm relieved to see he's holding my glasses. Taking them, I slid them on and am extremely happy not to be squinting all the damn time. He leans down by my ear and whispers quietly. "Ethan and Doc are running in your bloodwork to check and verify if it was just a sedative."

Exhaling, I nod. I'm hoping what Claudia said was true, that it was just a sedative and not Aphrodite's Kiss or whatever the other drug's name was that made someone go sterile.

The ladies come out and when they sit opposite me, I can tell they've all been crying.

"I'm so sorry, Mary. I still don't know how we didn't see them sneaking in last night. And for putting you through all of this. I hate that you had to go through something similar to me," Levi says in between sniffles.

'Talk to Smoke,' I mouth to her and her eyes widen before her face twists in anger. Instantly, she's up off the couch, heading across the room to Smoke. Well, as fast as a pregnant woman who's about to burst can get up off a couch, that is.

I know how Leon got in, or at least know almost all of what happened, Patch told me when I had asked, but I'm not saying anything around little ears. That and I don't know if I can tell Mae or not. Probably not. I'm sure if it's okay, Timber will tell her.

On the way home, Smoke had been frantically working on his computer, trying to figure out what happened. He was almost sure that someone wormed his way into the club's network, and when he found what he was looking for, he was fucking livid. Let's just say that unless the guy was coerced, there's going to be another man that works, or I should say worked, for **Abuelo** (Grandpa) joining the 'party' tonight. Surprisingly, a party I'm being allowed to attend, according to Thor. Regardless of what my family thinks.

That was when Patch told me it was **Abuelo** (Grandpa) and **Tío** (Uncle) Mateo who had requested I not be told about the trap they were planning. They hadn't wanted me to be exposed to more danger or have to witness what they might have to do. Honestly, I would have preferred to see what they and the club do to them. In a way, I feel like I need that for the closure of all the pain they've caused over the years.

As I shake off those thoughts, I yawn again and Mae chuckles.

"Hey, kiddos. How about we go and get you guys some breakfast? It looks like your mom and dad need a little shut eye," she says and I nod in agreement.

"Sleep would be divine," I mumble around another yawn.

The kids protest, but I give them all hugs and kisses, telling them that we'll all hang out later today after we've slept. Reluctantly, the kids follow Mae into the kitchen, but soon she has them excited and happy again with the promise that they can help her cook. They've all taken to cooking with us, but we only allow them to help when there's only one or two of us working in the kitchen, otherwise there's just too many people in there and I worry they'll get hurt as a result.

Patch steps forward as I use the arm of the couch to help me stand. He lifts me into his arms and carries me upstairs. I think if all of us hadn't been sleep deprived we would have gotten cat calls, but we're all fucking tired.

Once in our room, Patch closes the door and locks it before crossing the room to his bed, but then he pauses. "Fuck, I probably should have taken you to the med room first."

I shake my head. "The worst is my cheek and my wrists, but my wrists are from moving so I could get to the bracelets and then cutting through the ropes. My ankle hurts a little from the chain and later the rope, but it's just minor.

His brows dip in confusion. "But you were tied up when we came in."

"That's because Isaac tied me back up, though he wasn't too bright and didn't figure out that my bracelets were the reason why I got out of them in the first place."

He sets me down on the edge of the bed and then puts his gun and his knives away in the nightstand. Taking off his cut, he sets it on his dresser. Kneeling on one knee in front of me, he looks my legs over, gently running his fingers over the raw marks on my ankle from the chain. I shiver and my skin breaks out in goosebumps from his touch.

His green eyes darken as he looks up at me, and I can't help but notice he's hard for me. "I think I might need to do a more thorough examination."

"Do whatever you think you need to do." Even I can tell that my voice is breathy and huskier, which has his eyes darken even further and the bulge in his pants lengthening. I can already feel myself getting damp at the thought of him being inside me again.

Bending down further, he kisses up my leg, and when he gets to mid-thigh, he straightens as his fingers go to his hoodie before he's pulling it off me. My shirt comes with it, and I freeze when he scowls.

"Who did this?" he demands as his large hand splays across my side.

I look down and wince. The bruises had been healing, but now I've got another purple bruise blooming in the middle of the yellowish-green bruises.

"Fuck, I forgot all about that with everything else that had been going on. Eileen kicked me with those fucking pointy boots of hers."

His jaw ticks and I'm sure he's adding this to the long list of things Eileen's done to me throughout the years.

Leaning down, he kisses all over the bruise and then up my chest. He nibbles and nips up my throat and not being able to take it any longer; I pull his face to mine, slamming my lips to his. He slides his hands under my ass, scoots me back, and then leans me down on the bed. I moan when I feel his body pressing down on my own and I tilt my hips, needing friction on my core.

His kiss turns more forceful, and he grinds himself into me.

"Luke, I need you, please," I beg.

He nibbles slightly on my lip and then he's gone. I whimper, but then it freezes in my throat when I realize he'd pulled back so he could strip.

Reaching over and behind his head, he pulls his shirt off and at the sight of his rippling muscles, I rub my legs together, trying to get a bit of friction. Bending over, he unlaces his boots and slips out of them. He undoes his belt buckle and I moan as he strips out of his jeans and boxers.

He pumps his cock as I get on my hands and knees and when he presses the head of his cock against my lips, I eagerly open for him.

Taking his head in my mouth, I run my tongue through his slit and pull back before running my tongue up and down his length, teasing him slightly.

"Mary," he growls and I look up innocently at him. He growls again and a shiver runs through me, my juices already leaking down my thighs. I love when he gets all growly in bed.

When I reach his head again, I take him back into my mouth and my lips stretch wide around him. I know from experience, I won't be able to take all of him because of my gag reflux, so I grasp the rest of his length with one hand, pumping as I bob up and down.

After a few minutes, he suddenly pulls out, breathing hard. He manhandles me as he gets me back on my back and grabs my hips, pulling my ass just slightly over the edge of the bed. He hooks my left knee over his shoulder before he bites down on my thigh, not hard, but enough to send a slight jolt through me.

"Luke!" I cry out as he dives in, plunging his tongue into my pussy. My hands fly to his head and I thread my fingers through his hair, tugging slightly.

I squirm on the bed at the onslaught of his tongue. After not having sex for almost a week, not even oral, the pressure building inside of me is making my body tingle and my muscles coil tightly. He moves to suck on my clit and pushes a couple of fingers inside me. Then I feel his teeth lightly grazing my clit before he sucks on my clit again, and I explode, my vision turning white. When my senses come back to me, I realize he's pumping a finger in and out of my ass as he continues to suck on my clit.

Then he inserts another finger into my ass and I feel another orgasm building again. We'd been playing around with anal, but I've yet to take his cock. Judging by how he's stretching me, I have a feeling today might be that day.

Suddenly, he pulls out, stands up, and drives his cock into my pussy in one hard thrust. My breasts bounce from the force and he leans down, taking one of my nipples in his mouth.

"Fuck, yes!"

He bites down gently on my nipple and another orgasm rips through me, but he keeps up his torment, switching in between breasts as he continues to pound into my pussy.

"Right there, right there. Harder," I cry as I push back toward him, needing to feel him deeper in me.

Luke pulls out and flips me, sliding a pillow under my leg to better support my cast. His hands grip my ass cheeks, spreading them apart before driving back into me.

"Fuck, Mary. I love seeing my cock being swallowed up by your pussy."

A moment later, something cool lands on my ass and my body tenses, but I force it to relax.

"But it'll be even better seeing it sink into your gorgeous ass. Are you ready to give me this ass today, Siren?" he asks as he spreads more lube on me as and then I feel his fingers slipping inside of me again.

I moan at the feeling of his fingers stretching me while he continues to fuck me. I nod furiously. "Fuck, yes, Luke. I need it, please. More."

My body shakes as he pushes down on my back with his free hand as he adds another finger in my ass. A loud slap rings through the air as he spanks me, and it's just enough to send me over the edge again.

Luke takes that moment to pull out of my pussy and he presses his cock against my virgin hole. It stings a little, but if it's anything like how it feels after the stretch of adding another finger, I know I'm going to love the feeling.

Breathing deep, I force my body to stay as loose as possible as he slowly sinks into me, pausing whenever I hiss to let me get used to his size.

He moans when he's fully inside me and a shiver runs through me at feeling so full.

"Fuck, Siren," he hisses and I purposefully clench, wanting to feel his reaction.

He moans again and his hands tighten on my hips. Finally, he starts moving and again, it stings a little at first, but like I suspected, it soon gives way to pleasure.

I push back, meeting his thrusts and he finally gets the hint. For some reason, I need him hard and deep today.

"You want me to pound this gorgeous ass, Siren?"

"Yes, please," I damn near sob as I feel another orgasm building.

Luke grips my hips so hard I'll probably have bruises tomorrow, but I don't care. He pulls back and I cry out as he thrusts back in faster and harder than he had been doing before. I hope like hell no one can hear me, but soon all thought is wiped from my mind as Luke takes me hard. I'm sure I'm going to be feeling this later, but I don't give a fuck.

Another loud slap fills the air, then another, and another as Luke smacks my ass.

"Fuck, your ass looks good, all nice and red. Maybe I should get a flogger and really turn this ass red."

A shiver works through me as I imagine Luke tying me up and using a flogger on various parts of my body. With my history, it's surprising that I'm actually looking forward to it, but this is Luke. He'd never purposefully hurt me. The image of Luke using a flogger on me has me cresting once again and I vaguely hear Luke cursing before I feel the warmth of his cum filling me.

He slumps down over me but uses his hands to keep from crushing me. He kisses my spine which has me shivering again and him moaning as I clench around his sensitive cock.

Luke slips out of me and I collapse in a heap on the bed. He comes back in with a washcloth and cleans me up. I barely have the strength to climb under the covers, and when he wraps me in his arms, I'm out like a light.

A few hours later, we wake up and my stomach growls angrily at me. Looking over at the clock, I realize it's a little past one o'clock. Luke rolls me over and leans down, kissing me. I can feel myself getting wet again, but my damn stomach ruins it by growling again.

Luke chuckles. "Let's get cleaned up, grab some food, and go find our kids."

My heart warms at him calling them 'our' kids, but he must see something on my face because he sobers almost immediately.

"I'm so sorry I made you doubt me this past week, Mary. I meant it when I said you and the kids are my everything. My heart. My world. I'll do my best to never make you feel like that again."

I swallow thickly as I nod. "It cut me to the core when you suddenly started shutting me out. Before, you'd tell me if you could or couldn't tell me things, and if you could, then you'd give me the cliff notes version. I can handle it if you tell me I can't know something, but when you go radio silent... That's what I can't handle. We're supposed to be in this together."

He kisses me and when he pulls back, his fingers caress my cheek.

"Promise I'll do better. And if you're feeling like I may be slipping, call me out on it. I might not even realize I'm doing it like this past week. I don't ever want to hurt you, Mary."

Wrapping a hand around his neck, I pull him down for another kiss.

It quickly turns heated and he easily slides in between my thighs.

This time, we take our time, and he makes love to me nice and slow and tender as he worships my body.

When we both come together, he kisses me deeply before carrying me into the bathroom, his cock still inside of me. I rest my head in the crook of his neck, never wanting this to end. For Luke to be my one and only for the rest of my life.

Chapter 73

Patch

LOOKING OUTSIDE THE WINDOW, I realize we've gotten a fair amount of snow. Maybe a couple of feet, and it's still lightly snowing. We have an appointment at four o'clock at the bank, but until then we really don't have anywhere to be. Since we've got all the major players except for X, Thor said Mary and the kids could go back to life as normal and tomorrow, the kids will be returning to school, something they are really excited about because they miss their friends.

"Hey, kids." I call out as I lean against the door of the make-shift playroom. All four of their little heads pop up and look at me. "Who wants to build a snowman?"

You would have thought I told them they could have opened their Christmas gifts early with how much they're cheering in excitement as they tear through the clubhouse to their respective rooms. We still have to move our stuff back into the condo, since we haven't yet set up our rooms here for future lockdowns. Something we plan to do later this week. Also, I'll be moving my room up to the third floor. We've decided that anyone coming here with kids will get their rooms next to their kids' on that floor. That way, the kids are further away from what happens late at night. Though with the addition of our kids to the mix, I have noticed the guys have started to tame things down some in regards to the nighttime activities and the volume. Very rarely do the guys have sex out in the open anymore, and if it does happen, its usually when someone's had a fair amount to drink.

Following the kids to their room, I help them get into their snow gear and when they tear through the clubhouse down to the main floor and out through the back door, all of my brothers' faces soften into various degrees of smiles at their childlike innocence. And surprisingly, they all get up and head to their rooms, only to come out a few minutes after us dressed for the cold.

Noticing Mary has stopped right outside the door, I frown as it dawns on me she can't get down and play with the kids like she is. But then a smile forms as I think of a way she can be involved.

Grabbing a shovel, I start scooping a wider path around the door and then head inside for a stool that I know is kept in the original playroom. Then I grab some blankets and some supplies out of the med room. Heading back outside, I grin as I hold up everything for her to see. "Let's get you out there and making memories with the kids as well."

The blinding smile I get in return has me knowing I did the right thing.

I pack down an area by the kids and set her stool down. Walking over to her, I tape her cast over her heavy clothes to make sure no snow accidentally gets inside and carry her over to the stool.

For a moment, I just stand back and watch as Mary and the kids build the base of a snowman together.

"This is so much fun!" Cassie squeals. "Our first snowman!"

Instantly, my smile vanishes along with everyone else's. Mary looks down and I can tell by how her throat is working that she's trying her damndest not to cry.

As one, my brothers and I start getting to work.

"Well, if this is a first, then we're going to make it a fu—I mean, a freaking awesome snowman," Ryder says as he packs snow into a large snowball and starts rolling it around.

"To heck with just *a* snowman. Let's build a family of snowmen," Dragon says as he picks Cassie up and tosses her slightly in the air before catching her.

"Yay! A family of snowmen," she cheers as she hugs him.

And for the next two hours, that's exactly what we did. In the end, the kids made a snowman for each of them. Then our kids wanted to make one for Mary and I and Lindsey wanted one for Drae and Elvira.

Looking down at them, I realize we need to get the kids inside and warm. "How about we take a break for hot chocolate?"

The kids all moan.

"But we wanted to make Auntie MaeMae and Auntie Levi's snowmen families as well," Lindsey pouts.

Timber comes up and scoops up Lindsey and Cassie. "Well, how about we do those ones tomorrow?"

"Okay," they reluctantly agree.

Dragon and Thor come over to grab Ash and Isaiah and they head inside.

Picking up Mary, I give a chin lift to Axe who comes over and picks up the blanket and her stool.

"Thank you for getting those things so I could play with the kids, too. I don't know if I would have thought of that."

I kiss her temple. "Don't mention it, Siren."

Once inside, I help her strip off her gear and the kids', hanging them over a chair for now to dry.

"You kids hang out here for a bit and play. We'll get you your drinks."

"Okay, Mom," Isaiah calls out before he runs over to the pool table, and the others follow him. He loves playing pool any chance he can get. Timber even made stools for all of them so that they'd be able to be at the right height to shoot properly.

I turn and follow Mary into the kitchen, not surprised that Mae is already warming milk on the stove and is working on mixing something else in a pan as well.

"Oh, the kids are going to be beating down your door for the rest of the winter, Mae," Mary tells her with a laugh. "I've never made it homemade before, so we either made do with the powder packets or getting a tin of the mix."

Mae gives her a mock outraged look, but it's quickly ruined when they both laugh. "You and I both know that I love your kids and they are welcome anytime. Tomorrow, I'll show you how I make it."

"Sounds like a plan."

While Mae cooks, I get down some mugs and look around in the pantry for some marshmallows.

"Hey, Patch. Can you grab a couple of packs of chocolate chips out of there for me? Both the regular sized and the mini ones?" Mae calls out.

Grabbing them, I bring everything over to the island, but spotting the time, I kiss Mary on the forehead.

"I hate to say this, Mary, but we've got to get around to head to the bank."

Her head whips over to look at the clock on the wall and winces. "Crap, sorry, Mae. Can you guys watch the kids for us for a bit?"

She waves me off. "Girl, I was already planning on it. Now, shoo. Go do your thing." Mae winks at her and Mary grins in return. Once again, I'm thankful Mary gets along so well with the Old Ladies.

Heading back out to the main room, I slip off my cut and put my coat back on. We don't wear our cuts when we're in a cage.

"Ethan," I call out and he comes over to me, walking briskly. I hand him my keys. "Go grab my truck out of the garage for me, will ya? With it still snowing, I didn't want to grab it too early."

"You got it, Patch, Sir."

Slapping him on the back, I watch the kids play while I wait for Mary to be ready.

When Mary comes back down, she parks off to the side of the door and I plug in her chair to charge while we're gone. Picking her up, I carry her out to my truck and am grateful that Ethan left it warming since we'd only just came inside and Mary's still cold.

Sliding behind the wheel, I head into town.

About five minutes into the drive, I notice Mary wringing her fingers together and I reach over, taking her hand in mine. She's been wearing the sling less and less as her arm and shoulder grow stronger, but I know she always has it on her for if it becomes too much.

"What's going through that pretty head, Siren?"

She sighs and lays her head back on the headrest. "I just keep wondering if there's anything else in **πατέρα** (dads) safe deposit box. I hope it's just the daggers and Eileen's ring. I really don't want to add anything else to this confusing mess."

Squeezing her hand, there's really nothing I can say to comfort her, because those same thoughts have been roaming through my head as well.

We're silent for the rest of the ride and when I put the truck in park in front of the bank, she exhales heavily. Lifting her hand to my lips, I place a kiss to her knuckles. "Whatever is in there, we'll handle together."

Her body relaxes slightly as she nods. "Together."

Turning off the engine, I get out, slip my cut back on, grab her wheelchair out of the backseat and then get it set up on the sidewalk. Walking back to the truck, I help her out and carefully carry her over the slick streets and over the small mountain of packed snow by the curb.

Minutes later, we're in the lobby of the bank waiting for the manager.

"Hello," a deep voice calls from behind us. "I'm Earnest Young, the manager of this branch." We turn around and my gut clenches when I see his eyes roam over Mary with interest.

Mary and I both shake his hand, and I make sure my grip is tight. "I'm Mary Catarino and this is my boyfriend, Luke Morgan."

His gaze flicks to me, and I give him a hard look.

Mary's mine.

Keep your eyes to your fucking self.

He frowns slightly, but otherwise turns back to business. "Please, come with me. My office is just down the hall."

We follow behind him and once inside; I move the chairs around slightly so Mary can sit in front of him. He checks his notes and nods to himself.

"So, you wish to retrieve the items in a safe deposit box, is that correct?"

"Yes, it is." Mary reaches into her purse and pulls out a note and a key. "This is the box my father left for me."

His face softens and he gives her a sympathetic smile. "My condolences."

Mary gives him a tight smile, but says nothing.

"We have a room set aside for those depositing or retrieving items from their safety deposit boxes. My apologies for not leading you there right away, but I make a rule never to mention the boxes out in the open of the lobby. Please follow me."

It takes a little finagling due to the tight space, but once Mary is out of Earnest's office, we follow him down the hall to a small room with a table and a few chairs. Earnest gestures for us to go inside.

"Please wait here and I will return in a moment with your box."

I move a few chairs so Mary can comfortably sit at the table in her chair and take a seat beside her. Taking her hands in mine, I rest my forehead against hers.

"Whatever is in there, we'll handle together," I repeat to her, somehow sensing that's what she needs to hear right now. For her sake, I really hope it is just those three items in the box.

After a few minutes, Earnest returns with the box in hand.

"Please take as long as you need. To my knowledge, no one else will need this room for the rest of the afternoon. Just please be aware that the lobby closes at 5:30 pm."

"Thank you."

Once he leaves and shuts the door, both of our gazes go to the box.

I make no move, knowing Mary needs to do this herself.

A few minutes later, Mary exhales heavily, and with a shaky hand, unlocks the box.

Inside there are three boxes as well as a stack of papers, and a sealed envelope addressed to Mary.

Taking everything out, she first moves to the smaller box and opens it. Inside is a gold ring with the Vasquez family crest. She pulls out the ring and on the inside of the band, Eileen's name is engraved in fancy script.

Grabbing one of the larger boxes, she opens it and gasps.

Inside is a beautiful dagger and the blade is shaped like a large triangle, with the blade being wide by the hilt and then narrows down to the tip of the blade. The guard kind of arks down toward the blade on both sides. The hilt is intricately carved out some sort of dark wood and on the pommel is the family crest.

Looking closer at the blade, there's script engraved on the flat section of the guard, right at the base of the hilt.

Eileen Ines Vasquez.

She rotates the blade and on the back of the guard is her birthday, leaving room for the day that she dies.

July 26, 1976—

And the day that will be filled in for her death will be today, I think grimly. That is, unless Antonio disowns them all before killing them. Then I don't know what will happen.

Looking up at Mary, a myriad of emotions flit over her face as she stares down at the blade, running her thumb across the engraving of Eileen's name.

"I wish she would have been a better Mom. That I could have had a normal mother-daughter relationship with her. To share some of our hobbies—books, going out to get our nails done, little luncheons together, or just shopping. Why couldn't she have just been a good Mom?"

Her shoulders shake and I carefully slide the dagger out of her hands, setting it back down in its box, and pull her into my arms.

I'm not sure how long I hold her as she grieves, but I make no move to rush her or to pull out my phone to check the time. If she cries until they close the lobby, I'm sure Earnest will come back to get us before locking up.

Eventually, her tears taper off and she pulls back, wiping her cheeks. Sniffling, she reaches for the other box and reveals her dagger.

Mary Elizabeth Catarino.

March 14, 1996—

Other than the inscriptions, it looks exactly the same.

Setting it aside, she picks up the sealed envelope that is addressed to her and opens it.

Immediately, her eyes fill with tears again, and when I look over her shoulder, I realize it's a letter from her father. She clears her throat and begins to read.

Κορίτσι μου (My girl),

If you are reading this, then I am sorry that I have died before I could give your dagger back to you. If your grandfather, Antonio, hasn't already explained, this is your Vasquez family eared dagger. Your tie to the mafia side of the Vasquez family.

When a family member is of an age that they can learn the truth about the family history, the Don presents them with their eared dagger. It is a sign that you are trusted to know the truth and, in turn, trusted to keep the truth of the family's secrets. Even though Eileen and I are divorced, Antonio still looked at me as family.

When I found the daggers after the divorce, I went to Antonio, sensing that they were important, and he told me everything about them and about the family.

For starters, these daggers were not supposed to be in her possession, and to understand why, I need to tell you a bit about your mother's past in case you don't already know about it.

Eileen lost her place in the mafia side of the family shortly before I knew about your existence. She was trying to tie the family to the human trafficking and skin business. Something that one of your grandfathers a long time ago declared the family would no longer take part in.

Greed and power consumed her, and she lost focus on the family's purpose, goals, and beliefs. In essence, she betrayed the family. It was at that point that Antonio took back her eared dagger and her ring of the family's crest, telling her that she had to earn her way back into the family.

Her betrayal also cost her the man she loved, Raul Guerrero, the son of another Spanish mafia Don. As soon as he learned of Eileen's true nature and the path she wanted to lead the family down, he cut all ties with her.

With no other option, she came to me, and that was when I learned about you. At first, I had my doubts that you were my daughter. I wasn't sure if I could trust that she wasn't intimate with anyone else after me and that she had never been with Raul yet.

I knew that Eileen didn't want children other than to carry on the duty she would have needed to fulfill if she had married Raul, but since she was now with me, she especially didn't want to have you. However, I insisted she keep you. If she never came to love me or you, I told her she could leave and I would raise you myself, but I wanted my child, if you really were mine. Obviously, she agreed to carry you to term.

Then you were born, and my doubts on your lineage were immediately put to bed.

You looked just like my sister Catherine did when she was born. Black curly hair, your olive skin. Though your eyes, your blue eyes are all your mother. In my opinion, they are the only good thing you got from her. I just wish she could have come to love you and me as I had already come to love both of you.

In regards to your dagger, Antonio wanted to give it to you when you graduated from high school. He had it locked in his safe at his house. He had no idea that Eileen had stolen both hers and your dagger from his safe until I presented them to him. When he went to check, the boxes he thought contained your daggers were empty. The betrayal cut Antonio deep, and he asked me to keep them safe, along with Eileen's family ring, hence why they are in this safe deposit box. I knew there was a high chance of Eileen breaking into our house to get them, so I did the next best thing I could.

I have never forgiven myself for not seeing Eileen's true nature toward you until that fateful day we moved to Forest Creek. You were so brave to stand up against her, even though I know from later conversations that she threatened you with bodily harm if you ever told me the truth.

I wish I could take away the pain you have endured from her, but this isn't one of the fairy tales or the paranormal books you like to read. I had tried to shield you as much as possible from her hatred and poison throughout the years. Burning notes she'd left for you or sent to you so that you wouldn't ever have to see more proof of her hatred for you.

I'm not sure how much time will have passed between writing this letter and you finding it (or me giving it to you), but I hope that you have found the courage to rise above the pain Eileen has caused you and that you are able to live your life to the fullest.

Πάντα σε αγαπούσα και πάντα θα σε αγαπώ (I've always loved you and always will). *Please know this,* **κορίτσι μου** (my girl), *I will always be with you, even if I'm not there beside you as you walk through life's trials and accomplishments. Stay strong,* **κορίτσι μου** (my girl).

"Love, **πατέρας** (Dad)," she says before taking a shuddery breath and wiping another tear away. "Well, I guess that confirms what Eileen ranted about before Diego interrupted her. Her heart was as cold as ice. The only things she loved were power, status, and money. And really, all she had was money per what Carmen said last night."

In the van on the way back to the clubhouse earlier this morning, she had also told us Eileen's and Diego's plans. To sneak in after Mae and Levi have the babies, to steal all of the kids, not just the babies and kill all of us. Needless to say, we'll be upping our defenses and hopefully the feds will be able to bring them down. Smoke had apparently told Creed that when he got back to the clubhouse, he'd be able to send a bunch of encrypted information to him about Oasis.

Shaking off those thoughts, I cup her cheek and turn her to face me. "She may not have been the mother you always craved to have, but I can tell you without a doubt that you are a hundred times better than she has ever been. That much is evident in how much you care for your kids. How you treat your family. How you take care of everyone around you. Even though we made you doubt us this week, you are a member of our club's family, and we will always be there for you."

Her shoulders relax slightly. "What..." She pauses as she bites her lips and looks down and to the side.

I think I know where her mind is going, but it isn't something we can discuss here. I just hope she can wait until tomorrow for my surprise.

"Do you want to look through the last stack of things or do that later?"

She looks over at it and after a few moments, reaches for it and unties the ribbon.

A sob escapes her as she sifts through old notes, pictures, cards, and other little mementos.

"He kept them all."

It takes her a few minutes to sift through them all, and when she's done, she reties them and puts everything into the bag I brought with us.

"Ready to get out of here?" I ask her, and she nods, looking lighter than she did when we came here.

After thanking Earnest, we walk outside, and get back in the truck, heading back to the clubhouse.

It's time to end Mary's demons.

Chapter 74
Mary

AFTER HAVING A QUICK supper, we're on the road again. The kids weren't exactly happy with us leaving, but there's no way I'd ever allow them to witness what we're going to do tonight.

Well, unless one of them wants to work for **Abuelo** (Grandpa) or join the club at some point, then they might find out some of the things we do behind closed doors.

After the guard clears us, Judge drives the van up the winding driveway and straight up to the garage. Another guard lets us in and it isn't until the door is closed that the guys all file out of the vans. With the number of us present tonight, we brought three vans. One of them is holding our 'guests' who have been bound, gagged, and blindfolded. Four men that work for **Abuelo** (Grandpa) step forward and grab Stephan and Derrick before disappearing into the house.

Patch gets my chair out and once I'm situated, I follow him and Thor into the house as another man that works for **Abuelo** (Grandpa) leads us to the men who went ahead. While I know the upper levels from my times here before, I've never been allowed into the basement until now. Though something that's surprising is that Levi and Sasha are coming this time.

And can I just say... I want their boots!

They are both wearing killer boots, that overall look the same with them being red leather, but whereas Levi has the normal boot sole one would expect, Sasha's has what looks like metal stiletto heels. I wonder if the difference is because boots like Sasha's would be extremely uncomfortable for a pregnant woman. My gaze wanders over their outfits and I realize they are both dressed completely in black and their long hair has been braided and wrapped into a bun on the top of their heads.

I have a sneaky suspicion that they'll be getting dirty tonight.

Sasha sees me staring at her boots and winks. "I'll hook you up after this. Levi and I have these and some black ones that are like mine, whereas Mae just got some black ones. Right now though, with her being about to pop and all, she got regular boots but they have a compartment in the heel that has little metal spikes should she need them."

Choosing to ignore that little tidbit for now, I cock an eyebrow at her and concentrate on the rest of what she said as I feel my lips twitching as I try not to smile. "Red for work, black for play?"

Levi grins from the other side of Sasha. "Like I said before, I knew you were a good egg and a perfect fit for us."

Returning the grin, I feel a sense of belonging fall over me.

And this time, I don't question it, unlike I did in the past when I was still battling the demon voices in my head from Stephan and Eileen.

In a matter of minutes, we're led into a large room where we find **Abuelo** (Grandpa), **Tío** (Uncle) Mateo, and **Tío** (Uncle) Lorenzo. Half of the room is covered in plastic. In the middle of that plastic, Carmen, Eileen, and Phillip are strung up on one side, and on the other side are Diego, Carlos, and Isaac in a similar position. There's enough room between the two rows that our group will have no problems watching everyone's reactions, especially since they are angled slightly so that the two on the far ends are closer together than the two closest to us. Though, I am curious as to why they left a space between Diego and Carlos, but I'm sure I'll find out soon enough. All of them are stripped naked and I'm sure it's to make things easier tonight. I already know Leon is being held somewhere else here in **la casa de mi abuelo** (my grandpa's house) because we're saving him for the feds. Well, unless Creed has already been by to pick him up.

My gaze snags on a pile of bodies in the back corner of the room that are laying on the plastic and have already been, uh, handled it appears. My guess is it's the guards that Patch told me Diego had lured away from **Abuelo**.

Movement has me looking back toward my so-called family to find that they are stringing up Stephan and Derrick alongside the others—Stephan next to Carmen and Derrick opposite Carmen, between Diego and Carlos.

Raised voices have me turning and my jaw drops in shock when I realize Levi and Sasha each have a guard that work for **Abuelo** pushed up against the door with a knife to their throats. My gaze darts to Thor, Dragon, and Cowboy who are just barely holding themselves back from going to their women. However, I also see the respect and heat in their eyes toward their respective women.

"Maybe you should have talked to your fucking boss before putting your hands on me, you fucking asshole," Levi snarls as she presses her blade tighter against the man's throat.

"This is family business, no non-family women allowed," he grits out through clenched teeth.

"We are here under invitation to deal with matters the club way regarding the women. Again, you should have fucking talked to your boss before trying to manhandle me. Or maybe you thought I'd be too weak and easier to manipulate since I'm fucking pregnant."

"Since when are women allowed in MCs? You're probably just a piece of ass, the random flavor of the week."

"My sister is the President's and Enforcer's Old Lady, and our club's decisions are none of your concern," Sasha grits out as she tightens her blade against the man's neck. I'm not sure if the guy she's holding said something else or if she's replying to the guy that spoke.

A growl comes from behind me before **Abuelo** (Grandpa) strides past me toward them. Levi flings the guy around and removes the blade from his throat right before **Abuelo** wraps his hand around his neck.

"How dare you fucking touch my guests in this manner, Martin! They are here because I invited them and because the club deals with women a certain way. How dare you question my authority?"

Martin's eyes widen and he shakes his head as much as possible. "I was just trying to uphold the no non-family women rule we've always had, Boss."

"Well, that rule is forever going to be changed due to our ties with the Steel Archangel's. Any women they bring here, you are to consider them as my guests and you will treat them as such. Get out of my sight. Both of you."

Levi clucks her tongue. "Or they can stay and maybe they'll learn a thing or two about why they shouldn't fuck with us." She steps back and reaches into her cut. "Oh, and here, Antonio."

Martin scowls before patting himself down, growling when he realizes that she somehow lifted his gun.

"Why I outta—"

"Martin," **Abuelo** barks out before he turns and gives a curt nod to Levi. "Very well," he replies, though the glare he levels Martin and the man next to him that Sasha had just released would have made me extremely worried about how much longer I would be living.

Martin's gaze narrows when he notices the back of Levi's cut is the same as the other guys and a calculative look enters his eyes. I hope he doesn't try to do anything after this.

Thor and Dragon both go up to Levi, each of them taking turns kissing her senseless, and Cowboy does the same to Sasha. When they pull back, all three men send glares at the guards which has the guards shifting slightly on their feet.

Abuelo smirks, recognizing the claiming, and gestures to the cabinets behind him. Without a word, Levi, Sasha, Patch, Thor, Dragon, Ryder, Timber and Trip all walk over and take inventory of what tools are available. Though, I do notice Dragon and Ryder setting down some large boxes on the table. Guess they wanted to bring some of their tools as well.

While they decide what they want to use, **Abuelo** and **mi tíos** (my uncles) take off their suit coats and roll up their sleeves. All three of them are wearing sheaths that I bet contain their eared daggers. My own is burning against my side, and I hope Levi helps me with my one special request for tonight. Not even Patch knows about it, despite the fact that we discussed earlier what questions I wanted answered, if possible, and what I wanted to have done to everyone.

Patch walks up to Diego and then to Isaac before standing in the middle of them all.

"To quote something Dragon said during Leo's initial session, though I will be modifying it a bit, the only control you have right now is how much pain you endure. We can make your end *relatively* painless, or we can make your pain endless. Right now, that is the only control you have. How much pain you endure before you die. Those that tell us what we want to know will earn a less painful death. Refuse, however, and we will make it extremely painful until we get the information we need." He pauses and looks between Diego and Isaac.

"Which of you two killed Nikos?"

My eyes burn, but I refuse to let them fall as Patch asks one of the questions that has plagued me the most.

They both smirk, but neither one of them talks.

"Suit yourself."

Dragon steps forward and takes Isaac while Patch goes to Diego. They both begin to carve into each of their bodies and even from here, I can see both of them straining to not let on how much it hurts. Timber steps forward and starts working on Phillip while Ryder takes Stephan, Tripp takes Derrick, and Thor takes Carlos.

While they get to work on the guys, Levi and Sasha walk up to Carmen and Eileen, and as they pass people, they drop little wooden boxes on the ground in front of everyone. Levi looks up at the chains in the ceiling and follows it along the track to the control panel. Sasha walks over and lowers the women's arms until they are horizontal, when both women breathe a sigh of relief, Sasha grins wickedly and starts moving the chains out, stretching out their arms. Both of them cry out at the new pain and when Levi gives the signal, Sasha rejoins her.

"**Обычный** (The usual)?"

"**Да** (Yes)." Levi pauses as she tilts her head and studies the women. "**Заставим их извиваться** (Let's let them squirm)."

Soon the sounds of more harsh Russian words fill the room as Levi and Sasha stalk around the women while making contemplative gestures and looks. Sasha had told me what those three phrases meant earlier on the ride up here. Levi also shared that one of the techniques they use to make the guests squirm is to just talk about random shit in Russian. As Levi and Sasha continue, I have to give them credit—it looks like it's working just the way they wanted it to because it's not just the women getting on edge.

Then without warning, at least that I know of anyway since I don't speak Russian and I don't have one of the translator devices, they both pull out pliers and start bending Carmen's and Eileen's manicured nails back. Screams tear out of both women as they beg them to stop. My gaze stays on Levi and Eileen since she's the one I want to watch the most out of the two women.

Once the nail is bent back enough, Levi rips it off and drops it in the bin. She grins a wicked and dark grin at the sound of the nail hitting the bin. "I do so love the sound of my trinkets bouncing around my trophy boxes."

Glancing over at **Abuelo**, I see him and both **mi tíos** (my uncles) watching Levi and Sasha closely. Looking around the room, so are most of the men that work for **Abuelo**. And I don't mean that in a sexual way. I think the ladies may be starting to open their eyes to other ways of handling women traitors.

And they've only just begun.

When they are each done with one hand, they move to the next.

I also notice that Derrick is oddly interested in what's happening to Carmen. With every nail Sasha ripped out, he's been getting more and more agitated, ignoring his own injuries and focusing on hers.

A growl rips out of Derrick as he tries to thrash harder in his restraints. "Leave her alone," he yells, which surprises me, but it doesn't surprise the rest of the club or my family.

What's going on? Do they know something I don't?

Everyone ignores Derrick and they keep their focus on their person of interest, since Derrick isn't giving any useful information, just yelling threats.

The ladies continue ripping out each nail, one by one. When that's done, they raise the women's arms back to where they were before. Then they pull out their blades and begin slicing into their skin.

After a few minutes, and of Derrick's constant pleas for them to leave Carmen alone, **Abuelo** walks forward. When Tripp steps back, **Abuelo** draws his eared dagger, tracing the tip of it down Derrick's chest.

"Why should they stop, Derrick? Is there something you'd like to share?"

Derrick's jaw clenches as his gaze bounces between **Abuelo** and Carmen as Sasha continues to sink her blade into her skin, cutting her and sometimes shaving sections of skin off.

"How about the fact that you've been bedding my wife for the past five years?"

My hand flies to my mouth as both Carmen's and Derrick's gazes lock. Both of them pale slightly as they realize their secret is out. Then Derrick's face morphs into anger as he stares at **Abuelo**.

"You knew. You knew I loved her and yet you pursued her and married her. Flaunting your new family around in front of me every chance you got. Hell, you even assigned me to her security detail, which was fucking hell on earth until she told me she regretted her choice to pick you over me."

La cara del abuelo (Grandpa's face) face darkens. "I knew no such thing. I thought you two were just friends, not lovers. Your friendship is why I put you on her security detail, knowing you'd make sure she was safe when I was not with her. Why the fuck didn't you say anything to me? I never would have pursued someone that a person I had considered my friend also liked."

Derrick's anger falters some in his confusion, but he shakes it off. "No, I told you many times I wanted to make her my wife, and yet you still went ahead and courted her yourself. She felt pressured into saying yes to you. That she didn't have a choice."

"Not once did you ever tell me you loved her and wanted to marry her. You might have told others, but not me." Then, strangely, **Abuelo** chuckles darkly as he digs his blade into Derrick's skin. "As for pressured? She was the one that pursued me in the beginning. Not the other way around. Looks like you too have fallen to her manipulative ways. And since finding out of your dalliances, I took a closer look at the security cameras. You weren't the only one to warm her bed." He pauses and jerks his thumb over his shoulder at the pile of dead bodies in the corner. "Those assholes were also getting a piece of her. She was rotating all of you through her bed during the day and then slinking into mine at night."

Derrick's shocked gaze flies to Carmen's and he blanches at seeing the smug look on her face.

"Why else did you think I seduced you, Derrick? I needed to keep tabs on my husband so we could make sure our plans wouldn't be foiled. As for the others, my needs weren't being met, so I found willing men to do the deed." She pauses and turns, snarling at me. "However, you just couldn't ever stay down. You always had to keep pushing back and kept ruining everything. I should have just let Eileen kill you all those years ago, and then none of this would have gone to hell. My worthless, lazy-assed husband would have been dead and then Diego and I would have been ruling this family."

Abuelo walks over to her and she curls her lip at him, as she stares defiantly up at him.

"Was there ever a time that you loved me, Carmen? Or was it all just a game to you?"

She scoffs. "Of course, I never loved you after you choose Es over me. It was all about the power and money you could give me. Do you honestly think I would have killed my best friend over something trivial? No. I met you first. I should have been the one that you chose as your wife from the beginning. Maybe then I could have loved you, but no, you had to choose Miss Goody Two-Shoes and go on to have eight kids with her. All the while, you both rubbed everything in my face since Es just had to include me in everything. I took great pleasure in watching her life fade from her every day for months. I would have preferred to have done it longer, but the new doctor you brought in was getting suspicious. So, I had to end her earlier than I originally wanted to. That was her punishment for taking you from me."

La cara del abuelo (Grandpa's face) turns thunderous. "Sasha?"

"**Да** (Yes)?"

"Make it hurt, but don't end her. That's for me."

"It will be my pleasure," she purrs right before she walks over to the tool chest and comes back with a serrated blade and some other pincher-like pliers. As soon as she's back over by Carmen, she starts cutting into her even worse and periodically, she'll pinch and rip some skin off with the pliers.

Abuelo moves over to Eileen and Levi pauses before stepping back slightly.

"Why, Eileen? Is all of this still over the fact that I said our family would never again work in skin?"

Eileen juts her chin out at him. "Of course it is. With my ideas, I grew my clubs and Diego's ten times over. If we had been doing it since I brought us back into the business, we would have been rolling in money by now." This time, it's her turn to glare at me. "Then she came along and ruined it all. Because of her, I lost Raul."

"No, Eileen. You knew as well as I do that the Guerreros have an even larger hatred of the skin business than we do. They never would have stood for your involvement in the business."

She shakes her head. "No, I would have proven what could be had from it. Money drives everyone. Money, power, and status. I would have changed their minds when they saw what I was bringing in."

"That is not true, Eileen."

Chapter 75

Mary

"THAT IS NOT TRUE, Eileen," the voice repeats, though this time, it's softer and there's more sadness in his voice than before. No, not just sadness, but a mixture of emotions—disappointment, shame, pity, and there's a hard edge of anger underlying all of that.

I look around, trying to find the owner of the voice, when he steps out of the shadows and walks toward Eileen. She stares at him in shock, and I'm pretty sure I know who it is based off of her expression.

"R-Raul?"

He frowns as he looks her over. "Quite honestly, I had my suspicions for a few months before your father notified me of your deceit. I had also been suspecting that you never truly loved me, but rather loved the money and status my family could give you. Those two reasons were why I called off our wedding. My family has a long-standing hatred of the skin business. In no way would we have allowed you to continue what you were doing if we would have married. Thankfully, we found out ahead of time, but if it had been after we were married when the truth came out, there would have been no mercy for you. You would have been tortured and killed, like your fate tonight.

"However, if you had been with child when we learned of your betrayal, I would not have punished the child for its mother's betrayal. No one in my family would punish a child for their parent's sins. But after the baby was born..." He pauses as his voice trails off and stares into her eyes for a moment. "Were you even telling me the truth that night? When you said you couldn't wait to be a mother? To give me an heir?"

Eileen hesitates but eventually gives a slight nod. "For you, I would have done it. I loved you, Raul. I still do."

My chest tightens at her words, and that tightening increases as Raul looks up at me with sympathy in his eyes before returning his attention back to Eileen.

"And yet I've seen the proof that you couldn't even be a semi-decent mother to your own daughter. Why should I believe that you wouldn't have done the same if Mary had been my daughter and not Nikos'?"

"I... I..."

Raul shakes his head, cutting her off. "I will be forever grateful I did not end up married to you. To have found out too late the venomous snake that hid just beneath the surface." He pauses as he twists the wedding band on his finger. "Thankfully, after I cut ties with you, I eventually found someone who loved me, truly loved me, was a good fit for our family. We even just welcomed our first grandchild a few days ago."

The devastation on Eileen's face is plain as day as she learns the man she loved had found someone even better than her after her betrayal.

Raul turns to **Abuelo** (Grandpa). "Thank you for letting me put this last piece of my past to bed."

Abuelo (Grandpa) dips his head and Raul leaves as quietly as he came.

Turning back to Eileen, I'm surprised that a small part of me feels sorry for her as tears run down her cheeks as she stares at Raul's retreating back, but it quickly fades when memories of everything she has done to me over the years surface again. **Abuelo** (Grandpa) gives a signal to Levi who continues on with her torture on Eileen.

Patch stops cutting into Diego, and steps back and Dragon takes his cue to step back from Isaac as well.

"Who killed Nikos?"

Diego glares at Patch, but surprisingly, Isaac caves.

"D-Diego did it. My first k-kill was slotted for someone else who b-betrayed the family, according to Dad."

Somewhere deep inside, I knew that Diego was the one who had pulled the trigger, but knowing for sure puts that question to rest finally.

Patch walks over by Isaac, lifting his chin with the flat side of the tip of his blade. While he does that, Dragon switches places and starts working on Diego, trying to get him to crack.

"Why were you all really targeting Mary?"

"He v-viewed her as a t-threat."

"Shut the fuck up, Isaac," both Diego and Carlos yell as they squirm in their chains. Axe steps forward with some tape and tapes both their mouths shut before standing off to the side.

I tilt my head, watching Diego and Carlos. Diego seems more furious that Isaac's talking, where Carlos seems almost afraid. That if Isaac doesn't speak up, we might let him go. Not that we would. There's too much evidence against him and what he's done.

"Continue," Patch tells Isaac.

"Other t-than me, she was the next eldest g-grandchild. Aside from what the others have already said, D-Diego was worried even more p-power would be taken from him when Mary came of age and received her d-dagger. Diego hated that **Abuelo** (Grandpa) chose M-Mateo over him as successor. Like Eileen and Dad, Diego thought we could build our empire even b-bigger if we were in skin. Then when Eileen c-came back, and especially when she faked her death, we started g-growing our circles despite what **Abuelo** had ordered us not to do."

"What do you know about Oasis?"

Isaac frowns. "Not m-much. They didn't l-let me in those meetings very often. X is in c-charge of everything. Phillip has a homestead n-north of here on one of your woman's l-land. Eileen had p-plans that after both w-women had their b-babies, we were going to storm the c-compound, take them and the women, as well as M-Mary's kids and bring them into the fold as p-payback for what the club has done to X's stock and c-channels. Stephan had put the k-kids and her up on the black market website and Eileen finalized their b-buyers, but they know they won't get the kids till we get the b-babies. Also, X is f-furious that you lot are k-keeping him away from the woman he sees as his q-queen."

My blood runs cold as I look over at Timber as he leaves Philip and stomps up to Isaac. "And who does he see as his queen?" Timber asks, his voice lethal and dark.

"The one p-pregnant with t-triplets. Said she's of g-good stock that will h-help grow their p-product."

Timber turns on his heel, stalks over to Phillip, who's smiling smugly, and slams his fist into his stomach. Phillip sputters and coughs. After a few moments, he grins a bloody grin at Timber.

"Yes, enjoy your bitch while you can because she won't be yours for much longer," he wheezes out.

"We'll just see about that," Timber returns his grin and after a few moments, Phillip's grin falters.

"There's no way you'll find him. Hell, half the time he isn't even in the country."

Muffled cursing has me turning my attention to Diego, and Dragon rips off the tape that was covering Diego's mouth. Is Diego finally cracking?

"Shut up you fucking imbecile," Diego seethes.

My heart sinks as Dragon's face darkens, and at the same time, Phillip's face blanches as he realizes he just let some vital information slip out. My guess is that Dragon must have also hoped we'd get more information out of Diego, which was why he removed the tape.

Dragon pulls back and lands a hard punch to Diego's stomach and as he's sputtering, Axe re-tapes Diego's mouth shut, but the damage is already done. Phillip clams up and won't answer any more of Timber's questions. And not only does Phillip clam up, but so do the others.

"Time to up the ante, gents," Levi calls out after ten minutes have passed. So far, none of them have given us anything since Diego's threat.

Levi gestures to Bear, who brings over the boxes the club brought with them. She opens the boxes and when she pulls out a metal looking dildo, I know things are about to get a lot darker

"One of my buddies made these custom for me. I like to use these on assholes who abuse women or children and traffic them. This may seem like an innocent little dildo, but it's got a few surprises up its sleeves." She pauses as she hits a button on a remote and I swear everyone in the room cringes as metal spikes pop out of the dildo. "And there's one more feature." She hits another button and my eyes widen when the fucking dildo starts to move. "Oh, and I forgot to say that there are straps to make sure these babies don't work their way out of you.

She pushes a button and the spikes retract and the dildo stops moving. She puts the dildo back in the box and pulls out another thing, some sort of a ring.

"This little baby is for you men." She pushes a button and spikes pop out of the ring and it's only then that I realize it's a cock ring. "And yes, it also vibrates," she says as she hits another button. After a few moments, she shuts it off.

Moving to the other box, Levi reaches inside and I secretly wonder how many more surprises she has.

"And this is for the ladies. The metal bra claw as one of my brothers likes to call it." She presses a button that makes the spear-like ends shoot out from the center and then they start to rotate. She shuts it off and looks around, smirking at the looks of horror on our guests' faces. Taking a chance, I glance over at Martin and his friend who are protecting their junk and looking rather terrified of Levi right about now. Serves the assholes right.

"If I could please get some help, gents?" Levi asks and the guys who had been doing the torturing so far, all step forward and walk past my stunned family to grab the devices for the guys while Levi and Sasha handle the women.

It takes a few minutes, but soon everyone has the devices strapped to them.

Thor nods to **Abuelo** who jerks slightly as he comes out of his shock. Walking down the line, he rips the tape off of anyone who still has it covering their mouths.

Then he walks over to Carmen, glances at Derrick, and then back to her. "Despite what you thought, I did love you, Carmen. But then you disgraced our family by helping our children work behind my back in the hurting of innocents and most likely, causing the deaths of some of them. You were right, we do not divorce in our family. However, when we are betrayed, we silence them. No matter who they are."

He looks over her and nods to Sasha, who turns on her device to Carmen's metal claw bra and the dildo.

Carmen's wails fill the air and soon Derrick's cries mix with hers as he struggles against his bonds. A small amount of pity eats at me for him having to watch the person he loves die, and based on his reactions, he truly does love her, but I squash the feeling down. With everything he's done, he doesn't deserve any amount of pity.

Sasha cuts off the device when **Abuelo** gives her a signal and he walks around Carmen, sliding his dagger across her throat. "I brought you into **nuestra familia** (our family), and I take you out of **nuestra familia** (our family)."

Derrick weeps as the sound of her gurgling fades and then her body hangs limply in its chains. A sliver of remorse shines in **los ojos del abuelo** (grandpa's eyes) as he looks at Carmen one last time and at Derrick, but then his face hardens and he signals Tripp to turn on his device for Derrick. When **Abuelo** gives the signal to turn off the device, this time it's **Tío** (Uncle) Mateo who walks up to Derrick.

"You have betrayed the ways of **nuestra familia** (our family) as well as further betraying **nuestra familia** (our family) by hurting our own. By now, I'm sure you've already figured out the punishments for your crimes. To watch the woman you loved die and for you to be killed at my hand." Without another word, he steps behind Derrick and slides his dagger across Derrick's throat, slicing him open.

"**Mi Padre** (My Father) may have brought you into **nuestra familia**, but I take you out of **nuestra familia**."

A few minutes later, Derrick's body also hangs limp.

Thor walks up to Phillip. "Where is X?"

When Phillip doesn't answer, Thor nods to Timber, who turns on his device for a few seconds and then he turns it off. After a few moments, when Phillip is mostly just crying instead of screaming, he asks again.

"Where is X?"

"When he's n-not in the US. H-he s-splits his time between M-Mexico, Hawaii, and the C-Cayman Islands."

"Where is he right now?"

He shakes his head. "I don't k-know, just that when he heard M-Mary had left Stephan, he rushed b-back from Mexico, so I doubt he'd go b-back there. He'd probably g-go to one of his houses in the other l-locations."

"Who else is in control of the homestead north of town?"

"If I'm n-not there, the next highest-r-ranking person is Grant. He l-lives in the second l-largest thatch house."

"Why did Oasis put their homestead on Mae's land to begin with?" Timber asks him.

"B-Bruce thought that when everything was all s-said and done, he and X w-would have Mae and then they'd h-have the rights to the land. They s-sought out that land with the intent of always g-getting their hands on Mae. Then my idiot b-brother botched up their plans and didn't m-make sure that Mae was asleep before calling B-Bruce to sell her."

Timber's eyes rage and with a look at Thor, probably to see if he has any more questions. Thor shakes his head and Timber flips on the switch again. After a few moments, Timber hands the controller to Thor and steps around Phillip, slitting his throat even as the device still keeps tearing apart his insides and slicing through his dick. Only when Phillip's body hangs limp does Thor shut off the controller.

Patch, **Abuelo y mi tios** (Grandpa and my uncles) all step toward Stephan.

"You took my woman and son from me. You beat her and abused her for nine years. Tried to sell her children, which we shut down the website by the way." Patch pauses as Stephan shakes his head and mutters 'no' weakly. "No what?"

"I w-wasn't the one that p-put them on that s-site, d-despite what Isaac t-thought. T-That's Eileen's site. Sure, I t-threatened Mary p-plenty of times that if she didn't b-behave, that would be her f-fate, but it was always Eileen p-pulling those strings."

Patch narrows his eyes at him, but he must see something in Stephan's eyes that makes him believe him because he nods.

"Fine, that was Eileen, but you still beat her, made her bleed, broke her bones, and abused her physically, mentally, as well as emotionally. Not to mention stealing so many experiences from your own fucking kids. They've never even built a snowman until earlier this afternoon," Patch seethes and Stephan winces, whereas the faces of **Abuelo y mi tios** (Grandpa and my uncles) turn murderous.

"That w-was all part of the c-contract. I had to s-suppress as much as p-possible to try and make them as c-compliant as possible. If you don't b-believe me, look in t-the very bottom d-drawer in my d-desk. T-There's a false b-bottom. Remove t-that and you'll f-find all the v-variations of the contracts for Mary and the k-kids."

Thor looks over his shoulder and when I look around, I notice Smoke is on his phone, texting someone.

"Time will tell if you're telling the truth or not. Regardless of what we find, you still fulfilled the terms of that so-called contract with little to no coercion, you fucking piece of shit. No one twisted your arm to do any of that. That was all you, and you'll pay for what you've done," Patch growls out as he cuts deeply into Stephan's side.

He ignores Stephan's cries of pain as he moves from wound to wound, cutting deeper into each one. Wounds that I'm guessing Patch gave him during their first 'talk'. A small part of me baulks at enjoying the sound of Stephan's screams, but I squash the feeling. Stephan never responded to my pleas or cries for him to stop, and no one here is going to listen to his pleas he's currently crying out.

Abuelo y mi tios (Grandpa and my uncles) turn to face Diego, Carols and Isaac.

"You all have brought immense shame on the family. Your clubs, houses, cars, everything will be sold off. All the proceeds will go to helping those hurt by your greed." **Abuelo** pauses and looks at Carlos.

"In everything I have scoured, I have not found proof that Gianna was involved in any of this," and for a moment I see relief in Carlos' eyes. "But that said, I do not believe that she is totally innocent. Not with as many meetings as you were holding in your wing of the estate." He pauses again and the previous relief I'd seen in Carlos' eyes quickly dims. "Gianna will be cut from **nuestra familia**. The other ruling Dons will be warned about her to prevent her from worming her way back in. She will be cared for, but I refuse to allow her to continue living in my house. That said, I will not be supplying the same level of comfort that she is used to. By morning, family heirlooms will be moved out of the wing, and if there is anything missing, Gianna will return the items on penalty of death. The remaining items, she may do so as she sees fit with. Keep them, sell them, whatever. I don't care. However, her and her shit will be out of my house by the end of the day. A suitable house has been found and purchased for her. If she doesn't want it, then she's on her own to find her own housing. Is that clear?"

Carlos hangs his head. "**S-Sí** (Yes), **Padre** (Father)."

"Fucking man up, Carlos," Diego hisses, and Thor signals Axe before **Abuelo** even has a chance to. Axe steps forward and tapes Diego's mouth shut again before stepping back out of the way.

Antonio moves to Isaac next. "You had so much potential until you started taking more and more after **tu padre y tu tío** (your father and uncle). However, maybe if I had stepped in more, I could have saved you and diverted you on a better path. For that reason alone, I am granting you a quick death, but it will still be in the way **nuestra familia** handles traitors."

Isaac's face falls, but he quickly masks his emotions save for the guilt I still see shining in his eyes. **Abuelo** steps forward and defaces the family crest tattoo on Isaac's chest before shaving it off. Then he moves behind Isaac and quickly, but deeply, slices through his neck.

Carlos weeps as quietly as he can as Isaac struggles to breathe and a sob tears through him when Isaac finally stops breathing. For a brief moment, I see a shimmer of tears in **los ojos del abuelo** (Grandpa's eyes) before he blinks rapidly and his eyes clear.

When **Abuelo** stops in front of Carlos, he does his best to stem his tears as he looks up at **Abuelo**.

"Is there anything else you can tell us of X, Oasis, or the human trafficking?"

He nods. "X had p-plans to go to Hawaii n-next, but I don't k-know if he'll still do that s-since I'm sure he's figured out we were c-compromised." He pauses and turns to Thor. "Under Phillip's and G-Grant's houses, they b-built a bunker of sorts. If your t-tech guy is as good as they say, t-then he'll be able to get even more d-data about X. As for S-Sanchez, I'm sure r-retribution will come at some p-point. He's h-had his eye on Levi and Mary for q-quite some time now. He's even taken an interest in M-Mae after hearing X d-describe her. His daughter b-better get far, far away b-because when he finds out she w-was in on him losing his product all these years, he will t-tear everything and everyone apart to f-find her and end her. R-regardless of if she is family or not. He knew he had a m-mole, he just never s-suspected it was her. At least to my k-knowledge, anyway."

"Anything else?"

Carlos shakes his head. **Abuelo** steps forward and starts cutting up Carlos' family crest tattoo before shaving it off. When he's done, he gives the signal to

Thor, who switches on Carlos' devices, though as soon as they are on, **Abuelo** walks behind Carlos and slits his throat, fast and deep, like he'd done with Isaac. I don't know if he gave him mercy for being so honest at the end or what, but I think it might have been the case.

"I was part of bringing you into **nuestra familia**, and I take you out of **nuestra familia**."

Abuelo goes to Diego next and rips the tape off his mouth. They stare at each other for a while before **Abuelo** shakes his head.

"You don't regret anything, do you?"

"Only not killing you like I had wanted to and not killing that fat bitch that night along with Nikos. Money and revenge be damned."

"Thor, do you guys have any other questions for him?"

Thor looks toward me but I slightly shake my head, and when he looks at Patch, he shakes his head as well. "Nope, you can proceed with him however you want."

When **Abuelo** steps forward, Diego spits, but **Abuelo** is able to just barely jerk to the side to avoid it. He backhands Diego and when Diego grins a bloody grin, Axe steps forward and offers him the tape. **Abuelo** takes it and tapes his mouth shut before he starts cutting into Diego's tattoo and slicing it off like the others. He looks down at the device in Patch's hand and holds out his hand for it. He studies it for a moment before turning to Levi.

"Is there a speed option?" he asks to which she smirks and walks over to him.

"This knob right here dictates the speed. To the left is slower and to the right is faster."

His hand twists, and when I hear the device start, I realize he's turned it to the absolute lowest setting.

Patch reaches up and puts his fingers around Diego's wrists. It takes me a moment before I realize he's feeling for his pulse.

After a few minutes, Patch says something low to **Abuelo** who walks around Diego and slices his neck.

"I was part of bringing you into **nuestra familia**, and I take you out of **nuestra familia**," he says, repeating what he'd said for Carlos. Only when Diego slumps in his chains does he turn off the devices. When **Abuelo** turns toward Eileen, I wheel forward.

"Wait."

I stop a few inches shy of the plastic and at my voice, Eileen looks up. Seeing how broken she is surprises me, and I wonder exactly how much of Raul's visit and words destroyed her more than what Levi had done to her.

"What else do you want from me? You've already taken everything. My love. My husband. My house. My company. My family. What more do you want from me?" she screams.

I shake my head. "I never took any of that from you. It was your own actions that led to your downfall and the fact that you still can't see that says a lot about you. But then again, you are practically a mirror image of your own mother, so I guess the apple doesn't fall far from the tree, does it?"

She scoffs and shakes her head, but doesn't say anything.

It's then that the few things I was going to ask about don't matter anymore. Much like Diego, she really doesn't see anything wrong with what she's done. I hold my hand out, and when Levi hands me her controller, I'm pleasantly surprised when no one stops me.

Levi tells me what's what, and after I flick on the switches, I look over my shoulder and nod to Bear and Bones who come over. Locking the wheels of my chair, I stand with their assistance and loop my arms around them. They help me hobble my way behind Eileen, and when the guys help steady me, I'm not surprised to see Patch, **Abuelo y mi tios** (Grandpa and my uncles) are there, looking at me with concern as I pull out my own dagger.

"Are you sure, Siren? Taking a life changes you, but I get it if this is what you need to do to close this door. I just want to make sure you are positive this is what you want to do."

Pursing my lips, I nod. "I'm sure. I need to be the one to do this."

With a small nod in return, he checks her pulse since I put her controller on the lowest setting just like **Abuelo** had done with Diego. When he gives me another nod, I take a deep breath pass him the controller and reach around Eileen, slicing her throat as I say a variation of what **Abuelo** said earlier.

"You may have brought me into this world, but I'm the one who will be taking you out of it."

When her body sags in her chains, mine sags for an entirely different reason, and Patch quickly steps forward, wrapping his arms around me.

After a few moments, Eileen's gurgling stops and her body finally sags.

Someone clears their throat, and I look over my shoulder. Smoke holds up his phone.

"Stephan's story checks out. We have all the documents."

Patch steps forward, raising an eyebrow in question. Tightening my jaw, I nod. "Me."

He picks me up and sets me down in front of Stephan, whose head is hanging down, his chin almost touching his chest. After a moment, he raises his head, and for the first time ever, I see regret in his eyes. However, I don't know if he truly feels regret or if it's because he knows he's going to die.

"After today, you will never be spoken of again. The kids are already well on their way to forgetting you and have long since been calling Patch 'Dad'. For years I had thought of ways I'd make you suffer for what you've put all of us through, but now, I just want you gone."

Patch picks me up once more and sets me down behind Stephan. He hands me the controller, and like I had done with Eileen, I turn it on its lowest setting.

Patch reaches up, checking his pulse, and when he gives me a signal, I reach around Stephan's neck, but then I pause for a moment.

"You will never have control over me or the kids *ever* again."

Then I slice my dagger across his throat.

When his body finally hangs limp, my throat tightens with emotions, but I force myself to push them down for now.

Once again, Patch wraps his arms around me, and I lean into him.

"It's done. It's finally over and I'm free. My demons are dead."

I'm free, I repeat to myself internally.

I'm finally free.

For the first time in nine years, I can breathe deeply again.

Chapter 76

Patch

THE NEXT DAY, I'M a nervous wreck and I can tell Mary suspects something's up, but so far, she hasn't questioned me on it. Especially after the craziness of last night.

I had no idea that Mary wanted to be the one to end her mother and Stephan, but it shouldn't have surprised me. Even more so when I look back and realize she'd been talking to Levi a lot before we left to head to Antonio's house.

That night, though, I held her as she fell apart and was finally able to fully grieve. To grieve for Nikos, for the relationship she never got and would now never get with Eileen. However, mixed in with those tears, I knew there were also tears of happiness at finally being free from Stephan and to not have to constantly be looking over her shoulders out of fear.

Yeah, X is still out there, but Smoke was locked up most of this morning in his room with Thor and Phoenix as they updated Creed, our FBI contact, with the additional information we learned last night.

Also, this morning on the news, it was reported that Stephan's body had been found burned to a crisp when his car careened off a cliff outside of town. Uncle Sam and Brady had come out to tell her the news, and since it was in an official capacity, I thought she did a pretty damn good acting job. Even though he's dead, she'll still need to testify next month as a witness for the other cases she provided information for. And I'll be right there providing any support she needs after having to recount events again.

As for Phillip, we left his body in a place where we knew it would get found and serve as a message for X.

The homestead north of town.

And the message?

Continue to fuck with us and we'll make sure he gets the same treatment.

Shaking myself internally, I bend, helping Mary stand before picking her up and setting her down in my truck. Once Mary's buckled in, I round the front and climb up behind the wheel before turning on the truck and pulling out into the compound. However, she quickly notices I'm headed in the wrong direction.

"Uh, Luke?"

I hum.

"Where are we going?"

"All I'm going to tell you is that I've got a surprise for you."

"But what about Cassie?"

"Mae and Levi are grabbing her on the way back from their OB-GYN appointments."

"Uh-huh. And are you going to tell me what's got you acting like you drank three pots of coffee by yourself today?"

I huff but shake my head. "Nope, but you'll find out soon enough."

She pouts and this is why I have to be so damn secretive when planning a surprise for her.

My woman has no patience for this sort of thing and she hates surprises.

Thankfully, she doesn't ask me any more questions as we drive to our destination.

Her breath hitches and her face falls when I pull in front of a vacant building next to Levi's restaurant, Wallace's B&G.

With all our recent snowfall, I'm relieved that the parking lot and sidewalk have been recently cleared, so we won't have as much trouble as we had at the bank yesterday.

Getting out, I get Mary situated in her chair and walk toward the front door.

"Luke," she says, her voice laced heavily with confusion, and I'm betting she just spotted the 'sold' sign which has her pinching her lips together. She'd been looking at this place and had been devastated when Levi had mentioned it had been sold.

Ignoring her for a moment, I open the door and then wheel her inside. Once inside, she takes over and spins around to face me.

"What are we doing here, Luke? Are we going to get in trouble with the owners?"

"Trust me, Siren, we're not going to get in trouble." Pausing, I swallow down my nerves as I kneel down in front of her, clasping her hands.

"Mary, ever since I first met you, I knew you were special to me. I just didn't realize how special until much later in life. My heart beats for you and our kids, and I know it'll continue to grow and beat for any other children we may have in the future."

I pause, licking my lips. "What I'm trying to say is, Mary, will you please marry me? Marry me and make me the happiest man alive?"

Her hands fly to her mouth when I reach into my cut and pull out a little blue box, opening it to show her the perfect ring for her that I'd found all nine and a half years ago and feel that it still fits her today. It's a princess cut diamond surrounded by blue sapphires, her favorite gemstone, and on the band, there are a couple more diamonds on either side.

"Yes, of course I'll marry you!" she squeals as she throws her hands around my neck. When she pulls back, I slip the ring on her finger and grasp her hand again.

"I also wanted to know if you'll be my Old Lady."

Reaching into the bag I'd grabbed out of the backseat when I got her chair out, I pull out her cut with her road name 'Siren' stitched on the front and on the back, it has 'Property of Patch' stitched on the rocker.

"Yes, yes, yes!" she cries and I can't help my smile as I help her slip it on.

As soon as she has it on, cheers erupt from the back room and Mary jumps in shock as our family and friends come pouring out.

"What the heck? What are all of you doing here?"

"Well, witnessing your engagement, silly," Mae says as she spins the camera around, getting shots of everyone in here as she continues filming, because I still have another surprise for Mary but this next one is for the kids.

"Kids, can you come up here? I've got something for you three, too."

Levi hands me three boxes that I'm guessing one of the ladies wrapped for me. Handing them out to them, they immediately start digging into the wrapping paper, and soon, their cries fill the air.

"This is so awesome!" Isaiah says as he quickly puts on his cut with Mary's nickname for him, 'Sparks', on the front. Cassie's has 'Angel' stitched on hers and Ash's has 'Hawk'. All three of them have a rocker on their backs as well that say 'Property of Patch'.

When they have them all on, they all rush forward, hugging me and telling me thank you.

Looking up, Mary's dabbing at her eyes as she watches us.

After a few moments, I stand and walk back over to Mary while at the same time, Harris, Maria, Antonio and Luiza step forward as well.

"We have one more surprise for you as well, Mary."

She looks at me in shock. Then she looks around and her jaw drops again. When her gaze returns to mine, I nod.

"Yeah, um you see, ever since I found out that your *real* dream was to be a chef in your own restaurant, I started looking around for places. Then to get some opinions, I called in some help. Everyone agreed in thinking this would be a good place for you to start out. There's room to expand if need be because the club actually bought this restaurant and the strip of stores that were for sale. We're purposefully keeping the two stores nearest this restaurant vacant, but the others will be able to renew their leases if they want."

She stares at me in shock for a few moments before she finally speaks.

"This is my place now?"

I grin, knowing by the vibrations running through her and seeing her barely concealed happiness at the change, that I did the right thing.

"It is, Siren."

She cries out and pulls me toward her and down into a hug.

"Thank you, thank you, thank you," she whispers and when we pull apart to more sounds of cheering she looks around the restaurant.

Then she narrows her eyes at Levi. "Did you know the entire time?"

Levi smiles sheepishly. "Maybe," she squeaks out, but then Mary's also pulling her down into a hug.

Suddenly, Mary pulls back. "We're going to need to make sure we don't steal business from each other."

"Well, since I'm pretty sure you're going to focus on Greek and Spanish food, the only thing we might take a hit on is our tacos and fajitas but it'll be worth it to work next to you."

Mary's family swarms forward, and over the excitement, I'm relieved that she's finally able to spend time with Harris, Maria, and the rest of the Catarino side of the family. Most of whom are here today. Ever since that day in her old house, we had asked, for their safety, for them to keep their distance. Though if this mess with Stephan had gone on past Christmas, we would have made an exception for them all to get together.

Off to the side, I notice Antonio, Mateo, and Lorenzo are very quietly talking with Levi and I bet it's about her devices that we used last night. I wasn't the only one that noticed they seemed rather interested in them. I just hope they only use them when they are warranted, but as soon as that thought enters my mind, I banish it. None of them would torture innocents like that.

After a few minutes, Mary comes over and I bend down to kiss her again.

When we pull apart, she looks up at me with tears in her eyes. "Thank you so much, Luke. Thank you for loving me for me. Thank you for rescuing me, multiple times, and thank you for being the best fiancé and father a woman could ask for."

"Anything for you, Mary. Like I said before, **Υπόσχομαι ότι θα είμαι δίπλα σας σε κάθε βήμα** (I promise that I'll be by your side every step of the way.) **Πάντα σε αγαπούσα και πάντα θα σε αγαπώ** (I've always loved you and always will)."

Wrapping an arm around my neck, she pulls me close again, giving me a soft kiss. "**Κι εγώ σ' αγαπώ** (I love you, too)."

The end… until the Steel Archangel's MC plans a Christmas surprise to remember.

Author's Note

THANK YOU EVERYONE FOR reading *Steel Archangel's MC: Patch (SAFC3)!* I hope you enjoyed Patch and Mary's story. Next up is a surprise Christmas novella <3 Patch and all the club members set out to make the club's first Christmas with so many new family members one to remember :) A certain someone even don's a big red suit. Can you guess who it will be? :)

Then, it will be Reaper's story as he helps his Darlin' heal after a traumatic injury and works to claim his woman, his Neith, his hunter that owns his heart. <3 However, before he can do all that, he has to overcome his own demons. Can Reaper and his Neith save each other?

Reviews are very important for authors, and especially to new authors! Thank you to everyone that leaves a review, even if it is only a line or two or just leaving stars! Keep reading for info on how to contact me as well as other books by me. I'd love to hear from you!

About the Author

R. KNIGHT LOVES READING and writing romance novels, whether it be contemporary, MC, paranormal, reverse harem or menage. If you like strong women and partners surrounded by the men who adore and worship them, then follow me to hear about current and upcoming books that will satisfy your craving!

When R. Knight isn't reading or writing, she's spending time with her amazing husband, two kiddos, two cats and a dog where they live in Eastern Wisconsin. The usual shenanigans involve watching movies, camping, playing board games and/or video games.

https://linktr.ee/Author_R_Knight